AMONG
THIEVES

GEORGE CUOMO

AMONG THIEVES

Doubleday & Company, Inc.
Garden City, New York

*All of the characters in this book
are fictitious, and any resemblance
to actual persons, living or dead,
is purely coincidental.*

Surely the Lord is in this place;
and I knew it not. . . .

GENESIS

In writing this book I was helped by many people who generously gave me the benefit of their knowledge and experience. I should like to thank especially Warden John Molony of the British Columbia Penitentiary, Justice William R. McIntyre of the British Columbia Supreme Court, C. C. Dow and M. B. Gaw of the John Howard Society of Vancouver Island, and Mel Venter of KTVU, Oakland.

For their criticisms and suggestions concerning the manuscript, and for their patience and good wishes, I owe a real debt to Monica McCall, John Peter, Frederick Rebsamen, Donald Stanley, Samuel S. Vaughan, Robert V. Williams, and above all my wife, Sylvia.

AMONG
THIEVES

The living room was practically dark, with all the blinds down, but the way the sun was blazing away out there the room was like a furnace anyway, even with the cooler going. You could hear the cooler dripping away on the roof. Mel was stretched out on the couch watching the TV, with the kid standing alongside playing with Mel's buckle, the one he bought that time in the army, in a pawnshop in Columbus, Georgia, kind of gold with the field artillery insignia on it.

The kid started whining again.

Without taking his eye off the screen, Mel pushed out the little cardboard tray of the matchbox and took out a wooden match. Still watching the TV, he struck the match and held it in front of Chucky's face. Chucky blew, and Mel could feel little spots of wet on his hand, but the match didn't go out. He gave the kid another try, then smiled so the kid wouldn't feel bad and blew it out himself. He dropped the match in the tin ashtray, which was practically full from all the other matches.

A commercial came on, with a lion jumping out of a soap box and talking to this lady that was doing her wash, which the kid got a little interested in, but then it ended and he started scrootching again.

"What'samatter? The old breadbasket getting empty?" Mel got up and turned off the set. "Maybe the old lady's run off with the money, eh, Chucky?" He spread his legs and stretched: "Aggggghhhh! C'mon, we'll go see what we can scout up."

Mel shoved the breakfast stuff out of the way on the kitchen table and made some cheese sandwiches. Then he looked into the Yogi Bear mug to make sure it was dirty, and rinsed it out. He poured some milk in. "Chug-a-lug, kid. Make you strong."

Mel ate his own sandwich standing up, looking out the back window. Christ, it looked hot out there.

He could see himself in the glass, and took his comb out and ran it through his hair, which was all it ever needed. It was too curly to look much different before or after anyhow, except the hair in front that kept falling down if you didn't comb it back. Peggy liked it coming down. Girls in general did. It was very black, and kind of shiny, which made it look good too.

He heard the mug go and turned to see the milk spreading on the linoleum. From the table a smaller puddle dripped right onto the kid's diaper—which, let's face it, didn't need being any wetter. "Aw c'mon, be careful, willya?" There was some milk left but the kid didn't want it so Mel dropped the mug into the sink where Yogi Bear, smiling away, sank gurgling into the big pan of water. Mel laughed. Sure. Poor old Yogi.

"Mommy!" the kid yelled when he heard the car out front. He ran out in his bare feet, his diaper drooping all over the place. Mel dropped yesterday's sports section over the puddle and went out. Peggy was giving the kid a big kiss on the cheek.

"Hi," Mel said. "I'll get the bundles."

"Was he good?"

"Yeah, he was all right."

"Augh, Chucky!—you're soaking wet."

"I just changed him before," Mel said, bending into the back of the Dodge to grab the sacks.

Peggy carried Chucky toward the house, holding him away from her blouse. "I got some real good news," she called back over her shoulder.

"Yeah? What about?" Mel started up the path. The bags were heavy but he had a good grip on them. It felt all right, the weight of them. He clenched his arm muscles.

"Let me change him first."

Mel put the bags on a kitchen chair and dug down to get at the six-pack. He dropped the register tape on the table, then on second thought looked at it—$16.42. The hell, you gotta eat. He punched open a Coors and took a slurp.

"You should really put waterproofs over the diapers," Peggy said, bringing the kid in.

"I couldn't find any."

Peggy picked up the newspaper from the floor.

"The kid spilled some milk. I was gonna clean it up when he finished."

"Let me tell you the news."

"Yeah. Give me the good news."

"It's about a job," Peggy said.

"Oh?" Mel looked at her, at the way she was smiling. "A job, eh?" he said, keeping his voice even.

"It sounds real good, Mel."

He took a swallow and swished around the can. Chucky watched him doing it. "They all sound good."

"It's being a route man for a dry cleaning place. Best-Way Cleaners. They got places all over town—you seen them."

"How'd you hear about this anyway?"

"Ella's husband works on the counter in one of their branches. He's sorta like manager."

"Of the whole company?"

"No, just the branch, sorta. Where he works. But Ella gave me the name of the guy you're supposed to see."

Mel studied the label on the can.

"You pick up stuff to be cleaned and bring it back when it's ready," she said, real fast, like she was scared she wouldn't get it all in. "You get regular steady customers, Ella says, a regular route you go to all the time, and the more business you bring in the more money you get."

"You gotta be bonded," Mel said.

"She didn't say nothing about that. I'll put some of this away." She opened the refrigerator and started unloading the bags.

"Anything like that you gotta be bonded for," Mel said.

"Maybe her husband would give you a recommendation. Don't play with the mop, Chucky. It's all dirty."

"A recommendation got nothing to do with it. It's the bonding company."

"Will you try? She said you could go down this afternoon."

"This afternoon already?"

"Well, if you wanna try, you gotta get there before—"

"Okay, okay! I get the picture."

Peggy stopped putting cereal boxes on the shelf and walked over to where Mel was leaning against the wall near the window. He didn't move. She reached out and put her hand on his arm. "I'm sorry." She tried to bend forward to kiss him but he shrugged and stepped past her, looking for a place to stand, a place to lean.

She stared at him, then nodded and went back to the groceries and was quiet for a while. She came across a box of cookies and gave the kid one. He sat on the floor eating it while Peggy put away the last of the food. "We spent just over sixteen dollars," she said.

"I saw."

"I was just mentioning. You have anything left on you? You had a five and some change, didn't you?"

"A *five?*" Mel looked at her. "Do you know when you gave me that five?"

"I just wanted to know if you had any of it left."

"Some change maybe."

"I'll give you something to have on you." She waited a bit. "When do you wanna go down about the job?"

"I don't know. Right away, I guess. I mean, if there's such a big rush."

"You should shave and put on a tie."

"Christ, you gotta wear a tie on this job? In the goddamn summer?"

"It'll help when you go down. Ella said she thought of you because you looked so good all dressed up."

"She never seen me dressed up."

"She seen you a coupla times you came to pick me up."

"I wasn't dressed up."

Peggy kept quiet again for a while. "Was there anything in the paper?"

"The Blue and White cabs want a mechanic."

"No kidding? Did you call them up?"

"You gotta go down."

She sorta hesitated. "What about tools?"

"Maybe I can swing something on the tools."

"Well anyhow you got two things to try today. Maybe *one* of them—"

"Yeah. Maybe one of them'll say scram, and the other'll say come back in six years."

Peggy looked over at him like she was at a goddamn funeral.

"Look," he said, because he didn't want to get started on anything, "I'll run in and shave, all right?" He gave her a little smile and sort of tapped her chin. "I'll get a real early start." He took another beer and punched two holes in it. "C'mon Chucky. Watch Daddy shave."

The kid hopped to his feet and ran after him.

☐

He left with the five Peggy gave him in his wallet. He was all shaved and washed up and had on his one decent pair of summer slacks and a white short-sleeved shirt. He wasn't wearing any tie, and he wasn't wearing any jacket, and he could tell when he left that Peggy was just itching to say something about it, and when he got to the dirt sidewalk he made the mistake of looking back and there she was at the window, holding Chucky, and she had that kind of *good luck* look on her face that just sent chills through him. He scrambled into the Dodge.

Which naturally was like a goddamn oven. You could hardly touch the steering wheel it was so hot. A black car right in the middle of the desert—that's what the hell you needed, something black to soak up the sun, not to waste any of the heat. The car was eight years old and anything you could name that could be wrong with a car was wrong with it. He hated its guts.

Driving in past all the auto lots and drive-in stands and the big shopping center on Beradino Street, he kept thinking of, and trying not to think of, the five-spot.

He stopped at Rigoletto's and sat in a booth, fidgeting until the waitress finally dragged herself over. It was cool at least; the glare out there could practically blind you, even with sunglasses. He drank a coupla bottles of beer and then ordered another one and a ham on white. He didn't think he was really hungry but he felt better after eating it. Sometimes he wondered why he never got fat. He could always eat. Especially bread. He could live on plain white bread and wouldn't complain.

On the way out he picked up a pack of Winstons and dropped the five, sort of flipping it, on the little rubberpronged pad on the glass counter. He stashed the change in his pocket without even looking at it, then felt around for a quarter and walked back to the booth and left it for the waitress. He hated guys who didn't tip.

The Blue and White garage was one of these big underground deals, dark and cool and smelling of oil and gasoline and exhaust. He stood with the boss at the bottom of the concrete ramp and watched a coupla mechanics working on the cabs. He wouldn't have minded just hanging around awhile. But the boss told him about six hundred guys showed up first thing this morning and one already got the job.

He drove to the laundry and parked. In the yard there was a whole bunch of VW trucks painted in red and white stripes, like barber poles. He stood outside the wire fence looking at the plant, which was pretty big but all on one floor. Two big black chimneys on the roof were sending up smoke and the air had a funny smell, not like soap exactly, but like someone ironing, only stronger, like chemicals.

"Looking for something, Mac?" The guy was wearing a blue uniform and cap and he carried a clipboard over one arm and had a red and white striped badge on his shirt. No tie. Mel knew they wouldn't be wearing ties in the middle of the summer.

"Yeah. Do you know who I could see about if they need drivers?"

"Down the hallway on the left."

Mel went through this big steamy room, like a goddamn turkish bath, where a bunch of old ladies were working at pressing machines and this big nigger was pulling a rubberwheeled rack of shirts along the aisle. Then he walked along the hallway to the reception room, which was all air-conditioned and fancy, with all kinds of bright colored furniture and a girl behind the desk in a black dress with only very thin straps, what Peggy called spaghetti straps. Her arms and shoulders were all bare and her hair was heaped up in a pile with a big silver clip that had a kind of jewel in it.

"Yes?"

"The fellow outside, one of the drivers, said to come in here. I was wondering about a job, is what it is . . . I heard that maybe you had an opening somewhere for a driver."

She handed him a sheet of paper. Her fingernails were long and painted pink. He wondered what the hell she was doing all dressed up like that in an office, and somehow kind of felt sorry for her. How many people ever saw her all spiffed up like that?

"I was wondering," Mel said, "in case they don't have anything for a driver, if maybe they had anything in the mechanic line?"

"Just put down whatever you'd like to be considered for. There's a place on the form."

He printed everything very carefully. Actually, he got a kick out of filling out forms, writing down that he was 5'9" tall and weighed 142 pounds and was born in 1936 and everything. Also his printing was really good, so at the end the whole thing looked very neat.

It was question 17 on this form. He checked *yes* and printed on the lines below:

AUTO THEFT—1958—SENTENCED TO 9 MOS. AT ST. JOSEPHS INDUSTRAL SCHOOL. RELEASED AFTER SERVING 6 MOS.

BURGELRY—1961—SENTENCED TO 3 YRS. AT STATE PRISON FARM, KENSCOTT. RELEASED ON PAROLE AFTER 2 YRS. AND 3 MOS.

NOW ON PAROLE IN GOOD STANDING.

For references he gave the Warden at the Farm and Ken Muldoon at the Parole office. Some guys, of course, tried to fake it, but Muldoon told him a place that went to the trouble of having forms would probably go to the trouble of checking up, so you might as well put it all down and hope for the best.

The girl kind of glanced down both sides of the sheet and started to put it down, but then stopped, still looking at it. She tried to read the part so quickly you could tell she still hadn't got it all, but then she saw Mel watching and dropped it like a hot potato. "Yes—thank you . . . I'll see that the manager gets it when he comes in . . ."

And she was looking at him now. When he first walked in he could've had three heads and she never would've noticed. But now she was looking at him like she'd never in her whole life seen anything so goddamn interesting.

Mel pulled away with his tires screeching, the Dodge lurching first to the right, then to the left. He hit the brakes for a red light. The car strained, then tightened under him a few feet over the white line. On the cross street a squad car started slowly, the cop looking like he was trying to decide whether to bother swinging around. But he just gave Mel the eye and let it go at that.

It was almost four—Chucky would be getting up from his nap now and Peggy would be all finished cleaning up, just waiting for him to walk in so she could find out all the bad news and feel sorry for him because he didn't land nothing. Where the hell *were* the jobs?—that's what he wanted to know. Let's face it, he had about as much chance of landing a job as the man in the moon.

He went looking for Margolis.

☐

"Sure," Margolis said. "What the hell. Sit down. We'll buy you a beer."

Margolis finished his beer and the waitress brought a couple over. The place was empty but would crowd up at four thirty when the shift let out at Rohmann down the block.

"How's the sandwich business going?" Mel asked.

Margolis raised his eyebrows. He had these big heavy eyebrows. "There ain't no more sandwich business."

"I thought you was doing pretty good," Mel said.

"Times change, Mel. The world keeps spinning around."

Margolis was only twenty-six, two years younger than Mel, but looked older. He was heavier, for one thing, kind of thick through the middle and with a round face. He was also getting bald up front and spread the hairs sideways with goo, but that just made his face look rounder and even older. He looked like someone at least thirty or thirty-five. Margolis had been connected with Kroll for years now, first working here in the bar and then as a runner for the book and then eventually he got the sandwich deal, which was a very good deal. Kroll had bought off somebody in the front office at Rohmann Aircraft and also naturally the union, so had the lunch concession. Margolis would bring up the coffee and sandwiches and put in a coupla hours inside the plant at lunch time, and then again in the afternoon with coffee and doughnuts. It was hard work but Margolis made good money out of it, even though a lot of other people had to get their cuts too. Margolis also handled bets in the plant and ran the R.B.I. pool for Kroll, which was all part of the sandwich deal. And then of course he handled extra jobs for Kroll too, and in general made out. A few times Mel got in on deals with Margolis. They weren't any of them very sensational, but none of them rolled over and died either. Margolis was a very careful guy, and very thorough. The best Mel ever did with Margolis was this deal a few weeks back when they picked up fifteen Motorola TV sets from this warehouse at night, where Margolis had a contact. Mel got 107 bucks out of it.

"What're you doing these days, Mel?"

"Looking around," Mel said.

"The old lady still working nights at the bottling plant?"

Mel shrugged. "Yeah." They were quiet then, so Mel said, "I figure on lining up something pretty soon. Tell me, someone else got the sandwiches now?"

"Yeah, someone else."

Mel shrugged. Actually he wasn't exactly crazy about Margolis personally. But at least he didn't look at you like you had three heads. "While I'm looking around, you know, well, I could use a few bills. Now and then maybe you wanna stop somewheres for a beer. And the Dodge, you know—I could use a coupla tires for the Dodge."

"The rubber's no good, Mel?"

"The rubber's shitty, you wanna know how the rubber is."

"You're not interested in nothing regular?"

Mel didn't answer right away. "Nothing regular. Just something to tie me over."

"You still on parole, Mel?"

"What difference does that make?"

"How long you been out now, Mel?"

"Since January. Look, what am I supposed to do, fill out an application form?"

"Maybe something'll come up," Margolis said.

"Nothing too big," Mel said.

Margolis smiled.

"What I mean," Mel said, "is some kind of job'll turn up soon, so I ain't really in too bad shape."

"If you want something little and safe, you shoulda stood with that contractor you had there, hauling on the truck. I don't know nothing as safe as hauling sand on a truck."

"Anything safe enough for you will be safe enough for me," Mel said.

"Maybe I'll give you a ring sometime."

"Let me buy a round." Mel put down a single.

Margolis pushed it back. "We can't let the old lady pay, can we? We'll stand an old friend a coupla beers till he gets rolling, heh? Until something turns up."

□

Mel drove around a bit. It was hot as hell, naturally, with the sun blazing right down on you. You couldn't drive fast enough in the city to get any kind of breeze, so he headed north, out of Aurora on Highway 86, just to cool off. Somehow he felt kind of funny. Maybe he was hungry, he figured, so he slowed down at the bunch of gas stations and truck stops outside of town and stopped at a cafe there. It was air-conditioned at least. Everything around Aurora was air-conditioned, even the crummiest places. He sat at the edge of the counter near the side window and ordered two hamburgers and coffee. The food seemed to help, but still he felt funny, kind of very alert actually, very sharp and clear in his mind.

Through the window he watched the two guys working the Mobil station next door. "Used to work garages, gas stations a bit myself," he said to the guy behind the counter, who was leaning back dragging on a cigarette.

"Not a bad racket," the guy said. "These places out here do all right."

"Bet they do," Mel said.

The guy got busy and Mel watched the attendants in the station running around punching oil cans, wiping windshields, collecting money. He could almost smell the gas and feel the pump handle in his hand, thick and shiny and very heavy, and burning hot from the sun. He could feel the way the guy's shoulder moved when he polished a windshield with a paper towel.

An armored car pulled into the station. It kind of surprised Mel, coming out of nowhere like that, and for a minute he just stared at it with his mouth open, right on the verge of biting into his second hamburger. It was a Loomis car. It pulled past the pumps and stopped in front of the glass office. Mel put the hamburger down, lowering his hands slowly, still watching. The driver honked and one attendant left his hose in the tank of a Galaxie and hustled over. The driver, who wore a gray uniform and a pistol in a holster, followed him into the office and then came out a coupla minutes later carrying a moneybag. The attendant said something and they laughed and then the attendant went back to the pump and the driver took the money around to the back of the armored car, which Mel couldn't see, and then came back without it and got in behind the wheel.

Mel watched the armored car move slowly along the highway shoulder, past the cafe, and into the Chevron station on the other side. Mel got up and walked to the cigarette machine, which was near the window on that side. He fumbled in his pocket for change, keeping his eyes on the car as the driver went through the same procedure again and then headed for the Shell station a few hundred yards down the road.

Mel went back and finished his hamburger, but it seemed like he was just swallowing lumps now. He pushed his cup forward for more coffee.

"They sure must do all right," Mel said, motioning to the Mobil station. His voice was kind of thick and he cleared his throat, keeping his eyes on the guy's face. "They need an armored car to haul it away."

"Oh, it been by?" The guy looked at the clock on the wall. It was almost a quarter to five. "I guess so," he said. "They tried to get me to go along too, but I don't take in that kind of money."

"I guess not," Mel said.

The guy moved down the counter and Mel looked at the tab—$1.40. He put a quarter tip under his plate and left with eighty-five in his pocket.

He headed back to town. The thought of all that money in the armored car made him feel really strange, like the top of his head was just gonna float off, like he couldn't breathe, like he wasn't breathing air anymore but something so different it might leave him paralyzed, or really hopped up, or even dead.

The first thing he ever really learned about money was when he was eight or nine years old, because before that he never had more than a nickel or a dime in his hand at one time. But down the block a chink had this grocery that he worked alone and every night went out back to dump his garbage, just before he closed up at night. One night Mel charged in while the chink was out back and grabbed some bills from the register without looking at them and bolted before the chink ever laid eyes on him. When he stopped running he saw he had a twenty and a ten and two singles, and the first thing that hit him was how glad he was he picked up the two singles. They were real money. A kid could walk in a store and buy something with a single.

He blew the singles that night but carried the ten and twenty around in his pocket for days, wondering what the hell he could do with them. He thought of giving them to his mother, or even his old man, because the hell, they could've used it. But the old man would've just belted the shit out of him, because if there was one thing he couldn't stand it was any kind of wise-guy stuff. So Mel finally traded them off with an older kid he knew for five singles, which he spent but couldn't remember anymore what for.

He was driving like a bat out of hell but couldn't get himself to slow down. He was back in town now and was afraid he'd get picked up the way he was driving, or ram into something. He wasn't even watching. He wasn't even sure where he was. At the next corner he stopped to look. He turned right and drove downtown.

□

"Maybe," Margolis said.

"More than maybe," Mel said.

"Only just before you were so careful and everything. All you wanted was something small and safe. Now suddenly you wanna—"

"Because it's just sitting there waiting for us," Mel said. "I mean, Christ, we can't miss."

"I don't know," Margolis said. He held his Coors bottle up to the light and then poured what was left into his glass. There were a few guys in other booths but no one close. "I mean, are you figuring on packing some weight in this thing?"

"Guns?" Mel said. "We don't need no guns. Nobody mentioned guns. All we gotta do is figure out which station there pulls in the most. The truck comes a little before five. We move in, say, at four and pick up their whole haul for the last twenty-four hours. Some of them stations must gross a coupla thousand a day."

"But no guns?"

"What the hell do we need guns for? We just grab the dough and scram."

"You make it sound too simple."

"Look, you interested or not? I came because I figured you'd be interested. If not, I can find someone else."

"Something like this can get very complicated."

"Not if we don't let it. The hell, it'll be complicated to find us too. Those stations are all under two miles from town. I clocked it. And then there's a hundred different streets you can go on. I mean, you pull away from a warehouse with a truckload of TV's, and you're a sitting duck. And for what?—a coupla bills, tops. This'll get us a thousand each."

"I don't think that much," Margolis said.

"Look, I worked gas stations. I know what kind of business they do."

"I'll have to think about it."

"Well, I wanna know pretty soon."

"Sure. Anyhow, you say this tin can stops at all the stations out there?"

"Well, we could find out which ones for sure, but I think all of them. So all we gotta do is pick the one that looks best."

"Yeah. Well, I'll be thinking about it."

"All right. You let me know then."

"I'll let you know," Margolis said.

☐

He wasn't exactly keen on going home, but let's face it, what were you gonna do with eighty-five cents in your pocket? So he went home, and Peggy practically leaped all over him the minute he walked in the door. And what the hell it was when she finally calmed down enough to get it out was that the secretary from the laundry called, saying Mel should come down tomorrow morning because the boss, for Christ's sake, wanted to talk to him about a goddamn job.

Johnny chose a tie from his rack and knotted it before the full-length mirror, then picked out a sport coat. The closet held more than a dozen sport coats, perhaps two dozen slacks, eight or ten suits. Most he'd bought within the last four months. Before then he hadn't needed much of a wardrobe. Now he needed an even larger one, and added to it every week.

It'd been a problem finding a store in Aurora that carried his size. Being six-foot five meant not only that beds were never long enough, tables high enough or theater seats roomy enough, meant not only that you had to duck through doorways and stoop to sinks and bump your knees on steering wheels and give up short girls. It also meant you had to cultivate the sympathies of a local clothier. He had, and Kale's Men's Department now stocked 42 extra long.

He left the apartment and walked down the flight of stairs. It was ten thirty in the morning. The enclosed grass courtyard was shielded from the street by oleander hedges; on the other three sides it was bordered by the two-story apartment block. The walls were pink, the terrace railings white. The courtyard had a palm tree at each corner and a small swimming pool in the center. In Aurora, all apartment blocks had lawns and swimming pools. Those who came to Aurora, either as residents or winter tourists, expected swimming pools, demanded lawns: an unconscious distrust of the desert—a yearning for the reassurance of water and green growth, prompted by visions of gasping prospectors on hands and knees, cattle bones bleaching in the sun.

The visions, however, hadn't kept too many people away, nor had the fact that summer temperatures regularly broke one hundred degrees. But with air conditioning the hot, dry, unvarying desert climate became bearable, and the population of the city, having tripled since World War II, was now close to 300,000.

Downstairs Mrs. Warnsell was pulling a huge wheelbarrow full of garden tools across the lawn, like some industrious insect exhibiting its strength under glass. The sun was already oppressive, and she was no doubt sweating. Frail, small-boned, almost a miniature, Mrs. Warnsell was a woman who would sweat, if for no other reason, just to make bigger and stronger people feel lazy. But she was not a bad landlady, everything considered. She kept the place clean, asked a rent somewhat this side of outrage, and straightened up his apartment everyday without savoring any more personal papers than an experienced tenant had to expect.

"Good morning, Mr. Mancino!"

He waved over to her as he headed for the front.

"I'll be watching you again today," she called out, almost sternly, as if it were a threat. "I watch you every day." She twisted a faucet and halfway across the lawn a fine mist cascaded into the air, and the grass beneath it glistened.

☐

At twelve noon Johnny was sitting beside Madge in the flooding glare at the curved desk, waiting to go on.

"I see Hi-Valu's moved up to the second break," Madge said.

"Right," Johnny said. "And the safety spot's a VTR. I'll cue it in if you want."

"Okay."

"Stand by," the floorman called, touching his earphone. "Coming out on two."

The rush of the studio air conditioner stopped. The monitor dissolved to gray and then, as the theme music began, brisk and cheerful, the title appeared: caricature faces of a man and a woman, distorted by exaggerated smiles, with "Noonday" printed diagonally between them, and "Madge and Johnny" scripted across the bottom.

The floorman, standing between the two cameras with his clipboard, raised his right hand with his forefinger extended. He sliced at camera two as the red light on the machine glowed.

Seated behind his microphone, Johnny nodded soberly to the camera and made a little offhand gesture, not quite a wave. Madge came on smiling.

"Hello everyone! This is Madge Watson . . ."

". . . and Johnny Mancino . . ."

". . . welcoming you to 'Noonday,' a little bit of brightness and a little bit of fun . . ."

The show went well—as well as ever. He did his job; he was pleasant, he was informal, he kept things moving. The studio audience—ten or fifteen women soundlessly sealed off behind the long glass window on the studio wall—seemed to enjoy it, and the women at home probably did too. The sales department thought highly of "Noonday," which was doing considerably better now than when Johnny started on it four months ago. The mail was also good. (*Dear Johnny, I watch you every day and like especially the way you bring out all the interesting sidelights about your guests and the products you advertise and very amusing way about everything, please keep it up as I don't get out as much as I used to and appreciate everything very much. . . .*)

Today they had on a Salvation Army colonel and Nancy Meredith. The colonel talked about the Grand Old Army's new center on Hastings Street. He had come prepared to cite the square footage of each new room, hall and broom closet, and seemed determined to do so, with a bewildered, slightly apoplectic expression, as if his military collar were steel and had been bolted to his spine. Pleasantly, Johnny cut him off after eight minutes.

To Nancy Meredith he gave twenty. She was in town for only a few days and when Johnny called her yesterday she said she'd be too busy to make the show. But then Johnny phoned her studio in Hollywood and an hour later she called back to say she'd changed her mind.

She turned out to be very blonde, with long legs and a little girl's face and a low-cut dress.

Madge gloried a bit over her hairdo and her outfit and then Johnny got her to reminisce about her experience in the theater, her discovery by Hollywood, and her first two pictures, neither of which Johnny had seen.

"But truly, Johnny, I think this new one's going to be the one that will—well, you know—make it for me. I'm just in love with the script; really, it's just fabulous."

"And what's it called again?"

"Oh yes—let's get the plug in. It's called *Ranch Triple-X*—you know, three X's, it's the brand of this ranch, you see—and I play the part of a very *young* widow left alone on this ranch way back in the 1880s, and the whole film's going to be shot on location right around here, with all this lovely scenery and . . ."

The Salvation Army colonel, sitting rigidly on a little wooden chair back by the curtain, behind the cameras, watched intently, somewhat grimly, as if trying to learn how it was done, what the secret was that rewarded him with eight minutes and her with twenty.

They signed off at 12:44.

This is Madge Watson . . .

. . . and Johnny Mancino saying . . .

. . . it's been fun—and . . .

. . . see you tomorrow.

Have a great day everyone! Be good!

The kliegs browned and went out. The air conditioner started, moving the air immediately, chilling it.

"It was all right, wasn't it?" Madge said.

"It was fine," Johnny said. He bent down and kissed her on the cheek. "You were great."

The cameramen were rolling their machines back, kicking the big cables out of the way. There wouldn't be another local show until four, when "Kiddie Korner" came on. Johnny nodded to the cameramen, to the floorman, thinking *I deserve better; everyone deserves better.*

□

Johnny's schedule gave him an hour and fifteen minutes a day on KSUN-TV—forty-five on "Noonday" and thirty on his six o'clock newscast. At four that afternoon he began work on the news, going over the copy from the AP wire and their own reporters, then getting together with the editor and the producer in the projection room to time and cue in the network and local films and the stills. When they finished at five fifteen, the others went home. If anything broke at the last minute, Johnny would work it in himself.

He returned to his office, a cramped room that he shared with the news editor and the fellow who did "Kiddie Korner." A big bulletin board was covered haphazardly, everything overlapping, with old notices, cartoons clipped from somewhere by someone years ago, postcards, a sign that said THIS IS THE WAY TO GO, an envelope addressed to one of the other newscasters with his name incredibly misspelled, a list of instructions entitled IN CASE OF AIR DISASTER, a picture of a cactus drawn by someone's kid, stickers, posters, mimeo sheets, reminders, notes, publicity photos. Johnny got a sheet of paper from his desk and went down the hall to Arlanson's office.

"Hi, Johnny . . . I was just taking off. Is it anything pressing?"

Johnny dropped the paper on Arlanson's desk and sat in the leather armchair.

Arlanson studied the paper. He was small but solidly built. He wore a light blue suit with a narrow tie; even when he was sitting his suits always hung right, looked neat. He had a thin, graying mustache and steady eyes. "Yes, well what is it, Johnny? What's up?"

"That's three full weeks of a little bit of brightness and a little bit of fun all scheduled out there."

"So I see."

"I generally work two weeks ahead, but thought you'd like some leeway."

"It's been a long day, Johnny. I'm ready to go home and I need a chilled drink, full of energy and alcohol. Let's just say what we have to say, all right?"

"I'd like you to get someone to take over 'Noonday.' I've set it up three weeks ahead so the guy can step right in. I know it won't be easy to find someone as perfectly suited as the man you have, but if you're not committed to his being six-five and pure of heart, you might manage."

Arlanson made a little movement with the left side of his mouth. He touched the tab of the silver case on his desk; the cover popped up. "Cigarette?" Johnny shook his head; Arlanson lit up. "I see," he said. He paused. "I take it you're not interested in a raise."

"Not on 'Noonday.'"

"Maybe we could change it a bit—vary the format. . . ."

"No."

"What is it you want?"

"Something in the evening."

"What kind of something?"

"A news and feature show. Interviews, background on local stories, some treatment in depth, maybe an occasional series of shows on a single subject. But no housewifey stuff."

"We tried it a few years ago. It was a disaster."

"Maybe you didn't have the right man for it."

"Give me some time to think this over. It's too late in the day to make decisions."

"I'll drop back tomorrow morning," Johnny said.

"No—give me something on paper first—the kind of material you'd use, the things you'd be talking about. Do you have any ideas?"

"I've got some ideas."

"Good, let's see them. And if it doesn't work out, there's always 'Kid-die Korner.'"

"It'll work out," Johnny said.

3

This time the all-dressed-up-with-nowhere-to-go girl was wearing a skirt and a white blouse with ruffles in front so you couldn't see through.

Mel waited on the orange couch and tried to decide if he should look through the pile for a magazine or just take the *Time* on top that had some king or other from some country in Asia on the cover, or skip the whole thing and just sit there drumming his fingers. He didn't realize he was drumming his fingers. He stopped.

What the hell was he doing here anyhow?

The girl started to erase something and just then, when it was very quiet, a door banged open right next to the couch and Mel jumped like he'd been shot.

"Simmons?" the man said. "Come on in."

Mel took the chair the man waved at. He put his hands on his lap and tried to breathe very slow and when he had to say something he wouldn't sound winded. He straightened out his suit jacket. That was Peggy's idea, naturally, the goddamn suit. She even made him wait so she could press it, but let's face it, it still looked like something just this side of a rag pile.

The man sat in a big padded chair and leaned back, looking at him across his desk about the size of a football field, and then said, "I see you put in for a routeman's job. But that offers problems, of course, with the bonding company."

Mel nodded.

"Your record really isn't so bad, though. The main point, it seems to me, is whether or not you're ready to settle down and do some hard work for a change."

"Yes sir," Mel said, and it hardly sounded like him talking. "I really would."

"I'm not in the business of rehabilitating people, you know. But if you're willing to work, maybe we could use you."

"Sure," Mel said. "That's what I'm looking for. Work."

"Okay," the guy said. "As far as I'm concerned your record's a thing of the past. I'll trust you as much as anyone else, no more, no less. What I have is an opening for a sorter. It's hard work, loading and unloading, and it has to be done carefully. We pay $1.40 to start. Every three months you're eligible for a raise during your first year, every six months thereafter. Within a year you should be around $1.75, and after that we'll see. Are you interested?"

"Yes sir, I really am."

"Okay, you start tomorrow, eight o'clock. Ask for Mr. Coffey, he's the foreman. And bring some work clothes."

□

Christ, he was working with a nigger! There he was—black as the ace of spades and big as a bull. His polo shirt was all sweated up and his arms were black and shiny and about as thick as a tree stump.

"Jerrold, we got you a partner here," Coffey said when they came out to the platform where the nigger was working in the sun, hauling laundry bags off one of those VW's painted like barber poles. "Name's Mel Simmons. Mel, this is Jerrold Banks."

"Glad meetcha," Jerrold said. He had this deep gravelly voice that sounded like he was talking inside a box. His face didn't seem to show much feelings one way or the other.

"Same here," Mel said. Mel didn't have nothing against niggers, and in some ways even felt sorry for how they always got the wrong end of the stick. So it wasn't working with a nigger that bothered him. It was just that maybe he was *replacing* one.

When Coffey left Jerrold said, "You ain't done this before, heh?"

"No I ain't," Mel said. "I'll catch on though." He waited a minute, then said, trying to make it sound offhand, "Are you sort of head man out here then?"

"Coffey head man. I'll just show you what we do. Ain't hard once you get on it."

"I'm stronger than I look anyhow," Mel said.

So all morning Mel followed Jerrold around, getting the word. Actually there was a lot to remember, and if you weren't careful you could really screw things up. The hardest part was unloading. You had to lug these gigantic laundry bags in to the sorting table and then break each bag down into customer piles and each customer pile into section piles for the different parts of the plant. Loading was easier, just getting the right bundles on the right trucks. But what with trucks coming and going all day long, you really kept hopping.

Actually, Jerrold seemed all right, and not really too dumb, and Mel figured they'd get along. When Jerrold mentioned the guy who used to be his partner, Mel tried to figure out from how he talked whether the guy was a nigger or not, but couldn't.

□

That night he was beat. Christ, those laundry bags weighed a ton, and by the time Mel got home and grabbed a can of beer and flopped down he couldn't lift a bag of marshmallows.

He would've just gone to bed only he kept waiting for Peggy to go first, so she'd be asleep when he came in. Because let's face it, he was in no shape for anything tonight. But she was all cheerful and cozy and whenever he'd mention offhand about her hitting the sack so she wouldn't be so exhausted when she got up for work, because she had to get up at 3 A.M. for Christ's sake, she'd just shrug and say she felt fine. What it was, she was all hopped up about the job. It was all she wanted to talk about, what a great deal it was for him, and how happy he oughta be, finding such a sensational big-time job.

Of course the main reason she felt so great was *she* was the one that found it. Still Mel didn't want to spoil it for her by complaining, so he tried to keep up a good front.

"Sure," he said. "I think maybe it's gonna turn out all right."

"And the people are so nice, you said. That's really something, you know. Ella says her husband says the nicest thing about working there is all the nice people."

"Oh yeah," Mel said, keeping his eye on the TV. "Sure. The people are real nice."

Finally Peggy gave up and went to bed, and after waiting awhile to make sure she wasn't just laying in wait for him, he dragged himself to bed and went off like he was shot. Except he didn't really sleep too good, what with everything sore and aching, and all night long he kept waking up with these crazy dreams.

□

The next day he could hardly move. Shit, Jerrold didn't knock himself
out, so why should he? Only when he kept down to Jerrold's pace, the
time really dragged. Niggers, of course, were used to working that way,
kind of draggy and big-assed. They were born to it, it was their natural
pace. But it just made Mel itchy, because he liked to keep things moving, which was *his* natural pace.

"This ain't really my line of work, you know," he explained to Jerrold during lunch hour, mainly to have something to talk about, because Jerrold was about as big a talker as the nearest rock you could
kick. Mel brought along a cheese sandwich and a thermos of coffee and
some peanut butter cookies, and ate with Jerrold, the two of them sitting on the sorting table with their legs dangling over, surrounded by
laundry bags and wheelers full of dirty clothes. "Basically, I mean,
what I'm trained for is a mechanic."

"That so?" Jerrold said, chewing away. Jerrold chewed like he
worked, like a goddamn cow in a field, like he had nine hundred years
to live and nothing much pressing to do along the way. He was finishing the last of these three gigantic sandwiches he had in a paper sack,
and his third lemon and lime.

"Yeah. Lotta experience at it too—garages and stuff."

"Good line of work, I spect," Jerrold said after thinking it over for
five or six minutes.

"Oh yeah. One of the best, really, if you're good at it. Only you gotta
have tools, you see."

"Spect you do." Jerrold mulled this over for a bit too, and then said,
"Don't you have no tools?"

"Well, not any more, you see. Course I had a real good set at one
time, when I was working regular at it. But, you know. Things happen.
Maybe someday I figure I can get back in it."

Jerrold nodded, then picked at his tooth with a fingernail for a spell.

Mel finished his coffee and cookies and stretched out on the big table. He put his hands behind his head for a pillow. "How long you been
doing this, Jerrold?"

"Bout a year, I guess. Bout that."

"Like it?"

You got the feeling Jerrold never really considered the question before, and that it was a real toughie. "Not a bad job," he said finally.
"Course I ain't really trained in no special line of work."

"You oughta get yourself some training, Jerrold. I mean, it's none of my business, but a big strong guy like you, with a head on his shoulders . . . you could probably do real good with some special training. The hell, you gotta work for things, keep your eyes open."

"Pretty good work here," Jerrold said. And then he added, in what was a real burst of gab for him, "Used to be sweep-up inside. Year, two years. Then Coffey put me out here."

"Moved you up, eh? Well, that's all right, Jerrold. That's moving in the right direction."

Jerrold nodded, that big black head of his going up and down like a goddamn slow-motion movie. "Tain't bad work, really."

☐

Thursday Mel was supposed to report in to Ken Muldoon, which he usually did by going down to the Parole office. But of course he couldn't, seeing he had a job, so he asked Jerrold to cover him for a few minutes because he had a personal call to make and sneaked out to the phone booth down the block. Muldoon naturally thought it was great about him having the job.

"I can't tell you how pleased I am, Mel."

"Well yeah—I mean, I'm pleased too. Although the work ain't easy, of course, and you gotta keep jumping."

"Well, stick to it, Mel. I know you can handle it."

"Oh sure," Mel said. "I can handle it all right. There's no problem at all handling it."

☐

And it was true. By Saturday Mel had the routine down cold and didn't ache anymore either. But let's face it, he was bored out of his skull, and could see where he'd really go bughouse if he had to keep doing this the rest of his life.

Just before quitting time Coffey brought the pay, a bunch of envelopes standing in a shoe box. "Here it is," he said, picking out Jerrold's and then Mel's. "Nice clean money, fresh from the laundry."

Mel tore off the top and dumped everything in his hand. Since he only started Wednesday, what he got was four days' pay. After all the goddamn deductions, it came to $37.40.

Which wasn't too bad, really. For a full week he figured he'd take home better than fifty, which meant between him and Peggy they'd be clearing close to ninety, more than double what they had now, even with what they had to pay the lady to take care of Chucky every morning.

He felt pretty good, almost a little hopped up. So he dropped in at Western Auto and bought a chrome tail pipe for the Dodge, because it was rotting away under there and one of these days was gonna just drop off like a ripe banana. It came to $4.98 and he picked up a chrome extension for just another 98 cents. He also got a right rear-view mirror. "Fender or window mount," it said on the box. "Jet-styled for any car." Which was really some joke for the goddamn Dodge, but it was only $2.88 on special, and he figured it was worth the price just for the safety alone.

Christ, maybe the old heap could be fixed up after all. Because if you could just keep it running and not have to buy a new one, all these things you bought really saved you money in the long run.

The bill came to $9.11, what with tax and everything. What the hell did they do with all that tax money anyhow?

Peggy wouldn't even notice anything except maybe the mirror, although he wouldn't bet on that either. It killed him how Peggy never noticed anything about the car except that if you waited long enough the red light always turned green.

Anyhow, now that he had a job, Peggy wouldn't be using the car so much, because he'd need it, so she'd be riding to work with Ella what's-her-name.

Mel locked the stuff in the trunk and put another dime in the meter and walked down two blocks to Kale's. He really felt pretty good.

Kale's had four floors altogether and covered almost a whole block. Peggy shopped there a lot because their prices were okay and you could charge without getting a hard time.

"Go ahead, try one on," a salesman with a funny little mustache said. Mel was just looking at some lightweight suits on special for $34.99 when the guy popped up out of nowhere.

"I'm really only just looking," Mel explained.

"That's okay. You're about a 36 regular, eh? Here, try this one, see how it looks."

Mel went into the little cubby and put the suit on. It was light tan, which he figured would be very cool because it would reflect the sun.

"Like a glove," the man said when Mel came out.

Mel turned one way then the other in front of the three-view mirror. He needed a haircut in the back. The suit looked real good, though, and fit perfectly. Things always fit him good because he kept himself in shape. He wasn't very big or anything, but solid, and very trim.

"Terrific," the salesman said.

"Yeah," Mel said. "Not bad." And the hell, it was Peggy, after all, who was always bitching about him getting dressed up. When he was younger, before he got married and everything, he always dressed real good. Because people noticed. When you looked good, you felt good. You had more confidence.

He asked the salesman to charge it and left it to have the cuffs put on.

In the toy department he paid cash. He got Chucky a little cannon on a string that when you pulled it along it went *Pow! Pow!* and only cost $1.49.

He took the escalator and walked past all the plastic models without arms wearing brassieres.

"A lounging robe, you mean?" the lady said.

"Well, yeah. I mean, like a bathrobe . . ."

It came to $8.88, plus tax.

"Hey, Peggy! Chucky! Where are you? Surprises!" He stepped into the living room with the packages and Chucky came running in from the kitchen with Peggy right behind him. She kind of hesitated at first, but then turned all smiles, just beaming from ear to ear.

☐

Sunday morning after dropping Peggy at church, Mel worked on the Dodge in front of the house, in an old baseball cap to keep the sun out of his eyes and no shirt. Chucky played on the dirt sidewalk with the cannon while Mel installed the side-view mirror and hosed down the car. It felt good working around like that. Maybe one of these days he'd see if he couldn't get to use some tools down at Bingham's Texaco when they weren't busy and give the old heap a little tune-up, which Christ knows it could use. When he finished drying down the car he had to pick up Peggy, so he let the tail pipe go for another time.

"Hey," Peggy said. "You washed the car."

"Yeah," Mel said. "It really needed it." He waited a minute, then said, "I picked up a mirror for the right-hand side too."

"Oh yeah!" she said, noticing it for the first time. "Gee, that looks real nice." But you could see that iffy look come over her face, and practically hear the old adding machine clacking away inside her head.

"I got it real cheap," he said. "It's worth it just for the safety alone."

That afternoon they went on a picnic, which Mel suggested because he knew Peggy really liked picnics. It was too hot naturally on the desert, so they drove up on the San Juan Mountain and stopped at the first picnic area after the pine trees, which was maybe four thousand feet up. Mel didn't want to push the Dodge too much on any twisty mountain road.

There were about twenty tables near a little stream. Mel started a charcoal fire and Peggy grilled the franks, and for dessert they toasted marshmallows. Then Mel opened another beer and sat with Peggy on a blanket and watched Chucky playing in the stream. Mel was really impressed at how big Chucky was getting. He was still pretty skinny but he'd get his muscles before too long. Mel of course was a pretty fair ballplayer himself, and the first time he saw the kid, which was when Chucky was already over a year old because he was born while Mel was at the Farm, he could see he was gonna be a regular chip off the old block, with really good coordination and everything, and strong for his size.

Mel drank the beer and they talked about the kind of house they'd like. It was funny, but they never talked about houses except on Sundays. Anyhow, it felt good just shooting the breeze and taking it easy after working all week.

Peggy was sitting with her bare legs straight out and her arms stretched back with her hands on the blanket and the hell, she was still a lot better looking than nine-tenths of what you saw around. She really was, she was a real sweet-looking girl, which was how he remembered her looking when they used to go together. The pink shorts really did things for her legs and her blouse was pulled tight from leaning back and, well, Peggy had a figure, there was no arguing about that. Christ, it'd been a long time, what with one thing and another and him being so bushed all week from working on the platform, and he felt a little sad thinking about it.

"Hey, you know what?"

"What?" Peggy said. She'd been watching Chucky throwing rocks in the water.

"Maybe tonight after Chucky goes to bed we can send out for some pizza and beer and maybe watch some TV together. I mean, you know —it's Sunday and you don't have to go in, and we're not all so bushed and everything . . ."

She smiled and nodded quickly.

He pulled her down on the blanket and kissed her, soft at first but then real hard. But then she made him stop because of Chucky and everybody around, and they laughed because that was just how she'd been when they were going together, worried about people seeing them. Anyhow, Chucky hadn't even noticed. He was busy looking for another rock to throw.

☐

The way it turned out, they didn't send for pizza. Peggy said she wasn't really hungry and besides was trying to watch her weight. So she made a hamburger for Mel because the hell, *he* was hungry.

They were watching Ed Sullivan, who had on some foreign comedian with an accent you could cut with a knife that they flew over special after playing for all the kings and queens of Europe. He was supposed to be practically the funniest man alive, but Mel wasn't convinced. Instead of paying attention he somehow started thinking about how this was Sunday night already and figuring how many hours before he'd be back on the goddamn platform. Eleven, he figured. And nine and a half before he'd have to wake up for it. It seemed like he just *left* the goddamn place.

And this week he'd have six straight days of it, one after another, shagging ass back and forth hauling laundry bags.

And then Peggy started in on the goddamn beauty parlor business again. "You know, Ella said yesterday if I was really interested in that beautician school, maybe she'd go too. That way we could kinda go together."

"Well, you ain't interested," Mel said.

"But gee, Mel, they make terrific money. Ella knows this woman that pulls down a hundred a week."

"What is it with this Ella? She got nothing to do? She gotta spend all her time giving free advice about jobs for other people?"

"But Mel—it worked out just great for you, didn't it? I mean, you said so yourself, it's a terrific job."

"What's that supposed to do, make Ella some kind of genius? Look, I know what these schools are like. They take you for every penny you're worth. Besides, by the time you're finished you won't need a job anymore. I mean, you're not gonna spend your whole life getting up at three in the morning to work in a bottling plant. Your job's to stay home and take care of Chucky."

So that ended that. But then Peggy dragged up something else. The suit. She was just wondering, she said, if he still had the bill because she wanted to figure out the week's money and didn't remember the exact amount. Which was a lot of bull. When it came to money, Peggy had a mind like a steel trap. She could tell you what she paid for a box of Kleenexes back when Christ was a corporal.

"No, I don't have the bill no more, as a matter of fact," Mel said.

"Do you remember what it came to? About, I mean."

"About thirty dollars, I guess. I don't know."

"Well, don't get angry. It's just I gotta figure out what's due this week."

"Do you gotta figure it out now? I thought we were watching TV. I mean, that was my distinct impression."

They watched. Ed Sullivan was congratulating the comedian and saying how lucky all the poor slobs in America were that this guy was white enough to come over and let them see his stuff.

And then, all of a sudden, Mel realized he was just exhausted. He felt like he'd been worked over with a lead pipe. Christ, Sundays really killed you. You didn't do a lousy single thing all day long and you are bushed.

Peggy must've felt bad for starting in about the suit, because suddenly she was smiling at him and being cute. She leaned against him and he could feel she wasn't wearing any brassiere under the robe he bought her.

"I gotta go to the john," he said and hopped up.

But when he got back he just couldn't face it. He just couldn't. You spend your whole day driving up the goddamn mountains, giving up the one chance you had all week to watch the ball game, talking your head off just trying to be nice, just trying to keep everything on an even keel, and then it just turned to shit, just like that. He didn't know what it was but he'd explode if he didn't get out.

"I forgot," he said. "There's a poker game tonight I gotta go to. I promised."

She just looked at him.

"I forgot to mention it," he said. "But I promised."

Finally she said, "Where's the money?"

"The money? I got most of it," Mel said, very calm, very easy and friendly. After all, there wasn't anything to get worked up about. He made a promise, that's all, so he had to go. "I spent a little on the picnic stuff but—"

"Leave it here."

"Well now, wait a minute," Mel said. "After all, I worked for that money, you know. I worked my head off all week for that goddamn money."

"Don't I work for mine? Just leave it here, that's all. Then you can get wherever the hell you want."

"Now don't talk like that, Peggy," Mel said, real calm and easy again, keeping everything under control.

"Just leave the money here."

"Now look, I gotta have something to put on the table, you know. I mean, you can't go into a game if you don't have—"

"You're gonna spend it on some lousy slut."

"Peggy!"

"What d'ya think, I'm some kind of dope? Where the hell you been getting it? Tell me. Not around here, that's for sure."

"Aw c'mon now, Peg. What're you talking about?"

"You know what I'm talking about. What are you scared of? Are you sick or something? Can't you do it anymore? Can't you even—"

He grabbed her, not really hard, just to make her stop. She let out a little cry and jumped up clawing at him. She was trying to get at his eyes and was so wild he had to throw her back down on the couch. He broke for the door.

"Bastard!" she yelled. "Goddamn bastard!"

□

Mel called just about everybody he could think of. He was still pretty worked up, but by the time he hit pay dirt he was feeling a little better and explained—to Winnie, because it was Winnie who came through—that he wouldn't be too much of a drag on their juice because he'd already been to another party first.

"Broke up pretty early, didn't it?"

"Well no—I mean, it's after ten. But it was a dead crowd so I ditched them."

"All right then, come on if you want."

Winnie worked as a check-out at Safeway's and lived for a while with one of the guys who used to work at Bingham's Texaco, but Mel didn't know who she was shacking up with now. She had an apartment in back of a duplex and about a dozen cars were parked on the street when he got there. He could hear the party from the sidewalk. It was a very clear night, with a lot of stars. You could smell the flowers and everything.

He wondered if Dolin would be at the party. He'd called Dolin first because that's what he really felt like doing, showing Dolin a real time. Sometimes back when he used to go with her, and sometimes even now, he'd just be not thinking of anything in particular and he'd see himself with Dolin with a wad of bills in his pocket and dressed to kill and driving some real flashy sports car, and just knocking her eye out.

Only he didn't get any answer when he called Dolin earlier. Stevie and some of the others didn't answer either. Maybe the whole gang was at the party.

No one heard him knocking so he let himself in. The kitchen was so crowded and noisy no one even noticed him. Everyone was talking to someone else and he didn't see anybody he knew. You lost contact when you got married, because very few of the crowd were married. They were mostly just people who worked somewhere or other and hung out at the Rialto. They used to go bowling too when Mel was in the crowd. He didn't know if they did anymore.

The living room was just as mobbed, and some record was blasting away so everybody was shouting at the top of their lungs.

"Hey, there you are," Winnie said.

"How's it going, kid? You're looking good."

"You don't look too bad yourself. Ain't seen you around much."

"I been around," Mel said. "Good crowd you got here. Nice bunch." And Christ, it was true. Those were the days, with the old gang. You had fun, at least. You had something to think about once in a while besides all the goddamn bills you owed.

"Yeah, well dig in. Glad you made it."

"Yeah," Mel said as she moved off. "Lucky I called, I guess."

Actually it wasn't the world's greatest party. Mel hung around in the kitchen, slugging the beer and keeping an eye peeled for some of the old gang. Finally around midnight he spotted Stevie and practically trampled a dozen people getting over to him.

"What d'ya say there, Mel? Christ, where you been keeping yourself?"

"Around," Mel said. "Here and there. How you been doing?"

"Okay. Right now I'm cracking out, though."

"You heading anywhere? I wouldn't mind a little something."

"You tied up?"

"Well no," Mel said. "No I ain't."

"Yeah. Well, me and Mike Hutchins got a little something going. I mean, maybe one of them's got a friend."

"Well, sure," Mel said.

"You wait here, I'll sound them out. You got a few bills on you?"

"Sure," Mel said. "I got a few bills."

□

The six of them rode over to the Rialto in Stevie's Buick and got a big circular booth. The girl Mel got was Reena McKay, which was all right because even if she wouldn't exactly knock your eye out at least she wasn't a total stranger. Besides, she was kind of a kook with sort of orange-colored hair who played everything pretty loose. Anyway, she was all right.

Mel was telling her some pretty raw jokes and feeling her leg under the table. He got pretty worked up and Christ he was ready for it, and figured he could score if he just kept boozing her up because she had the reputation of not being exactly impossible to put on her back. He tried to remember the guys Reena used to run around with. She'd been married or something a coupla times too. She was no chicken but she had a good build. She wore a tight, low-cut dress, kind of shiny and greenish.

"Hey, what're you looking at?"

"The scenery," Mel said, giving her a wink. "Can't a guy look at the scenery?"

"Sure," she said. "Looking's free. Ain't that what they say?"

The band kept blasting away and Reena wanted to dance, so they did. He didn't mind the idea of rubbing up against her. He was really hot.

"Hey, whatcha gonna do, run a flag up it?" Reena said.

Mel laughed but stayed in close.

They had some more drinks and danced and the time went very fast, everything kind of woozy and loud and very fast.

On the ride back Reena sat on Mel's lap in the back seat and he got in some good feels. She was pretty much flaked out actually.

They stood on the sidewalk leaning together with their arms around each other.

"Hey, thanks," Mel yelled to Stevie.

Stevie pulled away and Mel eased Reena into the Dodge, then hurried around and got in himself. Reena leaned over against him and he started sliding one hand across the front of her dress, feeling for her nipples but mostly feeling just her brassiere. She bent one leg on top of his leg, so he put his hand under her dress.

"Let's go somewheres, all right?" he said. His voice was real hoarse. "Can we go to your place?"

She was squirming around on his hand and felt very hot and damp. "No," she said, kind of dreamy. "Your place."

Mel blinked. It took him a minute to catch on. Christ, she didn't even know he was married! "Why can't we go to yours?"

"Girlfriend lives there too."

"We'll go out in the desert a bit," Mel said. "C'mon."

The motor whined and groaned, turning over and over. It sounded like a dying cat. He waited and tried again. "Son of a bitch!"

Reena had her head on his shoulder and her eyes were closed. Her dress was practically up around her stomach.

Mel let the battery rest a minute. If the goddamn Dodge conked out now he'd put a match to it. He'd burn its frigging guts out.

He tried again. It almost started, but then coughed and died. He kept trying but the battery just got weaker and weaker and you could smell the goddamn gas. "Let's get out of here." He hopped out and went around and pulled her out. She didn't seem crazy about the idea, but he dragged her along. "I made a mistake," he said. "That was the wrong car."

He didn't wanna touch any car right near Winnie's because they might be leaving the party any minute. He picked a '64 Pontiac Laurentian with the buttons up a few houses down. He put Reena in and then got in himself, being very quiet on the doors. Reena just put her head back and died on the spot. She didn't know if she was coming or going.

He crossed the wires and drove away real quiet and headed north along Passmore Boulevard. There wasn't much traffic and he made good time. Actually, he was flying. The Pontiac moved along like a charm, swaying nice and soft on the curves. He always liked Pontiacs.

The desert was real dark and the few trees looked just like black globs but you could see the big cactuses pretty clear and the mountains of course, dark and far away and very cold looking. There weren't any houses so he pulled to the side and broke contact and just sat for a few minutes looking around at the instrument panel and the seat covers, which were leopard skin.

He put his arm around Reena and gave her a squeeze. He was a little dizzy but otherwise all right, and very hot. "Hey . . . wake up," he said quietly. "We're here."

She opened her eyes and stared up at him. Her eyes were wide open but blank.

She's wondering who I am! Mel thought suddenly. *She's trying to figure out what the hell my name is!*

"Hi," she said finally. Her voice was pretty thick. "Where are we?"

"Out a ways." Mel started sliding his hand along her thigh, slowly and not too hard.

"In the desert?"

"Well, kinda. But no one's around, don't worry. We're off the hell by our lonesome."

She was quiet a minute, then said, "I don't wanna get out in the desert."

"It's all right. There's no one around."

"You crazy? There's rattlesnakes out there. We'll fall into a cactus or something."

Mel held his hand where it was, on her knee, and looked at her. "Well, where the hell we gonna go then?"

"Just stay like this. Nice and comfy . . ."

"C'mon," Mel said. "Cut it. I don't want no just playing around."

She shrugged. She wasn't sore though, because at first when he put his hand between her legs she squeezed them together so he couldn't move between all that meat, but then she made a little sound and swung her knees wide and he cupped his hand right over her muff.

"Maybe the back seat," she said, still sounding pretty dreamy.

"I gotta have room. I'm all hot. I need a lotta room."

"There's room."

"All right," he said. "All right."

She got into the back seat and he pushed her down and slid his hand inside the top of her dress and got under her brassiere. "Hey," she said. "Easy now! Let's take off the dress, all right!" But he pulled down the brassiere and got her nipple, which Christ was practically like leather in his mouth and she was going "Oh . . . Oh . . . !" now because he had his hand up between her legs and he wasn't waiting for anyone to take off any dress, he just couldn't, he was going out of his mind he was so hot and she went "Oh . . . !" again, "Oh . . . nice—" and he said "Big cock!" and she said "Big cock!" and he could hardly breathe and the second he got into her he just went crazy, yelling and gasping and slamming down on her on the back seat of the god-damn Pontiac.

□

The goddamn Pontiac! They drove back along Warneke Road. It wasn't exactly light but it wasn't dark anymore either. It was a quarter after four, and the Pontiac felt like a noose around his neck.

"Jeez, take it easy already," Reena said. She was sore because she bumped against the door on the last curve, and also because it didn't turn out so good for her in the back seat, which was her idea, not his, so what the hell was she so sore about?

He braked to a rolling stop and then swung hard onto the highway and pushed the Pontiac up to seventy-five. When he hit town he stayed off the main streets.

"Last time I go to a party on a Sunday night," Reena said. "I gotta work all day now."

"Yeah, me too," Mel said. He was gonna ask her where she worked, but he didn't really care.

"Maybe we could stop for breakfast somewheres," she said. "You hungry?"

"No," Mel said. "I ain't hungry."

He parked in front of Reena's place. The sun wasn't up yet but it was practically bright as day. "Here we are," he said and leaned over and shoved her door open.

"Ain't you even gonna take me in?"

"Look, I gotta go. I'm in a big rush."

She got out and left the door hanging open. Mel pulled it shut and drove off.

Now what? He was about two miles from Winnie's and the Dodge, and had to decide what to do with the goddamn Pontiac. It wasn't five yet, so the owner probably was still asleep, so maybe he could just leave it where he found it. The guy'd probably never even realize it was gone.

Only what if the guy heard him last night and called the cops? What if he was a goddamn milkman or something?

He could just ditch it a few blocks away and walk over to see if there was any activity. If there wasn't, he could walk back and drive the Pontiac over and then try to start the Dodge. Or he could just leave the Pontiac where it was and try to start the Dodge. Only that would bring in the cops, if he didn't bring the Pontiac back.

He was about a mile from Winnie's, working the back streets, trying to take it easy, trying to keep everything straight.

Maybe the party was still on. Maybe it was just breaking up, with everybody strolling out just in time to see him drive up.

The nearer he got, the more the Pontiac felt like a goddamn bomb ticking away under him. He wouldn't be surprised if suddenly there was just this great big explosion and he got blown to bits.

He swung to the curb and broke the ignition. He'd had enough. He checked the seats, the floor, trying to think of everything as fast as he could. His chest hurt from trying to breathe and he was suddenly so scared he was shaking. He wiped off the wheel with his hanky and around the dash and the handles, working faster and faster, trying to breathe. He checked the streets and hopped out, leaped out, slamming the door without even looking back.

Christ, what was he, out of his mind or something, pulling stuff like that? And for what? For a pig that wasn't good enough to kiss the ground Peggy walked on. And Chucky. What if Chucky could understand, what if he could've seen his old man last night?

He worked up a story. He didn't exactly expect a cop to jump out of a doorway, but he worked up a story anyway. That was what the smart guys did, always had a story ready. He'd been at this party and left with a broad who lived nearby so they walked to her place and sorta played around a bit there but he wouldn't give her name because she was basically a good kid and he didn't want her dragged in. It was the only story he could think of. It wasn't any good.

But why should a cop jump out at him? He was just walking down the street. It was a free country.

And if there was any action near Winnie's—anything, some little old lady walking her goddamn dog—he wouldn't go near the Dodge. He'd just keep right on walking.

But there wasn't any. The street was dead, not a soul.

For a second he thought of going back for the Pontiac, but then said no, just get out of here.

He slid into the Dodge and dug in his pockets for the keys. Then he saw them still in the ignition. Christ, someone could've just walked off with the thing.

He turned the key and the motor started. It sounded like the garbage collectors grinding up old bottles and tin cans, but it started. *Now* it started. Shit.

But he was out of it now, the Pontiac was off his neck. He didn't need any stories, he didn't need anything. He pulled away and cranked open the window and smelled the air, which was still cool and clear as a bell, and he felt like breaking out singing or something.

He stopped at Al's Burgers and had some eggs and toast and coffee. While he ate he took out his wallet to see what he had left. He couldn't remember the exact amount he started with last night, but what he had left was six dollars and change.

It seemed like ages since Coffey handed over that envelope on the platform. And Christ, it seemed like years since he'd seen Peggy. He could suddenly see her again, on top of that blanket up in the mountains, in her pink shorts. When they were going together she used to wear a kind of very light blue dress with a white collar that Mel was just crazy about. He felt funny thinking about her. It really did seem like a long time since he'd seen her.

It was almost six now, and he had two hours before work. He could go home but this was the one morning of the week Peggy didn't have to get up for the alarm at three, and he hated to wake her. What could he say anyhow? I was out screwing some pig in the back seat of a Pontiac? He couldn't even believe it himself. Maybe he was just having nightmares, like when he was a kid.

Actually when he was a kid he was a very quiet kid, and never made any kind of trouble. The old man would've kicked the living daylights out of him for making trouble. The old man himself, he went through his whole goddamn life without ever making trouble for anybody, driving his beer truck and letting everybody shit all over him. And then the old lady would go around telling Mel why the hell didn't he get a good solid regular job like the old man, so he could make something of himself. *Something like that?* Mel always wanted to say. *Something for everybody in the goddamn world just to shit all over?*

Breakfast came to a buck and a half, including tip. He drove around a bit, killing time. His head hurt but he figured he'd be all right if he could just get through the day. He wasn't even sore at Peggy anymore. He felt sorry for her actually. He could see her side of it and didn't blame her one bit.

He got to work a few minutes before eight, and Jerrold was already on the platform.

"Morning," Jerrold said. "You bright and early this morning."

"That's right," Mel said. "Bright and early."

□

Actually, the morning went all right. At least that was one advantage of Jerrold, you didn't have to hold up your end of any snappy conversations.

The afternoon, though, really dragged. It was a struggle just to keep going. His legs were dead, his back hurt, and the goddamn sun was killing him.

Around two o'clock, he went to work by himself in the sorting room, organizing a batch of stuff for the Parkdale truck, which was due in at two thirty. Jerrold was off somewhere pushing a wheeler around. Just as Mel was finishing up, he noticed a bundle with a 7 ticket, which was the Olive Plaza number. He pulled it out, then noticed some more 7s, then a whole goddamn batch of them. The Parkdale number was 4, but the way some of these goddamn slobs wrote you couldn't tell a 4 from a 7.

Then he remembered the Olive Plaza truck pulled out right after lunch, with a full load. Shit, there must've been Parkdale stuff on it.

He started separating all the 4 bundles from the 7 bundles, wishing the hell Jerrold would get back and give him a hand for a change, when who the hell showed up, of course, but Coffey.

"Having trouble?"

"No trouble," Mel said. "We're doing fine."

Only Coffey naturally started nosing around and saw the bundles were all screwed up and began giving Mel this big song and dance about being careful which, let's face it, Mel was in no mood for today.

"Look," Mel said, "it was a little mistake, that's all. The world ain't gonna end. What's the big deal?"

Coffey didn't say anything to this. He just looked at Mel, then at the bundles. Then he left.

Which was just as well. Because if he'd stayed one minute longer, Mel would've just told him what he could do with the goddamn job, and all the goddamn bundles too.

What the hell did they want out of your life? You don't even get one lousy minute's sleep all night and then after all that you had to work like a goddamn nigger of $1.40 an hour, and *still* they weren't satisfied.

What was the use, he'd like to know, of being a white man in the first place if you still had to work like a nigger? You might just as well *be* one. Sure, that was it. When he was a kid somebody should've just seen they'd skipped him over by mistake when they were making niggers, and done the job with a little black paint, once and for all.

□

When he finally got off from work he was just ready to drop, so he stopped at Rigoletto's for a beer, just to catch his breath. Besides, he didn't really feel exactly anxious about facing Peggy. If only there was some way you could signal home and let your wife know what kind of a mood you were in. Because a lot of things had happened since he last saw Peggy. As far as he was concerned, she was just living in the past, probably still all bothered about him skipping out last night and everything, when really that part of it hardly even mattered anymore.

He would quit, he decided. Tomorrow. He would just go in and tell Coffey, very calm and collected, that he was just tired of the whole thing, that's all. No hard feelings, but he just wasn't gonna spend the rest of his life lugging around dirty laundry for no $1.40 an hour. It just wasn't his line of work. It wasn't what he was trained for.

He felt better once he decided. He paid the tab and bought a pack of cigarettes and left. It was nine thirty and dark and still hot out. He had a dollar and change in his pocket.

□

Peggy must've heard him pull up, because by the time he got out she was standing at the open door, with the light behind her so he couldn't see what kind of look she was giving him. He sort of nodded to her and walked up but she didn't move a muscle. "Hi," he said and kind of smiled.

She looked at him.

"Sorry I'm late," he said. "I can explain." He waited. Then he laughed a little, trying to draw her along. "Can I come in, heh?"

She turned and went into the living room and Mel went in after her. Only she didn't stop. She headed straight for the kitchen and Mel could see from the way she walked she was really sore.

"Hey, wait a minute! Where you going?"

"To make supper," she said, not even looking back.

"Now just *wait* a minute!"

She stopped and turned around. "Yes? What is it?"

"I wanna talk to you, see."

"All right."

Mel tucked in his polo shirt where it was coming out. He just did it to have something to do really, but then realized it was the same goddamn shirt and trousers he'd been wearing since the picnic yesterday. "What I mean is, it's all very simple and clear in my mind now, and I don't wanna get it all confused."

She didn't say anything.

"I mean, I just wanna say I been working very hard today and I—"

"Working?" She seemed really surprised.

"Yeah, working—what'd you think I was doing?"

"I—well, I don't know. You still got the job then?"

Mel was all set to tell her for Christ's sake of *course* he still had the goddamn job when he realized he'd just decided to quit. Shit. "Well, yeah," he said. "I mean, the hell, you work all day, it means you're working I guess, don't it? Only look—I'm tired, see, and I just don't wanna have any argument or anything. I mean, to tell you the absolute God's honest truth, I'm just too tired to argue. I'm just not interested, that's all."

Peggy was looking at him real funny. "All right," she said, kind of quiet.

"What I need is a little rest, is all," Mel went on. "I mean, the pressure's been on me all day, and I'm bushed."

"Don't you wannna eat first? Ain't you hungry?"

"Yeah, I'm hungry. I'm very hungry."

"All right. I'll make something." She started for the kitchen, then stopped. "Did you lose?"

"Lose?"

"In the game. The poker game."

Mel didn't answer right away. He wondered if she was trying to trap him or something. "That's right," he said. "I lost."

She stared at him but didn't say anything. Then she shrugged. "You got a call."

"Who from?"

"Margolis. He wants you to call him back."

For a minute Mel didn't say anything. Then he said, "I'll call him after. I'm too bushed now."

He waited until after they ate and Peggy finished up cleaning the dishes and came in to watch the TV and then said, "I guess I'll go give him a buzz now," and went into the kitchen and dialed. She couldn't hear, he figured, with the TV going.

"Hello," he said, keeping his voice low. "Margolis?"

"Yeah. How's it going, Mel?"

"All right," Mel said.

"Good. I ain't called you or anything, because I been thinking about this thing you mentioned last week. You know what I mean."

"Yeah."

"I think maybe, like I said, it has possibilities. With a few changes."

"Yeah. What kind of changes?"

"Well, I was talking it over with Kroll, and he—"

"What'd you go telling him for? I didn't say for you to—"

"Take it easy, Mel. He liked the idea."

"I don't care whether he liked it or not. If I wanted you to tell him I would've said so."

"Do you want out, Mel?"

"What do you mean, *out*? It was my idea, remember? I'm the one who says who's in and who's out."

"You want in, then?"

"What the hell are you talking about?"

"Well, what we figured is it's a pretty good idea, but with some weak spots. Like, a gas station out there on the highway, it don't pull in no three or four grand a day, like you say it does."

"It pulls in a bundle, I'll tell you that much."

"Okay, it pulls in a bundle. Only what Kroll figures is that if one station pulls in one bundle, then six stations pull in six bundles. There's six stations out there. We checked."

Mel looked over his shoulder. He lowered his voice. "What're you gonna do, go hopping down them one by one, for Christ's sake?"

"What we figure on doing, Mel, is opening up the tin can."

Mel didn't say anything.

"Look Mel, you take the same chance moving in on one station that you take moving in on the car."

"This ain't my idea no more, you know."

"I know. But you brought it all up, so Kroll says you can stay in if you want."

"Thanks."

Margolis didn't say anything.

"When are you planning to do it?" Mel asked.

"In a while. We wanna do some checking around first."

"I don't know if I wanna wait too long."

"I can't hear you. Can you speak louder?"

"No. I said I ain't interested in any six-month long-range proposition. To tell you the truth, you've been so slow about it already I practically forgot about the whole thing."

"What's the big rush, Mel? You got a job, you're working."

"I was thinking of shoving it. It's for the birds."

"Look Mel . . . are you interested in coming in with us?"

"I don't know. You've changed everything all around. I gotta hear more about it."

"You'll hear more when we got more to tell, when it's all worked out. But meanwhile, stay on your job. You hear?"

"Why?"

"Because. Because afterwards maybe somebody finds out you quit your job right before and suddenly, right after, you got money."

"Look, who the hell are you to—"

"You want out then?"

"It was my idea, remember. I don't *want* in. I *am* in."

"Then keep the job."

"I'll think about it."

"Okay. You do that. We'll get in touch in a week or so."

"Sure. When you get around to it, you let me know."

When he got back to the living room Peggy said, "What'd he want?"

"Some guy's out sick on the bowling team. He wanted me to fill in."
She looked at him. "What'd you tell him?"

"I told him I was too tired. The hell, I gotta work tomorrow."

"That's right," she said, and she was really smiling.

4

After his "Noonday" show Johnny drove downtown to Kale's department store and took the elevator to the fourth floor, where he found Kale's office.

"He'll be with you in a minute," the receptionist said.

Johnny sat and waited. He did not know Kale, but lately had used some items about him on the newscast. Kale was bucking for Attorney General and had been making a lot of speeches.

A buzzer sounded. "Right through there, Mr. Mancino."

Kale got up from his desk and shook hands. "Glad to meet you, Johnny. I suppose I could say I've watched you on television, but I guess that's what everybody says."

"Not quite everybody," Johnny said.

Kale's face was tanned and roughened; he appeared forceful, practical, sure of himself, rather handsome. In fact, he almost did look like a cowboy, and Johnny understood that he had a ranch, and could ride, and maybe even rope and tie and sing Western songs too, so even though he owned a department store and had gone through Michigan Law School you couldn't really complain about the publicity pictures he sent to the station, which showed him in a ten-gallon hat. He wasn't tall but was heavily built and had a strong baritone voice, an outdoor voice, and beneath his business suit he wore a tan vest that was almost a cowboy vest. His thick hair was graying. His brows were prominent enough to keep his eyes shadowed. He'd inherited the store as a thriving business from his father, and although he hadn't done anything to ruin it, he hadn't done much to improve it either. He had a reputation around town as something of a blowhard, overflowing with earnest, misguided convictions.

"Muldoon's the man you want," Kale said before Johnny finished explaining. "Ken Muldoon, down at the Parole office. You'll have to forget about prisoners, but he can line up some parolees for you."

"You don't think we could bring out a prisoner for—"

"No, of course not. These men are convicted felons. We're not going to give them a public platform."

"Maybe we could tape a show in advance, and you could—"

"Have you had any experience with prisoners?"

"No."

"Well, you're dealing with antisocial types, misfits. But I'm sure Muldoon can find you a decent one—one who's already out."

"Good. I'd like—"

"It's not for me to tell you what to do, but if it were handled right, I'd like to see you work in something on this whole business of parole and rehabilitation. We're really trying to help these men, and the Board could use a little public support. If nothing else, you might encourage a few businesses to give these fellows a break on jobs. That's a real roadblock. Anyway, you check with Muldoon for a start."

"Do you hire ex-cons?"

"I probably have more former convicts on my payroll than anybody in the state."

"How are they working out?"

"They're working out fine. If you'd like, I could come on the show and talk about my experience with them, or my work on the Board, for that matter."

"This is all still pretty vague, so I don't—"

"Well, if you're interested, just let me know. Only too glad to help out."

□

The newscast went well: ten minutes for national, eight for local, five for sports, three for weather, with four commercial breaks. Johnson—Goldwater—McNamara—de Gaulle—Sukarno—Saigon—the stock market—Mayor Briston—Governor Eberhart—a suicide, a rape, a bond issue, Koufax, Aaron, Mantle. For the weather summary he moved across the big board, announcing and chalking in the figures for Los Angeles and Boise and Denver and Winnipeg. He wrote the wrong figure for Pittsburgh, erased it with the heel of his hand, and put in the correct one. It had reached eighty-one degrees in Pittsburgh this day, and there were people watching who wanted to know that.

Johnny first got paid for talking into a microphone at the age of sixteen, on radio KLX in Oakland. (*KLX time is now three o'clock . . . official downtown temperature is seventy-four degrees, and it is sunny . . . tonight's projected high and low . . .* Ah—that rhythm, those cadences still echoed!) All told he worked for seven radio stations around the Bay area, paying his way through Berkeley. Radio was real to him. He was born in 1936, in Oakland, where his father owned a fruit and vegetable market, and as he grew up during the war the rest of the world boomed in (his grandmother was partly deaf) from the huge cabinet with the half-moon top, with a brown cloth over the speaker that smelled of ancient dust when you got close and was decorated with squiggles of curved wood. His only ambition had been to make his way on radio, and television somehow flawed this ambition and left it diffused. When he was twelve he talked a friend whose hobby was electricity into building a transmitter; they operated two hours a night from the kid's garage, Johnny as announcer, the friend as engineer. Johnny played records, read ads from *Look* and news stories from the Oakland *Tribune*. They had to stop finally because the neighbors were picking them up on their sets. The other kid's parents even got a formal cease and desist letter from the FCC.

It was only four years later that he got the job on KLX, but radio had lost its force before Johnny even got into it. He stayed with it anyhow, because he liked it in some kind of sentimental way involving that messy garage in Oakland. But when he heard about a TV opening in Aurora, he came out from San Jose and tested for it, hoping he wouldn't get it. But he did, and moved to Aurora, and had since decided that maybe he was lucky enough to be good enough on television to avoid some of the crap and do something worth doing, and maybe even enjoy doing it.

After the news show he drove out Beradino Street to the address Ken Muldoon had given him. The stucco house was a pale, faded green, square, flat-roofed. All the houses on the block were stucco, square, flat-roofed. Each had its cranking slatted air cooler on the roof, its plot of untended ground. Clusters of thin brown weeds sprouted from the hard ground amid the webs of crawling goathead vines, their green prickles ready to drop off, then to dry and harden in the sun and stick to shoes or stab into bare feet. In the rutted alleys stood the garbage cans. The street was paved, but the sidewalks were dirt. It was a little after seven now and still hot and no one was out;

the street was dull, choked, static. You couldn't look at this street and smile. You couldn't stand on this street at this time of day without weariness, without tasting a faint spoiled residue in your mouth.

("It's all set," Ken Muldoon called to tell him. "You can see him tonight—only I'm tied up; you'll have to go alone."

"Will it be all right?"

"I'm sure you'll be safe."

"You said he was nonviolent. You said he was pleasant and friendly."

"Well, people have funny ideas about ex-cons.")

Johnny stepped onto the cement slab raised a few inches from the ground and pushed the bell. Almost hidden in the weeds against the house lay a toy cannon on a string. He picked it up and the door opened. "Hi."

The woman looked at him. She was young, with a pretty face except for her eyes, which were slightly puffy, and lined with weariness. She had dressed for the occasion: her dress was clean, perhaps even new. It looked like the best dress of a woman who had one best dress. The woman—Muldoon said her name was Peggy—appeared self-conscious about it, as if she'd been determined to look her best and now feared she might have overdone it.

"My name's Johnny Mancino—does a Mr. Simmons live here? Mel Simmons?"

"Yeah, he's here. Hello. C'min." She backed from the door, hesitantly, staring up at Johnny's face as if she wanted to smile but wasn't sure she should. She had seen Johnny on television. You could always tell. You weren't a person recognized but an image brought to life.

Johnny stepped inside. The living room was small, the ceiling low. A young fellow, with a little kid on one knee, was slouched down at the far end of the flowered couch, watching the television set. Johnny couldn't see the screen.

The guy looked at Johnny long enough to show that he was impressed by Johnny's height, then glanced again at the screen, as if so engrossed he couldn't bring himself to turn away on such short notice— the type who'd expect you to carry on a conversation over the blasting of singers and commercials and love scenes from old movies, who would keep flitting his eyes at the screen, nodding absently at what you were saying.

The wife stepped over to the set and the noise stopped.

The fellow raised his eyes again. Methodically, perhaps to emphasize that this was his house and he owed no special consideration to un-

invited guests—and perhaps also to show the wife what he thought
of her obvious excitement, her deference, her dress—Mel Simmons deposited the child on the middle cushion of the couch and stood up,
buckling his army belt. He had not dressed: he wore jeans and a tee
shirt. Small and thin but wiry, well-muscled, Mel Simmons was
a remarkably good-looking kid. His face had a kind of youthful purity,
almost a sweetness in the way you'd say someone was a sweet musician
or a sweet ballplayer, not meaning effeminacy or softness but only a
kind of easy, unstinted smoothness, a kind of lightness and grace. And
the curly hair, intensely black, seemed both unkempt and shrewdly
mannered. He would photograph well, at any rate. Except for the hint
in his expression, not of stupidity but of a lack of real intelligence,
the fellow could pass in the right clothes for a pop singer.

"Hi," the fellow said at last, thickly, without inflection.

"Hi, Mel. Ken Muldoon said he'd call you today about—"

"Yeah, I know. He called. Well sure—sit down . . ." He motioned
vaguely. "What can I do for you?"

His wife hovered nervously, as if expecting something to go hopelessly wrong. "I'll go inside," she said. "I mean, if you two wanna
talk . . ."

"Please—stay if you'd like," Johnny said.

After a brief uncertainty, she moved quickly to the couch and sat
down, a little sheepish but obviously pleased at being allowed to stay.
Mel looked at her sourly but said nothing.

Johnny sat in a small armchair covered in the same flowered print
as the couch. Mel somewhat grudgingly returned to his end of the
couch. The little boy, between his parents, stared at Johnny.

"This yours, sonny?" Johnny held out the toy cannon.

"Go get it," Mel said.

The boy hopped off the couch. Shyly he accepted the toy and
bent to put it on the floor.

"Don't go playing with it here," Mel said. "Go inside if you wanna
play."

"I found it outside," Johnny said. "I thought maybe he lost it."

Mel said nothing.

"He's always leaving it around somewheres," the wife said. "Why
don't you go inside now, Chucky, and play there awhile?"

The boy shook his head; he climbed back on the couch and sat with
the cannon in his lap. As thin and small-boned as his father, with
the same tangle of shiny black hair, he looked like a duplicate, a
miniature. The kid shifted his gaze to the TV and kept it there. Johnny

realized it was still on, that the wife had only turned off the sound.

"What was it now you wanted?" Mel asked.

"Well, I don't know if you've ever caught a show I do on television— it's on at noon, so maybe you haven't had—"

"Yeah," Mel said. "I seen it a coupla times."

"Good. You know how it works then."

Mel nodded cautiously, reluctant to commit himself. He seemed to fear a trick.

"I've just started a new program," Johnny said, "every Wednesday evening, and I'd like to do a series on the problem of prisons and con- victs. I was talking to Mr. Kale about it the other day and—do you know him, Mel?"

"No, I don't think I do."

"The one who owns the store."

"Kale's, sure. That one. No, I don't know him."

"Well, as you probably know, he's also chairman of the State Prison and Parole Board."

"I didn't know."

Johnny took a breath. "Well, he was telling me about the work being done with ex-prisoners, and we agreed it was something people ought to know about, that the public ought to be aware of."

Mel remained silent, waiting for Johnny to continue. "Yeah," he said finally. "Sure."

"Kale sent me to Ken Muldoon and we talked the whole thing over. Muldoon was all for it. We went over the names of some men he's worked with, looking for someone who might fit in with this idea."

"And you picked Mel?" the wife blurted out, straightening up on the couch and looking back and forth between them.

"Let the guy talk, all right?" Mel said.

"That's pretty much it," Johnny said. "We figured you might be interested, Mel. We'd like to have you."

"I don't know if I get this exactly," Mel said. "I mean, what do you want from me?"

"We'd like you to come on and tell us something about yourself. That's all."

"Gee, Mel—you hear that?"

Mel glanced coolly at his wife, then turned back to Johnny. "I don't know that I really am too crazy about that idea, exactly. I mean, to be perfectly frank."

"Oh Mel—why not?" his wife said. "What's the matter?"

"I just don't know that I think it's such a great idea," Mel said steadily, not taking his eyes off Johnny. "I mean, did Muldoon say I was *supposed* to do this?"

"Not at all—that's your decision. He simply said you'd be a good man."

"How come Muldoon sent you to me? I mean, why me? He knows a hundred guys like me."

"For one thing, he said you were doing very well on your job. And of course we checked with the people at the laundry, and they put in a good word for you."

"They did?"

"Yes. They said you were doing fine."

"You oughta go on," the wife said. "Really. I think it's kind of exciting they picked you and everything."

"I don't know," Mel said, still staring at Johnny. "Maybe you can look around and come up with somebody else."

"Aw, Mel—go on, why don't you? I mean, why not?"

"Why?"

"Well, something like this is, well, something you oughta be proud of. I mean, they picked you and everything. And it'd look real good for you. It'll impress people."

"It'll impress people I'm an ex-con is what it'll impress."

"If that's the hitch, Mel, we could probably arrange to do it anonymously."

"What do you mean, like?"

"Well, this wasn't exactly what I had in mind, but we could have you behind a screen, or maybe just keep your face off camera. No one would know who you were then."

Mel seemed to consider this. His wife looked disappointed.

"I don't know," Mel said. And then he looked over at the television screen and studied it for a moment. Maybe he wanted to reassure himself about the basic principle involved, that one watched to see things, not to have them hidden. Maybe he was trying to imagine how he'd look on the screen, with or without his face showing. He turned abruptly to his wife: "Maybe Mr. Mancino'd like a cup of coffee."

"No I'm fine, thanks."

"Go put some on," Mel said.

"Sure." Peggy got up from the couch, and the kid, who'd been sitting quietly with his cannon, ran after her.

"A real quiet boy you got there," Johnny said.

"Yeah, he don't talk much. He ain't even two yet."

"I meant how well behaved he was. He seems like a real nice kid."

"Look, you got a minute? I mean, what say we go somewheres and talk this over?"

"Well—sure, if you'd rather."

Mel stood up quickly. "You set?"

"But, your wife's making—"

"That's all right. C'mon." Mel darted across the room. "Hey, Peg!" he called, leaning into the hall with his hands on the doorframe. "We changed our mind, all right? We're going out for a beer."

She appeared in the hallway, frowning, a metal pot in her hand. "I thought you wanted coffee."

"Look, you gotta put Chucky off now anyhow. Mr. Mancino's got something on tonight so I'll be back in no time."

"We got some beer in."

"We'll just be a coupla minutes. Bye now. *Night, Chucky!*" he called into the kitchen. "*Be a good boy!*" He started for the door. "C'mon," he said to Johnny.

"It was very nice meeting you, Mrs. Simmons . . ."

"Yeah . . ."

Mel yanked the door open and waited impatiently for Johnny to get out. He followed right after him and closed the door quickly, like a man escaping. "Can't talk with everybody around," he said. "Where you wanna go?"

"It doesn't matter. I don't really know the neighborhood."

"C'mon then." Mel hopped off the slab, his feet slapping on the path like a dancer's. He walked very fast. When they reached the dirt sidewalk he stopped and snapped his fingers. "Hell—I forgot. The car ain't been running too hot and—"

"We'll take mine," Johnny said.

"Well, I feel funny . . . I mean, it was my idea and—"

"Just point me in the right direction."

They got in and Johnny started the motor.

"It's kind of an old beat-up Dodge, you know," Mel explained. "A real cripple, if you know what I mean. Straight down the block and swing back to Beradino. A Rambler, heh? What is it, sixty-three?"

"That's right—sixty-three."

Mel shifted around on the seat to study the dashboard, to finger the armrests, the upholstery. He seemed unable to settle down, to absorb everything fast enough. You'd think he'd never been in a car before.

"What d'ya got, the straight six under this? How's it run for you?

I mean, you think it's a good car? Because you see we're thinking of ditching the old Dodge naturally and picking up something a little more dependable." He spoke rapidly, almost hectically.

"It runs fine," Johnny said.

"You think it's a solid machine, heh? As an investment, I mean. You know, something that'll get you where you wanna go."

"I haven't had any trouble with it, at any rate. I don't really know too much about cars."

"Yeah. Well I guess you could say that's the one thing I *do* know something about. Used to work as a mechanic, you see. Before I got all messed up and everything. Only naturally you gotta have tools for that."

"Don't you have tools?"

"No, no more. I'm working toward it though, trying to save a little something from the old paycheck every week. Course it ain't easy, I don't have to tell you that, especially since the job—that's it there, on the right, Rigoletto's. Sure you don't mind now? I mean, you got the time?"

"We'll have a quick one," Johnny said.

They sat at a booth. A few men stood at the bar; three or four other booths were occupied. The place was dim, with dark walls and heavy wood paneling. It smelled musty, with a hint of rotting dampness. The aluminum slats over the cooler vent high on the wall rattled.

Mel ordered rye and ginger, Johnny bourbon and water. Johnny put a ten-dollar bill on the table and Mel nodded to acknowledge it.

"To us," Mel said, raising his glass. "You let me know now when you gotta run." He took a sip, swished the liquid around in his mouth, then swallowed, his Adam's apple pumping. He lifted the glass again and drained half of it. He saw Johnny watching and shrugged. "You know what happened at home, don't you? I mean, when I heard you were coming I figured naturally we'd offer you a beer or something, but the wife puts the foot down and says no. Which is why, in case you're wondering, there wasn't nothing offered until we were ready to pull out. I don't know, she figured maybe you'd get the wrong idea or something. I don't know what the hell's wrong with her sometimes."

"I didn't expect you to entertain me."

"Still, you could offer a guy a beer, couldn't you? You got time for another quick one?"

"I've got a bit left. Order one for yourself."

"Maybe I'll make it a double, okay?—the one thing about this place— they don't exactly use the bathtub for a jigger."

The waitress took the money from the change on the table.

"Here's to you," Mel said, and drank. He seemed, in a curious way, more relaxed now, but he still talked rapidly. "Now look, since you probably ain't got that much time, maybe we oughta get right down to business, okay? I mean, I'm not trying to be pushy or anything, but what I wanted to ask you, because why beat around the bush, is exactly how much there'd be in this for me." He paused, then added: "Money, I mean."

"I'm sorry—I guess I didn't make that clear. But we don't pay our guests. We can't, actually. There's nothing in the budget for it."

Mel looked at him, his mouth pulled up at one corner. "You don't pay any of these people you get on, you mean?"

"I'm afraid not. You have to remember it's only a local show. I'm sorry I didn't mention this before."

Mel finished his drink and, after a questioning look at Johnny, called for another double.

"You too?" the waitress asked.

Johnny shook his head.

The waitress took it out of the change.

Mel drank, then put down his glass and looked steadily into Johnny's eyes. "You know, there's one thing I'd like the straight scoop on."

"Yes?"

"Why did you *really* pick me? I mean, *really*. You know, like I mean, I don't sing or dance or nothing—I can't put on no show for you. There's a catch in here somewheres."

"No catch, Mel."

"It just don't sound right to me—you know what I mean?"

"It simply came down to the fact that you sounded like the kind of fellow we were looking for."

"That's all, heh?"

"That's all."

Mel looked at his glass. He tapped it a couple of times on the table. "Only you don't think you could swing any money, heh? I mean, you don't think it'd be worth anything to get the kind of guy you wanted?"

Johnny almost smiled. Mel Simmons, as an operator, was so transparent that it was hard to be annoyed. Johnny looked at his watch. "I don't mean to cut this short, Mel, but I have to head on. Maybe we could talk it out on the way back to your place."

"Look, you don't have to take me back. I can pick up a ride, I know people around."

"No, I'll take you."

"Tell you what. It's not really in your direction, so instead of going way out there, just leave that to me. I'll get back. And that way we got time to talk this out here." He hesitated. "You ready for another?"

Johnny did smile this time. "Okay."

Mel signaled the waitress and gulped down what was left in his glass. "Now, like I was saying, you don't think there's much chance to make this worth my while, is that it? I mean, what I'd like to—" Mel stopped while the waitress put down the drinks and took the money from the change. He raised his glass when she left, then paused. "You know, I don't know what you think I make down at that laundry or anything, but do you know what it is? Exactly?" He drank, watching Johnny over the rim of his glass, waiting for the answer.

"No, I don't, Mel."

"A buck forty an hour. You know what that comes to? That comes to sixty-seven twenty a week—a *six*-day week, Saturdays included, without even figuring all the taxes and stuff they take out before you even see it." Mel nodded decisively. "I mean, that don't exactly make you a capitalist, does it? I mean, the bills alone every week . . . You know what I got on me right now? Do you have any idea?"

"Look Mel, I realize you—"

"Let me show you." Mel took out his wallet and extended it across the table, holding open the bill flap with his thumb. It was empty. "I mean, it's damn white of you to blow me to a drink like this, and I appreciate it . . . I really do . . . I mean that. But you know, it'd be nice too if I could buy *you* a drink. I mean, I'm no scrounge. I pay my way. And if you wanna know, I feel like a real schmuck just sitting here sponging off you."

"I'm glad to be—"

"That ain't the point, don't you see? I know you are. I can tell you're all right." Mel drank quickly. "You wanna know what happened to my tools?" he said, leaning forward and glancing around quickly.

"What happened to them?"

"My wife sold them is what happened." His voice was dry now, thicker. "When I was at the Farm that time. One day she just took the whole batch, even the goddamn box, and sold them without so much as blinking an eye. She didn't even ask me. She didn't even mention it."

"Maybe she needed the money, Mel."

"Well, sure she needed the money. I mean, the hell, you take a guy away from his family and stick him off like that, sure his wife needs the money. For Christ's sake, he ain't making any for her behind bars, is he? But what I mean is, these were my *tools*—I mean, after all, it was pretty dumb, don't you think, selling them like that?—for practically nothing, maybe half what they were worth. I mean, did she figure I was gonna rot in there the rest of my life and wouldn't need no tools? Because when you hit the bricks, you know, you gotta work, you gotta find a job. I mean, it wasn't like selling off something you didn't need—I mean, what happens to you then?—you end up breaking your back on a platform somewhere lugging sacks of laundry around when if you had a decent box of tools to your name you could be out working like a white man, instead of the wife bitching all the time because you ain't making the money."

"How much do you want, Mel?"

Mel drew his head back slowly. He didn't look pleased, or even surprised. He looked suspicious. "You really mean that? I mean, I ain't trying just to put the bum on you."

"How much do you want?"

"Well—it's up to you, I guess." Mel shrugged and let out a little laugh. "After all, I don't know what something like this goes for . . . what the regular price is or anything."

"There's hardly a regular price. We've never paid anyone before."

"Well, all right. What I was figuring on was maybe . . . well, I don't know, a coupla bills maybe . . ."

"A couple of bills?"

"You know—a coupla hundred dollars."

"This isn't the Ed Sullivan show, Mel."

"I was just trying to figure out a fair price."

"I'll give you fifty dollars, Mel. I think maybe I can swing that with the manager. I'll try anyhow."

Mel remained silent. Then he leaned forward and spoke earnestly, intensely. "You see, what I was figuring was, a coupla bills would be a real head start on getting a decent set of tools together."

"I can't do it, Mel. And look—I've got to go. I'd like an answer: yes or no."

"For fifty bucks?"

"That's right."

Mel studied him for a moment, then shrugged. "Well, all right. I mean, if you say that's the fair price, because I don't know myself how much these—"

"It's more than fair. I'd like to have you on next Wednesday, all right? I'll give you a ring in a day or so to set it up. You'll get the money after the show."

"Sure. That sounds fair enough. . . . You really gotta go now?"

"Yes." Johnny left a dollar bill near his glass and slid the rest—two dollars and change—across to Mel. "Here, buy yourself a cup of coffee on me, and then maybe you'd better head home. You sure you can make it all right?"

"Don't worry none about me, Mr. Mancino. And let me tell you something. Next time—I mean this—drinks are on me."

"Forget it."

"Besides, I'm perfectly all right. I want you to know that. What I mean is I don't want you thinking I go boozing it up like this all the time. I mean, when you're just sitting at home minding your own business and then out of nowhere someone pops in and you don't even know what the hell his game is or anything—well, I mean, on the outside you can be calm enough maybe, but you can get a little shook up on the inside. A little, well, you know—scared even, if you know what I mean. Especially if you ain't exactly any stranger to people popping in on you and bringing nothing but trouble when they come. I mean, usually when you think of something like this, what you think of is trouble . . ."

Johnny waited to see if Mel were planning to continue. He didn't seem to be. "You're sure you can manage now?"

"Sure, sure. I got friends around. I'm all right."

"Good enough," Johnny said.

□

"Fifty dollars!"

"That's right," Johnny said. "Fifty. Five-oh. Are you familiar with the term? Put it this way: if you take a hundred dollars and divide it in half, you'll—"

"Perhaps you're not familiar with the term *no*. Allow me to—"

"I'm painfully familiar with it around here," Johnny said.

"You lie," Arlanson said with a shrug. He pulled over a chair and sat alongside Johnny's desk. When he crossed his legs the crease in his blue trousers fell neatly down the center. Arlanson had come into the office carrying a white sheet of paper, which he placed on his lap, face down. "I treat you with a great deal of permissiveness, Johnny, out of respect for you imaginative powers."

"But you won't let me off 'Noonday.' "

"Sure I will. As soon as we find a satisfactory replacement. As soon as we see how your evening fling goes."

"How can it go if you won't pay fifty bucks for this fellow?"

"Why should I? You won't even tell me his name."

"What I'd like to do is a five- or six-part series on prisons, on the whole works, the people in them, the people who sent them there, the people who keep them there."

"Are you planning to put them on from their cells? In their striped suits?"

"Kale wouldn't let me."

"You've spoken to Kale about it?"

"Sure, he runs the State Board. And he's very enthusiastic."

"He's a jerk. Besides, he just wants some free publicity."

"He won't get it. He probably won't even like what I'm doing, once he finds out what it is. The whole system's rotten—I've been doing some research, learning a few things. But we're going to concentrate on the people, get a good look at them, and the real thing we've got working for us is that indefinable something you like to refer to as *human interest.*"

"I never use the term *human interest* except for satiric effect. What do you expect to do with this guy?"

"Get him to talk about himself. See what he's like. Find out what he thinks. I've already checked with Sol, and he said he'd give us a plug. That's fifty dollars' worth of publicity right there. I've also worked up a release to send out to all the ministers, for instance, the lawyers, the judges, the high school principals, the employment agencies, the service clubs. *Opinion leaders* is the term I think you use, for satiric effect, when you refer to them."

"If you worked this hard for 'Noonday,' you wouldn't—"

"If I worked this hard for 'Noonday' I'd be a damned fool."

"Do you really think this fellow's worth fifty dollars to us?"

"No. But I'd like to get him, and he's convinced we'd be depriving him of his just deserts if we don't pay."

"He has a finely attuned sense of moral fitness, this ex-con."

"Besides, he needs the money."

"So do we. Is there anything else you'll need? Armed guards? Handcuffs? A spotlight? Maybe a trained dog act to fill in the dead spots?"

"Nothing else. I'd work for free myself, to help you out, except the union wouldn't let me."

"Okay, have the fifty bucks. This time. Who do we make the check out to? Mr. X?"

"Make it out to me. I'll see that he gets it."

"See that he's worth it." Arlanson got up, holding the piece of paper he brought in. "Got a thumb tack?" He tacked it on the plasterboard wall, underneath the "Noonday" schedule and next to the Bank of Industrial Savings calendar. "I got it from a friend in Chicago," he said.

REMEMBER!

Every word you speak
Into the microphone today
Is heard by more people
Than heard President Abraham Lincoln
Deliver his Address at Gettysburg!

"I thought it would be good for us to remember that," Arlanson said.

"It's probably true in Chicago."

"It's true in Moose Jaw," Arlanson said. "It's true in Moscow, Idaho."

"My friend, the anonymous ex-con, will be pleased to know that."

"You know what I think of prisoners, Johnny?"

"What?"

"I think they ought to be in jail."

"You sound just like Kale."

Arlanson steadied his eyes. "I do not sound any more like Frank Kale than you do like Abraham Lincoln."

☐

They sent out three hundred dittoed announcements and the promised plugs appeared in Tuesday night's *Journal* and Wednesday morning's *Post*. Sol Perrin gave him top billing in his "Recommended Tonight" listing and four inches in his column:

> . . . When this department's favorite local TV personality gets the chance to spread his wings on prime time, it calls for some rejoicing. Those of you who aren't yet Johnny Mancino fans will get their chance to join the big fellow's rooting section when his new series debuts tonight (Channel 4 at 7). The betting here is that it'll be worth watching.

After "Noonday" Johnny went back to his apartment for a nap. He turned on the cooler, took off his shoes, and slept until the alarm rang at four.

Downstairs Mrs. Warnsell, a kerchief tied around her head, was sweeping the cement walkway around the lawn. Hunched to her broom, she jabbed away with quick, coiled strokes.

"I saw in the paper about you," she said. "This is really a real criminal you got on?"

"Honest and true."

"You should be careful. You shouldn't take any chances."

He got out to Mel Simmons' place fifteen minutes early, and as he turned off Beradino he saw a black car pull away. The low sun was in his eyes and he couldn't tell who was driving. There was no other car parked at the house. Johnny watched it speed off, then slammed down his accelerator.

The black car turned right, tires squealing. Johnny went through the stop sign and swung after it. It turned right at the next corner, toward Beradino. The sun was out of Johnny's eyes, but he was too far back to see the driver.

The car had a green light onto Beradino and veered left on the big boulevard; Johnny ran the yellow to keep up. The black car cut to the left lane to pass one car, then to the right to pass another. The traffic slowed for a red light and Johnny hit his brake. He was three cars behind and in the other lane. When the light changed the black car made a right turn. Johnny cut off a car to get over to the right, skirted a cluster of pedestrians on the turn and roared ahead.

The black car turned at the corner, and then turned again. It had to be either Mel or someone with a pretty guilty conscience. Maybe that was it: the whole neighborhood was populated by ex-cons and they were all jumpy.

The black car was approaching Beradino again, along a different street. It angled into the curb and parked in front of Rigoletto's.

Johnny pulled in behind. When he reached forward to turn the ignition, his hand was shaking. He closed his eyes for a moment.

Mel Simmons, in a tan suit and a dark tie and wearing dark wraparound sunglasses that masked half his face, stood near his car and watched Johnny walk over.

"Do you always drive like that?" Johnny said. His voice was dry; he cleared his throat.

"I left word with the wife," Mel said, his voice impassive, his eyes shielded behind the glasses. "What were you doing, following me?"

"You pulled out just as I came up. I didn't . . . Well, I thought perhaps . . ." He fell silent.

Mel shrugged again and ran his tongue over his lips. "I figured we could maybe have a beer first."

"Sure thing," Johnny said.

They took a booth near the back, under the flapping vents of the air cooler. Mel stared down at the table and didn't seem to notice the waitress. Johnny ordered a rye and ginger and a bourbon and water. Mel took off his sunglasses and placed them on the table. They faced Johnny with a kind of dark, vacant intensity.

"Well, how are we doing, Mel?"

Mel looked up, then wet his lips again. "All right, I guess." His voice was thick, subdued, very serious. When the waitress brought the drinks Mel straightened up. "On me this time, all right? I mean—well, it don't exactly square us, but let me pay."

Johnny let him.

"To the big show," Mel said cheerlessly and drank. He wasn't drunk but had the tight, dulled expression of someone who'd already had enough to feel it but didn't feel it. He took out a clean white handkerchief and wiped his face, then refolded it, his fingers moving stiffly, almost stickily. He looked good in his suit, in his white shirt and tie.

"We got time for another one?"

"Just one."

Mel signaled the waitress and Johnny reached for his wallet. "No, this is on me tonight," Mel said.

"Did you see the notice we got in the morning paper?"

"Yeah, I saw," Mel said after a moment. "*Unidentified ex-convict* —I got a big kick out of that. I'm gonna give everybody the big scoop, it says. I don't know, you know."

"Once we get under way it'll—"

"Yeah. Only I didn't really figure on all this noise. They had something in the other paper too."

"Have you told anyone about it?"

"Nah. I mean, the hell—who's to tell?" He drained his glass. "Anytime you're ready, I guess . . ."

"You feeling okay, Mel?"

"I'm feeling, you wanna know, like my bottom's gonna drop out. Let's *go,* all right? Let's get *out* of this place."

"Here—don't forget your sunglasses."

☐

"Good evening—this is Johnny Mancino, bringing you the first of K-SUN's 'Special Reports,' taking you behind the headlines for a closer look at the world we live in. . . .

"Ours is a stable society. We are a dutiful people. We work, raise our families, pay our taxes, support our schools, obey our laws. . . ."

His image dissolved from the studio monitor and was replaced by a shot of children playing in a sunlit schoolyard. He picked up the earphone to listen to the voices of children against a background of music on the sound track. The scene changed to a crowd at a football game, to the high school players on the field, to a PTA meeting, to a pan shot of men and women working in a large office, to a line of overalled men punching a time clock, to a man on a horse riding across a ranch outside Aurora, with the San Juan Mountains in the background. The music faded and Johnny put down the earphone. The red light glowed on camera two and his face reappeared on the monitor.

"This, at least, is the way most of us live. But here in Aurora, and throughout the country, an increasingly large number of men and women—from all economic and social levels, from all cultural and ethnic backgrounds—are rejecting these values and turning instead to crime and lawlessness. . . ."

The monitor now showed the glaring headlights of a patrol car racing through a downtown street; there was no music; over the earphone Johnny heard the scream of the siren. With quicker cuts this time, the sound track raucous with loud voices, running steps and the screech of traffic, the monitor showed a policeman chasing two men down an alley, a man running from a bank and roaring away in a car, a dark figure climbing through a window into a house, four youths following a woman down a deserted street, moving closer and closer, and then the woman screaming as they pounced. . . .

"The figures themselves are impressive. Only a small percentage of crimes are ever reported, yet last year over two *million* were committed. Put more simply, four serious crimes occur in this country every minute of the day and night. One expert, John Conrad, has written, 'In volume this country exceeds both absolutely and relatively the criminality of any other civilized nation.' Not many of these criminals are ever caught. Fewer are convicted, still fewer sentenced. Yet at this moment there are locked behind the walls of our prisons almost three hundred thousand men, women and—yes, children."

In silence now, with no music, no sound effects, the viewers were given a series of shots of prisons, of the walls, the buildings, of convicts marching past a row of cells, talking in a yard, working in a machine shop, eating in an enormous mess hall under the surveillance of uniformed guards.

"What happens to these people in prison? Are they helped? Are they returned to society better than they were? Are they made worse?"

Johnny paused, looking into the barreled lenses of camera two until the red light went off. The monitor now showed Mel from his collar to his waist. He sat alone at a small table, his arms encircling a cup of coffee. His left hand held a cigarette, his right a book of matches.

"It is with those who have heard the iron gates slam shut behind them, and have then seen them open again, that we are concerned to-night." The camera focused down to Mel's hands, to the smoking cig-arette that he held far back between his fingers and the match cover that he was slowly twisting into a tighter spiral. "Our guest is a young man, a former convict, whose name will not be revealed—and whose face will not be seen on your television screen. . . . For tonight, we'll call him Bill, and ask him to tell us something about himself. Bill . . . how old are you?"

There was a long pause. Mel was trying to twist the match cover even tighter. He did not seem to hear. Johnny was about to break in when Mel spoke hoarsely, eyes down, without emphasis: "Twenty-eight."

"And where were you born, Bill—where did you grow up?"

There was another pause, briefer this time. "I was born in Gary, Indiana . . . we moved to Aurora when I was ten. . . ." He spoke like a clerk reading a document.

"How many were there in your family?"

"There was three kids. But then my older brother . . . he got killed in the war. We moved out here after that. Then my sister, she mar-ried a fellow from Maynard."

"Are your mother and father still alive?"

"My mother is. She lives in Maynard with my sister."

"And you're married now, is that right?"

"That's right. And we got a kid. One kid."

"How old were you when you first got in trouble, Bill?"

"I don't know—I mean, what kind of trouble?"

"What was the first time you ever stole money?"

"Well, you don't really keep track of these things, you know. . . . I don't know—maybe around nine or ten."

"How much did you steal?"

"Thirty-two dollars."

"You remember exactly?"

"Yeah. There was a twenty, a ten, and two singles. I didn't expect to get that much."

"Were you caught?"

"No."

"Who did you steal it from?"

"From a store on the corner."

"Did you begin stealing money regularly then?"

"I never stole nothing regular."

"You never became a professional thief?—one who expects to make his living from his crimes?"

"That's right. I never became nothing like that."

"But you stole money again?"

"A few times, I guess. Yeah."

"Did you do it because you needed it? Was your family poor?"

Mel shrugged. He was speaking quietly, but in a more normal voice now. The match cover was in shreds. "Well, we weren't exactly poor, if you know what I mean. We could've used some more money, sure, but we weren't starving."

"You always had enough to eat, clothes to wear?"

"We ate regular."

"Your father had a steady job?"

"He had a real steady job. All his life."

"What was his trade?"

"He drove a brewery truck."

"Now, you were sent away the first time for auto theft, weren't you?"

"Yeah. Only we weren't really stealing it."

"You were out joy riding?"

"That's right. We were taking a little ride was all. I was just a kid then."

"You say we: who was with you?"

"Another guy."

"Did he get sent to prison too?"

"I wasn't sent to prison. I got nine months at St. Joe's."

"That's St. Joseph's Industrial School, right? Did the other fellow get sent there too?"

"He didn't get sent nowhere. He didn't get caught."

"How come?"

"Well, we kinda banged up the car when a squad car spotted us and started giving us the big chase. . . . I hurt my leg was what happened; the other guy beat it."

"Were you badly hurt?"

"Nah—I just couldn't run."

"And they gave you nine months for that, even though it was your first offense?"

"That's right. You see, well, I been in a little trouble before, and I guess what with trying to shake the squad car and then wrecking the car and not saying who the other guy was, they figured they'd give me nine months."

"To reform you?"

"I guess so."

"What kind of trouble were you in before that?"

"Well, once me and some other guys got picked up in a school—at night, you see. I mean, we were just horsing around but the cops showed and one of the guys was fooling around with a big can full of paper—matches, you know—and that sort of put the cops down on all of us."

"How old were you then?"

"I don't know. Fourteen, I guess. They didn't do nothing to me because I wasn't the one with the matches, but I guess they kinda got a good look at my face, if you know what I mean."

"Was there any other trouble?"

"Yeah—well . . . once they thought maybe I stole some car that was stole from the neighborhood, but they just picked me up because I was hanging around. It was just purely on suspicion, and they let me off."

"Anything else?"

"Another time I got sorta involved in a big fight in a bar. It was just my luck being there, actually, and before I knew it some guy was taking a swing at me. We all stayed overnight in jail on that, but they didn't file no charges—not on me anyway."

"And that was the only record you had before being sent to St. Joseph's for auto theft?"

"Yeah, that was all."

"Do you think the sentence was unduly harsh?"

"Well . . . of course, I don't know about that. I mean, that ain't exactly for me to say."

"Did it do you any good—being sent to St. Joseph's?"

"Well, I guess so. I mean, I worked some at being a mechanic there, so I guess, yeah, I got something out of it."

"Is that where you learned your trade? That's what you are, isn't it—a mechanic?"

"Yeah, that's right. That's what I am. And sure, I learned some about it there."

"Then you think the Industrial School is a good place for a young kid who's gotten in trouble? Or do you have reservations?"

"Well, I don't know that I should go shooting my mouth off here. . . . I mean, they're all right there. Of course it's crowded and there ain't much to work with or anything . . . but they're all right, I guess."

"Are they strict?"

"Well, of course they're strict. I mean, you're locked up."

"But they treated you decently?"

"Well, they don't go around beating you up or nothing, if that's what you mean. They leave you alone if you keep your nose—I mean, you know, if you do what you're supposed to."

"Did you?"

"Well sure—I had a blank sheet there. I got out after six months, as soon as I was eligible."

"Then what happened?"

"Well, I moved around a bit for a while."

"Did you have trouble finding work?"

"Not too much, I guess. I got jobs."

"Did you stay with any of them?"

"Well, no. Like I say, I was moving around. They weren't exactly sensational jobs."

"Have you ever held a job long?"

"Not real long, I guess."

"A year?"

"Maybe. A little less, maybe."

"But you're a trained man, a skilled mechanic—men like you are in demand, aren't they?"

"Sometimes they are, sometimes they aren't. It depends. I mean, you can't just walk out and pick up a job anytime you want one, just because you're a mechanic. A lotta guys are mechanics. At least they say they are. A lotta times too, the boss got a friend or his brother-in-law or something."

"You're not working as a mechanic now?"

"No, I'm not. It's like I say, you can't always just snap your fingers and get exactly the job you want."

"Tell us something about your schooling, Bill. How far did you go? Did you do well?"

"I guess I didn't break no records, you could say. I mean, I guess I did all right but—"

"How far did you go?"

"I went to high school."

"Did you graduate?"

"No, I didn't exactly graduate. I went for a while."

"After you got out of St. Joseph's, did you get in trouble again?"

"Yeah, I did."

"Did you get sentenced again?"

"I got sentenced to three years at the State Farm at Kenscott."

"What for?"

"For burgelry."

"Can you tell us something about the Farm—how you spent your time, what it was like?"

"Well . . . it was all right. I ain't got any big complaints, if that's what you mean."

"Did you stay in cells, were there bars?"

"Well, there was some, but no, you didn't stay in them regular. If you got in trouble, of course, they put you in the Block. The Cell Block. But no, I never spent no time there. We lived in barracks, like in the army—all these guys in this barracks. There was a great big fence all around, with barbed wire at the top, but no towers. Just this one guy at the gate."

"But within the grounds, you could come and go pretty much as you pleased?"

"At certain times you had to be in your bunk for bunk check, or with your work detail, and naturally for chow you lined up with everybody else, but there was times when you could move around, in certain places."

"Did you have movies? Television? Newspapers?"

"Oh yeah. There was a movie once a week you could go to, and they had a TV in the rec room, and different kinds of magazines and stuff. And a liberry of course, for guys that wanted to read. Things like that. And ball games too, regular leagues with teams and everything."

"But these, I imagine, were all privileges—you could be deprived of them."

"If you got demerits or anything, sure."

"Did you ever have any privileges taken away?"

"Oh no."

"Never? Not once in three years?"

"I didn't serve the whole three years, I got paroled, but no, never. You can look it up. I had a clean sheet."

"How is it, Bill, that someone like yourself, who's had some difficulty obeying the laws on the outside, doesn't seem to have the same problem in prison? Was it simply the smart thing to do, a way of seeing the movies and getting out early?"

"Well naturally a guy ain't gonna go cutting his own throat. After all, there ain't much percentage in that."

"Doesn't the same percentage apply outside?"

"Well, I guess it does, when you put it that way. But, well, it ain't exactly the same thing, if you know what I mean."

"How is it different?"

"Well, for one thing, they *tell* you. I mean, they say do this, and you know you gotta do it. If they say don't do it, well then you don't. I mean, it's clear-cut. You know where you stand."

"Isn't it clear-cut on the outside? Isn't it clear, for instance, that burglary is illegal, and that if you're caught you'll be punished?"

"Well yeah, something like that, sure. But it's not just that. I mean, you can make it all sound real simple and everything when you say it like that, but there's more to it . . . it's not just like one and one is two or something."

"Were you happy in prison, Bill? Were you contented?"

"Well now—I mean, I don't mean to, well—when you say something like that, it's just sort of funny, that's all."

"Nobody's contented in prison?"

"Nobody I ever known."

"The way you described it, with ball games, movies, TV—some people may think it sounds all right."

"Some people don't know then. It's a prison, you know. For one thing, it's boring. I mean, after a while you just get bored to death. Then there's this fence around it, eight feet high, with barbed wire. Maybe it don't look like a prison without a big thick wall, but then all right, it looks like a dog pound. That's what the guys call it, the pound. And the guards there, the staff—when they say do something, you do it. They don't exactly ask you for your opinion on whether or not you wanna do it. You hear everybody saying all the time that maybe because they let you watch a lousy TV show what a soft deal it is, but you know, on the outside, you don't have to ask nobody if you wanna watch a TV show, you just watch."

"You'd say then that the loss of individual freedom is the worst punishment in a prison?"

"Well sure I would. I mean, on the outside you never even think about something like that. Before you mentioned about the gates closing on all these guys and everything . . . well, I'll tell you—you don't know. You can't talk about any gates closing behind anybody, because you just don't know. It's gotta happen to you, and then you know. And I'll tell you, you don't forget it so easy."

"Did you work hard at the Farm? What did you do?"

"Well, I mainly did mechanic work, the same as St. Joe's. We had a coupla trucks and staff cars and one old beat-up tractor."

"Maybe we could backtrack a bit. You were sent there, you said, for burglary. Could you tell us exactly what you did, how you got caught?"

"Well yeah—if you want. What it was, was I went into this store—at night, I mean. I got in through a window."

"Was anybody with you?"

"No, I was alone. It was about three in the morning, and I was all alone."

"Were you frightened? When you break into a place like that, do you keep thinking of what might happen if you got caught?"

"Well no, you don't think like that. But you're frightened—I mean, you're not exactly very calm. It's dark and everything and very quiet and there ain't nobody around and—well yeah, sure, you're frightened."

"Were you armed?"

"Oh no. I never had nothing to do with anything like that."

"You've never carried a gun?"

"Never."

"You don't like violence?"

"I ain't never done no violence to anyone. I ain't never hurt anyone in my life."

"Can you re-create for us, in your own words, exactly what happened when you broke into the store? What did you do, what did the place look like, what were you thinking of?"

"Well, I don't know—like I say, it was real dark, and in this little alley next to the store you couldn't see your hand in front of your face."

"Did you use a flashlight?"

"Not out there. They had some garbage cans and I used one to climb up to the window, which was high on this wall, that went into a little bathroom in the back of the store."

"What kind of store was it?"

"An appliance store. Irons, toasters, things like that. Electric coffee-pots. I went in a few days before, you know, so I could see the layout. I told the guy I was looking for a glass knob for one of those electric coffeepots."

"This was all planned out then?"

"Well yeah—I mean, sure, you look around a little first."

"Did you get in the window all right?"

"I got in just fine, and then I was in the bathroom. It was really dark in there. I mean really dark. Anyhow, I found the door and let myself into this little hallway, which was just as black as the bathroom. There was some lights up front, of course, the part you could see from the sidewalk, because stores leave their lights on like that so nobody can go fooling around. Anyhow, I wasn't planning on doing anything up front, except just trying the register, because I knew the guy kept most of his stock in back. Naturally the register was locked, but I had some stuff with me and got it open."

"What kind of stuff?"

"Some little wires and stuff that you use. It's hard to explain. But registers ain't hard to open."

"I wouldn't know how to open one. How did you learn?"

"Some guy I knew at St. Joe's told me. It ain't really hard at all. Anyhow, I got it open—it was on a counter, and I was sorta kneeling behind it and reaching up so no one could see me from outside, in case anybody happened to be going by. I grabbed the bills and stuck them in my pocket and then went into the back again. There was a curtain over the doorway, so once I got behind it I turned on the light and looked around until I found these electric coffeepots."

"Why did you decide on them?"

"Well, see, I could get rid of them, for one thing."

"You mean you had a fence all lined up to dispose of them?"

"Well, I mean, he was gonna take them. What he did with them after, I wasn't in on."

"And you had contacted this fence ahead of time, and he told you he'd take electric coffeepots from you?"

"Well, yeah—more or less. I mean . . . well, I don't wanna go into that too much."

"Did he set the price he'd pay you beforehand too?"

"Well yeah. I mean, that's sort of standard anyhow. One-third."

"Of the retail price?"

"The wholesale price. Anyhow, let's just drop that part, okay? I don't wanna talk about it."

"All right. Go ahead."

"All right. Well, anyhow, I stacked these coffeepots by the back door and brought over some electric toasters, until I figured I had all I could handle. I only had my car, you see, and just wanted to take what could fit in."

"Where was your car?"

"Well, behind the stores on this block was like a little dirt road, which the delivery trucks used, so I parked the car right by this back door. When I got the stuff stacked by the door I knocked off the padlock—it was locked from inside, see—and loaded up as quick as I could and then threw these blankets over everything and headed down this little dirt road to the street, but with my lights off, going very slow. When I got near the street, I slowed down even more and cut the motor and just drifted toward it, very quiet, with my lights still off, so I could hear if any cars were coming along the street . . . and, well, I heard one. So I hit the brake, maybe ten feet from the sidewalk, and with buildings on both sides of me now, because at this end of the road you had buildings on both sides, little stores or whatever, I forget exactly what. But anyhow, I just sat there in the dark with my foot on the brake as hard as I could push, listening to this motor coming along the street, which seemed to take a very long time coming. And then I started thinking maybe somebody in the car could maybe see me sitting there behind the wheel. So right at the last second I ducked down very quickly, still keeping my foot on the brake, like I was right on the edge of a mountain or something. It was very uncomfortable all twisted around like that with my foot on the brake, but once I got down I didn't move a muscle. I just froze, and heard this car go by, real slow, with their headlights suddenly making everything very light but, well, in a kind of fuzzy way, and then suddenly the light was gone and it was pitch dark again. And then I heard the car stop. And it stayed stopped, with the motor idling very low, but with, I don't know, a kind of nervous sound somehow. I was still scrunched down on the seat, so I couldn't see anything, and I was beginning to think maybe I oughta sit up and try too see what was going on, or maybe even make a run for it. All this was going through my mind very quickly, and meanwhile all I could hear was this motor idling, real nervous like, edgy, and then the next thing was someone walking, his boots or shoes or whatever crunching on the dirt, and I remember thinking it must be a big man from the way he walked, because he sounded heavy, and very steady, like he knew exactly where he was going. And then I heard this real loud crackling sound suddenly, from nowhere, but very loud, and then this very loud voice, kind of crackling too. . . . I forget now what it said, but I knew right away then what I ran into was a godd—well, you know, a squad car. Because what it was, was their calls coming over. And it was funny, because I still never moved. I don't know how long it took, but finally I looked up and saw this cop standing there with his hand on the door, just standing there, looking at me, figuring, I decided after, that I must've been a drunk, passed out there on the seat. . . ."

Johnny waited. "And they arrested you then?"

"That's right. . . . They arrested me then."

"You didn't get very far with the loot, did you?"

"I guess I didn't."

"And it was all just a matter of luck—a few minutes, a few seconds . . ."

"That's right. I would've been all right once I got rid of the stuff."

"Is that where you were heading, straight for the fence?"

"Like I said . . . let's just leave that part out, okay?"

"Just one direct question—did you ever hear of a fence being sent to prison?"

"Well . . . no, I guess not."

"But the fellows who provide the stuff, for one-third of the whole-sale price—they end up behind bars often enough, don't they?"

"I guess so, yeah."

"Is it a case of the small fry getting caught and the big-timer going free?"

"I don't know. I ain't no expert on that sort of thing."

"During the time you spent at the Farm—what was it, three years minus the parole time?—did you often think about the way you were picked up, the way it was all determined by a piece of bad luck?"

"It was two years, three months. Well yeah, you think of something like that. What you think is that you had some pretty bad luck, that's what you think."

"Are most men in prison because of bad luck?"

"Well sure. Naturally. I mean if you're lucky, they don't catch you."

"Is it only luck? Could it be skill too? or money? or influence? What about the big-time criminals, the ones with brains and lawyers and organizations—you don't see many of them in prison, do you?"

"Maybe not. Of course I was only at the Farm. Guys like that get sent to the pen."

"Why did you decide to burglarize the store, Bill? Was it for the money?"

"Well yeah. It was for the money. Of course it was for the money."

"How much would you have made if you hadn't been caught?"

"About three bills. I had a hundred and seventy-one dollars from the register in my pocket when they booked me."

""But what you got instead was two years and three months at the State Farm. Was it worth it?"

"I guess not, the way it worked out."

"Were you in desperate need of money?"

"Well—I needed money, yeah."

"But did you need it desperately? Were you driven to steal for it? Did you have a job at the time?"

"No, right at that time I didn't have a job at the moment."

"Did you do it partly for the excitement, Bill? For kicks?"

"I don't know just how you mean, kicks. Everybody's always talking about kicks, but I don't know . . . I never talk about kicks."

"Some psychologists say that something like this is often just a means of expressing your discontent, of getting back at society because society has hurt you."

"Yeah. Well . . . like I said, I did it mainly for the money. I mean, you say three hundred dollars ain't so much maybe, but it ain't exactly peanuts either. Walking around with three hundred dollars in your pocket—well, that don't happen every day of the week."

"Did you have any special purpose in mind for the money?"

"I don't think I did, no."

"Tell me, Bill—do you have an ambition in life? What is it you hope to accomplish, what's your goal?"

"I don't know—I mean, you don't really think of it like that . . ."

"Can't you think of anything?"

"Well, you know—I mean, to get by, if you know what I mean. To make your way. I mean, that's all a guy wants, isn't it? For people to leave you alone . . ."

"Do you think, from your own experience, that the staff at a place like the State Farm are sincerely trying to help you do this, to help you get by, or are they just keeping you locked up until your time is served?"

"They're trying to help, sure. I mean, they tell you that, that it's for your own good and everything. Sure, there's exceptions, but mainly, no, they're trying to help."

"Are they usually successful?"

"Well, that I don't know about. I mean, I don't know none of the figures on things like that."

"The figures are pretty discouraging, Bill. A very high percentage of former convicts end up behind bars again."

"I guess maybe a lot of them do."

"Why? Is it the fault of the men themselves? Of the prisons, of society, our way of life?"

Mel paused. "I guess I just don't know the answer to that one, Mr. Mancino."

"We'll have to sign off in a minute now, Bill. But tell us—what about yourself? What are your chances for staying out of trouble now? You're still on parole, aren't you?"

"That's right, I'm still on parole. Well—I don't know what my chances are. I mean, I hope they're good. I'm trying anyway. I know that much."

"You've got a steady job now, haven't you, Bill? That makes a difference, doesn't it?"

"Oh yeah, sure. That makes a big difference."

"And a family to support."

"That's right."

"And you're really making the effort this time, aren't you?"

"Well yeah—I'm trying. I'm trying the best I know. I mean—well yeah, I'm trying very hard . . ."

"Well Bill, I'm sure I speak for everyone who's heard you tonight when I say we wish you every success. Thank you for coming and talking with us. And good luck."

"Well, really—thanks. Really . . . I appreciate it . . . I really do . . ."

The headless image faded from the monitor, and the City Center Tire commercial came on.

□

Five minutes later Johnny knocked at the door to Arlanson's office. "Did you watch it?" he said when he walked in.

"I watched it," Arlanson said from behind his desk, nodding toward the monitor in the corner. He leaned back in his chair, hands clasped over his vest. "I thought it'd be best to stay close—in case you needed a cool head around. Besides, I often work late. It's part of my ambition in life, to work hard, so I can make my way, so I can get by. That's all I want."

"Did you like it?"

"I liked it. It was quite good actually."

"Thanks. But we've run into a snag. The star's waiting for his money: he wants cash and all I've got is a personal check. Do you have fifty dollars on you?"

"No."

"You've got it in the safe."

"Where is he—inside?"

"He's not planning to hold you up."

"I know; he never touches guns. All right, come on." Arlanson led him down the hall to the accounting office and knelt down to open the safe. He removed a small green cash box and counted out fifty dollars. "Here. You can just give me our check back then."

"I banked it to cover mine," Johnny said. "I'll tear this one up and make out one to you in the morning."

Arlanson smiled. "An awful lot of paperwork to pay one man fifty dollars. Whereas the direct, uncomplicated route seems to be his specialty. Just spring the lock with a little magic wire and stick your hand in the grab bag. Finders keepers. That was all right, though, that part: robbing the store."

"What do you think of him? Not a bad kid, is he?"

"A fine fellow . . . I just wouldn't want him working for me, that's all."

Mel was waiting alone in the studio. The cameramen had left, the klieg lights had been turned off, the studio monitor was blank.

"Here we are, Mel. Fifty dollars. Cash."

"I didn't mean to cause no trouble . . . I just figured all along you meant cash when you—"

"No trouble. You did a great job, Mel, and I appreciate your coming on. If ever I can do anything, lend a hand in some way, you let me know, all right?"

"Sure thing, Mr. Mancino. I mean, I'll do that." He looked down at the bills in his hand. "And thanks a lot, Mr. Mancino. You know—for the money. . . ."

□

It took a few days for the mail to come in after a show, but when Johnny arrived at the studio the next morning the receptionist told him they'd received eleven calls.

"Good?"

"Just one wasn't. The others were very good. There was also a call from Mr. Winninger; will you phone him back?"

Bob Winninger was president of the Jaycees. He wanted Johnny to be a judge in the Miss Aurora Pageant.

"I'm a pretty shaky judge of beauty," Johnny told him.

"I don't know, Johnny—I've seen you squiring around some pretty impressive females. Besides, it's not a beauty contest. We never call it a beauty contest. It's beauty, talent, poise, character, intelligence—everything combined."

"Actually, I'm very busy these days."

"The Pageant's not till October; we're just getting things lined up now. If you're interested, we could probably arrange an exclusive appearance of the finalists on your show. The other stations will probably bitch, but I'll stick to that—if you help out, they're yours."

"All right," Johnny said. "I'll buy that."

"You're getting a bargain."

"I like bargains."

He had an hour before "Noonday," and spent the time trying once more to set up the third spot in the crime series. For the second he had a detective from the Juvenile Bureau, for the fourth the wife of a man now serving twenty years for armed robbery, and for the fifth Ken Muldoon from the Parole office. For the third spot he wanted the Warden from the penitentiary.

On Monday he'd called the pen and finally got the Warden, Wesley Griffing, on the phone. Griffing said he wasn't interested. When Johnny tried to talk him into it, Griffing cut him short: "I said no, Mr. Mancino. I meant it."

"Could you suggest another member of your staff? After all, if you people are interested in getting across to the—"

"I wouldn't want to commit another man. He might feel obligated to accept then."

"Could you just tell me who your top men are? I could speak to them directly."

"Deputy Warden is Tom Philson. Assistant Warden for Security is Jeff Dowler. Assistant Warden for Treatment is Sam Fleishman."

"Would you prefer I ask any one in particular?"

"You can have all three if you want."

"Thank you, Warden," Johnny said curtly. "I'm certainly pleased to have your support in this."

After a brief silence, Griffing said: "You're most welcome."

The Warden in charge of treatment sounded most promising, and Johnny tried him first.

"Dr. Fleishman is off today," the male voice told him when he dialed the pen again. It was the same voice he'd gotten before—probably a convict, assigned to the prison switchboard. It was odd talking to a man who was every night locked into a cell, and Johnny felt a vague obligation to be deferential. He wondered what kind of crime he had committed, how long he was in for, how much longer he had to serve.

"Could I get him at home?" Johnny asked.

"If it's a business call, sir, I think he'd prefer not being disturbed."

"It's important. Could you give me his number?"

"I'm afraid I can't, sir. It's unlisted and we're not authorized to give it out."

"Will he be in tomorrow?"

"Yes, sir. You could call him then."

"Is Mr.—let's see, Mr. Philson around?"

"No, sir. I'm afraid he isn't."

"And I guess Mr. Dowler isn't either?"

"Mr. Dowler's here, sir. Would you like to speak to him?"

Dowler wasn't as chilly as Griffing—he sounded less polished, less educated—but he was just as uncooperative. "Thanks, Mr. . . . er . . ."

"Mancino."

"Mancino. But I'm really not interested."

"Could you tell me why?"

"Nothing particular. I'm just not interested."

"I think it'd be a good opportunity for you people in prison work to reach the public and—"

"Maybe you should try the Warden."

"I did. He gave me your name."

Dowler grunted. "Well, I really don't think I'm your man. Sorry."

"Could you suggest someone who might be? I haven't reached Mr. Philson or Mr. Fleishman yet—do you think either of—"

"I think Dr. Fleishman might be your man."

"Could you give me his home number?"

"I'm afraid I couldn't. You try him tomorrow though. I think he's the man you want."

The next day, Tuesday, Johnny had called the pen three times. Fleishman, it seemed, was never in his office. At least the switchboard operator, the same one, seemed unable to locate him. The third time Johnny left a message asking Fleishman to call back as soon as convenient. He waited through Wednesday and then this morning called again, from his apartment.

"Dr. Fleishman isn't in his office right now," the same fellow on the switchboard told him.

"Is he ever?"

"Yes, sir."

"Did he get my message?"

"It was put on his desk, sir."

"Would you leave another one? Would you say that it is urgent he call me as soon as possible?"

"I'll do that, sir."

He checked now with the switchboard to make sure Fleishman hadn't called while he was on the phone with Winninger. He hadn't. Johnny asked for an outside line and dialed Frank Kale at his store.

"Yes, I did like the show, Johnny. I thought perhaps you bent over backwards to make the fellow seem a little more virtuous than his record suggests, but all in all it was a good job."

"We're going ahead with the series; maybe you'll like some of the other shows better."

"As I said, I liked this one. To be fair, though, I do hope you'll get the viewpoint of the Board presented too."

"Well, the whole thing's pretty fluid at this point. Right now I'm trying to get someone from the penitentiary staff and . . . well, I can't seem to generate much cooperation out there."

"I can't help much with Griffing. He can be pretty obstinate."

"I know. But he gave me the names of his deputies. One turned me down cold, and I'm getting the runaround from another. What goes on out there? What are they trying to hide? I always had the impression prisons were public institutions and—"

"Who's giving you the runaround?"

"Fleishman—Dr. Samuel Fleishman."

"Oh yes."

"Do you have any idea how I can reach him? He doesn't seem to take phone calls. Or messages."

"I'll see what I can do."

As soon as Johnny got back to his office after "Noonday" the phone rang.

"Johnny Mancino speaking." He leaned back and swung his legs up to his desk. He got settled, waiting for a response. His eye caught the paper Arlanson had tacked on his wall and he managed, somewhat absently, to read through the whole Abraham Lincoln routine before he got an answer.

"Yes, hello . . . I've just been watching you on television. . . ."

Johnny sighed. The same phrases all the time, with *I've just been watching you on television* probably the grand champion—followed by *This is the first time I've ever called anyone like you, You don't know who I am, but,* and *Hey, you sound just like you do on television!* The man's voice had a curious quality. Restrained, condescending, almost pompous, it sounded as if he were making a pronouncement and simultaneously passing a mocking commentary upon it. It was like listening to two persons speaking in unison—like the old radio routine in which one man imitated a duet.

"Well, it's nice of you to call . . . ," Johnny said, leaning forward now to spread out the mail that had been left on his desk and see if anything looked interesting.

"Nice?" the man said. "*Nice?* It was an act of sheer survival."

"Who is this, please?"

"Dr. Samuel F. Fleishman—at your service, it seems. Mr. Kale hinted, in his typically veiled manner, that you had some desire to speak to me."

Johnny dropped the envelope he had picked up and leaned back. "Oh yes—I've been having a little difficulty getting to you."

"I'm a very busy man. Hard to find. Devious in my comings and goings."

"Did Mr. Kale mention why I've been calling you?"

"I suppose so."

"Well, are you interested? I'd like very much to have you on."

"I've already been on television."

"All the better. I'm working up a series of programs on various aspects of criminal behavior and prison life. It's called the K-SUN Special Reports on Crime and Punishment, and—"

"Hallelujah!"

"Excuse me?"

"Nothing."

"Anyhow, are you interested?"

"Everyone else gave you the old goose egg, eh? Tell me, who've you tried?"

"Mr. Griffing and Mr. Dowler," Johnny said after a pause. "And frankly, I'd like to know why they turned me down."

"Me too. I could use the same excuse."

Johnny laughed. "Don't—I'm looking forward to having you."

"So Mr. Kale implied."

"Will you do it?"

"I don't know. When's it going to be? Maybe I'll be on vacation or something."

"When are you going on vacation?"

"Actually, I've already gone. I'm groping for straws. What are we going to do on this thing—the usual shit?"

"I hope not," Johnny said after a moment. "What I'd like you to do is just discuss some aspects of—"

"Of course. Aspects."

"Could you speak up a little please? I think the connection—"

"I was muttering. I frequently mutter. What kind of aspects will we be discussing?"

"Well, you could talk about what someone like yourself does in prison, what—"

"Suffer."

"Yes, well . . . and what kind of programs you have for the prisoners, the problems you face. It won't be scripted, of course. It'll be very informal. We'll ask a few questions and you'll be free to answer however you wish. Did you see our show last night, by any chance? It'll be along those lines."

"My wife saw it."

"Well—I hope she liked it."

"I hope so too."

"We had a pretty good reaction, and I think the programs will have an audience, and give you a chance to get your ideas across. Of course I'd be pretty disappointed if none of you were willing to do it, but I don't want you to feel that just because Mr. Kale—"

"Twisted my arm off? Ha-ha. Of course not. A man in my position pressured by a boob like Frank Kale? A man with a Ph.D.? The Assistant Warden in charge of Treatment, Rehabilitation and Education (TRE, as we call it, pronounced *Tree*) in the twenty-third largest state penitentiary in the nation? A man who has been on television all by himself twelve—count them, twelve—times? You can't think much of my integrity, Mr. Mancino."

"Will you come?"

"I have no choice, kiddo."

It was really weird last night after the show. He went to Rigoletto's just for a few beers to settle him down, but he was so worked up that they just didn't do anything for him, so he switched to rye and gingers and then suddenly jumped up, just like that, and went to the phone in the back and dialed Dolin's old number. He was amazed, he still remembered it after all this time.

He listened very calmly to it ring, but when he heard it being picked up he suddenly realized what the hell he was doing and his stomach practically dropped out.

"Hello—Dolin?" It kind of surprised him how funny he sounded. He cleared his throat. "Is this Dolin?"

"Yeah, who's this?"

"Hi, Dolin. . . . This is Mel."

"Mel?" There was a little pause. "Mel *Simmons*?"

"How you doing, Dolin? How's things going?"

"What are you calling me for?"

"I'm just calling."

"You crazy or something?"

"I just figured I'd give you a call."

"Well, don't figure, all right? You drunk?"

"No, I ain't drunk."

"Sure. Just don't be calling me, all right?"

"Look, I—well, I got a little jack, and I figured maybe—"

"Speak up, will you? I can't even hear you."

"I said I thought maybe I could pick up something and maybe drop over. For a talk. I was just feeling like talking to somebody."

"Look, talk to your wife, all right?"

"Don't be like that."

"You come up here, Mel, and I call the cops."

"Christ, Dolin . . ."

"You hear me? I mean it. You knock on my door and I call the cops." She hung up.

He had some more rye and gingers, really just downing them one after the other, but still didn't seem to be feeling anything, only when he got up to leave he thought suddenly he was going out of his mind. Just as he was coming to the door, reaching for the handle, he just froze solid. He was like a statue, he just couldn't move. Then he realized the whole goddamn world was like a statue and it scared the shit out of him because Christ, it might go on forever, with him never moving again or breathing or talking, having to spend the rest of his whole goddamn life like that, frozen solid and crazy as a frigging loon.

Finally it ended, like something red-hot cutting right through a bunch of nerves, and he got out the door, and got home.

□

Kroll's place was pretty empty now when he got there. In the front a couple-three guys were standing at the bar watching the TV, and in the back there were maybe six more in booths. Mel got himself a beer at the bar and asked if Margolis was around.

"He was around before; I don't know. I guess he left."

"Did he say he was coming back or anything?"

"I didn't even see him go. Thirty cents."

Mel bought a pack of cigarettes from the machine and took the beer to a booth in back and waited. Margolis said eight thirty, so he still had five minutes.

The five minutes went by. Mel got another beer and waited some more.

Margolis came at a quarter to nine. "Sorry," he said. "I got held up." Margolis watched the waitress pour his beer. "It's good to see you again," he said when she left.

Mel nodded. "What'd you wanna see me about?"

Margolis kind of smiled. "About nothing. I thought I'd be seeing you about our little deal, but what I'm really seeing you about is nothing."

"Whatd'ya mean, nothing? What's going on?"

"What's going on is you're famous, Mel." Margolis was still smiling.

"What kind of shit you handing me? What're you talking about?"

"I'm talking about how famous you are."

"I think maybe you're outta your goddamn head."

"You know, for a while I thought I was. I saw it with my own eyes, but I didn't believe it. So I called Kroll, and he saw it too, and he didn't believe it either."

Mel shrugged, looking at his hand on the glass. He lifted his fingers one at a time, then put them back one at a time. "You seen it, heh?"

"A lotta people seen it, Mel. I keep bumping into all kinds of people that seen it. And most of them were real—you know, complimentary. They think you did a terrific job."

"Cut the shit, all right?"

"No shit, Mel."

"Okay, because look, maybe you could tell it was me because, the hell, you know me. You know my voice and everything. But how the hell many people know my voice? How many?"

"You got more friends than you think, Mel."

"If they're my friends, they know me anyhow, don't they? I mean, the hell, I'm in the phone book, you know. Mel Simmons, it's right there, anybody wants it. What difference does it make that some guys who already know me anyhow know I was on TV?"

"Well, for one thing Kroll didn't like too much the way you were jawing about all this business with fences and everything."

"Whatd'ya mean? I didn't *say* anything! In fact, if he really saw the thing, he would've seen that the guy *wanted* me to say something, but I didn't."

"It ain't only that. For instance, how many cops know you around here, Mel?"

"What do you mean, cops? I ain't had nothing to do with a cop in years. I ain't even talked to a cop since I been out. What do you mean, for Christ's sake, cops?"

"Suppose the guy in the gas station, he seen the show. Suppose the guy driving the tin can seen it. Suppose maybe you open your mouth with them around—I mean, just suppose—and the guy goes away saying to himself, *You know, I heard that voice before somewhere, now where the hell did I hear it?* And suppose he happens to remember?"

"C'mon now, for Christ's sake. You don't even know what you're talking about."

"What I don't know is the same thing Kroll don't know, which is why the hell if you knew this deal was coming up, you went on the goddamn television."

"Because Christ, I ain't heard from you in weeks about this deal. Because as far as I could see, the goddamn deal might not come off for months the way you guys were dragging your ass on the goddamn thing."

Margolis smiled. "Look Mel—what do you wanna go messing around with these kind of deals for anyhow? I mean, look—you must've done all right on that show. And you got a steady job, like you said there, and you're on parole and trying real hard to go straight and everything —that part was real good, that and the part where you told how you got picked up that time with the coffeepots in the back seat. I never did know how you got picked up that time."

"All right, big joke. Only, you know, I didn't get any kind of sensational money out of that show, if that's what you're thinking."

"They paid you, didn't they?"

"They paid me fifty bucks."

"They paid you more than that."

"They paid the guy that runs the show more than that, but they didn't pay me more. Fifty bucks."

"You was rooked, Mel. You should get yourself an agent. That's what all these big TV stars have, an agent. A man with your background is worth a lot more than that."

"Never mind the shit, all right? All I wanna know is what's coming off now."

"Nothing, Mel. I been trying to make that clear."

"Are you guys figuring on pulling that job by yourselves? Because, you know, it was *my* idea."

"All right, tell you what. You like the idea so much, keep it. It's all yours. Only do me a favor, will you, and don't go getting any ideas about doing it yourself. You got a good job. Stick to it."

"I'd like to see how you'd stick to a job like that, Margolis. You ain't never worked like that in your life."

"It ain't my line of work."

"Well it ain't mine either, and I been sticking to it for weeks now waiting for you guys to get something going, and now you tell me there ain't nothing going. Well I'll tell you, I'm sick of sticking to that goddamn job. And I'm sick of everybody telling me all the time what a great job it is. It's a shitty job."

Margolis shrugged.

□

It was Thursday night that he saw Margolis. The next Monday he asked Coffey for a coupla hours off in the afternoon because his wife was sick and he had to take her to the doctor's. Coffey grumped a bit but finally said okay only not to make a habit of it. Mel drove out to the highway—his mind working like fury all the time, but very cool, very logical—and cruised up and down the stretch a few times, looking over the stations. There were six altogether, like Margolis said, three on each side, all bunched up within maybe a quarter mile. They were all pretty big, and he didn't see much to choose between. So he figured he'd just stick with the idea he first had, which was the Mobil station next to the cafe.

He drove in and pulled up to the regular pump. It struck him as kind of funny that maybe he'd end up robbing them on their own gas. But he wasn't laughing. He was looking everywhere at once and trying to remember every single thing he saw. He wasn't exactly nervous but really hopped up. He felt like he'd just gulped down about twenty cups of black coffee.

There were two sets of three pumps each under the canopy, and two guys working them. He waited in the car for the attendant who was getting change in the glass office for the Plymouth Belvedere at the hi-test pump. The other attendant was taking care of an Olds at the other set of pumps.

The sun was practically melting the paint off the Dodge, but Mel was too busy looking to worry about how hot he was. He noticed that behind the station there was a drop-off, because the highway was built up higher than the land around it. He seemed to remember a little country road ran along the highway out here, but all he could see past the drop was some cows out on the desert and some cactuses and a coupla houses pretty far apart, and way off in the distance the San Juan Mountains.

In maybe a coupla seconds he took all this in. He wasn't wasting any time now thinking about what he saw. He could do that after. Now he just wanted to make sure he saw everything and kept it all straight in his mind.

Through the glass he saw a back door in the office. It didn't lead to the johns because they were outside, on the side facing the cafe.

So it must be the storeroom. That gave him the whole layout—left front, office—left back, storeroom—right front, pits—right back, johns.

The attendant came out with the change for the Plymouth. It drove off and the attendant came over to Mel. He was maybe twenty-one or -two. He was bigger than Mel, taller and a lot heavier, but it was all flab. The guy put his hands on Mel's window and bent down.

"Afternoon . . . fillarup?"

"Yeah," Mel said. "Fillarup."

The kid cranked the pump and dragged the hose over. Mel got out and took a good look at the other attendant, who was finished with the Olds and heading for the office with a bill in his hand. Mel could see this second guy would be more trouble to tangle with than the kid. He was maybe thirty or thirty-five and looked more like the kind you'd expect to find working a station. You hardly ever found soft, flabby guys like the kid. This older guy wasn't any giant, but you could see he could be tough.

The guy passed him, and Mel turned to the kid at the pump. "You wanna check the oil and water too? I'm gonna go see what kind of maps you got, okay?"

"Sure thing."

Mel pushed open the glass door and went into the office, which was nice and cool. The older attendant had just rung up the register—$4.80 —and was making change with his back to Mel because the register was on a counter along the back wall. The rack of road maps was alongside the register, and Mel headed for them. The attendant looked around and nodded and then went on counting out change. Mel made believe he was studying the maps but got a good look at the cash drawer. It wasn't overflowing, naturally, because they must've had a cash box around to thin the drawer into, but all the slots were well stacked, even the ten-and-twenty slot. What with everybody carrying all kinds of goddamn charge plates now, a station didn't take in as much actual cash as they used to. But they took in a lot, you could see that.

The guy slammed the drawer shut and Mel reached for a map.

"Looking for anything special?"

"Just seeing what you got," Mel said.

"Sure. Help yourself."

The guy left. Mel stayed exactly where he was, his feet spread, his arms folded, his head back like he was staring up at the maps. Only, without hardly moving his head, he checked the open shelves under the register counter. They were stacked with Bardahl, window cleaner, radiator flush, STP. But the shelf right under the register had a door, plywood it looked like, and locked with a hasp and a key lock. That was it, he'd bet. At worst, there might be a small safe, but more likely just a cash box you could easy take with you.

He took an Aurora map from the rack and turned around slowly, looking for more locked shelves, and seeing if the attendants out there were giving him the eye. There wasn't anything else locked, and the attendants were both busy.

It suddenly occurred to him he could probably just walk over to the register right now, right this minute, and push down a key and hold the drawer so it wouldn't bang, and maybe just grab the ten-and-twenty stack and shove it in his pocket and maybe get away with it. The idea sent a shiver through him, thinking how close all that money was, and how easy it'd be, but right away he said *No!*, almost out loud. That'd be crazy.

He faced the back door of the office that he saw from outside before. It was open maybe eight inches, not enough to see in. He made a big show of looking for a sign, then pushed the door open and stepped into the storeroom. Guys were always doing that, looking for the john, and he needed only a coupla seconds. All he needed to know was how he could get in, where he could hide, and how he could get out.

What he saw was very good. The room had a big window in the back, toward the drop-off, and open. The storeroom wasn't air-conditioned, so the window was probably always open.

A door connected the storeroom to the grease pits but it was way back and you couldn't see much through it unless you were standing right at the back of the pits.

Mel turned around into the office again, making a big show of looking like he was trying to figure which way to go. The kid attendant outside made a kind of hooking motion with his hand, meaning for Mel to come out and go around the side. Mel smiled and waved thanks.

He went outside and around to the john. He noticed the drop-off was sloped enough so you could get up and down it without any trouble, and that the little country road was right at the bottom of the slope. He went into the john and tried to go but was too excited.

"Three-sixty," the kid said when Mel came out.

Mel gave him the last of the tens from the TV show and waited for the change. He really felt the heat and was sweating very hard. His mouth was dry as dust. He kept looking around but didn't see anything he hadn't seen already.

The kid brought him the change. "Get the map?"

"Yeah," Mel said.

"Come again now."

"Yeah," Mel said. "Sure."

He drove to Warneke Road, then pulled off to find the little country road on the map. It was called Ranchman's Road and squiggled in and out along the highway before swinging over to Turner Boulevard, which took you straight into town.

Mel drove along Ranchman's Road until he came to the mess of rusty oil cans on the slope behind the Mobil station. He stopped, waited for the second hand on his watch to get on the twelve, then gunned the Dodge. He rammed into second, hit the pedal, shifted into third and gave it everything it had, blasting up a real cloud of dust on the dirt road. He could taste it, raw and hot.

He got to Turner Boulevard in one minute and fifty seconds.

Back at the cafe on the highway, he sat at the end of the counter and drank two glasses of ice water and then took his time with the coffee and pie and watched the two guys working the pumps at the Mobil station.

He took off his sunglasses and rubbed the back of his ear, where sometimes the frame made it a little sore. He kept watching, but now the glare on the big plate-glass office was so strong it was almost like looking right into the sun itself, and you couldn't see past it into the office at all. He put his glasses back on. But his mind had started going like crazy when he first pulled into the station before, and it was still going. After a minute, more slowly this time, he took the glasses off again. He stared right at the big splash of glare on the window. He kept staring even after his eyes hurt and he could feel a little spot of pain behind them and couldn't anymore see a frigging thing.

□

Once he was definitely decided to do it, Mel wanted it done and over with as soon as possible. But the main point was he was gonna be very careful and not just get all hopped up and do something stupid. So he did some thinking to pick the best day. And the best day, from every angle, was Saturday.

It was the perfect day, actually, because it was a holiday, the Fourth of July. That meant, for one thing, that they'd have a pile of money coming in Friday night and Saturday morning at the station, what with all the extra holiday driving. It also meant he'd be off from work and wouldn't have to make any excuse to Coffey to get away which, if anybody checked after, might look suspicious.

So he decided. He'd do it Saturday.

That left him the whole rest of the week to get through on the goddamn platform, but if you were gonna play it cool, well then you had to play it cool.

The funny thing was that the week went all right. For one thing, him and Peggy were hitting it off pretty good these days, except for one night when she got on the goddamn beauty school again. So he just gave her the word, once and for all. She wasn't going to any beauty parlor school and that was that. He didn't care what the hell Ella said about the money she'd be pulling in. It was his job to be making the money, and she should worry about bringing up the kid right, that's all, which was her job.

Outside of that, they hit it off pretty good. And on the platform, although Christ knows it wasn't any vacation, things went pretty smooth too. Even Coffey was all right, and Mel got along with Jerrold about as good as you could expect with anyone that mopey. Jerrold was all right, actually, and Mel didn't hold it against him that he wasn't any ball of fire.

What really showed the kind of guy Jerrold was happened on Thursday. Mel forgot his goddamn lunch at home and naturally what he had in his pocket wasn't the kind of loot that bought you dinners at the Waldorf. What he had, exactly, was two dimes and three pennies. He felt kind of funny asking Jerrold for anything, so didn't, but when Jerrold sat down with his three sandwiches and his three bottles of lemon and lime, he naturally saw Mel was empty-handed. So he just reached right around to his back pocket—it took maybe a half hour all told to get his hand back there—and dragged out his wallet, which was all crummy and falling apart but so goddamn thick Mel's eyes almost popped, and handed him a buck. Just like that, with none of this *Remember where you got it from* crap. No, Jerrold just handed it over like you was his long-lost black brother and said, kind of serious and gravelly, "Can't work all day n'out something to eat."

"Well, I appreciate this," Mel said. "I mean, it's only a lend, you know—I'll pay you back tomorrow."

"S'nothing," Jerrold said.

So Mel had a good lunch out of it, and Jerrold never even said a word about it the next day, which was Friday and payday because of the holiday. Mel himself forgot all about it until after he left work. But he reminded himself then to definitely pay it back first thing Monday morning.

□

When he got home Friday night Peggy came out from the kitchen all smiles without even saying anything pulled out this great big envelope she'd been hiding behind her back and handed it to him.

"What's this?" he said. It was addressed to *Mel Simmons, Esq.* "What the hell is this?"

"It came for you. I'm dying to see what's in it. It's from the TV people."

Mel looked at the return address—*K-SUN, Aurora.*

"You think maybe they're sending money or something from being on the show?"

"In a bag like this? What're you expecting, rolls of bills or something?"

"I just thought maybe. Anyhow, open it up, all right?"

Mel turned the envelope over, studying it, weighing it in his hand. He shrugged and pulled open the flap carefully. He took out a batch of regular-size envelopes clipped together. There was a typed letter on top.

"What's it say?"

"Lemme read it first, will you?" Mel read the letter to himself:

Dear Mel,

I'm sorry these took so long getting to you. I asked the secretary to hold aside the ones for you and discovered today she was still holding them. I thought she had sent them along.

I hope they're as good as the ones we've received.

Did you see this week's Special, by any chance? It went over well, we thought.

Many thanks again for your fine work and cooperation.

Best,

Johnny

JM/lc

P.S. Perhaps I should warn you not to be bothered if you find a crank letter of two in the batch. We get them all the time, and the thing to do is ignore them.

AMONG THIEVES

"Huh!" Mel said. He handed the letter to Peggy, who practically yanked his hand off, she was so anxious to read it. Mel counted the envelopes. There were five. One was kind of light blue, with very thin, crinkly paper. He wondered if people sent in money. Maybe someone was offering him a job or something. Still, he felt funny about even opening them. They were all addressed to "Bill," or "Bill ——."

"You got fan letters!" Peggy said. "Gee—open them up."

He shrugged. "They're probably *all* from cranks, like the guy said."

"Oh, c'mon now."

"The world's full of cranks, don't you know that?"

"Open them up, I'm dying to see them."

So they sat on the couch and Mel opened the fattest envelope first and started reading it with Peggy practically stretching her neck off to read it too. The letter was typed, and it was three whole pages long. It just went on and on. He never read anything like it in his life. It wasn't even about him, or the show either. It was mainly about God. Mel began to get a little bored about halfway through the second page, waiting for the guy to get off God and on to something else.

"You gonna read all this?" he asked Peggy.

"I don't know. . . . Don't you think maybe we should. I mean, the person took the time to—"

"Let's just look at some of the others first, all right? We can come back to this one after."

The next one was from a lady. Mel figured she was one of those cranks, all right, because the whole thing was just one big lecture. It really was. How he should stop stealing and breaking the laws and everything. How if he listened to his mother and teacher when he was a kid and learned good behavior back then he wouldn't be in and out of jail all the time now. How he ought to know that crime doesn't pay. And then at the end she dragged in God a bit too, about how he should go to church regular and pray to understand all the ways he done wrong in his life.

After these two Mel wasn't exactly looking forward to the others. But the next one was a little better, and so were the last two. They were all from ladies, and they were all maybe a little drippy for his taste, but at least none of them just lectured him. The one on the crinkly blue paper he thought was the best of all. That lady said how it was a very moving experience and she could tell even without his face showing that he was a much finer young man than he gave himself credit for, and how she really hoped he'd get cracking because she was sure he could make a good life for himself if he just set his mind to it.

One of the others was pretty good too, except at the end where the lady went on about how it wasn't his fault, but hers and everybody else's because nobody ever made a good kind of setup for him to grow up in. Except for that part it was a good letter. In that part Mel had the feeling that she was trying to hand him a line or something.

"Gee, you're famous," Peggy said when they finished. "My husband's a famous man. He gets letters from people."

She said it sort of joking, of course, but you could see she was really impressed. Which was kind of funny, because before he left for the program that night Peggy was so goddamn worried he'd screw up she couldn't sit still. *Be careful what you say, watch your language, be polite, don't talk too fast, don't make trouble,* so that it was a miracle he could even open his mouth when he got there.

"That's right," Mel said, laughing a little, because somehow the letters made him feel sort of up in the air. "Sure. The old man's a big shot."

"He is!" Peggy said. "I think it's so nice for all these people to take the time and everything to write like that."

Of course in her whole life Peggy never wrote to anybody, except maybe a coupla times to her mother and to him at the Farm, so for her a letter was a real production. Actually he didn't know what the hell to make of four old ladies—he figured they were all old—and one guy who was a clear-cut case of some kind of nut on God, all sitting down with nothing better to do than write him a letter. To Bill. "Dear Bill," they all started. It made him feel a little funny, that's all.

"You hungry, Mel? You had anything to eat?"

"No, I ain't. You got something?"

"Sure, wait here. I'll go fix something." She went into the kitchen.

Mel picked up the pile, letters and envelopes all mixed up now, and started kind of browsing through them when suddenly it hit him again that for Christ's sake, tomorrow was Saturday. He could see it in his mind, the station, just sitting out there waiting for him, like in some way it was really very closely connected to him, only with all these letters in his hand and Chucky playing inside and Peggy banging pots around and Jerrold loaning him that dollar that he forgot to pay back, the station seemed kind of unbelievable and a thousand miles away, and for really the first time all week it just sort of hit him: *For Christ's sake, I'm really gonna do it!*

What it was, really, was that he was getting jumpy. Actually he'd been jumpy all week. Because let's face it, maybe sometimes things went all right there on the job, but he just didn't have the stomach for it. Sometimes he'd come across a handkerchief or someone's cruddy underwear and he could just puke. Every day he could feel it getting worse, kind of a pressure building up inside him. And no one could say he hadn't tried. He'd tried. He'd spent four weeks trying, working his balls off hauling people's dirty clothes, and he was sick of it.

Mel felt suddenly terrifically bored, disgusted, exhausted. The job, himself, all the messes everything always turned into. He just couldn't take it anymore. Every night he just prayed when he went to bed that he wouldn't hear the alarm go off at three in the morning, wouldn't have to make believe he was asleep while he watched Peggy get dressed and fix her hair and leave for work. But it never did any good, because every night he heard it, and woke up, and would just lay there clenching his teeth and watch it all again, the big special show put on every night just to make sure he didn't forget what a prize shit he was.

Christ, had he ever once in his whole goddamn life been really happy for maybe as long as a whole week running? Had any single thing ever worked out for him, ever really been right?

The army, maybe. Maybe if he'd just gone back in the army he'd have been all right. Christ only knows. Christ only knows what the hell he ever should've done about anything.

He thought about going back in that time after he broke up with Dolin, but then he started going with Peggy and it seemed like maybe the best thing to do was find a good kid like Peggy and settle down. So he did. And he had no complaints, it wasn't that. After all, Peggy was just great, she deserved a goddamn medal as far as he was concerned, and he loved her and everything.

What he needed right now though, was just somebody to talk to, to explain things to, so they could just go through everything together and then figure out one, two, three, the things he had to do, on a practical day-to-day level. Because that's where things got screwed up, day-to-day. *But what am I supposed to DO?*—that's what he felt like just yelling at people, like these goddamn ladies writing letters to him and everything. What he needed was just someone he could go up to and say, *Look, I'm all screwed up, see. And if you wanna know the God's honest truth, I'm scared too. I don't know which the hell frigging end is up. I mean, shit, here I am, I'm supposed to be a goddamn mechanic, and I never even owned a single frigging tool in my whole life!*

All kinds of things bothered him now that never used to. And at night now he kept having all kinds of crazy dreams and he'd wake up in the morning just exhausted, absolutely worn out, disgusted with everything, figuring what the hell's the use, someone pulled out the plug, everything's turned to shit.

A few nights ago he had this real weird dream he could still remember. Somehow he got captured in Russia and they told him they had this spaceship ready to go to the moon, and he was the guy going in it. He remembered thinking maybe he could just get crocked, so he wouldn't know what was going on until he actually got there. But then he thought of how it'd be being crocked with the goddamn spaceship whirling around way up there with all the stars and planets or whatever whirling around too, and he asked the Russians whether they were planning on getting him back and they said, *There was a chance*. He practically shit. He started carrying on like crazy then, talking a mile a minute at these goddamn Russians putting him in this space suit they had, telling them about his wife and family and everything and why didn't they at least pick a single man without responsibilities, and then he told them he had a broken arm so couldn't go, and when they wouldn't believe him he showed them his arm, and it was, it was broken right at the elbow, the bottom half just dangling back and forth like on a string. But they said it didn't matter and stuffed him into this space suit and started strapping him into this big rocket they had there, pointing straight up, and Christ by this time he was screaming his head off, crying like a baby right in front of all those Russians, thinking about just sailing off forever from the world like that, and how cold and black it would be out there, and of being all by himself on the moon, left to die way out in space like that, millions of miles away from anybody, out there on this great big black frozen rock or whatever the hell it was, and he kept crying and screaming at these goddamn Russians, *Why me? Why me?* but nobody even answered, and they just kept strapping him in.

Peggy was still banging around in the kitchen. What the hell was she making anyhow—a twelve-course meal?

He dropped all the letters and envelopes on the couch and headed for the kitchen to get himself a cold beer.

□

Saturday Mel left the house a quarter after two. He told Peggy he had to take the Dodge in to get the clutch adjusted. He didn't feel nervous. He felt kind of airy and floating. He felt like he wasn't touching ground, like all his nerves and everything had gone dead in a certain way, but in another way had become very sharp and alert. It was like everything he could see or hear or touch was suddenly strange and different.

He drove west a bit. You could get out all by yourself in just a few minutes in this direction, where all the houses just stopped and you were out on the desert. He pulled off the road and scooped up some dirt into the coffee can full of water he'd sneaked into the car and stirred it with a stick until it was thick and muddy. Then he slopped it over the license plates, not enough to cover everything but just to make it impossible to read the whole number. He slopped some more on the fenders and grill and the trunk, so it'd look like he went through a puddle somewhere, and then headed out toward the highway.

Most of the stores along Beradino were closed for the holiday and there were a lot of flags up. He passed a little neighborhood park where a bunch of people were sitting at these big wooden tables with kids running all over the place and a big sign hung up saying the American Legion was having a picnic.

He got to the highway and drove very steady at around fifty-five. There was a lot of traffic and it was very hot and dusty because the sun was really blazing down. The Dodge was like a goddamn black sweatbox.

He slowed up passing the Mobil station to get a good look. The same two guys were at the pumps, the fat kid and the older guy. The glare of the sun on the office window hit him just before he passed the middle of the station. It would be straight on the pumps, he figured, in about twenty minutes. It was ten to three now. Between five and maybe ten after he'd have to move in.

He swung onto Warneke Road and then onto Ranchman's Road and drove down to the rusty oil cans on the slope behind the Mobil station and pulled over and stopped. It was six minutes to three.

He crossed the dirt road and walked out into the desert until he could see the rear window. It was open. The bottom half was all the way up.

He walked back and sat in the car to get out of the sun and lit a cigarette and spread a map out over the steering wheel so if anybody drove by it'd be like he just pulled off to look at the map.

One guy drove by in a Comet. He went by like a shot, sending up a goddamn cloud of dust that practically choked Mel.

A coupla minutes later a kid, maybe twelve or thirteen, pumped by on a bike. Mel just made believe he was studying the map and didn't look up. The kid was heading back toward Warneke Road, which was good. Mel would be going in the other direction, so wouldn't have to pass him racing the hell away.

At two minutes after three Mel dropped the map in the back seat. He took off his sunglasses and put them in the magnet tray on the dash. He picked up the gloves from the floor and put them on. They were thin leather and fit very close. Then he checked to make sure the shift was in neutral and the hand brake off and the key in the ignition. Then he got out. He looked up and down the road to make sure no one was around, then picked up the small forked pry bar from under the seat and put it in his side trouser pocket. It stuck out, but just a little.

He left the door leaning closed so he could just pull it right open.

He wished he would loosen up a bit. Every time he moved or did something with his fingers it felt funny. It was like a motor working with a wrong oil, that was too thick for it.

He climbed the slope, careful not to kick any of the cans and start them tumbling down. The oil smell was very strong from the sun on all the empty cans. He was crouched low to the ground, and could even smell the hard dirt, the desert smell, very dry and hot, and the dry weeds too. He could even see the pebbles very clear. And then he stopped dead. He was looking right into the face of a goddamn Gila monster. It was right on the slope, heading down, and Mel was bent over so close his own face was about a foot from its face. The Gila monster was standing still too and looked like it might even be stuffed because it was so still. Its skin looked like black and pink beads, hard and leathery and covered with dust and not looking like live skin at all. Mel'd never seen one before except in the zoo once, and it looked like some goddamn shrunk-up dinosaur, with its fat tail and beady scales all over and even the shape of its head and the kind of dinosaur feet with claws it had. It was the deadest, ugliest-looking thing he'd ever seen in his life and at first, bent over like that looking at it, he didn't believe it was actually there. He thought maybe something snapped in his mind and he was seeing things. And very quick, in a real flash, he remembered hearing how these goddamn things were really deadly because they couldn't get rid of the poisons in their body because they had no way of going to the bathroom, and that if they clamped their jaw on your finger or something you could never get them open because their jaws were so strong they just locked together. But they were slow. They were very slow. This one still hadn't even moved. And then Mel thought *What the hell am I so scared for?*

He edged to one side, still crouched over. The Gila monster didn't move. It didn't even watch him move. Maybe it really was dead. Its eyes didn't even move.

Mel hurried past it, still bent over. He stopped when he got near the top to listen, then moved up onto the level ground, not rushing, keeping his eyes open. His eyes were burning. When he saw no one around, he walked straight for the back of the building, as easy and innocent as he could.

He was sweating like a pig. He leaned flat against the wall near the window, in the shade now. The window ledge came to his chest. He listened again. Then he inched his head carefully around the edge of the window to see if the door to the pits was open. It was. But he couldn't see or hear anyone working in there.

The door to the office was open a few inches, like the other time. He couldn't hear anybody in the office.

He took a deep breath but couldn't seem to get any air into his lungs. It felt like somebody sucked all the air out of the world with a pump. He could feel a kind of buzzing in his hands. He was afraid if he tried to move he'd just fall over, like a statue.

Only he had to move, he couldn't just stand there.

Very carefully, he put his hands on the window ledge. He swallowed hard, then boosted himself up. He swung one leg over, then the other. He couldn't get his feet exactly where he wanted, and he seemed to make a lot more noise than he planned to. He hesitated on the ledge a minute, then let himself down into the storeroom. His legs felt numb and very light, floating.

The room was so dark after coming in from the sun he was afraid he'd knock something over. He moved forward anyhow, away from the door that led to the pits. A thin slice of sunlight came through the little opening of the office door. He could see the dust dancing in it.

He heard the outside door open and somebody walk into the office.

He held everything clenched tight and pressed himself back against the shelves. He ached from how tight he was keeping himself. He was afraid to hold his breath because he might cough, so he breathed very quiet and even, through his nose. He could feel a little nervous spot in his stomach, right below where his ribs came together. It sort of fluttered and made the rest of his insides feel hollow, like some kind of empty shell around this little spot that kept fluttering. He held his hand over the spot.

Mel listened to whoever it was in the office walk across the floor, whistling, and ring up the register. Then it was very quiet except for the whistling, which sounded very thin and far away. Then he heard the register slam and the bell dinging very faintly in the air, and then some steps, and then quiet again, and then some more steps and the outside door opening and slamming shut.

It was perfectly quiet, except now Mel could hear the cars zooming by on the highway.

He waited a few seconds, still holding himself tight, and still fluttering inside. Then he moved his arm slowly—it was very stiff—and turned his wrist to catch the light from the slice of sun. It was four minutes after three.

He tiptoed to the office door, staying behind it, and inched his head forward until he could see around it. He could see only part of the station because of the angle. Staying behind the door, he bent down and put his eye to the keyhole.

It was a big keyhole, right through the door. He could see all the pumps. There were two cars out there, one attendant working each. Everything looked smaller than it really was, and sharper, and the sun was high enough so it wasn't in his eye. Somehow, the way his body felt bending over like that seemed very familiar, like something he'd done a thousand times before, even though he couldn't remember ever looking through a keyhole before in his life.

The flabby kid started for the office with a bill, his head to one side and his eyes down—the glare. Good. Mel straightened up but didn't move his feet. He stood very still behind the door and listened to the kid come in and walk over and ring up and then slam the drawer and go back out.

Mel crouched down to the keyhole again. A big new Continental pulled in. The kid gave change to the guy waiting and moved over to the Continental. The older attendant was cleaning the windshield of his car now, finishing up. This kind of timing wouldn't work. He needed them both starting on cars at the same time.

A guy in a light tan summer suit got out of the Continental. He was short and round and maybe fifty years old and looked like a goddamn boiled lobster he was so red in the face. He stood next to his car wiping himself with a big white hanky. Then, without saying anything to the kid, who was cranking the pump, the guy sort of wandered away, and still without saying anything, headed for the office. He stopped outside the glass door, looking around. The two attendants were working and didn't notice him. Mel was so pissed off at the jerk, and at the attendants for not noticing him, that he felt like yelling out himself that *For Christ's sake, the goddamn john is around the frigging corner!*

The man opened the glass door and stepped into the office. It was too late for Mel to straighten up, so he stayed bent over with his eye at the keyhole. The man looked around again, with a kind of dopey, put-out look, like it bothered the hell out of him the way people went around hiding the goddamn johns. With a shrug he moved toward the storeroom door.

The last thing Mel saw through the keyhole was the guy's white shirt stretched over his stomach. He didn't feel himself moving. The door swung open and the sun flashed into the room like a bulb being turned on.

Mel was about six feet from the door, his back to it, facing a row of shelves, holding a can of Wynn's Tune Up, looking at it with his shoulders hunched. He didn't move. The guy didn't move either.

"*Around the side!*" Mel said. He croaked it actually.

"Oh," the man said. He let out a heavy breath, like a sigh, like the heat was really getting him down. "Thanks." He went back through the office and out the glass door.

Mel was still staring at the Wynn's Tune Up in his hand, making believe he was trying to read the label. He *was* trying to read it, but the can was jiggling too much.

He finally looked around. The storeroom door was wide open. He leaped over. The older attendant was walking toward the office with money in his hand. Mel pushed the door back to where it was before and stood bolt upright behind it, his hand still on the knob. The guy came in and rang up the register. He slammed it shut and left.

Slowly, one finger at a time, Mel loosened his hold on the doorknob. The knob clicked when he took off the last finger.

He bent to the keyhole. Either the goddamn guy in the suit figured he was another attendant or else was the coolest bastard Mel ever seen. He waited for him to come out of the john. If anything looked funny then, if the guy said anything that made the kid look toward the office, even just glance over for a second, he'd just forget the whole frigging thing and run for it.

The red-faced guy came into view from around the corner where the john was. He was wiping his face again. The kid went up to him and said something and the guy said something back while he pulled out his wallet. The kid took the money and headed for the office.

Mel didn't move. He couldn't. He didn't even straighten up from the keyhole.

The kid took care of the change and left.

Mel closed his eyes. It felt like he hadn't blinked for an hour.

The older attendant was poking around at the oil cans on the rack out there because the only car at the pumps now was the Continental belonging to the guy in the suit. The guy got his change from the kid and drove away. The station was empty, but just for a second. An old blue Chev pulled in, and right behind it a Chrysler New Yorker.

Perfectly together, almost like a goddamn dance team, both the attendants bent down to the driver's window of the two cars and nodded and at almost exactly the same time moved to a pump, cranked, and dragged the hose over to the cars.

Okay. Either now or kiss it all sweet good-bye, the whole frigging business, money and all.

He pulled back the door just enough to get through. Then, without feeling stiff at all now, without feeling anything except a really surprising kind of easy smoothness, he slipped into the office, crouched over like a monkey on his hands and feet to keep as much below the bottom of the window as possible. Between keeping low and the glare, he didn't think anyone could see him from outside. So all he had to worry about was time. He had to work fast.

He scooted across the floor to the register. He felt very alert now and knew exactly what he wanted to do. He kept low and took a quick look outside. The older guy had his pump on automatic and was opening the hood of the New Yorker. The kid was still holding his pump. Mel reached up carefully and put one gloved finger on one key. He put the other hand against the face of the cash drawer and looked outside again.

The kid was cleaning the Chev's windshield. The older guy was looking at the New Yorker's oil stick.

Keeping his eyes on them, Mel pushed down on the key. The register clanged like a goddamn fire engine and the drawer slammed against his hand. Both attendants kept working without looking up.

Mel let the drawer ease open. He lefted out the cash tray and put it on the floor. He pushed up the spring loops of the slots and stuffed the bills in his pocket. Then he reached up into the drawer again and brought down a handful of all the checks and stuff they had laying under the cash drawer, because usually guys would put the really big bills under there if they got any, and he thought he might find a fifty or even a hundred, but all he got were checks, which he just dumped on the floor next to the tray.

He did all this very fast. Then he took the pry bar from his pocket and slid one prong through the hasp on the plywood door under the register. He pressed hard against the curve of the bar, using the door as leverage. It gave a little. He banged on the bar with the heel of his right hand. The hasp eased, then flew off, rattling across the floor. Mel looked outside. The kid was back jiggling the pump. The older guy was pouring oil into the New Yorker.

Mel put the pry bar in his pocket and opened the door. There were three shelves, filled mostly with papers and audit books. He grabbed the green metal box and scurried across the floor on all fours and lunged into the storeroom, bumping hard against the door. He straightened up, still moving, and leaped at the open window, almost like he really expected just to sail right through without even touching. Suddenly he hurt but couldn't tell exactly where and was tumbling without feeling anything except that everything was cockeyed and he was running downhill, all rubber, no joints, no bones, slipping on rocks and kicking oil cans that went clattering and then felt the jolt right up through his body, even in his teeth, like someone slammed up into the soles of his feet with a flat board, as he hit level ground and flung himself toward the Dodge and saw the kid there, looking into the car, his bike leaning against the front fender.

□

"Hello," the voice said, a woman's voice. "Hello—?"

"There's a fellow hurt," Mel said.

"Excuse me? Will you speak a little louder please."

Mel put his lips right against the mouthpiece. The little rubber fan in the booth wasn't working, and the booth was right in the sun, in the corner of the shopping center parking lot, and it was so hot he was afraid he was gonna puke. "There's a fellow hurt," he said. "He needs an ambulance."

"Who is this please?"

"There's a fellow hurt," Mel said. "On Ranchman's Road. Take this down, will you? Ranchman's Road, on the side. Right behind the Mobil station on the highway there. He's hurt."

"Can I have your name please? Where are you calling from? Has there been an accident or—"

"Did you get that? Ranchman's Road. Behind the Mobil station."

"Yes, I've got all that. But who—"

Mel hung up.

6

At ten minutes after five, with a final ambiguous nod, good old Dr. Samuel F. "Flash" Fleishman relinquished the responsibility he had held all day to the man who would hold it all night. Then he returned to his office and picked up some papers and said good evening to his secretary. His secretary was half a head taller than he was, with hands so large and fingers so gun-barrelly they seemed too gross for the typewriter and the poised pencil. But they were not. Harry, a prime fellow indeed, could secretary with the best of them.

Men, truth to tell, made ideal secretaries. You install a lithe, busty, lipsticked young wench in your office and next thing you know you're gaping slack-jawed when she crouches down to get some vital document from the file. Then you're pinching the backs of her soft thighs and where the hell are you for getting work done, or even wanting to? And who knows—you fall in love and there you are, amidst the assorted memoranda, commiting fornication on the Artmetal desktop, next to the Remington Noiseless.

After saying good evening to his secretary, whose face by this time of day was darkening roughly, making him look more than anything else like a moving-van loader, Flash left the office. By its thin leather handle he carried his thin executive briefcase, last year's birthday present from Jo Ann, who would dearly approve if he somehow managed to look a little more like an executive.

He walked down the long hall of the Quonset hut and then out the door and across the paralyzed, sun-struck yard. At the front gate, be-

neath the stone archway of the sally port, he performed his usual careless parody of military crispness in returning the guard's salute, signed
out, stepped through the small door in the barred gate, and walked
along the gravel path outside the wall to the parking area. From the
tower thirty feet above a guard waved down, holding his rifle in his
left hand and waving with his right. Flash waved back.

The reason he did not look like an executive, and his secretary was
half a head taller, was that he had to hold himself very straight, which
he rarely felt much urge to do, to be considered average height. He
was not short; he just wasn't quite average. Nor was he powerful,
fleshy, big-boned or muscular. He was narrow and small-boned and, in
all truth, weak. He could declare a paunch, but it was not a rollicking
paunch, not a lusty nor a hearty one. It was not Santa Claus's paunch,
or Churchill's, or Diamond Jim Brady's, or Falstaff's. It was, alas, Dr.
Samuel F. "Flash" Fleishman's paunch, and precious little to brag about.

He weighed 163 pounds, as of this morning. He kept a scale in the
bottom drawer of his desk, and every morning would place it upon
the floor, remove his jacket, shoes, wallet, eyeglasses, pocket change,
keys and hanky and weigh himself behind his locked door, getting on
the scale very delicately, very gradually, one foot at a time, and then
crouching over to squint at the magnified number. The scale at home
he never used. That was Jo Ann's scale, and she was welcome to it. He
wouldn't go near it.

No athlete, he. No physical culturist. No golfer, handball player or
tennis buff. A walker, though, but even that rarely now, for although
their *lovely almost new 5 bdrm 2 bth mdr ktn patio den frplce low
dwn easy pymts* house was exactly 1.3 miles from the salute at the
sally port, he drove every day back and forth because Jo Ann had declared—when they were reading listings every night the way pious
families used to read the Bible—that she would not live close to the
prison. "Close" came to mean walking distance, so he drove daily to the
walled and gated and patrolled fortress in which were imprisoned 1143
inmates, one warden, one deputy warden, two assistant wardens, a
comptroller, an accountant, a chief guard, a chief keeper, a dozen
guard lieutenants, over 150 guards and shop officers, a doctor, a psychologist, two chaplains, an educational specialist, a couple of dozen
social workers, classification specialists, interviewers, engineers, elec-
tricians, plumbers and assorted other professional and nonprofessional
helpers, fussers, doers, makers and changers, along with their duly appointed and engaged deputies and mortal enemies, over all of which

and whom, during the last eight hours of this festive holiday, Flash Fleishman had been in final, absolute and inviolable command.

Six days a year were recognized as holidays by the State Penal Code, the Fourth of July among them, and it had been his misfortune this holiday to be Acting Warden. He hoped that when Thanksgiving, Christmas, New Year's Day, Easter and Memorial Day rolled around, it would be someone else's turn. What profounder depths of despair could the human heart know than a holiday in prison? But it had gone well. He had sat in the seat of honor at the performance of the prison band. He had led the inmates and staff in the pledge to the flag, which had, God knows, been a moving and disturbing experience. Prisoners did not make light of Old Glory, and Flash thought of all those craggy veterans of World War II and Korea, those battle-hardened heroes that it was his sworn duty to keep locked up, he who had never served, who was flabby and cowardly and probably unpatriotic to boot. Afterward he personally inspected the holiday meal of turkey (standard every holiday; some friend of a key legislator was a turkey farmer) and manifold fixings, and had declared it excellent, which it was. He had authorized the traditional extra recreation period and the showing of a holiday movie—*That Touch of Mink*, with Doris Day and Cary Grant—which he understood the inmates enjoyed. But it was a holiday nonetheless, and nonetheless a prison, and Flash was exhausted and dismal, a beaten man.

He also did not look like an executive because he lacked the mien, the countenance. Not to him was given the glinty eye, the prominent chin, the decisive brow. What he did have was a moderately bushy mustache that might, charitably, be called significant; large, dark, deep-set and heavily browed eyes that he imagined, from the circus that went on behind them, usually appeared wildly inconclusive and may-be even harried; black hair brushed back and thinning miserably, giving him a bit more forehead than a man had any real use for. He also wore glasses with black frames—20/150 left eye, 20/200 right, with a pronounced astigmatism. Blind as a bat, in other words. He also had a larger than average nose: his Semitic feature, helpful in those situations when he chose to be a Jew.

And yet surely not an unattractive man. Never, truth to tell, handsome, not even in his youth. But he got by. Children did not laugh at him. No one threw stones. He photographed passably.

But only in his soul, he thought—turning the key to prompt the whining and scraping and then the *VHRRRRROOOOOMMM!* that announced to one and all that his trusty 1960 Volkswagen had plenty of 1.3 mile ferryings left in her yet—only in his soul could he truly be considered a thing of beauty.

And arrived home. The drive took approximately three minutes. The road from the gate led to Route 16, which led almost immediately to Mountain Acres. There were forty-seven houses in Mountain Acres. It was a development, a tract, a determined grouping, situated in as flat and unwrinkled a piece of desert as God ever created in all his green world. It was called Mountain Acres because, far off, through the fine haze of afternoon dust, one could in fact see not only one mountain but an entire range. The San Juans were eighteen miles away, north of Aurora, whereas Mountain Acres was southeast, but as the agent had no doubt also pointed out to the other forty-six families, they *appeared* closer. And by God they did, and lovely mountains they were too!

What the agent didn't mention was that the place was a lot closer to the prison than to the mountains, and could have more fittingly been called Penitentiary Acres or Jailbird Flat for that matter. But you couldn't see the prison; you could see only the backside of the hill it was built on, which except for a few bushes and a stray ironwood or two, was bare.

The whole bloody countryside was bare. You strolled a careless hundred yards from your back door, or twenty feet from any roadside, and there you were, out on the bone-dry desert. A hell of a place to live—or to build a prison, for that matter. And at night, driving into Aurora perhaps, or just gazing out from your patio, you were a bold and brave man indeed if you didn't feel a little shiver as all that vastness that had once been the bottom of the ocean spread out around you, black and flat and lonely, desolate, without decoration, without lushness, spare, sparse, true, cruel, eternal. It was a hell of a feeling.

And what had brought him here? What destiny led his steps from Austria (as a mere child) to London to Buffalo to Manitoba, and then here, to Aurora, to the heart and center of the biggest and best desert America had? Asthma brought him here: his oldest son, Walt, had asthma. Such the simplicities of our lives, the ease of accounting for our destinies. And for four years now they'd lived here where you could say, with only slight exaggeration, that there was no rain, no snow, no cold, where the sun shone every day and mercilessly, where all was, or could turn to, dust. It was like nowhere else in the world, this strange and blistering place where even some of the flowers bloomed only at night, and it was their home.

But it was all right. Aurora wasn't a bad city, big enough to offer advantages, small enough to let you move around, and they were only nine miles from its center. It had a fair university, a decent library, a good symphony, a passable drama group. And the place was booming, people were making their fortunes, money changed hands, all with a bravado that would have shocked all those dour and hearty Manitoba wheat farmers, and that shocked Flash. Every day—every hour probably —someone moved into Aurora and its environs, thousands every month. Who the hell they all were God only knew, but they came, and they kept coming—people who had kids with asthma, people who had arthritis or TB, people who liked heat and hated cold, who preferred air conditioning to furnaces, people who had grown weary elsewhere of rain and snow, people who had jobs in the electronics or aircraft plants, or at the SAC base, or on the ranches or citrus orchards, in the hotels and motels that milked the annual winter influx of tourists, people who wanted to make money selling cars or TV sets or real estate, or building houses, or making or selling plumbing or window glass or carpets to go into all those houses being built for all those other people who came for all those other reasons.

And, more to Flash Fleishman's interest, it had a penitentiary, an enormous fat old ugly outmoded overcrowded and poorly designed penitentiary, just what he was looking for, and luckily just what happened to be looking for him. Although personally he thought Griffing was crazy to hire him. If he were Griffing, he would have hired that other guy. But for some reason still beyond Flash, and probably everybody else in the place, Griffing offered him the job and down they came, all six of them (Jimmy was born here), to live perhaps forever on the desert which, when you gave it a moment's thought, was probably not such a strange place to build a prison after all.

In the carport he cut the ignition and the Volkswagen expired with its final deflating hiss. He got out and headed for the front door. He never locked the car, and locked the house only because Jo Ann insisted. If somebody wants to rob you he's going to anyhow, whether you spend your life locking things up or not. There you sit, thinking about bills, about Walt's asthma, Jo Ann's latest pregnancy, Marion's orthodontia problems, wondering what you're going to do Saturday and how many mistakes you made at work today that you don't even know are mistakes yet and why you have a funny little ache in your knee, while the thief watching from across the dark street has only one thought: how to get into your house. You can't beat him. All you can hope is he'll pick another house, that you'll be saved by the law of averages. Once he decides on yours, that's it. You can't beat the fanatic, the guy who's willing to spend all his time, to risk everything, to give up his freedom and maybe even his life to cart off your hi-fi set.

The lawns along Rio Brava Court were decorated with trikes, wagons, balls, bats, sneakers, dolls, carriages, plastic swimming pools, as if a low-flying cargo plane had sprung a leak. Some lawns, free of such paraphernalia, were being inundated by automatic sprinklers propelling figure eights. But few kids. It was dreadfully hot in the sun. Besides, Bugs Bunny was on now. Or Mighty Mouse, or Jonny Quest. Something. Along Rio Brava the families averaged 3.9 offspring each at last reckoning, although some swollen woman probably lay groaning at this very moment in the Aurora Hospital delivery room, ready to push the average up to new heights. This was it, Fertile Valley, where all the men played Daddy-O and the women took turns taking care of each other's children so they could take turns having more children.

Entering, placing his jacket on a hanger in the hall closet, he found all surprisingly quiet. Which meant he heard only the frenetic nickelodeon music and the enormous boom-boom bass of the TV set upstairs —no screams, no howls, no threats, no accusations over favorite dolls, lost comic books or stolen jungle knives, no screaming pleas to be picked up, listened to, played with. He poked his head into the living room. It was empty. He went into the kitchen.

"Has he called?" he asked. Jo Ann, his young and lovely and pleasant and intelligent and hopelessly once again—would it never end? was there no God?—pregnant wife, was stirring at the built-in electric stove. He kissed her, resting one hand on her bulging tummy.

"Hi," she said, brushing the hair from her eyes with the back of her wrist. She had sort of dark-honey-colored hair. "Who?"

"You know. The goon."

"Stop calling him that; that's terrible. He called before. He said he couldn't get you at work."

"What did you tell him?"

"I told him you'd be home tonight. How did it go? Was everything quiet?"

"Yes, it was quiet. Everything went fine."

It was always a problem deciding what to tell Jo Ann about his work. If he told her everything she became despondent and would suggest at the next opportunity that he wasn't getting any younger, that the future of the children had to be considered, and that perhaps they should start thinking (start! She had never stopped!) about finding some nice undemanding professorship at some nice secluded university. If he told her less than everything, she would assume he was withholding the really depressing news and so would become despondent and, at the next opportunity, would suggest that he wasn't getting any younger and perhaps . . .

"You look tired," she said.

"I am, a little." He opened the freezer compartment of the refrigerator, took out a handful of ice cubes, placed them in a large glass, added some vermouth and about three fingers of gin, stirred briskly with a fork and poured into a smaller glass, holding the ice back with the fork. He drank. "How was everything here? Was everybody good?"

"I guess so. The pedal broke off Terry's bike again. The one you fixed."

"Did you get to the pool with them?"

"Yes. It was mobbed. It was a madhouse. But they had a good time." Flash drank. "Are they all upstairs?"

"The little ones are. I don't know where Walt is. Janie and Terry are playing at the Bentons." Jo Ann took a bowl of jello from the breakfast bar and put it in the refrigerator. The jello was divided into three strips—red, white, and blue.

"Oh no," he said.

"The kids asked for it." She opened the oven and poked tentatively at the ham with a long fork. "I promised them a holiday dinner. We've got fireworks for after."

Flash drank. "You didn't tell me we had fireworks."

"I thought it'd be nice. Everybody else on the block has them."

"Did the goon say he was going to call tonight? He's not thinking of coming here, is he?"

"He didn't say. He just seemed pleased to hear you'd be around."

"I'm pleased he's pleased." He drank and then poured some vermouth and about three fingers of gin over the ice cubes still in the big glass. "I think I'll sit out on the patio and look at the paper."

"Okay. We'll be ready in about half an hour. I'm a little behind schedule."

"I don't have to eat that jello, do I?"

"It's mainly for the kids."

He finished stirring and poured into the smaller glass, holding back the ice with the fork.

☐

On the patio flagstones of their dark backyard Flash crouched match in hand to ignite firecrackers, Roman candles and a little cardboard house with a chimney wick. Jo Ann and the children sat on the webbed chairs or at the redwood picnic table and voiced their delight, except Walt, who was thirteen now and too sophisticated to be delighted by anything. The cardboard house was something new this year, and a special hit. It burned marvelously, flames shooting out of windows, the whole structure finally collapsing with hisses into charred remains and blackened rubble. *"House Afire,"* it was called, and it lacked only real screams and desperate second-story leaps.

In all the other backyards of all the other houses—or almost; he hated to overstate—the other fathers were no doubt similarly bent over, matches in hand. The night sky flared brilliantly and the usual evening quiet of Mountain Acres was violated by staccato cracklings and reverberating booms.

The crackling and booming continued as he and Jo Ann took turns going into the bedrooms to say good night to the kids.

"Good night," he said to Janie. "How'd the assistant mommy do today?"

"I learned a new stroke at the pool," Janie said.

"Good night," he said when he moved to Marion's bed against the other wall. "You like the fireworks, sweetie?"

"Tell me a story," Marion said.

"Good night," he called in to Walt, who had his own room, where an allergenic air purifier hummed away on the floor.

"Night, Dad," Walt called back without looking up. He was playing himself at chess.

On his way to the boys room he passed Jo Ann in the hall, who was on her way to the girls room. "Say something to Jimmy," she told him. "He made B.M. in the potty today."

"Jimmy made B.M. in the potty," he said, leaning over the crib in the boys room. "Good boy, Jimmy. Jimmy made B.M. in the potty."

"Song," Jimmy said.

"Good night," he said to Terry.

"Why do we have fireworks on the Fourth of July?" Terry asked.

Every night after getting all the kids off—Good God, soon they'd have six; there were only four cons in the whole prison who had more kids than that—he joined Jo Ann for her one drink of the evening, a gin and tonic. He had gin and orange juice in a large blue Mexican glass, his regular after-dinner drink. Usually they sat on the patio and observed the stars in the black sky and talked, but tonight they stayed in the living room. Flash had had enough rocketry for one evening, and things were still going off outside. Jo Ann sat in their purplish Freudian chair, he on the couch.

"Did Griffing check in with you today?"

"No," Flash said. "He was up in Maynard, boozing it up with the Governor."

"You didn't tell me that. Did Eberhart send for him?"

"More or less, I guess."

"Is it about your idea? The minimum thing?"

"I don't know. Maybe. Maybe it's about the poor state of Western Man. Who knows?"

"You're getting all nerved up again, Flash. Griffing doesn't get so bothered about everything. I don't see why you should."

"I'm perfectly relaxed. I'm just ready for another drink, that's all."

"Have one then."

"Thank you. I will."

Many are dying; there is suffering and despair everywhere. And I am weary, mainly from going to and fro in the earth, and walking up and down in it.

He slid back the door of the cabinet under the kitchen counter—a truly modern house; nothing opens, everything slides—and took out the White Bear gin, $3.19 a quart at Walgren's, and you can't beat that.

And whose idea is this? the Governor will ask—incredulous, outraged, flabbergasted.

It is, in truth, an idea shared by all of us down there at the big barred place, Griffing will say. It is the product of our combined wisdom and experience.

It sounds to me like the sort of thing Fleishman would dream up.

I didn't know you knew Dr. Fleishman, Governor.

I keep an ear to the ground, Warden. When you're governor of a great state and have a man like Fleishman working for you, no matter where, no matter in how menial and subservient a position, it's worth your eyetooth to keep tabs on him.

Your political acumen impresses me, Governor.

Thank you, Warden. And now this crazy idea of Fleishman's—is it sensible? Will it work? Does it claim the support of Reason and Logic? Is it pragmatically conceivable? Is it conceivably pragmatic? Can we afford it? Do we want it?

Yes, Governor. It is all those things, and more.

This Fleishman must be a genius.

He is, Governor. He is my strong right hand, my font of wisdom, my source of inspiration.

It sounds like mollycoddling to me. It sound like a piece of hair-brained liberalism. It smacks of—

Hare-brained, sir; not *hair*-brained.

How could you tell how I spelled it?

I had a feeling, sir.

As I was saying, it smacks of sentimental do-goodism, of Hottentot-ism and worse. The Legislature won't like it.

It's a good, realistic, tough-minded, hardheaded, two-fisted, down-to-earth, workable, conservative-in-the-best-sense idea, Governor.

The people won't like it.

The people, sir, is an ass.

Fleishman told you to say that.

No, Governor. I believe it.

It doesn't sound like you. Well, if this Fleishman's so damned smart, why isn't he up here presenting his crazy idea himself?

He is, sir. I brought him along with me—inside a footlocker actually, because our in-state travel money has run a bit short, what with all the Correctional Conferences and such I've had to attend. He's in the next room, sir.

Inside a footlocker?

He's out of it now, sir, although he's been complaining of a crick in his neck.

Well, bring him on then. Let the man speak for himself, if he's such a bullwhip genius. Let him win me over with his brilliance. Let him sway the Legislature with his sincerity and mesmerize the Board with his eloquence.

I'm sure he will, Governor. He's never failed me yet.

We shall see, Warden. We . . . shall . . . see . . .

He returned the orange juice to the refrigerator and the gin to the cabinet, sliding the door shut. On top of the cabinet, on the side of each of the six boxes of Girl Scout cookies Janie made them buy to fulfill her quota, he read:

> Worship God
> Seek Beauty
> Give Service
> Pursue Knowledge
> Be Trustworthy
> Hold on to Health
> Glorify Work
> Be Happy

And Stay Away from Dirty Old Men?

He returned to the living room.

"Are you going to have to work tonight?"

"A little."

"What do you have to do?"

"Go over some hearing requests. Won't take long."

At nine o'clock he went upstairs, fresh gin and juice in hand. He sat at his desk and removed from his executive briefcase the dossiers of the twenty-six men who had applied for parole hearings. He studied them for a half hour, jotting down occasional notes, and then noticed the light go on in the upstairs window of the house on the next lot. He had not planned this, of course. He had not even, back then, picked this room as his den. He got it because it was the smallest bedroom. Luck; that was all. Who could blame a man for the sin of good luck?

And beyond this it could be cited that he still had not so much as moved his chair. Note that, your honor, and ladies and gentlemen of the jury. He had not moved it one whit—whatever the hell a whit was—closer. And never once had he risen from the chair for a better look, nor used any device of visual magnification to obtain, or cause to be obtained, any advantage whatsoever.

Thus: Innocence. Acquittal.

Besides, he hadn't seen anything yet.

There were obstacles, impediments, forces in the world out to frustrate him. Time, though, would be on his side. Their neighbors were relatively new, having lived next door only three months.

A movement! And that, for a few moments, was all. He did not stir from his chair, nor swing it around. He merely turned his head slightly. It was uncomfortable; his neck grew stiff.

The main obstacle, of course, was the curtain. It was opaque, and covered the lower half of the window. But the upper-half curtains, meeting at the top but hooked to the side halfway down, left a roughly triangular area uncovered. Thus it was necessary that she stand in front of her dresser. If she merely walked past, it was hopeless, a blur.

And what did it matter if he ever saw those tart, grapefruity breasts or not, those poobly bumps, that crispy jointure, that pleasant view of thighs, belly, pudendum and assorted whatnot? (He would never think of violating her. Never. He would defend her purity to the death if some sex fiend, some pervert, tried to attack her—or even peek in her window.)

Still, why bother? Why not just pay attention to one's work and let the days pass as they would? After all, the world's full of beauty, it comes and goes, like air, boredom, crime, violence, suffering, and who gets raunchy now over Greer Garson? But don't laugh—for that very same abstraction Tristram lost his soul (and more), and Romeo, and poor black Othello, that bellowing bull, and was it all worth it, all for fat and flesh? Sometimes at those dim and grievous periods of the day, he doubted it. And yet, beauty was beauty after all, and so was sex, and it could take your breath away.

Thus contemplating the moral and philosophical nuances of the situation—his was indeed a restless and inquiring intellect—he was startled to see her appear at the dresser in a bra and half-slip. He leaned forward expectantly as her hands flowered suddenly behind her, fingering to unhook, and then he well-nigh leaped out of his chair.

"He's here," Jo Ann said. "What's the matter? Is something wrong?"

"*Who's* here?" he shouted.

"Him," she said. "Did I scare you?"

"I didn't hear you coming. I was engrossed. You mean *him*? The goon?"

"Not so loud."

"You didn't tell him I was home, did you?"

"Of course I told him you were home. Now come on down and be polite to him. He really seems very nice. He's cute too."

"What have you been doing—ogling him?"

"Somebody around here has to make him feel welcome."

And there he was, sitting on the couch. He got up—up and up and up—in lanky extended sections, smiling his wistful TV smile and holding forth at the end of his elongated arm an impressively oversized hand. "Well—Dr. Fleishman . . . ," he said.

"I hear you've been looking for me."

He smiled again. "For a couple of weeks now, on and off. I thought back then when I finally got you on the phone that—"

"That you had me, eh? You didn't know you were tangling with the slipperiest Fleishman of them all."

"Why don't you two sit down," Jo Ann said. "Would you like a drink, Mr. Mancino? Flash is having one."

"Sounds fine."

"Yes," Flash said. "Sit down. It's nice meeting you after all this time."

The goon folded himself sectionally into the sectional couch. His legs extended well into the room. His shoes looked about size 15. He appeared pleasant enough, he supposed, but Flash had actually seen him interviewing some woman pilot—really: a woman pilot who'd been in the Powder Puff Derby—on that fool show of his at lunchtime, and things like that weren't easily gotten over. As soon as Kale had called that day and machine-gunned him into playing along with the guy, Flash rushed up to the infirmary and shook the hell out of the inmates lounging around on the beds by turning the guy's program on and pulling up an old wicker rocking chair amid the broken arms and the formaldehyde and gaping at it, dumfounded, transfixed, incredulous.

Flash sipped from his glass. (He could see her now, facing him opulently, doing exercises perhaps, joggling up and down. The show of the year, probably. Never to be repeated.)

"I won't take up much of your time," the goon said. "But since you're on next Wednesday, I thought we should—"

"Is it *next* Wednesday?"

"Yes. You're coming, aren't you?"

"I guess so."

"Have you caught any of the shows since I talked to you?"

"I'm afraid I haven't. Sorry."

"Anyhow, they've gone well. We've gotten quite a good response."

"I saw them," Jo Ann said, bringing in a gin and tonic for the guy. "I thought they were excellent. Don't let Flash bulldoze you."

The goon smiled. "Thanks." He took the glass, looked at it briefly, and then raised it. "Here's to a good show."

"Good show," Flash said.

"I'm not interrupting anything by popping in like this, I hope. I just—"

"No, no—not at all."

"I just thought if you had any questions . . ."

"No. No questions."

"You're all set then?"

"Raring to go."

"Of course—you said you've already been on TV."

"Have I been on TV or have I been on TV? Tell him, Jo Ann— have I been on TV?"

She smiled at the goon. It wasn't just that she thought he was cute. Oh, no. He could forgive her that. But she thought he was nice too. She thought he was sweet. (Even worse, the kids, when they found out he was coming, were *impressed*. Here they were, with a man like Flash Fleishman for a father, being *impressed* by a man who went through life clutching a microphone.)

"Flash was a big hit on TV," Jo Ann said, talking in that cheerful tone she used on people she thought were sweet.

"Yes sir," Flash said. "Twelve times in a row, like beans in a pod. It was a series, you see. A thirteen-week series."

"Oh? How come you—"

"Ah, yes—how come. I'll tell you how come. They booted me out. You ever been booted out of a show?"

"No."

"Well I have."

"You've been booted out of a whole college," Jo Ann said.

"And without even being a Communist, either. The TV business was part of my professorial activity, you see. It was what people laughingly call educational TV. Oh well—bygones be bygones. Anyhow, tell me what you want me to say on your show."

"Anything you want."

"You don't want me to butter anybody up?"

"No."

"Do you really enjoy working on television? You seem like an intelligent man." And he did in his own way, although something of a cold fish too.

"I enjoy it."

"My wife keeps insisting you're very good."

"He is very good," Jo Ann said.

"How did you get mixed up in this prison business?" Flash asked.

"I don't know—I got interested in it. The whole idea of locking people up bothers me, I guess."

"What are you, anyhow, one of these misty-eyed reformers?"

"Flash," Jo Ann said.

"I was merely asking a question," Flash said.

"Most prisons could use a little reforming," the goon said.

"The world is full of things that could use a little reforming. Anyway, what do you know about prisons?"

"Very little. I'm learning, though. Actually, I'm not much of a reformer, to answer your question. I'm only trying to give people a chance to—"

"Never give people a chance."

"Flash is just kidding," Jo Ann said.

"And you really like television?" Flash said. "Have you ever *watched* anything on television?"

"Occasionally."

"Tell me, what was television's finest hour?"

"I don't know—the Kennedy assassination, I guess."

"That was it, eh? That was your big moment?"

"What was penology's big moment?"

"Jo Ann—you brought me downstairs to meet a wise guy."

The goon laughed and the phone rang and Jo Ann went in and answered it. She came back: "It's for you, Flash. Griffing."

"Excuse me." Flash went into the hall and closed the door behind him. "Hello, Flash. How'd it go there today?"

"I went fine, Griff. Very quiet. How'd your holiday powwow go? Did the Governor put on a good feed? Did you get a drink out of him?"

"It was all right. Look, Flash—they're serious about this business—about the Negroes. Kale was there too, and most of the Board. That's why I was invited up, so they could give me the decision in person."

"Is it definite?"

"Yes."

"In other words, they ignored all those arguments I spent days—"

"Everyone thought our arguments were very impressive. But incidental. We've got a month to submit a plan for handling this. So start thinking about it. Do you imagine you could give me a rough draft in a week or so?"

"I guess so."

"One thing, we might get some money out of it. I told them we'd need supplementary funds to do the job right. Kale backed me, and the Governor seemed to think it could be managed."

"Is this whole thing Kale's idea?"

"Probably. I'm sure he sees votes in it, especially up in Maynard, in the Negro areas. He's weak up in Maynard and could use some support. But the whole Board's for it, and the Governor too. I think it's just one of those things, Flash. It had to come."

"Never let it be said the penal system lagged behind in the battle for human rights."

"That's about it, Flash. Anyhow, the day wasn't a total loss."

"You mean they bought the minimum plan?"

"They didn't exactly buy it. But they didn't say no, either. What they want now—"

"Is another report."

"Yes. They want a complete breakdown, including names of actual inmates we'd assign to the new unit if the plan's approved. They suggested a hundred men as a start, but I told them it'd be uneconomical setting it up unless we could talk in terms of three or four hundred at least. Especially if they're going to be sending in two Negro hardrocks to replace every minimum man we send out."

"Christ, Griff, they're not actually going—"

"No, it won't be quite that bad. We agreed they'd only give us good ones—at least at first—and that twenty or thirty would be all we could handle at one shot."

"Is that twenty or thirty a week, a month, what?"

"A month."

"Starting when?"

"About a month from now."

"And when will we start moving men into the minimum unit?"

"After they approve it and we get it built."

"I detect an imbalance here, Griff."

"I got what I could out of them, Flash."

"Okay, Griff. I'll get on these things tomorrow."

"Good enough. I'll see you then."

In the living room Jo Ann and the goon were chatting pleasantly.

"Now where were we?" Flash said, picking up his drink.

"Did they accept it?" Jo Ann asked. "The plan?"

"It's all very vague," Flash said.

"What did Griff want?"

"Nothing important. Just checking in."

"I won't take up any more of your time, Dr. Fleishman," the goon said. "If you're set, then so am I."

"It was good of you to drop by," Flash said.

The guy said good-bye to Jo Ann, and Flash walked him to his car.

"You've got a very lovely wife," he said.

"Yes, I owe her everything. She keeps me sane. If it weren't for her, I'd probably be some kind of nut."

"I see you're expecting. Your first?"

"Our sixth."

"That's great."

"At best, children are only latent adults."

Fireworks were still going off, and they paused to watch a Roman candle burst overhead.

"Happy holiday," Flash said and shook his oversized hand. "I like you, Mancino. You're okay."

The goon smiled—could it have been bashfully? "I'll see you Wednesday then. We go on at seven, but we'd like you there by six thirty if you could manage it."

"I can manage it."

When he returned to the living room, Jo Ann put on her scolding look.

"He smiles too much," Flash said. "No reasonable man goes around smiling."

"You shouldn't give him such a hard time. He's all right; his heart's in the right place."

"I know," Flash said. "It depresses me."

"You're going to behave yourself, aren't you—on the show, I mean. You're not going to make trouble for him?"

"You can't make trouble for a guy like that. He has the strength of ten, because his heart is pure."

There was plenty of gin left but no juice, so he poured himself a little over the rocks. Why not? When they buried John, that good peasant pope, the cops arrested fifty pickpockets in the crowd at the funeral. What harm, then, to the ideal of man's perfectability, if Flash Fleishman has one more little drink?

7

It was the way he kept coming at him, grabbing, coming with his arms spread out and then his arms coming in, swinging, grabbing, and him thinking *this kid's a loony!—this kid's off his frigging nut!* And he did, he had a real crazy look. His eyes were stretched wide like he was swimming under water, and his face was all blank and twisted around, and his mouth was pulled open like he was screaming his head off although Mel couldn't remember hearing a sound.

What the hell was the kid doing there in the first place, nosing around somebody's car in the middle of the goddamn desert? Sure, on the radio it said the kid lived out there, because his family had one of those ranches. But it was Mel's hunch that the goddamn kid was just out for a quick heist.

Still, he felt kind of sick. He felt all sticky and hollow inside.

He couldn't remember actually hitting the guy. It was like bringing the bar down into some kind of foam, and all he felt was himself bringing it down. And the goddamn crazy kid just wouldn't stop coming at him, with his arms spread out and that crazy look on his face. That's when Mel stopped, when the look on the kid's face changed.

Fourteen they said he was, on the radio. Richard Wilders they said his name was.

Mel was pretty pissed off about the story on the radio. All right, you couldn't expect them to know the kid was just looking for a quick heist. But they could at least mention the call to the hospital. At least that showed he felt sorry for the kid, didn't it, taking a big chance like that just to give the kid a break?

And he didn't kill anybody—he wished they'd make that clear too. The guy driving the goddamn car killed him. Mel had his ideas on that part of it too. His idea was that the frigging guy in the car was barreling along so fast he hit the kid before he ever saw him. Christ, did the cops actually *believe* the kid was just standing at the side of the road and then, at *exactly* the right second, just staggered in front of the car like that?

Because it was Mel's feeling the kid wasn't doing any kind of staggering around at all. It was a *small* pry bar, for Christ's sake!

He wondered what it must've felt like when a car went slamming into you like that. He wondered if you felt anything at all. Maybe just one sudden smash and then blank. Maybe you felt it all over your body at once, everything just exploding, your head and your fingers and your stomach, everything just going *pop* like a balloon and all your insides suddenly busting loose.

He reached down for the beer bottle on the floor. He was sitting near the window and the room was dark and he could hear the firecrackers exploding and even see Roman candles in the darkness outside. He drank a little, then put the bottle down. He'd been drinking very slow, a sip at a time.

They say your shoes always flew off. Sometimes they'd find them a coupla hundred yards away.

In his pocket he had all the money. It came to $417, about 250 of it from the green box.

Which was another thing about the radio. According to them, six hundred bucks was missing. That really got him, the goddamn owner kiting up his take from the insurance. They made a frigging *profit* out of being robbed, the goddamn owners.

He dumped the green box down a sewer and the pry bar down a different one. So all he had on him that could connect him was the actual money itself.

The Roman candles seemed to be going off one right after the other, lighting up the whole room in different colors. It was almost ten, so he switched on the radio. After a song and the commercials the news came on. It was exactly the same as at nine. He turned it off and took a sip of beer.

A few minutes later he heard her footsteps in the hall and then her key in the lock, which sounded very loud in the dark. There wasn't anything in the whole goddamn world that sounded like a key in a lock.

The door opened. She stood in the doorway, kind of fuzzy because the light from the hall wasn't very strong.

"C'mon in already," Mel said. "Close the door."

She stepped inside and shut the door. He couldn't see her in the dark but had the feeling she was leaning back against the door with her hand still on the knob behind her.

"You just been sitting here in the dark?" she said.

"Looks like it, don't it?"

"It sure does." She was quiet a minute. "We could turn on the light, you know. I mean, the bill's paid."

"Sure. Anything you say." He didn't care. He didn't feel up to any big decisions.

The light came on and he closed his eyes.

"Sorry," she said.

He opened them slowly.

"How you been, Mel? Everything go all right?"

"Sure. Everything went all right." He waited, then said, "How'd it go with you, Dolin? It go all right?"

"It went all right."

The glare still hurt his eyes. The room looked about ten times as bright as you needed. A whole string of firecrackers went off like a machine gun somewhere. "I'd just as soon they cut that out and went home," he said.

"They're all over the place tonight," Dolin said. "A bunch of kids opened the door and tossed in a whole string of them. There were all these people at the counter, and these stupid kids—" She shrugged. "Somebody could've been blinded or something."

"Nobody got hurt?"

"No. Nobody got hurt. I just hope they get those kids and teach them a lesson."

"Yeah," Mel said.

Dolin was still standing just inside the door, looking very hard at him. She hadn't taken her eyes off him once. She started walking toward him now, but very slow. He didn't move. She sat on the arm of the chair and leaned over him. He could feel her big soft tit against the back of his head. For maybe a minute she didn't say anything, and then she said, "The whole time here, you just been sitting like this?" The words sounded funny, coming from above him like that. "You didn't eat or anything?"

"I ain't hungry," he said. His throat and mouth were very dry, but he couldn't move his arm the way she was leaning on him.

She squirmed around, her tit against his cheek now, just touching, then bent over and kissed him hard, her lips opening a little at a time. He felt her weight, because she slid off the chair arm onto his lap. All this while he just kept trying to keep his hands out of the way and thinking to himself *what the hell am I doing here, for Christ's sake?* Because he hadn't really planned to come. He just couldn't think of anywhere else to go. He hadn't even expected her to let him in actually, not after the way she shot him down on the phone that night he called her after being on the TV. And from the look she gave him when she opened the door this afternoon he could see she was all set to do it again, only then she must've seen how shook up he looked, because she let him in. He told her he had a few bucks on him because he cleaned up big in a poker game that went on all night and all morning, only he was in dutch with the wife for staying out and maybe could he just come in and say hello and maybe have a quick drink or something. At the time he hadn't even thought about staying overnight, and didn't know about her working the supper shift at the beanery now. All he wanted really was not even the drink but just a place to sit down and catch his breath. Only now he had to decide what the hell to do with his hands, because he was just sitting there like a block of wood, trying to keep them out of the way, and she was all the hell over him, and still kissing him.

So he put one hand on her knee. Her dress was all pushed up from sliding onto his lap but he didn't move his hand up, he kept it right on her knee. His other hand was kind of trapped behind her so he just left it there. She came up from the kiss and put her hand on his shoulder, squirming some more and making a little low sound right near his ear. Then he noticed she was unbuttoning her blouse and he just wanted to say to her *Stop, don't do it, that's not what the hell I came for!*

What he wanted, the only thing in the world he wanted really, was just to start the whole day over again from the beginning and this time keep everything straight and simple and under control so when he got back to this time of night again everything wouldn't be so goddamned screwed up.

Dolin reached down for his hand and put it inside her blouse, sliding it very slowly along her throat and then along the top edge of her brassiere. Then she pushed a strap off her shoulder and dragged his hand down hard to push the brassiere down and then put his hand right on this great big soft moon of hers.

For a long time he just let it stay there. He just wasn't interested, he really wasn't, but he just couldn't help it, he started getting hard anyhow and she was sitting with her leg right on it and could feel it getting big and she started purring in his ear and moving around on it.

In the dark bedroom, outlined against the window, she took her clothes off. There were still fireworks you could hear, but sounding far away now. He stood on the other side of the bed and took his clothes off. He felt funny about leaving his pants hanging over a chair with $417 in the pocket.

She came over and could feel how hard he was when she pressed against him, but when they got down on the bed he went soft.

He tried to stay away from her a little so she couldn't tell and ran his hand all over her trying to get it up again. But then she reached over and took hold of him and he must've jumped a foot.

"Hey, Mel . . . you all right?"

He didn't say anything.

"What's the matter, Mel?"

"I don't know."

She played with him, but it didn't work. Then she took his hand and put it between her legs but that didn't work either.

"I think maybe I ain't feeling so good," Mel said. "I think maybe being up all night last night . . . I'm just kinda bushed."

"Okay, Mel," she said after a minute. "Maybe we oughta sleep a little first."

"Yeah," Mel said. "That's it. I need a little sleep."

And he really must've, because he went off like a shot, like suddenly a big black cloud came down over him, like he'd been doped, only his mind was still racing away like fury except that everything seemed far off and mixed up but Dolin somehow seemed to be around and suddenly she must've had fifteen hands because she was all over him, touching him everywhere, only then he wasn't sure if it was really Dolin or maybe Peggy and then for a minute it was Reena in the goddamn Pontiac, but then it was Dolin again and he got so angry with himself because he was just begging her, crying all over the place for her to let him touch her, and now she was saying *No, beat it, get lost,* and laughing at him because she had all these big shots she was playing around with that Mel felt just like killing, and then he killed them by smashing their heads with something and then he had her legs spread a mile and was going into her and felt bigger and harder than he'd ever been in his whole life and she was screaming because it hurt and moaning and making noises like she couldn't breathe, like she was gonna faint from it, but then it turned out to be Peggy and he screamed *No!* but she screamed *Yes! Now!* and it was Dolin and he wanted more than anything in the world just to fuck her to death, to make her cry from fucking her so hard, only he went soft again and couldn't.

He was wide awake. His eyes were open. He was still on top of her in the dark, still in her, and he remembered the kid coming at him, and the look on his face.

"You all right, Mel?"

"Yeah." His voice was so thick he could hardly talk. It was like his whole throat was just glued together. "I'm all right."

"You must've really had a hard day . . ." She said it very drawn out, in a kind of sleepy whisper. "You must've really wore yourself out . . ."

He rolled off her without saying anything and in a few minutes he could tell she was asleep. Only he was even wider awake now, and thinking of Peggy, and Chucky, and even for some reason, he didn't know why, of Jerrold, and he didn't fall asleep again until it was almost light outside.

□

Mel listened to the nine o'clock news by himself in the living room. He had trouble even finding news because it was Sunday and the stations all had church sermons. Dolin didn't seem to get the Sunday paper and Mel didn't want to ask about it. She was in the kitchen making breakfast, and he played the radio very low so she couldn't hear it. He was dressed. The money was still all in his pocket. He counted it before in the bathroom.

The radio mentioned the kid dying pretty much like last night, except now the cops said the kid was probably fatally injured—that's what he said, *fatally injured*—before the car even hit him. Only how the hell could they tell after a car got through with him whether a kid was *fatally injured* before, for Christ's sake? The cops also said they didn't have any idea who pulled the robbery because nobody saw the guy except the kid, who was dead.

Mel wasn't really worried that anybody saw him. The only two that actually did were the fat red-faced guy in the storeroom and the guy who flew past in the Comet while Mel kept his nose buried in the map. Neither one got any kind of look at his face. Besides, the red-faced guy was probably five hundred miles away by now, where the papers and the radio probably didn't even carry the story. So as far as all that was concerned, he just didn't see that he had anything to worry about. And thank Christ, because he'd had it. He'd had all the excitement and worrying he ever wanted. He was tired of being scared shit all the time and he just wanted a little peace, that's all, just everything nice and quiet for a change and everybody leaving him alone, because let's face it, he couldn't take it anymore, he couldn't stand the gaff.

They ate breakfast in the kitchen, on a little table squeezed between the refrigerator and the wall. Dolin had on a white bathrobe and he didn't know what underneath.

"Who'd you rack up in the big poker game?" she asked. "Anyone I know?"

"Nah," Mel said. "No one you know."

"I know a lotta people."

"It was no one you know," Mel said.

She went on eating her toast. She made him bacon and eggs but just had toast and black coffee herself. She must've fixed her hair before she woke him. It looked pretty good, with a white hair band holding it back behind her ears. Looking at her sitting there in her white bathrobe drinking coffee on a Sunday morning with her hair tied back like that and looking so nice and fresh, Mel thought what a shame it was someone like Dolin never really got married and settled down.

"What's the big plans for today, Mel? Any big plans?"

"No," he said. "No big plans."

"I gotta go in again tonight, you know."

"Oh?"

"I get Tuesdays off."

After a minute Mel said, "I thought maybe I'd just head on. I mean, it was real nice of you to—well, you know, put me up and everything. I mean, I appreciate it, Dolin, I really do. But I think maybe I better just head on."

"Go patch it up with the wife, eh?"

"Well, yeah. You know how it is."

"How's Peggy doing these days?"

"Peggy's doing just fine. We got a kid, you know. He's almost two."

"I know." Dolin poured herself another cup of black coffee. Mel still hadn't finished his first cup. It was very strong. "You're working now, eh, Mel?"

"Oh yeah, sure. I'm working now."

"You doing all right?"

"Oh yeah. I'm doing all right."

He tried to think how to handle the money bit. He figured he really should leave her maybe a twenty, for being so decent and taking him in, but felt funny about just handing it to her. Maybe he could just leave it where she'd find it after. She could buy herself a dress or something. The hell, she didn't make no money punching beans.

"How you gonna explain to the wife all the dough you got?" Dolin asked.

Mel shrugged. "Tell her I won it at poker," he said. Dolin said nothing, but gave him kind of a look. "I mean, you know—just tell her the truth, just tell her what actually happened." Dolin still said nothing. "The hell," Mel said, "you come home with a few bucks in your pocket, chances are the wife won't be *too* put out."

"Who'd you say you was playing with?"

"I said nobody you knew."

"It was a real big game, huh? I mean, you really cleaned up?"

"I did all right, I guess. But I mean, nothing sensational."

"How much is all right?"

Mel hesitated. "Sixty-seventy bucks. Something like that."

Dolin said nothing.

"I thought," Mel said, "that since you been so decent taking me in and everything that maybe it'd be only fair you got cut in on the winnings too. I mean, not to pay you for anything, but just, you know, because you were decent and all."

Dolin said nothing.

"Look, I gotta go to the john," Mel said. "I'll be right back, all right?"

In the john he took two twenties from the wad and put them in one pocket and the wad in the other. He made it forty because from the way Dolin was looking at him he had a hunch she might've took a quick look in his pocket when he was sleeping.

Dolin was sitting just the way he left her except her cup was full again. She had a great big electric coffeepot and was on her fourth or fifth cup. You'd think all that coffee would hop somebody up, but Dolin seemed very quiet and, he didn't know—serious.

He sat down and smiled over at her but she didn't change her look. He shrugged and took out the two bills, which he had folded over a coupla times. "I figured . . . well, I figured maybe you wouldn't mind if we sorta split it like this," he said. He looked down at the bills in his hand, wondering what the hell to do with them now. She didn't show no signs of reaching for them. So finally he just slid them under the plastic butter dish. She didn't even look down at them but kept looking right at his face. "That's forty bucks there," he said.

"A tip, eh? Under the plate."

"C'mon now, Dolin. Don't be like that."

"What'd you do with the other two hundred?"

Mel sorta blinked at her. "What other two hundred, Dolin? What're you talking about?"

"Out of the six hundred."

He stared at her. He wet his lips. "*What* six hundred?"

Dolin was quiet for a while, just looking at him. Then she said, "You been reading books about playing poker, Mel? You been taking lessons?"

"What're you talking about, Dolin? I'm just not following at all what you're talking about."

"You ain't never in your life won ten cents at poker, Mel. Who you kidding?"

"I won at poker. Plenty of times I won."

"I must've missed out on the news those times."

"I guess you must've."

"All the times I heard about, you didn't do so well. And now you come around with four hundred dollars in your pocket. Who were you playing—Donald Duck?"

"That four hundred ain't all from the poker. I mean, Friday was payday, you see. And well, we only get paid every two weeks there, and naturally what with overtime and—"

"You should have six hundred, Mel—not four hundred." She waited a little and then said, "The guy on the radio last night said six hundred."

"Are you crazy or something? I mean Christ, what're you trying to pull here?"

She didn't answer. After a while she pushed back the sleeve of her bathrobe, very slowly, and reached for the money under the butter dish. And then, very slowly, she unfolded the bills and looked at them and then just sort of let them flutter down to the table. "Forty ain't half of six hundred," she said. "Three hundred is half."

"You know, you're talking crazy. I mean it."

"Tell me, how could you blow two hundred dollars so fast? It was a little after three when it happened and—"

"When *what* happened? What the hell are you talking about?"

"—and hardly after four when you got here. So at most you had maybe an hour. That's pretty fast spending, ain't it?"

Mel stared at the two bills on the table, then leaned forward. It felt like he was stretching. He could feel the pull in his neck muscles. "Dolin, there *ain't* any other two hundred. I'm giving you the straight scoop now—there just wasn't any, and I don't give a shit *what* the guy on the radio said. The goddamn owner is padding the take, can't you see that? They do it all the time, to rook the insurance outfits."

"Oh," she said. "Sure, I see that. Why didn't you just say so in the first place? I would've believed you, Mel. I trust you."

He said nothing. She was still staring at him, so he looked at the chrome sink with a red dishrag hanging over the faucet. On the sill over the sink she had a pack of Salems and a little yellow flower in a pot and a piece of steel wool.

"In that case, Mel, let's just say that half of four hundred is two hundred. All right?"

"What's come over you, Dolin? I thought we were friends. I thought we were real good friends."

"We all make mistakes, Mel. I told you last week when you called to stay away. Long before that I told you to stay away. You should've took my advice."

Mel stood up.

"Where you going, Mel?"

"I gotta be going. I said so before."

"Only tell me what you think of my arithmetic first, okay? Ain't two hundred half of four hundred?" She picked up the coffeepot and filled her cup again. She was smiling. "Aw c'mon, lover boy—show us you can count, all right?"

Mel stood for a long time looking at her with her hair tied back and her white robe closed up at the neck. And it went suddenly through his mind that he could kill her easy enough. And he could tell by her look that she knew exactly what was going through his mind, and wasn't worried.

He shoved his hand into his pocket.

☐

It was a little after ten. There wasn't much traffic and he kept the Dodge moving along. He went over a big bump along Beradino where they'd been fixing the street and heard the exhaust pipe he bought that time rattling around in the trunk and thought maybe this afternoon he'd get around to putting it on.

Only just now he didn't feel like doing anything. He felt very lazy. The air blowing in the window was very hot and dry and had a funny flavor. It seemed heavy, kind of doped, and made everything seem very strange as he drove along.

You'd think when someone just screwed you out of two hundred bucks you'd be pretty pissed off, pretty worked up. But the whole business seemed kind of dull and far away. Everything seemed far away in the heat and the glare of the sun, and very still and quiet, like nothing was moving, nothing was happening.

When he got home Peggy and the kid weren't there. Peggy must've gone to church and left Chucky with someone. He looked around for a note, but couldn't find any. The rooms looked funny to him, like rooms he hadn't been in for years. They had a different feeling somehow.

He took the money out of his pocket and put some on the shelf of their closet under the boxes they kept there, and some with his underwear in a drawer, and some in the back of the TV, between the tubes, and some in a big crack way up the cement wall of the utility room. He kept thirty dollars in his wallet.

All this took only a few minutes and he was coming out of the utility room through the kitchen when he heard the bell.

For a second he didn't move. He wasn't really scared, but just very alert. His mind was working very fast. And right away he decided the thing to do was answer it. The thing to do was act exactly like anyone else would act because no one had a thing on him and he couldn't go through the rest of his life not answering doorbells or hiding in the closet whenever anybody came by.

So he answered the door. There were two guys there. The first thing he thought was that they were just a coupla Mormons coming around to try and sign him up, because they had a sort of religious look on their faces and a few months back a coupla Mormons actually did come around on a Sunday morning. Only the Mormons were practically kids and wore these very dark black suits and these guys were older and one wore a blue suit and the other a brown one.

8

"Good morning," Arlanson said cheerfully when Johnny picked up the phone Monday morning. "Did I wake you?"

"No," Johnny said. "I was just on my way out."

"I've got news for you. It's about that protégé of yours—Mr. No-Name, the nice clean-cut kid that goes around opening tills with little pieces of magic wire that he always keeps close to his heart. That one."

"What happened to him?"

"He's in jail. I haven't heard the details yet, but my guess is that he probably got a register open somewhere and the drawer slammed shut on him and that's how they found him the next morning, still trying to get his hand out."

"Very funny," Johnny said.

□

The jail was a wing of the police building, thick gray slabs and barred windows and oak doors. Johnny followed the signs and entered through the side of the building, on a blind alley with a decaying wood fence. He stepped into a narrow room with a cement floor and a long desk that divided the room in half. A sergeant was talking across the desk to a woman. Another policeman was writing on a pad, a third going through a file cabinet. No one else was there. A big fan whirled in a corner, aimed at the ceiling.

The sergeant glanced at Johnny. Neither of the other policemen looked up.

"But where is it?" the woman demanded. She looked about fifty, small, with gray hair and a whining voice. "What did you people do with it?"

"We didn't do anything with it, lady," the sergeant said wearily, his eyes lidded. "We never saw any dog. No one ever mentioned any dog."

"But she had it with her. I'm sure she thinks you're holding it for her. Who's going to take care of it wandering around the streets like that? What's going to happen to it?"

"Look lady, I wasn't driving around with any dog; your friend was. Ask her what happened to it. She'll be right out." The sergeant stepped around the policeman writing at the desk. "Help you, mister?"

"My name's Johnny Mancino. I'd like to see—"

"Oh yeah—sure. Sure. How are you, Mr. Mancino?"

"Fine. You've got someone booked here by the name of Mel Simmons. Can I see him?"

"Sure, if you want. Is there some kind of story on him?"

"No story. I know him, that's all. He was on my show a while back."

"You're kidding."

"Can you tell me what he was picked up for?"

"Car theft. Joy riding."

"Oh—is that all? Well . . . that shouldn't be too bad."

"Bad enough. We pinned him first on a Pontiac but there were some others too. Eight, I think it was. And then it's a parole violation, so—"

"You mean he stole eight different cars?"

"Yeah—isn't that something? You'd think a guy his age would—"

"Can I see him?"

"Right through here."

The sergeant led him into a gray, dimly lit area from which two wide corridors of cells extended at right angles. The place was bare of furniture except for a single desk, and the cement floor was lined into big squares like a sidewalk. A uniformed jailer, his shirt open at the neck, stood up from the desk, a ring of keys jangling on his belt. (They actually had rings of keys!) The sergeant nodded and left.

The jailer led Johnny toward the corridor on the right. From the other corridor a police matron appeared, helping along a heavy-set woman with bleached hair. The woman wore a loose knit blouse, a wrinkled skirt. Her hair hadn't been combed and she wore no make-up; her face was gray. She walked steadily but precariously, in fear of traps, impediments, obstructions, not ashamed of her hangover but somewhat humbled by the circumstances in which she was having it.

Her expression was pained, vaguely uncertain. The matron led her toward the door.

The corridor had three cells on each side, and crowded into the first cell on the right were fifteen or twenty men, sleeping on cots, sleeping on the floor, sitting on stools, slumped against the back wall. A few held on to the bars, looking out. Two men whispered together. One man sat on the floor staring at a piece of paper in his hand. The smell of alcohol was stale and sweetish, but the smell of vomit was stronger.

"A real bunch of beauties," the jailer said across his shoulder.

The other cells held only four or five men each. Mel was in the last one on the left, with three other men. He was sitting on a cot, leaning forward with his elbows on his knees and his head down. He wore a white tee shirt that hung outside his trousers. As they approached he raised his head slowly and looked at Johnny without recognition, without pleasure or displeasure. In the high-ceilinged cell, he seemed smaller and slighter than Johnny remembered. He got up and moved to the front of the cell and stood there with his arms at his sides until the jailer unlocked the barred door and slid it open. Mel then took two steps into the corridor. He executed the maneuver like a soldier on a drill field, not as crisply perhaps, but doing exactly what was expected of him, no more, no less. The jailer slammed the door shut and the clanging reverberated through the corridor, raw and unabsorbed, physically shocking.

"Hi," Johnny said, holding out his hand. "How are you, Mel?"

Stiffly, Mel shook his hand.

"Down there," the jailer said, motioning toward a wooden table at the end of the corridor, past the cells. "How long do you want?"

"I don't know," Johnny said.

The jailer shrugged and headed back to his desk at the other end of the corridor.

"Should we sit down?" Johnny said.

Mel turned obediently and walked with him. Johnny slid onto a bench and Mel sat opposite. The table and benches were bolted together, like a picnic table. The stone walls were blank except for a barred window near the ceiling. The area seemed oddly dimensionless. There was no color anywhere, everything appeared depthless and gray.

Mel sat with his hands clasped and stared at a spot on the table between himself and Johnny. He seemed almost to be waiting for instructions. But he didn't look at all uncomfortable. He looked very calm, very settled, perfectly at home.

"I heard this morning," Johnny said. He kept his voice low; they weren't far from the cells. At the other end of the corridor the jailer was back at his desk, watching them. "I was sorry to hear it."

"Yeah," Mel said. His voice was uncertain, as if he hadn't spoken in a long time. (What did you talk about in a cell? What did it feel like to be locked up with three men you'd never seen before, who'd been arrested for God knows what?)

"The sergeant said it was car theft—joy riding."

"Yeah," Mel said without looking up. "That's right."

"I came down—well, to see if there was anything I could do. Do you have a lawyer, Mel?"

"I don't want no lawyer." After a moment Mel wet his lips. "I don't really figure on needing any lawyer, Mr. Mancino." His gaze was direct now, steady, without expression. "Maybe the best thing all around is just that you don't get mixed up in any of this."

"Are they treating you all right?"

"Sure. They're treating me very good."

"What's going to happen this time, Mel?"

"I guess maybe that depends on the judge."

"Why'd you do it, Mel?"

Mel looked at him. "Sure, that's the question, I guess, ain't it?"

"You seemed to be doing all right, Mel. You seemed to—"

"You ain't never worked on a platform I guess, Mr. Mancino. You ain't never just lugged around dirty clothes all day long."

"Does it make it any better to go driving around in someone else's car?"

Mel was silent.

"Well, maybe it does," Johnny said. "Maybe that's what you need after working like that—to go racing around in a flashy car."

"Maybe," Mel said. "Sure."

"Did being on the show get you picked up, Mel?"

"Oh no—no, nothing like that. It was fingerprints or something, they said."

"*Or something?* Don't you even know what evidence—"

"Fingerprints. That's what it was. Sure . . . fingerprints."

"I'd think you'd be pretty careful to—"

"It was fingerprints, I tell you. They had the fingerprints. You can't buck fingerprints. They got them on file at the FBI and everything."

"Well, it could be worse, I guess."

"That's right," Mel said. "It could be worse."

They were silent awhile. "Are you sure I can't help, Mel? I know some good lawyers around town."

"Mr. Mancino, look—don't go stirring anything up, all right? I don't want any lawyers. Let's just forget about lawyers."

"What about your wife? Can I give her any help finding a job or something?"

"She already got a job." Mel paused. "You know, I don't really get this, Mr. Mancino. I mean, what the hell am I to you?"

"I don't know—the first person I've even known who's in jail."

"You never knew nobody who got sent away before?"

"Not really."

"That's kinda funny." Mel laughed quietly.

They were silent again. Johnny looked at his watch without noticing the time. He stood up. Mel stood up too and stepped back over the bench and waited for Johnny to make the next move.

"Can I get you anything—from outside?"

"Well, maybe if you got some extra cigarettes on you. I wouldn't mind having some cigarettes."

"I'll send in a couple of packs. Can I just give them to the jailer?"

"Give him a couple extra, all right? I mean—a couple for him, you know. Winstons, all right?"

"All right. I'll send them right in."

□

When Johnny got to his office at the studio he dialed police headquarters and got Detective Radigan.

"This is Johnny Mancino—K-SUN News. Could you give me some information about a Mel Simmons? He's in for auto theft."

"What do you want?"

"Has he confessed to all those jobs?"

"That's right. Eight of them."

"In writing?"

"In writing."

"How come you picked him up?"

"Hold on."

Johnny drew circles around Radigan's name on his pad.

"I'll read you the report. 'At some time during the evening of Sunday, June 14, or the early morning hours of Monday, June 15, a 1964 Pontiac Laurentian sedan disappeared from in front of the dwelling of the owner, Michael Canberry, 2177 Territory Street. Its absence was discovered by the owner at approximately eight A.M. on the morning of June 15 and reported to the police. The vehicle was located at 1:25 P.M. of the same day, parked on Brisbane Street, five blocks from the dwelling of the owner. There were no apparent signs of damage. The vehicle was taken into custody and subjected to routine inspection after surveillance seemed to indicate that it had been abandoned. No damage was found. According to the testimony of the owner, the mileage indicated that the vehicle had been driven for an approximate distance of twenty-five miles during the time it had been missing. Investigation also revealed that the rear seat of the vehicle had been used for the purpose of sexual intercourse. A routine—' "

"What was that again?"

"On the seat," Radigan said. "You know—spots—semen." He resumed reading after a pause. " 'A routine check of fingerprints taken from various parts of the vehicle indicated that one set belong to Melvin Simmons, who had previously been convicted of auto theft and subsequently convicted for—' "

"Do you usually check out cars this thoroughly?"

"It's not really very thorough; just routine."

"But this was over two weeks ago—how come it took you so long to pick him up?"

"Well, like you say, it was just joy riding, so there wasn't any big push on it. And by the time we sent the prints out and—"

"Did you find his prints on all the other cars too?"

"No."

"How do you know he was involved then?"

"Well, when we pick up someone like this we naturally check the open files—to see if there's anything similar that might tie in. Do you want me to read the rest?"

"No, that's all right. What made you think these tied in?"

"A few things. They were all taken off the curb in the same part of town, about every two or three days over a period of a few weeks. They were all hot-wire jobs, and were all abandoned the next morning pretty close to where they were taken from."

"Did he realize you had no actual evidence when he confessed, that you were simply—"

"There was no shoving around, if that's what you're getting at."

"I'm not suggesting there was. I'm just wondering why he confessed when he had nothing to gain from it."

"Well, I'll tell you—guys do that. They worry sometimes about getting caught and then when they do they just want to get it all off their chest. I don't know—maybe it makes them feel better."

Johnny called K-SUN's legal counsel.

"Yes, I follow. But what is it you want me to do?"

"I just wanted to know if it sounded fishy to you."

"Fishy? In what way?"

"I don't know. Do you think anything can be done? He seemed pretty set against bringing in a lawyer."

"Why not let him have his way then? The court will assign a lawyer. All he'll have to do is enter a guilty plea."

"I'd like to help him."

"It's a little late for that, I'm afraid."

Next he called Ken Muldoon at the Parole office.

"Yes, I heard," Muldoon said. "Too bad."

"What will they give him?"

"A few years—two-to-five's a good guess. It's his third time around. Parole violation."

"Do you think that'll do any good? Spending a few more years behind bars?"

"Do you think it did him any good crossing wires on other people's cars?"

"He didn't hurt anyone. He didn't even really take anything. Maybe if they gave him a chance—"

"They've given him a lot of chances. He fell into a good job and—"

"He doesn't seem to think it was such a good job."

"What was he looking for—the presidency of a bank? Look, Johnny, I know this guy. I've worked with him. I even like him. And I'm sure I feel just as sorry for him as you do. So we both agree: it's a damn shame. But what do you want me to do? Remember on the show last week—that list I mentioned, those fifty-three ex-cons I'm supposed to be keeping an eye on. Well, right now half of them are probably—"

"Did you know about the girl? The police say there was a girl along —at least in one of the cars."

"What'd they do—find pecker tracks on the seat?"

"Yes. Maybe that's how he got messed up, with some girl."

"Well, I didn't know about any girl, but I guess it's possible. That's the way to do it, isn't it?—get yourself a nice little wife at home and then go screwing around with some broad who likes driving in the moonlight."

"Do you think I could do anything to help him?"

"No."

"Could Frank Kale?"

"Do me a favor, all right? Do Mel a favor. Don't mention it to Kale. Use your head. You don't run for Attorney General by helping ex-cons who go around picking up loose cars."

"Okay," Johnny said. "I guess that's about it, then."

"Yeah, that's right. That's it."

When he hung up he swung around angrily in his swivel chair and slapped the desk. Then he saw Arlanson standing in the open doorway.

"How's it going with your friend? The fellow with his eye on the prize. Old sticky fingers."

"He's in for auto theft."

"They got the goods on him?"

"It seems so."

"What'd he do? Get his shirttail caught in the power window?"

"His neck," Johnny said.

□

Tuesday evening Johnny reported on his newscast that Mel Simmons had been arraigned on eight counts of auto theft, had pleaded guilty, and had been remanded for sentencing the following week. Normally he wouldn't bother with a story like that—there were too many of them every day—but he somehow felt obligated to use it. He read the item without emphasis and then turned the sheet over and placed it on top of his nightly pile of more newsworthy disasters.

□

After driving past a mile of fenced land, Johnny pulled into the entrance—"The Bar K Ranch"—and drove along the paved road to the house. The sun was low in the sky now and the San Juan Mountains, which were about thirty miles away, on the other side of the city, were turning red and orange in the sunset. He parked in the paved area behind the ranch house; there was room for thirty or forty cars. It was about half-filled.

At the door Johnny was greeted by a man in a bright red jacket, a flecked silver tie and shiny black trousers, who led him past the carpeted staircase and through a large sitting room. He ushered Johnny into a living room that must have been three times the size of his whole apartment. There were about thirty men present, no women. At first glance, Johnny recognized no one. Halfway across the room Kale excused himself from a group, patting one man lightly on the back as he stepped away, and walked over. He wore a brown suit, with a bright green shirt and a dark green linen tie. His Mexican silver tieclasp was a replica of a cow's horned head.

"Johnny—glad you could make it," Kale called out heartily. They shook hands. "Come in and meet some of the boys." Kale got him a drink from a waiter and introduced him to five men who were talking in front of a marble table. He neither recognized nor remembered their names. The doors swung open again and Kale went to greet the new guest.

Johnny listened to the men talking about the Governor's recent proposal for a water resources study. They seemed pretty knowledgeable about it, and discussed it in detail.

Johnny saw Arlanson across the room and left the group without anyone seeming to notice. As always Arlanson looked neat, unruffled, just this side of dapper. He was standing alone, holding a drink and smoking a cigarette in front of the fireplace. There was no fire.

"I didn't know any of my announcers were privy with our future Attorney General."

"He's still hoping to get some publicity out of me," Johnny said. "Who are all these people? Do you know them?"

"Sure. The political crowd."

"Tell me—why on earth did they ever pick Kale for Attorney General?"

"It was all very logical." Arlanson didn't look at Johnny as he spoke, but at Kale, who was booming out a joke in the middle of the room. "Eberhart's too liberal for half the Democrats in this state. His whole ticket was too liberal last time, and he almost lost. So the right-wing crowd, the money boys, gave him the word. They wanted their spot."

"And now they've got it?"

"Now they've got it. *Who do you want?* Eberhart asked, and they said, *Kale,* and then he, reportedly, said something on the order of *Heaven protect us all!* But that was it, that was the deal."

Kale left four or five men laughing heartily behind him and came over to join them by the fireplace.

"How's the series going, Johnny? I was out of town last week." His voice was deep and mellow, with a faint Western drawl. It was a good voice, almost professional.

"Just fine. We've got that warden on tomorrow—Fleishman."

"Ah—you finally got through to him. I hope now he doesn't make a damned fool of himself. And now what about us—are you planning to give someone from the Board a chance?"

"I'm afraid our schedule's gotten pretty tight. But I appreciate your help along the way."

Kale seemed disappointed, but determined to be friendly. "Let me introduce you to a friend. He's got to be leaving, but wants to meet you."

"I'll have to be going too," Johnny said.

Kale shrugged. "Want to come along, Paul?"

"No, you two go ahead," Arlanson said.

Kale took him to a group of men standing, as if arranged that way, in a near-perfect circle. The conversation stopped as Kale came up, his hand on Johnny's arm.

"Roy," he said, addressing a small, thin man with glasses and a dull complexion, "I've got a friend here who's in a big hurry to leave. He's something of a celebrity around these parts, you know, busy all the time, and won't give me the chance to show him off to everybody. So the honor is yours alone."

The man smiled. "I'm flattered," he said quietly, without irony. "Pleased to meet you, Mr.—Mancino, isn't it? I watched your news program in my hotel room." He had a soft voice, a reserved, almost scholarly manner. He was shorter and slighter than he appeared in his pictures.

"Glad to meet you, Governor," Johnny said.

"Tell the Governor some of your ideas, Johnny," Kale said. He turned to Eberhart. "The big fellow here's been running a smashing exposé of our penal system, Roy. Really been stirring things up."

Eberhart smiled patiently. "I think that's a fine idea."

"It wasn't an exposé," Johnny said. "I was just trying to learn a few things."

"I'd be interested in reading the transcripts." Eberhart turned to Kale. "Have you seen the programs?"

"Most of them. I helped Johnny set them up, gave him a few contacts."

Eberhart nodded, then looked at his watch. "Now I'm afraid I'm the one who has to go. Did you say your were leaving too?"

"Yes, I was on my way," Johnny said.

Kale accompanied them to the door; the man in the red jacket handed Eberhart his hat, brushing off the brim with his sleeve. Eberhart thanked him. From an alcove off the vestibule a chauffeur appeared.

"Don't bother coming out," Eberhart told Kale. "I'll see you in the morning then. Thanks for the drink."

The night was clear and balmy, the stars bright. They started along the path to the parking area. Eberhart looked up at the sky. "It's very pretty," he said. "And it doesn't come with the rest of the state, which is perhaps why I appreciate it."

"The air's nice too."

"But that I have to worry about. We can fill that with smog."

When they reached the parking area the chauffeur, who had been following silently, stepped ahead and opened the rear door of the black limousine.

"Your programs aren't shown up in Maynard, are they?"

"I'm afraid not."

Eberhart smiled again, with that same show of patience, of mildness. "It's been nice meeting you," he said, extending his hand.

□

At a quarter to seven Wednesday evening Johnny slammed down his phone and hurried out of his office.

Fifteen minutes to broadcast. Fifteen minutes.

He started for the studio but stopped abruptly and headed toward the reception room. Maybe he was hiding behind the couch in there, on his hands and knees, enjoying the hell out of himself.

"Is he around?" he asked June. "Has anyone heard from him?"

From behind her desk at the switchboard, June dutifully surveyed the empty chairs and couches. She raised her eyes to Johnny and shrugged.

Johnny looked around too. Maybe he had camouflaged himself as a rubber plant. Maybe they should search the broom closets and stairwells.

"Should I drop a net over him if he shows up?"

"Yes," Johnny said.

In the studio, Max was peering into his camera, testing his settings. Willy, standing with one foot on the base of his machine, was lighting a cigarette.

"How we doing?" Willy asked.

"Lousy."

A network show was coming over the studio monitor. The air vents rumblingly pumped in a refrigerated breeze.

The floorman came over, adjusting his headset. "All ready now."

"Good. Thanks." Johnny looked up and saw Stan Terrace behind the big window of the control room, shrugging at him. Johnny shrugged back. What the hell was he supposed to do? It wasn't his fault. He hurried across the floor and into the control room. The engineer was sitting at the board, both hands outstretched to dials.

Stan Terrace, standing next to him, removed his headset and gazed up at Johnny. "We're ready with the sub, anyhow."

"I hate to use that 'Noonday' backup. Can't they find anything else?"

"We've got a public service film from the National Forestry Service. There's also a travelog, on the Andes, I think, that no one seems to think we've used before. You ought to tape some undated backup for the evening show."

"Use the forestry thing, okay? Or the other one. I don't care."

"You want to try it alone—maybe he's just late and you can keep it alive until—"

"Can we cut into either of these films if he shows up?"

"Be kind of tricky."

"Is Arlanson around?"

"No. I tried his home before. He's out somewhere. Haven't you heard anything at all from this guy?"

"His wife said he left an hour ago."

"Maybe he's walking. I'll get the forestry film set up."

"Ten minutes to broadcast. Ten minutes."

He should have picked the guy up. Maybe then he could have at least spotted him trying to get away, like Mel Simmons, and could have chased him through the city to his favorite bar, or wherever the hell wardens went to hide. He should have put a leash on him and tied him to a camera stand. And this was the guy that ran the prison, or practically did, or helped do it, or something. From the beginning he had his doubts. Trust Not Nobody—that was Arlanson's advice, and that, not Abraham Lincoln, should be framed on the wall. That was the answer: that would protect you from all the nuts and jokers, all the dandelion brains, all the Samuel F. Fleishmans of the world. Trust Not One Damn Soul.

"Mr. Mancino. Telephone please."

Oh Christ—the guy was lost, he took a wrong turn somewhere and ended up out on the desert. Johnny ran into the nearest open office and grabbed the phone.

"Johnny? Hi . . . Bob Winninger here. I was hoping I'd catch you still—"

"What? Who is this?"

"Bob Winninger. What's the matter? Is that you, Johnny?"

"For Christ's sake—I'm practically on the air!"

"Oh, did I get you at a bad time? I just wanted to check with you on the Pageant schedule and see—"

"Call me tomorrow." He whirled around and saw him standing in the doorway. Over his little potbelly his hands were clasped, and he held the tag end of his tie between his thumbs. He was smiling. The comical qualities his face normally possessed were made ludicrous by the smile. What with his false-looking mustache and those gigantic black eyeglass frames that you wouldn't be surprised to learn had no lenses (you expected him at any moment to demonstrate by poking a finger through them), he looked like a third-rate vaudevillian—or a soused haberdasher portraying a third-rate vaudevillian at an annual Rotary Club revue. He needed only the cane and straw hat and maybe a few barber-pole stripes on his jacket, doing a Shuffle Off to Buffalo, chopping headlong toward the stage exit, his eyes gleaming, twinkling . . .

Johnny grabbed the phone again. "Give me Stan Terrace. . . . Stan? We're on."

"I know. June buzzed me. You've got six minutes."

Johnny hung up and looked at Fleishman again. His smile was gone. His lips were puckered in an exaggerated frown.

"Of course we're on," Fleishman said. "I agreed, didn't I? I said I'd be here."

"You said six thirty. It's almost seven."

"I was fortunately delayed. It was fabulous, really. You see, I happened to be passing this drugstore and—"

"Come on—we have to get in there."

"Okay; I'll save it for after. How long did you say this show lasts?"

"A half hour."

"Oh well—it could be worse."

☐

"I'd like to begin if I may, Dr. Fleishman, by quoting from the National Commission on Law Observation and Enforcement. In discussing the success of our prisons, the Commission wrote, 'The treatment accorded law violators does *not* tend to make them law abiding . . . to produce that adjustment which permits them to rejoin the community without the desire, or compulsion, to commit further crimes.' In other words, they seem to be saying that prisons have failed to do their job. Do you agree?"

"That's a terrible question to ask a warden. But yes, I guess I agree."

"Why have they failed?"

"I don't know for sure. I don't think anybody does."

"Can you tell us something about the men you get? How would you describe the typical convict?"

"Well, first of all he's young—probably not yet thirty, often not yet twenty. At the same time I guess we can say that he's old. He comes to us after having been subjected his whole life to all sorts of dreary influences and experiences over which we have no control, and about which we know practically nothing. The third fact is that he's probably had several previous convictions. He's not only a veteran criminal; he's a veteran prisoner. The fourth fact is that he's undereducated. He has, let's say, completed seventh grade. His intelligence is probably also below average. The fifth fact is that he—"

"Is that true as a general rule—that criminals are below average in intelligence?"

"We're talking about inmates, not criminals. Yes, their average IQ is well below normal."

"What else can you tell us?"

"Well, he's probably had trouble with either alcohol or narcotics or both, and more than likely comes from what people call a problem home. He's probably been poor most if not all of his life, and generally has a bad work record—few jobs, much shifting about, long periods of idleness and unemployment."

"Anything else?"

"If we really want to grab this thing, we can add one more characteristic, as a summary of all the others. That's that the men we get can be classified as dedicated failures. The only choice that life—society, whatever—seems to offer them is the choice between different kinds of unsuccess. From their earliest recollections, life around the home has been unsatisfactory, and they often look upon this as their own fault, their own failure. Then they have failed in school. They have failed at work. And it is the sum total of all these failures which is acknowledged in their turning to crime. And then, to top all this off, they've failed *even as criminals*. They've been caught, not once but several times. They've been convicted. Thus they arrive at the penitentiary, and we greet them."

"What happens then?"

"Well, we're supposed to do two things, to hold them and to help them. To keep them in custody, and prepare them for their return to society."

"Which is more important?"

"We have to do both. But the second's certainly more difficult. In addition, there's a third reason a person is locked up, and that's to hurt him, to punish him for his sins, to exact revenge."

"Is that still an important factor today?"

"To the public, it's the obvious and logical reason for putting someone behind bars. And to the inmate himself, of course, imprisonment *means* punishment."

"Do you think that's one reason for the failure of prisons—this confusion about their proper function?"

"Yes. So does James V. Bennett, Director of the Federal Bureau of Prisons. What he says is that we imprison men to punish them, and yet hope to reform them. We discipline them rigidly, yet hope to teach them self-reliance. We regiment them and depersonalize them, and yet hope to make them respected individuals. We suppress initiative and independence, yet must teach them initiative and independence. We isolate them from normal, law-abiding citizens, yet claim our goal is to make them normal, law-abiding citizens. We won't let them make any choices about the way they live, yet later expect them not only to make choices, but to make the right ones. And on and on."

"Isn't there some way we could resolve all this, eliminate some of these contradictions?"

"One would hope so, I guess. One reason for our difficulties, however, is that we're trying to accomplish a lot more than we used to. The easiest way to simplify the whole mess would be just to execute all criminals. It wouldn't reduce our crime rate, but it'd sure solve the problem of rehabilitation."

"Is there any other way we could solve it?"

"There are lots of ways, but there are also lots of problems. Our job, basically, is to teach these men something, but it's hard to know exactly *what*, to say nothing of how we should do it, or their ability to learn, their willingness to listen to a bunch of finks and square johns like us. Especially when the whole thing gets mixed up with our desire for revenge. Capital punishment is the ultimate example of this: when we execute someone we're making it pretty clear we aren't interested in his reform. Of course we're moving away from capital punishment now—at least for white men—so I guess you could say we're also moving away from the idea of pure punishment. But we still punish, and we still punish more for a major crime than a minor one, the assumption being that the sentence *is* punishment. An eye for an eye. Tit for tat."

"Do you personally oppose this concept?"

"Let's say I'm personally not very crazy about it. Take the case of a man who fires a gun at another man, and it jams, or his aim is so bad he misses. Suppose the gun had worked, or his aim had been better. What determines the way we treat someone like this has nothing to do with *him* at all."

"The punishment should fit the criminal then, not the crime?"

"Actually, the whole idea of punishment fitting anything strikes me, if I can interject a personal note here, as just so much ringading and chit-chat."

"Someone's said the real reason we send criminals to prison is that we haven't been able to think of anything else to do with them. Do you agree?"

"Yes. Even if we assume the courts are convicting the right people—pretty doubtful in itself—I think we can still say they're sending them to the wrong place, for the wrong reasons, for the wrong length of time, and with the wrong expectations. After all, if the great and good and free social forces on the outside have failed after twenty or so years to lure these men into the path of righteousness, how on earth are we poor jailers supposed to do it behind bars?"

"You said the average prisoner considers his sentence to be punishment, pure and simple. Does this make your job harder?"

"Of course. But the mind of an inmate, alas, is no more rational than anyone else's. To some extent, the criminal *wants* to be punished. Many criminals are examples of stunted emotional development. Even the basic rationalization of their behavior is essentially childlike: society has hurt them and they want to hurt it back."

"Then the criminal's attitude toward society is the same as society's toward him—each wants to get back at the other?"

"I think so. At least that's a thought that has occurred to me during some of my more depressed moments."

"But then society is merely doing what the criminal wants it to do—because he feels guilty and *wants* to be punished?"

"Within reason. I'm not talking about the rack and the thumbscrew."

"What about the whole question of penal reform? Isn't it a frequent complaint that the newer, more advanced prisons are coddling the prisoners?"

"This complaint has always been raised, and to tell you the truth, I'm pretty weary of it. It was raised in the days of the water torture, of the lash, of hanging men by their thumbs. No one in his right mind can use the word *prisoner* in the same breath with *coddle*. When you lock a man up, you're punishing him enough to satisfy even the most ravenous and bloodthirsty revenge-seeker, if he only had the imagination to realize it. And I'm not just talking about the loss of freedom, though God knows that's punishment enough. What you accomplish when you put a man behind bars is quite simple, and quite vicious. You obliterate his image of himself as a man."

"Is there any hope then, of saving these people?"

"Many, as far as we can tell, do better afterwards. Unfortunately, the term ex-con fits very neatly into a headline."

"Do you have any figures on the men who do better, Dr. Fleishman?"

"I have all kinds of figures. They just aren't any good. We have, for instance, what we call a recidivism rate—a return rate, the percentage of released inmates who eventually get sent back. Certain institutions even brag about their low return rate. But it's impossible to develop this figure with any pretense of accuracy. Once a man's released it's very hard to keep tabs on him until he dies forty or fifty years later, and that's what you have to do."

"Then you have no idea how successful you are?"

"Very little, except on an individual basis."

"Before, you mentioned that the average prisoner is in his twenties. Isn't this a sign of your success? What happens to ex-convicts over thirty, over forty?"

"The pressures change. Men now in their twenties have always lived in a period of general prosperity. And after all, the surest way to produce a criminal is to expose him mercilessly to all the rewards our society can offer—cars, homes, clothes, prestige, power, leisure—and then deprive him of any legitimate means of attaining them. Everywhere today someone is telling us to buy something, and convincing us by extremely effective methods that we *must* buy it, that we need it, that life is weary, stale and flat without it. You do it yourself all the time, on television. Well, some of this fades by the time they're forty. Then too, their resentment often lessens. They don't feel so compelled to hurt people because people have hurt them."

"Could you tell us a little about how you go about trying to reform these men?"

"Sure. Speaking in general terms, prisoners exhibit antisocial attitudes, combined with—and probably caused by—an inability to perform successfully in society. There's no point trying to change an inmate's attitude without also eliminating its cause, so our main push is to give him the education and training he needs to get on the trolley that all his life's been clanging past him. It's a long haul for a lot of them. Much of the schoolwork, for instance, is at the fourth or fifth grade level. If a parent wants to keep his kid out of prison, he should send him to college. He may turn out to be a crook, but the chances are he won't get caught, or at least not sent to prison."

"Why not?"

"The obvious reasons. Basically our system of justice—I mean here the whole choreography of police action, of legal and judicial ceremony, of punitive incarceration—is a kind of ritualistic program designed by the haves to keep the have-nots under control. What we call justice is really a means of protecting *us* against *them*, of keeping the Romans from being overrun by the barbarians."

"Can you give us some examples?"

"Let's pick just one—narcotics. It's estimated that over thirty per cent of all users are professional people. Yet professional people are involved in less than ten per cent of the arrests—and even fewer of the convictions. Unless, of course, we don't want to believe these statistics either."

"Generally speaking, Dr. Fleishman, would you say more or fewer people should be sent to prison?"

"Fewer. Many fewer. I think we need to make a clear distinction between the menaces and the nuisances. I'd say about fifteen per cent of our inmates absolutely have to be in prison. They're the menaces. They're dangerous and unstable, and show little sign of changing. Maybe another twenty-five per cent are borderline. But the rest, the other sixty per cent, the nuisances, should never have been sent away. They should be handled outside, placed on probation and provided with counseling, job training, education, within the context of a normal society. There's even a good hard-money argument for this. Probation costs about a hundred and fifty dollars a year per man. The pen costs two thousand. Probation also avoids the problem of institutionalization."

"What's that?"

"It's a thorn in our side. Let's face it, the ideal inmate is the one who fits most quietly and cheerfully into prison life. But the more this happens, the harder it is for him to readjust to the outside world when his time is up. One of our real troubles is that we worry only about the inmate's past and his present—his record, and his ability to adjust to prison life. The future seems like an irrelevance, a bothersome intrusion."

"Why is this?"

"Because the public wants it. The public sees prisons as warehouses, not social hospitals."

"You hear a lot these days about the growing crime wave—'crime in the streets' seems to be the phrase. Do you feel the increasing amount of crime is a major national problem?"

"Well, Mr. Hoover seems to think so—but I yield to no man in my lack of admiration for J. Edgar Hoover. Every year his P.R. boys publish a little book of statistics proving that crime is increasing at a phenomenal rate, the point being that to throttle this monster we need more money for the FBI, that we need more arrests and more convictions and tougher sentences. I confess to being unconvinced, even slightly appalled."

"Are you saying his statistics are phony?"

"I would say they're being used to present his case in the best possible light. All law-enforcement agencies feel frustrated at not being able to wipe out crime, especially since the public is always clamoring for them to do just that. So they're always pleading for more money, more power, more authority. And I don't necessarily blame them. I'm no cop hater. If I were a cop, I'd feel exactly the way they do. But this whole viewpoint seems to me irrelevant, if not actually absurd."

"Why?"

"For one thing, the whole business of crime statistics is a hopeless jungle. There are thousands of law-enforcement agencies in the country. Some keep good records, some don't. Terminology varies; classifications are often vague and overlapping. In general, however, these records are getting more complete and accurate every year. Which means that maybe the so-called increase in crime really reflects better records, not more crimes. And then of course all we can even hope to record is the number of crimes *reported*. We have no idea in the world how many are actually committed, a great many of which are never reported."

"Do you think stricter law enforcement would reduce crime?"

"It would increase the number of arrests, I grant that. But arrests won't solve the problem. It's like standing near an insect-breeding swamp and swatting at the mosquitoes as they fly out."

"Would this serve as a deterrent though—cracking down on offenders?"

"In talking about deterrence we're running at a real windmill. One hates to go against the confirmed wisdom of both the masses and J. Edgar Hoover himself, but I don't think capital punishment, for instance, is a deterrent, or ever was. No matter how cruel or inhuman or excruciating a punishment we devised, I don't think it would affect our murder rate one whit—assuming, of course, that we could figure out what the hell our murder rate actually was. Are you allowed to say *hell* on this station? Hell. . . . Hell. . . . Are we still on?"

"We're still on."

"Good. The deterrent theory, I suspect, merely discourages certain crimes—not because the punishment is severe, but because the chance of getting caught is great—and encourages others, where detection is less likely. And if we assume that much crime is at least partly a means of getting back at society—of defying the comfortable rule-making people the criminal hates and resents—then the threat of punishment is what assures him the act is wrong, and it's because it's wrong that he wants or feels compelled to do it."

"Are you saying then that what's intended to deter might actually do just the opposite?"

"In psychological terms, yes—although I don't know anything about psychology. No one does. But what keeps *you*, for instance, from crime is not the threat of prison. It's the constraining forces of the stable social situation in which you exist. Crime doesn't speak to your condition, whereas socially acceptable behavior does. Naturally, under that term *social acceptability* we include some pretty creepy activities, along with many that are technically criminal. But they're so widespread, so hard to detect and prosecute, and so conventional that we don't consider them criminal. Neither does our law-enforcement apparatus, which obviously doesn't accurately reflect our laws, which in turn don't reflect our stated beliefs, which in turn don't reflect our actual beliefs. The man we call a criminal is not the man who has broken a law. He's not even the man convicted of breaking a law. He's simply someone whose basic attitudes contradict our comfortable group feeling, not of what a person shouldn't *do*, but what he shouldn't *be*. Thus the murderer, if he has defied our precepts in this one instance only, may not be considered a true criminal, because he's still one of us. What society fears most from the criminal is pollution. He is loathsome to us. He is what the Jews were to the Nazis, the witches to the churchgoers of Salem, the heretics to the courts of the Inquisition. He's our leper, and our reaction is to banish him so he won't be able to contaminate us, and to punish him so he'll be made to feel the power of our terrible swift sword. We put criminals in prison the same way we put evil thoughts out of our minds, and for the same reason, to keep ourselves pure. To be considered a criminal a person must challenge our most cherished and necessary faiths. He must threaten to destroy them unless we first destroy—or banish—him."

"I hate to put a stop to this, Dr. Fleishman, but I'm afraid our time has run out. Thank you for joining us tonight. It's been a pleasure."

"Anytime."

□

Johnny got up and reached across to shake Fleishman's hand. Fleishman, seated as he had been through the whole broadcast—with his hands clasped on the table and his head settled into his shoulders, peering at the microphone through his big glasses with owlish imperturbability—turned to gaze up at him. He smiled abruptly, as if trying to be nice, to be understanding. He rose and accepted Johnny's hand briefly.

"You were just fine," Johnny said.

"It's time for a drink," Fleishman said.

They drove separately to the Hotel Aurora, Johnny following Fleishman's Volkswagen into the sunset through the evening traffic. They sat at one of the small cocktail tables in the Longhorn Room.

"Let me," Johnny said when the girl brought his bourbon and Fleishman's double martini.

"Okay," Fleishman said, eyeing the girl's low-cut blouse. He took a long, slow sip of his drink, casting his eyes to the ceiling in mock ecstasy, then darted his glance sideways to watch the girl walk away in her black mesh stockings and short black skirt. He stared soberly, coolly, with a kind of skeptical concentration. (Here's the man Winninger should have gotten to judge his beauty contest!) Fleishman turned to Johnny and smiled. It was a strange smile, a glittering, unabashed smile. His expressions changed so abruptly, and each seemed so incongruous in respect to the one that preceded it, that the effect was somewhat startling. "I'll buy the next round," he announced. "You did all right tonight. You're a good straight man, Mancino. You could go places."

Johnny laughed. "Well—I hope we had a good audience. Maybe it'll do a little good for some people to—"

"It won't do any good," Fleishman said. "Anyway, what happened, you see, was that I actually witnessed a crime. Incredible, but it's the first time in my life I've seen one actually take place." Fleishman's expression had sobered as he spoke; abruptly the smile returned.

"Excuse me?"

"On the way over. The drugstore. I promised to tell you about it—remember?"

"Oh yes—of course. Sorry—it slipped my mind in all the—"

"I was just driving by, you see. Minding my own business, as we say. An innocent bystander, expressing neither fear nor favor, giving no quarter and asking none. And the eerie part was that I had already driven past the drugstore when I became aware of an overpowering compulsion to turn around and go back. *Why?* I asked myself. I am not, you understand, the kind of man bullied by irrational compulsions. Just because one little voice in my head says *Stop! Go back to that drugstore!* is no reason, as I see it, to stop and meekly go back. I must have a reason. And so I asked myself *Why?* And then I realized it was because I did not have a cigar on me. Now, normally, I am not much of a cigar fancier; occasionally, however, I indulge. But why this sudden desire for a cigar? Was I simply rationalizing? No, I realized; of course not. It was in honor of the occasion, like a bottle of wine. After all, it's not every day in the week a man appears on television. A man like me, I mean—not a man like you. Do you appear on television every day of the week?"

"Except Sundays."

"Honor the Sabbath. So there I was, zooming along Beradino Street —I hate that street, you know. *Zoom, zoom, zoom,* all those furious, snarling maniacs. I hate all streets actually, but between you and me" —Fleishman leaned forward over the little table and glanced suspiciously to each side—"Beradino Street really scares the shit out of me. I am a physical coward of long standing, you see, especially behind a wheel. Anyhow, before I knew it, I found myself making a spectacular death-defying U-turn—on Beradino Street, no less!—in the middle of the rush hour! And there I was, sliding in between the white stripes in front of the drugstore in that big shopping center there and stepping from my trusty Volkswagen in a kind of brisk and monomaniacal trance, like a man obeying orders from beyond, my mind wholly fixed upon that single idea of purchasing a cigar. With my hand still on the door handle, having just slammed the door shut with my usual crispness, the way automobile salesmen on TV always slam doors, although in my case the *élan* results from a sense of profound gratitude at having once more emerged alive from that death box, I paused to study the drugstore, as if expecting to see something miraculous there. Remarkably enough—or not, depending on your feelings about the occult—I did. A man. A large man, emerging from the drugstore. What immediately caught my eye was that he was holding, as if suffering from a cold or about to sneeze, a handkerchief fluffed over his mouth and nose in such a way as to conceal the lower portion of his face. That and the fact that he was, if not actually running, certainly moving faster than usual for a drugstore patron. And the eyes. For he saw me, this man;

he looked right at me, piercingly, vibrantly, fatally. Our gazes met for no more than an instant, but I was overwhelmed. The sensation, of course, was indescribable. These things always are, aren't they? So I simply can't do justice to what I felt, to what I saw in this man's eyes, the unearthly fusion of terror—a sheer and ultimate terror such as, believe me, one does not frequently see in the eyes of one's fellow man— and defiance, and pride, and abject humiliation, and a kind of electric alertness, and confusion, and anguish, and determination, and about ten other things. What I should have done, of course, as a good citizen, was immediately cry out *Stop thief!* But I was stunned, immobilized, frozen. I could neither move nor speak—no doubt partly because, as I said, I'm a coward. But it was more than that. It was the impact of this man's gaze, and the turmoil behind it. Beyond that there was the rather startling realization that here I was, a penologist, a student of crime and punishment, an expert, a man who's spent the better part of his maturity working with and trying to understand criminals—here I was for the first time in my life actually witnessing a crime, actually *seeing it happen,* actually, so to speak, coming at last face to face with the primal root source of all this flibbery-gibber, seeing the whole thing bare, like Euclid gazing upon his isosceles triangle, or Moses falling to his knees upon hearing the thunderous voice from the mountaintop. I, however, maintained a standing position. Anyhow, I didn't yell *Stop thief!* To be perfectly frank, I would have felt like a damn fool yelling it. No one really believes that people go around yelling things like that, do they? My own suspicion has always been that they would probably yell something on the order of *Hey!*—or maybe *What the* ——*!,* which is what people in Dick Tracy usually yell, if you've ever noticed. Then again, I've never really understood the grammar, the syntax, of *Stop thief!* Is there a comma in there somewhere? Is it a plea—which seems rather ridiculous in the circumstances—for the criminal to stop, to simply chuck the whole thing over and come slouching shame-facedly back? Or is it a command for him to stop?—in which case one would need both a gun *and* a comma. Or is it supposed to be a cry of alarm?—a request, perhaps, that somebody *else* stop the thief? This would seem rather presumptuous—in effect saying that there's a dan-gerous man running loose but *I'm* sure as hell not going to risk my sweet neck trying to stop him, so would somebody else please do it? Here they are. Fine—on me this time."

Fleishman, in silence, watched the waitress come and go. When she was out of sight, he said: "So what I did during that split second was say nothing. I stood transfixed. The man, after concluding this briefest of indescribable glances in my direction, raced to the end of the buildings. The drugstore, as you may know, is next to the last building in that corner, with only a toy store between it and the border of the shopping plaza. He raced past the toy store and lurched around the corner, almost sideways, not so much turning as *pulling* himself in that direction, and then, I presume, leaped into a waiting car. At any rate, I saw no more of him—although who knows, maybe some day I will. The next moment, though, I saw the proprietor emerge in his white pharmacist's jacket and—uncannily—pause to look straight at me. I began to feel as if I were ten feet tall, the way everybody seemed to be drawn to my presence. Anyhow, *his* eyes revealed to me a very different but equally complex and, in my ignorance, equally amazing insight. For in this case it wasn't only something I'd never been exposed to, but something I'd never even considered. The other, yes; this, never. Yet it was verily the other side of the coin. *My God,* I thought, *what a revelation!* And what I saw this time, equally indescribable, was not only outrage, but a kind of awesome shock, and disbelief, and fear—but not terror this time, interestingly enough; not that strong— and determination, but again of a less passionate form, not so absolutely resigned to the risking of everything, or anything, to carry out what had to be carried out. And I remember thinking, *All these years, and now at last I'm beginning to realize the depths of my ignorance.* Meanwhile, of course, the pharmacist, staring at me like that, seemed to be expecting a response, a reply, an answer to his unspoken question. The temptation, naturally enough, was to cry out gleefully 'He went thataway!'—which is at least grammatically intelligible. But I wasn't up to it. I merely pointed. Reluctantly, I might add . . . as if somehow I didn't want to spoil the purity of this pantomime, this ballet, that I had been privileged to witness—or maybe because I wanted the guy to get away. It occurred to me that perhaps I was secretly rooting for him, or maybe even reacting to a deeply instilled contempt for snitchers. At any rate I did, although with reluctance, point, and the pharmacist charged past the toyshop and stopped to peer—somewhat cautiously—around the corner. He relaxed then, and seemed relieved to discover that the man was nowhere in sight; and so, of course, for whatever the reason, was I." Fleishman drank. "Anyhow, that was why I was late."

Johnny smiled. "You said it only took a few seconds."

"I stayed to chat with the pharmacist, explaining my interest. He was practically incoherent, poor fellow, and insisted I wait for the police to give them the benefit of my professionally competent description of the thief. So I did. I told them he was of larger than average size, and had intriguing eyes. . . . Did you know I was once hired to be a thief?"

"No," Johnny said. "I didn't know."

"It was back in my days as associate professor of criminology and penology. This firm that manufactured toll collection equipment paid me an outrageous sum to beat their system. They were troubled, you see, by the fact that certain toll collectors, despite the company's numerous safeguards, were sitting out there in their lonely toll booths with nothing better to do than think up ways to pocket part of the take. So they hired an expert on the criminal mind, me, to sit for hours with nothing better to do than think up ways to beat their system, so they could then think up ways to keep the ways I thought up from working. I'll tell you, it was one of the most enjoyable and satisfying jobs I've ever had. You should have heard my shrieks of joy when I came up with a new way to rob them blind. . . . Here, by the way—have one. I bought two when I finally got around to it."

Johnny laughed. "Much appreciated," he said, taking the cigar. "Tell me, how much did the guy get?"

"Eighteen dollars and change," Fleishman said, stony-faced. "Want a light?"

☐

While working up his newscast the following Tuesday afternoon, Johnny saw that the report of Criminal Court proceedings received in the K-SUN newsroom noted that Melvin Simmons had been sentenced to the state penitentiary for three-to-five years. He didn't use the item.

9

Good evening, ladies and gentlemen—welcome to "Profound." This is your genial host, big Johnny Manservant, friend to all and eight feet tall. Cute as a boot. Our guest tonight is the Old Flasher himself, joining us here in Televisionland with a few juicy anecdotes about life in your nearby and neighborly state pen. Tell us now, Flash old boy, how's it going out there in the old Big House?—as the hardened cons refer to it in their colorful argot.

It's going dandy. Soon, among other things—thanks to the humanitarianism of our next Attorney General—All Hail Kale!—we'll soon be able to hear all those darkies singing, their humble faces wreathed in smiles as they march off in lock step to their—

But tell us first, is it really a *big* Big House?

We boast 1172 souls, as of this morning's soul count.

And is that considered big, as Big Houses go?

It will, sir, suffice.

Don't mumble, just talk right into the microphone there. And now I'm sure our viewers would like to know exactly what you do out there. I mean, you *do* do something, don't you? You can't just sit around all day long jangling keys, can you?

Well, I've devised this wonderful plan that will transfer four hundred deserving inmates to a specially designed—

What else do you do?

I devise other, equally doomed and wonderful plans. And then when my plans are aborted, I improvise. When I'm too busy to improvise,

I react. When I'm too tired to react, I yell. When I no longer have the strength to yell, I sulk. What about you, Mr. Manservant—what do you do?

I neither create nor produce, I neither sow nor reap nor gather into barns. I influence.

Glory be to God.

You will have your little joke, won't you? But we didn't come here tonight with all these lights and cameras and coaxial cables just to talk about big old me. So would you briefly summarize for us exactly what must be done to halt the scourge of crime and sin infecting our fair nation?

Good question. Though as we say, the church is near but the road is icy, whereas the den of vice is far but I'll walk carefully. Or who could have told that honest pharmacist in his white jacket that the Finger of God was upon him, that out in a dark alley, his eyes aflame, someone was lying in wait, plotting, scheming, organizing—just yearning to remove by illegal means a sum of eighteen dollars and change from his cash register, thereby to alter the very core and fiber of two lives, and perhaps even three? But who am I to deny the criminal his meager share of the world's loot. He has a greater investment in the stolen goods—of time, energy, intelligence, dedication, fear, danger, commitment—than any owner can claim. So maybe we should just chalk up the whole thing to the theory of Just Deserts, in which we all so fervently believe. But, as I was saying, this plan of mine to transfer four hundred—

Isn't it true—admit it, you beast! you barbarian! you *jailer!*—that the weak and disadvantaged are mercilessly crushed by our so-called justice, that they—

Ah yes—piles for the poor, as my doctor friend says, and hemorrhoids for the haristocrats.

Alas, Flash, but time, as it inevitably does, is running out. So let me thank you for guest shotting with us tonight on "Profound," and bringing along all those vivid insightful glimpses into that prison of yours out there amid the rocks and the cacti, that suppurating, bleeding sore, that bleak monument of man's inhumanity to man, that—

The phone rang.

"Manson wants you in the shoeshop, sir," the operator said. "I think there's some trouble."

"What kind of trouble? Put him on . . . Hello? Hello? Manson? Where the hell's Manson?"

"He's in with them, Warden. This is Canwell."

"In with who? What's happening?"

"With those inmates, sir. I can see him from here; he's sort of in the corner with them."

"What's he doing with them?"

"I don't know—sort of talking to them."

"How many are there?"

"Four, sir. They're against the wall and he's got his back to us in the office here."

"Are they threatening him?"

"They don't seem to be, sir. We started in before but he waved us back out. Murray and Bostick are here with me. Do you want us to move in? We've alerted Warden Dowler."

"Where are the rest of the men in there?"

"At their machines, sir. Their regular places."

"Are they working?"

"They're just standing, sort of watching. Do you want us to move in?"

"Not if Manson's got it under control. I'll be right up."

Flash left the Warden's office and hurried along the narrow cement hallway and down the staircase and out under the arched stone sally port of the main entrance, where an officer was closing the big gate behind the departing garbage truck. Flash slowed to a more normal pace as he stepped out into the glare of the late morning sun. He buttoned his jacket. Ahead on his right he saw Jeff Dowler coming out from the Quonset hut, moving with the same sense of carefully restrained urgency. Flash motioned for him to wait. Dowler did so, but reluctantly, his broad face set and his meaty hands behind his back, still leaning, straining forward, impatient to be moving again, and foully muttering God only knew what. But Griffing was on his vacation and Philson on his day off and it was Flash's turn, not Dowler's, to be Acting Warden. Thus, having been told to wait, Dowler waited.

"I can handle it," Dowler said as Flash came up.

"I told them I was coming," Flash said.

Dowler fell in step on Flash's left, a pace behind, not out of deference but out of twenty years' habit of making sure that if you got slugged it wouldn't be from behind. *Keeping the spoons out of your back,* the guards called it. It was a habit you observed even when walking with Flash Fleishman who, as God and even Dowler knew, wouldn't hurt a fly.

They moved up the path, between the wide expanses of sloping lawn at the foot of the hill, toward the Cell Block at the top of the rise. The gravel path gave way to flagstone steps as the incline steepened. They climbed rapidly but steadily, with no outward show of excitement. On the lawn an inmate work detail puttered about in the blazing sun, mowing, raking, trimming the grass into neat circles around the base of small trees. Another detail worked on the flower garden. In turn, in apparent randomness, each inmate looked up briefly and then resumed his work. An inmate was not allowed to stare, but did not have to. He learned—as a guard learned to walk behind his companion—to see everything he wanted to see in one glance. And what they saw now, undoubtedly, was the excessive haste that Flash and Dowler were trying so hard to disguise.

They turned left at the top of the hill, along the path that circled the Cell Block. The barred windows and gray, stained walls were on their right.

An officer stepped out from the booth and saluted as they approached Post Two, at the corner of the Cell Block. Flash returned the salute; Dowler started to, his hand flicking, his arm stiffening, but caught himself in time and let his hand drop as casually as possible.

"There's some trouble in the—"

"We know," Dowler grumbled before Flash could speak. Dowler's voice was deep, almost hoarse; it sounded always as if it had to struggle up through some great congestion. "Just stay on your toes. We'll handle it."

They turned right again and headed for Post Three at the rear corner of the Cell Block. The officer at Post Three saluted. "I've got telephone contact with Canwell. It's still quiet."

"Okay," Flash said without stopping. "You stay here on phone contact," he told Dowler. "I don't want us both in there."

"Maybe it'd be better if you stayed and I—"

"No. You get on the phone here."

Dowler hesitated only long enough to advertise his disapproval, then headed for the concrete booth.

Flash turned the rear corner of the Cell Block and started toward the Shops Building. Back here the dry, cracked ground was bare, with no grass, no flower garden: visitors seldom got this far.

The building housed eight shops. It was two hundred feet long, two stories high, and sixty-three years old. The roof was slanted and gabled, the dark windows barred. The shoeshop was on the upper floor and could be reached either by the inside stairway or by the exterior metal fire escape that clung to the front of the building like a dark angled scar.

Flash started up the slatted fire escape, running his hand lightly along the metal handrail. He heard no noise from above. At the top he mounted the metal landing. The bolted door in the wall swung open.

"They're still in there," Bostick said. Flash stepped inside; Bostick locked the door behind him. "We haven't moved in."

"Good."

There were five other officers and one inmate—Manson's secretary—in the glass-enclosed office. One officer had the phone; the four others were standing at the glass, staring into the shop. They turned around as he entered and nodded. They would, no doubt, have been happier to see Dowler, but managed not to make it too obvious. They stepped aside to make a space for him at the glass. He walked over and looked in, with two officers on either side. They were bulky and composed. They shuffled protectively.

In the shop the inmates stood motionless at their places. Some held tools—awls, knives, hammers, shears—but not threateningly. In true inmate tradition, they held them casually, as if they had simply neglected to put them down. They were all looking toward the far corner of the shop, where Manson stood with his back to the office, facing four inmates who were lined up shoulder to shoulder against the wall. The shop machinery partially blocked Flash's view, and he couldn't see whether these four still held their tools.

"How long have they been like that?"

"About fifteen minutes, sir."

"That's long enough, I guess." He turned to the officer on the phone. "Have you got contact with Dowler?"

"Yes sir."

"Okay. I'll go in and see what's happening."

"I'll go with you, sir," Bostick said.

"No, stay here. If any trouble starts, get the rest of the men out. Don't let them mix in."

Flash turned the knob and pushed open the glass door. The inmates at their machines and benches turned to look. The four men against the far wall looked up too. Manson, slightly hunched, did not turn around.

Flash walked steadily between the narrow rows of wooden benches cluttered with leather cuttings, nail boxes, partially assembled shoes. The room was stifling and smelled richly of sweat, of leather, polish, volatile glues, fresh-cut rubber. In the silence against the background drone of the two large fans he listened for noises, for movement, but heard only his own footsteps, rhythmic, heavy, the left one louder and more shuffling than the right. (Did he always walk that way, or only at moments like this, when he was scared to death?)

He turned past the row of stitching machines. The four inmates watched him approach. Two he knew: Rogers and Verdun.

Manson still did not turn around. Three of the inmates, all except Rogers, held tools. Verdun had a chisel. The third had a knife, the fourth a hooked leather cutter.

Manson yelled without taking his eyes off the men: "I told you to stay out!"

"It's me," Flash said.

Manson stiffened, then backed up a step as Flash came alongside. Manson was tall, a once-lean man now thick in the waist, with large and roughened workman's hands. His lips, thin and red, always moist, were clamped shut. He had a fleshy, bulbous, faintly discolored nose unbalanced to the left side. He did not look frightened now but looked as if he had been frightened.

"They tried to get wise," he said to Flash, jerking his head angrily toward the four men.

Flash touched Manson's arm, nodding for him to stay where he was, then moved toward Verdun, steadily, his expression sober. He stopped two paces from Verdun and held out his hand, palm up. He kept his eyes on Verdun's face while Verdun looked down at his open, extended hand, maybe to see if it was shaking. "Come ahead," Flash said. "We've finished with our tools for today."

Verdun did not move.

"Let me have it," Flash said.

Verdun shrugged—theatrically, aware of his audience—to make it clear to all the other men in the shop that he didn't mind giving up his chisel because he never planned on using it anyhow. He offered it to Flash blade first, then quickly pulled his hand back in mock apology, smiling to see if he had sucked Flash in.

Flash rolled his fingers, beckoningly.

With exaggerated propriety, Verdun presented the chisel to Flash handle first.

Flash nodded.

Verdun shrugged to show his boredom.

Flash held out his other hand toward the inmate alongside Verdun. *Orninski*, according to his name tab. *Orninski*: a name he vaguely recalled having heard before. Orninski gave up his knife, handle first, without any carrying on.

Flash accepted the leather cutter from the other man: *Terrence.*
He looked at Rogers. "You have any tools on you?"

"No, sir."

Flash turned about, putting his back to the four inmates, and spoke
to Manson. "Would you ask Officer Bostick to come in, please."

Manson scurried clumsily down the aisle and waved to Bostick.

"Would you return these four inmates to their cells until I call for
them," Flash told Bostick when he came up.

"Yes sir. Come ahead now, step lively."

The four inmates, led by Verdun, marched in a line up the aisle.
Bostick waited for them to pass, then fell in behind.

"The stupid sons of bitches," Manson said. "I warned them if they—"

"Carry on until lunch," Flash said. "Then report to me in the Ward-
en's office, please."

□

On the big polished desk stood a vase of fresh-cut red and yellow
flowers, the names of which Flash did not know, brought in this morning from the garden by the Warden's inmate orderly.

"What do you mean, got wise? Be specific, will you?"

Sitting behind the desk, leaning back, Flash had his hands crossed
over his stomach. His suit jacket was unbuttoned now; when there
were no inmates around for whom you could set a bad example, you
were allowed a little more sneaky sloppiness.

Manson stood awkwardly in the middle of the room, like a gawky
bird. His gray-blue uniform was buttoned, he held his cap under his
arm, and his tie was knotted up to a collar that was too tight for the
folds of his neck. Manson was a singularly unattractive man. When he
wasn't scowling he could produce only a servile, wet-lipped grimace.
He could make shoes, that much could be said for him. He was a good
man with a claw hammer and a piece of cut leather. Whether he was
good at anything else—even the thing he was paid for, which was
teaching other men to make shoes—was a different matter. As shoeshop
foreman, Manson was a member of Flash's staff, his little box on the
organizational chart connected by a line up to Flash's box. Prisons,
however, were no places for a theoretician. Flash could not, even in
his most gracious moments, bear either the sight or the thought of Manson. But he was stuck with him. In Flash's four years at the pen, not
one training officer had quit or retired or been fired. Nor had a single
new position been created. Thus Flash hadn't yet had the opportunity
to choose a single one of the twenty training officers under his authority.

Whether, given that opportunity, he could have found anyone willing to take the job who'd be better than the average man he had now was doubtful. But God knows he could have found someone better than Manson, better than this—

"It was Orninski—he was the one who started it," Manson said. "So I told him to shut up and do his work or—"

"Orninski? Not Verdun?"

"That's right. Orninski."

"How did he start it?"

"Well, I was telling him how he wasn't doing something right—he works on the uppers, pinning them to the last—and he right away got wise so I told him to shut up and get to work or I'd charge him. And then Verdun and Terrence, they work right next to him, they started putting their two cents in. So I just told them to get against the wall."

"What about Rogers? How come he was with them?"

"Well, he works right there alongside them. And, I don't know—he sort of got in on it too."

"What do you mean—*sort of*? Did he or didn't he?"

"He did. Everybody started chickenshitting around then, razzing and blowing off, so I got these guys out of the way before I had the whole shop on my neck."

"Rogers is coming up for parole."

"That ain't my worry. I just didn't want the whole shop on my neck. Your friends over in Classification don't exactly send me the sweet ones, you know. When everyone started chickenshitting around like that, I wasn't about to turn my back on any of them. And Rogers was right with them, in that same row, so I put him over with the others."

Flash nodded. Manson's reputation was so bad that few inmates ever asked for the shoeshop. The ones who got sent were usually pretty far down the list, because an inmate who kept clean could eventually get the assignment he wanted. Manson's version, however, was that he got the tough ones because no one else could handle them.

"We'll have to charge all four of them," Flash said. "If you're sure Rogers was involved."

"He was. I told you that. He was giving me static right along with the others."

"No one's ever charged him with anything like that before."

"Well, I'm charging him. What am I supposed to do—let myself be pushed around by a bunch of wise guys?"

"Did any of them push you? Did anyone touch you?"

Manson thought a moment. "No."

"Okay. Now tell me what you were doing standing there for fifteen minutes with those men against the wall. I'd like to know what you said to them during that time, and what they said to you. I'd also like to know why in God's name you didn't take their tools away."

Manson shrugged moodily; he shifted his feet.

"Did you ask them to turn over their tools? Did they refuse? If they did, you realize, they're going to face a very serious—"

"No, I didn't."

"Why on earth not?"

"Well, I didn't figure there'd be any trouble, that's why. I mean, they weren't threatening nobody or anything. There wasn't anything like that at all. They were just wise, just blowing off."

"Why didn't you let the officers in?"

"Because I had it under control. I can handle my shop. There's no use making a big thing of this."

"All right. I guess we'll have to transfer these men out when they get off punishment. Where are they in the training program?"

"Orninski's finished—I had him on his last set, a few years ago. Verdun I think is about halfway along, and I think Rogers is finished. The other one, Terrence—"

"What do you mean, *think?* Don't you even know which men—"

"Sure I know. They're where I told you they are."

"What about the other one—Terrence?"

"Well, he ain't none too bright anyways, and he's just sort of started. They had him in the tailor shop before and then they buck-slipped him over to me."

"All right. Now, as I understand it, Orninski started talking back and then Verdun and Terrence came in, and then, more or less, Rogers. Is that correct?"

"Yeah. Only Rogers came in all right, as much as the others. I don't see why he should get any special treatment."

"We'll take care of the treatment, Manson. You just tell us what happened."

"I told you what happened."

"Okay. That'll be it for now."

☐

It was almost one o'clock by the time Flash got to the staff lunchroom. Dowler was alone at the senior officers' table when Flash joined him.

"Seen Manson yet?" Dowler asked.

"Just now," Flash said, taking the linen napkin from the place setting and tucking one end between the third and fourth buttons of his shirt.

The inmate orderly appeared at his left. "Good afternoon, Warden."

"Good afternoon," Flash said.

The orderly put the plate down in front of him: fried chicken, Spanish rice and salad. The staff did not eat inmate food. The orderly placed a basket of hot rolls on the table and filled the coffee cup from a metal pitcher. He moved the cream and sugar over. "Will there be anything else, sir?"

"That'll be just fine. Thank you."

The orderly left.

Flash tentatively probed at the half of chicken with his knife, then sliced a piece from the breast. "We'll have to charge at least three of them—insubordination, I guess, which is all I can get out of Manson. Rogers didn't seem to be particularly involved. Orninski is supposed to have started it."

"That figures," Dowler said. "Orninski, I mean."

Flash shrugged, chewing, and sipped his coffee. The coffee was dreadful, as usual, because the man who could brew a decent cup of coffee inside the walls of a prison hadn't yet been born, but the chicken was excellent. The food was almost always excellent, and fattening. "I would have figured Verdun myself. I don't know much about Orninski."

"Verdun doesn't waste his time on stuff like that. He's got more important things on his mind."

"Like what?"

"He keeps busy. He's a bright guy, Flash. He's got a hand in a lot of things. And he keeps out of trouble."

"What about Orninski?"

"Psycho."

"What's he in for? I haven't checked their files yet."

"Bank robbery. Armed."

"Same as Verdun?"

"The same. Only when Verdun goes into a bank, it's to get money. Orninski goes in because he's loco."

"Orninski's been here before, hasn't he?"

"That's right. Bank robbery. Armed."

"What's he on now?"

"Twenty-to-life."

Flash ate a moment in silence. "What about Rogers? Do you have anything against him?"

Dowler looked up smiling from his apple pie. "I don't have anything against anybody, Flash. You know that."

"I'd like to get Rogers out this time. He's ready; he's worked for it."

Dowler shrugged. "Just recommend loss of privilege then."

"I'd like to keep him off charge entirely. He comes up next month."

"Then maybe he should've stayed out of trouble."

"I think he just happened to be standing there."

"That's what they all say, Flash. Have you interviewed them yet?"

"After lunch."

□

When he got back to the Warden's office he sent for the files on the four inmates and returned a call from a state legislator in Maynard, who wanted to arrange a visit for a group of clergymen from his district.

"They're very interested in prison reform," the legislator said.

"Well, that's just fine," Flash said. "So are we. We'll be glad to show them around."

After he hung up and marked the date of the visit on the Warden's calendar, he jiggled the cradle and asked that the four inmates be brought over. He glanced through their files and then called Ted Reed in Classification. Reed had little to add, except about Terrence, the dumb one.

"Maybe we should just put him on cleanup and forget about it," Reed suggested. "I thought he might get something out of the shops—he's pretty good with his hands, actually—but it looks like I was wrong."

"Okay. We'll see what we can do. Thanks."

"Wait—you got a minute? I was just going to call you."

"What is it?"

"We just got word that one of the inmates—Bryher, I don't know if you know him—"

"No."

"In the powerhouse . . . two-to-five for breaking and entering. His wife smashed up their car yesterday and she's in the hospital—in Phillipsburg. She's not too badly hurt, but his kid's all banged up. Do you think we could manage a furlough?"

"What do you think?"

"I think maybe. Thirteen months good time. Not a bad guy."

"Do you want to send him clean?"

"Could we? The kid's nine, and I'd just as soon his old man didn't have to show up in bracelets."

"Today?"

"The kid's in bad shape; they're afraid he might not pull through."

"I have to have clearance from Security."

Reed paused. "Is it absolutely necessary?"

"Yes; you grab Dowler and let me know what he says."

□

Bostick stood out in the hall, holding the door open, while the four inmates marched in.

"Okay," Flash said.

Bostick backed out and pulled the door shut. He would remain in the hall, his ear against the door. Flash didn't see much point in it. If anything happened it'd either be loud enough to hear anyhow or so quick it wouldn't matter.

The four men stood in a row, hands behind their backs, feet spread, eyes not at him but straight ahead, past him. Flash looked at each in turn, taking his time. He had no expectation of learning anything. If he had, he would have called them one at a time. But no inmate could be charged without an interview. This was their interview.

"Orninski?"

"Yes, sir."

"Did you have a dispute with Officer Manson?"

"No, sir."

"He reports that you did."

"I just asked him to leave me alone. I was doing my work. I wasn't bothering no one."

"Did you speak to him in a disrespectful manner?"

"I just asked him to leave me alone."

"In what way was he not leaving you alone?"

Orninski said nothing.

"You're expected to obey all officers and to treat them with respect at all times."

"Yeah—I know."

"And to address them by their proper titles."

"Yes . . . Warden."

"Verdun: how did you get involved in this?"

"Involved in what, Warden?"

"In a dispute with Officer Manson."

"I didn't notice any dispute, sir. I was busy all the time working."

"Did you speak to him in a disrespectful manner?"

"No, sir."

"Terrence."

Terrence straightened quickly, his eyes pale and terrified. You could believe he wasn't bright enough for the tailor shop, or for the shoeshop either. Looking at him, you even wondered if he could make the grade on cleanup—if he could ever truly master the mop and pail. His IQ was fifty-three, and his face showed not even animal shrewdness. His eyes were dull, his mouth soft. His expression was bland and aimless, vague, confused.

"What about it, Terrence? What were you doing in this thing?"

"I wasn't doing nothing . . ."

"Warden."

"Warden. . . ."

"Rogers: were you involved in this?"

"No, sir."

"The officer said you were."

"I didn't do anything, sir."

"How did you get involved?"

"I wasn't involved, sir."

"Okay. Do any of you have anything to add?" He glanced from face to face. "That will be all, then." Without raising his voice he said, "Bostick—come on in," and the door opened immediately. "Return them to their cells. They're to remain confined until further notice. Full rations, though."

□

Flash picked up the recommendations for tomorrow's Classification meeting, part of the stack of TRE work he brought along with him this morning to the Warden's office. Usually he served as Acting Warden only three or four days a month—his menses—but with Griffing on vacation he'd be pulling it five times in three weeks. As Acting Warden he was expected "to visit every part of the Penitentiary and observe the conditions and activities thereof, to make his presence known to inmates and staff, to make himself available en route for consultation and comment, and to pay special attention to inmates in the infirmary and on punishment." He had done so this morning, and between that and Manson's Folly in the shoeshop, he had done little else.

Every one of the thirty-seven new inmates from Induction who were coming up for classification tomorrow had already been interviewed by a Classification officer, the prison doctor, the prison psychologist (and in some cases, on his recommendation, the visiting psychiatrist), a social worker, a training officer and an education officer. Each filed a report, with recommendations. The reports went to Ted Reed, who summarized them and added his own recommendation. The whole file then went to Flash. As secretary of the committee, Flash presented each case to the group, which was chaired by Philson and further composed of Jeff Dowler, as Assistant Warden for Security, and the Chief Training, Education and Classification officers. The meetings of the Classification committee were invariably calm and businesslike. The members were all rational men, and they arrived, in general, at rational decisions. Thus was each new inmate, without prejudice, without furore, in the most objective and reasonable manner possible, assigned his place in the savage and debased jungle of the penitentiary.

Of the thirty-seven coming up tomorrow, thirty-one were repeaters. One was starting his seventh term, although only his third in the pen. The shortest sentences—given to nine men—were one-to-three years. Most had two-to-four or two-to-five, although one had twenty-to-life for second-degree murder, and another had straight life, for the assault and murder of two ten-year-old boys. He was one of the first offenders, twenty-five years old. He had two years of college, worked for a brokerage office in Maynard, and had never before been in trouble.

Dowler phoned. "Did you see those men? They have anything to say?"

"Not much—the usual. I still don't think Rogers was involved."

"Well, let me talk to Manson and see what he has to say. This guy Bryher, now, the one with the wife and kid that got hurt. Reed's here right now—what do you think, Flash?"

"I thought maybe we could give him twenty-four on an arrival and departure check-in with the Phillipsburg police, and then see what happens with the kid, if he pulls through or not."

"You know this guy at all?"

"No. Reed says he's all right. Record's clean."

"Because we don't serve nothing here. He's a bottle baby, Flash."

"Oh—I didn't know that. Well . . . would you feel better if I saw him first? Maybe if we made it clear to him that—"

"I can do that," Dowler said. "I just wanted to know how keen you were on signing him out."

"I think we ought to, in a case like this. But I need a release from Custody."

"Well, I don't know if I want to stick my neck out for this guy, to tell you the truth. I could give the okay on Reed's say-so, if you want, but then if anything happened, Reed would be—"

"Give it on mine then," Flash said.

"Okay," Dowler said after a moment. "If you're sure that's what you want."

"Only talk to him before he leaves, will you? Talk to him real good."

Flash took up the weekly report from the Chief Training Officer from his pile of TRE work. He approved seven inmate requests for job transfers—after calling the Chief Training Officer about a couple—and disapproved of three. He initialed all five requests from shop officers for reassignment of inmates. He accepted an accident report from the laundry: a man had scalded his hand on one of the big driers, and was now in the infirmary.

At two thirty, right on schedule, the orderly brought in a tray with the Warden's afternoon pot of coffee and a glazed doughnut. (Sure, Griffing could sit here all day eating doughnuts, the son of a bitch. *He* didn't gain two pounds every time he opened his mouth.) While eating the doughnut—it was delicious; they had an excellent pastry cook, serving three-to-five for assault—Flash went through the requisitions from the shop officers, countersigning all but one of them, which he wanted to check when he had time. The coffee was sour, gritty, filmy, and lukewarm, but he drank it anyhow.

After knocking and waiting for Flash's answer, Reverend Millard R. Traceman stepped in, wiping his forehead with a handkerchief. He was a big man, florid, of considerable girth. (*He* could eat doughnuts. A doughnut wouldn't cause even a ripple in that great Protestant equatorial belly. It was only the poor slobs with *little* potbellies who had to worry.)

"Hot out there, eh, Padre? And you know what it is?—it's those black suits God makes you wear. And He made the sun, remember—the sun, the heat, the desert, the dust. It's all His fault."

The chaplain dropped heavily into a chair, breathing hard. He was in his sixties and short-winded. He folded his handkerchief into a square on his lap. "Busy?"

"Nothing Philson can't do tomorrow. Just having a cup of slop, actually. Join me?"

"I think not, thanks."

"Shakes your faith a bit, doesn't it, to realize He made the coffee too?"

"It would, Flash, if I let myself dwell morbidly upon it. How'd it go today? I hear you had some trouble in the shoeshop."

"Just Bubblebrain up to his usual tricks—and now don't go telling me God made *him!*"

Traceman crossed his bulky legs and settled lower in the chair. "One of the men in upholstery—Jerry Coughlin—would like to see you, Flash, if you think you can manage it."

"What about, do you know?"

"It's pretty vague, but he's obviously bothered about something. I think it might help if you could talk to him."

"Okay, Padre. I'll see him."

"Thanks." Traceman was silent a moment, still with his folded handkerchief on his lap. "You haven't been around to see Rodriguez today by any chance, have you?"

"No, as it happens, I haven't been around to see Rodriguez today by any chance. Why must you pick the one lousy day I'm stuck in here to decide it's time for the Warden to trade jollities with Rodriguez?"

"Actually, I guess it's too late for today anyhow. I'll mention it to Philson in the morning."

"Sure—first thing. Hide behind his desk and leap out with it as soon as he walks in. That's what a fellow likes to hear when he gets back from his day off. In fact, if I were you, Padre, I'd hit Griffing on this too, the minute he gets back from his vacation."

"You wardens are all alike. You leave the dirty work to us."

"You can't complain, Padre: the last three were Catholics."

"I figured Rodriguez for an R.C. too. It's not easy to find a Mexican Protestant."

"Especially one who's shot his wife and mother. How is he these days?"

"Same, I guess. How would one expect him to be?"

"Scared," Flash said. "That's how I'd be."

"I think he's beginning to have some doubts about his lawyer."

"The Governor will commute anyhow, I expect. After all, Eberhart's one of the six men in the state who don't believe in capital punishment."

"Why doesn't he just do it then? What's he waiting for?"

"The election."

"He didn't commute for Calder."

"There were complications then, and besides, Calder was black. The ones he commuted were white. Rodriguez is kind of cinnamon brown, so I figure he's got a fifty-fifty chance."

"Most of the times I've seen him he's been pretty white. What's this I hear, Flash—about bringing more Negroes in."

"Ah yes. It's all logical enough, I guess—what else would a rational man expect but that someone like Kale, who lives in a restricted all-white neighborhood, would—"

"I didn't know that."

"Hell, they don't even allow Jews up there in Old Trail."

"What's your neighborhood like, Flash?"

"It's crawling with foreigners—niggers, kikes, wops, poles, chinks, the whole show, the rainbow, from A to Z. And it's great, Padre, it's the American way. I don't want my kids growing up prejudiced. 'You be nice to those black sons of bitches down the block,' I tell them."

"No you don't, Flash."

"Anyhow, Kale's decided it's our job to solve in our six-by-eight cells all the messy social problems that great humanitarians like himself are too chicken to even *try* to solve in their own backyards."

"Perhaps Kale doesn't understand some of the problems you people face."

"Kale doesn't understand anything. He's a nincompoop. What he knows about the operation of a prison a hummingbird could pass unnoticed in its wee-wee while flying."

"You have to admit those Negroes up at Raintree have it pretty dreadful, Flash. They deserve something better."

"Of course they do. I'm all for burning down Raintree and firing nine-tenths of the staff. Those guards up there are practically a Ku Klux Klan unit. But meanwhile, I'd just as soon not see us inherit any more problems here. I think we have enough problems. I think maybe we deserve a moratorium on new problems for a while."

Traceman shrugged. "We've always had Negroes here."

"A few, in their own tier, working on the service details."

"What's going to happen now?"

"We're going to get more, some transferred down from Raintree, some sentenced directly. And they're all to be given an equal opportunity to participate in all our programs, activities and uplifting influences."

The chaplain said nothing.

"Maybe you shouldn't spend so much time with Rodriguez, Padre. It depresses you. It quenches that great Protestant *joie de vivre* that we all find so appealing. I'll make a deal; you skip it this afternoon and I'll go up instead. I'll even mumble a few Pater Nosters for him— or is that one of the other team's cheers? Okay—I'll sing 'Rock of Ages' then."

The chaplain shook his head. "I promised I'd come every day. But it might be nice if you went too."

"Sure, to help the time pass. Do you think, Padre, he really wants the time to pass?"

"Yes and no—it's something of a unique feeling, I imagine."

"I'll bet the hell it is," Flash said.

Fifteen minutes later an inmate was ushered in.

"Sit down, Coughlin. What's on your mind? The Padre said you wanted to see me."

Clutching his cloth cap as if he feared Flash was about to seize it, Coughlin backed hesitantly into a chair: a small pasty-faced man with a nervous mouth. His eyes—extremely small gray eyes—showed a clearly recognizable kind of fear, and Flash wondered how Coughlin, or any of those who came for the same reason, managed to keep the other inmates from also seeing it.

"I don't know exactly how I oughta put this, Warden . . . What I'm saying is I don't want you thinking I'm figuring on getting anything out of this or anything but, well—Youngdahl's got a shiv is what it is, pure and simple. It's hid in his bed, under the frame somewhere."

Flash looked at him impassively. "Why are you telling me this?"

"Well, I'll tell you . . . It's because I happen to know—only I don't know why, because I never done anything to him—that he's out for me. And well, I can take care of myself all right, but not someone coming at me with a blade."

"Has he ever done anything to you?"

"Well no—no, he hasn't. Not actually."

"Has he ever threatened you?"

"No. But I been around, Warden. I think I know the score. And I tell you he's out for me."

"Is that all you have to say?"

"Well, yeah—except that I was wondering—well, maybe if you didn't think it'd be an idea if maybe I got transferred out of the tier."

"What tier are you in?"

"South 4. Youngdahl and his boys are all over the place there." He paused. "I heard there's some empty cells down in 1, and I thought maybe—"

"Who do you know in 1?"

"It's not that, Warden. I mean it. Put me anywhere you want and it'll be okay with me, just so I get away from where I am. I only thought of 1 because I heard they had some empty—"

"Have you put in a request for transfer?"

"Well no—no I ain't. I was thinking maybe it'd look better, you know, if—"

"Is there anything else?"

"No, Warden, that's all." Coughlin got quickly to his feet, still throttling his cap. "I really appreciate seeing you . . . it's not any joke, you know, when somebody's on you like that. Otherwise I woulda never come in and—"

"Okay. That'll be all now."

A few minutes later the phone rang. The operator said a gentleman wanted to speak to him.

"Who is this gentleman, may I ask?"

"He wouldn't say, sir. He just said to tell you it was an old friend."

"Okay, put him on."

There followed a nerve-shattering explosion in his ear. (Even the best of inmates, sadly enough—even the switchboard operator, as decent and harmless a man as you'd find behind any set of bars in the country—harbored certain subconscious resentments against their jailers.)

". . . finally cornered you, I see. After those other times I thought I might be better off not—"

"Excuse me, but I don't think I caught the—"

"Johnny Mancino. Remember? We shared a pleasant half hour on the airwaves a few weeks ago."

"Oh yes. Mancino. Yes; I remember vividly."

"You really *do* work there, don't you? People really can get you on the phone."

"I'm a public servant, Mr. Mancino—available to one and all, rich and poor alike, the destitute, the homeless, the ill-at-ease—all humanity is my parish. So what can I do for you?"

"I'm calling for a friend, actually. I don't know if this is the way to do it, but—"

"What kind of a friend?"

"One of your prisoners."

"You should avoid friends like that. A clean-cut fellow like you."

"I thought you might be interested—he was on the show a couple of weeks before you—and was almost as big a hit."

"But not quite, I trust."

"Well no, not quite. Even though he turned out to be more expensive. But anyway—"

"What do you mean, more expensive?"

"He couldn't get it out of his head that the rest of us were cleaning up, so he insisted on getting—"

"How much did you pay him?"

"Fifty dollars, actually. But—"

"Fifty dollars! And you never even offered *me* one lousy red cent?"

"You never asked for anything, Dr. Fleishman."

"Sure—that's how it is—the crooks and the loudmouths of the world clean up while the humble self-effacing types get the bird. Sure, Flash Fleishman comes cheap. You can keep your hands in your pockets when dealing with him. Who is this guy?"

"Maybe I shouldn't tell you now."

"Tell me. I'm not the one to harbor a grudge. Who is the son of a bitch?"

"His name is Simmons—Mel Simmons."

"Oh yes—I just ran across his name somewhere. He's coming up for classification, I think. When did he arrive?"

"A few weeks ago. I was going to call you earlier but—"

"That's the one. I've got his file right here. What about him?"

"Well, I don't know just how to put this, but I think he's basically all right. I don't mean he's necessarily innocent, but he strikes me as someone who could be helped. I thought maybe if you could—"

"He's on three-to-five, it says here. Auto theft, eh?"

"Joy riding—that's right. Naturally you know a lot more about this than I do, but I think—"

"Two previous offenses, eh?"

"That's right. Pretty minor ones, though. I really thought he was all straightened out this time when he fell into this."

"Fell? Into eight different cars?"

"You know what I mean."

"What is it you want me to do with him?"

"I'm not really sure. But I thought maybe you could give him a hand in there, if you would—or maybe there's something I could do for him out here, helping him toward a parole or something."

"He's asked for the garage—that's a pretty popular assignment, you know. It's not easy to put a new man on that right away."

"Well, I'm certainly not trying to push him for anything. I just thought you might be—I don't know, interested in him, since you were both—"

"You know what that comes out to? Over fifteen quarts."

"Excuse me?"

"Fifty dollars. I get it at Walgren's for $3.19, and I'll never forgive you. Okay, though, I'll have a chat with him. But I can't promise anything."

Flash called Induction and asked to have Simmons brought over. Then he called the South wing and asked the keeper if anything was brewing between Coughlin and Youngdahl in tier 4.

"Nothing I've noticed, Warden. Want me to keep an eye on them?"

"Yes—especially Coughlin."

Then he phoned the upholstery shop.

"This fellow Coughlin—how's he doing?"

"All right, Warden. He does his work."

"Has he got a boyfriend there? Someone in the shop?"

"Well, I been wondering about that, to tell you the truth. I didn't want to say anything until I was sure."

"Who is it?"

"Young kid—fella by the name of Grieg. But I'm not really sure yet. That's why I haven't said anything."

"Do you know his tier?"

"Wait a minute—I got it right here . . . South 1."

Flash made a note to transfer Coughlin out of upholstery to get him away from Grieg. He'd probably have to be moved out of his tier too, in case there actually was trouble between him and Youngdahl, or in case Youngdahl learned who turned in the knife. He could be shifted tomorrow as part of the general reshuffling when the inductees were assigned regular cells—to North 2, as far as possible from both Youngdahl and Grieg. Flash also decided to keep an eye on the upholstery officer, to make sure he wasn't being bought off by the homosexuals. He didn't like the idea of his knowing about Coughlin and Grieg and not saying anything.

He called Dowler.

"I haven't had a chance to see Manson yet," Dowler said.

"That's not what I'm calling about anyhow. Did Bryher leave?"

"He's getting ready. We'll put him on the bus and the Phillipsburg police will meet him and take him to the hospital."

"You told them to let him go in alone, didn't you?"

"Yeah, I told them."

"Okay. That's not what I'm calling about either." Flash gave him a rundown on Coughlin.

"We ought to move right in on the blade," Dowler said. "If there is one."

"The only thing is, I'm afraid that might really set Youngdahl on Coughlin. Maybe we can shift Youngdahl tomorrow too, and not tell him till he gets back from work, so he won't have time to get rid of it. A guard could stay with him while he's getting his stuff together to make sure he doesn't take it with him. Then we can have the guard discover it during a routine search before the new man arrives."

"No go, Flash. I'm not going to ask one of my men to stand around sucking his thumb in a cell with a guy we think's got a blade handy."

"I guess you're right. You want to send someone over there now?"

"I think we have to, Flash."

"Okay then. Coughlin will just have to take care of himself."

□

"It's all right, Simmons. Relax. Sit down if you'd like."

Although theoretically standing at ease, Simmons was rigid. He was clenching his teeth so ferociously he seemed unable to speak; the muscle along his jaw bulged like a whipcord. Most inmates, even the cockiest, were a little nervous coming into this office, but Flash couldn't remember ever seeing one as profoundly *scared* as Simmons seemed right now. He was a good-looking kid, and you could see why Mancino had picked him. There was something appealing about him, a kind of reassuring sense of uncomplicated inadequacy. His curly black hair and pleasant, boyish features would come over well on a TV screen.

"Go ahead; sit down. I just got a call about you and—" Flash leaped from the chair and grabbed Simmons just as he seemed about to topple. The color had drained from his face; he wavered, his eyes fluttering. "Good heavens, man—are you all right? Here, sit down—that's it—*sit*. Put your head down—put it between your knees."

"No . . . I'm all right . . ."

"Are you sick? You haven't been on anything, have you?"

"Huh?"

"Drugs? Have you been on drugs?"

"Huh?—Oh no . . . I ain't been on anything . . ."

Flash put a thumb on his forehead and pulled up one eyelid.

Simmons twisted his head away. "I'm all right . . . really . . ."

"Do you want a drink of water?"

Simmons shook his head.

Flash stood over him, watching. The kid still looked pretty shaky, but some of his color was returning. After a moment, Flash went behind the desk and sat down. The kid stared at him uneasily for a few moments. Flash smiled, trying to get him to loosen up, but the kid just lowered his eyes, as if in final resignation to something—hopelessness, futility, something.

"What is it? I realize you're new here, but we're no worse than any of the others. We don't bite."

Simmons tried to wet his lips; he looked up, as if Flash too might be amazed to realize how dry his tongue was. He swallowed after much effort. "What was it . . . you wanted me for?"

"Oh, is *that* it? I'm sorry, really. I should have realized. But it's nothing to worry about. You haven't done anything. We're not after you."

Simmons waited. He didn't seem prepared to believe this. What in hell could he have done to get so shook up? Nothing, probably. He'd probably been sitting down there in Induction when suddenly the door screeched open and somebody yelled, *Get a goddamn move on, boy! The Warden wants you!* You had to keep reminding yourself. After a while, with twenty or thirty or forty new men arriving every week, the whole process began to seem pretty natural to you, inevitable, and you kept forgetting what it must be like.

"Let's get this straight now, Simmons—there's nothing to worry about. You're not in trouble. The only reason I sent for you was that I got a call from a friend of yours—a mutual friend, actually—asking how you were getting along, and I thought I might as well meet you and see. That's all."

"A friend . . . ?" Simmons said finally. His voice was still unsteady.

"Yes—the TV fellow. Mancino. He said you were on his show." Simmons narrowed his eyes. "He called you? About me?"

"Yes. You see"—Flash smiled, chuckled—"I was on one of his shows too. So as he said, we were more or less costars, the two of us."

Simmons ignored the playful smile, the friendly chuckle. His expression remained unchanged. "But—well, what did he call *about?*"

"I told you—to ask how you were doing. To put in a good word for you, to see if he could do anything. You've got a real booster there, Simmons. I'm not saying, you understand, that he can do anything for you here. But it looks good when someone in a responsible position goes out of his way to speak up for you."

"Well yeah . . . I guess it does. But I mean . . . well—that's what he called about, you mean? That's what he said?"

"What did you expect him to say?"

For the first time Simmons cracked a smile, almost shyly. "Well, nothing, if you know what I mean. I mean, you know, I never expected him to say anything—I never figured he'd ever call."

"I'd say you had a real friend there, Simmons."

"Yeah . . ." Simmons seemed awed by the idea.

"I certainly hope you don't let him down. He's got a lot of faith in you."

"Oh no—I mean, well, if you wanna check or anything, you can see I had a clean record at St. Joe's and at the Farm and everything. I never got one mark on my sheet in either of those places."

Flash blinked once, watching him. According to his package, Simmons had been on punishment for ten days at St. Joseph's for attacking another inmate with a chair leg. No reason for the attack was discovered. Flash waited, still looking into Simmons' face, giving him a chance to remember, to correct himself, but the fellow didn't even seem aware of the fact that he was lying; his face was all innocence and steadfastness, all confidence in the truth as he saw it. He believed in his own lie and that saved him, that made it all right, and far be it from Flash Fleishman to mess up another man's precious vision of his own innocence. So what Flash said was, "Let's keep it that way, Simmons. Let's keep that sheet clean."

"Well—that's what I figure to do," Simmons said, with a truly impressive earnestness.

"And remember, no friend on the outside, no matter who he is, can serve your time for you. You understand that, of course."

"Oh yeah. Sure—I understand that."

"And Simmons, you're expected to address the staff by their appropriate titles here."

"Yes, sir—Warden." He jumped up, his hands stiff at his sides. It could have been mimicry, a real hardrock's joke, but it wasn't. "I'm sorry, sir. I was just—you know, all mixed up. I won't forget, sir."

"Okay, that'll be all. I'll be looking forward to hearing good reports about you."

"Yes, sir. You will, sir. You'll see."

Ted Reed had earmarked Simmons for the tailor shop, where they had some openings, and Flash had already initialed his okay. Now he crossed that out and wrote *Garage* instead. What the hell, he seemed like a decent enough kid. "Anxious to please," the Classification interviewer had written, "but very uneasy, unsure of himself—seems content just to be left alone—surprisingly little resentment or bitterness."

Oh well, maybe if the committee could be convinced that Simmons knew as much about fixing cars as he obviously did about stealing them, they'd go along. Unfortunately, the garage crew was always overloaded, not only because practically every inmate considered himself an automotive engineer, but also because Delft, the garage officer, was better than most at handling troublemakers. That meant that a lot of men like Simmons got shunted to other assignments to make room in the garage for inmates who'd screwed up somewhere else.

Flash once more looked over the dossiers of the four inmates from the shoeshop. He shrugged. Maybe Dowler would get something out of Manson that made sense. If anyone could, Jeff Dowler was probably the man. A former semipro fullback, a former high school football coach, a former border patrolman, a former guard corporal and guard lieutenant and chief keeper in the federal system, Dowler was about as good a security man as you could hope to find. Dowler and Flash were equal in rank, pay and status, and theoretically in power. The organizational chart showed a big box at top center for Griffing, a smaller box directly underneath for Philson, and below that, to the right and to the left, two still smaller identical boxes for Dowler and Flash. But everyone knew, including Flash, that Dowler more often got what he wanted, that his opinion counted for more, that his agreement was needed to get anything changed. Flash did not mind, too much. It wasn't a matter of personalities; it was always this way, everywhere. Security outranked Treatment. You could rehabilitate a hundred men—a thousand—and get no more than a yawn from the public and a shrug from the reporters. But let one man escape . . . Then too, Dowler had over twenty years in prison work. Flash had four. And there was no question about it: Dowler knew just about everything there was to know about his job. He was what the inmates, in the highest compliment they could pay a staff member, called *stir-smart*. He knew what was going on, and why, and could scratch out in the sand as neat an organizational chart of the inmate power structure as that unknown civil servant had years ago drawn up for the staff.

"How do you do it?" Flash asked him once, casually, not wanting to appear too serious. "What do you do all day? How do you spend your time?"

"I just walk around," Dowler said, full of seriousness. This was his life he was talking about, his soul, and that square rugged jaw of his didn't have a casual line in it. His ears were large and rather turned out, so that on someone else they might look funny. They didn't look funny on Jeff Dowler. "That's why you don't know anything, Flash. You're always *doing* something. Shuffling papers. If I had my way I wouldn't touch a piece of paper from Christmas to Christmas Eve, except paychecks. I'd just walk around. And if I could do that, you know what? Then I'd *really* be able to run this place."

And he probably would. Dowler had come up against and survived just about every conceivable challenge a prison official might face, short of earthquake, flood or damage by artillery fire, and he had no doubts about continuing to survive.

Unfortunately, he had some doubts about Flash. Not that they didn't get along. They got along fine, all things considered. But Dowler had reasons for looking upon Flash as an outsider, an interloper, an amateur—among them that Flash's main claim to qualification for his post was that he had spent twelve years lecturing co-eds—he had taught at an all-girl college, a fact that Dowler cherished—about the theory, history and practice of penology. He had also written a book on the subject. Actually, it had been his dissertation, turned into a book by the excision of a few reams of footnotes, and it was now used, at last count, by twenty-seven colleges as a text. A supplementary text, for small advanced classes of serious, bespectacled students, and thus no money maker. *A World Behind Bars: A Source Study of Non-Formalized Inmate Attitudes*, Prentice-Hall, 1959, $7.50, slightly higher in Canada.

When Flash joined the staff four years ago, as Chief Classification Officer, Griffing had purchased out of institutional funds three copies of the book and had suggested in a memo that all staff members avail themselves of the opportunity of reading it. Dowler, not being one to ignore his Warden's suggestions, must certainly have done so, although he had never admitted it. But back then the whole thing probably hadn't bothered him much, because as Classification Chief Flash was one step below Dowler, and in prison all steps are giant ones. You might almost as well be ten steps below—Recruit Guard Officer, Probationary—as one step. But two years later, when Flash moved up to Deputy Warden for TRE and to a (very, very) theoretical equality, the book and the professorship and the co-eds and the Ph.D. all assumed for Dowler the coloring of some special form of Faustian damnation, not for himself, but for Flash. This was the ultimate affront, the primal sin, from which there could be no salvation.

Ah, if Flash had his way, he would like to invent some *really* special form of damnation—something like hanging by the thumbs, but subtler and more penetrating—for that hammerhead in the shoeshop. With any other shop officer except Manson, Flash would have been willing, albeit reluctantly, to shrug off Rogers' shot at a parole next month. But Manson was an idiot, a moral and intellectual dinosaur, a lout, a slob, a liar, a millstone around the trachea of the state penal system, a jackass. He'd obviously been as much at fault as any of the inmates, but one thing you did not do in official reports was criticize staff members, especially when such criticism might be interpreted as an endorsement of an inmate's point of view.

And so tomorrow Flash would privately tell Philson that Officer Manson was an idiot, a moral and intellectual dinosaur, a lout, a slob, etc., etc., and that he had unforgivably mishandled the incident and was lying to boot, not only about Rogers but about everything. No officer of Manson's experience—no matter what his claim to oafishness—

would let three disorderly inmates stand against a wall for fifteen minutes without insisting that they put down their tools.

What probably happened was that Manson did order them to drop their tools, and they refused, perhaps at Orninski's lead. And so Manson had just stood there, afraid to turn his back and equally—more—afraid to force the issue. And the only way he could be found out would be for the inmates themselves to admit a greater degree of guilt than they were being charged with. It was a pretty safe bet this wouldn't happen much short of the next millennium.

After explaining all this to Philson, Flash would then inform him that, under his duly constituted authority as Assistant Warden for Treatment, Rehabilitation and Education, and after much serious deliberation, he was forced to recommend that Officer Manson might be more valuable to the institution as Recreation Officer, assigned to the athletic field. The post offered the same pay and perquisites as his present position and thus should not be viewed as a demotion. Officer Manson's new duties, however, would involve no responsibility for any part of the inmate training program, and that, is his respectfully submitted opinion, was a consummation devoutly to be wished.

And Philson, paring his fingernails while waiting for Flash to finish, would suggest he bring the matter to the attention of Warden Griffing, as soon as the Warden returned from his vacation.

And then Griffing, tanned and rested from his well-deserved holiday, would listen placidly while Flash repeated it all, word for word.

And now where is it you want to put him? Griffing would ask, paring his fingernails.

The athletic field, Flash would respond.

I see. Do you think he's qualified to handle the athletic field?

I'm sure he is, Warden. And it would be good for him, out in the sunshine and fresh air, throwing balls, swinging bats, rubbing neat's-foot oil into baseball gloves, overseeing the distribution of volley-ball equipment in an alert and responsible manner.

But then who would run the shoeshop?

I'm sure we could find someone, Warden. There are people around who can run shoeshops. America is a hotbed of talent. There are men around who can do all manner of things. Many are just waiting for their chance, their big break.

I'm not wholly convinced, Griffing would say.

Either that lout goes, or I go. That's it. That's my final word. I can't stand him one day more. If he's still working here tomorrow morning, I will—

Cigar, Flash?

No thank you, Warden. I'm serious. I'll quit. I'll pull out. I'll move on. My wife would leap for joy if I resigned this very minute.

How is Jo Ann these days? When's she due, did you say?

In October. She's fine. And if I quit now the child could be born within a stone's throw of some green and pleasant tree-lined campus, where the co-eds' skirts blow in the autumn breezes, instead of—

To be perfectly frank, I don't see just how we could manage a transfer right now, Flash. For one thing, it would overload us in Recreation. And let's admit it, Flash—Manson is a good shoe man.

A superb shoe man. He can clench a line of tiny nails between his teeth with the best of them.

Exactly. And in that case I think you'd have to agree the smart thing would be to keep him right where he is.

I don't think I'd have to agree. I am absolutely, unequivocally—

I knew you'd see it my way, Griffing would say, smiling his mystical Warden's smile.

□

"How is he today?"

"Okay I guess, Warden. Quiet."

They began climbing the last flight of metal stairs at the end of the East wing. The stairway was open and if you looked down over the guardrail, which Flash did only once because heights made him giddy, you could see the four flights of gray steel cells and catwalks stretching out below you at a distorted angle, a couple of hundred barred doors, everything metal and concrete, every gloomy leaden image duplicated again and again, like a hall of mirrors in a horror house. It was enough to make anybody giddy.

"The Padre been by yet?"

"No sir, not yet."

"Anyone else?"

"Warden Philson was in yesterday."

"Is he eating any better?"

"He didn't take much lunch, but he did all right by breakfast."

They reached the metal door to the small landing at the top of the wing. Flash paused, holding on to the railing, and let the officer slip past to unlock the door. Flash was puffing a bit. The officer swung the door back and stepped inside. Flash followed. The landing measured ten feet by twelve. The walls were cinder block and there were two doors, the one they had entered and the one opposite it, each of heavy-gauge tool-proof steel with a small porthole of mesh-reinforced unbreakable glass. The Special Detention Unit was isolated from the rest of the Cell Block, and the only way you could get up here, no matter who you were, was to call up first and have an officer come down and unlock the doors for you.

After relocking the first door, the officer walked across the landing and unlocked the second with another key from his ring. He swung this door back and let Flash into the S.D.U. exercise room.

The three guards standing together in the center of the area turned smartly to face him. Flash returned their salutes.

"How's it going, men?"

"Very well, sir."

"You fellows are lucky—this is the coolest spot I've hit since I left Mr. Griffing's office."

They laughed. "I wouldn't have left, if I were you, Warden."

"That's a warden for you," Flash said with a shrug. "No common sense. It's one of the things they test you for on the exam."

They laughed again. Why not? To a man, the officers hated the Special Detention assignment. Four officers had to remain on duty here all day, two all night, and there was bugger-all to do. They were glad to see anyone, pleased at the least diversion, ready to laugh at the feeblest jokes.

Each tier of the Special Detention Unit was locked off from the exercise room by identical steel doors at the four corners of the room. Within each tier the inmates were locked in individual cells. (That was the joke the officers liked best: when you came up, you asked very soberly if anyone had escaped recently.)

Tier 1 included the two death cells and ten cells for protection cases, men removed from the general prison population for their own good. These men had either attacked a fellow inmate in such a manner as to ensure retribution, or had been convicted of a crime so gruesome as to outrage the moral sense of the other prisoners. Usually it was the murder or sexual assault of a child. One man, on life, already had spent over three years in Special Detention. He had raped and then killed an eleven-year-old girl, and had been caught, bloody as a butcher, the ax in his hand, in the act of dismembering her in his cellar, parts of her body already in the furnace.

Tier 2 housed psychotics.

Tier 3 housed inmates who were, or might readily become, violent.

Tier 4 housed inmates on punishment.

The S.D.U. exercise yard was twenty-five feet square. The floor was cement, sloped toward a drain in the center. The walls were gray cinder block. The ceiling was merely two layers of heavy wire mesh, five feet apart, thus classifying the yard as an outdoor exercise area. It was shaded from the direct sun by adjustable sheet-metal louvers on the roof. The inmates were brought into the area twice a day for twenty minutes each time. A volley-ball net was then strung up and the men could play if they desired, or simply stand around and talk. During these periods the officers re-deployed. Two remained in the area. One climbed a ladder to the ceiling and positioned himself between the two layers of wire mesh, crouching there with a rifle across his knees. The fourth guard locked himself out on the landing and spent the period peering in through the unbreakable glass porthole of the toolproof steel door.

"You want to go in now, Warden?"

"Might as well. You men seem to have everything under control out here."

They laughed.

The officer led him to the farthest corner of the room, selecting another key from his ring. He glanced through the window of the door marked TIER I, then unlocked it. Flash stepped inside and the officer followed, relocking the door. Unlike the regular cells downstairs, the cells here had full steel doors with small barred portholes. Each porthole, large enough to frame a man's face, framed a man's face.

Flash walked down the twelve-foot-wide cement area in front of the cells. Depending upon their behavior and the cause of their assignment to S.D.U., the inmates were allowed to work, play cards, or indulge their hobbies for two hours a day in this area.

Flash followed the officer around the cinder-block partition that partially separated the death cells from the protection cells. The first death cell was vacant. In the second, behind the barred door, Joey Rodriguez sat on his bed reading a magazine which he held straight out to the length of his forearms. He turned and looked at Flash.

Flash was careful—it was easy—to show no hint of excitement, of cheer. "How are you today, Joey?"

Rodriguez continued studying Flash's face as the officer unlocked and slid back the door. Then Rodriguez shrugged and lowered his magazine (*Sport World*—"Can Tittle Lead the Giants All the Way Again?"). He did not get up. He did not have to. He possessed, by tradition, privileges beyond those of the ordinary inmate. He could not, of course, show disrespect, but neither was he required to exhibit the standard shows of rigid discipline, and he could even presume a casual equality—a real joke, that—with the Warden or his assistants. He also had unlimited access to library books and periodicals, again solely by custom. In the corner of the cell stood a television set. Three years ago a previous inhabitant had pleaded with the Warden, with the Padre, with his lawyer, for a television set. That was the only special concession he desired, but he desired it passionately. The Warden granted it, and since then every man sent to either of these cells assumed he would get a television set, and did.

The cell was larger than standard and more comfortably furnished. The bed was an actual bed. The desk was large and there were two soft chairs and an oversize bookshelf, which held a Gideon Bible, several books, and a haphazard pile of sport, girlie and detective magazines.

Flash nodded for the officer to leave and sat on the padded rocking chair, perhaps six feet from this unprepossessing cinnamon-colored youth who, one among a thousand, was both the best and least known convict in the place. Few had ever seen him, but the other inmates talked of him all the time, uneasily, with a kind of hoarse respect. Their attitude toward him was almost religious: they recognized a touch of the eternal about him. Others had committed more heinous crimes, were more violent, more vicious, more dangerous—including some Flash would not walk into a cell with for all the riches of this world and the next combined—but Rodriguez towered above them all: to him alone had the state paid the ultimate acknowledgment, and so he alone was hero, martyr, saint and poorest son of a bitch in this whole walled city of poor sons of bitches.

Flash crossed his legs and rocked himself gently back and forth. He was still careful not to smile, so Rodriguez would not think he had come with good news.

But Rodriguez asked anyhow, as he always did. "You have not heard?"

"No. There's been nothing to hear that I know of."

"You have heard from my lawyer?"

"I think Warden Philson has; I think they were in touch the other day. But nothing special, you understand—I think they were just conferring. As far as I know, nothing is up."

"Something is up," Rodriguez said stiffly, with a kind of Latin formality that he liked to affect. Rodriguez was not uneducated; he had been to high school and was proud of his intelligence and his manners. His family, he was convinced, contained no Indian blood at all—or at the most, no more than, say, Jefferson or Albert Einstein. "My lawyer is working."

"He is working his head off, Joey. We all know that."

"But you do not believe he will get anything done?"

Flash shrugged. "It's not for me to say, to make guesses. I don't have anything to do with that part of it."

Rodriguez fell silent, having for the moment exhausted the only subject that interested him.

"Not watching the TV much anymore, eh, Joey? What's the matter—bad reception? Programs no good?"

"There is nothing on today."

"The Series will be on soon. You still like St. Louis?"

"I still do not like Philadelphia. Philadelphia will not win, I don't think."

"I guess that means St. Louis will."

"We will see," Rodriguez said.

"How are you feeling these days, Joey? They tell me you're no longer eating like a horse. They say you're eating like a bird now."

"I am not always hungry."

"The doctor's been up this week, hasn't he?"

"Every week. He says there is nothing wrong with me. I am in very good health."

Flash nodded. State law did not allow a man to be executed unless he was in good physical and mental health. If something were wrong with him, the state would generously spend whatever sums necessary to restore him to physical and mental health, so that they could then kill him. "And the Padre?"

"Every day. We play rummy now."

"I'd have figured he'd be against gambling."

"We use little torn pieces of paper."

"Do you beat him?"

"Sometimes I win. Sometimes he wins."

"He's a good man, the Padre."

"He is very nice."

"The pro football games start soon now. Do you like watching them too?"

"I like baseball better. Do you know if the lawyer said anything about when he will come again?"

"I don't, Joey. I guess he figures there's no point coming unless he has something to tell you."

"The Governor, he says, always stops the sentence before it is carried out. The Governor, he says, does not believe in it."

"I can't speak for the Governor, Joey. I don't know about that."

"You know if he stops them or not."

"Sometimes he stops them, sometimes he doesn't. It's not just a matter of what he believes in. There are laws that he—"

"The lawyer says that since the Governor is running for election again, he will be even more ready to stop it. He says he will probably stop it before the election gets too far along."

"I don't know, Joey. He might want to wait until the election is over before doing anything."

"The lawyer says he will probably do it before."

"I hope the lawyer's right, in that case."

Rodriguez shrugged, as if to say it didn't really matter what Flash or anyone else hoped.

"Is there anything I can get for you, Joey? Would you like me to see if thay can work up some special dishes? Is there something you'd like to eat for a change?"

"The food is all right. I am just not always hungry."

Flash stood up. "I have to go now. I understand the Padre hasn't been by yet; he'll probably drop in later."

"He said he would come."

"He will, then. I hope you have good luck with the cards today."

"Sometimes my luck is good," Rodriguez said.

☐

When Flash got back to the Warden's office Dowler called in to say that Bryher was on his way to Phillipsburg.

"Did you give him a good talking-to?"

"I gave him a real humdinger, Flash."

"Well—Godspeed to him then. Have you seen Manson?"

"Yeah. He said he doesn't have anything more to say."

"Well, what do you think, Jeff—can you back me on Rogers?"

"It's gonna be hard to single out one man for special treatment."

"Well, on the basis of Manson's story, none of them have to get rammed too badly."

"You want to let them all off?"

"No, of course not. But Rogers was the only one who didn't have a tool in his hand. We could cite that."

"Then you'd have to cite the others for having them, and then all three will be in pretty bad shape. I'll tell you something, Flash, just between us. I don't see any real advantage in coming down too hard on Verdun, especially since Orninski seems to be the guy who started the whole thing."

"Oh?"

"Yeah. Verdun's no prize, I mean, but he keeps his nose clean and he knows what's going on. He probably does a better job of keeping things quiet back there than another guy might."

"You'd like to protect him, then?"

"That's not what I said, Flash. If he gets in trouble, he'll get rammed just like anybody else, and he knows it. All I'm saying is I don't see any point in jumping on him unless he deserves it. And I'm not sure he does."

"You want to get Verdun off then?"

"I don't think we can do that, Flash. I mean, he knows the score and I don't want him to start thinking he's got any kind of suction here. I'm just saying let's not overdo it."

"What would you say, then, to a report on Orninski for insubordination, and just disrespect for Verdun and the other fellow—the dumb one—Terrence?"

"And what about Rogers?"

"I really can't report him on this, Jeff. I just don't think Manson's made a case."

"Okay, Flash. It's your report. You were there."

"Will you back me on it?"

"I guess I could buy that, Flash. Only Manson's gotta—"

"I'll take care of Manson," Flash said.

Flash wrote up the report in longhand and took it to the staff office down the hall to have it typed up. Then he called Manson at the shoeshop.

"I've just written up the report," he told him. "It's being typed, so I don't have a copy before me at the moment. But I'm sure you'll be satisfied with it."

"Okay," Manson said. "I guess so."

"Orninski will be brought up on a charge of insubordination," Flash said. "Verdun and Terrence will be charged with disrespect."

"What about Rogers?"

"Neither Warden Dowler nor I, I'm afraid, can see any basis for a charge there." He paused, but Manson said nothing. "Of course, if you're absolutely convinced that all four men should be charged, we'll just have to reopen the whole investigation. We'll get Warden Philson to look into it, and you can explain to him in more detail exactly what took place."

"I guess that'll be all right then," Manson said after a moment.

"What will be all right?"

"What you said. The report you made."

"Fine. I'll send you a copy when it's typed up."

□

At a little after four Flash called the Aurora police. He had been meaning to call them for some time, but never got around to it. Talking to the TV fellow had reminded him.

"Hello, Radigan? This is Fleishman, out at the pen."

"Hi, Flash. What's up, lose your key or something?"

"I was wondering, old pal, if you could check on something for me. You had a case on the books—let's see, it'd be almost a month ago now. Here it is: Wednesday, July 8—a robbery at that drugstore in the big shopping center on Beradino."

"Fletcher's?"

"That's it. I was just wondering if you ever picked up the guy."

"Hold on a minute . . . yeah, here it is. No, we haven't pulled anyone in on that. Why? Do you want us to put some heat on?"

"No—I was just curious."

"The guy only got eighteen bucks, you know."

"I know. I was just wondering if you happened to catch him."

"Have a heart, Flash. We can't get them all."

"Just as well, I say."

Dowler phoned in as soon as Flash hung up. "There's nothing there, Flash. No blade, no nothing."

"Did they check the bed good?"

"They checked everything. I sent Bostick in; if he didn't find it, it's not there."

"There probably never was one. Do you think Youngdahl's really out for Coughlin—or was that just part of the bluff?"

"I don't know," Dowler said. "But he'll be out for him now if he finds out who sent us up there."

"Okay—we'll just go ahead on those transfers, and see if we can't shuffle enough people around to cover up for him."

At a few minutes to five Flash signed the four thirty head count. God was in his place and so was everyone else, 1172 men, all satisfactorily accounted for. (Four years ago, when Flash had come, there had been 864.) He greeted Lieutenant Timmins, who seemed cheerful and fresh, and who would be in charge until seven thirty tomorrow morning. He informed Timmins of the trouble in the shoeshop and gave him the names of the four inmates. He briefed him about Coughlin and Youngdahl and Grieg, and told him that Bryher was en route to Phillipsburg.

A few minutes later Flash left the office and walked down the stone steps and out under the stone archway of the sally port. The gate officer saluted crisply. Flash returned it, not exactly crisply, and signed out. He stepped through the gate into the still-blistering sunlight, paused to contemplate the arid world that spread out before him with neither leaf nor blade nor flower to commend it, and then headed, with a little *carpe diem* shrug, for his Volkswagen.

10

1. Your first duty is STRICT OBEDIENCE to all rules, regulations, requests, directives and orders of the officer under whose charge you may be placed.

2. Strict SILENCE is to be maintained while marching in line through Cell House, Dining Area, Infirmary and all Grounds and Buildings of the Institution.

3. You are not to speak to visitors, nor give or receive presents from visitors, except by permission of The Warden or his Deputy. At no time are you to approach, talk to or communicate with STATE OFFICIALS, ADMINISTRATIVE OFFICERS, or VISITORS without approval of the officer in your immediate charge. GAZING AT STRANGERS passing through the Institution, or at Officers, Officials or FELLOW INMATES, is strictly forbidden.

4. You are expected to apply yourself diligently to your duties, and to do the same work as would be expected of a Citizen.

5. You will be subject to Report and Punishment if you JOSTLE or BRUSH AGAINST fellow inmates with the intent of provoking or angering them. MAKING FACES or INSULTING GESTURES will not be tolerated. Provoking fellow inmates to break the rules is Punishable.

6. Your person and your quarters are to be kept CLEAN and TIDY at all times.

7. Under no circumstances are you to carry away TOOLS, KNIVES, PAPER, MATERIALS or any other objects from work areas or from any

other areas or depositories. Possession of such items will be accepted as proof of disobedience of this rule.

8. Writing notes to, receiving notes from, or carrying or dispatching notes to, or from, other inmates is forbidden.

9. Careless or wanton or purposeful destruction of State property is Punishable.

10. You are not allowed money on your person. Any money found will be confiscated and will be Punishable. TRADING or BARTERING between Inmates, or with Officers or Citizens, is strictly forbidden.

11. Money received in your name will be placed on your Credit in the office of the Chief Clerk, to be dispensed only upon your request, with the approval of The Warden or his Deputy, or upon your Discharge.

12. If you wish to approach the Officer in your immediate charge, you will speak in a respectful manner at all times, in the fewest possible words, and in a clear and distinct voice, confining yourself to the matter at hand.

13. All Officers are to be addressed as "Officer," or as "Sir." INSOLENCE or DISRESPECT in any form will not be tolerated.

14. When you approach, with permission, any Administrative Official of this Institution, or any State Official, you are to use his appropriate title in addressing him, and to stand in the prescribed ("At-Ease") manner, with cap in hands and hands clasped behind the back. Be BRIEF, CLEAR, RESPECTFUL and ALERT at all times.

15. If The Warden, the Deputy Warden, or an Assistant Warden approaches you at any time, you are to remove your cap and stand at "Attention" unless he gives you permission to stand "At-Ease." You are to answer all questions briefly, clearly and respectfully.

16. Upon entering administrative offices, Dining Area, Cell House, Infirmary, Chapel or Theater, you are to REMOVE YOUR CAP.

17. All inmates who cannot read or write will be required to attend School.

18. You are required to shower once a week, oftener if your work requires it. You will receive a change of clothes and bedding once a week, oftener if your work requires it.

19. You are not allowed to possess or wear clothes except as officially furnished.

20. You are responsible for the care and maintenance of all clothes, bedding and materials furnished to you. Do not ALTER your clothing, or CUT your shoes.

21. You are not to write letters to, or receive letters from, unacquainted persons except on legitimate business. All letters sent and received will be examined for approval by the Mail Censor.

22. You are permitted to receive newspapers and magazines, if approved, and SENT DIRECT FROM THE PUBLISHER.

23. In your first letter, inform your Family of the rules regarding letters so no confusion or unnecessary worry will result. Those unable to read or write may approach the Officer in their charge for assistance and guidance in the dispatch of letters.

24. Smoking is prohibited in restricted areas.

25. At the sound of the Morning Bell, rise promptly, wash, dress, clean Cell, make bed neatly and be in readiness to march. At Signal, open door, step out, close door WITHOUT SLAMMING, form line and wait for order to march.

26. Upon entering Cell House, march directly to your Cell, enter, close door WITHOUT SLAMMING and stand with one hand on door until Count is completed, if Count is to be made. Remain in Cell at all times except when authorized to leave.

27. Your Cell is subject to search at any time. Lack of neatness and tidiness will result in a Report.

28. Possession of tools, weapons, files, money or ANY CONTRABAND ITEMS will be considered as proof of intent to do bodily harm or injury, or to escape, and will be treated accordingly.

29. Possession of drugs, alcoholic beverages, or any unauthorized and unfurnished substance is STRICTLY FORBIDDEN.

30. You are to maintain strict silence AT ALL TIMES in your Cell, except during authorized Talk Periods. Laughing, loud talk, reading aloud, shuffling of feet, drawing benches or chairs or beds across the floor, or shouting, is prohibited at all times. Do not tamper with electric light, radio headphones or connections.

31. You are entitled to one of each of the following items in your Cell: Bible, dictionary, cup, towel, soap, toothbrush, comb, blankets (2), pillowcase, mattress, pillow, bed, chair, small table, library shelf, library catalogue, mirror, copy of prison rules, and other articles approved by The Warden or his Deputy. You are also allowed in your Cell recent issues of approved magazines or newspapers, three authorized Library withdrawal books and authorized School books and materials.

32. At his discretion, the Officer in charge of your Cell Unit is authorized to furnish you with writing materials for a period of one-half (½) hour. Permission may be granted for a longer period of time due to school work or other authorized reasons.

33. Inmates wishing to exchange Periodicals, may do so as follows:
   a) Mark on front top of margin the Register Number and name of Inmates you wish to receive the Periodical.
   b) Drop it in the Exchange Box at the foot of stairs.
   c) After reading Periodical given to you, cross your Register Number out and put Periodical in Box. Do not erase or add any other numbers.
   d) Writing or drawing on, or mutilating or damaging in any way, will not be permitted.
   e) Papers will be allowed to circulate one week, Magazines one month.

34. When Lights Out is designated, go to bed at once and remain quiet. Sleep with your head uncovered at all times. If you are ill, or an emergency arises, tap LIGHTLY on bars to call Officer. This privilege must not be used unless ABSOLUTELY NECESSARY. Abuse will be punished.

35. Upon entering the Dining Hall, join the tray line, take your assigned seat promptly, place tray upon table and with eyes to the front and hands in lap, sit erect until the signal is given to commence to eat.

36. Strict silence is to be maintained at all times in the Dining Hall. TALKING, LAUGHING, GRIMACING (Making Faces), or GAZING ABOUT is strictly forbidden.

37. Do not place food or eating utensils directly on the table. Do not pass food back or forth with other inmates. DO NOT TOUCH OR TAMPER WITH THE FOOD OR UTENSILS OF OTHER INMATES.

38. Eating or drinking before or after being told to commence or cease is forbidden.

39. Do not remove FOOD or UTENSILS from the Dining Room.

40. Wasting food is NOT TOLERATED. Do not ask for or accept more than you will eat. Do not leave crusts or small pieces of bread on your tray.

41. Should you desire additional food (seconds), make your wants known to the waiter as follows:
   Bread: hold up right hand
   Soup: hold up spoon
   Vegetables: hold up fork
   Coffee: hold up right hand with thumb and index finger extended
   Water: rub hands together over head
   Illness or Emergency: hold up left hand

42. Do not under any occasion RISE or STAND UP during meal.

43. Regular attendance at Chapel is STRONGLY RECOMMENDED AND ACTIVELY ENCOURAGED FOR ALL INMATES.

44. Strict attention to Chapel Service is observed. Sit erect and face the speaker. Do not gaze at others, make faces, signal or provoke other Inmates.

45. Strict silence is to be maintained in the Chapel. No whispering, coughing, whistling, humming or talking is tolerated.

46. Reading, shuffling of feet, unnecessary noise or spitting on floor is strictly forbidden in the Chapel.

47. All matters of a religious nature should be taken up with the Chaplain. Permission to see the Chaplain is to be requested of the Officer in your direct charge.

48. The following list of OFFENSES are Punishable:
Altering Clothing
Bed not properly made
Clothing not in proper order
Communicating by signs
Contraband articles on person or in Cell
Creating disturbance or unnecessary noise
Crookedness
Defacing anything
Dirtiness of Cell, of possessions or of self
Disobedience of orders
Disturbance in Cell House
Drinking alcoholic liquids, or being under influence of same or possessing same
Fighting
Gazing
Grimacing (Making faces)
Hair not combed
Hands in pockets
Hiding things
Ill manners
Impertinence or Insolence to Officers or Officials
Impertinence to visitors
Inattentiveness
Insolence to Inmates
Lateness
Laughing or fooling around
Leaving place of assignment without authorization

Littering

Loitering to or from place of assignment

Loud talk

Malicious mischief

Mischief of any kind

Neglect of assigned study

Not being shaved

Not out of bed promptly

Not out of Cell promptly when brake is drawn

Out of place in shop or line

Profanity

Pushing, shoving, jostling, tripping, blocking or interfering with
other Inmates

Quarreling

Refusal to answer

Refusal to obey

Shirking

Spitting on floor or grounds

Staring

Stealing

Striking anyone

Talking when not authorized

Throwing away food

Trading, bartering or exchanging

Using unauthorized drugs or substances, or being under influence of same or possessing same

Vile, obscene, vulgar or dirty language

Wasting food

Wasting anything

Writing or receiving unauthorized letters, notes, messages or com-
munications

49. Punishment for any violation will be determined by The Warden
or his Deputy. An Inmate violating any of the above rules, or ANY
OTHER RULES, or BEHAVING IN A PUNISHABLE MANNER, may be placed
in Grade 2, may be deprived of privileges, may be placed in Special
Detention, or any combination of these. On a Detention Report, Time
lost is designated by the State Penal Code. In addition, an Inmate
loses a number of days of Honor Time as designated by The Warden
or his Deputy.

50. A Grade 1 Inmate will be allowed all normal privileges, will be
able to receive all mail approved by the Mail Censor, will be able to

write one letter every two weeks at the expense of the State and other letters, at his own expense, as authorized, and to receive visits from close relatives and approved friends once a week for a period of thirty (30) minutes, at the discretion of The Warden or his Deputy. All Inmates, when they are received, will be placed automatically in Grade 1.

51. A Grade 2 Inmate will be deprived of the following privileges: recreation periods (except after dinner on Monday), Canteen, Library, radio headset, Movies, mail (except certain incoming letters approved by the Mail Censor), Pay for Work, and such other privileges as designated by The Warden or his Deputy.

52. Inmates with a Clear Record for two months from the date they are received, will be given Honor Time. Honor Time will reduce their future time to be served by one-fourth (¼). Honor Time may be lost, and previously earned Honor Time may be removed, at the discretion of The Warden or his Deputy, in case of rule violations. Men returned from escape or attempted escape must go one year with Clear Record before being eligible to receive Honor Time.

53. If one or more Inmates commit, or attempt to commit, or organize, or in any way become involved in, or act as a party to, or force other Inmates to engage in, ANY IMMORAL ACT, or any act CONTRARY TO THE CODE OF HUMAN DECENCY AND MORALITY, it will be considered a GROSS VIOLATION of the rules and will be subject to the strictest disciplinary measures.

54. The State, The Warden and the Officials of this Institution, and all the Officers and Staff, wish each Inmate the enjoyment of all privileges and benefits. All Inmates who obey the foregoing rules and directives, and who approach their work with the Proper Attitude, will find opportunity for self-improvement in many directions. The best of luck and good fortune is wished to each and every Inmate.

55. If you have any questions concerning the meaning or interpretation of any of these rules, or any doubts concerning the proper behavior required in any circumstance, you may request clarification from the Officer in your direct charge. Ignorance of these rules, or of any other rules, directives or regulations, or of the proper behavior required in a circumstance, will not be accepted as an excuse.

56. All rules are subject to change without notice.

☐

Gee, it was terrific. It was just beautiful, it really was. He could stay in forever, and he wouldn't complain. He could just close his eyes and not give a good goddamn about anything, just turn his head up with his eyes closed and feel the warm water pouring down his face and off his body. It was like something warm and soft all over. It was just great. You didn't even have to think. Thoughts just didn't come into your head. It was like you didn't have a brain at all, like you had nothing in the world to think about, nothing to worry about. All you were was just something smooth and clean and warm and wet and smelling of soap.

"Okay, men—time! Let's move!"

The guy behind him poked his back to get him moving, so he moved, and bumped against the guy in front of him, because the guy in front of *that* guy wasn't moving. The screw on the platform must've figured somebody was holding the line up just to be wise. So he turned around and twisted the big metal knob.

You couldn't believe the screams. The goddamn water was suddenly like ice, and everybody was screaming their head off and jumping up and down like they just picked up a loose electric wire, the screams bouncing and echoing like crazy off the tin walls.

Mel was way back in line and it took his breath away before he got out, what between leaping and yelling and the water hitting you like icy needles. He was gasping and had a pain in his chest from screaming. He grabbed a towel and rubbed himself as hard as he could. He was shivering and his skin was rough and turning red and full of goosebumps. The towel was like a butcher's apron or something, like canvas practically. He kept rubbing to dry himself off and warm up and got in line for clean clothes.

"Quit the fucking shoving," one of the guys yelled.

"Fuck you," one of the other guys yelled back.

"Who's making the fucking racket?" the guy behind the window yelled. "Let's keep it down, all right?" He was only a con that worked in the laundry, but the screws got on him if there was a lot of noise.

"Go fuck yourself," someone told him.

The guy at the window didn't pay no attention.

Mel got to the window. "Simmons," he said. "47163."

The guy pushed out a wire basket with the clean clothes. Mel carried it over to the dressing area and started getting dressed. All the clothes had labels on saying Correctional Industries, meaning they were made by cons. There wasn't any place to sit and the cement floor was full of puddles from guys still dripping, so you had to be careful not to get your new stuff all wet. Sometimes, because it was so crowded, a guy trying to get into his pants would bump into another guy and make him get his clothes wet, which naturally got the other guy pissed off, so there was always a lot of yelling back and forth. The screw on the platform let it go usually, except when it got too loud. Then he'd yell over for them to shut the fuck up. He wouldn't get down off the platform and come over unless it was practically a riot. Most screws were world's experts at not moving unless they absolutely had to. The guys said you could always tell a screw because he didn't move when he got laid. He made the woman move.

Mel got dressed and threw his towel into the wheeler and got in line at the OUT door. Across the room by the IN door another bunch was getting undressed and putting their dirty clothes in wire baskets and lining up by the showers. They took fifty at a time.

When everybody was in line to leave, the guard that brought them over unlocked the door and they filed out. Even though it was still early, the sun really packed a wallop, especially after that ice water. They started marching and stopped at the Cell Block for the kitchen workers to fall out, then marched to the garage.

Delft took over then, and the guard took the guys that were left to the hobby shop, which was right across this empty space from the garage. Then he'd head back for the next bunch at the showers. Christ, walking back and forth in the sun all day long, taking lines of guys to the showers. Lots of screws had jobs like that. The one on the platform in the shower room, for instance, what he did all day was just turn the water on and off and hustle the men through.

Nobody liked Delft much, although actually he wasn't too bad if he didn't just decide to ride you. He figured himself for a big joker and liked riding guys. "Everybody all nice and clean, heh?" Delft said, standing in the shade of the big open side of the garage and looking up and down the line and rubbing his hands together in front of this great big gut he had. Delft was probably the biggest guy in the whole pen, including the cons, except for this one con who must've been seven feet tall but was kind of diddly in the brain, so nobody paid much attention to him. Next to him, Delft was the biggest. He was six feet three and weighed 254 pounds. You knew exactly because he told you, although most of the guys figured he actually lopped a few pounds off when he told you. Anyhow, whenever a new con got assigned to the garage Delft would tell him that he was six feet three and weighed 254 pounds, and that if the guy thought he was gonna fuck around with him, he was crazy. Actually, you didn't have to be told. Even though Delft was maybe fifty years old and had a gut like a rain barrel, he was pretty solid. The only fat he had, the guys said, was between his ears.

"Okay, in your places for roll call, kiddies. All this goddamn showers and business makes us late. We got lots of work to do."

This was one of Delft's regular jokes, that you heard about twenty times a week. There were forty guys assigned to the garage. They had enough tools for maybe twenty, and when they were lucky, they had work for ten. Outside of taking care of the cars and trucks that belonged to the pen, they were supposed to get cars from the guards and the staff, because anyone who worked there could have stuff done on his car if he just paid for the parts, wholesale. But right before Mel came in some guard's car got kind of queered up being fixed, and since then they had trouble getting much to work on. Delft bitched to the Warden about not having anything to do, so the Warden made a big show about sending in his Monterey, even though it ran like a clock and was still on factory warranty anyhow, and made all the other big shots up front do the same, to set a good example for the guards, but they still didn't get many, except around the end of the month, when the screws were short of money. And naturally Delft was very hairy now about who he let touch anything, because he didn't want any more cars ruined if he could help it, so the only guys that ever really did anything were the ones that already were mechanics. The ones that were supposed to be learning how to be mechanics just mostly stood around and held tools, or maybe cleaned off a windshield or something.

They marched into the garage and took their places on the numbers painted on the floor. Mel was number 23. He stood looking straight ahead like you were supposed to while Delft walked along checking to make sure everybody was there. Mel was glad to get in out of the sun. One of the best things about the garage was it was open but shady, so it was one of the coolest places you could work.

Everybody was there, on their numbers, so Delft gave out the assignments. They had a Corvair with generator trouble and a Dart that needed linings that both belonged to guards. Then there was a penitentiary sedan and the Buick that belonged to the Deputy Warden, Philson, that was put in for a motor tune-up which it probably didn't even need.

Delft put Salmando on Philson's Buick. Salmando, even though he was a Mex, was the best mechanic they had, so he always got the jobs Delft wanted to be most careful about not screwing up. That part was all right with Mel, because he was willing to admit Salmando knew his business, and maybe even knew more than he did. Only he wasn't so sure anyone else there knew any more, and that was his one real bitch about Delft, that he never gave him the kind of work he oughta be doing. Like today. Today what he gave Mel, with five other guys, was rotating the goddamn tires on the penitentiary sedan.

And naturally Delft didn't put Orninski on the same crew with him. He never did. All the screws were like that. When they saw you got along with anybody, the first thing they did was split you up. You'd think they'd be happy you made friends, that you got along with the other guys. But no, it was the worst thing you could do, let a screw get wind you had a friend. Christ, there were guys who were good friends that got so split up they never even *saw* each other again for years.

Orninski, of course, had Delft's number, because Orninski was one shrewd cookie. It was Orninski, for instance, who figured out why Delft wasn't giving Mel any breaks. Orninski was really great at that, at figuring things out and organizing things in his mind.

"Because he knows about your contact, see. That's the bind. Because Delft, he don't like anybody thinking they got lines up to the front, to say nothing about lines even outside too, with guys on the TV and everything. I mean, he don't like that at all. He likes all their lines to stop right here with him. That way he can take care of who he wants and not worry about anybody up front nosing in."

Mel explained to Orninski, of course, that the contact up front wasn't *his* idea, for Christ's sake. It just happened, because of the goddamn TV guy, and there wasn't anything he could do about it.

"Sure," Orninski said. "I understand. Just don't play it too big, is all. Because what the Fish Man probably did, you see, after the TV guy leans on him about you being his friend and all, is he comes up to Delft one day, all innocent and everything, and he just says *How's things going with this Simmons fellow? He working out all right?* And naturally that's all Delft has to hear, and ker-boom, you're on his shit list."

And he was, no question about that. Christ, rotating tires! Any goddamn kid you picked up off the street could rotate tires.

Anyhow, Mel went to work, him and the five other guys, jacking up the car and taking off a tire and checking the pressure and then letting the air out and taking it off the rim and taking the tube out and checking the tire for breaks and cuts and checking the tube in the bath for leaks and then putting the tube back in the tire and putting the tire back on the rim and pumping it up and checking the pressure and then putting it back on a different hub and starting in on another tire.

The main thing was to do it slow enough. This was the job for the day. But you couldn't just stand around, because that didn't look good. So you worked very steady, and very slow. Like the guys said, you earned your pay. Your pay was fifteen cents a day. They put it in the Canteen fund for you.

Orninski was working two cars down, one of the seven or eight guys supposedly helping the Mex, Salmando, tune up Philson's Buick. Usually they could get together a coupla times a day if they watched their step. What they'd do would be hit the drinking fountain together, or the tool board, or one would go from his gang to the other's to borrow a tool or something. They really got along, him and Orninski, and it wasn't easy, naturally, finding anybody you really got along with in a place like this. Most of the guys, let's face it, you wouldn't go out of your way to be friends with. A lot, for one thing, were just plain dumb. They just didn't have nothing to say. And for Christ's sake, they were the goddamndest greatest collection of *mumblers* you ever heard in your life. They knew maybe ten words altogether outside of fuck you, which was how interesting those guys were to talk to. And most of the others, all they wanted was someone to sit around and listen to them bitch, how the world was screwing them. That was it as far as they were concerned—bitch, bitch, bitch. That was their idea of something to talk about.

One guy in his tier actually could hardly talk at all, but just make these kind of grunting sounds. Of course there was something wrong with him. There was something wrong with a lot of the guys, all kinds of scars on their faces, and one guy with a big chunk of his hair gone where he got a piece of his scalp sliced off one time in a fight, guys with only one eye, guys with tattoos all over them, with a piece of their ear bitten off, guys that were cross-eyed and had harelips and everything. And a lot were just fishy-eyed, with nothing really *wrong* with them that you could see, but *strange*-looking, like they were some kind of nut or something. Those were the ones that really made you feel a little creepy.

So it wasn't easy finding someone you could talk to, especially a guy like Orninski, who actually was one of the smartest guys Mel ever knew. When Orninski opened his mouth, it was because he had something to say. He wasn't just airing his tonsils, like most of the guys you met.

Orninski, though, wasn't any kind of car mechanic at all. He was one big joke of a mechanic, actually, and hardly knew which end of the wrench to hold on to. The point was, *most* of the guys in the garage—and *all* the apprentices—were just as bad. The difference was they wouldn't admit it, and were always trying to bullshit you. Orninski wasn't like that at all. If he saw you were actually a mechanic, a real one, he respected you for it.

The way they got to be friends was kind of by accident. It happened right after Orninski came down from S.D.U. and got put in the garage on the apprentice program. What happened was that one of the wolves, whose name was Penney and was still working in the garage but goddamn careful now to stay out of Mel's way, figured he was going to move in on Mel. He probably figured that since Mel was still a fish he'd be a soft touch. He'd been in almost five years, this guy Penney, and was real stir-bugs, only at the time Mel didn't know this because nobody told him. It was only afterward he learned, from Orninski, that he was like that and at one time actually pulled a goddamn knife on a guy to make him go down.

What happened was this son of a bitch came over to Mel in the corner of the garage this one day when the pickup was in there for some work on the air filter. Delft was up at the other end, so he couldn't see anything because the pickup blocked them off. Mel at the time just happened to be leaning against the wall back there, taking a break to dig out a cigarette paper and some tobacco, when Penney comes over with this look in his eyes and sort of leans over suddenly and puts one shoulder against him, kind of pinning him to the wall, and the next goddamn thing he knew the guy had his hand inside his fly. All this happened in about one second. The guy worked like a goddamn pickpocket, pulling Mel's zipper down and getting his hand in all in one motion. But then it was all over in about two seconds more. Penney was bigger than Mel and supposed to be a big muscleman and everything, but it wouldn't have mattered who he was, because Mel hit him, right in the face, harder than he ever hit anyone in his whole life, and that really took the starch out of him. But Mel was so wild he kept hitting him anyhow, until suddenly the guy was down all crumpled over in the sawdust.

And then Mel heard Delft from the other end yelling, *"Hey! What's going on down there?"*

So Mel grabbed the son of a bitch under the shoulders and yanked him up and sort of propped him against the fender of the pickup with his head hanging forward under the hood to make it look like he was checking the motor or something. Then he leaned in himself, like he was checking too, just as Delft came charging up yelling, *"What the hell's happening here? What's going on?"* Mel kind of shrugged, keeping his head under the hood, and Penney, not looking up at all, just said, very thick and mumbly, "I tripped . . . nothing happened . . ."

Delft just stood there with his hands on his hips, looking at them. He naturally knew about Penney and could easy figure out what happened, especially with Mel still breathing hard and Penney sort of gasping, practically choking, trying to keep himself from puking all over the motor, where he already was dripping blood from his nose. As it turned out, he puked a minute later, in the sawdust in the corner, as soon as Delft walked away.

Anyhow, Delft just stood there looking things over for a few seconds. Then he said, to Penney, "Watch where you're going next time," and walked away.

The thing is, a shop officer don't like charging anybody unless he really has to. It looks bad if he's always having trouble in his shop, so they naturally try to settle everything on the spot and not put anything down on paper.

Anyhow, this was how him and Orninski got to be friends. Even though Mel didn't realize it at the time, Orninski, who'd just been sent down from S.D.U. to the garage, was right nearby and saw everything and afterward came up and told Mel who he was and how impressed he was with the way Mel put Penney in his place like that and got away with it too.

Actually, like Orninski said, it was to your benefit that someone like Penney tried to fag you early, as long as you could cut him down. That way word got around, and people left you alone. Because as soon as a new fish walked in there'd be fifty guys sizing him up, looking for a stooge maybe, or a patsy to muscle tobacco and stuff out of, or like with the wolves, like Penney, a new fag. And there were even guys just looking for somebody to push around when they felt like pushing somebody around, the gorillas.

This morning Mel got to talk to Orninski around ten o'clock. He was pulling a tube out when Orninski strolled over like he was looking for a tool. He came up from behind and Mel didn't see him until he was right alongside. Mel kept working, stooped over the tire, and Orninski stood there, talking kind of low and casual while keeping his eye on the other end of the garage where Delft was.

"How's it going, kid?"

"All right," Mel said. "How's it going with you?"

"All right." Orninski waited, looking down at the other end, ready to fade if he had to. "I hear Verdun was blowing off over there last night again," Orninski said.

Mel shrugged. Verdun was in Mel's tier, and since Verdun was one of the wheels, and no friend of Orninski's, Orninski was always interested in what he was doing. Orninski himself wasn't any kind of wheel, but he was one of the real smart guys around, and the wheels naturally were always worried about some smart guy trying to take over from them. So Orninski had to keep an eye on Verdun because he knew Verdun was keeping an eye on him, especially since that trouble in the shoeshop.

"I didn't catch no noise," Mel said. "If there was any."

"I hear he's talking very big these days," Orninski said.

"I didn't hear none of it," Mel said.

"It looks like he's really pushing. That's what I hear."

Mel was feeling around inside the tire for breaks and cuts. He found a little pebble and threw it off to one side. "If he doesn't look out, maybe he's gonna be stepping on Westerman's toes."

"Nah, he don't have to worry about that," Orninski said. "Westerman, he don't get involved in any pushing."

"I guess maybe not," Mel said. Mel didn't really know too much yet about who was pushing who, and who was running what, but Orninski knew, so Mel was learning. What it was, was that Westerman, who had eighteen months for some kind of license violation or something, was on the outside a very rich guy, with all kinds of friends and some pretty big deals working for him, so naturally he had the use of a lot of money, both inside and out, and a lot of suction. So it was probably true, like Orninski said, that Westerman didn't have to do any pushing. His money pushed for him, and his suction. But a guy like Verdun, without all this, had to really work at it if he wanted to score. And he had to keep his eyes open, and watch his step, because there was naturally always guys around who wouldn't mind muscling in on the kind of deals Verdun had going for him. Verdun had deals with the different merchants mainly, but also with the guys who had lines into the kitchen and the infirmary, and that made the brew in the tannery.

"And you know what the big joke was?" Orninski said, stretching up on his toes to see what Delft was doing. "That son of a bitch, Verdun, he's telling everyone he can really start spreading out now. You know what he's saying? He's saying the way he got off so light was that he got everybody's number now, not only Manson's but Dowler's too, which was why he got off so light. Ain't that some joke?"

"Yeah," Mel said. "Some joke."

It was too. Because it was Orninski that told Manson off, not Verdun. Verdun didn't even open his trap, which was why he got off so light, with just privilege, and not because he had anybody's number. Verdun started it, of course, by trying to step on Orninski, who naturally wasn't gonna let him, so there was some noise and when Manson came over what he did right away was jump on Orninski, so Orninski told him to go fuck himself. The way the whole thing worked out, naturally, left Orninski pretty pissed off, especially at Verdun, who was the guy that started the whole thing, while Orninski was the guy that got rammed. But, like Orninski said, at least that showed he wasn't sucking up to anybody, like Verdun, who ended up being transferred to the goddamn hobby shop. The hobby shop was just about the softest go there was, and you couldn't even get near it unless you had suction, like someone like Westerman, who'd been assigned there the whole time, or like Verdun, who sucked up to everybody up front.

"See you later," Orninski said, and was gone.

Mel pumped up the tube with the air hose and took it over to the bath to test it for leaks. He saw Delft at the other end, watching him. Mel pushed the tube down into the water and didn't look up until he was finished, by which time Delft wasn't watching anymore.

At eleven Delft yelled it was time and they stopped for the morning and everybody returned whatever tools they were using and Delft checked all the tools against their numbers on the shadow board, and all the guys against their numbers on the floor. Then Delft marched them over to the Cell Block. There were always a whole bunch of lines coming from the different shops and work details, so you usually had to wait out in the sun awhile, because they only let in one line at a time. Today they waited about fifteen minutes, out in the sun.

They marched into the dome, which was this great big open area, open all the way up to the roof, and was the center of the building, which was shaped like an X. There were four wings, one for each leg of the X. When they marched you in for dinner or back to your cells at night, you were supposed to fall out of line when you got in the dome and go right away without running or talking or making any noise to your wing, and then to your tier and then into your cell. To see that you did, there were screws all over the place. LaSala, who was Cell Block Keeper and a real loudmouthed bastard, always stood like one of those great big beefy traffic cops right in the middle of the dome, watching everybody coming in and yelling at them to make sure they didn't run or make any noise, and naturally making more noise him-self than all the goddamn cons put together. LaSala was really a slob, old fuck-ass everybody called him, and he was always yelling and screaming at you. The guys didn't actually mind too much though, be-cause you could yell right back. He expected you to. The way he figured it, it was the thing for people to do, to yell at each other all the time.

And then there'd be the wing keepers standing at the entrance to each wing. Each wing had five tiers, and at the front of each long tier there'd be a screw standing by the big brake that worked the locks for all the cells.

Mel was in the West wing, in tier 1, cell 12. It was the ground-floor tier, which was a very good deal. You didn't have to climb up and down a lot of stairs every time you went in or out of your cell.

All the cells were unlocked when you came back for lunch. The tier guard would unlock them all at once with the brake, a great big metal wheel like the wheel for steering a boat, which there was one of for each tier. It could be set to open any cell you wanted, or all to-gether. When you got to your cells, you slid the door open and then closed it behind you, without slamming it too hard because the guards got pissed off if there was too much noise. So what you did was just slam it enough to let the guard know you weren't his patsy.

Then you washed up and went to the john and laid on your bunk or looked at a paper or something until they called your tier for lunch.

The cells were six by eight, and about eight feet high. They were supposed to be for just one guy, but they all had two, with one bunk riveted on the wall over the other. It was a little crowded naturally, but it wasn't too bad if you had a decent guy in with you. Mel heard of worse places. There were places where they packed three and four guys in cells built for one. Actually, the more you heard about other places, the more you figured this one wasn't too bad. That's what practically everybody said who'd been around.

Of course that didn't mean they didn't bitch. The only cons that didn't bitch, everybody said, were the ones in tier 21. That was be-cause the Cell Block had only twenty tiers, and 21 was what they called the cemetery. It was right outside the wall and Mel had never seen it.

The guy Mel celled with was really a creep, and he always gave Mel a very funny feeling, but never any trouble. So as far as that went, they got along. The guy, though, hardly ever said a word. He was probably the quietest, creepiest guy Mel ever knew. His name was Fenster, and he was twenty-three years old and wore glasses and had a lot of trouble with his teeth. This was the first time he'd ever been sent away. He somehow got involved with some guys looting a big liquor store up in Maynard and the cops moved in and one of the other guys had a gun and there was some shooting. Nobody got hurt, but still the judge gave it to them all pretty rough, including Fenster, who got three-to-five. He'd been in fourteen months when Mel moved in with him.

All this Mel learned the first day, because naturally he was interested and so asked a few questions. He hadn't learned anything since, except that the guy worked in the furniture shop and was always going to the dentist for his teeth and coming back with his face all swollen up. He didn't even know, for Christ's sake, if the guy was married or not, because the guy *really* never said nothing. He just sort of moped around, with this real dark kind of droopy, dopey, faraway look on his face. And Fenster never even asked Mel one single question about himself, who he was or anything.

Today Mel got back to the cell before Fenster and after going to the john and washing up he climbed up on his bunk. He had the top bunk because the rule was the first guy in a cell got the bunk he wanted, which was always the bottom one, because it was set on the floor and had better springs. The top one was only an iron frame riveted to the wall with chains attached to the outside corners.

Mel had about fifteen minutes before lunch so he took up to the bunk with him the book for the class he was taking in school. It was called *The Magic of Numbers, #6.* When you were down in Induction, they gave you about three million kinds of tests and told you what kind of stuff you should take in school and everything. The guy said Mel should take this arithmetic class because a good mechanic really had to know his arithmetic backwards and forwards. He got the #6 book because he did pretty well in the test—most guys in the class were doing #4 or #5.

What it meant was going to this class two afternoons a week and the guy there trying to explain things to everybody and have them do examples on the board. It was really a drag, actually, and all Mel wanted to do was just get through with it. Then maybe they'd get off his back and leave him alone.

He wasn't doing exactly sensational in the class. He was doing sort of average, he figured. But he always got his homework in—you had to, or they put you on report—and sometimes when he had the chance he'd read over the lesson. He read a little now in this week's lesson,

all about measuring distances from point A to point B and the different time zones in the country. Parts were pretty thick going, and let's
face it, none of it seemed exactly like the kind of stuff a mechanic had
any terrific need for.

What really got him about the book was how old it was. It was practically falling apart, and all taped up. The pen must've got their books
about ninth-hand when regular schools on the outside were finished
with them.

The door slid open and Fenster came in. Fenster was pretty tall, but
very skinny and very gray. His skin was really kind of dead-looking,
like some guy who figured he was gonna die of some fatal disease or
other and felt kind of bad about it. One time Mel just came right out
and asked him if he was sick or something, and Fenster just looked
at him with that real mopey faraway look and said, *No.* That's all.
He didn't even bother, for Christ's sake, to ask *why* Mel figured he
might be sick.

Fenster closed the door behind him. He closed it quieter than most
of the guys, mainly because he probably wasn't interested in bothering
to slam it. Then he stopped for a second to look up at Mel on his bunk
and sort of nodded, making a kind of grunt, and then went to the
back of the cell to go to the john. Then he washed his hands and sat
on his bunk, not reading or anything but just sitting there looking
down at his feet. He usually sat like that, looking at his shoes. Maybe
he thought a lot, Mel figured.

A few minutes later a big bang—kind of a *slap-clank!*—sounded in
the door. That meant the guard had locked all the doors and you were
supposed to get up and stand with one hand on the bars for the count.
So Mel got down from the bunk and stood with one hand on a bar,
alongside Fenster, who even though he was standing now was still looking down at his goddamn shoes, and the guard came clumping by,
looking in, and then after a bit came clumping back, and then you
heard the *slap-clank!* again, which meant you were supposed to slide
the door open without slamming and step out on the catwalk and wait
for the signal to march, meanwhile closing the door behind you without slamming.

So Mel pulled their door back and they stepped out with all the
other guys from the tier, everybody then pulling their doors shut,
slamming just a little bit, which all together naturally made one hell
of a racket. That was something else about Fenster. Even though you
both had your hands on the door, he'd never be the one to slide it open.

When he heard the *slap-clank!* he'd just drop his hand to his side and wait for you to pull it open. He'd expect you to shut it too.

The guard gave the signal and they all marched in a line along the catwalk, but not in step because you didn't have to be. The catwalk was about five feet wide with a wire fence from the edge of it up to the catwalk on the tier above.

They marched across the dome and then down the stairs to the dining hall. The dining hall was really huge, with great big long white wooden tables, one for each tier. Still they could seat only five hundred at a time, so you ate in shifts. Mel's tier was on the early shift, which meant they ate lunch at eleven thirty. The other five hundred guys had to wait in their cells until you were finished, and then you had to wait in your cells until they were finished.

The meals went very quick, because everything was organized. You picked up a metal tray and a fork or whatever and then slid your tray along past the steam tables and had the guys behind the counter put on the stuff you wanted. Today they had mashed potatoes and gravy, peas and carrots, macaroni and cheese, bread and butter—which was really margarine but everybody called it butter—and marble cake. The macaroni and cheese was the main dish. You got meat at night, except Fridays when you got fish. You could have seconds on anything you wanted except the main dish, but no thirds, except that you could take all the bread you wanted. You had to eat everything you took, though.

One of the ways guys sometimes rode a new fish was to pile a whole stack of bread on his tray. The new fish naturally weren't used to eating that much, and since you only had about fifteen minutes to eat, the old guys would get a big kick out of watching this new guy trying to get a whole loaf of bread down in fifteen minutes, along with everything else. The cons who worked behind the steam tables sometimes played along and piled extra big helpings of everything on the guy's plate too.

It was the kind of joke, of course, that you could only pull on a new guy. After somebody'd been there a few weeks, he'd be eating practically that much regular, at every meal. What the guys said, of course, was that you learned to swallow everything fast so you wouldn't have to taste it. But it really wasn't that bad. The worst of it, actually, was just that it was the same all the time, so you got tired of it. And the guys that'd been there five or ten years, naturally, *really* got tired of it.

But still, everybody ate like horses. Mel himself always took seconds on everything and generally put away five or six slices of bread at each meal. Some guys put away ten and twelve. He could never understand why you were so hungry all the time in prison, because, let's face it, nobody worked hard enough to build up any kind of appetite. Still, practically no one was fat. The guys said it was because they bought a very special kind of food there, which they took all the vitamins out of first.

Fenster, who always sat beside Mel at the table because they kept their places in line, was an exception. He hardly ever took seconds, except maybe on dessert.

The rule was that you couldn't talk at the table, but you didn't need any rule because there wasn't time anyhow. Everybody was always rushing like crazy just to get the food down, because to get seconds you had to be finished with your first helping of whatever it was.

So what you did was gulp down your coffee first thing, even though it'd burn your goddamn tonsils out, so you could right away lift your hand with your thumb and finger stuck out for another cup, because the coffee was usually the first thing to run out. Actually, it was really pretty shitty, the coffee, but almost everyone drank their two cups.

There'd also be other waiters moving around with big metal pots of seconds of other things, so what you did was start by eating everything more or less at once at the beginning, meanwhile keeping an eye peeled to see which waiter was gonna hit your table first. If the guy with the potatoes seemed nearest, you quick ate up the rest of your potatoes so you'd be ready for him, and then looked to see which waiter was coming next and finished off whatever he was bringing.

After you got the seconds from the main part of the meal, you quick polished off the dessert so you could get your seconds on that, and then went back to the vegetables or macaroni or whatever and saved your second piece of cake for the end.

Sometimes the waiters came up from behind you and you couldn't see them, so you always had to watch the guys sitting across from you. If they all suddenly jumped on the peas and carrots, you did the same.

When your table had five minutes left, the mess officer would come over and say, "Five minutes," and if you weren't already finished you stuffed down whatever was left. Usually though, everyone was finished.

Then the mess officer told you all to stand and file out, which you did, taking your tray over to the big opening in the wall where you slid it in to the dishwashers. A screw always stood there checking to make sure everybody turned back all their silverware.

Then you marched back up the stairs to the dome and then back to

your cell to wait for the late shift to go down and get done. This was
called cleanup period, but there wasn't anything to clean up because
you had to have everything cleaned before you left in the morning,
so you just hung around. What Mel usually did was plug in the earphone and listen to the radio. They got four stations, three from Aurora
and one from Maynard. Sometimes, like today, when he felt a little
drowsy, he'd just lay out on the bunk and catch some shuteye. He'd
fall asleep pretty quick generally, even though it didn't seem you ever
did anything during the morning to wear you out. But it was like always being hungry. Christ, you ate and slept more in prison than you
ever did anywhere else in your whole life, but you were always ready
for another go-around.

☐

He was back at work and actually feeling pretty good, because today
was his wing's turn for rec period and his tier's softball team was playing tier 4, and he was looking forward to it because he was right fielder
for his tier. But then around two o'clock, when he was sitting on the
sawdust with his legs spread out, tightening bolts on a wheel, a screw
came into the garage and went over to Delft. A few minutes later
Delft came over, the screw with him. Mel got up from the ground, kind
of slowly, looking at them.

"They want you up front," Delft said. Then he said, making one of
his big jokes, "Maybe you done something bad, heh?"

"Nah," the guard said. "They just wanna see him."

"Sure," Delft said. "Simmons here is a very nice boy."

"Come on," the guard said. "Let's go."

Mel walked out into the sun, with the screw walking alongside but
a little behind. He could feel Delft's eyes on him, watching him go,
and then noticed Orninski standing next to the Buick watching too.
Mel kind of shrugged to let Orninski know he didn't know what the
hell was coming off either.

"Just keep walking there," the guard said. "Just keep your eyes front."

So Mel kept his eyes front and kept walking. "Where to?" he said
after a minute.

"Quonset hut," the guard said.

They walked down the steps and the path to the bottom of the hill
and over to the Quonset hut, where Mel stopped at the door to let
the guard reach ahead and open it. Mel had been to the hut before,
because this was where they did all the interviewing and testing when
you were in Induction. There was a very narrow hall down the middle

of the hut, with little offices on both sides. It was nice and cool in there though, and after the long walk in the sun it felt pretty good.

"Down there," the guard said, and Mel walked down the hall, passing about a half-dozen closed doors. "Hold it," the guard said and Mel stopped. The guard knocked on the door. It had a little card that said DR. S. F. FLEISHMAN, and underneath that, ASSISTANT WARDEN, and underneath that, TREATMENT, REHABILITATION AND EDUCATION.

All Mel could think of was *Oh shit.*

Someone inside said, "Come in," and the guard pushed the door open a little and said, "Simmons here."

"Okay," the voice said. "He can wait in here."

The guard shoved the door all the way open and motioned for Mel to go in. It was a very small office with plasterboard walls and a desk and a small wooden bench and a file cabinet, and sitting behind the desk was this con.

"Have a seat, Simmons," the con said, nodding to the bench. Mel sat down. Then the con turned to the guard, who was still standing in the doorway, and said, "Dr. Fleishman said it'd be all right to leave him here."

"Well . . . awright," the guard said, kind of grumpy, and then left and closed the door, banging it a little. You could see he was pissed off, because no guard liked being told anything by any con, not even Come in. But naturally all the cons that worked for wardens and everything always made it sound like an order from the guy they worked for, so the guards had to go along.

Christ, if Mel was a guard, he wouldn't want any goddamn con telling him what to do. He didn't even like the idea of a con telling him now. All the guys felt the same. Certain cons who just because they went to high school or maybe could type good—this one had a typewriter on his desk—got soft jobs working for the staff, and right away started feeling they were pretty hot shit, and not just another con. They were even celled separate from everybody else, in tier 1 of the North wing, probably mainly to give them enough chances to congratulate each other all the time on what hot shits they were.

What Mel wanted to know was if they were so goddamn smart and had such high-class sensational educations, what the hell were they doing in the goddamn pen?

Mel sat on the bench and watched the con behind the desk, who was typing away like a frigging hurricane, his fingers flying all over the place. He was a great big guy who looked like he hadn't shaved and wasn't, if you asked Mel, so goddamn educated-looking.

The other door opened and Fleishman poked his head out, looking at Mel through those great big milk-bottle bottoms that he wore and that made his eyes seem ready to pop out, which was maybe one reason besides his name and the fact that he was in charge of all the new fish that everybody called him the Fish Man, and said, "Come on in, Simmons." Then without waiting for an answer he turned and went back into his office.

"Go ahead," the con said, when he saw that Mel didn't just leap off the bench.

Mel gave the con a dirty look. He could've slugged the son of a bitch. But the guy was typing away again and didn't even see the look. Mel got up and went in.

The office was a lot smaller than the other time, when Fleishman scared the holy shit out of him by calling him in, because all Mel knew that time was that he was being called right into the goddamn Warden's office, and the only reason he could think of why the Warden would want to see him was that somebody must've tied him in to the gas station. But you could see now that this was Fleishman's regular office, and let's face it, it wasn't much.

"Sit down, Simmons," Fleishman said, poking around through the papers on his desk and not looking at him. His desk was very small, and a mess. That other time, behind that great big wooden desk in the Warden's office that must've been ten feet long and had hardly any papers on it at all, Fleishman looked kind of small and funny, like a duck sitting on a goddamn pond. Here he looked more at home. It was really a chintzy office.

Mel sat down on the wooden chair.

Fleishman seemed to find what he was looking for in the mess, a bunch of papers clipped together. Mel figured they had something to do with him being called in, but evidently not, because Fleishman just looked at them for a minute and then dropped them into a drawer and then, finally, sat back in his chair and put his hands over his stomach, like an old lady in a rocking chair, and looked at Mel. Mel's grandmother always used to sit like that, snoozing in her rocking chair with her hands over her stomach.

He had a funny kind of face, this Fleishman, what with the mustache and the milk-bottle glasses and the funny way he looked at you. He was more or less smiling, but you got the impession he was probably thinking about something else entirely—that bunch of papers he just dropped in his drawer maybe.

Actually, none of the guys were very sure about Fleishman. You could ask anybody what the score was on the Warden, for instance, and they'd tell you, because they knew. They'd tell you Griffing was very strict, that he liked his boys to be good boys and was very tough on people who made trouble. And for someone like Dowler—well, for Dowler you could get a whole book, the cons knew him so good. And what it boiled down to was Dowler was very rough, and you had to be always ready for him, because he was all over the place. He ran the show, actually, and he ran it very tight. He didn't just sit around and wait for you to make trouble before he'd ram you, like the Warden. He'd ram you if he figured you were just *thinking* of making trouble. Not that he put a lot of muscle on the cons, unless of course he had to. If you tried to get tough or anything Dowler didn't see nothing wrong with giving you some of the same right back, and knew how to do it. What Dowler was, actually, was practical. He didn't care about stories, or reasons, or any kind of explaining. All he cared about was what you did, and you knew this, so you knew where you stood.

But now with Fleishman, you just couldn't get a line like that, that you could depend on. About the only thing everybody agreed on was that he was kind of a funny egg. They weren't even sure *how* he was funny, but just that he was. The guys said he used to be some kind of professor in a college. Well, all right, maybe he was. You could believe it. But he wasn't like the doctor or the psycho guy or the guy that ran the school. Those guys probably all went to some college too, but Fleishman was a *warden,* one of the four top people in the whole goddamn place. That's what got the guys. What they figured was a guy like that should stay where the hell he belonged, with the headshrinker and the school stuff, and all those goddamn tests and everything, and leave the actual running of the place to real wardens, like Dowler and Griffing and Philson, who at least knew what the hell was going on, and weren't always just thinking up new ways to screw everything up and change it all around and bother everybody with a lot of dumb tests and everything.

And then there was all that doctor business. What the hell *kind* of doctor, for Christ's sake? Orninski said not the kind that could treat you for anything, but something you got after going to college, or at least that some guys got. Well, maybe so. Only most guys would bet he was some kind of goddamn headshrinker himself, a special kind maybe, that probably couldn't cut the mustard on the outside and so got stuck in the pen.

For a minute or so, all the time giving him this funny little head-shrinky look, Fleishman just sat there with his hands on his stomach, staring at him like maybe he was some new kind of animal he never seen alive before. Finally he said, "Well, how are we doing these days, Simmons?"

"I'm doing all right, Warden. I got no complaints."

Fleishman made like a little twitch with his mouth, and looked at him some more. "You're on your third month now, right?"

"That's right, Warden. Nine weeks."

"This is an important time, you know. You get to know your way around, get used to the way things are done. It's important now that you keep moving in the right direction."

"Well, like I said, Warden, I don't really have no complaints."

"Are you getting anything out of your work in the garage?"

"Sure, it's going very good there, Warden. I'm learning a lot."

"You're attending school too, right?"

"That's going very good too, Warden. I'm learning a lot there too."

Fleishman made that little twitch with his mouth again, like he had something caught in his teeth and was trying to get it loose without having to go in after it with his finger. "I take it you're pretty much satisfied with things, then?"

"Well, yeah—I mean, like I say, I got no complaints about anything. If anybody's been saying I been complaining, Warden, they—"

"Oh no, nothing like that. Actually I asked you to come for two reasons. In the first place I'd just like to say, simply and frankly, that in a place as large and as overcrowded as we are, it's a good idea for a fellow to keep his eyes open . . . not to get too friendly with the wrong kind of people."

"Now Warden, I don't know what you—"

"Let me finish. I just want to make sure you realize that not everyone you meet in here is necessarily a good choice to, well, to get tied up with. This isn't St. Joe's, you know. These men aren't kids."

He stopped talking to look at Mel, but Mel just kept quiet.

"All right, that's all I have to say about that. Now the second thing is quite different, and a little more positive." Here Fleishman smiled that kind of funny, fishy smile he had. "You've heard, I guess, of the group counseling program that we've had here for the past few years . . ."

Mel kind of squinted at him. "Well, no, I can't say I—"

"Well, the program's been quite successful, by and large. Each of the Classification officers has a group, nine men. They meet once a week and—"

"Oh yeah—I heard about that. Oh yeah, sure. Those."

"Well, I'm starting up a new group for myself, and I'm looking around for qualified men who'd be interested in joining—on a strictly voluntary basis, of course. I want to stress that: no one *has* to join. The whole idea is that the members *want* to belong, that they think it'll help them. . . . Now, do you think you'd be interested?"

Mel sort of looked at him. "You want *me* to join one of those things?"

"If you'd like to."

"But—well, what I mean is—well, I mean, there ain't nothing *wrong* with me, you know . . ."

"No one said there was. The program's for our best men, not our worst. It's for the men we have the most hope for."

Mel wet his lips. "Yeah, well—I hope you don't mind me saying so or anything, Warden, but . . . well, the general impression I get is that these things are for guys who . . . well, maybe are kind of a little off . . ."

"Well, that's simply not true. These groups merely offer another way of—"

"I don't really think I'd like to join, Warden. I mean, not right now. I mean, if it's all right with you."

"Maybe I could explain a little more fully . . ."

"No, it's all right—really. I mean, if like you say, I don't really *have* to join."

"Maybe you'd like to think it over for a while. Maybe you could talk to some of the men who already belong."

"Well yeah, sure. But meanwhile . . . well, I don't think you really oughta count on me. I mean, unless I'm *supposed* to join or something . . ."

"No, not at all. No one is forced to join."

"Yeah, well, okay then. Then I'd just as soon not—I mean, if it's all right with you."

"Okay then. Let's just forget it, Simmons. It's up to you."

"Well yeah, sure. I mean, thanks a lot, Warden. I mean, sure . . . I appreciate it . . ."

□

When the screw brought him back to the garage, Delft waited until the screw was gone and then said, "What'd they want you for?"

"For nothing," Mel said. "They wanted to know if I wanted to take some more classes."

"That's all?"

"Yeah, that's all."

"Who'd you see?"

"Mr. Fleishman."

"What else did he say?"

"Nothing. That's all. They're starting up some new kinds of classes or something."

"How come you took so long?"

"I had to wait to get in to see him. I was only with him a coupla minutes."

"He must've said something else to you."

"I'm telling you, that's all he said. Go ask him yourself."

Delft gave him a look and then said, "Okay, get back to work," and Mel went back to work.

The other guys had gotten to the last wheel while Mel was gone and were working on it now, so Mel started wiping the car down with a shammy, taking off the top dust to kill some time before they hosed it down.

He knew it wouldn't be long before Orninski came over asking questions too, and about ten minutes later, there he was. "So what was the big deal?" he said.

"No big deal," Mel said. There was some crud stuck on the hood and he rubbed hard at it with the shammy. He shrugged. "What he wanted was for me to join up one of those bullshit groups—you know, where the guys sit around and blow off at each other." He'd decided not to say anything about the other part, the wrong kind of friends.

"You mean A.A.?" Orninski said.

"No, not A.A., for Christ's sake! Those classes or whatever the guys from Classification run. I think Webber's in one of them."

Orninski raised his eyebrows and kind of twisted up his face, like he was very impressed with the information and giving it a lot of hard thought. "What is it, Mel—the Fish Man think you're a loony or something?"

"I don't know *what* that guy thinks," Mel said. "If you know, you tell me, all right? Then I can pass the word around and everybody'll know."

"Hey—come on now, Mel—don't go getting all pissed off."

"I ain't getting nothing. It's just I don't like it too much when some goddamn joker tries to pull that kind of shit on me, that's all."

"Well sure, man—I don't blame you." Orninski waited a minute. "Are you joining?"

"No, I ain't joining."

"You just shut him off?"

"That's right. I just shut him off."

"Well, that's all right, Mel. That's the way you gotta handle those people. I mean, shit, you don't want everybody thinking you're some kind of loony."

Mel stopped rubbing with the shammy to look at Orninski. "I ain't ever known anybody that ever thought I was any kind of loony."

"Well Christ, Mel—I ain't ever thought it."

"Okay. I just don't like taking that kind of shit, that's all. From anybody."

"Well, all right, man. I'm with you there. I'm with you all the way."

□

It really kind of bothered him the rest of the afternoon and even through dinner, what Fleishman said, and the more he thought about it the more pissed off he got.

For dinner they had meat loaf and mashed potatoes and creamed corn and banana cake and after it the tiers in his wing got marched out to the athletic field for their rec period. It was five o'clock then, and still hot as hell, although the sun was beginning to go down a little.

There was a big gate in the back wall that they unlocked and you went through into the athletic field, which was outside the wall and surrounded by this high wire fence with barbed wire. The guys from the South wing, which also had their rec period today, were already throwing balls around when they got there. They had three softball fields out there and a track you could run around, and mats to use for boxing and wrestling, and some basketball and volleyball and badminton courts, and a place where you could do weight lifting and even places where you could play checkers or dominoes if you wanted. The field was pretty well kept up, because about thirty cons had the job of just taking care of it, but still it was hard as a rock from being baked in the sun.

There wasn't anything Mel liked more than rec period, which they had three times a week. He could spend his whole day out there and it'd be all right with him. For one thing, it was the only place where you could see out, because you had only the wire fence instead of the wall, which you couldn't see over. Out here you could see the desert, and the mountains way off in the distance, the San Juans, and even— pretty far away, because the pen was stuck out in the desert by itself —some houses and lawns and what looked like a big street with trees and some stores.

But what really gave Mel a kick out of rec periods was that he made the team. He moved into the tier from Induction just when the last tourney ended—they had about five tourneys a year—and so Mel went all out in the pickup games, and when they posted the roster for the tourney, Mel was on it. And then when the starting lineup for the first regular game came out, Mel was on that too, for right field and leadoff. He went out there that day feeling like a million dollars. And he did all right too, with two solid hits.

For the first thirty minutes of the period, the guys on the teams warmed up, while the guys not on the team played basketball or volley-ball or whatever they wanted, or just stood around. Then for the last hour they had the tourney game, which most of the other guys watched.

Today Mel came out still feeling kind of crummy about that business with Fleishman, but the minute he got his glove on for the warm-up and went out to shag some fungoes he forgot all about it. Just the hard ground under you made you feel better, just pulling down that first ball. One of the real bitches Mel had about things on the outside was that everybody just figured having a good time, like playing ball or something, was for kids. Sure if you were a kid, you could play till the cows came home, in all these Little Leagues and everything. But what about if you weren't a kid anymore? What then? You had to be a goddamn con then to ever get a chance to play any ball.

Sometimes the whole deal on the outside seemed, to tell the truth, pretty shitty. Not that he was saying prison was *better*, but let's face it, it wasn't all bad either. Christ, even take something like the job they gave you here. So all right, they paid you fifteen cents a day. Sure, big joke. But the hell, they fed you, they put clothes on your back, they gave you books to read if you wanted books. They gave you a radio you could listen to and a place to sleep, and if you were sick or had bad teeth, like Fenster, well Christ, they had a doctor or a dentist to fix you all up. They let you play ball if you wanted to play ball, and they gave you the gloves and bats and balls to play with too. Sure, maybe none of what they gave you was exactly high class, but still, when you considered all these things, the fifteen cents a day wasn't really such a goddamn joke after all.

You didn't have to break your back working either, or go around kissing ass just to *get* a job in the first place. And when you started figuring up all the goddamn things you had to buy with the lousy $1.40 you made on the outside, and all the frigging deductions they took out before you even saw it, well Christ, fifteen cents a day looked pretty good. The money on the outside, let's face it, was just a headache, just something else to get all screwed up with. Because you knew, no matter what they paid you, it wasn't ever gonna be enough. It wouldn't get the worries off your back, it wouldn't pay the goddamn bills, it wouldn't let you ever just relax. You always had to be pushing, grinding your nose in the goddamn dirt, killing yourself for a frigging $1.40 an hour while other guys just sat on their ass and cleaned up.

When the players finished warming up, most of the other cons started crowding around the foul lines to watch the game. Mel was leadoff, so he picked up a coupla bats and loosened up with them off to the side and studied the delivery of the pitcher to see what stuff he had. And then the umpire, who was a con that worked for the rec officer, called *play ball* and Mel dropped the extra bat and dug in at the plate. All the guys from the other tiers started razzing him, and all the guys from his own tier yelled *meet the ball, hit it good, this guy out there's no pitcher, no pitcher.* Everybody's always hopped up at the start of a game, so the leadoff man gets all the static, but it didn't bother Mel. Once he got in a game nothing bothered him. They could set off firecrackers behind him if they wanted.

He took the first two pitches, a ball and a strike. The next one came in shoulder high and a little outside. He stepped into it and knew right away he got the good wood on it, and the ball skimmed over the first baseman's head and landed just fair and then bounced away from the right fielder. Mel was sliding fadeaway into second before the throw came in, and then he got up and dusted his pants off and sort of nodded to the guys along the foul lines that were all cheering and then got set, with his foot touching the corner of the bag, to take his lead on the next pitch, and cupped his hands over his mouth and called in to the batter, "*Come on now—we can hit this guy! We can take him! No pitcher here, no pitcher at all!*"

☐

After rec period they marched you back to your cells. It was seven o'clock then and still light, so actually you could've played another hour, but seven o'clock was when you had to be back, so that was it. You had free talk period then until a quarter to eight, unless your tier was on restriction.

The game went six innings, and they won, 6–2. Mel got a single and a double, two for three. He also made a pretty good catch knee-high coming in full steam on a sinking liner. So all in all, he felt pretty good.

In the five games so far he had 6 hits in 16 at bats, for .375. In the newspaper, which came out every other week, they gave the top hitters and their averages, like the regular papers did for the big leagues, and Mel figured he had a good shot at making it next time. If he did, he thought maybe he'd clip it out and send it to Peggy. She'd like seeing his name in the paper and everything, and seeing that he was doing all right.

Usually Mel didn't yak too much during free talk. You couldn't talk to Fenster naturally, and Mel wasn't too friendly with most of the guys around him. A lot were just tools of Verdun, for one thing. But Mel was all hopped up tonight, so he gassed around more than usual. Most of the guys had seen the game and were pretty impressed the way Mel came through.

He was really having a good time—not *all* the guys were Verdun's tools, and one guy a coupla cells down was the third baseman, and real nice actually—and was thinking maybe he oughta make a little effort to get to know some of these guys better when the bell rang for quiet time.

The way it was, you could still talk if you wanted, even though you weren't supposed to, but you had to keep it down, which meant pretty much just talking to the guy in your own cell, so Mel didn't bother. Fenster probably hadn't even seen the game. He probably didn't even know there *was* a game.

So Mel climbed up to his bunk and put in his earplug and got the Maynard station, which picked up the Giant games from S.F. The game wasn't on yet, just music. He looked through the *Motor Age* magazine he had out from the library. He already read the whole thing about four times, but didn't have much else around.

The sun was down now and there wasn't much light coming in from the big windows high up on the outside wall, so everybody had their cell light on. Even with the plug in one ear, you could still hear guys whispering around, but all in all it was pretty quiet, with now just the voice of Russ Hodges on the pre-game warm-up coming into your one ear. That was something Mel still wasn't used to, the sound right there in your ear, instead of all around you. Some of the hopped-up feeling was fading a bit now, although he didn't really feel tired yet. But he wasn't exactly interested in the magazine either, and began to wonder what time it was. It was always around now that the time started going kind of slow, when it got dark and you were just laying around waiting for lights out, and everything was pretty quiet and empty. It was a funny feeling, because in some ways you could *feel* a whole mob of guys around you in the other cells and over you in the other tiers. But it was really pretty quiet and except for the lights in the cells, pretty dark. They weren't very strong lights, 60 watts. The big windows on the outside wall got darker and darker, kind of purplish-black. What it was, was that you were really part of a very big crowd, but the crowd was all separated off by themselves, lying on bunks reading maybe, or working on hobbies the way some guys did, and almost all of them listening to the radio, hundreds of guys all around you listening to radios and not a sound from them, except right in the guys' ears. It was a funny time of day, and kind of a letdown, with the time moving very slow and draggy, and all the good things you felt during the day just sort of draining out of you, and all the crummy things, not only from the day but just in general, somehow gradually sneaking back in.

It was worst, of course, when you didn't have rec period. Then you'd be locked in from five o'clock till breakfast the next morning. It was a long stretch. It was four and a half hours just until lights out, when maybe you'd get to sleep, although usually not right away. Sometimes, afterward, Mel would wonder what the hell he did during those four and a half hours, how he made the time pass. Because along the way it would seem very, very slow, but afterward you couldn't remember what the hell you could've done for four and a half hours.

Sometimes he'd read over letters from Peggy. Peggy wasn't any great shakes of a letter writer, but she wrote twice a week, and usually tried to fill up a page or so. There wasn't a hell of a lot she could write about, because she came every week too and they talked for a half hour.

The game started. Bobby Bolin was going for the Giants, against the Cubs.

In some ways, actually, Mel would've been just as glad if sometimes Peggy didn't come, if he just had the letters. But of course you couldn't explain this to her, because she'd take it the wrong way, but seeing her like that through the wire screen and everything—well, what it was, was that you looked forward like hell to seeing her but then you had a pretty rough time thinking up anything to say. Usually the half hour went pretty slow, because the whole time you were straining like hell just to think of something to say, and then after she left and they took you back to your cell, well, you just always ended up feeling pretty lousy.

She got all dolled up when she came, and when Peggy got dolled up she naturally looked very good. But then that made you feel a little funny too, seeing her looking so good and watching her walk out when the time was up and the guard there sort of giving her the once-over. Not that he worried about her. Some guys maybe had to worry—actually, a lot of guys worried—but he didn't, not about Peggy.

In the letters what she usually wrote about was Chucky, which was generally what they talked about when she came. And she'd always ask Mel how he was doing, and he'd always say he was doing just fine.

The car, she said, the old Dodge, was still running. Mel got a big kick out of that. The goddamn old Dodge, for Christ's sake. And Peggy probably not even bothering to put any oil in until she saw smoke coming up from the hood. But in some ways it wouldn't surprise him if the goddamn thing was still running when he got out. It wouldn't surprise him if it ran forever. It was like these old dogs you saw, blind and crippled and all twisted up, but still dragging theirselves around, just too goddamn dumb to die.

She said one time she found this thing in the trunk that she didn't even know what it was, and asked him about it. He told her it was this tail pipe he picked up for a song, for practically nothing actually, that he never got around to putting on. She was just wondering, she said, if it was something the car needed to run. Well Christ, he said, it's running *without* it, ain't it? So she asked him what she should do with it, should she just leave it there in the trunk, and Mel said well, he didn't see much else she could do with it, unless she wanted to put it on herself, seeing that she was always so mechanical and everything. He figured maybe it'd be a kind of joke and she'd get a laugh out of it. But she didn't laugh. She never laughed when she came. Well, maybe she could get someone to put it on for her, she said, if the car really needed it. Who? Mel said. She didn't know, she said, somebody in a garage maybe that knew how to do it. Look, Mel told her, don't bother. It ain't worth it. Just leave it where the hell it is and forget about getting anybody to do her any big favors in putting it on.

He wondered what the new models were like. They were coming out already, and he saw the ads in the papers. He hadn't actually seen one yet, though. Someone said Dowler just bought a new Impala, and Mel and the other guys in the garage kept hoping he'd bring it in for a wash or something, so they could get a look at it.

Christ, by the time he got out there'd be another whole year's models out already, maybe even two years', if the Parole Board didn't come through for him.

But the hell, like everyone said, you couldn't go around thinking all the time about getting out. You'd just bug up. The only way to serve time was not to think of it, because no matter how long you had, you had to serve it one day at a time. You had to settle down if you wanted to make it. You had to hang loose.

Once in a while he'd suddenly, out of nowhere, get a picture of himself out on the street again—free, you know, just off by himself doing whatever the hell he wanted with no one around to stop him, and it gave him a real funny feeling. Actually it kind of scared him, this picture of himself out there. It gave him a little chill. Because the point was, what the hell would you do if you just got out like that, just suddenly, without any warning or anything. Sure, you could be with the wife and the kid again and everything, and of course that'd really be something, because naturally you missed them. But still that wasn't the whole thing either. What *would* you do, for Christ's sake?

The bell clanged and Mel practically hit the ceiling. Christ, it was loud. What the hell were they trying to do, give everybody a goddamn heart attack?

He tossed the magazine down to the desk and took off his shirt and trousers and crawled under the covers in his skivvies. It was still warm but it chilled up during the night. He left the earplug in. The game was in the sixth inning now and he figured he'd listen to the end, because he didn't usually get right to sleep anyhow. The Giants were behind, 2–1.

The lights went out. It was nine thirty.

You couldn't hardly hear a sound now, except maybe someone climbing into a bunk or something, or some springs creaking. The place was really dark, although a very weak kind of glow came from the lights in the dome. But right around you, in the cell itself where the glow didn't reach, it was dark. The big windows on the outside wall seemed lighter, by comparison.

This was the time of day you were really glad you had the radio, when it was dark and quiet but you still weren't asleep. Without the radio it really felt pretty creepy.

He wondered how Dolin was doing. He wondered what the hell she'd done with all the goddamn money she screwed out of him.

The rest of the dough, that he spread all around the house and then told Peggy about afterward in the jail, Peggy said she'd spend on some bills and some she was just saving. Mel told her all the places to look for it. He said he won it in a big poker game that Saturday night and was going to tell her about it eventually but hid it around that Sunday

morning because he figured she'd be sore at him for staying out overnight and it might be better to wait a few days before telling her. He
didn't know if she really believed him, but anyhow it didn't seem to
stop her from snatching it all up quick enough and doing whatever she
did with it. She never told him exactly what bills she was talking about
or anything, and kind of just shrugged and changed the subject when
he asked her, which pissed him off but you gotta be careful about making a fuss when someone's visiting you, so he let it go. The hell with
it.

He was sorry he never got the chance to pay Jerrold back that dollar
he loaned him that time for lunch. He could still remember what he
bought with it that day—soup and a ham and cheese. Bean soup. It was
funny, but Jerrold was one of the guys he thought about sometimes,
and kind of missed. He didn't actually think about him maybe, but remembered him a lot. He felt bad about that dollar.

Shit, let Dolin have the goddamn money. Because for Christ's sake,
she was the one that saved his goddamn ass, let's face it, and she
probably never would've done it except for the money. Actually Reena
was the one that screwed him, not Dolin. Reena and the goddamn
Pontiac. A quick piece in the back seat and there you are, sitting out
three-to-five. Well, there were guys worse off. One guy down the tier
had five-to-eight for something that didn't take him two minutes. What
he did was kill a guy, in a fight in a bar, with a knife. So in some ways
the judge went pretty easy, considering he killed a guy. Still, the whole
thing took maybe two minutes.

If nothing else, Dolin had what you could call common sense. She
knew if she put the finger on him he'd just put it right back on her,
and she could be booked for receiving stolen money, or even being an
accessory. So she backed him, and told the cops sure, he'd been with
her all day Saturday and then stayed overnight too. It really worried
him when they started asking about where he was on that Saturday,
because he was beginning to think maybe they had some kind of lead
tying him to the gas station. But then he saw they were checking out
every single guy in the jail, everybody they could get their hands on
actually, drunks, bums, everything, like they always did on something
like that, and didn't have a clue in the world who really did it.

Actually the only time he was *really* scared was when the cops first
picked him up Sunday morning, when he didn't know yet it was just
for the goddamn Pontiac. When he opened that door and saw those
two guys standing there he thought he'd just drop in his tracks, stone
dead. He really did. And then when they were driving him to the

station one of them said, "Ain't you ever gonna learn, Mel? Still gunning around in cars, for Christ's sake—ain't you getting a little old for joy riding around like that?" It just stunned him was what it did. He just couldn't think of anything to say. The cop didn't say no more either, and by the time they got to the station he had it figured out, and could play it cool, and not look so scared shitless that he might just drop dead in his tracks.

What the hell happened to you when you were dead, anyhow? Sometimes he felt like he really knew, that he could really *feel* just what it would be like, but other times the whole thing seemed very funny and kind of unbelievable. Sure, you were dead and everything, but what the hell did that mean? You got cold as ice, of course. Guys who'd touched dead people—Christ, he'd never touch one!—said you never in your life felt anything so goddamn cold as a dead person's skin.

Mays doubled and it looked like they were gonna get a rally going, but then McCovey flied to left and it was two away.

What it was, of course, was the way the goddamn kid just kept coming at him. What the hell were you supposed to do when a guy just came at you like that, with this crazy look on his face?

Even Orninski said so. He said he'd do exactly the same thing himself. What it was practically, Orninski said, was a case of self-defense, with the kid coming at him like that, which was what he tried to explain. At least you could count on Orninski, that he'd understand. At least there was somebody in the whole goddamn world who understood. After he told him, actually, he wondered if maybe he shouldn't have. But Orninski, of course, was the only guy he ever mentioned it to, and he really didn't worry about it, because let's face it, Orninski at least knew how to keep his mouth shut.

Christ, that was a hell of a way to go, smashed to pieces like that. What did it feel like? You could just imagine, a car like that barreling into you.

Well shit, he was in prison, wasn't he? What difference did it make what they called whatever they sent you away for? So all right, so he hit the kid a coupla times. He didn't *kill* him—the goddamn *car* killed him. He just did something he shouldn't, that's all, and now he was in prison, so as far as he could see, that was that, they were even.

And let's face it, he wasn't no worse than anyone else in there. He'd like to know some of the things some of those other guys did that nobody ever caught them for, or even knew about. He'd like to know, for Christ's sake, some of the things that guys on the outside did that no one ever caught *them* for, and that they never even got sent to jail for, no matter what they called it.

Davenport grounded out to end the game and Mel turned off the radio and took the earplug out. Sometimes he listened to music till pretty late, but he was tired now and never got to sleep unless he turned off the radio.

Down below, he could hear Fenster at it. Every night. Christ, no wonder the guy was a creep. I mean, what the hell, that wasn't good for you, not every night like that.

He tried not to listen, but the little squeaky sounds seemed very loud with everything else so quiet. It made him kind of sick. He wished the hell the guy would at least wait till he figured Mel was asleep.

Sure, who wouldn't, who didn't? It was just the every-goddamn-night part that got him, and the guy himself being such a creep that you wondered sometimes what the hell was wrong with him.

After all, what the hell were you supposed to do, let the guys fag you? Was that supposed to be better?

He hadn't started it, for Christ's sake—it hadn't been his idea. He didn't even know what the hell was happening until he got all involved and was so goddamn mixed up he didn't know what he was doing. Because Christ, you take a kid and send him off to St. Joe's where it's just crawling with guys like that, and the kid doesn't know what the hell is coming off when a guy like that starts buddying up to him. Because he hadn't ever done anything like that before in his whole goddamn life. He'd just like to see somebody try to say he had.

After it was all over he went just sort of crazy. He was really just out of his mind.

Well, a guy like Penney sure as hell wasn't going to say anything like that about him, that was for sure. And no one else better get any ideas either, or he'd get what Penney got. Or what that goddamn guy at St. Joe's got.

Christ, the things you heard about guys like that, the places they'd do it and everything.

With Dolin you never had to worry, you always came through like a trooper with her.

Because, for Christ's sake, the whole thing wasn't as simple as some guys wanted you to think. All this *screw them, fuck them* routine, and what kind of sensational cocksmen they were. Like the whole thing was just like snapping a goddamn whip or something. Well, it just wasn't that easy, that's all. It just wasn't that simple.

That's the way people were always trying to bullshit you, that everything in the whole frigging world was so goddamn simple. So it was always your fault then, if anything got screwed up.

I mean, all right—so he wasn't the greatest mechanic that ever lived. So was that his fault? Was it his fault that nobody ever took the goddamn time to *teach* him anything about it? Was it his fault that he never in his life owned even one single goddamn tool?

Reena of course was just a pig, so you didn't give a damn with her one way or the other. Now Dolin, she kept herself in shape. It was something to see, it really was. Christ, but she had a body. You could just feel it, her whole body under you, her legs and her belly and those great big tits of hers pressing up against you.

He could hear Fenster breathing very regular.

He tried to keep it going as long as he could, thinking of Dolin spread out like that with her knees up, but he couldn't, and then at the end—he shouldn't be doing it again! He did it last night, for Christ's sake!—he just couldn't keep the picture of her in his mind and wanted to stop only it was too late.

He tried to breathe easy, and not too loud. He tried not to move.

It wasn't his fault, for Christ's sake. He'd kill anybody who said it was. He was just a kid back then, and didn't hardly know what the hell was going on. He lost his head.

He couldn't see the face of the guy at St. Joe's at all. He just kept seeing the face of the other kid, coming at him.

They both had crazy looks. They were both bleeding, and he kept hitting down on them.

What the hell was wrong with that fucking Fish Man?

Did big shots ever do it? Did the President ever do it?

He wouldn't have gone near that kid if he had any idea what he was looking for. He thought he was just looking to be friends. What was wrong with trying to be friends? But that was it, that was the way it went. You try to be decent, just try to be friends with somebody, and it all turns to shit.

Let's face it, it was probably all spent months ago. Christ, someone like Dolin could just go through money like water if she got the chance.

You didn't know with Peggy. Maybe she really *was* saving most of it.

He wondered if Chucky was asleep now. Sometimes when Mel wasn't home, Peggy'd let Chucky stay up late for company.

What guy, for Christ's sake, in what gas station? Who the hell did she know who knew anything about a goddamn tail pipe?

Maybe there was something *inside* the body that made it get that cold. Because otherwise it wouldn't get colder than anything else, would it?

He got up and dusted off his pants, very offhand and casual, and nodded to all the guys that were cheering, and then put his foot on the corner of the bag and got set to take his lead on the next pitch.

It wouldn't only be the cold. The dark would get him too.

He hoped Chucky was asleep. It was too late at night for a kid his age to be up.

ONE VIEWER'S VIEWS
by Sol Perrin

Finding a local TV personality anywhere in these United States who's worth watching is no easy chore. But loyal Aurorans have something to brag about in this respect. A big something, because the fellow could pass for a pro basketballer.

Johnny Mancino, who's been touted here before, notably for his series on Crime and Punishment a while back, has happily moved up another notch at K-SUN. He'll give up his straight news show for a new five-nights-a-week program next Monday, and it should provide some of the best local viewing to be had in these parts.

In addition to dropping the newscast, the big fellow won't be seen anymore on his popular "Noonday" show, so it's pretty clear the powers-that-be at K-SUN are expecting success with the new offering.

The show will be called "Report" and it sounds well-suited to Mancino's talents. The program will open every night with an "in-depth report on an important, although perhaps neglected, local news story," according to the release. Following this, Mancino will bring on a guest for fifteen or twenty minutes of "free and frank discussion," which may or may not tie in with the earlier report.

We're also promised sessions with national figures from "the entertainment world, government, science, the arts, business, and the professions."

Not a spectacular or very original format, but one that figures to provide a little more bite than the housewife-oriented "Noonday."

Johnny Mancino's popularity stems from a number of good reasons. Most important, over the long haul, is his intelligence. He has a head on his shoulders. And it's obvious that he bones up beforehand on the special fields of his guests. It doesn't take much in the way of brains—or work—to ask someone, in that immortal line of television interviewing, to "tell us something about your work, Mr. Hollowhead." Mancino's questions are pointed, thoughtful, and clear.

What really sets him above his fellow practitioners, however, is that *he listens to the answers.* A simple thing, but it makes all the difference. Mancino knows that in order to get your viewer interested in somebody, you have to be interested yourself.

He's also well-mannered. He doesn't try to show off. He avoids the smart-aleck approach and the tasteless pushiness of his inferiors.

Tune in and see if you don't agree. That's "Report," with Johnny Mancino, 7 P.M. nightly on Channel 4, starting Monday Sept. 28.

□

Late Friday afternoon Johnny got dressed for the formal dinner, putting on his rented trousers and white dinner jacket. Tonight, mercifully, would be the end of it. He was sick of looking at the girls, of talking to them, of having tea and ice cream and cokes in their company; he was sick of their perfumes and their hairdos and even their two-piece bathing suits.

Actually, all things considered, they weren't a bad bunch. They were young—God knows, they were young!—and inclined to silliness and breathless chatter, but they were good-looking and full of vitality, and a few had at least a suggestion of intelligence and perhaps even talent. If he were five years younger he'd be interested—for a while. Until he could find someone better.

The Queen of the Aurora Fall Pageant! How many queens did they elect each year in Aurora, to say nothing of the whole country? The University alone probably turned up a couple of dozen, each dutifully crowned by some assistant dean or other, each assured of a photograph from the *Post* or *Journal* for her scrapbook. The Pageant Queen fared better than most, for the Jaycees had come up with a staggering list of prizes for her. Still, you couldn't take it seriously. The girls, however, did. And so did Winninger, who must have spent hundreds of hours on it, neglecting not only his family but even his appliance store, to make sure the Big Prize went to The Girl That Deserved It. That was Winninger's line and he stuck to it, and might even have believed it.

Johnny could just imagine the hand-wringing that would go on at the Arena tonight, when the Queen finally got called up to collect all her prizes. Thirty-seven girls had entered the contest, and he got some idea of the emotional commitment involved when they cut the original crowd down to the ten finalists. As the names were read off by Winninger, there were shrieks from some contestants, tears from others, outraged cries from parents. One girl collapsed and had to be revived as she lay sprawled on a chair, her legs twisted grotesquely, her mouth slack.

The next day at the studio Johnny received a phone call: "You don't know who I am, but I have a couple of things I want to tell you. I—"

"Why don't you just tell me who you are?"

"It doesn't matter. What I have to say is what's important." He paused, and Johnny could hear him breathing heavily into the phone. "You don't think anybody's really going to believe you actually picked those girls honestly, do you? I *saw* those girls. I . . . I even happen to know some of them personally. And I want you to know you're not going to get away with it."

"I don't understand—what's your complaint? What's wrong with the girls we picked?"

"Are you kidding? And just who the hell are you to set yourself up so high and mighty? To judge and . . . and *write off*, just like that, a whole bunch of girls you never even saw before? Why, there were girls in that contest that—" The man choked on the words. "What a crummy . . . what a *lousy* deal that was," he blurted, his voice cracking. "There were girls in that contest that were *ten* times as—"

Johnny had hung up then.

He wished now he'd never got involved. He'd done it only to get the girls for "Noonday," but now he no longer had "Noonday," and didn't want them on "Report." The new show had done well its first two weeks, better than Arlanson had expected, better than Johnny had hoped. They had an audience, they'd gotten good coverage, they had sponsors. It was, at any rate, a better show than "Noonday," and he had no desire to bring on ten giggling girls in bathing suits.

He'd called Bob Steele, who worked with Madge now on "Noonday," and offered him the girls, and they'd gone on last Monday, the day the Pageant began. Johnny didn't watch.

Every night this week Johnny had gone to the Arena to sit in his little judge's booth and watch the performance, with all ten girls modeling gowns, bathing suits and sports outfits, to watch them presenting their talent routines. Tonight after the dinner the three judges would get together in a locked hotel room and decide which of the ten girls would be the new Miss Aurora.

He clipped on his wine-red bow tie and looked at himself in the mirror. The dinner jacket didn't quite fit. It wasn't easy renting clothes, and after trying all three rental stores in Aurora, he had to have the outfit sent down from Maynard. It was a little short in the sleeves, but would do if he didn't stretch his arms.

He drove downtown. It was almost six; it had been an unusually hot day, and was still hot, with the air getting muggy now. He parked near the Westerner Hotel and walked. Even in the shade the pavement seemed to be broiling. You could smell the tar melting in the streets and your eyes smarted, your lips burned. The big neon sign in front of the Aurora *Post* building flashed the temperature: 110.

The refrigerated air of the hotel lobby was like a reprieve. He took the elevator—equipped with Muzak—to the third floor and walked along the red carpet to the upholstered double doors of the private dining room. A man in a gold jacket checked Johnny's name against his clipboard list, then pulled back the doors.

On the huge oval table beneath the glass chandelier the white tablecloth sparkled with glasses, with silverware, with polished china. Candles flickered and the air was like incense. The girls' gowns were brilliant, their faces fresh and smiling, stunning, incredibly attractive. It was all light and color, fragile opulence, fantastic brightness.

Winninger got up from the table and walked over, looking in his dinner jacket like the owner of an appliance store in a dinner jacket.

"Am I late?" Johnny said.

"No, you're fine," Winninger said, shaking his hand. "Only somebody's been trying to get you on the phone."

"Was it important?"

"I don't know, but they've been trying every five minutes. Here—here's the number. There's a phone in the checkroom."

"Okay," Johnny said. "I'll be right back."

12

He felt fine. Not too much, that was the secret of his emotional balance, his cool analytical view of the world. Never too much. And stick with gin. Avoid colored whiskey, red wine, anything that bubbles. True, some unfortunates after a friendly drink, or perhaps a lonely one, a desperate one, flubbed their work, lost their friends, suffered hangovers. But not Flash. In the morning, it was true, he might cry out aghast at his mirrored image—at the pudgy, pasty face, the life-in-death mask, the wrinkles, the squinting pink-shot eyes, the hair that looked professionally dried, thinned and devigorized. He might cry out, *I remember when I ran up steps three at a time!* But that was not the whole story either. For, appearances aside, he was perfectly clearheaded and free of morbid aftereffects. It was not merely to a sober world that he awoke; it was to a world of porcelain clarity, a silent winter world (in the desert?) with bell-bright air and a crystalline landscape visible to the horizon, every object (as soon as he got his glasses on) brilliantly defined, poignant, full of significance, steady, and he himself on his way again, crisp and full of foolish confidence.

> *Oral, anal, genital,*
> *All our trouble's men-i-tal . . .*

And now, in his boxer shorts and sleeveless undershirt, clean-shaven and mildly deodorized, he walked from the bathroom to the bedroom, admiring as he went the Klee and Modigliani prints in the hallway, and the Janie Fleishman original. It was eight fifteen and downstairs

Jo Ann was screaming breakfast at the kids, indestructible buggers that they were. Three more quarts of milk shot to hell, and God knows how many boxes of Kiddly Krunch and Sugar Popped Tiddly Bits. A lot of open mouths to feed, when you sat them all around a table three times a day—not counting their midmorning, pre-nap, post-nap, after-school, before-supper and before-bed snacks, which they took on the move, like channel swimmers.

But the noise, the screams and shrieks, the threats, the tears and howlings that distinguished breakfast at the Fleishman's from any normal form of human activity—loud and clear though it all came to his ears as he buttoned his shirt—did not bother him this morning. Let Marion rave at Terry, who probably deserved it. Let Walt sulk, let Jimmy fall off his chair. Let Janie go with God in claiming that Terry was making faces at her. Let them spill their milk, soil their school clothes, disseminate their crispy bits of wheat and oats upon the floor of the dining nook, to be ground forever into the fibers of the rug. Let the noise level rise ever higher. It mattered little, and worried him not at all. It was his morning off. He, damn it all, was going to have breakfast *served* to him on the patio, after the big kids had raced off, still chewing, for the school bus, and the little kids had been enticed into the playroom and there bound and gagged. It was his payoff, his kickback. His palm was being greased, and let no man deny he deserved it!

Usually, of course, he joined Jo Ann every morning in facing, side by side and shoulder to shoulder, the massed and numerically superior foe. But today it was all her agony. For yesterday had been his (oh, God!) day off, and he had agreed to take care of the kids for the day, the whole day, from seven in the unholy morning until nine in the embittered night, while Jo Ann went off to Maynard for an outing in the big city, to visit the museum, shop in the stores, see the sights and have dinner out. He did not begrudge Jo Ann her last holiday before she would once again have to rush off to the maternity ward in the middle of the night to begin for the sixth time that dreary cycle of birth and responsibility. She deserved her fling; God knows she deserved it. But still, from seven in the morning until nine at night he had been sole custodian of five healthy children, and it had not been much of a day.

"When do we eat?" was their battle cry, piercing and persistent. "Where's breakfast? Where's lunch? Where's supper?"

"Do not," Flash had solemnly replied, gritting his teeth, "bug thy father or mother."

He had hustled the big kids off to school, had wrestled the little ones down to their naps, had borne stoically the endless and deafening *rat-a-tat-tat* of Jimmy's Smithereen Gun, had given Janie two aspirins and a dirty look when she decided, late in the afternoon, that she was beginning to feel ill, had listened, rigid and grimacing, to Walt's trumpet and Terry's flute lessons, and had kept Marion's dead goldfish in a jar in the refrigerator until she got home from school, when he helped her bury it out back in the caliche.

He had started drinking—beer—at ten thirty in the morning. He switched to martinis at four, and later eased onto gin and juice. It had helped. It muffled the noise, gave the "I wanna eat!" cries an illusion of distance, and dulled the rasping edge of his nerves. He got the kids finally bedded down (except for Walt, who was dispatched to his silent room) at eight thirty ("All right—nighty-night! Nighty-night, for Christ's sake!"), staggered to a chair and downed quickly two glasses of gin and orange juice while waiting for Jo Ann.

Should he be casual, blowing on his outstretched nails? (*Oh no— no trouble at all. A cinch, actually. No strain.*)—thus subtly and forever undermining her conviction that her job was tougher than his, and at the same time illustrating the superior male talent for efficient personnel management? It was a temptation.

Or should he tick off for her, factually, the whole ugly business in all its deadening horror, and thus receive the appreciation and sympathy that God knows he deserved?

She had returned, glowing from the carefree joys of her day, at a few minutes after nine. He stared at her numbly, and said nothing. Not a word. His heart was too full; his spirit overfloweth.

Shirts and trousers on now, he knotted his tie.

> *Shine, Lovely Maid, in Needlework,*
> *But Shine not only Here*
> *Know that Thy muft for Thyfelf*
> *A Better Place prepare.*
> *Maud Wefton SOWED thif Sampler*
> *In the Yr. of our Lord 1793*

Decorated with intricate curlicues, swirls, loops, flowers, dogs, cows, a tree and a house, all with colored thread. He was no great Sampler fancier, truth to tell, even if Jo Ann's great-great-whatever actually had SOWED it, but there were worse things to have hanging over your head every morning when you tied your tie. Especially if the sentiment got you. It got him. He wasn't much on lineages, but a sucker for sentiment.

Alas, who knew the real Flash Fleishman, that man of flesh and bone and quivering sensitivity? Not his kids. To them, he was a shaker-out of cereals, an assembler of toys and $4.98 patio chairs, a grumbler and a growler, a thundering, pudgy lawmaker. Just as well: it was right that they should grow up to be independent and call him Fatso and Bubblehead. Son, Daughter: set forth in the world alone, as you muft, and for Thyfelf a Better Place prepare. Go off to your appointed trysts and rendezvous with your grubby lovers, of whom we won't approve, and who will (along, alas, with you) consider us ancient and unbending and sexless. Think nothing of it; it is meet and just. But let no man thrust false banners in your hand, nor shit all over you. Love and distrust thy fellow man, and respect always the Imp of the Perverse. *Ave atque vale!*

Tie knotted now, jacket over his arm, he went into his den to pick up his briefcase. The shade was down across the way. He didn't even care. The whole thing was hardly worth the effort—not, of course, that he put much effort in it. He had met her once, on the sidewalk while he was watering the lawn. She had stopped to chat. She snapped her gum. She was not even, close up, good-looking. She wished she lived, she said, in California, so she could ride a surf board. Her voice was nasal, whining and juvenile. She made him feel three million years old, and tired. Was this all the reward a man got for his efforts, his idealism?

He took his briefcase and went downstairs—he didn't have to, it wasn't part of the deal—to say good-bye to Walt and kiss Janie and Terry when they took aim for the bus stop and ran, and to jest paternally with Marion and Jimmy for thirty or forty seconds, until all three of them wearied of it and Jo Ann, conscious of her pledge, hustled them into the playroom and manacled them to the TV set.

Taking this morning's *Post* with him, he pushed back the sliding glass door and stepped out to the patio, where he sat on a metal chair at the round metal table, under the striped plastic sun umbrella, greatly cognizant of his leisure, and admired the early morning sunlight on the distant slopes of the San Juan Mountains. He liked it here—here on this patio, here in this house, here in sun-drenched Aurora, where the lime and the avocado grew and where, in the spring, even the cactus bloomed. True, when you walked into a neighbor's house it was all *déjà vu*, like walking into your own, only quieter. And true, they would probably never live to see the end of the mortgage on their glassy five-bedroom house with its seven thousand feet of tangled garden hose, but what of it? Let who would rant at suburbia, and condescend to its faceless inhabitants. He, Flash Fleishman, took his comforts where he found them. The voice of God, as we all knew, could speak to one as clearly here, in our tract homes, on our lawns, as anywhere else—yea, even in our rumpus rooms and on our patios—and the voice of Doom too, for that matter, and the chilling cry of Recognition.

He unfolded the *Post* and studied briefly the ten girls in evening gowns on the front page; checked the weather forecast, noting there would be a full moon tonight; turned to an inside page to read Peanuts; and had just pulled out the sports section when Jo Ann, who had gone upstairs to get out of her robe, came out carrying breakfast on a tray and wearing the new maternity dress she had picked up yesterday in Maynard—for a song, she assured him, since she'd only have a few weeks to wear it. It was a charming outfit, white and powder blue and ballooning all over.

"It's charming," Flash told her, salting and peppering his eggs. They ate in the bright, steady, but not yet pulsating sun. "Hot again," Flash said, which in Aurora, where it was hot nine months of the year, meant only that it was hotter than usual. And for the past two days, for October, it had been hotter than usual.

"The radio said it'd break a hundred again," Jo Ann said. "It set a record yesterday."

"That's what must have worn me down. The heat."

"Oh?" Jo Ann said. "Were you worn down?"

"Well, not really," Flash said. "Not enough to show."

"It was awful nice of you to take them all day. I had a grand time."

"That's what counts," he agreed grimly. "That you enjoyed yourself."

After some further chit-chat Jo Ann asked, as he was finishing his second cup of her excellent coffee, "Do you think Griffing's inviting us over for anything special tonight?"

"I suspect he's inviting us over because he hasn't invited us over for a few months now and doesn't want his key man, his ace, his tower of strength, bearing grudges. Besides, he's inviting everybody over."

"I wish he didn't feel he had too. You can see he doesn't enjoy it, everybody drinking till two in the morning."

"It's part of his job. It's a lousy job, all in all."

"We should leave early and let him get some sleep. He doesn't want to stay up all night partying any more."

"He never did, not even when he was young and feisty like me."

"Maybe that's why he's still so healthy."

"He's not so healthy."

"What's wrong with him?"

"Nothing's wrong with him. He's just getting old, that's all." Flash looked at his watch. "Time to go."

Jo Ann walked out to the carport with him. "Wasn't that nice having breakfast out there by ourselves? We should do it more."

"Yes. What happened to the kids? Are they still alive in there?"

"They're watching Captain Kangaroo. Have a good day now."

"You too," Flash said. He kissed her, pinched her cheek, patted her swollen tummy and climbed into the Volkswagen.

□

It did get hot. It got hot as hell. As he walked up the hill after lunch, up the path and the stone steps, the sun burned through his porous summer suit with a kind of pure, businesslike objectivity, and scorched the back of his neck. Usually by October you got what the natives called fall, which meant warm days and chilly nights. But today it was blistering, with the air as dry as alum, so that your tongue seemed swollen by thirst. Your eyes grew raw and watered from the heat. A cool breeze—that was all, that would suffice. Just one sweet wisp of a cool breeze.

"Afternoon, Warden."

Flash nodded and stepped into the shoeshop office. The officer had been sitting reading a newspaper, which he quickly dropped as he jumped to his feet. Well, it wasn't the most interesting job in the world, hanging around here all day. That was one of the battles Flash lost—or at least only half-won. He wanted to remove all custodial officers from the shops, to reduce as much as possible the atmosphere of repression, of imprisonment, from those areas that were essentially educational and rehabilitative in nature. He had no illusions as to any great advantages accruing from this, but it was, as he had argued to Griffing, at least a gesture, at least a modest attempt to make things modestly better. And there would be no real loss in security: the officers could be kept nearby in case of trouble. Dowler, of course, had argued equally reasonably against the idea, and poor old Griff, faced for the millionth time with the impossibility of paying homage to both God (Flash, of course) and the Devil (who else?), agreed to remove the guards from all shops with fewer than twenty-five men, and all shops separate from the main building. But the big ones, and the ones in here, would retain them. And so this guy sat here all day reading the newspaper and doing heaven only knows what else to pass the time.

"How's it going here? Everything under control?"

"Everything's fine, sir."

"Good. Is Manson around?"

"Out in the shop. I'll get him for you."

"No, I'll find him." He turned to Manson's inmate clerk, who was checking time cards at the desk. "Hello, Samuels. How are you doing?"

Samuels, who had been careful to keep his eyes down, rose and snapped to attention. "Very well, sir."

"Keeping all those numbers straight, I hope."

"Trying, sir."

"Got a minute to spare?"

"Yes sir."

"Come along then." Flash opened the glass door to the shop and went in, letting Samuels follow.

One good breath and you got used to it—that incredibly rich, fruity odor of ripe leather and sweet-smelling rubber, of glue thick enough to float horseshoes on. Christ, it was hot. The two fans cranked away drearily at the ends of the shop without doing a hell of a lot of good. The men in their aprons, glancing up qucikly from their machines and workbenches as he walked by, were steaming. You could see the sweat on their faces, hanging in drops from their noses. You could see the salt-reddened bleariness of their eyes. The place was so hot it smelled hot; you could smell the heat along with the leather and glue.

The solution was simple, of course, and had been proposed by Griffing every year for the last five or six years: have the inmates build some simple evaporative cooling units for all the shops, thus with one stroke saving the state money, giving the inmates some useful work and good training, and making life more bearable for prisoners and staff alike.

But the Board would first have to ask the Legislature for funds to expand the present machine, electrical and sheet-metal shops, which had neither the space nor the equipment to do the job. Such an expansion was needed anyhow, because all three shops were wholly inadequate for an institution this large. Nevertheless the Board would reject—as it did every year—Griffing's request. After all, a man wasn't sent to the pen to familiarize himself with the Good Life. If he liked air conditioning and similar creature comforts so much, he should stay out of prison.

Of course, the Board members (led by Old King Kale himself) would assure Griffing that they *personally* favored the idea, since in a place like Aurora an air-cooling system was hardly a luxury, even for convicts. But they had enough trouble as it was getting funds from the Legislature, and asking for something like this might put more important requests in danger. The politicians were always eager to cut out frills, and once you gave them something they could cut, once they started cutting, heaven only knew where they would stop.

Besides, the state had contracted to purchase all air-conditioning units from a single distributor who, as it happened, was not wholly without friends in the Legislature. Thus, even if they were to provide air conditioners for the prisoners (which of course they couldn't, because it would be coddling), they'd have to buy them from this distributor (which of course they couldn't, because it'd be too expensive). That meant that the only solution was to have the inmates build the units themselves (which unfortunately was out of the question, in view of the state's contract with the distributor). However, if the Warden merely wished to request funds to expand the shops as part of a general upgrading of the whole prison training program (which the Board members *personally* favored), and without any reference to the matter of air coolers, he should of course do so. However, there was no chance the Legislature would approve such a request—unless, of course, it could be shown that some specific and immediate need could be served by the expansion—such as, for instance, the manufacture of evaporative cooling units . . .

It was all reasonable enough, actually, once you got the swing of it, once the irrefutable logic of it seized you, jaguar-like, by the throat.

Manson was yelling at an inmate, an older, weary-looking man, and Flash was upon him before Manson realized he had a visitor. He flushed and stepped forward quickly, his eyes darting. "Good afternoon, Warden . . . I didn't realize you—"

"Afternoon, Manson. How are you today?"

"Just fine, Warden. Everything is going just fine here."

"What's this fellow doing wrong?"

"Nothing wrong, Warden . . . I was just showing him something."

"I'd like to see Rogers for a moment if it's convenient."

"Oh, sure. You want to take him outside?"

"No. I'll speak to him here."

"Sure, come ahead. Right this way." Manson glanced at his inmate clerk, who was still behind Flash. The clerk's presence obviously disturbed him. It set his so-called mind working. *Why is he along? What's happening? What have I done now? Who's trying to screw me?* Looking back every couple of steps to make sure he hadn't been deserted,

Manson led them along the aisle between the workbenches. Rogers was spreading glue on rough-cut leather soles and laying them out to dry. Two men worked alongside him at the same job. The fumes from the glue were pungent, and somewhat toxic, so that a six-inch fan, as required by the safety code, rotated back and forth over their bench.

"Rogers—report to the Warden!"

Rogers dropped his brush into the gluepot and came to attention. "Inmate Rogers, sir."

"At ease," Flash said. And then, raising his voice a bit: "We've just received the Parole Board's decision in the matter of your application, Rogers."

For a moment, Rogers' expression remained unchanged. Then he seemed to lose control of his facial muscles. His eyelids fluttered, his lips loosened. "Yes, sir . . ."

"I'm very pleased to report," Flash said, even louder, "that the Board has approved your application. You will report to Mr. Reed in a few days to make arrangements for your release at the end of the month."

Flash extended his hand. Rogers did not move. Then tentatively, self-consciously, he extended his hand, as if not even sure which one he was supposed to use. Flash shook it vigorously. "Congratulations, Rogers. I'm delighted."

He headed for the glass door with Manson and the clerk scurrying along behind him.

☐

When he got back to the Quonset hut he came upon Dowler and Ted Reed talking in the foyer.

"The goddamn automatic transmission was all screwed up," Dowler was saying. "So I went to the dealer and waved the warranty in his face and I said to him, 'The goddamn automatic transmission is all screwed up, and I'm not about to pay this kind of money for a piece of junk.' So he fixed it up, in one day. Like that. Now it runs great."

"My Volkswagen always runs great," Flash said. "Like a charm, a watch, a billiard ball down an inclined plane."

"You're driving a heap, Flash. You should buy yourself a new car. Live a little. Get rid of that old kraut-box."

"What kind did you get, Jeff?"

"Impala."

"What kind is that?"

"A Chevrolet, Flash."

"Why don't you say so then?"

"I'm going to have to run," Ted Reed said. "Will you see that fellow after, Flash?"

"Sure, send him along."

Reed left.

"Who you gonna see?" Dowler asked, edging nearer. When Dowler spoke to you he stood very close, and leaned even closer, jutting forth his rugged jaw and keeping his voice low, gravelly, grim. You felt always a compulsion to back away, to put more space between you. It was a habit, no doubt, that Dowler picked up from interrogating inmates, a way of putting them on the defensive. It worked. He stared straight into your eyes, breathed in your face—this broad, phlegmatic bull of a man—and kept you always precarious and uncomfortable, leaning back, struggling with vague, nagging visions of your inferiority.

But Flash was used to the treatment and, all things considered, held up well under it. "New Classification man," he said.

"College boy?"

"Yes. Sounds pretty good."

"Uh-huh," Dowler said. "How come you need him?"

"Wentham's leaving. Got a personnel job at Rohmann Aircraft."

"Just as well. Never thought too much of him, to tell you the truth."

"He would've worked out fine with a little more experience behind him."

"Uh-huh," Dowler said. "That's what you'll be telling me about the new guy too—that he'll be just great in ten or twelve years. I might be dead by then, for all I know. The only thing I worry about, Flash, is what the guy can do now, today."

"Christ, Jeff—you're an existentialist."

"Call it what you want, Flash. It's all the same to me. Have you seen Griff? What are we gonna do about that list?"

"Give him four hundred names. That's what he says he wants."

"I went over that list, Flash. I can't find four hundred."

"I'm afraid you'll have to, Jeff. Griff stuck his neck out to get the Board to okay four hundred. He can't go back now and say we don't have them."

"We don't."

"I think we do. I think we have six hundred."

"I saw your six hundred, Flash."

Flash shrugged. "If I'm willing to cut my six hundred down, you should be willing to fatten your two hundred up."

"I gave you more than two hundred. It was two hundred and thirty-one."

"Griff wants four hundred."

"You want four hundred, Flash."

"I want six hundred. But I'm willing to compromise."

"Then you can be the one that rates them minimum."

"I'm not authorized to."

"I've been rating inmates a long time, Flash, and if any guy in that dormitory or whatever the hell you wanna build is gonna slug one of my guards and crash that little toothpick fence you're gonna build, it's gonna be some guy you rated minimum, not me."

"We've got to take a chance now and then, Jeff. We can't—"

"We took a chance on Bryher."

"He came back," Flash said.

"He needed a little help, only. A couple more drinks and he might've lit out for Timbuktu."

"The man was under a lot of strain. His kid almost died. His wife was all banged up."

"I see you left him off your list."

"That's right," Flash said.

"Only if his wife hadn't wrecked the car and got him the chance to get out and crank up the elbow a bit, you would've put him on, wouldn't you?"

"I guess so. He had a good record. Christ, Jeff, we can't just rate the blind and the bedridden minimum. If Griff's willing to take the chance on four hun——"

"He'll have to do it on your say-so then. Not mine."

"Good enough," Flash said. "I'll tell him that."

Flash went to his office. Harry, good old Harry with his darkening beard and his oaken fingers, was going at the typing machine like a man possessed. He stopped and looked up. "Warden Griffing called before, sir. He asked that you call him back."

"Anything else?"

"No sir. I'm almost finished with these cards you wanted—the cross-analysis Mr. Reed worked up."

"Okay, fine." Flash unlocked the door to his office and went in, unbuttoning his jacket. He sat behind the desk and put the call through. "You want me, Griff?"

"Yes. You people are coming tonight, aren't you?"

"Of course we're coming. You're serving drinks, aren't you?"

"Only to friends. Look, I'm leaving early today—I have to see somebody downtown. I don't know how much time I'll have; could you manage to pick up some ice for us? We're having twenty people; one of those big sacks should do."

"Sure. Anything else?"

"No, that'll be fine. Did you see Rogers?"

"Yes. Did you get to the others?"

"They've all been notified, yes. The Board didn't really do too badly this time."

"I was hoping they'd go along on Reasoner too. What'd they have against him?"

"I don't know, Flash; he just didn't make much of an impression. He sounded surly somehow. We'll have to prime him better next time."

"Will they let him come up again in December?"

"Yes, I asked them to waive the six-month set."

"Good," Flash said. "I was just talking to Dowler; he's really not very anxious to give us those names."

"I know. I'm going to see him about it later. I'll handle it."

"Did you get a look at the chapel bench?"

"I was over before. I don't know, Flash; I guess we might just as well replace the whole bench. It's gouged in pretty deep."

"I noticed. They have any idea who it was?"

"Dowler thinks a number of them must have worked at it, taking turns. Evidently whoever sat there got passed the knife and was expected to do his bit."

"I didn't think we had that much talent here," Flash said. "It was actually pretty artistic, I thought, all those curlicues and everything."

"Dowler's going to sit the men by tiers now, in the same row each time."

"I think Traceman felt rather bad about it."

"I know," Griffing said. "Dowler offered him extra men to patrol the place during services, but he said he wasn't sure he really wanted them."

"He was always something of a sentimentalist."

"Dowler?"

"The Padre."

"Okay, Flash. We'll see you tonight."

"Good. I'm in the mood for a party."

Actually, he wasn't in the mood for much of anything. Maybe it was the heat, or the mid-afternoon lull—or yesterday, fourteen hours with five kids, seventy kid-hours—but he felt weary and ambitionless. He felt lazy. It was a good day for it, at any rate. Most days he had a dozen inmates and fifteen staff workers leaping at him out of doorways with agonizing, insolvable and unintelligible problems. He'd have a foot-high stack of papers to read and another of reports and letters to write, and all day long the buzzer buzzed and the telephone shrieked. Lately it was even worse, what with Griffing and Dowler taking their vacations and now Philson away on his. But at the moment, incredibly, everything was quiet.

It was what he needed, a respite, an interlude of peace, a few pleasant hours with a reed of grass in his mouth and a bamboo pole between his toes. Huckleberry Fleishman, in a battered straw hat. But he lacked finesse and conviction as a loafer. He couldn't even keep a clear conscience when he worked. Some lurking guilt-shrouded voice was always badgering him to work harder. After all, breath was rare; you held the universe in your trembling hands for only the briefest span.

He took out the carbon of the minimum list he had submitted to Dowler, 600 names, with Dowler's firm red check next to 231 of them, and aimlessly flipped through it. Then he put his feet up and stared at the ceiling, which needed a painting.

It wasn't Dowler's fault, after all, that his whole world seemed to be composed of 1223 proven liars, swindlers, sociopaths, rapists, burglars, murderers, thieves, traffickers, addicts, strong-arm men, bank robbers, larcenists, muggers, sex perverts and child molesters, all spending their days plotting new and more insidious assaults upon the custodial purity that it was Dowler's sworn duty and greatest satisfaction to uphold. Flash understood—at least a little.

And sure, maybe this year, or the next, or the next, they might get the minimum unit approved, and maybe two or three or five years after that even get it built. Meanwhile, next year, instead of getting a six-bed psychiatric annex for the infirmary; two more classrooms, two more psychologists; a full-time psychiatrist; three more caseworkers to set up a prerelease program; three more Classification officers; more money for the library; more money for textbooks; more money for a staff training program; more money (a lot more, an incredible, impossible, hopeless but necessary amount more) for an expansion of the whole job program, so the 150 men for whom they now had no work could be relieved of their idleness; more money to improve the shops they already had, to put a cement floor in the garage, to purchase up-to-date equipment so that a man would not have to be trained, for instance, to operate a type of lathe that was no longer used anywhere in the civilized world except in the penitentiary machine shop; more money for a study of their whole classification system in the hope (nay, the assurance) of developing a better and fairer system—instead of all this and the fifteen or twenty other things he had asked for, Flash would get, if the stars were favorable and the omens good, a couple of crates of discarded schoolbooks, one Classification officer, and a folding screen to be used to partition off the quieter patients in the infirmary from the screaming psychotics.

Dowler, of course, had a list equally long, and would get equally little of it, or perhaps, because legislators were more afraid of prisoners escaping than of prisoners not being rehabilitated, a trifle more.

And what did Griffing want? Griffing wanted a whole new prison. Every day the last thing Griffing did before leaving was to make a single heavy stroke in the ledger book he kept in his desk. When a page filled up, he added the strokes on that page to the previous total from all the other pages and wrote the new grand total at the top of the next page. The tally was started by the Warden-before-the-Warden-before-him on the day when the penitentiary, according to a specific, public promise by the Governor, would be torn down and replaced by a new and modern institution. That date was July 1, 1937. The promise had been faithfully reiterated, with new dates, by every Governor since. The book now contained over ten thousand strokes, and thanks to the foresight of the man who purchased it, still had a good many blank pages left.

Christ, Fleishman, but you have settled down and fizzled out! Do you even remember that scowling revolutionary, that youthful flame-thrower, that devourer of mad texts?

He remembered. Had ever a man entered the penal service of his country more fired with enthusiasm, more stirred by ideas and ideals, more confident of being the radical Moses who would lead not only the prisoners but the whole of society out from behind the stone walls of ignorance and bestiality?

And now?

Yes: where is that Flash Fleishman of yesteryear, what is he doing now, that rowdy unkempt youth who climbed tabletops in beer halls and banged on lecterns at campus rallies? Ah yes, Samuel F. Fleishman, now Assistant Warden for Treatment, Rehabilitation and Education (or TRE, pronounced *tree*)—and let's admit it, it was a hard enough banner to wave, a lot harder than the ones he used to wave. That was why radicalism wore thin after a while. It was too easy, all conviction and adrenalin. It was the simplest thing in the world. Maybe it was the best too, and the purest, the noblest, the grandest, the most neces-sary and commendable. Maybe it was all these things. He for one didn't doubt it: who'd want to do without Christ or Bolívar or Thomas

Mott Osborne or even, for that matter, the most illogical and tiresome street-corner orator?

But still it was easy. What the hell, he could carry placards. He could march, he could protest, he could win enough debates to stretch from Aurora to Plato's Athens and back again—and he'd feel one hell of a lot better afterward than he usually did after a soggy day of slugging it out in good old dependable TRE. And he'd probably even be able to pick up a few useful scars or a limp or something for his grandchildren. *Yes sir: see this slash mark up here over my left eye? Policeman's saber, 1963.*

It had its rewards, all right, which he wasn't exactly sure TRE did. (Although he did have a scar: two inches long, on his calf, having slipped one day on the metal stairs in the Cell Block after completing a cleanliness inspection, during which he reprimanded three inmates for untidy quarters.) No doubt about it, one cut a lot more mustard in the history books convincing people the world was no goddamn good (true enough, God knows) than by doing anything else you could name offhand. If you just did your job and sat home nights drinking like a normal man, the world passed you by. The clarions did not sound at your approach, nor the mournful bugle at your departure. You had to wear buttons and hate cops and support experiments that expanded your consciousness.

SHRINK YOUR CONSCIOUSNESS!—that was Flash Fleishman's grubby little motto, that was the button he'd wear. He'd have it made into a sign and hung on his wall, along with IF YOU LOVE EVERYBODY SO MUCH, WHY DO YOU HATE ME? And that good line of De Voto's: WE DON'T NEED FREUD TO TELL US THAT OUR LIFE IS DREAM-BOUND, DEATHWARD AND IN THE DARK.

Along with maybe STOP THE WAR IN FLASH FLEISHMAN'S SOUL! Yes, one of the great struggles of our era, along with Vietnam and the Gaza Strip and wherever the hell else the world will decide to go to shit again. Let us all devote a moment of silent mumbling to wish Flash Godspeed and success, along with all those young black and brown and white and yellow men destined to fall and rot in the gangrenous jungles for some stupid reason or other, and the people being decapitated by windshields and mutilated against dashboards for even less reason, and the kids who get leukemia and cystic fibrosis for no reason at all.

Yes, we Jews, we have known suffering, we have known despair and heartache, and have seen the glory of the Holy Land trampled into the dust. It is our heritage, suffering. It is the jewel of our navels.

I thought you weren't Jewish, Flash. What are you trying to—

That was last week, sir—whatever the hell business it is of yours! It's a strain being a Jew, or even a fraction of one, all the time, week in, week out. A man has a right once in a while to be free of all that persecution, those long bloody centuries, to join the winning team for a change. Every man has a right to be a gentile, even if he is a Jew, or vice versa, depending on your point of view.

(Only we're all of us, hebe and goyim, white and black and yellow, members of the same sad team—the losers, the ones that never win the pennant, that have to play with their bare hands and will never be able to afford uniforms with numbers on them. We're the guy that late on election night goes before the TV cameras and concedes, tearfully, while his disheartened followers and hangers-on shout *No! No!* and his wife weeps, his children weep, his campaign manager weeps. And then the crowd starts singing "For He's a Jolly Good Fellow!" They never sing that for winners. When they start singing that for you, you're finished.)

Reed phoned to ask if he were free to see that fellow.

"Of course. I'm just sitting here twiddling my thumbs, killing time. Send him in, your protégé, your great white hope."

He talked with the kid for fifteen minutes. He was twenty-one, with a psych major-soc minor B.A. and a mild speech impediment. He planned to get his master's in penology and wanted a job where he could help people. He was getting married in January, which was why he decided on prison work instead of the Peace Corps. His family lived in San Francisco where his old man piled up the coin importing Japanese knickknacks. He wore a gray suit and a very narrow tie that he kept touching as he talked, and he seemed to perspire subtly but steadily. He was five feet eleven inches tall, wore glasses, and weighed, the skinny son of a bitch, 147 pounds. He played chess. He allowed that Freud was a brilliant man, but perhaps more of a philosopher than an empirical scientist, and that his theories, although insightful, could no longer be considered viable in the light of quantitatively established data. He smiled a good deal to foster the impression of self-assurance and general all-around neighborliness. When questioned, he agreed that a flexible, nonaligned and undogmatic approach was best in treating individual cases, but Flash decided to hire him anyway.

He would start at $5165 a year, a few thousand less than his predecessor would get shuffling personnel cards at Rohmann Aircraft, but $470 more than a new guard got. This was a sore point with Dowler, who figured all Treatment men were fags anyhow and wouldn't have paid a red cent to hire a one of them. Flash was often tempted to point out how unfair it was to castigate a whole group of dedicated hard-working men on the basis of an unfounded popular misconception—especially since everyone knew that all *guards* were sadists, and probably bull queers in the bargain.

There were times when Flash almost wished Dowler *was* a sadist, or at least a homosexual. Unfortunately he wasn't either. True, he'd never married and had no houseful of kids to befuddle and bedraggle him—he had instead his 1223 children right here, and was working hard to teach them manners—but no matter how sweet it'd be to make something ominous of this, in all honesty you had to admit that Jeff Dowler was at least as normal as the next guy—especially when the next guy happened to be Flash Fleishman.

He buttoned his jacket, told Harry he'd be back shortly, and walked through the midafternoon sunlight to the Administration Building. He was just about to enter the staff office when the door to the Warden's office down the hall swung open and Bostick leaned out.

"Sir—aren't you coming in here?"

Flash looked at him. "No. I was going in here."

"Didn't you get the message, sir? The Warden wanted you in here."

Flash walked down to Bostick, who stepped into the hall and closed the door behind him. "What message?"

"Just a minute ago, sir. The Warden called in and told me to get the operator to get you up here."

"It must have just missed me." Flash shrugged, then smiled at Bostick, who seemed somewhat confused. "Anyhow, here I am, at the Warden's service. What does he want me to do?"

"I don't know, sir. That's all he said."

"Is he in there?"

"No sir, he's not."

"Where is he then? Where did he call from?"

"I don't know, sir. But he wanted you in here."

"All right then," Flash said. "I'll go in. I'm not a hard man to get along with." He opened the door and stepped into the Warden's office. He paused and looked back at Bostick, who was hovering, somewhat indecisively, in the hall. "Maybe you can find out where the Warden is. And maybe even what he wants me to do."

"All right, sir. I'll try."

Flash made himself comfortable in the big cushioned chair. Griffing was a clean-desk man, and generally left damn little around worth prying into. He glanced up at the framed prints of old English prisons and the plaque Griffing had been presented by the American Prison

Association in 1957, and then considered the September issue of the *American Penological Review,* which lay on the desk next to today's vase of fresh-cut flowers. A single pink petal had fallen upon the issue's amber cover, one of those breath-taking God-sent images you hesitated to disturb. But he tired of admiring it and slanted the magazine toward the wastebasket, sighing a brief haiku sigh as the petal slid in, and started flipping through the dull gray pages of doubtlessly leaden prose.

The phone rang. It was the operator. "Excuse me, sir—but is it all right to put calls through?"

"Of course it's all right. Griffing's not here, though, so you might just as well—"

"I mean about the alert, sir."

"The what?"

"The alert. I think we're on a standby alert, sir."

Flash was silent a moment. "You *think* we're on a standby?"

"That's right, sir. I was told we're on standby."

"Who on earth told you that?"

"One of the officers, sir."

"Is Bostick out there?"

"Yes sir, I think so. He was around a minute ago."

"Send him in, please. If you can't find him, send another officer. Right away."

A moment later Bostick opened the door and looked in.

"What in hell's going on?" Flash said.

"I don't know, sir. Evidently we're on standby."

"Says who?"

"I don't know, sir. I was calling around trying to locate the Warden for you and then somebody said we're on standby."

"Who the hell is somebody?"

"Officer Sylvester, sir."

"Who told him?"

"I don't know."

"Why in Christ's name didn't anybody tell me?"

"I don't know, sir. This just—"

"All right. Get that inmate off that switchboard. Get on it yourself if you have to. Keep this line clear then and find out what the hell is happening."

"Yes sir."

Flash waited a minute or so and then picked up the phone. "Bostick?"

"Yes sir. We're on yellow alert now, sir."

"Good Christ—when did that happen? Why didn't you—"

"It just happened this minute, sir. I was just going to—"

"All right. Clear the inmates out of there and set up the circuit. Take the circuit yourself. Put someone else on the board. Go ahead now."

"Yes sir."

"Wait—where's the trouble, do you know?"

"No sir, I don't. Post Four called in the yellow, sir."

Flash hung up and plugged in the yellow socket of the intercom. He waited until the secondhand on his watch made one full sweep and then depressed the talk button. "Bostick—are we on yet?"

There was no answer.

He waited another minute and pressed the button again. "Bostick?"

"Yes sir," came the response, along with an incredible amount of electronic crackling.

"Is the circuit on?"

"Just about, sir."

"Get me Post Four as soon as it's open. Can't you cut out this static?"

"I don't exactly know what's causing it, sir. I think maybe you could try Post Four now."

"Am I on the circuit?"

"Excuse me, sir. The static is pretty—"

"*Am I on the circuit?*"

"Yes sir, you're on. Go ahead."

"Fleishman here. Post Four, come in."

There was no response.

"They should be on, sir," Bostick said. "Try them again."

"Fleishman here. Post Four, come in."

"—us, sir?"

"What was that? Hello—who's there?"

"Are you calling us, sir?"

"Is this Post Four?"

"Yes sir. Post Four."

"Did you call in a yellow alert?"

"I'm sorry sir, but the reception here is very—"

"*Did you call in a yellow alert?*"

"Yes sir, we did. On Warden Dowler's orders."

"What's happening?"

"Nothing seems to be at the moment, sir. They're still in the—" The connection broke: no static, no sound. Abruptly it resumed, first the shattering interference, and then, barely audible over the racket, a voice: "—left, I think."

"Give me that again, I missed it. Who's in where?"

"The inmates, sir. In the hobby shop. The Warden and Mr. Dowler tried to approach but were driven back."

"What do you mean, driven back? What are you talking about?"

"The men started throwing things out, sir. Chunks of wood, things like that."

"Was anyone hit?"

"I don't think so, sir. They were yelling something but we couldn't catch it over here. I don't know, but I think Mr. Dowler's still up here. Everything seems quiet."

"Where's the Warden?"

"He left, sir."

"Where was he going?"

"I don't know, sir. He was heading down the hill."

"Everything seems to be under control then?"

"I think so. It seems to be."

"Let me know right away if anything happens."

"Yes sir."

Under a yellow alert each man had a specific and clear-cut responsibility. The plan had been devised years ago by Dowler, and it had impressed Flash as being eminently practical and ingenious. He wished the hell he could remember how it went.

He got Bostick again on the circuit. "Can't you get rid of this static? We'll all end up going deaf."

"I'm trying, sir. But I just don't know why it's—"

"Are there any more inmates still in there?"

"Yes sir. A couple."

"They should be cleared out."

"Where are we supposed to send them, sir?"

"Hell, I don't know . . . put them in the visitor's room, I guess. And get someone to round up all the other inmates in the building too."

"Yes sir."

"And send an officer—two officers—in here right away. Can I get Reed on this thing?"

"I don't really know, sir. I guess so."

"Fleishman here. Reed—Ted Reed? Come in, Ted Reed."

There was no answer.

"I'll try the phone," Flash said. He picked up the phone and jiggled the cradle. "Who's this now?"

"Officer Jennison, sir. Bostick told me to take the board."

"Do you know how to work it?"

"I think so, sir. I think I can manage."

"Can you ring Reed for me?"

"Yes sir. I'll ring him."

The phone rang twice.

"Mr. Reed's office, good afternoon."

"Fleishman here. Who's this?"

"Inmate Settleman, sir."

"Is Mr. Reed there?"

"Yes sir. He's in conference at the moment with—"

"Put him on."

The inmate hesitated an instant. "Yes sir."

There was a knock and Flash yelled, "Come in!"

Two officers stepped in. "Did you want us, sir?"

"Yes, wait a minute." He spoke into the phone again. "Are you getting Reed?"

"Flash—is that you? Did you want me?"

"Yes, what the hell are you doing there? Why aren't you on the circuit?"

"What circuit, Flash?"

"The alert circuit, goddamn it. We're on yellow alert."

"We are?"

"For Christ's sake, get on it, will you. And get all those inmates rounded up—get someone to hold them in the conference room. You're supposed to be in charge there during an alert."

"What's happening, Flash? What's going on?"

"I don't know. But we're on alert, and I don't want any goddamn inmates answering the phone. Get your men together and stay on the circuit in your office."

"I don't have any circuit, Flash."

"What do you mean, you don't have any circuit?"

"I never had one. My intercom doesn't have that connection. It never did."

"Why the hell didn't you ever say so?"

"Well—I don't know. That's the way it was when I got here, so I figured—"

"Okay, use my office. But get moving."

"I don't have a key for your office, Flash."

"Oh for Christ's sake—never mind then. I'll get you on the phone if I want you. Just get moving."

Flash turned to the two officers. "Do either of you know what on earth's going on?"

They looked at each other. "I'm afraid not, sir."

"Okay. One of you get down to Alden at the gate and make sure they know we're on alert. The other go check with whoever's on as tower lieutenant. Fast."

"Yes sir." They turned sharply and pulled open the door and almost ran down Griffing. "Excuse me, Warden!"

"Where are you running to?" Griffing said.

"I'm sending them to make sure the alert's in effect," Flash said. "We're on alert, aren't we?"

"Okay, go ahead," Griffing said. The officers left and Griffing stepped inside, pulling the door closed behind him.

"What's going on?" Flash said.

Griffing eyed him, tilting his head, raising his eyebrows. He was biting his lower lip; not hard, but soberly, meditatively. For a sixty-six-year-old man who didn't have the world's liveliest endocrine system anymore, and whose whole goddamn prison had just gone on yellow alert, Griffing looked pretty good, although hardly cheerful. "Is the alert out?"

"Mostly," Flash said. "I think so anyhow. I've got Bostick on the circuit and I've been trying to make sure everyone's got the word. I haven't checked the dome or the kitchen or any of the shops yet."

"We sent word to them from up there."

"What's happening, Griff?"

"Some inmates from the garage moved into the hobby shop, and took Delft with them."

"They *took* Delft?"

"Yes. We don't know who yet, or even how many. Cloninger's in there too."

"Are they armed?"

"I don't know. Possibly. Probably, I guess."

"What are they trying to do? What's the point of it?"

"I haven't the slightest idea." Griffing motioned to the intercom. "Is this thing working?"

"More or less."

Griffing bent down and pushed the button. "Bostick? Are you there?"

"Yes sir."

Griffing jerked up. "Good heavens!—what's wrong with this thing, Flash?"

"We seem to picking up some interference."

Gingerly, Griffing pushed down the button. "Get this immediately to all duty officers: all inmates are to be returned to their cells at four, at the regular bell, and kept there until further orders. No one is to

go by the hobby shop, or even within sight of it. Make sure they understand that, especially in the powerhouse and the East wing shops.
They're to take the long way around. If anyone strolls into that area
with his men I'll have his skin."

"Yes sir. I think someone's trying to get you, Warden."

"All right; put it through." Griffing blinked as they were subjected
to an unbelievable electrical battering. "—here. Calling Warden Griffing."

"Is that you, Dowler? Go ahead."

"Are those weapons on the way? I haven't seen them."

"They're coming. Is it still quiet?"

"It's quiet. Nothing's happening. Do you want me to approach them
again?"

"No, stay where you are. Give a pistol to one man on each side of
the building and take one yourself. Keep everything else in the garage,
out of sight. And under guard."

"What are the orders on use?"

"Your men are *not* to use anything except on specific command.
Make sure that's clear; I'll hold you responsible."

"What if they start shooting from in there? Do I have emergency
fire authority?"

Griffing hesitated. "Discretionary. But I'll want absolute proof of
necessity. And make sure your men understand this. They don't have
the authority. You do."

"Okay."

Griffing straightened up and looked at his watch. "It's twenty to four,
Flash. I want you to get up to the hut and do some interrogating. We
sent all the inmates left in the garage up there; take over and find out
what happened. If we're going to move in, I want to do it before
supper, while the men are in their cells. It doesn't give you much time."

It was a good hundred-yard run to the Quonset hut. He pushed open
the door and stepped into the foyer. It was pretty small—everything in
the hut was—and mobbed. About twenty inmates and probably that
many officers and staff members were packed in there. Everyone seemed
to be yelling at everyone else. It was like a train station scene in some
old movie, as the troops were shipping out to the front. Ted Reed was
in the middle, looking frantic.

Flash nodded at the nearest officer. The officer blew his whistle and
bellowed: "Ten-*shut!*" The inmates and officers drew quickly to attention. The staff workers seemed indecisive. The room was silent.

"Line the inmates against that wall," Flash called to an officer. "All staff members report to the staff room. Mr. Reed, stay with me. Let's go."

"They just got here," Reed said, hurrying over. "I—"

"How many do we have?" By twos, Flash counted quickly down the line of inmates. "Thirty-four. Is that it?"

"I don't know," Reed said. "All they told me was—"

"Okay." Flash looked at the officers. "Renderman—get on the phone and get me the head count on the garage crew today from the training officer. And for the hobby shop."

"Yes sir."

Flash turned to the inmates. "All inmates assigned to the garage crew step forward. Now!"

All of them stepped forward, their eyes straight ahead, their faces sober.

"None of you are from any other crews? Answer *yes* if you are." No one said anything.

"Step back," Flash said. "Who brought these men down?"

"I did," an officer said. "The Warden told me to."

"Are these all the men who were left in the garage?"

"As far as I know, sir."

"You didn't see the trouble, did you?"

"No sir."

Flash looked at Reed. "How many men do you have available right now?"

"I don't really know. I—"

"Find out."

Reed hesitated, then hurried toward the staff room.

Flash counted the officers; there were seven. "You two stay here with the inmates; get me a list of their names as fast as you can." He led the other five down the hall and ushered them into the staff room. He went in after them and closed the door.

"We have eight men here, counting myself," Reed said. "I don't know where the others are."

"That makes fifteen with the officers—no, sixteen counting Renderman, seventeen counting me," Flash said. "Have you got someone on the circuit in my office?"

"Well no, I haven't yet . . . this all happened so—"

Renderman pushed open the door. "There were forty-one in the garage, sir. Seventeen in the hobby shop."

"Here's my office key; get on the alert circuit and stay on it. Take another man as runner. Report to Griffing that it appears—appears, mind you—that there are twenty-four inmates in the hobby shop, seven from the garage, seventeen from the hobby crew. We'll give him the names as soon as we've got them."

"Yes sir."

Flash turned to the men crowded together in the staff room: Classification men, social workers, interviewers, guards. "We've got to find out very quickly what happened. I want each of you to take one inmate into a room and make it clear to him that you want information. Make it very, very clear. There are two guards being held by those men. We want information. We want it right now. Find out what happened, and how, who started it, who's running it. All we know is that some inmates from the garage took Delft with them to the hobby shop and are in there now, with both Delft and Cloninger. Find out if they're armed. Find out if anyone got hurt. Find out who's giving orders. If anyone starts talking, pump him dry and let me know as soon as he's finished. If he seems ripe but you can't get anything out of him, let me know. Reed—get these men in separate rooms; I'll send the inmates down."

Flash ran back to the foyer. "Have you got their names?"

"Right here, sir."

"Take it to my office and tell Renderman to get the Training Officer to check it against the garage roster. Tell him to use the phone and not tie up the circuit. Then have him get Griffing on the circuit and give him the names of the men who are *not* here; as far as we know they're the ones in the hobby shop."

"Yes sir."

"You ready?" Flash called down the hall.

Reed was standing in the hall. "Yes."

Flash faced the inmates lined against the wall. Most of them came to attention; a few seemed uncertain.

"Ten-*shut!*" an officer commanded.

"At ease," Flash said. "As of now, none of you are in trouble. There's been some trouble, but you were smart enough to stay out of it, so you're in good shape, all of you. But if you want to stay that way, you're going to have to answer some questions, and answer them honestly, and without any stalling. I'll charge any man who refuses to cooperate, and I'll do it good and hard. You are now under direct orders from the Warden, every one of you, to answer all questions put to you. I hope that's clear. It better be. All right, officer, send them down —fourteen of them. You stay here with the rest."

The guard ticked off the men at the head of the line, sending them down one at a time, about twenty feet apart. Reed directed them into rooms along the hall.

The tenth man in line was Walker, one of the dozen civil-rights Negroes they'd sent down from Raintree a couple of weeks ago, and the only one assigned to the garage. At least they'd been spared that; at least he'd managed to keep out of the mess.

Flash hurried down the hall into his secretary's office. Through the open door to his own office he saw Renderman and the other officer leaning over his desk, checking the rosters. "Get those names to Griffing as soon as you can," he said, and went back into the hall and stopped the inmate who was walking by and directed him into his secretary's office. *Welcinak*, his tab said; a big slope-shouldered, bullet-headed guy.

"Stand there, Welcinak, face me." He looked at his watch. It was four minutes to four. Flash sat on Harry's straight-backed chair, behind his small desk. A sheet of paper stuck up from the typewriter: this week's training survey, broken off in midsentence. "What are you in for, Welcinak?"

Welcinak stood with his feet outspread and his work cap clasped behind his back. He swallowed. His broad flat lips moved slowly, as if not wholly familiar with the shapes required of them. "Burglary, Warden. They give me three-to-five."

"How old are you?"

Again the slow, uncertain response. "Twenty-four, Warden."

"Where were you when the trouble started?"

Welcinak opened his mouth, then hesitated. He ran his tongue along his upper lip. "I was up front. You know, the front part, near the tool board."

"What were you doing there?"

"I was working. On Salmando's crew. We were working on the Plymouth Fury. It belongs to one of the guards. I think it was the points that—"

"Is Salmando here?"

"Yeah, he's here. Yeah, I saw him."

"Where did the trouble start?"

"I never saw no trouble, Warden. I was just working there, you know, and then . . . well, suddenly everybody was saying Delft wasn't there. That he was gone, and some of the guys too."

"Who was saying this?"

"I don't know . . . I mean, everybody was saying it."

"Did you see the men go? Or Delft?"

"No, I didn't see nothing."

"How did you know they were gone?"

"Like I said—everybody was just saying they were gone."

"What were they working on at that end—where the trouble was?"

"I didn't see no trouble, Warden. I didn't see nothing. Well—they were working on the garbage truck, I think."

"And they were the ones that left with Delft?"

"I don't know who those ones were, Warden. I didn't see anybody go anywhere. I just heard about it, when everybody started saying it."

"Who were the men working on the garbage truck?"

"I don't know. I mean, you get different assignments every day, you know—different crews and everything. I never keep track where—"

"What were they working on next to the garbage truck?"

He wrinkled his brow. He wet his lips. "The bus. You know—the Econoline."

"Come on." Flash took Welcinak back to the foyer. "He's finished," he told the officer. "Keep the finished ones separate." He approached the first inmate in line, stopping directly in front of him. "What was your assignment today in the garage? What were you working on?"

The inmate blinked. Flash waited impatiently. That was something all inmates learned, and that you learned to put up with: Don't answer too fast, don't open your trap before you figure out what kind of trouble you can get into. "I was working on the sedan, sir. The prison limousine. We were giving it a—"

"Okay."

Flash went down the line, like an officer inspecting ranks, taking one sideways step for each man, asking each the same brusque question. Two of the inmates said they'd been working on the Econoline. He responded to them exactly as he did to the others, with a single sideways step to the next man. Nobody said he was working on the garbage truck. When he reached the end of the line he swung about and asked the officer: "Hasn't anyone finished with any of the other men yet?"

"No sir."

He ran down to the first door and pushed it open. A Classification man sat facing a standing inmate across a desk.

"Are you getting anywhere?"

"Well, not exactly. He doesn't—"

"Come on," Flash said to the inmate. "You're finished; move on out." He sent him back to the foyer and waved for the first inmate in line

to go into the room. "Try this one for a while," Flash said to the Classification man and slammed the door.

He did the same at the next three doors. One of the two men
from the Econoline crew was now first in line. Flash opened Reed's
door and sent away the inmate he had been questioning. It was
Walker, the Negro.

"Get anything out of him?"

"No. He doesn't seem to really—"

"Okay. Look, it happened at the far end of the garage, the guys
working on the garbage truck. This man coming was right alongside
them; he must have seen something. Get it out of him."

He stepped into the hall and waved the inmate in.

He took care of the next three men and then sent the next one—
the other Econoline man—into his secretary's office and went in after
him. It was almost four fifteen; the inmates would be back in their
cells. He sat again on Harry's hard chair and stared at the inmate.
Sasher.

"What are you in for, Sasher? What's your sentence?"

Sasher thought briefly before answering. "Bad checks, Warden."
His voice was brisk and clear, with a hint of ready cheerfulness.

"How old are you?"

"Twenty-six, Warden."

"What did you say you were working on today?"

"The Econoline, sir. We were giving it a—"

"What were they working on next to you?"

"The limousine, sir."

"And on the other side?"

"I think it was the garbage truck, sir," he answered brightly after
a brief hesitation.

"Who was working on it?"

"I don't remember exactly. I wasn't paying too much attention, sir,
and—"

"Is that where the trouble started, with the guys working on the
garbage truck?"

Sasher lied pleasantly and earnestly. "I didn't see any trouble,
Warden. I didn't see anything."

"When did you realize that—"

The door from his own office opened. "The Warden wants you on
the circuit," Renderman said.

"Stay with this fellow." Flash went into his office and bent over the
intercom. "Fleishman here."

"Have you got anything yet?" Griffing asked, his words broken by the static.

"Not really. Can you give me a few more minutes. We might have—"

"I think you'd better get back here."

"Is anything happening?"

"No—it's quiet. But you get up here."

"Okay." He straightened up. "Stay on the circuit," he told the officer. "Reed'll be in charge here; I'll send him down."

In the secretary's room, Renderman and Sasher, both standing, were eying each other silently. "Come outside," Flash told Renderman. They went into the hall, Renderman closing the door. "He was working next to where it started," Flash said. "He saw something. Get what you can out of him and pass it on to Reed."

Flash hurried down to Reed's office and pushed open the door. Reed and the inmate turned abruptly, startled. "I'll be in the Warden's office," Flash said. "You're in charge. Move down to my office so you can stay near the circuit. Find out what this fellow knows and then check with all the others. I want a report in five minutes—ten at the latest."

He ran again, the hundred yards or whatever it was, and was puffing (just a bit, hardly noticeable) when he stepped into the shock of the air conditioning.

Griffing was standing next to his desk, his hands behind his back. "I'm going up there," he said. "We're holding off supper till five."

"Are you going to move in on them?"

"It's either now or after supper. We can't keep those men in their cells without food too long."

"Did you get the names?"

Griffing handed him a sheet of paper.

Flash looked down the list, written in Griffing's small, almost European handwriting. "Orninski," he said.

Griffing shrugged. "Have you seen the hobby shop roster?"

"Who's in there?"

"Verdun."

"Oh Christ, yes. Do you think they pulled it together?"

"It's possible, I guess. You didn't find out if anyone was armed, did you?"

"I didn't have time to find out much of anything. It doesn't seem like there was much trouble, though. It evidently happened very quickly—quietly too. It must have been pretty well planned out."

"Maybe there was a gun then," Griffing said. "I can't see Delft going along quietly otherwise."

"They might have had knives. Tools. Delft's not crazy."

"Is Orninski?"

"Dowler seems to think so," Flash said. "And his psychiatric report seems pretty shaky; I checked it out after that trouble in the shoeshop."

"What do you think he'd do if we sent a dozen officers charging in there?"

"I don't know," Flash said.

"What if we used the gas? What do you think he'd do? Or Verdun, for that matter. Or whoever's running the show."

"I'd like to know why they're in there before we do anything, Griff. Why don't you stay here and let Dowler and me go in. We'll see how far we get and then—"

"If I were Delft or Cloninger, I think I'd rather the Warden thought I was important enough to come himself. You stay here; we'll keep in touch."

"Let me come too," Flash said. "If Dowler goes in with you, there should be someone else around. I'll take the walkie-talkie."

"All right. Meet me up there."

Griffing left and Flash got the two walkie-talkie units from the Warden's closet. He put the shoulder strap of one over his head and went into the staff office and gave the other one to Bostick. "I'm going up there," he told him. "Griffing and Dowler are there too. Get us on this if you need us."

He ran up the hill, hoping to catch Griffing, but didn't. As he rounded the rear corner of the Cell Block he saw Griffing and Dowler talking together just outside the big open wall of the garage. The garbage truck, the Econoline, the limousine and the Plymouth were still lined up inside the garage. A dozen or so officers stood in a cluster between the garbage truck and the Econoline. Other officers were deployed about in pairs, in the little alleyway between the garage and the storage shed, behind the Post Four booth, in the powerhouse entrance, behind the powerhouse. The hobby shop stood by itself, a small cinderblock building with four small windows, all on this side. The windows were closed, and from this distance seemed opaque. Scattered on the ground in front of the shop, out to a distance of thirty or forty feet, were chunks and small blocks of wood.

Flash went up to Griffing. "Are you going over now?"

"Yes, the two of us. The officers will cover."

Flash switched on the walkie-talkie and held it to his mouth. "Bostick —any word from Reed?"

There was no answer.

"Bostick! Are you there? Do you have any word from Reed?"

There was no answer.

"Shit," Flash said.

"Let's get going," Griffing said. He looked at Dowler. "Do you think you should take that pistol with you?"

"If you let me go alone, I'll leave it behind."

"All right," Griffing said. "But keep it out of sight. Flash, you stay back now; I don't want the three of us together."

"Why don't you take the megaphone," Flash said. "You won't have to go so close."

"That electronic thing, you mean? You can hear it all over kingdom come."

"Take a regular one."

"It still carries too far. Keep those two officers with the rifles out of sight."

"Do I have emergency fire authority?"

"There shouldn't be any need for it."

"I'm not going to let them pull you in."

"I may want to go in," Griffing said.

"Signal me then."

"All right," Griffing said. He and Dowler started walking steadily, in step, across the dry, rutted ground. The hobby shop was perhaps seventy yards away. Griffing, taller and narrower than Dowler, walked somewhat stiffly, his arms at his sides. Dowler swayed; his shoulders sloped alternately with each step and his short, thick arms swung with a kind of powerful looseness.

Flash motioned inside the garage to the two officers with rifles. "Stand there," he said, pointing to a spot in the sawdust alongside the garbage truck. The men held the rifles loosely in their right hands, the barrels resting on their left forearms, muzzles down. "Keep the safety on."

Griffing and Dowler halted about twenty yards from the hobby shop. Griffing cupped his hands at his mouth, bunching his gray suit jacket across his shoulder blades. "This is the Warden—give me your attention!" He did not yell, but Flash heard him clearly. "It is my duty to warn you that you may face very serious charges for this disturbance. For your own benefit, I am ordering you to release the officers and come out quietly and in good order." He dropped his hands deliberately to his sides. He waited, then raised them again. "I will give you one minute to obey this order. If you fail to do so, I shall declare this to be an insurrection and act accordingly."

Griffing waited, his hands at his sides, his jacket hanging smoothly across the back. There was no movement at the windows. The door remained closed. Griffing folded his arms across his chest. Dowler shifted his weight from one foot to the other.

"Bostick here—calling Warden Fleishman."

Flash lifted the walkie-talkie to his mouth. "Go ahead."

". . . Bostick here—calling Warden Fleishman."

"Go ahead! Fleishman here! Go ahead, Bostick!"

"Come in, Warden Fleishman. Bostick calling Warden Fleishman . . ."

"Shit," Flash said, letting the walkie-talkie drop. It dangled at his waist from the strap.

"The time is up," Griffing called. "Are you coming out?"

There was no reply.

"I'm coming in," Griffing called. He and Dowler began walking slowly toward the door.

"Be ready," Flash said over his shoulder.

When Griffing and Dowler were about ten yards from the building a window opened noisily from the bottom, with no face showing, no hands. Griffing and Dowler stopped short, Dowler's right hand jerking to his pocket, hovering over it, poised.

"Get out here," Flash said without looking around. "Keep your weapons down."

The officers moved forward quickly, one on each side of him.

"Watch that open window," Flash said.

"Are you coming out?" Griffing called.

Something flew out the open window. The two officers swung up their rifles.

"Down!" Flash yelled.

The object landed about ten feet to Griffing's right and bounced twice, erratically. It looked like a piece of two-by-four, about a foot long. The window remained open; nothing else came out.

Dowler went over and picked up the wood. He examined it, turning it over, then yanked something off it, a piece of paper, and handed it to Griffing. Griffing held it, staring at it. Dowler stared too. Griffing put it in his pocket. "If you want to talk, you can talk to me," he called toward the shop. "I'm coming in."

He started for the door again, with Dowler on his right. A man's face appeared at the open window. The two officers jerked up their weapons.

"Get them down," Flash said.

It was Cloninger. Only his face showed, his head, just over the sill. He must have been kneeling on the floor. "Don't come in!" he shouted.

Griffing said something that Flash couldn't hear.

"Stay away!" Cloninger yelled. "Do what they say!" Abruptly his face disappeared.

Griffing, still looking at the window, did not move.

"Bostick here—calling Warden Fleishman. Come in, Warden Fleishman."

"Fleishman here!" Flash screamed. "Fleishman here! Go ahead!"

"Warden Fleishman—come in please. Bostick calling."

Flash pulled the strap over his head and threw the thing to the ground.

"Bostick calling Warden Fleishman—come in please."

He kicked it aside.

Griffing was hunched close to Dowler, talking. He turned and faced the window again. "I want assurance that my men are safe," he said loudly. "I want assurance that they haven't been harmed, and won't be harmed." He waited. "If I don't have that immediately, I'm coming in."

Cloninger's face reappeared. "We're all right," he called, his voice shrill. "Do what they say." His face disappeared.

After a moment, Griffing looked at Dowler. Neither seemed to speak. Griffing turned sharply and started walking back to the garage.

"Stay alert," Flash said to the two officers.

Dowler remained where he was, his eyes on the building, until Griffing was most of the way back, then started back himself.

"Okay—inside," Flash told the officers.

Griffing approached, walking steadily, his eyes down.

"What is it?" Flash said.

Griffing came up to him. He closed one eye, his left, as he had a habit of doing, to fix you somewhat solemnly with the other. "They want to speak to Manson," he said.

"What?"

"They want to speak to Manson," he said in the same flat tone.

□

Manson—surprisingly, considering it was Manson—was where he was supposed to be, in the Administration Building, having reported there after returning his men to their cells. While they waited for him to get up the hill, Flash ran over to Post Four to get Bostick on the circuit.

"What were you calling me for?"

"Oh, there you are! I was trying to get you on the walkie-talkie before."

"I know. What did you want?"

"I just wanted to check and see if it was working."

"Well, it's not. Use the circuit. Have you heard anything from Reed?"

"No sir. And I haven't been able to locate Mr. Kale. He's somewhere in town but I can't find out where."

"I didn't know you were looking for him."

"The Warden asked me to, sir. I'll keep trying."

Flash rejoined Griffing and Dowler in front of the garage. It was six minutes to five. A few moments later they saw Manson coming, bumbling his long, ungainly body over the rock-hard ground. His shoulders were narrower than his waist and hips; he vaguely reminded one of an ostrich. As he ran he glanced furtively from side to side, as if fearful of ambushes. He stumbled in a rut a few feet from them and staggered up to the Warden. He made a clumsy, rather indecisive salute. He seemed unable to decide whether the gravity of the situation made the salute mandatory or ludicrous. He was breathless and bug-eyed, his face flushed, his bulbous, lopsided nose a glossy purplish-red.

"Yes, sir," he gasped. "You—you wanted me, sir . . . ?"

Griffing stared at him wordlessly. His gaze was cool and rather steely. He coughed quietly, glanced at Flash, then studied Manson's steaming face. "Perhaps you'd better catch your breath first," he said. "Wait over there."

Manson seemed about to say something, then wheeled about and scurried into the garage to join the officers alongside the garbage truck.

"What do you think?" Griffing said after a moment of silence.

Flash cleared his throat. "I admit to certain doubts."

Again Griffing was silent. He looked over at the hobby shop and then, for some reason, up at the sky. Some clouds had formed, but the sun was still bright. "Why on earth do they want *him?*" Griffing said.

"Verdun and Orninski might both have it in for him—after that business in the shoeshop," Flash said.

"Do you think they want to take him and let one of the others go?"

"If that's the case . . ."

Griffing was displeased. He said nothing, didn't even frown, but you could tell by the tightening of his jaw muscles.

"Flash doesn't think much of Manson," Dowler said.

"What do you think, Jeff?"

"I don't know . . . He's Flash's man."

"I know who's man he is. I'm asking you if you think I should send him in."

"I can think of men I'd rather send," Dowler said, somewhat grumpily. "But if that's who they—"

"The man's frightened out of his wits," Griffing said. "And he doesn't even know what we want him to do yet."

"Let's not send anybody then," Dowler said. "Let's just tell them to get the hell out, and if they don't—"

"Why should they ask for him in the first place?"

Neither Flash nor Dowler answered right away. Finally Flash said, "Maybe they just want an intermediary—someone to bring out a message to you."

"If they've got anything to say to me, why can't they just say it?" Griffing looked at his watch. "It's almost five—we'd better tell them to hold off a while longer on supper." He noticed the walkie-talkie on the ground, about twenty feet off to the side, where Flash had kicked it. "What's it doing there?" he demanded.

"It's not working too well, I'm afraid."

"Didn't you check it out first?"

"I guess I didn't. I was in a rush to—"

"Officer!"

"Yes sir."

"Get on the phone in the garage and tell Bostick to hold off supper call until he hears from me."

"Yes sir."

"Manson!"

Manson hustled over. He was breathing easier now but looked, if anything, more harried. "Yes sir."

"Do you know what's going on here, Manson?"

"No sir. I was just—"

"There are twenty-four inmates in there, most from the hobby shop, some from the garage." He paused. "They're holding Delft and Cloninger hostage."

Manson's eyes wavered. He inhaled noisily.

"The inmates evidently have something they want to discuss," Griffing went on. "I don't know what, because they won't talk to me." He paused again. "They said they'll only talk to you."

It was a moment before Manson spoke. "I—don't understand . . ."

"Neither do I, frankly," Griffing said. "But I'd like you to go over and see what they have to say."

Manson's lower lip drooped. He turned his head slowly to gaze at the

hobby shop. Then, again slowly, almost cautiously, he returned his eyes
to Griffing.

"Are you willing to go over?"

Manson hesitated.

"I think we're out of our bloody minds," Flash said. "Sending this
man in . . ."

"What would you suggest?"

"Anything. Let me go. Maybe they'll talk to me."

"They didn't ask for you."

"We'll tell them Manson's not here. We can say he went home, that
he fell down a well, that we can't find him."

"I'm sure they saw him coming." Griffing looked at Manson. "What
do you say?"

Manson swallowed. "I—don't know . . ."

"I can go with him," Dowler said.

"I don't think so," Griffing said.

"They asked for *me*?" Manson inquired, leaning forward a little.
"Yes. Alone."

"Well I—what would I do? I mean—what am I supposed to say?"

"You don't have to say anything. Just find out what they want, what
the trouble is, what's happening with Delft and Cloninger. Just see
what they have to say and then come out."

"Suppose they won't let me come out?"

"They don't need any more hostages."

"Who's in there, did you say?"

"I told you; twenty-four inmates, as far as we know." Griffing remained silent a moment. "We're not certain, but we think the leader
is either Orninski or Verdun, or possibly both. At least that's our
guess."

"*They're* in there?"

"It appears so."

Manson looked at Flash, then faced Griffing again. "They got it in
for me—those two. We had that trouble that time."

"Will you go or won't you, for God's sake? We've got two officers
hostage in there and a thousand men clamoring for supper. We can't
stand here all night talking."

"Go ahead," Dowler said. "You'll be all right."

"You don't have to, of course," Griffing said curtly. "I won't force
you."

"He's an officer here," Dowler said. "He goddamn well better."

"Okay," said Manson quietly.

"You're sure now?"

"Yes . . ."

"All right. I'd like you to get inside if you can. If they insist on talking through the window you'll have to go along, but I'd rather you got a look around. At any rate, keep your eyes open. Listen to what they say, make no promises and come right out. Do you have something to write with?"

Manson blinked, as if not quite comprehending, and then began fumbling through his pockets.

"Here," Flash said.

Manson held the pen and notebook in his hand like a schoolboy, like a kid without pockets.

"Go ahead," Griffing said. "If you get inside and any trouble starts, we'll move right in."

"What kind of trouble?"

"Any kind. We'll be ready to move in."

Manson nodded without much show of conviction.

"Go on now. And walk like you mean it. Don't go crawling up there."

"Yes sir. All right." Manson turned, somewhat tentatively, and started walking toward the hobby shop. He tried to generate a brisk pace but failed. He moved jerkily.

Griffing moved a few steps forward and cupped his hands. *"Here he comes!"*

Before Manson got halfway across a cry went up from the hobby shop—a hoot, a howl, derisive, mocking. Manson faltered, then stopped. Without shifting his feet he twisted around to look imploringly back at Griffing.

"What the hell's wrong now?" Griffing muttered.

"Christ, I don't know," Flash said.

Dowler waved Manson on with an angry push of his arm.

Manson started forward again, hesitantly. The cry came again, more drawn out this time, a sort of throaty hillbilly yelp. Before it stopped other cries rang out. It sounded like a dozen men—none of them visible —jeering and howling inside the shop, like a barnyard cacophony.

"No!" somebody shouted over the other noises. *"Noooooooo—"*

Manson stopped, his head and shoulders pulling back, as if unable to move against the force of the cries, which were growing even louder and more raucous.

Through the open window a piece of wood sailed out, turning over and over in flight. It landed a few feet from Manson. The three other windows were shoved up and more wood flew out. Manson ducked; one piece struck his upraised arm and seemed to bounce off his shoulder. He lurched about and bolted for the garage.

They rushed forward to meet him. Blood was running from a cut over his eye; it trickled down both sides of his nose. He still held the pen and notebook in his hand. "They don't want me!" he blurted. He seemed almost crazed with relief. "They don't want me!"

Griffing grabbed his shoulders and held him—he was shaking—to look at the gash. "Take him to the infirmary," he told an officer. The officer gave Manson a handkerchief and started to lead him away, stooped over, stumbling, his hand pressing the handkerchief against his brow in a stylized posture of injury and grief.

Griffing put his hands on his hips and looked across as the hobby shop. The barrage had stopped but the windows were still open. The wood, mostly rough ends from lumber cuttings, lay about on the dry ground. "What in *hell* is going on?" Griffing said.

Neither Flash nor Dowler answered.

Griffing pulled out the crumpled note and read it again. He shrugged in disgust.

Flash leaned over to peek. Griffing shoved the paper at him. He seemed glad to get rid of it.

"Well," Flash said, "they certainly did a neat job of—Good Christ: they don't want *Manson!*"

13

Well, Jesus Christ, they just couldn't believe it. They really couldn't. You could see that even Orninski—well, he was just buffaloed. And then Preston, who was crouching down next to Orninski at the window, said, "What the fuck!—it's *Manson!*"

Orninski himself didn't say anything at all. He just kept watching Manson coming across. But you knew he was thinking, because Orninski was always thinking. So when Manson got close enough Orninski just crouched up a little tighter and put his mouth right over the window sill and let out this real crazy yell.

And leave it to Orninski, it was the right thing to do. Because then naturally the other guys, when they heard this, they figured everything must be okay, and not real trouble, so they just joined right in, everybody hooting and hollering to beat the band, having a hell of a time giving old Manson the bird.

Because by this time they'd been holed up there a coupla hours already, and some were beginning maybe to have a few second thoughts, and get a little cold feet. And something like that, just letting loose and laying into old Manson, who everybody agreed was a shit—well, it was just what they needed. It took the edge off, and you could see everybody felt better after.

And then Orninski hauled off and tossed out this piece of wood. And then everybody just started falling all over theirselves to grab a piece too and get into the act, and they really got a good laugh out of it, seeing Manson running off howling like a big-assed bird.

"I got him!" Ferrucio yelled. "It was my piece got him!"

A coupla other guys argued, of course, that it was *their* piece that got him, and you could really see everybody was suddenly feeling pretty lively, and full of oats.

The main thing, of course, was that it showed the Warden he couldn't pull any fast ones, or whatever the hell he was trying to pull, sending that goddamn Manson in like that.

After a while, though, the guys starting bitching and grumbling again about it being way past suppertime and they were starving to death. And Fledgett said how Orninski should've put that in the note too, about their food, and not talking to anybody until they got it.

"What the hell am I supposed to throw out, for Christ's sake—a whole book? Besides," Orninski said, sort of motioning over to Delft and the other one, "they ain't eating either. So don't you worry. We'll get plenty of chow when we want it."

"I want it now," Preston said. "I'm hungry, man. I could eat a fucking horse."

"All right then," Orninski said, very cool. "I'll see you get one when the time comes, being that's what you especially want."

Of course Verdun and the others from the hobby shop, they didn't say nothing—about being hungry or anything else. They just sort of sat clumped together on the floor against the wall without saying a word but just watching Orninski, not taking their eyes off him for even a second.

Actually, if Mel'd been handling the thing, he wouldn't have come to the goddamn hobby shop in the first place. He wouldn't have come —or gone—anywhere. If it'd been up to him, the whole damn thing would've never started in the first place, because let's face it, when you dragged the goddamn Warden in, you dragged in trouble.

That was what he tried to tell Orninski before it all started, that maybe there was some other way they could handle it.

"It won't work no other way," Orninski said then. "The guy, you know, he thinks he's hot shit. He ain't gonna listen to no other way."

And of course he was probably right, but still Mel didn't like it. He just didn't, that's all.

But still, like Orninski said, the important thing was to show them up front right now, at the beginning, that they couldn't pull this kind of stuff, because if they kept it up there'd be real trouble. Because this guy Walker, you could just see he thought he was one slick son of a bitch. And instead of just putting him in the kitchen or on cleanup with the rest of the spades, they had to go assign him to the goddamn garage, which they never assigned any kind of nigger to before. And if that wasn't bad enough, everybody started saying they were gonna put the son of a bitch in *charge* of one of the crews.

That's when Orninski said they had to do something, before it went any further. After all, he said, white guys got their rights too.

Now Mel's feeling was it didn't bother him any that this nigger was a mechanic, or even a good one—although Mel had his doubts about that too. But anyhow, that didn't bother him. What bothered him was why the hell did they have to send him down here to take away jobs from the white guys. That's what he wanted to know—whose goddamn great idea was that? According to Orninski, the word was that it was the Fish Man's, because he was the guy that assigned guys to jobs anyhow, and because of how the Jews always stick up for the niggers against the white man anyhow. Well, it wouldn't surprise Mel at all. That was just the kind of thing Fleishman would dream up, some goddamn brilliant idea to screw everything up instead of just leaving things the way the hell they are.

After all, didn't they have a garage up at Raintree too? Didn't they have trucks up there to take care of, and cars? So why couldn't the guy just be sent up there, where the hell he belonged? It didn't take any great brains to figure that out, did it? It was just common sense, for Christ's sake. And if he was so goddamn good, well let him teach some of those jazzbos up there how to hold a goddamn wrench then, because let's face it, Mel hadn't yet met a nigger that knew which end went in your hand.

Naturally, Orninski agreed. Because the real problem, he said, was if they let this one guy move in without doing anything, before they knew it the whole goddamn prison would be crawling with them, and every white guy in the place would be fighting off fifty niggers just to hold onto his job. And let's face it, Raintree was nothing more than a goddamn jungle. Everybody knew that. There weren't *that* many niggers in the state, but for Christ's sake they were always getting picked up for one goddamn thing or another, taking the needle in the arm or cutting up their buddies or something, shooting their broads, so naturally Raintree was one very crowded place, with four or five guys in one cell, and like everybody said just a goddamn jungle. What else could you expect when you crowded that many niggers together, especially the kind that got sent to prison? The guys said that up there at Raintree the screws had to actually walk back to back so they could watch everywhere at once, or they'd get a spoon between their shoulder blades the first time they blinked. And the screws themselves, they said, were either all gimpies or else a little stir-bugs too, because who the hell in his right mind would want to work in a place like that? Or else they were the kind that got a big charge out of knuckling guys up, which they naturally got plenty of chance to do, because those niggers, half of them were crazy anyhow, hopheads and muggers and pimps and everything, so things got pretty hot some-times. For rec periods up there, the guys said, the screws staged razor fights between the cons, which maybe was supposed to be a joke, but maybe not.

And so what would happen if they let Walker move in, Orninski said, was that the people whose brilliant idea this was would start bringing them in by the frigging truckload. Soon you'd be getting every nigger in the state that was being sent away, plus all the hopheads and gorillas already up at Raintree, getting their Jew lawyers pulling strings to get them sent down here, and before you knew it you'd have three and four goddamn cons in one cell here too, half of them big buck nig-gers with razors in the sole of their shoes.

And then what was to stop them from sending white guys up *there?* Christ, can you imagine what the hell that would mean, with the things that went on in that place?

So everybody agreed, something had to be done. Especially with this guy Walker being such a wise guy. Not that he said much, because he didn't. But you could tell from the way he looked, from the way he walked even. You could just see him out on the streets somewhere, strutting around in a goddamn straw hat and a yellow striped suit with about six purple rings on his fingers, licking his chops over all the white meat that went by.

But still Mel didn't like the idea of working him over. He never in his life set out to hurt anyone like that, ganging up on some guy and pounding the shit out of him. It could really get rough, cutting up a guy's face, giving it to him in the nuts and everything, and Mel just didn't have the stomach for it. Just a few weeks ago some guy got it out on the athletic field, a guy named Coughlin, that everybody said was one of the wolves. Suddenly a whole bunch of guys were all around him, without a screw near enough to stop them, and everybody else running over to see what was going on, which made it even harder for the screws to do anything. By the time they finally broke it up this guy Coughlin was really a mess. Some of the guys even used bats. Mel saw him, real close up, when they carried him away. It made him sick, it really did. Even thinking about it now make his skin creep.

So he tried to tell Orninski that maybe there was some other way they could take care of Walker. Maybe just give him the cold shoulder or something, or just threaten him. But Orninski said no, if they didn't want half the goddamn niggers in the state moving in, they had to do it his way. Or else one day they'd wake up and find some big black bastard in a fancy uniform standing over them saying, *Get yoah ass movin', white boy, I'se in charge now.*

And when Mel said he still didn't really like the idea too much, Orninski said, all right, he was tired of hearing it. "If that's the way you see it," he said, "I'll tell you what. We'll try it your way."

So what Orninski suggested was for Mel to go up to Delft and say he thought he oughta be the next crew head—not saying anything about Walker, but just asking for it himself. Because this guy named Pettibon that was a crew head now was getting very short and would be out in a few weeks, and that was the deal everybody said Walker was gonna get. Then if Delft said no, Mel was supposed to explain, sort of privately, how all the guys felt about Walker, him being a nigger and everything, and just sort of let on how it might make trouble.

"Go ahead," Orninski said. "Talk to Delft. See how it goes."

Actually, Mel wasn't really crazy about this idea either. Sure, he probably deserved to be head as much as anybody, because as far as he could see—and Orninski agreed—there wasn't any better mechanic around except maybe Salmando, who already was a head. But let's face it, Mel was used to being screwed out of things he deserved. What he figured would happen, before Walker even showed up, was that Delft would just hand it to some buddy of his, some suck-ass that didn't know an exhaust pipe from an ignition key. After all, wasn't that what always happened? So why make a big stink?

And then too, he didn't like the idea of saying anything to Delft about maybe there being trouble, because then if there *was* trouble, Mel would be the first guy blamed.

But shit, he was backed into a goddamn corner. So he said okay, he'd try it. What the hell else could he say?

So yesterday afternoon he kept an eye out to get Delft alone, without a lot of guys around. A little after two he saw him sitting at his desk having a smoke. Mel left what he was working on, which was tightening up the bumper that rattled on a Galaxie that belonged to one of the guards, and went up front, passing Orninski on the way, who gave him a kind of hard, squinty look.

"Yeah?" Delft bellowed, swinging around that great big horse head of his. He was sitting with his back to the garage, making believe he was looking over some papers, but actually just taking a break. "What is it? What's the matter?"

Mel came right up close against the desk and bent over so he could keep his voice down. But when he got up close like that, practically nose to nose with this goddamn overgrown slob who, let's face it, was out to get him from the beginning, he had a little trouble keeping straight just what the hell he was supposed to say. He'd gone over it six thousand times in his mind and practically memorized it, but everything now just suddenly left him, and there he was, practically breathing into Delft's face, zeroing right in on him, and he couldn't think of a single goddamn thing to say, not even hello.

"For Christ's sake, stop leaning all over me!" Delft shouted, loud as hell. He yanked his head back, and just stared at Mel like he was very pissed off at him for coming over and ruining his goddamn break. "Well—what is it? What do you want?"

Mel tried to clear his throat and then said, practically in a whisper, "I wanted to say something to you—private . . ." He was still leaning over with his shoulders hunched up.

Delft kept his head pulled back and just looked at him. He had one hand on his knee. The other hand, which held the cigarette, was on the desk. The cigarette seemed to be smoking like a goddamn volcano, and it looked very skinny in Delft's fingers because he had a hand like a goddamn monster.

"Well, what it was," Mel went on, a little faster now but still very low, talking out of the side of his mouth in a kind of confidential way, "was, well, that open crew . . . I mean, what I was wondering was, you know, whether, well, maybe there'd be some chance, you know, with that open crew and everything, of maybe, well, getting it . . ."

"What the hell are you talking about?" Delft yelled. "What open crew? We ain't got any open crews."

Mel swallowed and leaned even closer, talking under his breath. He was sweating like a pig now. "You know. The crew Pettibon got. I mean, he's going soon. That crew."

"You wanna work on that crew?" Delft said, still screaming like a goddamn bull. "What do you mean, for Christ's sake? You can't just work on one crew."

Delft had a very loud voice anyhow, but by now he was practically roaring. Mel felt this real itch to look around, to see if everybody was watching, but he fought it off. He knew they were anyhow.

"I don't wanna be *on* it," he said, straining to keep his voice down.

Delft still had his head pulled back and he was looking at Mel now like he was standing on his goddamn foot or something. "What I mean is—well, what I thought was I could maybe, you know, be *head* of it. You know—*run* it. I mean, I got a lot of experience on the outside and—"

"What's that? What?"

Mel drew in his breath between his teeth. "I *said* I wanted maybe to be *head* of it."

"What the hell are you talking about, boy? You crazy or something? What the hell you bothering me for?"

Well, shit, how can you explain anything to a guy like that. Mel was ready, he really was, just to chuck the whole thing. He just wanted to get out, get away. He just wanted to go somewhere where not a single guy in the whole frigging world could ever find him. Only now Delft for some reason got all worked up and started screaming like a goddamn maniac. He just wouldn't let Mel go. He just sat there at his goddamn desk with his great big sloppy gut hanging down between his knees, this goddamn baboon, yelling his head off at him in front of everybody.

Finally Mel got away. He just kind of stumbled back to the goddamn Galaxie, not looking at anybody, his eyes all fuzzy and funny anyhow so he could hardly see where he was going, and right away started working and didn't even look up to see if anyone was watching him, although he could feel their eyes. He worked like that for a long time, without looking up. Not a soul came near him. All those things Delft said really sank in now and he was so goddamn angry he could hardly see to keep the wrench on the nut. He could have just killed Delft, he just wanted one chance to get at that fucking slob without his fucking uniform on. He'd kill him. His hands were shaking he was so angry.

Then he saw somebody's legs right next to him. He kept bent down working on the bumper and didn't look up. But the guy didn't go away. Finally Mel looked up and saw it was Orninski, but didn't say anything. Orninski didn't either. They just sort of looked at each other for a coupla seconds, and then Mel shrugged and went back to working. His eyes were still all fuzzy.

"Didn't turn out so hot, heh?"

"No," Mel said. He waited a little, because his voice sounded funny. He swallowed. "It didn't . . ."

"I guess we're gonna have to do it like I said then."

Mel shrugged without looking up. He kept working at the same goddamn nut and bolt he'd already tightened and loosened about three hundred times.

"Well, whatd'ya say, Mel? I mean, I gotta know—you agree or you don't agree?"

"I agree," Mel said.

"I figured you would," Orninski said. "Unless you got some more ideas you wanna try . . ."

"No," Mel said.

"Okay then," Orninski said. "We're all set then."

And so today, this morning, Orninski passed word around that after lunch they were gonna take care of it. The way Orninski set it up, it all depended on who worked at the far end today. Well, it turned out that neither Orninski or Mel got there, but Walker did, to work on the garbage truck. That was perfect, because they needed Walker at that end, and this way he'd already be there.

Mel got put on the Econoline and Orninski on the prison sedan. Orninski then came over and asked Mel what part he wanted to do —take care of Walker or help keep Delft busy and out of the way. With the other guys, Orninski said, he just told them what to do. With Mel, being he was a friend, he was giving him a choice.

Actually, the only thing Mel wanted was to stay out of it. Only he couldn't. So he just said he appreciated having the choice, and could he think about it a bit?

"There ain't time," Orninski said. "We gotta get set up. We gotta know."

"Oh," Mel said.

"Come on, Mel. What's it gonna be?"

"I'll keep Delft busy."

"That's what you wanna do?"

"Yeah. Just tell me how I'm supposed to do it."

"Okay," Orninski said. "I'll tell you."

So this afternoon, a little before three, Mel got the signal from Orninski. The signal was just Orninski nodding to him. Mel left the Econoline then, and started up front. Orninski, who was working on the sedan, starting moving in the other direction, toward the garbage truck at the far end, where Walker was. It all had to be timed just right, and so Mel was a little nervous, and tight in the stomach. Orninski didn't look nervous at all. You could see he was hopped up, but not nervous, just anxious to get going. He had a kind of excited look in his eyes. It wasn't like any look Mel ever seen in his eyes before.

Mel walked along the open side of the garage, out on the ground a few feet but still under the shadow of the roof. It was hot as hell, really blistering, and just being *near* the sun out there you could feel how hot it was, like the middle of the goddamn summer. He went past the sedan and then came to the guard's Fury that was being worked on by Salmando's crew. The Fury was at the front of the garage, right near Delft's little desk. Lamperra was talking to Delft, like he was supposed to, and laying in the sawdust under the front end of the Fury was Welcinak, with his legs stuck way out. Mel walked into his legs and fell down.

Welcinak scrambled out from under the car and jumped to his feet. Mel jumped up too.

"Watch where you're going!" Welcinak yelled.

"Keep your goddamn feet out of the way!" Mel yelled back.

"I'll knock your fucking head off!" Welcinak said. "You talk to me like that—"

"Hey—what's going on?" Delft shouted.

Mel didn't look around but kept his eyes on Welcinak. Welcinak was built very solid and strong, and a lot heavier than Mel, which was why Orninski picked him, so it'd look all right that Mel acted scared.

"You son of a bitch!" Welcinak said, and let go with a right that missed Mel by a good foot. He wasn't really too bright, Welcinak.

"*Hey—*" Delft said.

Welcinak swung again and Mel ducked under it and then, like he was really scared, turned to run. He was supposed to run outside, around the side wall there, with Welcinak chasing him like he was gonna beat shit out of him. Then Mel was supposed to keep dodging around out there, with Welcinak chasing him and Delft chasing the both of them, finally letting Welcinak catch him so they could scramble around a bit and put on a good show. The main thing was just keeping Delft busy at that end while Orninski and the others were taking care of Walker around the corner at the other end, in the little alley between the garage and the storage shed.

Only Delft, instead of heading right at them from his desk, for some goddamn reason went out wide, out the open side of the garage to sort of circle in on them. So when Mel turned to run, he ran smack into him.

Delft went "*Ooooff!*" very loud, and before Mel could untangle himself, Delft grabbed his arm. Welcinak, who was about to tear after Mel, was just as surprised as Mel, so for a second none of them

moved, Delft holding Mel's arm, and Mel just standing there, not knowing what the hell to do, and Welcinak just standing there too, with all
the guys in that part of the garage stopping work to watch, like they
were supposed to.

Then Mel tried to yank free, suddenly, to catch Delft by surprise.
But Delft had a hold on him like a goddamn vise. Mel yanked again,
then started jumping and stamping and twisting around, doing every
goddamn thing he could think of to get loose except actually hauling
off and slugging Delft. But Delft was like a frigging mountain. Mel
just couldn't budge him. Actually Delft wasn't even paying any attention to Mel, even with all his jumping around. He just kept this
hold on him with one hand and kept his eyes on Welcinak, who was
still kind of leaning forward, like he wanted to slug Mel.

Then Welcinak got a brainstorm. He jumped and grabbed Mel
around the neck—kind of hard, actually—and started scrambling
around with him, probably figuring Delft would have to let go of Mel
to get them apart, and then Mel could run out, like he was supposed
to. Only Delft didn't let go. He just put his free hand on Welcinak's
chest and shoved. And Christ, Welcinak, who was supposed to be so
strong and everything, just went sailing backwards with his arms flying out. He bounced off the fender of the Fury and landed on his ass
in the sawdust.

"And stay there!" Delft said to Welcinak. "Stay right there!"

And Welcinak did. He stayed right there.

Mel couldn't think of anything else to do, so he started jumping
around again, trying to get away, so Delft turned on him and yelled,
"Stop that! What the hell you afraid of now? He ain't gonna hurt
you!" Then Delft grabbed Mel's other arm and yanked him around in
front of him and shook him hard and said, "Stop it now! Stop it!"
because Mel was still sort of squirming around, although actually he
didn't have his heart in it anymore, the way everything had got so
fucked up.

All this happened very fast, maybe thirty seconds altogether.
They were supposed to keep Delft busy at least a few minutes. Maybe,
Mel hoped, Orninski had enough sense to wait and make sure everything went right with Delft before trying anything with Walker. He
was just dying to look up there and see, although naturally he didn't,
but the funny thing was just when Mel was *thinking* of looking,
Delft *did* look.

"Hey—" Delft said. And then, a lot louder: "*HEY!*" He let go of

Mel and shoved past him and headed for the far end. *"Hey! What's going on? Get back in there!"*

For a second Mel just went blank. He couldn't think of a goddamn thing. Then Welcinak got up from the ground and Mel took a coupla steps like he was gonna run away, but then stopped because shit, Delft was barrel-assing toward the other end and not even looking.

Then Mel got a brainstorm. "C'mon!" he told Welcinak, and ran after Delft, who was practically at the other end already. Welcinak tore after him and Mel ran as fast as he could after Delft, both of them yelling their goddamn heads off. Delft swung around and Mel cut into the garage then, between the Econoline and the limousine, dodging the guys that were standing there watching. He hoped maybe Delft would chase them in there and then chase them all the way up front again and then outside and around that wall, where they were supposed to be in the first place. But Delft only yelled, "Cut that out or I'll have your ass!" and turned away and hustled around the wall at the far end and into the little blind alley there, between the garage and the storage shed.

Mel stopped short and Welcinak ran right into him, and for a coupla seconds the two of them just stood there, right on top of each other, alongside the Econoline. Everybody else in the garage was standing too, listening to hear what the hell was happening around in the alley. And something was happening all right, because you could hear Delft bellowing, *"What! Hey!—stop that!"* You could hear other voices too.

"Let's go," Welcinak said. "Let's get out there!"

Now why the hell he said a stupid thing like that, Mel just didn't know. Because shit, it was too late to do any good, and for Christ's sake, what was the point of getting in any deeper? But Welcinak said it very *definitely*, like it was an order, like it was something anybody with half a brain would know they *had* to do, and it must've been how he said it, because suddenly Mel was running again and Welcinak was running after him, yelling like he was gonna kill him. And then there they were, in that little blind alley there, and Christ it was a mess, a goddamn free-for-all.

And the first thing Mel saw, the first thing he really noticed in all that mess, was the goddamn nigger Walker, sort of ducking out from the middle of this whole bunch of guys swinging and punching and leaping around. And before Mel could even blink, the son of a bitch was gone, just moving like a goddamn cat right past Mel and back into the garage. He didn't have a mark on him. His goddamn shirt wasn't even mussed. He looked as cool as a goddamn guy out for a stroll.

Then Mel saw that the guy everybody was on top of was Delft, and suddenly Delft was down, right in the middle of all those guys—one had a wrench, Mel saw—and then Orninski, whose face was all red and swollen on one side, and bleeding around the mouth, said, "Okay —stop! Stop for Christ's sake!"

After a few more kicks and punches and stuff, with Orninski trying to pull the guys off, they stopped. Delft was just sitting on the ground, and his face looked like a goddamn pulp. It was way worse than Orninski's. It was really all cut up and there just seemed to be blood everywhere. And all this happened in maybe a coupla seconds. That really got Mel, how fast it happened.

"Keep him there," Orninski shouted at Preston, who had a goddamn knife in his hand. "Stick it right in his gut if he makes a move."

Preston bent over and put the goddamn knife right up against Delft's throat. Only Delft, who was sitting on the ground all spread out like a great big mound, his legs bent kind of funny, didn't seem to even realize the knife was there. He really looked out of it. He had a very kind of dopey look. The blood was running down his face and dripping onto his shirt. It was even dripping onto Preston's hand and the knife.

Orninski ran right past Mel too, just like the nigger did, and Mel figured naturally that was what he was after, the nigger. Orninski didn't even seem to see Mel standing there. He went by like a shot, looking kind of wild and frantic. He had blood all around his mouth and chin, but not as bad as Delft.

Suddenly Mel felt his brain snap into place. He suddenly said to himself, very fast, all in one flash, *Shit, I didn't do any of this. I didn't beat up any screw! No one ever said there was gonna be anything like this!*

So he just turned and scooted right back into the garage. Only he no sooner got in when he practically tripped right over Orninski, who was crouched down near the wall, digging into the sawdust with a big screwdriver. Mel stopped short and Orninski jumped up and what the hell did he have in his other hand but a goddamn gun.

"C'mon!" Orninski said, and you could see how hopped up he was, because he really looked wild, especially with his face all bloody like that. He gave Mel a shove that spinned him right around and then, like he was in some kind of crazy dream, there he was, running out into the sun again with Orninski jabbing his back with the goddamn gun trying to get him to move even faster.

"Get him up, he's coming with us," Orninski yelled at Preston as soon as they swung into the alley.

Delft was still sitting just the way they left him, and Preston yanked his arm and said, "Get up, for Christ's sake! Get off your ass!"

But Delft was too big for one guy to pull up. So Orninski waved Mel over, waving this goddamn gun which Mel wished the hell he wouldn't. "Help him, for Christ's sake! Get him up!"

So Mel grabbed Delft's other arm and him and Preston and O'Neill, who pushed Delft from behind, got him to his feet. He was really very dopey, swaying and everything, and they had to hold him up.

"We gotta move," Orninski said. "Get him going. Make him run."

Mel didn't know what the hell he was talking about, but suddenly everybody started running and so Mel, who had Delft's arm over his shoulder now to hold him up, had to start running too. Preston still had Delft's other arm and O'Neill was sort of pushing from behind. Delft was like a goddamn ton of bricks, hardly even moving his feet, just sort of letting them drag him along. Anyhow, the bunch of them started, barrel-assing across the ground with Orninski leading the way, waving the goddamn gun in the air like it was a flag. The suddenly Mel realized they were heading for the hobby shop.

It was a long run. There was maybe only fifty-sixty yards between the buildings, but dragging Delft along it felt like about five football fields, end to end. Mel must've walked that space a hundred times, and must've seen it maybe a thousand, because whenever you looked out from the garage, what you saw was this stretch of ground. But it seemed different now, running across it. For one thing, it was so bare, and it seemed so goddamn big. It was like running across a whole desert. He never in his life had such a feeling of being off in the goddamn absolute middle of nowhere, just miles and miles of nothing. He ran and ran, puffing and sweating in the sun that was hot enough to melt the hair off your head, dragging Delft along and sometimes tripping in a rut and almost falling, losing more of his breath each time, really gasping and wheezing. But at the same time, it was crazy, he felt like he was running on air. Christ, it felt good. Maybe Delft weighed a ton, but in some ways it didn't feel like no weight at all. Mel felt like he was running along at a picnic or something. He felt like he could just run like this for hours and feel better and better the more he ran, like he was a goddamn kid leaping and romping around in a park, feeling like a million dollars and without a worry in the world.

Then they reached the hobby shop door and Mel snapped out of it. Orninski barged in and the others pushed in after him and then

Mel and Preston and O'Neill shoved Delft through the door like he
was a big crate and scrambled in themselves and Orninski slammed the
door shut.

It was just then, Mel figured, that if Orninski hadn't actually thought
of Verdun before, he suddenly did. Because when Orninski turned
from the door and started waving that gun around, he didn't seem to be
waving it half so much at the screw there, whose name was Cloninger,
as he was at Verdun, who was sitting at one of the big wooden work-
tables, sanding down the outside of this goddamn little toy wooden
sailboat.

"Okay, stand up!" Orninski said. "Everybody—stand up! And don't
take nothing with you! Move!"

There were about fifteen guys working at the three tables when
they barged in, one guy at the jigsaw, and one guy up front getting
a tool from the shadow board. Cloninger himself was bending over a
guy at the middle table, like he was showing him something. The closest guy to Orninski was Verdun, who was at the first table, so of
course maybe that was why Orninski seemed to be waving the gun
especially at him, although Mel didn't think so. You could really smell
the wood in there, kind of a very sweet smell, like fresh wood always
smells.

Naturally it must've been a shock to all those guys to see Orninski
with a gun in his hand and his face all banged up and Delft looking
like he fell head first into a meat grinder, and when Orninski told them
to get up, nobody moved.

So Orninski just jumped right over to where Verdun was sitting and
poked the goddamn gun into his ribs, hard, and said, *"I said get up!"*

For a second it looked like Verdun was gonna slug him, gun or
no gun. But he didn't. He got up. But he did it very slow, keeping his
eyes on Orninski's face, getting up just the way he would for a screw,
as slow and draggy as he could get away with.

"The rest of you too," Orninski said. "Come on. *Up!*"

And so the rest of them got up.

"And leave that stuff down."

A coupla guys that still had tools in their hands dropped them.

Cloninger meanwhile hadn't said or done anything. He was a real
old-timer but probably hadn't never in his life seen any con with a
gun, and maybe still didn't really believe it. Mel didn't really believe
it himself. Anyhow, Cloninger stepped out from between the tables and
started walking toward Orninski with one hand raised a little in front
of him. Cloninger was kind of an old guy, and everybody called him

The Perfesser because he once used to teach shop or something in a school and was kind of a quiet, easygoing old guy, very different from Delft, for instance. Actually, he was kind of an old lady, but the guys mostly liked him. He was maybe average size, but looked small because he was sort of stooped. He had glasses and was bald on top, with white hair over his ears.

"Hold it!" Orninski said. "Stay right the hell where you are!"

Cloninger stopped, but kept his hand raised a little like that. "What are you doing here?" he said. He had a very quiet voice that he couldn't make very loud, sort of a weak voice, and he said this like he really *couldn't* figure out just what the hell Orninski was doing there.

"Just get over there and sit down," Orninski said, waving with the gun to the other wall, alongside the jigsaw.

Cloninger didn't move, but just kind of squinted at him. Then Mel realized Cloninger didn't know who this con with the gun was, and was trying to read the name tag. "Orninski . . . ," Cloninger said, sort of to himself.

"That's right, Perfesser. Now you just get over there like I say."

"What happened to Mr. Delft?" Cloninger asked, kind of very seriously, in this real soft voice of his.

"He got himself a little hurt was what happened. Now you just be careful because we don't want nobody else getting hurt."

"If you'll just let me have that gun there," Cloninger said, "and let me get you and Mr. Delft to the doctor, I think everything will—"

"Get *over* there!" Orninski went right up to him and jammed the gun into his gut, like he was trying to punch it right through to his backbone. Cloninger let out a little cry. "*Move!*" Orninski yelled. "You ain't taking nobody no place!"

Cloninger's gut must've really hurt, the way he was kind of closing one eye, and when Orninski jerked his hand like he was gonna give it to him again, Cloninger backed away a little, sort of looking around, and then, keeping his eyes on Orninski, backed over to the wall, right in the corner.

"Sit down," Orninski said.

Cloninger sat down on the floor, kind of holding his hand over the spot on his stomach where Orninski'd rammed the gun.

Orninski smiled and let out a little breath. He turned to Mel. "Him too," he said, motioning with the gun to Delft.

Mel and Preston walked Delft over and lowered him down, with his legs straight out on the floor and his back against the wall, right next to Cloninger. Delft's eyes were open, but he was still really out of it. He just stayed the way they put him, looking straight ahead but not like he was taking in much of what he saw.

Mel and Preston came back to stand with the other guys from the garage.

Then Orninski started giving orders all over the place, rattling them off one right after the other, like he had everything all planned out ahead of time. It really got Mel, how fast he could organize things just on the spur of the moment. He stationed Akar and Larrobee at the windows to keep an eye out, told Preston and Fledgett to watch the two screws, and told O'Neill, Ferrucio and Quinlan to collect all the tools and put them back up on the shadow board and then take batches of lumber ends from the bin and pile them on the floor under each of the four windows. Then he put all the hobby guys against the long wall without windows, had Cloninger's keys taken from him and the front door locked, had all the windows shut, and gave out knives and stuff laying around to the guys from the garage. Mel got a thick-handled knife that was used for carving. He put it under his belt. Then Orninski took Cloninger and Delft's wrist watches from them and put one on, Mel couldn't tell which. Then he surprised hell out of Mel by giving him the other one. Everybody saw this, naturally, and it made Mel feel a little funny, because it looked like Orninski was showing them that Mel was number two man, next to himself, which struck Mel as real crazy because Christ, he wasn't out to be any kind of number two man in anything like this. As far as he was concerned he still didn't even know what the hell was going on.

But Orninski didn't ask if he wanted the watch, he just gave it to him. So Mel took it and put it on. It had one of those silver metal straps that stretch out and then pull back tight on your wrist. It was eight minutes after three. He saw for he first time there was blood on his sleeve, about a half-dozen spots, all very small except this one that was about the size of a quarter, near his cuff. They were dry already, kind of dark brown on the blue sleeve.

Orninski told the guys at the window to yell if anyone showed up outside, and walked between two tables to the opposite wall where the cons from the hobby shop, including Verdun, were all standing together very quietly, just watching things. The whole place actually was very quiet.

"All I wanna know," Orninski said to the hobby guys, "is if you guys are with us, or you ain't with us. That's all."

None of them answered. You could see they just didn't know what the hell he was talking about. Except for the garage crew, nobody was supposed to know what they planned today for the nigger, because Orninski said the fewer that knew about it the better.

Orninski waited, looking around at their faces. Still nobody said anything. One or two guys sort of shifted from one foot to the other, and a couple gave a little shrug.

Then, just when it looked like Orninski was gonna go ahead and explain to them about the nigger and everything, Verdun piped up with, "What the hell's going on? You off your fucking nut or something?"

Orninski turned to look right at him very slow and steady. "I ain't asking you," he said. "I'm asking the others."

"Good," Verdun said. "Because between you and me, I don't want any part of it. I don't even wanna know about it."

"Get over there," Orninski said, jerking his head to the corner where Delft and Cloninger were. "Get over there with them, where you belong."

You could see this really caught Verdun off guard, because the worst thing you can say to another con is that he's in with the screws. So he tried to cover up by smart-assing. "Sure," he said, kind of shrugging and giving Orninski this big smile. "Glad to." And he sort of swaggered over there, like he was feeling very chipper about things, and plopped himself down on the floor next to Delft, leaning back against the wall and bending his knees up and looking straight ahead, smiling like a goddamn idiot.

Orninski, who watched Verdun along with everybody else, then turned back to the rest of the guys from the hobby shop. "We're gonna be staying right here where we are for a while, and I wanna know if—"

"Do I have to stay too?" Verdun yelled over from the corner, making his voice sound sort of whiny, like a kid's. "Can't I just let you guys stay?"

Orninski whipped around and leveled the goddamn gun right at Verdun, and Mel kind of shrunk up a little, like when you expect a big noise to suddenly go off, because he thought sure Orninski was just gonna pull the trigger, then and there. But he didn't. Orninski kept looking at Verdun for a long time though, the gun aimed straight at him, just waiting for him to open his mouth once more.

Verdun kept smiling, but didn't say anymore. Actually, the smile looked kind of phony now, because Verdun could see how close Orninski was to pulling that trigger.

While Orninski was standing like that, Mel got his first good look at the gun. You could tell it was something somebody made, and not

Orninski, because Orninski couldn't make anything if his life depended on it. Either someone else made it for him, or else he just happened to learn where it was hid under the sawdust. You heard all the time about guys making guns from scrap—and you could do it easy enough, if you could handle tools at all—but this was the first one Mel ever actually saw, and it sort of interested him. Only it suddenly hit him again, looking at the gun, what a crazy idea this whole thing was.

"You got anything else to say?" Orninski said to Verdun.

"I only wanted to know if it'd be okay if I left," Verdun said, "since you guys were planning to stay anyway." There was still some of the wise-ass sound, but less. He didn't want to exactly look chicken, but he didn't want to push Orninski too far either.

"Well, it ain't okay," Orninski said. "That answer your question?"

"Sure, boss."

"That's it," Orninski said. "That's the word—boss. You remember that word."

"Okay, boss."

"That's it. That's perfect." Orninski turned again to the guys from the hobby shop and said, "All right then. Any of you guys wanna join us, just say so. If you wanna join, you can, but now's gonna be your last chance."

None of the guys said they wanted to join. None of them said anything, actually. Which Mel didn't really see how you could expect them to, because let's face it, they still didn't know what the hell Orninski was talking about.

And then Orninski said, "Okay—that's how you want it. You just stay where you are then. You just stay out of the way and keep quiet and don't give us any trouble."

"Heads up!" Larrobee yelled from the window. "Griffing's out there."

Orninski ran over and peeked out. "Okay," he said. "Get ready with that wood. Mel, you take that other window."

"What're we gonna do?" Mel asked.

"We're gonna keep him away is what we're gonna do."

And they did, first by tossing out wood and then, when he kept coming anyhow, by making Cloninger yell from the window to stay away. Griffing went back then, over to the garage, which by this time was a real mob scene, with a whole bunch of screws running around in circles bumping into each other. In a way it was kind of funny, and a few of the guys even laughed.

Then Orninski told Akar and Larrobee to keep their eye peeled and went with Mel up to Cloninger's desk, which was at the front of the room away from where everybody else was, and said, "What the hell went wrong before? You were supposed to keep Delft busy, for Christ's sake!"

It sort of took Mel by surprise. That part of it seemed so far away now. So he shrugged and said, "We couldn't get him outside was the trouble." He waited a little and then said, "I thought you were gonna make sure he was outside before you did anything."

"I didn't say nothing about doing that," Orninski said. "I figured you could take care of it, you and Welcinak."

And for the first time Mel realized, with all the running around and everything, that Welcinak wasn't with them. He must've just headed back into the garage and stayed there, and now probably wasn't in any kind of trouble at all. "Anyhow, what happened was we couldn't get him outside," Mel said. "What happened with you in the alley?" He sort of motioned to Orninski's face, which wasn't bleeding now but was pretty swollen on the one side, including his lips on that side, which made him sound kind of thick when he talked. Some blood on his chin and around his mouth was dry now, and kind of crusty. Some was still wet.

"What happened with us," Orninski said, "was that Delft showed the hell up."

"He the one that slugged you?"

"Who do you think did it? After all, I wasn't exactly expecting him just at that minute, you know."

"Yeah," Mel said, kind of shrugging. "Anyhow, the nigger got away then, heh?"

Orninski sort of made a face. "Look, we got other things to worry about now—the nigger ain't exactly our biggest worry anymore, you know what I mean? Let's find some paper here to write on."

So Mel got some paper from Cloninger's desk and wrote down as neat as he could what Orninski told him to. But when Orninski got to the part saying the only guy they would see was this television guy, Mel stopped and looked at Orninski and didn't write that part down. "What the hell do we wanna see *him* for?"

"Because he's a big friend of yours. I mean, he is, ain't he?"

"That ain't what I mean," Mel said. "I mean, what the hell do we wanna *see* him for?"

"Use your head, Mel. Whatd'ya think's gonna happen, we try and talk to the Warden? We gotta have somebody else, from the outside, that we can talk to."

"The Warden ain't gonna like this thing about Delft, you know, no matter who we talk to."

"Look, he hit me first. He loosened my goddamn tooth. I can feel it jiggling around in there, and it hurts like hell. Now for Christ's sake write down what I tell you, will you?"

So Mel wrote it down, about them only talking to the television guy, and then they just waited around for almost an hour, which was pretty slow going, because there really wasn't much to talk about, or anything really to do, and it was hot as hell with all those guys in this one little room.

About four thirty the Warden started across again, with Dowler right alongside this time, and yelled in about how they better come out because what they were doing was an insurrection and they'd get in a lot of trouble if they kept up. Orninski threw the note out then, taped to a piece of wood, and dragged Cloninger over again and made him tell the Warden to stay out and do what the note said.

After that, there wasn't much to do again except wait some more, and some of the guys, especially Preston, started bitching about Orninski not saying anything in the note about food.

And then, at a little after five, they saw that of all the people in the world to send over to talk to them, that for Christ's sake they sent over *Manson*. Which was when Orninski gave him the old hoot and holler and they all got a big kick out of throwing the wood and everything, which made them all feel better, because up to then everybody was just kind of draggy and moping around.

But then as soon as Manson went running back to the garage, Orninski turned to Mel and he said, "What the hell did you *write* in that note, for Christ's sake?"

"Whatd'ya mean, what did I write?" Mel said. "I wrote exactly what the hell you told me to!"

"Then what the hell are they sending *Manson* over for?"

"How am I supposed to know? Maybe they can't *read!*"

"Send out another note," Preston yelled from where he was keeping an eye on the two screws. "Tell them we gotta have food. Tell them we're starving."

"There ain't nobody close enough to get any note," Orninski said.

"They'll get it," Preston said. "Tie a fucking flag on it."

Everybody else started saying then how starving they were too, so Orninski said okay, okay, and had Mel write out another note, putting down exactly what he said.

Bring us food NOW for 24 of us, plus 2 guards or they
won't eat the whole time. No guards bring it up only inmates to pass it in the window. The *only* one we talk to
is JOHNNY MANSNO of *television,* no one else!

They didn't put down his first name the other time, or mention the
television, which Orninski said was maybe how they got it screwed up.
Mel had Orninski check the note over so he couldn't blame Mel if anything went wrong again. Orninski read it over a coupla times and
said, "Okay. It'll be better this time, mentioning the television," and
taped it to a piece of two-by-four and tied on a piece of white rag.
He yelled *"Get this!"* and tossed it out the open window. Dowler came
and got it and read it and went back to the garage without yelling in
to them or even looking in their direction, except just once to sort of
glance over.

After a while Cloninger said from where he was sitting in the corner, "Why don't you let me wash him up a bit, maybe he'll feel better."
Meaning Delft, who seemed to be coming out of it now, sort of squirming around a bit and moving his head slowly from side to side and
moaning a little.

Orninski looked at Delft, thinking it over. "All right," he said.

Cloninger helped Delft over to the sink and washed up his face.
He couldn't get all the dried blood off because Delft's face was too
sore for him to scrub with the paper towels, but when he got finished
Delft did look a lot better. It seemed to make him feel better too,
although he still seemed pretty dopey.

At about a quarter to six they got food. Three nigger cons in white
aprons from the kitchen crew came across the ground pushing these
rolling tables with slots for a whole batch of trays, that were used to
bring meals up to the men in the infirmary. Everybody let out a big
cheer.

"See," Orninski said. "They're listening out there. They're paying
attention."

The cons rolled the tables over the bumpy ground right up to a window and then passed the trays in one at a time to Mel and O'Neill
while Orninski stood nearby keeping an eye on things.

"What's going on out there?" Orninski asked one of the niggers. "What are they doing?"

"Jeez man, I dunno," the con said, his mouth moving around into different shapes like it was made of rubber. "What you got going on in *here?*"

"We're on a strike," Orninski said. "You pass the word around, all right? You tell everybody we're on strike here."

"What the livin' shit you on strike for, man?"

"Look, just pass it around, all right? Don't get wise."

"Shit man, *I* ain't getting wise," the nigger said, real cheerful, like it wasn't any skin off his black ass that a bunch of other guys might be in all kinds of trouble. "I just doing what the big boss says. I just follying orders." They kept passing the trays in and the nigger said, "Whooosh, man! You got a motherfuckin' army in there!"

"You just remember," Orninski said when they got near the end. "You pass the word around." But you could see he didn't have too much faith in the nigger doing it.

"Sure man," the nigger said, giving Orninski the big jazzbo smile. "Anything you say, man. You got enough food now? You got enough to fill up all your old tummies?"

"All right," Orninski said. "Don't get wise."

The niggers left, having a great time steering the empty carts back across the ground, like a bunch of kids playing with wagons.

The guys from the garage crew, who were the only ones Orninski let roam around, came over and grabbed trays for themselves and set them on the tables and started eating like food hadn't been invented up till then. Orninski then let the hobby shop guys come over one at a time to get a tray and take them back and sit down and eat on the floor. There was one spoon on each tray, but no knife or fork. And no dessert. Everybody bitched about this naturally, but Orninski said they had more important things to worry about than what kind of shit pudding they would've got, and they should be glad they got what they did. What they got was stewed chicken and vegetables cooked together—which was mostly vegetables actually, and not too heavy on the chicken—and mashed potatoes and six slices of bread with no butter. They didn't get no coffee either, but the guys didn't bitch about this as much as the dessert. Preston, who was a great chow hound and the world's expert on what you were supposed to get with what on the different menus, said today's dessert was supposed to be dutch apple cake, which made everybody bitch more, because everybody liked dutch apple cake.

Orninski let Cloninger take a tray over to Delft and then come back and get one himself. Everyone had trays then except Verdun and Orninski himself. Orninski said he'd wait and keep an eye on the window while everyone else ate. It didn't look like he'd have to wait very long anyhow, the way the guys were shoveling it in.

Without turning his face from the window, Orninski said, "You gonna have some supper too, Verdun?"

"Sure," Verdun said.

"You wanna eat, huh?"

"Sure, why not?"

"Okay. You ask me for some then. You ask me real nice."

"Fuck you," Verdun said.

"What'samatter, you ain't hungry?"

"That's right. You got the story. I ain't hungry."

"Okay then. No use wasting food on you then."

In about three minutes just about everybody was finished, and Preston started in again about there being no seconds.

"There's an extra tray here," Orninski said. Orninski himself was starting to eat at a table now, because Akar and Larrobee were back at the windows. "Eat that if you're hungry."

"Nah," Preston said.

"You don't want that? It's extra."

"No thanks."

"Okay then. Anybody else wants it, he can have it."

No one else said they wanted it.

"Okay then," Orninski said. "I guess we just throw it out then." So when he finished eating he took Verdun's tray and went into the john there and flushed it down the toilet. Everybody could see him doing it, because the toilets didn't have doors so the screws could watch for funny business. "It's a shame," Orninski said when he came out with the empty tray, "wasting food like that." Nobody else said anything.

Actually, Orninski could be a real nice guy when he wanted to. But he had this thing about Verdun, and it made him act like that, in a way he wouldn't ordinarily act. It seemed to put everybody in a kind of edgy mood, and for a minute or so the room was very quiet, with nobody even looking at anybody else. And then Cloninger, who was the one guy still eating, leaned forward to look across the front of Delft to Verdun and said, "You can finish mine if you want. I'm not much of an eater."

Everybody looked over then, first at Cloninger's tray to see what was left—which was most of the potatoes and maybe half the chicken and vegetables and four slices of bread—and then at Verdun, to see what he was gonna do. Because everybody saw he was in a tight spot again. Cloninger just meant it to be nice, and of course Verdun was probably starving, what with it being way past mealtime and having to watch everybody else eat and smell all the food, but still no con likes to take favors from a screw, even one like Cloninger. And it was especially touchy for Verdun, because he already looked bad just being over there with the screws in the first place.

"Thanks," Verdun said after a while. "But I really ain't hungry."

"Go ahead," Cloninger said, with everybody in the room leaning forward to hear him, because he spoke so low all the time. "I never eat much of a meal."

And you could believe it, because Cloninger was a kind of frail old guy that you could probably knock over with a feather.

"Nah," Verdun said. "You eat it."

Cloninger shrugged finally and leaned back against the wall and went on eating with his spoon. He probably realized the spot Verdun was in and didn't want to push him.

It was after six by this time, when usually it cooled off this time of year, but it seemed to be getting hotter instead, even though they had all four windows open. You could feel it in the air, and it was dark for this time of day, with heavy clouds all over. It wasn't like night, but there was a real kind of shiny blackness in the air, and everything felt close and damp.

"It's gonna blow up a storm," Orninski said to him, kind of quietly. They were sitting side by side at the first table, facing the wall where Verdun and the two screws were. The guys from the hobby crew were on their left, against that wall, and the windows were on their right. No one else was sitting near them.

"Yeah," Mel said, looking at the wrist watch he had on. He must've looked at the goddamn thing twenty times in the last ten minutes. "It's gonna be dark soon too. What're we gonna do about lights in here?"

"We got lights," Orninski said.

"Maybe they're figuring on sneaking up on us when it gets dark," Mel said.

"I don't think so," Orninski said. "I don't think they'll do anything crazy like that."

Mel shrugged and didn't say anymore about it. They were quiet a few minutes, and then Mel said, "How's your tooth? Still hurt?"

"It hurts like hell," Orninski said. "My whole mouth hurts."

They were quiet again for a while. The whole room, considering there were twenty-four guys in it, twenty-six counting the screws, was really very quiet. Maybe it was just getting some food in their stomachs, but since supper nobody seemed to have much to say. A few guys in the hobby crew were talking low to each other, but that was about it.

Then Preston, who was sitting at the back table watching Verdun and the screws, came up front and sat alongside Orninski. "You know what?" he said, speaking low too, and huddling close.

"What?" Orninski said.

"I think maybe we got ourselves fucked," Preston said.

"You think that, heh? I mean, that's what you think?"

"Yeah. That's what I think."

"Okay," Orninski said. "Whatd'ya planning to do about it?"

"That's what I'm asking you. What are we gonna do?"

"We're gonna get ourselves un-fucked," Orninski said.

"How we gonna do that?"

"Maybe by letting me handle it," Orninski said. "Unless you got better ideas, in which case it's all right by me, you can handle it."

"You ain't worried, heh?" Preston said.

"I ain't worried," Orninski said. "I think we're sitting pretty myself. We got a nice place here, we get our chow sent in special by a coupla nigger waiters, just like in a fancy restaurant, and we got the Warden running around out there picking up notes and doing whatever we tell him. All the time everybody bitches because they get shoved around. Well, now nobody's shoving you. Maybe you oughta try to enjoy it a bit. I enjoy it."

"You think that guy's gonna come? That TV guy?"

"Sure. He's gonna come."

"When?"

"Soon," Orninski said. "They gotta find him first, you know. He's not just sitting out there waiting."

Preston went back to keep an eye on the screws again and Mel and Orninski didn't say anymore but just sat there waiting. The time went very slow. And the worst thing was, it didn't rain. The rain would've cooled things off. But it just stayed up there and kept everything very hot and close, with your clothes sticking to you.

Everybody was beginning to feel very edgy, without cards or a radio or anything to do. O'Neill and Ferrucio played tictactoe on a table, drawing it out right on the table with a marking pencil. Preston got a piece of wood and started carving with the knife he had. Quinlan saw him and started doing the same himself.

Akar gave everybody the biggest laugh because he just sat down on the floor by the window and started building things out of the lumber ends piled up there, like a kid playing with blocks. The guys all razzed him of course, but he just said, "You got something better to do?" and went right on. He built a castle first with a big wall around it, and then all kinds of different houses and a big bridge, knocking each one down when he finished it and using the same pieces to build the next thing. He was really pretty good at it.

What Orninski did to pass the time was write down some stuff on a paper. Orninski, of course, didn't have a lot of schooling behind him, but he could write things out for himself without any trouble. It was just the spelling that bothered him, he told Mel one time, which was probably why he had Mel write out the notes.

Mel himself didn't feel like doing much of anything, so he just sort of sat there, near Orninski. He tried to think of something he could say to the TV guy when he finally showed up, if he ever did.

Delft, sitting on the floor and leaning back against the wall, was sleeping. A coupla times, out of nowhere, he'd let out a snore like a goddamn baboon, and everybody would laugh and razz him. All the commotion woke him up one time and he mumbled a little, but dozed right off again.

Verdun sat next to him with his legs stretched flat on the floor and his hands folded in his lap and his eyes closed, but you could tell he wasn't sleeping.

Cloninger, on the other side of Delft, had his hands folded in his lap and just kept watching Orninski, without much of an expression on his face one way or the other.

Most of the hobby shop guys just sat, a few of them whispering together, but most of them just sitting, or maybe dozing.

By about seven o'clock it was really getting dark, and Orninski had a coupla guys from the hobby crew go around and pick up the trays that were still lying around and pile them on a table, because he said he didn't want nobody breaking his leg in the dark later.

Then he fixed up the lights, and did it very shrewd. You could see he'd been thinking about it. First he took the gooseneck lamp from Cloninger's desk and put it on the floor under the first table, which was as far as the cord would go. He bent the gooseneck over so the light would shine down at the floor and then turned it on. That way the light spread around the floor but not in anybody's eyes, and didn't show in the windows. Then he took the extension light hooked to the top of the jigsaw and hooked it facing down on a chair, and put the chair between the second and third tables. Then he poked around in Cloninger's desk until he found the flashlight. Shop officers all have a flashlight for emergencies. And then he said: "Okay, now. We got light. We're all set."

And then they waited some more. It was getting darker by the minute, and muggier and more uncomfortable too, and kind of eerie-feeling.

"Something's happening over there," Larrobee said.

Orninski went to the window, and Mel went too. It wasn't completely dark yet outside, and you could see people moving around by the garage, but couldn't tell one from another anymore. The way they were moving around looked like something was up.

"He must be here," Orninski said. "They must've found him."

"He's a great big guy," Mel said. "Tall."

They looked some more, but couldn't tell. A bunch of guys in front of the garage were all crowded together.

"You keep an eye," Orninski told Mel and then turned to the other guys in the room. "Now listen to me," he said very loud. "When this fellow comes in here, we don't want any funny stuff. I don't want nobody to say even one word. You understand that? Nobody. I'll do all the talking, and Mel here, because Mel's a friend of his."

"They got flashlights now," Mel said. He could see a couple of spots of light flicking around out there.

"All right," Orninski said, still facing the other guys. "Now I ain't kidding here. I mean this. Anybody opens his mouth, he's gonna be sorry. And Verdun—this goes for you double. I don't wanna hear a goddamn word from you."

Mel was watching the lights in front of the garage, but noticed it was very quiet and looked over at Verdun, who was still sitting there with his head slumped down like he was asleep.

"Verdun," Orninski said.

Verdun didn't move.

"Kick him," Orninski told Preston. "Wake him up."

"He's awake," Preston said.

"He better answer then."

There wasn't any answer.

"Kick him."

Preston leaned over and jiggled his arm. "Hey, wake up. Come on." But Verdun didn't move.

"Kick him."

Preston sort of nudged his foot against Verdun's leg.

"I said *kick* him!" Orninski yelled. It was more than a yell, actually. It was like a scream.

So Preston kicked him in the meaty part of his leg, hard enough for him to feel it. But that Verdun, Christ, he was a crazy bastard, and he didn't even twitch. He just kept right on like he was fast asleep.

Delft, meanwhile, who *had* been sleeping, woke up when Orninski screamed and was watching Verdun now, along with everybody else. The room was pretty dark, with the lights just on the floor, and everything was kind of shadowy.

Orninski waited about one second and then charged, like a goddamn maniac. He shoved Preston out of the way and let go a kick that would've sent a football fifty yards, right in Verdun's ribs. It might've glanced off his arm too, but mainly it was right in the ribs, and this time Verdun really let out a yelp. He practically jumped off the floor.

"You awake now?" Orninski said. He was breathing very hard, kind of gasping.

"That's right," Verdun said. The way he talked you could tell he was really hurting, but still he managed to make his voice sound wise at the same time. "Wide awake, boss . . . What can I do for you?"

"You can keep your trap shut."

"I ain't been saying anything, boss. I been sleeping. I been very quiet."

"Well, *stay* that way. And I ain't kidding. I ain't kidding at all. And you too," he said, looking at Delft, then Cloninger, like he was ready to jump on them too. "I don't want anybody in this corner saying one goddamn word."

Like everybody else, Mel was watching all this, but then he glanced out the window. "Hey! Here he comes!"

Orninski ran over. The guy was halfway across the ground, carrying a lighted flashlight although you could still see enough to walk without one. "That him?"

"Yeah, that's him."

"You sure?"

"Yeah. That's him."

"Go over by the door," Orninski said. "Here." He gave Mel Cloninger's key ring. "Get the right one but don't open it yet."

Mel fumbled around with the keys, trying the different ones in the lock. There wasn't much light to see by there, but finally he found the right one and put it in. There wasn't a sound in the room now. He could actually hear the guy walking out there on the hard ground. He sounded very close.

"You got anything on you?" Orninski yelled out the window.

The walking stopped. "Excuse me?"

"You got a gun or anything?"

"What? No, I don't have a gun."

"Leave the flashlight on the ground there."

"I can't see very well without it."

"We got one in here. You won't need it."

Mel heard the flashlight hit the ground.

"Okay," Orninski said. "Let him in."

Mel unlocked the door and swung it open. The guy was standing about ten feet from the door. He was wearing one of those light blue raincoats all the screws had, that were part of their regular uniform, and had it all buttoned up even though it wasn't raining. It looked kind of funny because it was about a foot too short.

"Come on in," Mel said, kind of quietly.

"That you, Mel?"

"Yeah," Mel said. "It's me."

"Let's get in and close that door," Orninski said.

For just a second the guy didn't move. Then he came ahead. He came slow and steady, and maybe a little careful. When he got to the door he stopped, for just a second, then ducked his head down because he was so tall and stepped in, looking around very quickly. Mel closed and locked the door and Orninski flicked on the flashlight and put it right in the guy's face. The guy, his face suddenly lighted up like that, and probably blinded by it, stood very still. He didn't look scared—actually he was standing very calm, very steady, with his mouth closed tight and breathing very quiet—but the way his face looked you got the impression that he figured he could just as easy get shot dead right this minute as anything else he could think of.

14

The cop who drove him out had been polite, casual, full of mild jokes. He seemed to enjoy the ride; maybe it was a pleasant break in his routine. He appreciated Johnny's white jacket, his wine-red tie.

"First time I ever took anybody out there dressed like that," he said as they raced along with the siren shrieking. He darted from one lane to another and challenged red lights as the traffic divided to let them roar by.

Johnny sat alongside him in front. The back seat was caged in by a thick wire screen, and the inside handles had been removed from the rear doors. The radio under the dashboard croaked, raucous and insistent.

"What's happening out there?" Johnny asked.

"I don't know," the cop said. "They just said get you out there four-one."

"What does that mean?"

"Fast," the cop said.

□

What got you first, and most, about the prison was the wall. It was unbelievably high, shadowed in the growing darkness, massive, oppressive. He'd seen it before, from the highway, but going inside, being escorted through the huge barred gate, you were visited by the unsettling thought that *you might never get out again*: the criminal in us all, the deep-seated conviction of guilt. *They've found me out at last!* It was the shock of moving so simply through a single locked gate into a world where everything was locked, where every man was either guard or guarded, a world of uniforms, guns, turrets, salutes, distant patternless lights, keys on metal rings hanging from belts, of dark gothic buildings honeycombed with unseen cells full of hopeless men.

The vision was so complete that it didn't linger: you felt perfectly natural standing in the sawdust of an open garage, not ten feet from a stack of firearms and a pile of little bloated projectiles, talking to the men who ran this dark and absurd place. You listened quietly, nodding, wiping your forehead in the damp heat. The white-haired Warden looked like somebody's stern grandfather, and his voice was sharp, astringent, all edges. In the shadowy light of the garage, among the cars and trucks, the tools hanging on the wall, the uniformed guards standing about in twos and threes—amid all this the white-haired Warden loomed like some mythical ruler, some medieval tyrant rattling about his somber castle.

"Are you clear now, Mr. Mancino? Have you got all that?"

"Yes. I've got it."

"You'd better take a flashlight."

The other one, the third one, Dowler, handed him a flashlight.

"I think I'll take this off if you don't mind," Johnny said.

"Yes," the Warden said. "Take that off."

Johnny folded the dinner jacket inside-out and placed it carefully on the fender of the car alongside them. "It's not even mine. I'd hate to get it messed up."

"I'll guard it with my life," Fleishman said.

Johnny unclipped his bow tie and slipped it into the jacket pocket. He unbuttoned his collar.

"You'd better put something else on," the Warden, Griffing, said. The Evil King. The guy who couldn't even refuse civilly when Johnny called him up that time to ask him to come on the show. And he looked, and acted, as cold and impatient as he had sounded then. "Get him a coat or something."

"I don't know if we've got anything that'll fit," Fleishman said.

"Aren't there any raincoats up here? They brought some up before."

It came halfway down his thighs, over his dress trousers.

"You look like a million dollars," Fleishman said.

"Are you nervous?" Griffing asked.

"Of course he's nervous," Fleishman said. "He's not crazy."

"Be careful in there," Griffing said. "Don't take any chances."

"They won't hurt you," Fleishman said. "We wouldn't let you go in otherwise."

"Give him a whistle," Griffing said. "Put it in your pocket. If there's any trouble, anything at all, we'll move right in. Just blow this—loud—or yell. Anything. But make it loud. Then get down on the floor, get out of the way. We'll be ready to move right in."

The whistle was silvery, barrel-shaped, about three inches long. He put it in the raincoat pocket. "I'm sure there won't be any trouble."

"Of course not," Fleishman said.

"Just be careful," Griffing said. "Just don't take any chances."

And the walk across. It was the last thing in the world you'd expect to happen, expect to feel, inside a prison. The wall you could have imagined, but this, an absolute aloneness, walking in the near-darkness across a bigger stretch of empty ground than you ever suspected prisons had, in more silence than you thought existed. The raincoat seemed to stick to him in the dampness. He wiped his face as he walked across; he didn't want to go in there with the sweat pouring off.

"Maybe you could take the light out of my eyes." His voice was steady, loud but not too loud. For someone used to klieg lights, he was impressed at the way a single flashlight could pulse so whitely, could so completely obliterate your awareness, your sense of place, even balance. He was afraid he was tottering.

"Okay," the voice behind the light said, the same voice that had spoken to him from the window. The light dropped to Johnny's feet, but it was a while before he could make anything out. Then he realized there were lights, somehow shrouded under tables, shining down on the cement floor but not reaching the walls where, in the darkness, he could vaguely distinguish men crowded together, dim and motionless, like actors poised about a stage, waiting for the curtain to go up.

"We're glad you came," the voice said. It was an odd voice, nasal, insinuating, almost formal. Yet the words were muffled, as if the person had a speech impediment. "We were counting pretty heavy on you coming, Mr. Mancino."

"Who am I talking to?"

"Well, you see how it is, Mr. Mancino, it don't make any difference what my name is, because what I'm just doing, you see, is speaking for everybody here. I'm just the guy speaking for them, is all."

"I'd still like to know who I'm talking to."

"Is that what the Warden said for you to say?"

Johnny said nothing; he waited.

"Sure, okay. The name's Orninski. That okay?"

"That's just fine," Johnny said. At least that much was encouraging. At least the Warden knew enough to have guessed that part right.

"Good. We can have our little talk then, all right? Because, you see, we got a lot to talk about. Let's just make ourselves comfortable, all right? You can sit over here, if you want." Orninski swung the flashlight beam to a big wooden table. "Just like friends, you see."

"First I'd like to see the two guards you're holding."

Orninski was silent a moment. "The Warden, he gave you a kind of big list of things to say, heh?"

Johnny said nothing.

"What if I say you can't see them?"

"Then I guess I'll head back."

"If we let you?"

"That's right."

Again there was a pause, with not another sound in the room. He had the impression, though, that he could hear the sound of breathing. It was getting dark so rapidly that he could no longer distinguish individual shapes.

"Sure, Mr. Mancino. You wanna see the officers which are in here with us, you can see them. We're not the ones trying to hide anything. We're the ones trying to let people know. You come and I'll take you on a regular tour."

With this Orninski shone the beam into the face of Mel Simmons, who was still at the door. The light gave his face a grayish cast. He looked heavier than the last time Johnny had seen him, older, with the boyish quality somehow gone from his face. His eyes bugged and glistened in the light.

"How are you doing, Mel?"

"I'm doing all right, Mr. Mancino."

Orninski led Johnny between two tables to the other side of the room. He moved the light quickly back and forth across the faces of perhaps fifteen men in gray-blue convict uniforms. They were sitting on the floor, looking up, none of them moving, none speaking.

"Now these here, Mr. Mancino, are various different guys that have been sentenced to this prison for different amounts of time. I won't bother listing for you all their names or anything, because there is so many of them and I don't want to waste your time, because I know you must be a busy man. But anyhow, these are some of the men with us here, and since you want to see everything, here they are."

Johnny remained silent.

Orninski led him back between the tables to the wall with the windows and shone the light in the face of a convict standing there. "This is inmate Larrobee," Orninski said.

"Hello," Johnny said.

"Hello."

In turn he aimed the light at the other convicts whose names Johnny had seen on the list—Ferrucio, Akar, Quinlan, O'Neill, Fledgett, Preston. One of them—Preston—had something in his belt that glinted when the light caught it for an instant.

"Who's that?" Johnny said as the light flashed over a convict sitting against the wall, his head slumped forward on his knees.

"Just one more of the fellows in here with us, who like you saw is just catching a little shut-eye, so we won't bother him. And this here next to him is one of the prison officers, which you are especially interested in seeing, which is Officer Cloninger, who is a good officer and well-liked by all of the men."

Cloninger, a small, mild-looking man, older than Johnny had expected, squinted up into the light. His eyeglasses flashed.

"Are you all right?" Johnny asked.

"Go on," Orninski said. "Tell him if you're all right or not."

"I'm all right," Cloninger said.

"Have we touched a single finger on you, Mr. Cloninger?" Orninski asked in that peculiar stiff phrasing of his.

"No," Cloninger said.

"And this here next to him, who you can see is maybe not quite so much all right, which is something I want to talk to you about, is Officer Delft, who is in regular charge of the automobile garage, which is where Mel and myself and some of the rest of us are assigned."

Johnny drew his breath sharply. "What happened to him?"

"I want to tell you all about that, Mr. Mancino. That is exactly one of the things I want to talk to you about."

"Are you all right?"

Delft, a huge man with an enormous spread of stomach, sat with his head down, not looking into the light. His arms hung limply, his hands touching the floor. It was hard to tell if he were even conscious. His shirt was stained with blood.

"We washed him up good so he would feel better," Orninski said. "He is maybe bruised up a little, but otherwise all right. We have been taking good care of him since he got hurt."

"He doesn't look all right," Johnny said. He bent down to look at Delft's face but Orninski blocked him quickly with the hand that held the flashlight. The spot of light skimmed crazily over the walls and ceiling.

"How do I know you're not trying to pass him a gun or something?"

"I've got nothing to pass. I told you that. I didn't come in here with any gun."

"Well, you just stand back a little then and I will shine the light on him and you can see. I just don't want you getting too close."

Johnny bent down again as Orninski stood between them and shone the light on Delft. The guard lifted his head slowly and stared, unblinking, into the glare. Johnny felt his stomach muscles contract. "We've got to get this man to a doctor. What on earth happened to him?"

Orninski abruptly swung the light to one of the big white tables. "Let's us go and sit down now, Mr. Mancino. Then we can talk about these things."

"This man's got to be taken care of."

"Let's us just go talk about that now, okay?" Orninski took his arm and led him to the table farthest away from the two guards and gestured for him to sit. Johnny swung his legs over the bench and then under the table, cracking one knee on a hidden leg. Orninski sat next to him. "Mel, you come sit with us too," Orninski said, and Mel Simmons walked over and sat opposite them. Orninski put the flashlight down on the table, the beam illuminating a large circle on the front wall next to where, according to Fleishman's sketch, Cloninger's desk should be.

"Now you are probably very much bothered," Orninski began, speaking with that same thick, clotted stiffness, "about how Officer Delft looks."

"That's right," Johnny said. "I'm very much bothered."

"Only you shouldn't be too fast jumping to the wrong ideas, because there is still some things here you haven't seen yet."

"What haven't I seen?"

Orninski picked up the flashlight and shone it into his own face. "What happened to you?"

"One more thing, first. I don't like to ask you to look, because it is still very bloody and messy, but since you want to see everything, I will go ahead and ask you to." Orninski stretched back his head, opened his mouth as wide as he could with his swollen lips, and shone the flashlight in. With a finger of his free hand he poked at a tooth about halfway back. It wiggled in the swollen and bloody gum. Johnny looked. Mel leaned across the table to look too. Orninski removed his finger, wiping it on his shirt front, closed his mouth and put the flashlight down, turning it off. He spoke more quietly now, satisfied with his performance. "So you can see, Mr. Mancino, what the tooth is like in there, and maybe will believe me when I say that it hurts. So you don't want to be jumping to any kind of concludings, about what happened to Officer Delft back there."

"All right. Just tell me what happened."

"Sure," Orninski said, leaning close again and lowering his voice. "I will tell you exactly what happened. And what happened was that I make a mistake today. What I did was to step in front of the garage for a breath of fresh air, after working for a long time over a car motor. Because, you see, a convict is not supposed to do that, not even when it is as hot as today. And before I knew it, Mr. Delft, he was all over me. And like you noticed I'm sure, Mr. Delft is a very large article, and very strong, you can believe me."

Johnny hesitated, staring at Orninski's face. He couldn't distinguish his features in the darkness, couldn't see his expression. "You don't mean to say the guards beat you up for no reason at all."

"I am not saying what guards will do, Mr. Mancino. I am saying what Mr. Delft did. Now the other one back there, Mr. Cloninger, he wouldn't hurt a fly."

"What happened then? Did you hit him back?"

Orninski laughed quietly. "Mr. Delft back there, he weighs two hundred and sixty-five pounds. Am I lying to Mr. Mancino, Mel?"

"No, that's right," Mel said. He seemed surprised at being called upon. "Two sixty-five."

"Did you see all this happen?" Johnny asked Mel.

"Huh?"

"I said, did you see it happen?"

"What Mel here—"

"Let him answer," Johnny said.

"Well—I mean—no. No, I didn't. I mean, well, I was in a different part of the garage, you see, and—"

"But he saw what happened after," Orninski said. "The part I haven't told you about yet."

"Well, yeah—I saw that part," Mel said.

"What part?"

"The part I am trying to tell you about, Mr. Mancino," Orninski said. There was an edge in his voice now.

"All right," Johnny said. "Tell me."

"All right. What I was going to say, when you asked me what I did to Mr. Delft, was that I didn't do anything." Once again he sounded cautious, earnest, almost disingenuous.

"Who did it then?"

"Some of my very good friends, Mr. Mancino, were afraid that the way Delft was going at it, I might get killed or hurt for life before he was finished. Because, you see, that has happened in prisons. Prisoners have been killed like that by guards. So my friends tried to help me, like Mel here, which is the part that he saw, and knows about. And it is only because of my friends that my life was saved today, or I might right this minute be a dead man."

"So they beat him up and brought him here?"

"He got himself some few cuts and bruises was what it was—and then, that's right, we came here."

"Why?"

"Because we knew the only way we could get ourselves protected from what otherwise would happen was to see that somebody from outside, not just the Warden, could hear our story. Because, you see, one of the big troubles in a prison is that the Warden, he can do anything he wants, and nobody outside ever even knows."

"The Warden, in other words, wouldn't believe your story?"

"The Warden would believe Mr. Delft's story, which would be very different from what really happened. And even if the Warden, he knew for a fact that our story was the truth, he still would say he has to protect his guards. The rule is any prisoner that touches a guard, no matter what the reason, is in very bad trouble with the Warden. That is the rule, you see."

"What do you want me to do about all this?"

"We want you to see that our side of the story gets on the outside."

"That's all?"

"Mostly that is all. Just see that people know, so the Warden can't give these friends who helped me the kind of punishment he would otherwise give."

"What kind is that?" Johnny shifted position on the bench and stretched out his legs under the table.

"That would depend, Mr. Mancino. But he would naturally—*Hey!*"

The lamp under the table clattered and the light flared in their faces.

"Oh—I'm sorry. I must have—"

Orninski leaped up and yanked Johnny to his feet. "Don't move!" He jammed something hard into his side. "Mel—get that lamp—pull the goddamn plug out—quick!"

Mel lunged from the bench and yanked out the cord.

"Are they coming?" Orninski yelled toward the windows. "Is anyone out there?"

"No—I don't see nothing."

"Watch this guy!" Orninski shouted at Mel. "Don't let him move!" He ran to a window and peered out.

"Nothing's happening," Johnny called over to him, rubbing his side. "It was an accident. I'm sorry."

"Just be ready," Orninski yelled over his shoulder to the others. "Keep your eyes open."

"Nothing's going to happen," Johnny said. "I only—"

"Just keep quiet," Orninski said.

The room was silent, everyone alert now, poised.

After a minute or so, Orninski turned from the window and flicked on his flashlight. He directed the beam at Johnny. "If that was a signal, Mr. Mancino, that will be a very bad thing for you."

"It wasn't any signal, for God's sake. It was an accident. I have long legs."

"All right," Orninski said after a moment. "Fix the lamp up, will you, Mel?"

Mel plugged in the cord and righted the lamp.

"There," Orninski said. "Now we are all set again."

"What were you poking in my ribs?" Johnny said.

Orninski had started toward the table; he stopped and switched off his flashlight. "You don't have to worry about that, Mr. Mancino. No one here is planning to hurt you."

"For a minute I wasn't so sure."

"Maybe you don't understand our situation here, Mr. Mancino. Maybe you think that the Warden is leaving us alone and letting people come in to see us because he wants to be nice to us."

Johnny said nothing.

"Will you sit down again now, Mr. Mancino, and let us be friends again, and talk about things."

"All right," Johnny said. He sat down.

Orninski sat across from him this time, next to Mel. "And now you were asking me, I think, what kinds of punishment the men would get from the Warden. Well, I will tell you what kinds. Of course it depends on different things, but the first thing the Warden would do right away is take away everybody's good time—which is the amount of time a prisoner earns by good behavior and lets him get released early. So everybody would lose all his good months, maybe even years in some cases. And then next everybody would lose their jobs and their place in the training program, which is a very bad thing, because these men, like Mel here, are just trying to become better mechanics so they can get a decent job someday on the streets. And of course they would take away your right to go to school and get yourself a better education."

"What else?"

"We have just started. Next, there are different kinds of privilege they can take away from you. They can take away your mail privilege, so you can't write letters to your wife or anyone, or get them. And other things. They can take away your privilege for the radio in your cell, for the movies, for the TV ball games that they show sometimes, for the canteen, for the liberry and your newspapers, for the rec periods. The Warden can take away all of them by just snapping his fingers, anytime he wants to."

"What else?"

"Well the main thing, of course, is that everybody would get some kind of sentence in S.D.U. That is what they call our Special Detention Unit—S.D.U. It is like what they used to call solitary, or the hole. In some places they call it the shelf. Here they call it S.D.U. and they put you in a very small cell up there without a mattress and put you on B and W—which is bread and water—and naturally you don't have any—"

"Bread and water?"

"If you don't believe me, Mr. Mancino, when you go back out there you just ask the Warden what they feed men on punishment in S.D.U. Just ask him. But the ones on punishment—ask about those, because otherwise he will tell you what they feed the other men up there that are not on punishment, which is the regular meals."

"What other men?"

"The ones up there for other special reasons. Like the psychos, that have different kinds of trouble with their mind or something, according to the psychiatricist."

"Aren't those men sent to a mental hospital?"

"Those men are sent exactly where I tell you they are sent, Mr. Mancino. You can ask the Warden about this too."

"How long do they send you there for punishment?"

"If you do something small and they are only teaching you a lesson, just a week or two. If you do something worse, maybe a month. But if what you did is serious, like putting a finger on a guard, no matter what he did first, you will get maybe two, three, four months."

"I expect to check all this, you know."

"Haven't I been telling you to check it?"

"All right. Is that it, then?"

"Yes, that is mostly all that they do—officially. I will tell you about the unofficial side now, but you don't have to bother asking the Warden about this, because he will just say there isn't any such thing. Only there is. Now we are not saying every single guard in here is bad. Some—well, they are all right. Some. But there is also a number that like very much to use the knuckles, and are very good at it, like right between the legs with a knee. Things like that. And when we get out of S.D.U., then the fun starts, according to these kind of guards, because we come out practically with a sign on us saying *this here guy is a guy that likes to beat up guards*. And from then on, I tell you, the prison records will have a lot of entrancies about all of us having various different kinds of accidents, like falling down a stairs or tripping over something and hurting our head. And all this will not just be for a week or so. These accidents will keep happening the whole time we are here, because every time a guard, he's feeling a little mean because maybe he had a fight with his wife that morning, well he just gives one of us the works, because any con that beats up guards, well he deserves whatever he gets. He tells himself, after all, it is just another way of keeping up dislapin."

"Excuse me?"

"Of keeping up dislapin—you know—making you behave."

"All right. Now what do you want me to do about all this?"

"We would like you just to tell the people over the television what we are telling you, our side of the story, so people will know our side."

"What good will that do?"

"It can do a lot, just for people to know. Because now, nobody knows, and that is one reason for a lot of the troubles we have."

"If I do it, will you free those guards?"

"Well, that is not exactly all of it, Mr. Mancino. The Warden will have to—"

"I thought you said it was all."

"It is all, for you. But there are other things, for the Warden."

"Let me tell you what the Warden said about that."

"Sure. Go ahead."

"He said to tell you that I can't make any agreements or enter into any kind of negotiations. He also said I should warn you that you're risking severe punishment, and the longer you—"

Orninski was laughing quietly. "Like I been saying, we don't need the Warden to tell us what kind of risks we're taking."

"He also said that if any harm came to either of the guards, you could expect—"

"Mr. Mancino, we know what we could expect."

Johnny waited a moment. "All right. What do you want me to tell him?"

"I'll give you a little list, Mr. Mancino. You can write it all down and then give it to the Warden." Orninski turned on the flashlight and placed it so that the beam shone along the length of the table. "Do you have something to write this all down with?"

Johnny took out the pen and notebook Fleishman had given him. "Write neatly now," Fleishman had advised him. "Spell everybody's name right." He opened the notebook and put it flat on the wooden table, in the cone of light.

Orninski took a piece of paper from his pocket and held it to catch the light, hunching forward to read it.

"If you've got it all written down already, I can just—"

"This is very rough," Orninski said. "I'll just tell it to you and you write it down."

"All right."

"First, you can tell the Warden that we don't mean any harm to anybody and are treating the guards all right, and nobody will be hurt as long as nobody tries to rush us or anything. Tell him we are not making any threat, but only trying to keep people from getting hurt, and protect ourselves and see that we get our rights . . . Don't you wanna write any of that down?"

"I'll remember it. Don't worry."

"All right—if you say so . . . Anyhow, then you can tell him that we will be very happy to let the guards go free and come out ourselves if he will just agree to give us certain rights. But he has to agree so that the people outside, the public and everything, *know* he has agreed. It has to be put on the television or the radio that he has agreed before we will come out."

"What's he supposed to agree to?"

"I will give you the list. I won't make a long list, but just the main points . . . I think maybe you should write this part down, to make sure you don't forget it."

"All right. Go ahead."

"First, he has to agree to let a group of people come in and investigate all the conditions we have in the prison, and one of the people has to be you."

"Me?"

"That's right. We want to make sure it is not just a whitewash. We want there should be three people on it—one to be you, and one choosed by the Governor of the state because this is a state prison, and one from outside the state, from the Osborne Society."

"What's that?"

"That is the society interested in making reforms so the prisoners are treated decently. Now, will you agree to be part of it?"

"If the Warden agrees, yes."

"Okay. And then we want a promise that whatever the group reports in their findings will be made public, and that they can investigate anything they want about the prison, but especially these certain things: brutality and sadisticisms on the part of some of the guards . . . men getting cut out of the training program, and also the educationist program, the schoolwork, if they get in any kind of trouble . . . men getting charged—that is the report they write up if you do anything wrong—for doing even the littlest things, that nobody should get charged for . . . the food that is served, which is terrible, and always the same, and some days not even good enough to eat . . . the bread and water you get, and the way prisoners are treated in S.D.U., and getting very hard sentences for very little things. . . . Am I going too fast?"

"No, it's all right."

"You're not writing much down."

"I'm abbreviating. Go ahead."

"Okay." He glanced again at the paper in his hand. It was only the second or third time he had looked at it. "The dining room being too small, which means everybody has to eat in two shifts and just sit in their cell with nothing to do while the other shift is eating . . . the athletic field not being big enough, which means guys only can have their rec periods every other day, and on the other days just have to sit in their cells . . . there not being enough shops and equipment for everybody that wants to work and learn a trade, which means a lot of guys have nothing to do, and there's nothing for them to learn . . . no air-cooling or anything in the shops, which in the summer get too hot for men to work in them, and a lot of men get sick just from the heat . . . the infirmary not being big enough, which means guys have to stay in their cells when they should be in a hospital. . . . Yeah

—and the guys I told you about before, that were up in S.D.U. and should be, like you were saying, in a hospital for people like that—you know, a mental hospital."

"Is that all? You said it was a short list."

"Well, I got more. The training the men get as guards, and the shop officers that are supposed to be teaching you a trade—whether these men really know anything about this kind of work or not . . . and the nurses for the infirmary, because they use just inmates for nurses, that don't have no training at all and are always giving people the wrong kind of pills . . . and the guys that work in the kitchen—that could be part of the food, that we mentioned before. That they ain't even cooks in the first place, which is why the food is so bad, and do not keep the place clean, so that there is always flies and bugs in the food . . . and the guards, which are always bootlegging food for theirselves, which is supposed to be for feeding of the inmates, taking home chickens and hams and things like that. All the guards do it, the same way all the guards take money from the friends and relatives of a man that is a prisoner here, in order for the guards to promise that these men will not be mistreated badly. And then just one more thing, which was to do with us, my friends that helped me mostly. And that's that this group to investigate the prison, that you will be on, has to sit in on the Warden's court about what happened today, and know what punishment we get. Just so you know about it, that's all, so we don't get shafted, if you know what I mean."

"Is that it?" Johnny asked, looking up from the notebook.

"Yeah, that's it, if you got it all. If we really wanted to pile it on, we could go on all night."

"This is pretty impressive as it is."

"It is only a small part, Mr. Mancino. Believe me."

"That may be. But I still think it's too much. You might do better by concentrating on the important things."

"They're all important, Mr. Mancino."

"You want me to give him this whole list?"

"That's right. The whole list."

"All right. The other thing is that if you really want the Warden to pay any attention to all of this, you'd be smart to let that guard back there, Delft, come out with me and get to a doctor."

Orninski was silent a moment. "I don't think we can do that, Mr. Mancino."

"You'd still have one hostage; what's the advantage of two?"

"The advantage is that we got them. That is the advantage."

"Let me take his place then. I'll give the list to the Warden and come back so you can let him go."

Orninski seemed to consider this. "He ain't hurt that bad," he said finally. "And maybe if the Warden is in a hurry to get Delft out, he will be in a bigger hurry in agreeing to things."

"Will you let me bring a doctor in?"

"What doctor?"

"I don't care what doctor. Any doctor. He can fix you up too."

"I don't want any doctor fixing on me. But all right—maybe you have a good idea there, to show people we are willing to help a man that's been hurt. When you come back with the Warden's answer, you can bring along Dr. Angiotta, which is our regular prison doctor, but no one else, that we don't know."

"Why can't I bring him over right away?"

"No. When you come back with the answer. Not before." Orninski moved his hand into the flashlight beam and pulled back his sleeve. "It is now eight thirty. You can tell the Warden he can give his answer by nine thirty, one hour."

"What does that mean?"

"It means if he doesn't answer by then, we don't talk again until after breakfast in the morning."

"That's not much time."

"All right then—ten o'clock. But that is the latest. And you come back with the answer, no one else."

"What about the broadcasting part?"

"If he says yes, first come back and tell us, and bring a radio or TV so we can hear what you say. Then when we hear it, we will come out."

"Is that all?"

"Except one thing. Mel, I want you to say to Mr. Mancino here, who is your good friend and knows you, whether you agree one hundred per cent on everything I have said."

Again Mel seemed surprised to be called on—it took him a moment to answer. "That's right," he said. "I agree."

"On the show," Johnny said, "you didn't seem to think prisons were so bad. You didn't mention any complaints like this."

"That was before he ever been in the penitentiary, Mr. Mancino. This is not just another prison, it is the penitentiary. Ain't that right, Mel?"

"Yeah," Mel said. "That's right."

"So tell Mr. Mancino—do you agree with everything I been telling
him? Do you go along one hundred per cent?"

"Sure . . . one hundred per cent."

"Okay," Orninski said. "I guess that is it then."

And they let him go; he got out.

☐

"Is that it then?" the Warden said, raising his eyes, his hands clasped
on the table. "Is that all he wants?"

"That's it," Johnny said. He paused. "At first he wanted an answer
by nine thirty. Then he agreed to hold off till ten."

"That was kind of him," the Warden said.

They sat around a wooden table. On the table stood a lamp, ashtrays,
pencils, an intercom box, a telephone, an opened pack of Pall Malls.
It looked like a conference of executives of a small, unpretentious
business, except that the room was an open garage, with no lights
except for a table lamp. Behind Griffing in the dimness there were
three cars and a garbage truck, and not far away uniformed and
armed guards and that pile of rifles and tear gas bombs, and beneath
their feet a layer of sawdust over the bare ground.

The air was humid and oppressive. Regularly Dowler wiped his face
with his handkerchief. Fleishman did the same, but less often. Griffing
didn't seem to perspire. His face was dry and sinewy.

Johnny had taken off the raincoat and sat now in his shirt sleeves,
his collar open. He smoked a cigarette, his third or fourth since coming
back from the hobby shop. He felt both spent and exhilarated. At any
rate, his voice was steady again (had it sounded as shrill to Orninski
as it had to himself?) and the tightness in his stomach was almost gone. He could still feel the spot in his ribs where Orninski had
pressed the gun against him. It didn't hurt, but the pressure still
seemed to be there. Looking at the others, he decided he'd probably
held up as well as anyone. Even Griffing seemed irritable and frustrated. Even Fleishman—the nut, the clown—seemed sobered.

"You're positive now that he's got a gun?" the Warden asked.

"Well, it was pretty dark. But it felt like a gun. I assumed it was a
gun."

"Could it have been a wooden model?"

"It could have, I guess."

"I realize you're not a medical man, Mr. Mancino, but could you
be more specific about Delft—the injured officer. Exactly what would
you say is wrong with him?"

"Well, his mouth is cut and swollen. One eye is very puffy, practically closed. One ear seemed to be cut or ripped. He's got some nasty bumps and at least one cut on the head. The hair is matted over but it doesn't seem to be bleeding now."

"Would you say these were serious injuries, or primarily superficial?"

"I don't know. He seemed pretty dazed; maybe there's a concussion."

"Jeff, what's Orninski going to do if we send this fellow back with a flat no?"

"He'll make a lot of noise maybe, but I don't think he'd really do anything." Dowler sounded sullen, his voice thick. "Especially if we make it clear enough what'd happen if he did."

"That should be clear enough now," Griffing said.

"Well—maybe," Dowler said. "But what I think we oughta do is let him stew in there till morning, and if he won't come out then, just move in. We could get in through the roof, we could even break through the back wall if we had to. We could put men on both sides of the building, where he couldn't see them, and get them inside in a couple of seconds. We could use the gas—that'd get them out."

"Suppose they came out shooting?"

"You let me arm a dozen men and put them where I want, and you won't have to worry about him shooting."

"Suppose we use gas and he comes out behind Delft or Cloninger, uses them as a shield?"

"The minute he got out far enough, we could get him from behind."

"I don't know that I'd want to risk that. Mr. Mancino—would you say Orninski appeared rational? Did he seem to be in control of himself?"

"He certainly wasn't ranting and raving. He seemed precise enough about what he wanted; even rather logical."

"Our records indicate a—well, a potential of instability."

"The psychiatrist thinks he's a nut," Fleishman said.

"He is," Dowler said.

"Do you think Delft or Cloninger are in any immediate danger?" Griffing asked. "Did Orninski give any indication, for instance, what he'd do if we rejected his demands? Did he make any threats?"

"Only what I mentioned—that he wouldn't be responsible for what happened if you tried to rush him. Actually, I got the feeling that he has this whole business pretty well thought out; he knows what he's doing, what he wants. I don't think, for instance, that he expects you to accept his list whole-hog. I think he's enjoying this—the demands, the bargaining, his importance. I think if you simply accepted him on his own terms for the moment, as representative of the other side, and bargained with him, he'd be more than ready to be reasonable."

No one spoke.

"Did I say something wrong?" Johnny inquired.

"Not at all," Griffing said stiffly. "I appreciate your help. All of us, we're very indebted to you for coming here like this."

"There's one more thing," Johnny said. "My impression was that of all the things he mentioned, he's most concerned about what will happen to him—and his friends—after this is over. If he got some assurance on that, he might—"

"He oughta be concerned," Dowler said.

"The story he told you," the Warden said, speaking rather drily now, "conflicts somewhat with the version we've pieced together. Tell him what you've got, Flash."

Fleishman was sitting alongside Johnny, doodling on a pad. He dropped his pencil and looked up, producing one of his normal, weird smiles. "Our mutual friend, Mr. Simmons, apparently got in some sort of ruckus with several other inmates. Whether it was a real fight or a staged incident we don't know. But when Delft tried to break it up the men overpowered him."

"Where'd you get that story?" Johnny asked.

"From the other men in the garage. We got it independently from enough men to think it might bear some relationship to the truth."

Johnny shrugged. "Anyhow, Orninski isn't worried so much about your believing his story as he is about what you'll do with him afterward. He envisions a few months on bread and water."

"Yes, you mentioned that," Griffing said.

Johnny waited a moment. "Do they actually get that in solitary—bread and water?"

"It's not solitary, Mr. Mancino. But yes, for breakfast and supper they get bread and water. For lunch they receive the regular meal. They're kept on it only a week at a time, under the observation of the doctor. Then they get full meals for a week." His voice seemed devoid of any show of personality, any emotional commitment to what he was saying. It was as if, in his eminence, he couldn't allow himself the luxury of human involvement.

"I really didn't think the bread and water business was still in favor," Johnny said.

"How would you suggest we punish inmates who violate the rules? They're already in prison; would you rather we flogged them?" The Warden didn't wait for an answer. He looked at his watch and announced flatly: "It's after nine now. There's no need to wait any longer that I can see. Are you willing to go back in, Mr. Mancino?"

"Yes. What do you want me to tell him?"

"Tell him I can't make any promises in regard to his punishment. He'll be brought before the Warden's court, under the normal prison procedure, with which he is already amply familiar. You can also say that I reject the whole idea of any kind of broadcast of the terms of settlement. He wants me to make a public confession, at least by implication, and I'm not going to do it. So that part is out."

"He seemed pretty set on that part."

"Well, it's out. I'm also rejecting his list of complaints to be investigated by this commission he's dreamed up. That too implies that I accept these complaints as legitimate. But you can tell him that if he will immediately release the hostages and surrender, along with the other inmates in there, that in due course a commission will be formed to conduct a general survey of the prison—a free and open study, conducted in whatever way the commission sees fit, with no predetermined areas of inquiry."

"Will the report be made public?"

"That would be up to the Prison Board. But I would assume so."

"What about the membership?"

"I have no serious objections to the membership he suggested. You can also tell him this is my final statement. There'll be no more negotiations, and I'll receive no more demands. If they reject these terms now, they won't get another chance to accept them. If they don't release the guards immediately, I'll hold them all responsible for whatever happens afterward, and they'll receive no protection or leniency whatever." He looked at Dowler and Fleishman. "Do either of you have any suggestions?"

They both shook their heads and the Warden was about to go on when Fleishman said: "Maybe we ought to leave ourselves some elbow room, Griff. Maybe instead of definitely saying this is the final—"

"No. This is it. I'm not going to have him toying with us. Is the doctor ready?"

"I'll get him," Fleishman said. He headed outside.

"I should warn you, Mr. Mancino, that Orninski might not be quite as gracious this time. If you'd rather not go back, we certainly—"

"I'll go," Johnny said. "Only I ought to mention that you can't expect me to go along with you about not putting Orninski's side of the story on the air. I can see your point, of course, but I don't feel I—"

"You mean you intend to make public that fellow's demands—that absurd list?"

"If it's absurd, you can point that out. You can come on yourself and—"

"We didn't ask you to come in here so you could get a story, Mr. Mancino. Why didn't you mention this before?"

"Before I went in? Because I had no idea it'd come up."

"We're all set," Fleishman said, returning with the doctor.

"No we're not," Griffing said. "Mr. Mancino's not going in."

Fleishman raised his bushy eyebrows, causing his big black eyeglasses to ride up his nose. He contorted his face into still another ludicrous grimace. "He's not?"

"He wants to use all this on the air. He's just out for a story."

"I don't see why you should assume everything you do is privileged," Johnny said. "This is a public institution."

"I don't wish to discuss this," Griffing said. "Jeff, you take charge here. I'm going over myself. If they don't want to listen, that'll be their business."

"Wait a minute, Griff," Fleishman said. "Maybe we can just—"

"No, I'm tired of this. We'll handle it ourselves."

"They won't talk to you," Johnny said. "They won't even let the doctor in if you go."

The doctor, a short man with sloping shoulders who had been standing silently alongside Fleishman, raised his head, but did not break his silence. In his right hand he held his small black bag.

"Maybe he's right," Fleishman said.

"I am right," Johnny said. "And I think I can get him to accept your terms. I think at least I have a chance. You don't. Besides I'm going to use what Orninski said no matter what you do now. You're not gaining anything this way. And if you're really interested in getting those men out, you—"

"He's right," Fleishman said. "Let him go in."

"No, I've had enough of him."

"Give him one more chance. The hell with his story—let him put it on the air. Let him shout it from the rooftops. He'll be on that commission anyhow, so what difference—"

"He's not going to be on the commission."

"That's not what you said two minutes ago," Johnny said. "Is that what your word's worth? Is that what you expect the men in there to—"

"Will you please go outside for a minute?" Fleishman said. "Will you please let us talk?"

"No," Johnny said. "If you don't want me, I'll leave now, and for good—but you'd better have a way of settling this yourselves then, because I'm not covering up for you. If anything happens to those guards you'll—"

"Have an officer escort him to the gate," Griffing said.

"I wish you luck," Johnny said. He turned to go.

"Wait," Fleishman said.

"No, get him out of here," Griffing said. "He's in the way."

"Will you please be decent enough to let us talk in private for one minute?" Fleishman said.

"No. If I'm staying, I'm going to know what's going on."

"Oh shit," Fleishman said. "Listen Griff, what do you care what he says on television? He can say what he wants. But let him go in and see if he can't get those men out. It's going to be one hell of a mess otherwise. If we try to rush them we'll just—"

"We can rush them," Dowler said. "I'm with Griff. Let's just give them the word."

"Why? Why not at least try it this way first?"

"But I'm on the commission," Johnny said. "That was part of the deal."

"Oh for Christ's sake, put him on! Put Ed Sullivan and Jack Paar on too, for all we care. Who gives a shit?"

"I don't see any reason why we have to deal through this man," Griffing said. "He's just out for what he can get."

"I didn't ask to come here," Johnny said. "You sent a cop to *bring* me here."

"Be quiet, will you?" Fleishman said. "What do you care what he's out for, Griff. If we can use him, let's use him. Maybe he can pull it off. If he doesn't, all right, we'll send him home."

The Warden waited a moment. "Do you really believe he can do something with them?"

"At least there's the possibility. Because if this thing blows up, he'll go on every station in the country and say he could have done it only we wouldn't give him the chance."

Griffing stared at Johnny. Johnny stared back.

"Maybe you're right," Griffing said to Fleishman. "Maybe it's worth a try."

"Sure it is, Griff. There's nothing to lose."

Griffing turned back to Johnny. "If you go in, will you agree to tell them exactly what I said, nothing more or less?"

"Am I on the commission?"

"Let him be on the goddamn commission."

"All right," Griffing said. "I'll stand by that."

"Okay," Johnny said. "Let's go."

They moved out from the garage and stood for a moment looking across to the dark windows of the hobby shop. Several guards stood nearby with rifles, or maybe shotguns. Johnny put the raincoat back on and took the flashlight from the pocket.

"Get a light for the doctor," the Warden said, and one of the guards brought over a flashlight. The doctor took it without comment. "Perhaps you should repeat to me what you're to say," Griffing said.

"I'm not an idiot," Johnny said.

The crackling of a voice over the intercom sounded from the garage, loud but unintelligible.

"I'll get it," Fleishman said. He hurried inside and they heard more crackling, and then Fleishman called: "Warden, it's for you."

Griffing headed into the garage and Johnny started in after him.

"Wait here," Dowler said, touching his arm.

Johnny shrugged. They waited. In a few minutes the Warden and Fleishman returned. In the dark, Johnny couldn't make out their faces.

"We're going to hold off a bit," the Warden said.

"What time is it?" Johnny said. "We don't have much longer."

"It's nine twenty, and we're waiting."

"Why?"

"Because I said so, that's why."

"Until when?"

"Until I say you can go in."

"What's the matter? What's up?"

"I've just spoken to the chairman of the Prison Board, and he—"

"Kale?"

"Yes. Do you know him?"

"Yes, I know him."

"Well, he's coming out. He's on his way."

☐

As they waited, the rain began. It came down with a great roar, the drops huge and slashing, the puddles forming on the hard ground almost instantly. The noise was tremendous, and the night closed off before them. They could see out only a few feet now, and the only sound was the crashing of the rain; it was the sound of a waterfall, magnified enormously on the tin roof of the garage.

"Between you and me, kiddo, this is the craziest goddamn weather I have seen in all my adult life." Fleishman had to shout to be heard.

Johnny nodded. The two of them were alone at the far end of the garage, watching the downpour. They stood alongside the prison garbage truck, a clumsy gray monstrosity, metal barrels hanging by hooks from its side. The Warden had gone up front to meet Kale, taking Dowler with him. They had beaten the rain, but just barely. It was twenty to ten, and they'd been gone about fifteen minutes.

"Why didn't the Warden take you with him too?" Johnny said. "I got the impression you were his trusted advisor."

"You know what I am? I'm the court jester. Worse. I'm the resident intellectual. I'm the Arthur Schlesinger Jr. of the state penal system. I give the place tone."

"What's Dowler then?"

"Dowler? He's the Old Pro. The guardian of our collective virtue, the man with the crest, the cross, the shield."

"And Griffing's the Evil King," Johnny said.

"Oh?" Fleishman said. He mused on this for a moment. "And what does that make you—Prince Charming?"

Johnny laughed. "Tell me, do you know Kale?"

"That's a point—what the hell is he? It's too awesome even to contemplate. But yes, we're acquainted."

"What do you think of him?"

"I think he's my duly appointed superior."

"You don't get along?"

"We rarely meet."

Johnny looked out at the rain. The hobby shop might as well be twenty miles away for all you could see. "How come you don't have floodlights or something? Suppose they try to get out?"

"You can see the lights from the Cell Block. They won't try to get out."

"Has anybody ever escaped from here?"

"A few. Not recently. The last one sneaked out on the laundry truck about six years ago, and headed into the desert. They got the bloodhounds after him, and tracked him over craggy and crack for two days, into the mountains and through the valleys and dry arroyos. They were closing in on him out there, and there wasn't anyplace else to hide, so he climbed into a mesquite tree and I guess tried to look like a withered branch or something. The posse and the dogs and the guards dragged him down—it was like an early Western, I hear tell. The guy was starving and dehydrated, his beard was scraggly and he was nearly delirious. He'd covered something like twenty-five miles, the last bit of it evidently on his hands and knees."

Johnny said nothing for a moment. "Everybody keeps talking about that fellow in there, Orninski, as if he's ready to blow his top. Is he?"

"Shall I quote? From his classification report? It was made over a year ago, but we had the occasion to look it up a while back, and again tonight, so I can quote: 'The subject presents no well-defined mental condition, but there is some evidence of distortion of personality, along with the possibility of a persecution syndrome, perhaps paranoia.'"

"Then what's he doing in a prison?"

"Spending fifteen-to-twenty of the best years of his life for armed bank robbery, during which he beat a teller unconscious with the butt of his gun. And since he's got some thirteen years to go, he doesn't have much to lose. What the hell, what's a few more years? All we can do is put him on punishment—which you and he seem to agree is inhuman."

"Doesn't a psychiatric report like that make any difference?"

"A report like that? You should see the bad ones."

"The ones that get locked up in your special cells?"

"That's right. They're the real lulus."

"Why aren't they put in a mental hospital?"

"Because the mental hospital won't take them. Because they're even more crowded than we are, and have their own problems. Because, if you will promise not to send my words ringing over the airwaves, the only way we can transfer a left fielder over there is to accept, in exchange, one of their first basemen."

"You mean you have to *trade* with them?"

"Body for body. Of course the ones they send us have to have a conviction, but they've got no shortage of those."

"What about Mel Simmons? What did his report say?"

"Nothing. Simmons is just fine. A good levelheaded clean-cut kid. As sane as apples are round."

"He's in real trouble now, isn't he?"

"It's that fifty dollars you paid him. It destroyed his sense of values, getting that kind of dough while a man like me wasn't considered worth a plug nickel."

"I guess I gave you a bum steer on him . . . asking you to help him out."

"We try to help everybody out."

Johnny sat on the running board of the garbage truck; it smelled damply of fruit skins and stale cooked vegetables. Fleishman remained where he was, hands in pockets, leaning one shoulder against the wall, looking out at the rain. It seemed to hold a great fascination for him.

Well, of the three of them (Winken, Blinken and Nod? The Three Blind Mice? The Butcher, the Baker, the Candlestick Maker?) Fleishman would have to be the one, at least by default, you'd prefer being marooned in a prison garage with on a rainy night. The other two—Good God, no wonder they had trouble, no wonder the convicts every so often felt like beating a guard to a pulp. What was annoying was that Griffing, by his own pigheadedness, forced you into making excuses for Orninski. For God's sake—bread and water! But only a week at a time, and not including lunch. Humanitarians all. Well, if mental cases like Orninski were the kind that got sent to prisons, and martinets like Griffing the kind that ran them, what could you expect?

It'd be interesting to know what psychological aberration influenced the man who first decided that the proper Christian treatment for a lawbreaker was to lock him up behind a wall. And the guards, the wardens—how could anyone, having once seen that wall, want to spend his life working inside it? You needed a kind of moral anesthesia, a lack of imagination, an inability to project yourself into another's sensitivity. Even then, over the years, something must happen to you. In some way it had to corrupt you; in some way you had to degenerate.

"Flash? Where are you?"

It was the Warden's voice, from the other end of the garage. The rain was still pounding and they hadn't heard or seen him return. Just as well no one seemed to think Orninski had any ideas about escaping. In this rain he could march an army by without anyone noticing.

Johnny hurried after Fleishman toward the other end of the garage. It was ten to ten. Standing near the wooden table, the Warden was talking quietly to Dowler. Both now wore raincoats and flopping rain hats that came down to their shoulders. A guard stood nearby with additional coats and hats over his arm. The Warden was wiping his face with a white handkerchief as they approached. He looked up and nodded, then folded his handkerchief and swung his hand under his dripping raincoat to put it away. He seemed intent upon getting the handkerchief properly smoothed out in his pocket, and the others waited in silence while he fussed with it. Then he looked up, almost as if surprised that there were people nearby, waiting for him to say something.

"Did Kale get here?" Fleishman asked.

"He's up front, trying to get in touch with the Governor." He paused. "I hope it won't further weaken your faith in my word, Mr. Mancino, but Mr. Kale and I have decided on a somewhat altered course of action."

"Am I going in?" Johnny said after a moment.

"If you're still willing to."

"What am I supposed to tell them now?"

"That their demands have been rejected."

"All of them?"

"All of them." He paused. "Under the circumstances, I'll understand if you'd rather not go."

"Am I supposed to tell them anything else?"

"Only that we won't receive any more demands from them."

"Good Christ," Fleishman said.

"You have a comment, Flash?"

"No, Warden. I was just stifling a sneeze."

"Is the doctor coming with me?" Johnny asked.

"Yes. Isn't he here?"

"He was around before," Fleishman said. *"Doc? Where are you?"*

The four of them looked down into the darkness at the other end of the garage. They heard a door open and Dr. Angiotta got out, hunched over, from the back seat of one of the cars. "Just catching a little rest," he said. "You ready for me now?"

"Yes. You two are going in; I guess you'd better walk fast—it's five to ten. I'm sending Dowler halfway over with you—with five armed officers. They'll be ready to move in if there's any trouble. Have you still got that whistle, Mr. Mancino?"

"Yes."

"You'd better take one too, Doctor."

Angiotta took the whistle Dowler produced, unzipped his black bag, and dropped it in.

"If you're gonna blow it, blow it good and loud," Dowler said.

"Be careful," the Warden said. "Don't get involved in anything. Just get Delft taken care of and then tell them what I said and get out. Don't stay in there talking; there's nothing to talk about. Here, you'll probably want these hats."

Johnny and the doctor put on and buttoned the visored rain hats.

The five of them moved to the open side of the garage. They paused before the dripping wall of water.

"Let them get about fifteen feet ahead, then follow after them," Griffing told Dowler. "Go close enough to see the building, then pull back a few feet. If the rain stops, back up some more. We don't want them seeing you."

"They won't see us."

"Okay," Griffing said to Johnny. "If you're ready."

Johnny flicked on his light, then ducked his head against the rain and moved out quickly, the doctor at his side. It was quieter out in the open; the rain flashed silver in the moving beam. His right hand, holding the flashlight, was already soaked. He kept the other hand in the raincoat pocket, fingering the whistle.

15

The full moon: that was it. Because Flash Fleishman was no dope, he knew a real live omen when he saw one. You wouldn't catch him being snippy toward those occult roots, those savage primacies. And that could do it: the full moon not in its pristine presence but worse, in its latency, hidden behind clouds. So Simmons felt a little unruly, and Delft gave in to a dark urge to throttle Orninski, and Orninski *et al.* decided to show Delft that even the clipped claws of the caged tiger eventually grew back and honored still the instinct for blood—well, what else would you expect?

It was as good an explanation as the next. Even Flash himself—as rational and civilized man as you'd hope to meet, a gentle man, a kindly man, long free of those base, brooding instincts—even he would feel better if, for instance, he could have booted the Charming Young Guy with his Head in the Sky in the ass. The goon. The one with the large white teeth. Him. Old Icewater, fearless and undismayed. Our lanky savior, in there now dispensing blessings upon the poor and the meek, making hallowed that very ground upon which those noble and unfortunate victims stood, consecrating for all time that humble hobby shop as a sacred relic. *Here stood Orninski against the world, Smithereen Gun in hand! Kneel, good men, and pray!*

Good God in heaven, why Johnny Mancino? One hated to be glib and sociological—but a television announcer!

"How long does it take to say no?" Griffing said, not raising his voice enough to carry over the noise of the rain clattering on the roof, so that Flash, standing next to him, caught only a few words and had to reconstruct the sentence, in retrospect, before answering.

"He's only been in ten minutes," Flash said.

They stood near the garbage truck. They could see nothing through the rain, not even Dowler and his cohorts crouched out there faithfully somewhere in the mud, their rifles poised and dripping.

"What's Kale doing up front?"

"Still trying to get the Governor, I guess," Griffing said.

"Maybe he won't be able to."

"That's what you said when we were trying to get Kale."

"Hope springs eternal."

"Kale was giving a speech in town when they found him," Griffing said. "I'm afraid he thinks this is a Republican plot."

"It's the moon, tell him. There's a full moon up there somewhere, behind those clouds."

Griffing said nothing. He didn't even seem to be listening. Wasn't it always thus? The voice of wisdom drowned out by the press of daily affairs.

But then he realized Griffing was listening to something else—the sound, amidst the pouring characterless rain, of someone approaching behind a hazy light.

"Who is it?" Griffing called.

"Us," came back the voice of Dr. Angiotta, and a moment later two dark figures materialized amid the downpour. Figures of normal, human proportions: an officer, rifle lowered, seemed to be escorting the good doctor back. The doctor hurried into the garage and shook himself, water flying. The officer turned and headed back grimly into the slosh.

"What happened?" Griffing demanded. "Where's Mancino?"

"He's still in there," Angiotta said in his best unruffled manner.

"What on earth is he doing in there?"

"Talking," Angiotta said, unbuttoning his raincoat. The cuffs of his trousers were soaked, and he studied them, rather wistfully, in the beam of his flashlight, lifting and turning one foot for a better look.

"Damn him," Griffing said. "What about Delft? Is he all right?"

"They wouldn't let me near him."

"Then what have you been doing all this time?"

"Waiting. The television fellow—what's his name, again?—was arguing with the inmate about it. Then the inmate said either I'd have to leave or we both would. So the television fellow said it'd be best if I did."

"What the hell did you listen to him for?"

Angiotta looked at Griffing, steadily. "It wasn't a matter of listening to him. There was nothing I could do there, and they both seemed to agree I might as well leave."

"Damn him," Griffing said. "How long is he planning to stay in there?"

"He didn't say."

Undoubtedly he had planned to stay for a while, because fifteen minutes later he was still inside.

"Do you think they're holding him?" Griffing said.

"Don't suggest the idea," Flash said.

"We should never have let him go in," Griffing said. "We shouldn't have taken the chance."

"He'll be all right," Flash said. "God protects his kind."

An officer came hurrying toward them from the other end of the garage. "Warden—we've got someone on an outside line who wants to talk to that fellow there—Mr. Mancino. He says it's an emergency."

"Tell him he's busy, for God's sake!"

"He said he absolutely had to speak to him, sir. I tried to—"

"See what you can do, will you, Flash? He's your friend."

Flash went down to the other end and picked up the phone from the table. *He is not my friend, goddamn it. He is Mel Simmons' friend.* "Fleishman here."

"Johnny—? Is that you—?"

"Unfortunately Mr. Mancino is tied up at the moment. You're speaking to Dr. Samuel F. Fleishman. At your service."

"Can you speak a little louder? There's an awful lot of noise coming through."

"It's raining here. Is it raining there, wherever you are?"

"What? Yes, it's raining here. What are you doing—standing right out in it?"

"My window is open."

"Can I speak to Johnny Mancino, please?"

"Not right now. But we have an officer here named *Manson*. Would you care to speak to him? He's also fairly tall, and their names are practically the same."

"Look, this is important. What's going on there? What's he doing?"

"Who knows, I always say."

"Can you get a message to him?"

"Can I get a message to him? Well, I guess you didn't catch before just who you were speaking to. You're speaking to Dr. Samuel F.—"

"Tell him to call Bob Winninger *immediately*. Will you do that? He knows where I am, I'm at the arena. Tell him to—"

"The arena?"

"Yes. In Aurora. Never mind—he knows where I am. Tell him we've been holding up the contest for an hour now and we have to make the announcement right away. Have you got that? This is very important. We've got to get word to him and—"

"Don't you fret. The minute I hang up I shall seek him out, and *what Fleishman seeks, Fleishman finds!* You're probably not familiar with that saying, but it's quite common around here. Anyhow, I shall find him, and I shall say, 'Officer Manson, you are wanted at the arena immediately. The Romans are impatient, the lions are hungry, the—' "

"Oh for Christ's sake!—Mancino! Johnny *Mancino!*"

"Of course. How stupid of me."

"Look, what the hell is going on there? Are you sure you're—"

"It's raining. Yes, that is the news here. The big rain is coming down. And if it weren't for that, the moon—"

"Will you give him that message?"

"Why not?" Flash said and hung up. "Some nut or other," he confided to the officer, who had been standing aside pretending not to listen.

He headed back to the other end where—wouldn't you know it?—all hell now seemed to be breaking loose. That's what happens—you turn your back for one minute and Chaos strolls in. Even Kale was there, large and damp and impressive, with a blue officer's cape wrapped dashingly around him. And the goon. And five officers, wet to the skin and armed to the teeth. And Dowler himself, the Biggest Officer of Them All, with a .30 caliber rifle caressed in his blunt hands. (Oh Christ, what might the moon do to *him?* No—he didn't need it. It was for nights like this that he really yearned, not for all those quiet years spent avoiding trouble. Dowler was not at heart a peacetime general, inspecting bored troops on dusty parade grounds. He was a combat infantryman who happened to have a couple of stars on his helmet. What he loved most of all was the enemy—armed, dangerous, hidden, committed. What he desired most was the moment when all the vague words and galling ambiguities could be brushed aside, the bloody stump of battle here at last.)

They must have just piled out of an express train—how else could they all have gotten there so fast? Ten all told, crowded between the wall and the garbage truck. A convention. They should have hired the arena away from Mancino's pal and set up folding chairs. Invited in people off the street who might come up with a few more bright ideas about settling prison disturbances.

Mancino unbuttoned his raincoat and shook the water off. When he noticed he was shaking it on everyone else he stopped. Dowler sent his five officers away, thinning the crowd somewhat. Another officer arrived with a Coleman lantern ablaze, holding it awkwardly at arm's length, whitening their faces to ghastly hues and sending grotesque shadows sprawling upon the walls.

"What happened?" Griffing demanded. "What took you so long?"

"Nothing," Mancino said.

"Did you tell him there'd be no more negotiations?"

"I told him. He said he didn't plan on any more until after breakfast anyhow."

"Breakfast?" Kale said. "Whose breakfast?"

"Theirs, I assume," Griffing said.

"Were you planning to serve them breakfast in there?"

"We gave them supper. There are two officers in there—one of them injured." Griffing turned back to Mancino. "Does Orninski still seem to be in control?"

"Oh yes."

"Was he the one who refused to let the doctor see Delft?"

"Yes. He insisted on hearing your answer first. Then he wouldn't let the doctor go near him."

"What took you so long? What have you been doing in there?"

"It didn't seem so long," Mancino said, rather casually, standing in the glare of the Coleman lantern with his TV face turned on. "I was trying to get him to let the doctor see Delft. Then I tried to talk him into letting Delft go. Anyhow, I did find out something."

"What did you find out?"

"That they'd accept the terms you were ready to offer before."

It was quiet for a stretch. Very quiet. Except for the rain, of course. Then Griffing said, in his best knife-edge voice: "You told them about that?"

"I didn't say you suggested it, of course. I simply asked if he'd be willing to accept something along those lines."

"You weren't authorized to do that."

"Well, I did it. And he seemed to think it was a reasonable compromise, although he didn't actually commit himself. But I think you can get him out on those terms."

"What terms?" Kale demanded. "Did you offer those men terms?"

"You overstepped your authority," Griffing said to Mancino.

"All right, I overstepped my authority. I apologize."

"What's he talking about?" Kale said. "Did you or didn't you offer anything to those men?"

"We didn't," Griffing said. "We simply discussed among ourselves various possibilities. I told you that on the phone."

"Then just what did you say to them?" Kale asked the goon.

"I told you—I just sounded them out. I didn't mention the Warden at all. I just—"

"He did it entirely on his own," Griffing said.

"But you told them all their demands had been rejected, didn't you?" Kale said to the goon.

"Yes, I told them."

"How did they seem to take it?"

"Quite well. He didn't seem at all disturbed. Or even particularly surprised."

"You don't think they're planning any trouble for tonight?"

"They seem content to wait until morning."

Kale was silent for a moment. Conceivably he was thinking. You never could tell. "How did you get in on this, Johnny?" he asked abruptly, as if the oddness of the whole thing had just occurred to him.

"He's a friend of one of the inmates in there," Griffing said.

"The leader?—what's his name again?"

"Orninski," Griffing said. "No, not him. Another one. Mel Simmons."

"They're willing to talk to him, is that it?"

"That seems to be it," Griffing said. "Although I think perhaps his usefulness has ended. We can arrange transportation back to—"

"No," Kale said. "Let's keep him handy. Can you arrange a bed or something for him?"

"A bed?" Mancino said.

"You might as well get some rest," Kale said. "It doesn't look like we'll need you before morning."

"He's planning to use all this on television," Griffing said.

"All what?"

"What the inmates told him. He plans to put all their gripes on the air."

"Well, we'll worry about that when the time comes. What do you say, Johnny? Will you stay?"

"What are you planning to do in the morning?"

"We'll have to work that out," Kale said. "But I'd like you to stay, if you would. We might need you."

"All right," Mancino said.

"Fine," Kale said. "I appreciate that. Is that all right with you now, Griff?"

Griffing gritted his teeth and said nothing.

"Before you go nighty-night," Flash said, "you got a call before. Somebody at the arena; he wants you to call him back."

"Oh, that," Mancino said.

"Will you show him where the phone is, Flash," Griffing said.

"I know where it is," Mancino said.

"If you don't mind, Flash will go with you. I'll have to ask you not to say anything about what's happening here. The men in the cells have radios."

"I won't say anything," Mancino said. "This is just that beauty contest thing." He glanced down at his dress trousers, evidently by way of explanation, or possibly illustration.

"That what?" Griffing said.

"Beauty contest," Mancino said. "I'm a judge."

"I see," Griffing said, with impressive restraint.

Flash took him down to the table at the other end, where an officer was lounging on a chair, staring at the cigarette in his hand. He stood up. "Any hot news over the handy-dandy circuit?" Flash asked.

"No sir. Nothing."

Flash picked up the phone. "See if you can dig up a Mr. Winninger down at the arena in Aurora, will you? He's running a beauty contest and wants to talk to Mr. Mancino."

"A beauty contest, sir?"

"That's right. Go to it now." Flash put the phone down.

"What are you people going to do in the morning?" Mancino asked.

"You know as much as I do."

"If the Warden had any guts, he'd have gone through with that offer. Those men would be out by now."

Flash glanced at the officer standing nearby, and Mancino at least had the sense to shut up.

When the phone rang Flash motioned for Mancino to pick it up, then backed a few feet away to listen at a more polite distance.

". . . Well yes, I guess so. If you want them . . ." He looked at Flash, uncomfortably. Flash looked down at his shoes, which were muddy. "All right—first, Margo Weisner . . . Yes, that's the one. I thought she showed a good deal more—well look, let's not go into all that now, okay? I'll just give you the names. Second, Ann Marshall . . . That's right, the colored girl. And third, Jenny Goodrich—you know, the singer . . ."

When the goon finished, Flash led him back to the other end of the garage. Kale and Griffing were gone. Dowler was talking to Bianco, who eyed Mancino steadily.

"Johnny Mancino," Flash said. "Paul Bianco, our Chief Keeper, Mr. Dowler's right-hand man."

"We're putting everyone on four-hour shifts," Dowler said. "Bianco and I will split shifts up here."

"I can take a shift," Flash said.

Dowler shrugged. "Griff said he wanted a Security man here."

"All right," Flash said. "If that's what he wants."

It was logical enough, after all, and nothing too feel slighted about. Bianco was trustworthy. One thing about Security people, they were trustworthy. They could shoot. They did their jobs. They wore uniforms (except for Dowler, who somehow managed to make street clothes look like a uniform). They knew whereof they stood, and they stood foursquare. It was not in the ranks of Security that you found sentimentalists, would-be poets, do-gooders, intellectuals, fragile souls or stutterers. You found that sort in Treatment. Treatment men had to be handled. You didn't have to handle a Security man. You just had to tell him what to do, and he did it.

"What you wanna do," Dowler told Bianco, "is keep enough men close enough to make sure nothing's happening in there. If anything happens, or looks like it's gonna happen, buzz us, and fast. You do not, repeat not, have fire authority, but you can shoot back if they shoot first, or to protect those men in there. You got that?"

"I got it," Bianco said.

You knew he had.

Dowler turned to Flash. "The Warden wants me up front now. He said for you to set up Mr. Mancino here for the night—he said maybe you could fix up a cot in the library. Then I don't know—I guess you should head up front too, in case he wants you for anything."

"I'll do that," Flash said, as pleasantly as he could manage, and started off with Mancino.

Sure; in this moment of crisis, on this night of portent, he was left to slosh through the mud and rain with an overgrown TV announcer in tow while the others were gathering in Griffing's dry and lofty office to plot grand strategy. He had to bend his intellect to the problem of finding clean sheets while they, tight-lipped and beady-eyed, discussed the value of one man's life, the chances of another's death. He played nursemaid, while they played God.

"Where on earth is this place?" Mancino muttered.

"We're almost there," Flash muttered back. *I* didn't ask him to come. He's not *my* friend. It's eleven o'clock at night, six agonizing hours after cocktail time and every minute setting a new world record, the rain is still coming down as if it had something personal against me, I am being slighted and shat upon by superiors, equals, inferiors and outsiders alike, and see no reason in the world why I should be nice to *any*body, let alone him!

And they were supposed to go to the Griffings' tonight, for a party. Somewhere out there in the real world there was gin to be drunk, and music, laughter, good fellowship. Somewhere bands are playing, somewhere people shout . . .

They arrived at the Quonset hut. A drenched officer stood outside the door, huddled up against the rain.

"What are you doing out here?" Flash asked.

"Mr. Reed put me here, sir. He thought somebody should be standing guard."

"I don't think we're in any imminent danger down here," Flash said. "Why don't you just stand guard inside for a while?"

"That sounds just fine, sir."

They stepped into the dimly lighted foyer. On cots lined in double rows along the walls about a dozen officers were sleeping. Flash didn't see any of his own staff; God knows where the hell they were. At a table, four officers were playing cards. Some were sitting on the cots, talking quietly.

"Is anyone in the library?"

"I don't think so," the officer said.

"Would you do me a big favor?" Flash said in a sudden inspiration. "Would you kindly take Mr. Mancino and introduce him to Mr. Reed, and tell Mr. Reed that the Warden would like Mr. Mancino set up for the night in the library, with a cot and any other conveniences and creature comforts that he might desire." He turned to the goon. "If you'll excuse me then . . . Do have a good night's sleep."

"It's still pretty early for that."

"I'm afraid we can't have you wandering around. This is a prison, you know."

"I've noticed."

Flash left, considering the fact that maybe there *was* something after all to the idea of locking people up, that maybe it too had its virtues, its logic.

He walked to the Administration Building. The rain was fading; the violence had gone out of it. It now seemed merely boorish and implacable.

The staff office was deserted, the desks unmanned, the files locked, the typewriters covered. No one was there except Bostick, who sat rather forlornly at the switchboard with the intercom unit on the chair beside him. A Styrofoam cup with some cold-looking coffee stood on the switchboard.

"How are things up here?" Flash said, unbuttoning his raincoat and removing the absurd Gloucester fisherman's hat. "Been quiet?"

"Well, it's quiet now. But it's *been* busy."

"What's been going on?"

"Wives, sir."

"Oh Christ. What have you been telling them?"

"What the Warden said: that the men would be on duty through the night."

"What about Delft and Cloninger? They're both married, aren't they?"

"The Warden spoke to their wives, sir."

"Has mine called?"

"Oh yes, sir. Some time ago."

"What did you tell her?"

"The same as the others, sir."

"Can you give me an outside line?" Flash sat on a desk and dialed. Mrs. Moore said Jo Ann was at the Griffings'. Sure, boozing it up, all the wives partying gaily, like the night before Waterloo, doing quadrilles, while their husbands, grim, harassed, bone-weary, caring not for their own safety . . .

He dialed the Griffings'. "Hi—Rosa? Flash here. Is my wife sober?"

"What's going on there? Has anything more happened?"

"No, everything's very calm."

"What's happening with those guards in there?"

"Nothing. But everything is under control. Your husband's fine; I'm fine; the guards in there seem to be fine. We don't want all you women worrying now, and ruining your party."

"I had all this food in, Flash, and I didn't see any reason why we should all sit home chewing our fingernails by ourselves. Griff isn't planning on staying up through the night, is he?"

"I'm sure he's not. He'll probably be in bed before you, if that wild party doesn't break up soon."

"It's like a funeral here, Flash. Tell me a good joke to pass on and liven things up a bit."

"I'll try to think of one. Put on Jo Ann, will you, like a good Warden's wife."

"Hold on."

Flash couldn't think of a joke. He never could. He was an atrocious joke teller. He didn't believe in jokes.

"Flash, are you all right?"

"Of course I'm all right. I gave Rosa all the news; you can get it from her. Just wanted to say hello. How's everything going?"

"Everything's all right *here,* for God's sake."

"Sure—your kids aren't locking themselves in broom closets and throwing stones out at you."

"Is that what's going on there? Are they throwing things at you?"

"I was being metaphorical."

"Is it really bad? Are you people in trouble?"

"No, I don't think we're in real trouble."

"How are you going to get those men out?"

"We'll manage, don't worry. Anyhow, it's very quiet here now; how's the party going?"

"I've been to livelier ones. They were just having the senior staff— no outsiders. So it's all girls now, plus a few gallons of liquor and about three tons of food. I never realized the share of eating and drinking you men handled."

"Well, don't hang around all night waiting for news. If I were you, I'd have one more stiff drink and head home to get some sleep."

"I'm going to stay over with Mrs. Cloninger. Rosa just arranged it; she's going to stay with the other fellow's wife—"

"Delft."

"That's it. She figured they might be having a pretty rough time of it, so—"

"I don't envy you."

"What should I say to her, Flash? I've never even met her."

"Tell her everything's going to be all right, but not to expect any news until tomorrow. Are you going to stay with her all night?"

"I guess so—if she wants me to. I've already checked with Mrs. Moore; she said she'd stay over for us and give the kids breakfast."

"Okay. Try to be cheery with Mrs. Cloninger."

"All right. And you be careful, Flash."

"I will, don't worry. And tell Rosa to try the one about the stripper and the chiropractor."

"What?"

"It's a joke. Good luck with Mrs. Cloninger. Maybe you can both get some sleep there. We'll let you know the minute he's out."

"Okay. Be careful now, Flash."

"You already said that. Sweet dreams, sweetie."

"Okay. Just be careful."

Flash hung up and remained sitting on the desk for a moment, staring at Bostick at the switchboard. Bostick was pretending to be writing something down, as he had been doing throughout the phone call. "Has anybody arranged to relieve you here?"

"No sir."

"Call the hut and have Mr. Reed send someone over who knows how to work this thing. You go up there and get some sleep then, and come back on in the morning."

The door opened and Dowler leaned in. "Oh—here you are."

"Yes, just got here. Does Griff want me?"

"They're finished now; I just wanted to tell Bostick that the Warden's going to try to catch some sleep in his office. Don't put anything through to him without checking with Flash or me up at the garage."

"Am I going to be at the garage?" Flash said.

"Yeah. The Warden wants Bianco in the dome. Kale's coming too— oop, here he is." Dowler stepped out of the doorway and a moment later Kale appeared, pausing to gaze in at Flash. He still wore his blue officer's cape, dark blue now from being wet. Perhaps he liked the flair of it—a sort of F.D.R.-on-the-deck-of-the-flagship look, cape flying in the Mediterranean breeze: the Commander-in-Chief, eyes steady and off to the horizon. No sir—no little ruckus in any little old penitentiary was going to ruffle the self-assurance or muddy up the clear vision of Frank J. Kale.

"Let's go," Kale said, and the three of them walked down the hallway, Kale leading. He paused at the end of it, uncertain whether to turn right or go down the stairs. Dowler gestured soberly and Kale, cape floating backward ever so gently, led them down the stairs and out to the sally port. The two wall lamps burned under the stone archway, casting a faint yellowish light. Everything was still dripping, and the smell of wet earth seemed stronger than ever now, but it was quiet; the rain had stopped.

The officer on duty at the gate, who had been talking with three other officers, snapped about and saluted. Kale nodded in acknowledgment. "We'll be heading up to the garage for a final look-see before I turn in," Kale told him. "The Warden's catching a little sleep in his office."

"Yes, sir," the officer said after a brief pause, puzzled as to why the hell Kale was telling him this.

The three of them headed up the hill along the flagstone path. The air was cool now, very fresh, and the sky was already beginning to clear. Flash looked up as they walked. Here and there he saw a star between the clouds, but no moon. That old debbil moon. Way up in the sky. Ahead of them the Cell Block, with small lights glaring down from the corners of the roof, stood with dismal and obscene massiveness. Flash, as a warden, never pulled night duty, and rarely saw the place after dark. Just as well; it was sufficiently depressing in the daytime. The lines of dark windows in the Cell Block and the lighted booths spaced along the top of the shadowed wall were enough to drain the marrow from your bones. But at least it was quiet. They had managed to get all the inmates down to supper and back without any difficulties and now it was well past Lights Out, which meant they were probably home free for the night. What nicer, more reassuring vision could any humanist ask for—a thousand men jacking off in there and now sleeping comfy as babes behind their bars.

They reached the top of the steps and swung left along the gravel path, Kale in the middle. "I certainly hope you men realize how much I'm counting on your full support tomorrow."

Neither of them answered. It wasn't a statement that exactly cried out for a response. Dowler did, however, sort of nod.

"The Warden tells me," Kale said, favoring Flash with his gaze as they trudged along the wet path, "that you were in charge of interrogating the prisoners from the garage. I was wondering . . . well, if it came to your attention whether or not that colored boy—you know the one I mean, what's his name?—was involved?"

"Walker."

"Yes, that's the one. I was going to ask the Warden but it slipped my mind."

Indeed. Here was his chance. He just wished the hell he could say *Look here, bubblehead—THAT was the cause of the whole goddamn mess! Yes!—you and your fellow vote-sucking boobs up in Maynard brought this agony upon us! You slobs who probably wouldn't let Ralph Bunche move into your neighborhood!*

But alas, the truth was never that logical, and the truth must out. So Flash said, "No. He didn't seem involved at all. Of course we've only got a sketchy—"

"Well, I'm glad to hear that. It certainly would have set us back if he'd been involved. You men, I assume, are doing everything you can to see that these colored boys are being absorbed into the mix without any trouble."

"Of course," Fleishman said.

They turned the corner of the Cell Block and the two officers at Post Three—all booths were double-staffed for the night—stepped forth and saluted.

"That's the way, men," Kale said, pleased as hell. "Stay alert now."

But he was deadly—you had to keep reminding yourself of that. You could no more laugh him off than any other mortal enemy, sneaking up on you with a knife between his teeth. True, he didn't even know enough to be scared, and had about as fine a grasp of the day-to-day operation of the pen as their other great helpmate this evening (our saviors—the goon and the boob!). And Kale was a boob, all right, but a special kind. The kind that won, that got what he wanted, that ended up in charge. The kind whose ideas—although stupid, immoral and wrong—worked. Whereas what the hell ideas did Flash Fleishman ever have that worked, or that ever got him anywhere?

At the garage they found Bianco standing out on the soggy ground at the far end. Two officers were with him, several more within view, and presumably a dozen or so more lurking about. All off-duty officers had been called in, so that hidden about in nooks and crannies, sleeping on cots, sitting on wooden stools, standing around somewhere talking in the vast recesses of the prison grounds, were over two hundred uniformed men.

"The Warden wants you over in the dome tonight," Dowler told Bianco. "The radios are all cut off, so if you get any gripes, tell them the electricity's on the bum."

Bianco left, walking off into the darkness. They looked around for Kale. He had wandered fifteen or twenty feet away. They joined him.

"Which building is it now?" he asked as they came up.

"The one over there, sir," Dowler said.

"Oh yes. Couldn't make it out before in all the rain. Are those the only windows?"

"Yes sir. Four of them."

"Do you think your men could get the shells through them? The gas shells, I mean—you know, tear gas."

"We could get some in, sure."

"How long would it take for the gas to get them out? How much time would they have to react, to organize themselves to do anything?"

"If we moved close enough, we could probably get some in on the first try. Once they get in, they'd work right away."

"But they'll realize something's up, if you go close."

"That's right, sir. But if we fire them from here, say, the chances of getting two or three in on the first try wouldn't be so good." Dowler paused. "Is that what we're planning to do in the morning, sir?"

Flash blinked; he gazed at Dowler in astonishment. What do you know—he hadn't been in on the big powwow either! A warm feeling for good old blunt Jeff Dowler coursed through him: his trusted friend, his comrade, his equal in ignorance.

"The Warden and I discussed a number of alternatives," Kale said. "The main thing is that we've got to make it clear to those men that they can't use this as a means to embarrass us."

"Excuse me?" Flash said.

"It seems obvious that they're aware there's an election on. Why else would they have picked this time to pull something like this? Anyway, tell me—what would you say to the idea of moving up under the cover of darkness—say, like right now—and putting those bombs in? That would let you get a lot closer, wouldn't it?"

"*Now?*" Dowler said.

"I'm just asking. I'd just like your opinion."

"Sure . . . Well, I guess yes, it'd let us get a lot closer. But we wouldn't be able to see much, and of course if there was any shooting, it'd be awfully hard to—"

"Of course," Kale said. "We've notified the State Police, by the way. They'll be standing by in the morning if we need them. We'll have all the manpower we can use." He continued to stare out across the ground at the hobby shop. "Do you think I could move up for a better look?"

"There's not really much to see," Dowler said. "I don't know that we'd want to get too close."

"I'd just like a better look, that's all. I won't go too close."

"Well, all right sir . . . if you want. I'll go with you."

Kale started out at a brisk, arm-swinging pace. Dowler took off after him, hesitating only long enough to glance hopelessly at Flash, who shrugged hopelessly back.

Flash stayed where he was and watched Dowler fall in step alongside Kale. They kept walking. They kept walking and walking, fading into the darkness.

For one ghastly moment, Flash envisioned Kale walking straight across without a pause or a doubt and flinging open the door and announcing, in a commanding voice, *All right now, enough of this*

foolishness! Let's just march out, two by two. Come on now—let's go!
And then—and this was the spine-tingling horror, the thing that really
unnerved him—he could see the whole gang of them, Orninski sheep-
ishly leading the way, trudging out with their hands up. (Stranger
things had happened, even in the dreariest of lives. Idiots often enough
stumbled onto the only path through the forest while wise men were
strolling blissfully off cliffs, quoting Spinoza.)

But thank God, no. That much Flash—all of them—would be spared.
About halfway over, Kale stopped. Flash could no longer distinguish the
two figures, but he didn't have to. He could see it clearly enough in his
mind's eye: Stonewall Kale with his aide-de-camp, surveying the terrain on the evening before the battle, his mouth a thin line, his eyes
hard as gems.

Kale and Dowler returned. They walked rapidly, and Kale's cape
fluttered. He was probably planning to sleep in it.

"Well, how is it out there, sir?" Flash inquired.

"I think we'll be all right," Kale said.

"I suspect the terrain will be a little firmer in the morning, sir."

"Yes," Kale said, drawing the word out indecisively and finally letting
it hiss off into a kind of disapproving silence. And then, looking at
Dowler: "Do you think we could set up a cot here?"

"Here?" Dowler said.

"Inside I mean. In the garage. I'd like to stay close in case anything
breaks."

"Well, I don't really—I mean, sir, it'd be—"

"Anything will do—just a folding cot or something, if you can manage it."

"You could use your cape as a cover," Flash suggested. "It gets pretty
cool out here at night."

"Yes—no need to worry about blankets or anything. What time does
everyone get up around here? The men in the cells?"

"Five thirty, sir."

"That early? Well, yes, fine—you wake me at five then. And now
if you people have everything under control, I promised the Governor I'd call him before I turned in."

Flash waited outside while Dowler took Kale to the phone in the
garage. Dowler then rejoined him, so Kale could conspire with the Governor in privacy.

"Flash?" Dowler said quietly. "What is it this guy's running for?"

And in one of those rare illuminations that open everything up for
you, Flash cried out to himself: *Aha, this is it!* And it was—the epitome

of Jeff Dowler. Because obviously Dowler would know Kale was running for something (he wasn't that ignorant), but not what it was (he wasn't that interested), and yet was shrewd enough to realize that Kale's candidacy for *something* (who cared what?) might just possibly be influencing everything he did. Flash felt pleased. It was always nice working things out.

"Attorney General," he said.

"Is he gonna win, you think?"

"Looks like it," Flash said, and then added: "He's running for the Democrats."

Dowler nodded but didn't say anything.

Flash wondered if Dowler were a Democrat. Or a Republican, for that matter. They never discussed politics. They never discussed anything.

"Did you get something to eat tonight?" Flash asked.

"No, I didn't. Did you?"

"No. Do you think we could scrounge something from the kitchen?"

"Christ, it'd be worth a try. My stomach's been rumbling all night."

"I guess maybe we should wait and ask Pooh-brain if he wants something."

"I guess so," Dowler said. And then after a rather long pause he said: "The old man's kind of taking it on the chin, it looks like, doesn't it? I mean, with Kale moving in and—"

"Any man who decides to make the penal system his life's work doesn't get any sympathy from me," Flash said.

Kale emerged from the garage. "We've got the full backing of the Governor on this, men," he announced, as if either of them knew what the hell that meant. "He's with us one hundred per cent."

"Yes . . . ," Flash said, trying to imitate Kale's performance with the word but not managing, not getting quite enough sibilant, lip-curling distaste into it. "Would you care for a little bite now, sir? A little food?"

"Not now—but can you get hold of Johnny right away?"

"Johnny?" Flash said. "Johnny *Mancino?*"

"Yes—the Governor's still on the line. He wants to talk to him."

16

The room was small, square, no larger than an ordinary living room. It had no windows and the air was stale, smelling of dust and yellowed paper and bindery glue. The cot had been set up in front of the desk, in the only space large enough to hold it; everywhere else books were stacked to the ceiling on metal shelves: old books, worn books, books for boys, technical manuals, detective stories, sports stories, adventure stories.

Johnny had removed his shoes and turned off the overhead lights, but left the desk lamp on. He lay on the cot, his legs bent up, and tried to get comfortable enough to sleep. At least the game of musical chairs was over, which started when Kale told the Warden to put him up for the night, and the Warden told Fleishman, and Fleishman told that guard to tell that other fellow, Reed, whoever he was, and Reed told some young kid, some assistant of his probably, and the young kid, who didn't seem very certain of anything, palmed him off on the first guard he bumped into. It stopped there. They ran out of subordinates—no scrubwomen, no apprentice office boys . . .

His eyes were closed and he must have been almost asleep; the pounding startled him; he leaped off the cot. "What—? Who is it—?"

"Fleishman! Open up!"

"They locked me in. Don't you have a key?" Johnny looked at his watch. It was twenty to twelve.

A key scraped and the lock snapped. The door opened inward and Fleishman, clutching the knob with one hand and struggling to extract the key with the other, looked up at him, eyes wide and magnified behind his huge black-rimmed glasses, his expression not quite baffled, not quite outraged, not quite comical, but some kind of weird Fleishmanesque combination of the three, like an old Marx Brothers movie, where Groucho would plunge buoyantly into the wrong hotel room, occupied by the society dowager in her corset, a towel clasped to her bosom—only Fleishman looked too weary and rumpled and disgusted to carry off the rest of the scene.

"Come on," he barked, short of breath, his voice raspy. "The Governor wants you on the phone."

Johnny followed Fleishman down the hall and into a tiny office with a single desk and a file cabinet. Fleishman jiggled the phone impatiently. "Hello!—Hello! Anybody there? Where the hell is everybody?" He jiggled some more. "Yes—*hello!* Fleishman here. I've got Mancino—" Fleishman listened, blinking. "Well, what the hell did you do with him? . . . No, I don't know his number! He's on a goddamn line somewhere waiting to— Hello, Governor! Good evening! I understand you— Yes, he's right here. I'll put him on." He thrust the phone at Johnny.

"Governor Eberhart?"

"Hello, Johnny. I hear you've been helping out down there. It sounds as if they've run into some trouble."

"It seems that way," Johnny said.

"I just wanted to tell you how much I appreciate your help." Eberhart sounded exactly as he had that night at Kale's: quiet, calm, with that same hint of scholarliness in his voice. "I understand you've already gone in and talked to those men several times."

"Just twice."

"Well, we all appreciate it. I realize the danger involved."

"There hasn't really been much of that. That's not what I'm worried about."

"What are you worried about?"

Johnny looked at Fleishman, who was sitting on the hard-backed chair behind the desk, one foot resting on the other knee, his arms crossed over his chest. He gazed steadily at Johnny with morose, objective displeasure.

"I know it must sound pretty lame, coming into a place like this and second-guessing the people who run it—but I'm the only one here who's talked to those convicts since this started, and frankly, I think they're now sorry they got into it. I'm sure they'd be willing to work out a reasonable settlement."

"Well, that's the best news I've heard all night, Johnny. That's exactly what we're hoping for, of course."

Johnny looked again at Fleishman, arms still crossed and resting now on his little potbelly, expression unchanged. "Have you told the Warden then—or Mr. Kale—to press for some sort of settlement?"

Eberhart was silent a moment. "No, Johnny, I haven't. I'm two hundred miles away. I can't overrule the men on the scene."

"But if they won't agree to a settlement, they'll have to go in after those men, and if that happens—"

"I'm sure Warden Griffing knows what he's doing."

"And he was ready to settle—until Kale pulled the rug out from under him."

"That doesn't seem possible. I say this with all due respect, Johnny— but I talked to Kale not five minutes ago, and to Griffing earlier. They've both agreed not to do anything until morning, until things clarify, which seems to me quite reasonable. And if you say the convicts are ready to give up, I'm sure they can work out something then. Neither Kale nor Griffing is particularly bloodthirsty."

"Then why didn't they settle tonight? That guard could be in a hospital, where he belongs, instead of having to spend the night sitting on the floor with some convict pointing a gun at him."

"Surely you're not suggesting that Mr. Kale and Warden Griffing are unconcerned about those guards?"

"I'm asking you to urge them to make some effort to settle this thing before—"

"There's no need to urge that. That's exactly what Kale wants to do. And of course I'm behind him—one hundred per cent. Johnny—take a little advice from a sage old politician. Let the professionals do their job. Believe me, I'm as concerned about this thing as you are. But that doesn't mean I'm going to start throwing my weight around. Can you imagine what shape we'd be in if I tried to tell every bureau head in the state what to do?"

"All right. Okay."

"I'm sure they'll work this out—with your help. You've already done far more than we have any right to expect, and I'm grateful."

"Okay," Johnny said. "Thanks."

"Good luck now. And please—watch your step. We don't want anyone else getting hurt."

When Johnny replaced the phone, Fleishman uncrossed his arms and observed the back of one outspread hand. "Tattletale." It was just the sort of thing—the exact word, in fact—you'd expect from him, only there was an edge to it, a hint of touchiness.

"I kept expecting you to cut the wire," Johnny said.

"Who am I to interfere with the Governor's freedom of information? Are you ready to go back to the library?"

"What are the chances for some food? I was just sitting down to dinner tonight when you people called, and haven't eaten anything since—"

"C'mon," Fleishman said, with as little grace as possible.

Johnny followed him out the building and up the hill. He hadn't taken the raincoat; he walked along in his dress trousers and dress shirt. The air was clean and invigorating, but it didn't seem to do much to improve Fleishman's mood. He trudged in silence, head down, shoulders drooping.

Kale, talking to Dowler outside the garage, turned to watch them approach. Fifteen or twenty guards were standing about, all at a respectful distance. Wardens—and Kale—seemed to exert a curious kind of magnetic force. They always attracted clusters of bulky men in gray-blue uniforms to them, but never close to them. About ten paces away the magnetic pull seemed to reverse itself to produce a kind of buffer zone, a ring of undefilement.

"Did you get to talk to him?" Kale asked. Unlike Fleishman, Kale was still full of zest.

"Yes," Johnny said.

"We're heading over for something to eat," Fleishman said. "Can we bring back something? Or maybe you'd like to join us?"

"Oh no—I've eaten. But you men go ahead."

Fleishman nodded, and he and Johnny turned to go.

"Wait," Kale said. "Aren't you going?" he asked Dowler.

"Flash'll bring me something back, Mr. Kale. I couldn't leave without somebody—"

"I'll be here," Kale said.

In the silence Dowler swallowed noisily. Fleishman was rigid, staring at Kale. He probably blinked a few times too, although it was too dark for Johnny to tell.

"I don't know if that'd be . . . appropriate," Dowler said uneasily. "The Warden told me to—"

"There's nothing to worry about. I'll keep an eye on things."

There was another awkward silence. "I'm really not that hungry," Dowler said.

"Don't be silly. You must be starving. Go on now."

They went, somewhat hesitantly. In silence they marched back to the main building, turned a corner and approached a big wooden door, set into the side of the building with a huge dimly-lighted stone archway. It was all reminiscent of a castle or fortress from an old movie.

Dowler knocked and a guard peered out through the barred window and unlocked the door. It was solid wood, oak probably, and at least six inches thick. They stepped into a brightly lighted stone hallway and the guard locked the door behind them. They walked down the hallway past a series of wooden doors: Dentist's Office, First-Aid Room, Sick Call, Chief Keeper, Officer's Lounge, Assistant Keeper. At the end of the hall they came upon another guard at a barred gate. He let them through and relocked the gate. They went down a flight of stairs and through a plain wooden door which, miraculously, wasn't locked. The kitchen was brightly lighted in one area; the rest was dark, full of shadowy suggestions of sinks, stoves, gigantic refrigerators. Two men in chef's hats were sitting at a chopping block playing cards; six other men lounged around, all in white aprons, except for a lone uniformed guard sitting at a desk with a cup of coffee. Everyone, including the guard, jumped to attention.

"As you were," Dowler grumbled.

"Anything to eat for a few starving friends?" Fleishman said.

"Sure thing," the guard said. "Monihan!" he barked.

One of the men in a chef's hat came running. "Yes sir. What would you like, sir?"

"A sandwich or something," Fleishman said. "Whatever you can manage fast."

They left the kitchen through another door, which the guard unlocked for them. He reached in to flick on the lights and stood aside to let them enter. "The staff dining room," Fleishman announced. There were perhaps a dozen wooden tables, the size of card tables. They sat at the nearest one.

"What would you do around here without keys?" Johnny said.

"Not very much," Fleishman said.

They waited in silence. Johnny lit a cigarette after offering one to the others, both of whom declined. "Kale seems to have the Governor in his corner," Johnny said. "Or vice-versa."

"So I gathered," Fleishman said.

"Kale's all right," Dowler said. "I was talking with him. He's got the right ideas."

"Why were you so reluctant to leave him up there alone then?"

"That's different. I'm just saying he's got the right ideas."

"Sure," Fleishman said.

"Does that mean he wants to rush those men?" Johnny asked Dowler.

Dowler glanced at him. "I guess you'd have to ask him about that."

"I know what Mr. Mancino's worried about," Fleishman said. "He's afraid we're going to fuck up."

"Well, we ain't," Dowler said.

"Ever hear of St. Vincent de Paul?" Fleishman asked Johnny. "A prison in Canada?"

"They had a riot there," Johnny said. "A couple of years back."

"You mean you actually remember what you read on the air? I'm impressed. Only it wasn't exactly a riot. You newshawks call everything a riot. Two inmates held a guard hostage in a cell. The Warden and two guards charged, firing into the cell. They killed one of the prisoners. They also killed the guard. Afterward the Warden was found criminally negligent, even though the guard had already been knifed, and they could see his blood dripping out from the cell. They still found him criminally negligent."

"Who's they, Flash?" Dowler asked without raising his eyes.

"The coroner's jury, as I remember."

"Maybe the coroner's jury made a mistake."

"Maybe the Warden made a mistake."

"I wouldn't know," Dowler said. "I wasn't there."

"Who's going to decide tomorrow?" Johnny asked. "Kale or the Warden?"

Neither of them answered.

"Skip it," Johnny said.

"There's nothing to worry about," Fleishman said. "Mr. Kale's a dedicated public servant, and has all the right ideas. And Jeff here's got all his men sleeping around in offices, ready to be unleashed at a moment's notice."

"At least I know where my men are," Dowler said.

"That's true," Fleishman said. "I haven't the slightest idea where mine are."

"Well, they're staying out of the way, anyhow."

"They weren't hired to parade around with rifles, Jeff. We don't test them to see if they're crack shots."

"I know," Dowler said.

The door opened and the young fellow in the white apron and cook's hat wheeled in a serving cart. He placed a linen napkin and silverware in front of each of them and then a plate with a sandwich cut in fours and two scoops of potato salad. In the center of the table he set down a plate holding a whole loaf of sliced white bread standing on end. He poured coffee from a large metal pot and set out a pitcher of cream and a bowl of sugar cubes. "Will that be all?"

"That'll be fine," Fleishman said. Both he and Dowler had been sitting stiffly, avoiding each other's eyes. The fellow left, closing the door behind him. Fleishman poked at his potato salad. Dowler picked up a piece of his sandwich and took an abrupt, enormous bite.

Johnny also tried the sandwich. The sliced chicken was at least an inch thick, with practically another inch of mayonnaise. "Is that fellow a convict?" Johnny asked after a few moments.

"Yes," Fleishman said.

"What's he in for?"

"I don't know," Fleishman said.

"Breaking and entering," Dowler muttered.

"There—there's your answer," Fleishman said. "Mr. Dowler is the man you should ask about these things."

Dowler was already on his second triangle of sandwich. He paused to glare across the table at Fleishman, who countered by devoting his attention to the potato salad. Dowler resumed eating.

After a minute or so Johnny nodded toward the loaf of bread, which no one had touched. "Do they always serve bread with sandwiches?"

"They serve bread with everything," Fleishman said. "Including water, on occasion."

Johnny smiled. Fleishman didn't. Neither did Dowler.

"You ever get the chance to check out those guys in the hobby shop?" Dowler asked, putting the last piece of sandwich in his mouth. He didn't seem to be rushing, but managed to get the food down with amazing speed. "The ones from the garage, I mean."

"I've seen their names," Fleishman said.

"Didn't happen to notice any from your list, did you?"

"There were four from my list," Fleishman said. "Out of six hundred."

"You only need four," Dowler said. "Four is plenty." He checked both sides of his fork to make sure it was clean, and started in on the potato salad. "Did you notice, one of them on your list, Simmons, is the guy they say started it."

"What list are you talking about?" Johnny asked.

"Orninski seems to be the fellow behind it," Fleishman said. "Or maybe even Verdun. But not Simmons."

"I didn't have *any* of those on my list," Dowler said. "I didn't have one guy over there on my list."

"What list?" Johnny said.

"Not even Verdun?" Fleishman said. "I thought he was your friend."

"None of them are my friends, Flash. I don't make friends with in-mates."

"Simmons belonged on that list," Fleishman said.

"He even got in trouble at St. Joe's," Dowler said. "It's on his sheet. Besides, no buddy of Orninski's belongs on that list."

"Bullshit," Fleishman said.

"No bullshit, Flash. I ain't the bullshit guy around here. I ain't the guy that took the guards out of the shops."

"What the hell is that supposed to mean?"

"You know what it means, Flash. It means if we still had guards in the shops, like the garage for instance, maybe Delft, who's your man, not mine, would still be in one piece."

"Anything else, Jeff? The guys on my list started the trouble, my man couldn't handle it, and because of me your man wasn't around to snap his fingers and keep everything under control. I've got all that, I think. Is there anything else?"

"Yeah, there's something else. It's that it's all right for you to go around playing games here, Flash, and getting all kinds of cute ideas, because when we get stuffed up to the gills with these ideas and the whole fucking place starts falling apart, you just say your guys ain't trained to use guns, what with them being too smart and delicate for that kind of work, so it ain't your problem, you say, it's our problem. I mean, thanks. Thanks a lot. Only if you and your guys are gonna go around fucking things up, Flash, maybe you just oughta remember sometimes who's gotta straighten it out. Because I'm the guy in the middle when there's trouble, not you. Sure, you can sit around on your ass saying the goddamn Warden in Canada shouldn't've went charging into the cell with any guns and shooting up people. Sure, it's all his fault. Only I wanna know whose fault it was maybe that they *had* the trouble in the first place, who then said to the Warden okay, now it's your baby, you take care of things now, because I don't know nothing about shooting any guns. Sure, Kale, he's all wrong, he's a horse's ass. And naturally I'm all wrong because, I mean, what the hell, I never even went to college. And of course Griffing's all wrong too, except when he listens to your bullshit ideas. Everybody's all wrong but old Fleishman, the guy with all the brains and the big high-powered staff of all these brilliant kids that went to college and got good grades from all their teachers. Sure, you know all the answers, you got all the ideas. And I know what the hell your idea is, Flash, with those guys in there, and I'll tell you something. It's a shitty idea. Because you ain't kidding me, Flash. You wanna go in there and kiss their ass, that's your great idea. You wanna play footsie with those guys in there, and ask them real nice if maybe please won't they come out, because after all it ain't their fault, they're not really bad guys, they're just misunderstood, that's all, and it's really all our fault, all the guards that push them around and won't even say sir to them or nothing, when all they ever did was maybe rob a bank or just put a knife in somebody, not meaning no real harm. I've been seeing all these great ideas of yours all over the place for four fucking years now, and I'll tell you something, I'll say it again, they're shitty ideas, every goddamn one of them, and the shittiest of them all was taking the guards out of the shops, and the next shittiest is wanting to go in and kiss Orninski's ass to get him out of there. And I'll tell you something else, Flash—I think maybe it ain't the worst thing in the world that Orninski and those guys blew their goddamn top. Because you can go around saying Kale is a dope all you want, Flash, but he's got his eyes open, and maybe he's gonna begin to see that maybe some other people besides you got some ideas about how things oughta be run, and that maybe these people's ideas might even work, because they've worked other places and didn't come out of no book, and ain't exactly based on the idea that everybody in here is just an angel and oughta be given toys and everything to play with to keep him happy, and let run around loose wherever he wants to, or put in any goddamn fancy dormitory with nothing more than a matchstick fence around it, but maybe instead are based on the idea that everybody in here, he got sent to prison, which maybe means he's like what they call a criminal, you know, and maybe not the nicest guy in the world, and maybe not the kind of guy, if you had any brains in your head instead of just ideas, you'd ever be deaf, dumb and blind enough to trust."

Fleishman had stopped eating during this, the color draining from his face. Although Dowler had become loud and excited, he knew exactly what he was saying and was enjoying the release, enjoying his outburst the way an athlete enjoys sweating. But Fleishman couldn't control his rage enough even to express it, let alone enjoy it. "Anything else?" he said finally. His voice almost cracked. He was struggling to produce an air of steady, casual condescension, a refusal to be touched, but couldn't manage.

"Yeah," Dowler said, speaking more quietly now, with a kind of thickness. "There's more. Maybe one of these days we'll all have a chance to talk about some of these other things too."

"I'll be looking forward to it," Fleishman said after a moment.

Dowler had finished eating. He shoved his plate away and got up. Only he shoved too hard. The plate slid across the polished wooden tabletop and knocked Fleishman's plate onto his lap. Dowler was already turning to go. He stopped short, astonished. And maybe Fleishman didn't realize it was an accident, or didn't care. Maybe he had just been straining too hard to keep control. The plate tilted off his lap and crashed to the floor as he leaped up and in the same unbroken lunge, uttering a kind of fragmented cry, flung himself over the table at Dowler, seizing his jacket with both hands and clutching to it frantically, his body stretched out full-length across the table, rigid and desperate, like a man clinging to the edge of a cliff. Dowler swung about abruptly, whiplashing Fleishman off the table and scattering bread slices in a billowing, flower-like pattern. Somehow Fleishman managed to land on his feet, stumbling, still hanging on. He let go with one hand, his right, and swung. He swung clumsily; the blow wouldn't have ruffled Dowler much, even if it had landed. About all you could say for it was that it showed a kind of incredible presumption that you had to admire. Dowler caught it like a first baseman, gloving Fleishman's clenched fist effortlessly within his hand, holding back the whole force of Fleishman's arm, frustrating his frenzied assault into a kind of static helplessness.

Johnny skirted Fleishman's overturned chair and jumped between them and tried to push them apart. Dowler let go of Fleishman's fist and Fleishman went stumbling backwards.

"Get your hands off me!" Fleishman yelled.

Johnny didn't move; his hands were already off Fleishman. After a momentary embarrassment, Johnny dropped his arm from Dowler's chest. Dowler nodded in acknowledgment. Fleishman shrugged his jacket angrily back into place. He was puffing. He adjusted his glasses, which had gone askew on his nose, and glared through them at Dowler.

"It was an accident," Dowler said grudgingly.

Fleishman looked down at his grease-stained trousers. A piece of potato salad had somehow managed to adhere to one leg through all the scuffling. Fleishman swiped at it vengefully. He looked again at Dowler.

"I said it was an accident," Dowler said.

Fleishman swallowed to get his breath. "Okay," he said. "Forget it."

"Sure," Dowler said. "Let's forget it." He paused. "I'm going back up. You oughta get some sleep—you're supposed to come on later." He turned and walked out, pulling the door shut behind him.

"Why don't we sit down?" Johnny said quietly. "Let's have some of that coffee."

"I don't want any." Fleishman's voice was still unsteady.

"Come on," Johnny said, touching his arm. "It'll do you good."

Fleishman yanked his arm away. "That son of a bitch," he said. He slammed his chair down on its legs, kicked away slices of bread, pieces of potato salad, broken dinnerware, and plopped down.

Johnny returned to his chair. There was a large puddle of coffee absorbing a smaller puddle of cream on the table. It dripped off one side, just missing the seat of Dowler's chair. "You don't want to get in a fight with him. He's twice your size."

"I don't like having things thrown in my lap."

"I think it *was* an accident." Johnny righted Fleishman's cup and poured coffee from the metal pot, which had somehow remained standing, along with his own cup.

"I don't give a shit," Fleishman said. When he tried to lift his cup he couldn't hold it steady. He put it down. He accepted the cigarette Johnny offered; it trembled as Johnny lit it for him. Fleishman tried the cup again, seizing it and drawing it abruptly to his lips. He slurped down half of it and made a face. Johnny stared at the ceiling; it was stucco, painted off-white.

"I'm forty-four years old," Fleishman said.

"He provoked you."

"You know what kind of place we'd have if he had his way?" Fleishman demanded. His voice was getting stronger, but the tremor was still there and the pitch was high.

"I'm glad at least you don't agree with him. I'm glad somebody here doesn't."

"Shit," Fleishman said.

"You've both been working too long, under too much strain."

"I know. It's past midnight. Fleishman has turned back into a pumpkin."

"Tomorrow you'll both have forgotten all about it."

"Shit," Fleishman said.

Johnny picked up his coffee.

"It's probably ice cold," Fleishman grumbled.

"It's all right," Johnny said and drank. He sputtered, gagging, then forced himself to swallow and gasped for breath. It was the most incredibly bad coffee he'd ever tasted.

"It's no better hot," Fleishman said, and then: "I try not to despise Jeff Dowler."

"I don't know if I'd try too hard," Johnny said after a moment.

"Don't be a cop hater. It doesn't befit a liberal turn of mind."

"Dowler's not a cop."

"The principle's the same," Fleishman said. He spoke breathlessly, in a frantic, hectoring tone. "If you have the largeness of heart to remember that Orninski is a human being, maybe you ought to do the same for Jeff Dowler. And if you think Dowler's bad, you should have seen the guy before him, who was here when Griffing took over, who Griffing spent two years getting rid of. You know how he used to punish inmates? He'd have them stand for six hours in an eighteen-inch circle painted on the floor. You ought to try that some day. He also used to handcuff them to the bars, high up, so just their toes touched the floor. He kept them that way for four hours. And when that didn't work, he used a leadtipped cane, or sometimes a high-pressure hose."

"Jeff Dowler doesn't do these things?"

"No. Jeff Dowler doesn't do these things."

"This must be one of the more enlightened prisons in the country."

"It is."

"And Jeff Dowler's a gem. You certainly show a remarkable ability to sing the praises of a guy who—"

"I hate the son of a bitch."

"But you try not to."

"I even try not to hate the guy before him. But you hate him, don't you? You'd be willing to put *him* on bread and water, even though you hate anyone who'd put Orninski on bread and water. Dowler's at least consistent. His approach is Biblical—Old Testament. Mine's New."

"What was this list you were talking about before—that Mel Simmons was on?"

Fleishman shrugged, bored. He would have preferred something more philosophical—a discussion, perhaps, of moral relativity. "We're working up a list of inmates who might qualify for a minimum security unit. If we ever get a minimum security unit."

"And Mel was on the list? Was it because of me, because I pushed you about him?"

"It was because I thought he belonged. Along with five hundred and ninety-nine others."

"What kind of trouble did he get into at St. Joe's?"

"Nothing serious. Stop fretting, it wasn't your fault."

"Mel Simmons shouldn't even be here. You said that yourself on the show. Half your men shouldn't be here."

"Meanwhile they are."

"How did Orninski get that gun? Where'd it come from?"

"Christ only knows. There's a lot of hardware stashed away in here. I guess you never heard the story of the Warden who learned that some inmate had a knife. He told the whole tier they wouldn't see the movie that week unless the knife were turned in. Twelve knives were turned in."

"They're going to try to blast those men out of there tomorrow, aren't they? Dowler, Kale—they're going to get their way."

"I don't know."

"What about Griffing? Which side is he on?"

"Griffing's not on any side. He's the one all the people on all the sides hate."

"I'm not much more impressed with Griffing that I am with Dowler."

"Leave Griffing alone."

"You understand and sympathize with him too, is that it? And even with Kale, I bet. What gets me is how you can put up with this. How can you believe what you do and still work in a place run by people like Kale and Dowler?"

"I am all heart, I guess. Let's go; you're not going to drink any more of that slop anyhow. I'll take you back to the library."

"Are you feeling all right?"

"I'm feeling shitty, to speak the God's honest truth. Maybe we'd better bring back some hot coffee for Kale in case he's still up there scanning the horizon for periscopes. It'll serve him right."

They went back through the inmates' dining hall, up the broad stairway, across the floor of the dome, down the stone hallway, and out onto the dark grounds. Johnny counted this time: four locked doors to cover perhaps a hundred yards.

Kale was standing in front of the garage with Dowler at his side. Dowler ignored Fleishman. Fleishman ignored Dowler. "Here," Fleishman said brusquely, thrusting the container of coffee at Kale.

"Well—thanks. Yes, that sounds fine; it's getting kind of chilly." He removed the plastic lid from the container and looked around for a place to drop it.

"I'll take it," Dowler said. He shook the lid a few times to dry it off and dropped it delicately into his jacket pocket.

Kale watched with great interest, then raised the container to his lips. Johnny bent forward in expectation. Kale paused. "By the way, the Governor rang me back again, while you were eating."

"Oh?" Johnny said.

"Yes. He was *very* pleased with the report you gave him."

"He was?"

"Yes. I didn't want to get his hopes up too much when I first spoke to him, but of course you've been in there, talking to those men, so that's a different matter." Kale smiled, still holding the container of steaming coffee just below his chin.

"I'm not sure I understand," Johnny said.

"Well, just between us, I was a bit worried about the Governor—being up there in Maynard, I mean, not right on the scene. But whatever you said to him, it certainly did the trick. And of course he's behind us all the way." Almost as if in a toast, Kale raised the container high, then drank. "There!" he announced heartily. "That certainly hits the spot!"

17

It was really a funny kind of dark. The lights were just the same as earlier but everything looked different. It felt different. It was practically perfectly quiet, for one thing. Almost everybody was asleep, and all the guys breathing in their sleep made the room very *heavy*, besides being so dark and quiet, and so late at night.

The only ones awake, as far as Mel could see, were O'Neill and Ferrucio, whose shift it was at the windows, and Orninski himself, who said he wasn't planning on sleeping. Mel had already pulled his shift at the windows, from midnight till two, so this was his sleep time, only he was wide awake.

It was two thirty, or was the last time he looked. It felt funny wearing a watch again. It was one of those things you never thought about.

He was sitting on the floor up front, near Cloninger's desk. He had his knees up and his head back against the wall. The knife stuck in his trousers felt funny too. The hell, he hadn't carried anything like that since back in Gary, when the kids used to play pirate with wooden knives.

The lamp under the table lighted the front part of his legs up to his knees, but not his face. He was really trying to sleep but his stomach kept twitching, kind of a hungry, fluttery sort of sick feeling, and a coupla times just from the crazy things running through his mind he'd get all hot and sweaty, even though the room was pretty chilly now. It really cooled off after all that rain. But still his shirt smelled from the sweat. The whole room smelled pretty bad, actually.

He could just imagine what was running through Orninski's mind. Although maybe not. You never could tell with a guy like that. After all, who would've figured on him being *glad*, for Christ's sake, to hear that the goddamn Warden wouldn't even listen to those things he wanted?

Christ, when Mel heard that, his heart dropped about twenty feet. Sure, the Warden wanted his two guys back in one piece, but a goddamn screw just signed his life away the minute he stepped into this place anyhow. The Warden actually made them sign a paper saying if there was any trouble and some screw happened to be in the way, well, that was just too bad. So when the TV guy came in and said the Warden said no to everything, well then it looked to Mel like they were just ass-end up and that was it, sad movies.

But Orninski didn't even bat an eyelash. Actually, he seemed pretty chipper.

"You see, what it is, Mel, is that the Warden's gotta make some noise first so it don't look like he's being pushed around by a bunch of cons. What he's doing is just having this TV guy sound us out with this plan he's got, this offer. Because that was the Warden's plan, not any TV guy's plan. So now he knows we're interested, and now we know he's interested, so if you ask me, Mel, everything looks like maybe it's gonna work out all right."

Frankly, it seemed to Mel that if that's what the hell the Warden was getting at, he could've made it a little clearer. As far as he was concerned, the whole thing was just one hopeless frigging mess. Everything that was supposed to be so important at the beginning nobody even talked about anymore. The only things anybody talked about now were things that never would've entered anybody's mind when it all started.

Mel put his hand down on the floor and turned his wrist to catch the light from under the table. It was ten to three. Whenever he moved at all he could feel the keys in his pocket, like a lump. They were on a little ring and there were maybe a dozen all told. He wondered what they were for—closets and stuff around the shop probably. He wondered if he had a key in his pocket right now for the front gate. He didn't think so. Maybe some of them were for Cloninger's car and house and stuff. He wondered what kind of car Cloninger drove. He somehow couldn't see him driving a car, he didn't know why.

If anything happened tomorrow, the first thing he'd do would be ditch the keys.

Actually the time was going very fast, which you wouldn't think it would. That always got Mel, how the time went. He'd been in three months less a few days now, and in one way it seemed like a hell of a long time, years and years, like he'd been there forever and couldn't even remember being out anymore. But in another way the three months went very fast, and didn't seem long at all.

It kind of frightened Mel to think of what was gonna happen when this thing ended. It seemed like it was happening off by itself. Sometimes everything seemed that way. You'd be just sitting in the dining hall eating your goddamn mashed potatoes or something, and suddenly out of nowhere you got the feeling that it wasn't real, because all at once you could see everything that ever happened to you, from when you were so small you could hardly remember, and you couldn't believe it all could've happened the way it did, and that now it was all over and didn't even matter anymore, because here you were, sitting in the goddamn dining hall, eating your mashed potatoes.

Orninski stood up. He'd been sitting at the middle table, on the side nearest the windows, sort of hunched over. He walked over to the guys at the windows and whispered something. Mel could see Orninski against one window, sort of a black shape flat against the fuzzy light from outside, from the moon maybe or whatever. Then Orninski walked very quiet, like he was on tiptoes, up to the front of the room, waited a minute, then sat down very quiet next to Mel on the floor and leaned back against the wall. There was maybe six inches between them. Mel kept his head straight and didn't look over and kept his eyes mostly closed. For a while Orninski was very quiet, not moving at all. Then, very softly, like the sound came from real deep inside, Orninski gave a kind of little low moan.

"It still bothering you?" Mel whispered.

"You awake?"

"Yeah. Sorta."

"I figured you was dead out by this time." Orninski was just whispering too, practically right in his ear. He sounded kind of fuzzy because of the way his mouth was so swollen up, although Mel couldn't actually see his face with the light not coming up that far.

"I'm sort of awake," Mel said. "Is that tooth giving you trouble?"

"My whole head's killing me."

"That's really too bad." He waited a bit. "I think everybody else is pretty much asleep."

"Yeah." Orninski was quiet a minute. "How you feeling, Mel? I mean, you feeling all right?"

"Sure. I'm feeling all right."

Orninski was quiet again. "You scared, Mel? This thing got you scared a little?"

"I don't know."

"It's kind of creepy in here, ain't it?"

"It gives you a kind of funny feeling," Mel said.

"Yeah," Orninski said. They were both still whispering. "And you know, it really gives you a funny feeling when you're the guy with all the responsibility and everything."

"Sure it does," Mel said.

"I mean, in the morning, I gotta be wide awake, because Christ knows what the hell they're gonna try to pull or anything. It's not like these other guys. I mean, I wouldn't say this to anybody else, but the guy with the responsibility, he's gotta play it cool all the time, but he got worries too. You know what I mean?"

"Sure."

"And who can you talk to? You can't talk to these guys. They don't give a shit what happens to you. Sure, everybody thinks I'm some kind of fucking nut that don't even know enough to know what it means when you pull a gun. But I know what it means, Mel. And sure, tomorrow, if anything goes wrong, all these other guys they can just jump under the table and wait for it to blow over. But there ain't nowhere for me to jump. I'm the guy with the gun in his hand. And you know, I ain't crazy, Mel. You know that."

"You ain't crazy," Mel said.

"Not that crazy," Orninski said, his voice very grave and low in the dark, and kind of slow, like it hurt even to just talk. "I could tell you right now exactly what it's gonna feel like if they start shooting, because I know what it's gonna feel like, just thinking about it. And then you stop and say to yourself, *What the fuck am I doing this for? What the hell's wrong with me?* And you start thinking well maybe I *am* nuts, maybe there's something very bad wrong with me, to be doing something like this. I mean, I never in my life said anything like this to anybody before, but after a while what happens is you just don't know what the hell you're doing things for, because everything just gets all screwed up in your head and you can't keep anything clear anymore, and the more you try to figure it out, the worse it gets. You ever get that feeling, Mel?"

"Sure. You get that feeling sometimes."

"I mean, what it is, is that sometimes you get the feeling there ain't anybody else in the whole goddamn world that knows what you really feel. And if there's trouble tomorrow, you know what everybody's gonna say? They're gonna say it's all my fault. Orninski fucked up, that's what they're gonna say."

"I thought before you said there wasn't gonna be any trouble."

"I just mean if there *is* trouble."

"Sure," Mel said. "Only I just mean there probably won't be any. Because I mean, if the Warden's ready to go along, well then the hell, *we're* ready. I mean, as far as I'm concerned . . ."

"As far as I'm concerned too," Orninski said. He was still speaking very low, whispering, but his voice was getting rough now, like a guy with a sore throat. "Only sometimes it ain't that simple. I mean, who knows, maybe what the TV guy said before was just some trick the Warden dreamed up to make us put our guard down or something."

"You think that's what he's doing?"

"I don't know what he's doing. I ain't no mind reader."

"I thought before you said you knew."

"You gotta be ready for anything, Mel. Half the people in the world, you know, they're crazy, they don't know what they're doing themselves. I mean, after all this, I'm not gonna just play patsy. I got my neck stuck way out, and you do too, all you guys, and I'm not gonna let the Warden or anybody else ruin it now. Because I know what I'm doing, and you gotta know, because if you don't you're just another piece of shit for them to step on. But if you really believe in what you're doing, and know you're right, well then you're ready for anything."

"Sure," Mel said.

"You believe in it, Mel? You think what we're doing here is right?"

"Well, sure," Mel said. "Sure—I believe in it."

"Good," Orninski said. "I'm glad. I really am." He was quiet a minute. "You tired, Mel?"

"I don't know."

"I think maybe I'm tired. Even my arms and legs, they just feel dead. And this goddamn tooth is killing me. It feels like a guy in there with a fucking sledge hammer."

"Maybe we could do something for it."

"Well Christ, I'll tell you something. It better go away. I'll be climbing the goddamn wall if it keeps up like this."

"You oughta try to sleep. I'll keep an eye on things. I ain't very sleepy."

"I don't think nothing's gonna happen till after breakfast. We both oughta sleep, so we're not so all worn out then. I could sleep like a log, you know, if it wasn't for this fucking tooth." Orninski moaned again, very low, and moved his head from side to side, like a guy who was dopey.

"Maybe you could rest it on something," Mel said. "We could fix up sort of a pillow or something."

"Christ, I don't know. Even my neck hurts now. My whole head hurts." Orninski moved his head some more, sort of hissing in air between his teeth.

"Maybe you can kind of rest it against me," Mel said. "I mean, if it'd make it more comfortable."

"I don't know," Orninski said.

"Yeah, well . . . I just thought . . ."

"How're you gonna sleep that way, then?"

"It won't bother me none," Mel said. "It's just if it's any better for you that way."

"Maybe we could try," Orninski said. "It really hurts."

"Sure."

Orninski moved a little closer and sort of scrunched down and put his head over against Mel's shoulder—against the top of his arm, actually. They were both quiet for a minute.

"Is it any better that way?" Mel asked.

"Yeah, a little."

"Maybe I should take my arm out of the way," Mel said.

"I don't wanna make it uncomfortable for you."

"We could try it," Mel said. Orninski lifted his head enough to let Mel get his arm out from between them and put it over Orninski's shoulders. Orninski put his head down again, very easy, sort of against Mel's chest now.

"That's a lot better," Orninski said. "I appreciate this."

"Sure," Mel said. His mouth was dry and he felt kind of a little funny, but it was comfortable. He felt like he could really sleep this way. For the first time all night, he felt like he could just forget everything and drop right off to sleep.

"Are you sure it's all right for you?" Orninski said.

"Sure," Mel said. "I'm half asleep."

"Me too," Orninski said.

And they must've been, because they didn't say anymore and it seemed like only a minute before Mel could tell that Orninski was dead to the world, and then it seemed like right after that he went off too, like a shot, and they must've slept like that without moving a muscle, because when he opened his eyes again, waking up very suddenly, Orninski's head was still resting on his chest. And then he realized, for Christ's sake, that the room was bright as day, and there was the goddamn sun, streaming right in the windows.

18

In due course Dawn, in all its splendor, arrived at the penitentiary. Even the penitentiary. We in our petty hypocrisy might avert our eyes from the grim wall and the toolproof bars, but not Dawn, not the Big Eye Up There. No matter what slobby depths you descended to under the cover of darkness, no matter what shameful lusts or vilenesses you courted, Dawn came to you anyhow, even as it did to the best of men.

"It's dawn," Flash said.

"That's right," Dowler said, standing like all good Security men are trained to stand (although who knows, maybe they were born that way, the stance being, so to speak, *ex utero*), with his legs spread and his meaty hands clasped behind his back, as indestructible as Gibraltar.

Neither had slept. Neither was in particularly good spirits. Yet they were behaving again toward each other with politeness, moderation, even a somewhat stiff show of respect. The reason, of course, was that each could afford to be magnanimous: Dowler because he had boorishly shouted Flash down in their trivial little spat in the dining room; Flash because he had brilliantly outwitted Dowler in the fiery debate that had followed.

—Ah yes, Jeff old man, well-said, and far be it from me (calmly, blowing on his fingernails) to deny the germ of truth, however distorted, in what you say. But let us remember too that he is freest of mistakes who takes no chances, purest who sits on his ass and does nothing. True, you have never in your many years of penal service been accused of trusting an inmate too far—you have never trusted one at all. Nor have you ever been corrupted by the softening influence of a book, a hope, a dream. Your world is here and now, standing square and solid with its hands behind its back.

—You should go back to your old goshdarn college, Flash. Using big words to all those co-eds in short skirts.

—The temptation, believe me (stifling a yawn, with just a touch of condescension) is overwhelming. Those co-eds *were* rather cute in their knee-knocker outfits. Further, they rarely cursed at me, did not mumble answers, and never used knives, guns, fists, clubs or lead pipes to make philosophical points. My most nagging annoyance was the notes I continually got from the Dean for using the wrong space in the faculty parking lot, although once I got lectured about taking a short cut to class across the campus lawn. *I would not love thee, Dean, so much,/ Loved I not green grass more.* There were, of course, other minor abuses, such as being fired from my TV show in its twelfth week for, in a most dispassionate and scholarly manner, detailing some of the barbarisms being practiced in the nearby state prison. That was when the Dean, in our last friendly chat, suggested that perhaps since I was such an expert on what was wrong with prisons I might be happier out there somewhere, trying to improve them. (Odd, isn't it, how he always insisted I belonged here, whereas you always insist I belong there?) I think he perhaps only meant it as a joke, although I didn't bet on it. And so here I am, Jeff, back to my first love, making the prisons of the world a better place for all of us to live in.

—Which is the reason, like I said, that we got this dangbatted trouble here. Because of all your horsefeathers ideas, turning this place into a mollycoddling bed of roses.

—Perhaps. But studies such as McCorkle's ("Resocialization Within Walls" and "Guard-Inmate Relationships," both in *Sociology of Punishment and Correction*, edited by Johnson, Savitz, and Wolfgang), although in some ways agreeing with you, by admitting that humane treatment does not in itself bring about rehabilitation, also points out that neither does *in*humane treatment, and that in all probability most prison disturbances result neither from repressiveness nor permissiveness, but from a random fluctuation between the two, and thus we can say, along with Osborne (in *Society and Prisons*) and good old Fleishman (in *A World Behind Bars: A Source Study of Non-Formalized Inmate Attitudes*) that since the object of prison is not to produce good prisoners but good citizens, a consistently humane and enlightened approach might very well—

And on and on, with casual confidence and startling éclat. The victory was decisive enough to allow Flash to be generous and high-souled toward poor defeated Jeff Dowler.

Thus when Flash relieved Dowler at two fifteen he greeted him, if not pleasantly, at least not unpleasantly, and Dowler had responded in kind.

"Hi," Flash had said.

"Hi."

"How's it going?"

"It's going okay."

"Well . . . you can take a break, I guess. I'm relieving you."

"Yeah. Okay."

"Anything special to keep an eye out for?"

"No—nothing special."

"Getting a little chilly, eh?"

"Yeah, been getting a little chilly."

Dowler went off for a cup of coffee, killed some time shaving and washing up, and then came back up the hill to keep Flash company at the garage—possibly because he didn't trust Flash there alone, but more probably because he just didn't feel like sleeping.

Earlier, during Flash's off-duty stretch, he had also killed some time shaving and washing up—after finally getting the goon locked safely back in the library—and then went to his office to spend the half hour he had left sitting in his chair with his eyes closed and his arms folded and his stockinged feet on the desk.

That was when he heard someone walking down the hall. Then he heard the door to his secretary's office being slowly and quietly pushed open. Cautious, assassin-like steps approached his own door. The handle turned very slowly and the door inched open.

"Oh—" Griffing said. "I didn't wake you, did I?"

"C'mon in, Griff. I'm wide awake."

"They told me you just got here. If you're planning to sleep I won't—"

"C'mon, sit down."

Griffing sat on the other chair. He undid his collar and loosened his tie. It was not a characteristic gesture. Griffing's expression was scarcely characteristic either, and nothing to brag about. He looked like he'd had it. He looked exactly like a guy in his sixties who'd been working too hard for too long under too much of a burden of frustration and disgust, who hadn't quite reached final exhaustion but was approaching it, and knew it, and was searching for some hidden source of energy, something to stave it off, and hadn't found it. He looked somehow *skimpy*; not the Evil King, but the Sick King.

"Where's Kale?"

"Sleeping with his troops. In the garage."

"In the sawdust?"

"We forced him to accept a rude cot. He's got a cape to throw over him if it gets cold."

Griffing shrugged. "I don't know why I came bothering you. I was just taking a walk and thought you might be up." He fell silent a moment. "I've never had trouble like this before, Flash. Never had an officer taken hostage. Never had a politician coming in telling me what to do."

"Or a TV announcer."

"That man. He's a dreadful person, Flash. How can you be a friend of his?"

"Christ, Griff—I only went on his show because *you* wouldn't. Don't keep saying he's my friend."

"I thought he was."

"He's not. But he's not really too bad, I guess. I mean, he's just a little—"

"Don't defend him."

"Okay."

Again Griffing paused. "I don't think we deserved this, Flash. We've done our job. Look at Raintree, for God's sake—you'd think they'd have something like this every week up there, the way that place is run."

Flash shrugged. "You just need one guy to start it."

"I think maybe I've become too remote from things. I think maybe that was part of it, that I've lost touch, and maybe let the place go soft."

"Good Christ, that's Jeff's theory—not that you've become soft, but that I have. The guards being removed from the shops, the minimum plan . . ."

"Well—naturally, he'd feel that way. Don't let it bother you."

"It doesn't bother me."

"Although I expect it *will* be a little tougher now to get the minimum plan through. For a while at least."

"Why? Just because four of them were on my list?"

"Really—four of them?"

"Out of *six hundred*, Griff."

"Of course. Well, yes—that's not really too many, I guess."

"Actually, Jeff's probably got a better case, on the surface at least, about the guards in the shops. I mean, to someone on the outside, it'd seem logical enough to connect—"

"We'd have to put those guards back anyhow, no matter whose idea it was."

"I don't see why, Griff."

"Can you imagine what we'd look like if we didn't, and had a repeat of something like this?"

"But it seems a shame, just when we try—"

"Let's worry about that after, all right?"

"Okay. Sorry."

"Did Kale have anything to say to you people before?"

"Not really," Flash said. "He called the Governor though, and then the Governor called Mancino, and then the Governor called Kale again. I think that was the sequence. Something like that."

"The Governor called Mancino?"

"They're old buddies, it seems."

"What did Mancino tell him, do you know?"

"It just so happens I was within earshot. He told him the inmates are ready to make a deal, and urged him to urge you and Kale to go along."

"Do you know what the Governor said?"

"He said *no*. I didn't actually hear him say no, but it could be gathered."

"Why did the Governor call Kale back then?"

"Unfortunately I didn't overhear that conversation. But for what it's worth, Kale *said* Eberhart called again because he was so pleased at Mancino's report that he wanted to tell him—Kale—again how much faith he had in the way things were being handled. It really didn't make much sense to me, to tell the truth."

Griffing said nothing.

"What's Kale planning for the morning, Griff?"

"I don't know. I'm not convinced he knows. His main point seems to be that we'll play it by ear. He mentioned that two or three times." Griffing paused. "Tell me, Flash—what do you think would happen if I told Kale he'd have to leave and let us handle this ourselves. And then when it was all over, if he didn't like what I'd done, he could fire me."

"What if he won't leave?"

"Then I'd resign."

"That'd put Jeff and me in a ticklish spot. We couldn't very well leave Kale here without any—"

"Oh no—that'd be out of the question. You two would have to stay."

"To have the pleasure of working hand in hand with Kale? Besides, if we stayed, it'd look like we were taking his side."

"No it wouldn't. After all, I'll be ready to retire one of these days anyhow. I'm not as strong as I used to be; I don't know if I can hold down a job like this much longer."

"That's rank idiocy, Griff. You can hold down this job as long as you want to, and you know it."

Griffing remained stony-faced and silent, but was pleased. An understandable vanity. Maybe when Flash got old and tired and sick and daily imbibed collections of pills, potions and fizzy tablets, some young whippersnapper would be kind enough to flatter him a bit too.

"At any rate, I'm not really thinking of pulling out," Griffing said. "I couldn't in the middle of something like this. I just thought the threat might get rid of Kale."

"I doubt it. He's got nothing to lose by staying. He'll take all the credit if things work out, and blame us if they don't. Take my advice, all right, Griff? Go back to your office and get some sleep. This too shall pass."

Griffing shrugged. "Your wife's with Cloninger's wife, did you know?"

"Yes. And yours is with Delft's."

"It was my idea," Griffing said. "I thought it might make it easier for them."

"It was a good idea, Griff."

Griffing laughed briefly, without humor. "Here they were, all set for a party . . ." He stood up, fastened his collar, slid up the knot of his tie, and checked to make sure his jacket was buttoned.

"So was I," Flash said. "C'mon, I'll walk you over. I'm heading up to relieve Jeff anyhow."

And so he put his shoes back on and walked Griffing to his office and then climbed the hill for what must have been the twentieth time that night (why do they always build prisons and colleges on the tops of hills?) and relieved Dowler, who then returned to keep him company an hour later, and together they passed the dull and dismal hours under the fullness of the moon—rather quickly, all things considered—until there it was: good old Dawn.

The air was cool and unbelievably fresh. And in that first light of day, that brilliant, beautiful, incredibly dishonest flood of orange light, the prison looked pleasant, congenial—almost, God forbid, pretty. All the harshness seemed gone from the gray and monstrous buildings. The walls took on a faint rose color, and then a warm coppery glow. The big ugly Shops Building looked good for at least another hundred years of shoemaking and sheet metal work: the light seemed to hold promises, it drugged your senses and lured you into absurdities. The tough lifeless ground in front of the garage, still damp from the rain, dotted with odd-sized ends of wood, looked now as if it might conceivably become green, as if grass might someday flourish even there.

A few minutes later, Griffing arrived—straight as a ramrod, neat as a pin and sick as a dog. It was easy to see that he had not slept, despite the entreaties of all and sundry. His eyes were dry and without luster. His words were forced, hoarse, toneless. His expression was that of a man with a stomach cramp.

"Morning Flash, Jeff—how'd it go?"

"It went fine, Griff."

Griffing joined them for a few minutes of silent contemplation of the early morning scene and then, not without some reluctance, dispatched an officer into the garage to tap Kale gently upon his cape-covered shoulder. And so, at a few minutes after five, there they were, the four of them, gathered together on the fateful morning to face whatever the furies had in store for them. Kale, looking well slept and bubbly-bright, quickly asserted his easy sense of command by making his first decisive move of the day. He ordered breakfast.

While they sat around the wooden table in the garage, some few feet away from the nearest car, waiting for the food, Kale used the phone there to call some flunky of his up front, whom he'd summoned last night to come out and take care of all the newshawks who, after racing here in the wee hours and leaping from their screeching cars only to be shunted into the inmates' visiting room, were now clamoring to photograph Kale standing with one foot upon the chest of the prostrate Orninski. But without his cape, for he was not wearing it this morning. He wore his gray business suit, and his somewhat rumpled white shirt and his tan silk tie. The four of them, in their suits and ties, formed a pretty drab and unimaginative collection of derring-doers, all in all.

"The morning paper?" Kale said into the phone. "No, we haven't. Send a copy, will you?"

Breakfast came and they set upon the foul coffee and the excellent scrambled eggs and bacon and toast. Why not? A hearty meal. *Te salutamus* and all that.

An officer arrived with the *Post*. Kale and Griffing looked at it together.

"About as good as we could expect, I'd say," Kale said. Griffing said nothing. Kale passed the paper to Flash, who looked at the front page, nodded at the side-by-side photos of Kale and the goon, and at the lead headline—

TWO GUARDS HELD HOSTAGE
BY ARMED CONS AT PEN

—then leaned toward Dowler, holding the paper so they could both read. Dowler, he assumed, read the story. Flash didn't. Instead he studied the picture at the bottom of the page of the beauty queen and her princesses. He tried to recall the names the goon had given the guy over the phone last night, but couldn't. He did, however, remember him saying something about a Negro girl, and one of these—the first runner-up —was a Negress. Of the three, she was the snazziest. She had a fine dusky complexion, high cheekbones, vivacious eyes. There was even a suggestion of haughtiness in her face that appealed to him. The queen herself was a dog.

"Finished?" Dowler said.

"Oh yes," Flash said. "I'm finished."

"Well, we might as well get down to business," Kale said, lowering the thick, crude-handled prison mug and establishing it solidly upon the table. "First of all, Warden, let me say that I talked twice to the Governor last night after you went to bed . . ." Kale paused. He seemed to regard this as a minor triumph, talking to the Governor while the Warden was off sleeping like a babe. ". . . And he was as straight-forward and understanding as you'd expect him to be. He said he'll back us all the way."

Griffing looked at him, a bit blearily, and said nothing.

"The main point, to my way of thinking," Kale said, "is that we can't under any circumstances let ourselves be bullied—or even *appear* to be bullied. We've got to make a clear show of our authority. At the same time, we've got to get this thing settled with a minimum of fuss—and of course without any bloodshed."

Flash blinked. Griffing studied the scrambled eggs on his plate. He had barely tasted them, but appeared to be finished. Dowler cleared his throat and took a sip of coffee.

"As you all know," Kale continued, "I've always insisted that control of our institutions stays where it belongs, in the hands of the wardens. But if we can't put this thing down quickly and firmly, we're going to absolutely ruin our chances for continuing the support we've been getting from the Legislature. Heaven knows, we have few enough friends up in Maynard now. What it boils down to is that we've got to get those men out. The main risk, of course, is what might happen to the two guards. Although, if my guess is right, the danger's not as great as it might seem. I don't think that fellow in there—what's his name again?—"

"Orninski," Griffing said.

"Yes, Orninski. Well, I just can't see him killing those men in cold blood. I think we've got to call his bluff. We simply can't allow ourselves to be pushed around by every convict who's got a gun or a knife hidden somewhere. The Legislature would be only too happy to find an excuse to make us clamp down here, to turn this place back fifty years and wipe out all the advances you men have made." He paused. "What I'd like to hear now, Warden, is some of your ideas on how we want to go about this."

"Getting them out, you mean?"

"Yes. Just how do you think we should handle it?"

"I'm not sure all of this is very clear," Griffing said, speaking more slowly than usual. "Am I to understand that we're to bring them out by force? Is that the basic assumption?"

"No, not necessarily force," Kale said. "We want to use as little force as possible."

"But we're not negotiating?"

"We can't let those men dictate terms. Don't you agree?"

Griffing was slow to answer. How he would have loved to tell this oaf that he did NOT agree! But, of course, the poor guy, he did. And so, unhappiest of men, Griffing said finally, hopelessly, "Yes; I agree."

"Then we all see eye to eye. All right, let's get to it. Let's work this thing out."

"Very well," Griffing said quietly, steadily. "My main concern at the moment is the matter of breakfast. The inmates are normally brought to the dining hall in shifts between six and seven o'clock. I would strongly oppose any delay this morning, and—"

"That's what I want to hear," Kale said. "Specific suggestions. What you want, what you don't want. Okay—the men start eating right on the button."

Griffing lowered his eyes for a moment, like a man resigned. "The question, then, is whether we prefer to make our move before or after breakfast."

"Which way do you want it, Warden?"

"If we tried anything out here before breakfast," Griffing said evenly, "I think we'd need help from the State Police to keep control in the dining hall. The men in the cells are obviously aware by now that something is going on. If we make our move out here before breakfast, and run into any trouble, we couldn't take a thousand men out of their cells to the dining hall with only the officers we have on hand."

"You think they'd start acting up?"

"I wouldn't be surprised," Griffing said without emphasis. He was bringing it off fine, disguising his contempt with all the sweet reasonableness in the world, and Flash was pleased.

"Well then," Kale said, "the obvious solution is to wait until after breakfast."

"In that case," Griffing went on, still speaking deliberately, "we face the problem of feeding the men in the hobby shop."

"We're not feeding them," Kale said.

"Are you hoping to starve them out? I'd suggest that would take several days at least, during which time—"

"That's not what I'm suggesting," Kale said. "We're going to end this thing today."

"Fine," Griffing said. "But then there seems no advantage in denying them breakfast. I see, however, two disadvantages. It would create further unnecessary discomfiture for the two officers, one of whom is injured, and both of whom have been under the severest kind of strain since yesterday afternoon. It would also unnecessarily aggravate the mood of the inmates. After all, they've been under some strain too, and might easily become overwrought, even under a minor provocation."

"That's why I want them out of there," Kale said. "Before anything happens."

"I'd suggest, then, that we give them breakfast."

"I can't buy that, Warden. I'm not ready to provide catering service for every convict who decides to tie up a guard. It's embarrassing enough, it seems to me, that—"

"In that case," Griffing went on in the same flat tone, "we'd have two choices. We'd have to inform the inmates in there—either directly, or through our lack of response to any request for food—that they won't get breakfast; or we'd have to try to stall them off by promising something we had no intention of delivering. In either case, we'd have to be prepared for violence, for serious threats against the officers, for any number of unpleasant developments, at a time when the rest of the inmate population is crowded together in the dining hall. Without reinforcements we'd have a—"

"I just don't see any reason to call in the police as long as we're on top of things. They're standing by; that should be good enough. The minute we call them in everyone will assume we've lost control."

"We'd be taking too much of a risk, not calling them in," Griffing said. "I couldn't support that."

"Why on earth didn't you explain all this last night?"

"You suggested we leave the details for morning."

"Well yes, but—well, we'll just have to work something out, that's all. You're not suggesting we just throw up our hands and quit, are you?"

"I'm suggesting that we give the men in the hobby shop breakfast."

"It seems to me you're putting an awful lot of emphasis on just what and when these men eat. The world's not going to come to an end just because a few convicts are deprived of their morning cornflakes. And if I'd been here last night, those men would never have seen that dinner you sent in either. What are we supposed to be doing, rewarding troublemakers with opulent meals?"

"It was scarcely opulent. There was no dessert, no coffee even."

"What on earth was that supposed to prove?"

"Nothing—except that they received the standard noon meal given to inmates on punishment."

"Well—I hope they saw the significance of that. I hope they felt properly chastised. Look, let's just leave this point for a moment, all right? How do you feel we could best move in on them when the time comes? That's the big question."

"I can't leave this point, Mr. Kale. Anything we do afterward will be affected by it. If we're not going to feed those men, and aren't going to call in reinforcements, I simply can't support any action."

"What does that mean?"

"That would be up to you. Or the Governor, who's empowered to re-move me."

"Well, I can tell you right now the Governor has no intention of removing you. You have his complete confidence."

"Perhaps I wouldn't if he realized how inflexibly opposed I am to what you're suggesting."

"*Inflexible* isn't one of the Governor's favorite words. Inflexible men don't respond well to unusual situations."

"That is a point," Griffing said drily, "I have been trying to make."

"You think we ought to feed these men? Is that the question at issue here? Is that the whole argument?"

"Yes."

"Well—I don't think we should. In fact, I don't think we can."

"You'll have to take the responsibility then for what happens."

"I will anyhow," Kale said. "And now we've discussed this backwards and forwards, and I've heard you out, and the decision's been made. Are you ready to go along with it?"

Griffing didn't hesitate before answering; he simply chose not to hurry. "All right," he said at last. "We'll try it your way."

So that was that, at five thirty in the crystal-clear morning.

"And now which way do you want it?" Kale asked Griffing. "Should we make our move out here before or after those other men are fed?"

Griffing turned to Dowler.

"After," Dowler said.

He turned to Flash.

"After."

Griffing nodded. "After."

The unanimity pleased Kale, and astounded Flash. He couldn't remember offhand the last time he and Dowler had agreed on anything.

"That's it then," Kale said. "We'll sit tight till we get those other men fed and safely back in their cells. Then we'll give that fellow in there one last chance to come out quietly. If he doesn't, we'll use the gas. Maybe we should get ready on that now."

Griffing nodded to Dowler. "You can start by rounding up all the extra men—anyone who's not needed somewhere else. How many do you think we have?"

"I don't know—maybe fifty."

"Send half of them up to help Bianco run the men through breakfast, and bring the rest back here. Keep them behind the garage, so they can't see them from the hobby shop. Pick the ones you want to work with you—you'll handle the gas, and the rush too, if we're going to have to move in. Make sure the men know exactly what they're supposed to do; explain everything to them very carefully."

"Okay," Dowler said, and left.

"Are you going to arm any of the men in the dining hall?" Kale asked. "Maybe it'd be a good idea if—"

"There's no place to fence them off," Griffing said. "We don't want any weapons where someone could grab them."

"What about Mancino?" Kale asked. "Do you think he can help us in any of this?"

"I really don't see how," Griffing said.

"All right, we'll leave him where he is then. Where is he?"

"In the library."

"Okay. We'll leave him there."

At twenty to six the inmates in the hobby shop hung a large white poster board from a window:

BRAKFAST.

"Do you want to respond?" Griffing asked Kale.

"How long will it take to turn off the water and electricity in there?"

"Excuse me?"

"I think that might be the best answer."

"That might just provoke them to—"

"I don't see why you keep talking about *us* provoking *them*. They're the ones who've done the provoking. And maybe this is the time to let them know how we feel about it. How long would it take?"

"A few minutes, I guess . . . I don't know."

"Okay. Put the order through. The water and the electricity."

"Why the electricity? They don't need it now anyhow, and—"

"Maybe it'll convince them we mean business. Is there anything else we can turn off?"

Griffing and Flash exchanged a dismal glance. Flash was tempted: *The heat?* But he resisted.

God knows what Griffing was tempted to say, but whatever it was, he also chose to forego the opportunity.

"All right then," Kale said. "Just the water and electricity. Give the order."

Griffing nodded to Flash. Flash went into the garage, where a line of perhaps a dozen officers moved past the rifle stack, each man taking a weapon. Flash got Bostick on the intercom. "Orders from the Warden. Get this straight now: have the *water* and the *electricity* in the hobby shop cut off immediately. Have you got that?"

"Yes sir. The water and the electricity."

"Let me know when they're off."

"Yes sir."

Flash told the officer at the intercom to let him know the minute word came through, then went back outside. "They're going off," he told Griffing.

"All right."

They waited, watching the hobby shop. The sign still hung from the window. There was no breeze, and the early morning coolness was already gone; the day would be hot.

"Will we know when they're definitely off?" Kale asked.

"We'll get a confirmation," Flash said.

"They might not notice in there until someone turns on a faucet," Griffing said.

"We're in no rush," Kale said.

They watched for several minutes, waiting for a reaction, an outcry.

"Are you sure they're going to confirm?" Kale asked.

"Yes."

They waited a few more minutes.

"I'd better check," Flash said, and went into the garage. "Nothing from Bostick?"

"Not a word," the officer said.

Flash leaned over and pushed down the intercom switch. "Bostick? Fleishman here." There was no reply. "Bostick? Where are you? Alert center, come in! Alert center—Bostick—come in!"

"Something's wrong," the officer said.

And it occurred to Flash that he should have slept. It was not only that his joints ached, that his legs weighed a ton each, that his throat felt ragged and his eyes raw. It was simply that, at this moment, he was ready to concede that no pudgy forty-four-year-old gives up his night's sleep to run up and down hills and sport about in front of garages without paying a further and subtler price too.

"Of course," he said, realizing now that he'd been aware something was wrong. "The thing's dead." He poked the button up and down several times: no harsh electronic screech, no static, only the clicking of the button.

Flash grabbed the phone and banged the cradle. From the hearing piece pressed against his ear came nothing at all, pure voided silence. "Shit," he said, and slammed down the phone. He grabbed an officer from a group of four alongside the nearest car. "Get up front to Bostick at the switchboard. On the double. Tell him the *hobby shop—not the fucking garage!* Have you got that? *The hobby shop, the hobby shop!*"

The officer gave him a look of almost disembodied terror and confusion, then took off at a run.

Flash rejoined Griffing and Kale, strolling up to them as casually as he could manage as they stared, dumfounded, at the officer who had just raced past.

"Just a little hitch in our communication system," Flash said cheerfully. "Have it straightened out in a jiffy."

"Is the water off in there?" Kale asked.

"Will be instantly, if it isn't already," Flash said.

At ten to six the officer at the intercom came out to tell them that the electricity and the water had been turned off in the hobby shop.

"See," Flash said. "I told you."

The three of them watched for some reaction in the hobby shop. None came.

"They probably don't realize it yet," Griffing said.

"Maybe not," Kale said.

"Should we go ahead on breakfast in the dining hall?" Griffing asked. "It's almost time."

"I don't see why not," Kale said.

"Let me check with Bianco and see how it looks up there," Griffing said and headed inside.

Flash and Kale waited, staring at the hobby shop. The sun was high enough now to make the hobby shop, the Cell Block, the Shops Building, the dead ground, all look as normally and believably drab, ugly, colorless, bestial and depressing as ever. At the window the sign remained: BRAKFAST.

Griffing returned. He was looking worse by the minute. The little set-to with Kale at breakfast seemed to be the turning point. "You'd better go over and give Bianco a hand," he told Flash. "We'll need Dowler here, and I think Bianco could use some help."

"What's the problem?" Kale demanded. "Are they having trouble?"

"No. But they'll have more to do than we will. And they won't be able to get all the men through by seven. It'll probably be seven thirty."

"The longer we have to wait here, the more chance—"

"I know," Griffing said. "And the more they have to hurry there . . ." He shrugged and turned to Flash. "Keep an eye on things up there, will you? Play it carefully."

Bianco was standing in the middle of the concrete floor of the dome, talking with LaSala, the Cell Block Keeper. Along the circumference of the dome, officers waited in pairs at the wire mesh entrance to each of the four wings. It was just six now; the convicts were still in their cells. The Cell Block, all cement and steel, echoed and magnified and reverberated every sound, so that except when the inmates were sleeping and the officers motionless, the place was always a bedlam. But now it was unnervingly quiet.

Bianco turned at the sound of Flash's footsteps. He nodded. "We're just about ready."

"Who's doing what?"

"LaSala's gonna handle it up here. I'll be down in the dining hall. We'll bring them out every three minutes."

"I'll stay up here too," Flash said.

"Give me a minute to get down," Bianco said. "I'll let you know when we're ready."

Bianco went down to the dining hall. Flash and LaSala walked over to the Keeper's standing desk, between the East and South wings, in front of the big nail board with its rows of white discs.

"I'll stay here," Flash said, nodding to the intercom on the desk. "Which wing are you starting with?"

"North," LaSala said. LaSala was fat, rather ugly, loud, coarse. He always appeared to be in the worst of all possible moods, and always was. There was something almost simian in the length and thickness of his arms, the sloping mass of his shoulders, the bushiness of his brows. And one didn't have to be a snob to assume that LaSala might not be a raconteur and a wit, an intellectual, a genteel clubman. But no Security man had a dirtier or more difficult or more important job. He controlled and organized—through a combination of shrewdness, bullying, bellowing, and brute force—the movement of a thousand men in and out of their cells several times a day. No one liked him, but he was as close to being indispensable as any man on the staff, and for this reason Dowler admired him. Dowler admired any man who did a good job.

"You handle it and I'll just stand by," Flash said. "Are your men ready to seal off if we run into trouble?"

"If I yell, we seal everything off," LaSala said.

"Can you put another man at the stairway? If anything happens here I want one free to get down to tell Bianco."

"Okay," LaSala said. "Let me know when you wanna start." LaSala moved to the center of the dome and sent an officer to the double doors of the stairway to the dining hall. He turned then, hands on hips, to gaze inquiringly at Flash.

Flash depressed the intercom switch. "Fleishman here. Come in at garage."

"Yes sir."

The crackling, the enormous static was gone. Somebody must have fixed the damned thing: a good omen perhaps. "We're ready to start feeding. I want a final go-ahead from the Warden."

"One moment, sir."

An officer came up the stairway from the dining hall and signaled Flash that they were ready downstairs. Flash nodded but held up his open hand to tell LaSala to wait.

"The Warden said to hold on a bit, sir."

"Why?"

"I don't know, sir. He just said to hold on."

"All right." Flash shook his head at LaSala and shrugged. LaSala stood with his hands still on his hips, in what appeared to be the exact center of the dome. He looked like a Japanese wrestler staring, through heavy-lidded eyes, at his opponent.

The Cell Block remained astoundingly quiet, with hardly a sound from the cells.

The intercom startled Flash. "The Warden says you can start now, sir."

"What was wrong? Is anything happening there?"

"I don't think so, sir. I really don't know. But the Warden said to start feeding."

"Tell him we're starting." Flash nodded to LaSala.

LaSala thrust his right arm straight out, his forefinger extended to point at the officer on the ground-floor tier of the North wing. The officer spun the metal brake on the wall. The whirring and clacking of gears and metal teeth sounded through the dome. The officer adjusted the brake to General Open, then looked back over his shoulder. LaSala nodded. The officer pulled the lever and stepped onto the walkway. *"Tier 1—breakfast call!"*

The slamming of twenty-five barred gates blasted terrifically—a fantastic screeching and clattering. The inmates stepped from their cells and slammed the gates shut.

"March for breakfast!" The officer turned sharply and marched through the wing door and onto the dome floor. The inmates followed in silence, passing single-file within a few feet of LaSala, who had not moved, had not altered his perpetual scowl. He stared ferociously, with undisguised contempt, into the face of each inmate who passed. It was not a special tactic, devised for the occasion. It was simply the physical embodiment of his theory of institutional control.

The lead officer began walking sideways, then backwards, staying abreast of the first inmate and watching the ones behind. When the last inmate stepped onto the dome floor, a second officer fell in at the rear. The first inmate reached the stairway door and was halted by the lead officer. The line compressed neatly; the inmates stopped.

"Take 'em down!" LaSala commanded.

The two officers took them down. None of the inmates had looked around. None had even tramped or scuffed his heels.

One of the officers returned from downstairs and hurried back to the North wing to help take the next tier down. When three minutes were up, the second tier brake was spun and the men stepped out and slammed their doors and were led down the single flight of caged metal steps to the dome floor and then across to the stairway. They were as quiet as the first group. From the men still waiting in their cells came no sounds at all. As the odors rose from the kitchen and dining hall—you could smell cooked cereal now, coffee, hot bread—the men usually showed their hunger and impatience by banging on their bunks, scraping chairs, clapping, stamping, hooting behind their hands.

The officer who took the second tier down returned. Flash beckoned him.

"Everything okay down there?"

"They're eating. They're quiet."

After three minutes, LaSala signaled for the third tier.

Every three minutes another tier was escorted across the floor and down the stairway, the inmates walking soberly, their eyes down, their faces gray, expressionless. Faces of inmates, no matter how much sun they got, always seemed gray, and the quieter an inmate became, the grayer he looked.

At six twenty, the fifth and last tier from the North wing marched down for breakfast. That meant approximately two hundred and fifty men were downstairs eating. The other seven hundred and fifty were still waiting in their cells. Three minutes later the first tier of the West wing was sent down, three minutes later the second, three minutes after that the third.

At six thirty an officer came up from the dining hall and told Flash that the first tier had finished eating and was now ready to return.

"Okay. Bring them up."

He waited until the tier got back into their cells before signaling LaSala to send the next group down. He continued alternating the groups coming and going. That meant one tier every five minutes instead of every three. He got the garage on the intercom. "Tell the Warden we won't be through feeding until ten to eight at the earliest."

A few minutes later Griffing's voice came from the box. "Flash, what's up? Are you having trouble?"

"We've got men coming back now too. I don't want them crossing."

"All right. Is ten to eight the best you can do?"

"We may pick up a few minutes after everybody's down there and we only have groups coming back."

"All right, do your best. Everything's quiet here."

"Do they know the water's off?"

"They must by now. But they're not saying anything. I think they're waiting for us to bring in breakfast."

"Do you think they'll wait until ten to eight?"

"No," Griffing said.

By seven o'clock, at which time all men were normally finished eating and back in their cells, only eleven of the twenty tiers had gone down. Only four had returned. The fifth was coming up the stairs and starting across the dome. From the East wing came a scream: "WHERE'S THE FUCKING FOOD!"

Flash stood rigid: a sudden vague plummet took his breath away.

When the lingering, reverberating echo died, the place was absolutely silent. No one even looked toward the East wing, not LaSala, not Flash, not even the men marching across the floor, who had merely stopped, their eyes down. Everyone seemed to be waiting for some signal to break their locked stances, some confirmation that the cry had been real, that they had actually heard it.

The men coming up the stairway, however, evidently hadn't heard it, or else didn't realize the men ahead had stopped. They kept coming, piling up on the landing.

"Quit shoving!" an inmate said, elbowing the man behind him.

"Get those men moving!" Flash called.

"Go on! Move!" LaSala yelled at the lead officer.

"C'mon!" the officer shouted, angrily waving the inmates ahead. "Get moving!"

The man at the front of the line moved, but hesitantly. The middle of the line remained motionless; it had thickened and lost its shape. The men who were piled up at the end spread out aimlessly onto the dome floor.

LaSala ran to the stairway. Just then an inmate swung at another. He missed, and the other, with a yell, swung back. He also missed. LaSala charged up in a heavy, clumsy, almost sideways stride and grabbed one of them and flung him aside. An officer jumped on the other from behind. The inmate struggled and kicked back at him.

"Get back in line!" LaSala yelled at the inmates.

"WE WANNA EAT!" someone bellowed from the South wing.

Two or three others yelled, and the cries became so numerous they were unintelligible, the screams and their echoes riding over each other like waves, shrill and hysterical. And then even these sounds were overwhelmed. It sounded as if every man in the place was banging on the bars or slamming his bed down. The noise intensified so much you could not hear it; it was no longer sound, not even noise; it was sheer brutal shock; it staggered you.

The men clustered at the stairway entrance seemed oblivious to it.

They continued to shove at each other, to mill about. LaSala and the two officers struggled to get them into line.

The inmate at the head of the line, frantically prodded by the lead officer, reached the wing entrance. The officer shoved him through and grabbed the arm of the next inmate to do the same. But the first whipped around and charged back out and leaped on him, knees first, bringing him down. Grappling clumsily—and seemingly in silence, a dumb show amid all the noise—the two of them whipped about on the floor, locked together. Another officer ran over and grabbed the inmate's arm. He was knocked sprawling by two inmates battering into him from behind.

Three officers, hurrying over to help LaSala at the stairway entrance, saw the trouble at the front of the line and stopped, hesitating for a moment, and then swung around and ran in that direction. Eight or ten inmates were now pummeling the two guards. Both were on the floor. One was struggling to break free from a hammer lock. The other, scrunched over like a fetus, was trying to protect his head.

The convicts at the back of the line broke ranks and charged across the floor, their mouths open with shrieks Flash couldn't hear. LaSala, whose back had been turned, suddenly found himself alone.

"Riot call!" Flash screamed into the intercom, his lips against the grill. The yelling and banging continued from the cells at an unbelievable intensity. "Riot call in the dome! Riot call!"

LaSala lumbered over, head down, sideways, to plunge into the melee at the door to the wing. It now included everybody in the dome except Flash—fifty inmates and maybe a dozen officers. Half seemed to be on the floor, kicking and writhing. The others were all either wrestling or throwing punches. Every officer was surrounded by gray uniforms. The inmates who couldn't get close to an officer fought each other. One inmate, seeing another on his knees, his arms sagging, stepped forward deliberately and smashed his fist into his face, sending his head looping backwards.

Flash ran to the double door to seal off the stairway to the dining hall. He slammed one double door but then, in reaching for the other, realized that part of the noise he heard was coming from downstairs, funneled through the staircase, pulsating, echoing. He stepped onto the landing and pulled the second door shut behind him and locked it. He scrambled headlong down the stairway. A metal food tray clattered against the wide barred gate at the foot of the stairs and dropped ringingly to the concrete floor.

The gate was locked. The tables in the dining hall were overturned, their crossed white wooden legs sticking up in the air. The floor was spattered with trays and food; trays, cups, silverware flew through the air; men leaped yelling over tables and benches. Everyone he could see was fighting, running, screaming, throwing something. He could not see Bianco; he saw only two officers in the whole mess, each flailing against six or eight inmates.

Flash unlocked the gate, waited until three awkwardly wrestling inmates stumbled past, still fighting. He shoved the gate open and slid quickly through and relocked it and put the keys in his pocket.

He hesitated, looking for a place to start. Most of the trouble, most of the men, were at the other end of the huge room. Forty or fifty were down at this end. One inmate, waving a jagged table leg overhead like a tomahawk, bulled into the edge of the crowd at the other end. Flash took the keys out again, unlocked the gate and left it open. He pounced on the three convicts who were still wrestling nearby and got a strangle hold around the neck of the nearest one and yanked him back. Before the man could respond Flash shoved him toward the open gate.

"*Get in there! Stay there!*"

He turned without waiting to see if the man would obey. The other two convicts were gone. They didn't want to touch a warden; they didn't want to be seen by a warden.

Flash moved toward five inmates who were pulling out the large metal food containers from the serving tables and dumping great steaming blobs of oatmeal onto the floor. He grabbed the first one by the back of his collar, twisting it tight, and jerked him back. He spun him around and pointed to the stairway entrance.

"*Get in there!*"

He took the arm of the second inmate and sent him stumbling after the first. He quickly got the next two moving without trouble. The fifth man was trying to upset the milk dispenser, rocking it violently back and forth, straining the bolts that held it to the steel counter top. He hadn't seen Flash coming, and when Flash pulled him away from behind he tore free and swung. It was a wild, roundhouse swing; Flash saw it coming and followed it all the way, dulled, abstracted, unable to move. It landed heavily on his shoulder. The inmate stiffened, wide-eyed.

"Go ahead!" Flash yelled, pointing to the stairway. "Over there!" Flash turned him around and pushed. The man went, running with a stiff, indecisive stride, picking his way over the trays and the slop on the floor.

An officer appeared, sleeve flapping, hustling four inmates toward the stairway, and Flash thought *This is it; we've got them moving now.*

Then he glimpsed a blue uniform in a maelstrom of gray. He lunged forward and was staggered by an inmate leaping over a fallen bench. The inmate disappeared. Flash slipped on a slice of bread and lost sight of the officer. The crowd from the other end seemed to be expanding, surging closer. Two inmates hurled a third to the floor and leaped on him. One held his arms while the other ripped off his trousers and clawed at his underwear.

"*Hey!*" Flash yelled.

Someone crashed into him from behind, taking his breath away. Flash whipped around angrily and collided with a shoulder. There was no space, just arms and faces. Everything lurched fitfully, grotesquely; men shouted into his ears. "*Hey!*" he yelled, groping, trying to keep his feet, rocked violently from all sides. "*Hey!—Hey!—*"

He stumbled clear, not knowing what had propelled him. He straightened up to stare into the face of an inmate, who stared back, too astonished to move. The inmate's expression, feeble, almost squeamish, did not change as a mug smashed into his face. For a long time, it seemed, it did not change. Then his nostrils flared red; terrified, he ran.

Two inmates wrestled for control of a metal pitcher that one held high overhead, his wrist gripped in the other's hand.

An inmate, as if pitching sidearm, sliced the edge of a metal tray into another inmate's neck, then watched him crumple.

Something knocked Flash down. He slashed backward with his arm at an inmate sprawled over him. He drove him off and got up.

An officer lay on his back on an upright table, motionless, his head turned from Flash, his arms and legs outstretched, his hands limp over the edges. He lay amid trays and broken mugs and spilled milk and blotches of cereal, and his shirt front was dark and wet. An inmate, his back to Flash, leaped from the crowd alongside the table and flung himself upon the officer, bringing down his arm like a man jamming a stake into the ground. He withdrew the knife, bloodied, from the officer's stomach, and lurched into the crowd.

Flash charged after him, lost him, and stopped suddenly facing three convicts abreast. The one in the middle held a ring of keys.

"*Give me those!*"

The inmate's eyes bulged. He turned and ran, followed by the others. Flash raced after them but lost them in the crowd. He whirled around and headed for the officer on the table. He dropped heavily to his knees, his arms clutched over his head. Holding his arms up exhausted him; he fell forward onto his face. A smothering weight materialized on top of him; he was paralyzed; he could not breathe. His mind remained clear, very precise, except that it leaped frantically. The weight evaporated, but roughly, and he was on his knees and his eyes were open although he wasn't sure if he was seeing anything. For an instant the silence was absolute, then the noise returned like a radio suddenly switched on full-volume. His left hand, outspread on the floor, was in a blob of cereal, cold and watery.

He cringed, arching his back, as an inmate hurtled past.

Enough! he wanted to cry out. Fair was fair, and he deserved better! At least some understanding—at least a glimmer of acknowledgment . . .

He got one foot planted on the floor and tried to pull himself up, using his knee as a fulcrum. This time whatever hit him was precise and astounding, as emphatic as a small, contained explosion at the base of his skull, and he just felt, *Oh shit,* but blissful too, sinking sweetly into a pure and luxuriant softness.

19

It could have been noon for all you could tell in there, but it felt like the middle of the night. The aisles between the bookshelves were shadowy; only the light on the desk burned. He looked at his watch: a quarter to seven.

"Sir—the Warden wants you!"

"Is there a bathroom here? I'd like to—"

"I don't think there's time, sir."

"What's happened?"

"I don't know—but they want you right away."

They ran up the hill in the brilliant morning sunlight. They rounded the Cell Block and ran along the bare ground, damp and slippery now. Griffing and Kale were huddled near the garage. Five guards, their entourage, their fluttery retinue, stood at the standard discreet distance.

"What's up?" Johnny asked. He was puffing.

"We'd like you to go in again," Griffing said. He looked about twenty years older than last night. His eyes were raw and bloodshot. His voice was lifeless.

"What for?"

"To talk to them."

"What about?"

Griffing hesitated, then deferred with a glance to Kale. Kale looked fresher, but at the same time more harried. "I don't know," he said. "Sound them out, see what they're thinking."

"I did that last night."

"They're waiting for their breakfast," Griffing said. "You can tell them it's coming."

"They put that man out the window," Kale said.

"What man?"

"The guard in there," Kale said. "The old one."

"Cloninger," Griffing said.

"What do you mean—put him out the window?"

"They held him upside down," Griffing said, without emphasis. "Hanging by his feet."

"Tell them they'll have the food within ten minutes," Kale said.

Johnny looked at his watch: five to seven. "What else should I tell them? Are you going to make some kind of offer?"

Neither seemed eager to answer.

"What's the use of my running back and forth if you won't even—"

"They asked for you," Kale said. "Just hold them off till they get their breakfast."

"Don't make any offers," Griffing said. "Don't negotiate."

"If that's all I'm supposed to—"

"They were threatening to kill him," Kale said. "The guard."

Johnny paused. "How did they do that?"

"He held a gun between his legs," Kale said.

"All because their breakfast was late?"

"Will you just go in and assure them it's coming," Griffing said. "We don't want them doing that again."

"All right," Johnny said.

"They've boarded up the windows," Kale said.

Johnny turned to look. Each of the four windows seemed opaque; the sun glistened off the panes. A big white sign hung from one window: BRAKFAST. "What'd they board them up for?"

"To keep us from getting any gas in," Kale said.

At that moment one window, next to the one with the sign, suddenly cleared. Johnny saw a man inside, his back to them. The top pane slid down, opening the upper half of the window. The man seemed to rise from the floor, still with his back to them, as if by some form of levitation.

"They're putting him out again—" Kale cried.

"Get over there!" Griffing said. "Hurry!"

He was already running. "Wait!" he yelled ahead. "I'm coming!"

They lowered Cloninger out head first, his face in the sun, his back against the lower part of the window and the wall, his knees hooked over the window frame. His head did not reach the ground. As Johnny raced closer he saw that Cloninger's eyes bulged in terror. His face seemed to be burning; his lips were parted; he groaned breathlessly, straining to arch his neck and shoulders.

"We'll get you right in!" Johnny shouted and ran up to pound on the door, but it swung open as he approached. He ducked quickly inside and stopped, looking for Orninski in the strange half-light of the room behind the boarded windows. He whipped around quickly as the door slammed shut; Mel Simmons relocked it immediately, as if afraid someone might suddenly materialize out there, a whole armed posse, and force their way in. The handle of a knife showed over his trousers.

Orninski stood to one side of the open window, near the two ropes knotted around Cloninger's ankles and tied to a leg of a wooden table, stretched taut, like guy wires. He had a thick, snub, crudely made gun in his hand. His face was grotesquely swollen, lopsided, and the shiny purplish-red flesh seemed covered with a stretched translucent membrane. His right eye was so puffed it was closed. He had to turn his head to look at Johnny with the other eye.

"What's wrong with you?" Johnny said. "Have you lost your mind?"

"Now look—" Orninski started to say, but Johnny hurried past him to the window, reaching up to take hold of one of Cloninger's legs, trying to figure out how to get him in, how they had managed to get him out.

"Hey—!" Orninski yelled.

Johnny felt a hand on his arm and was flung around, away from the window. He stumbled against the ropes.

"Get back!" Orninski was only a couple of steps from him, hunched forward. The room was quiet. Johnny looked at the gun, then at Orninski's face, almost in profile, the left eye wide and unblinking.

"That's better," Orninski said, very quietly. His words had a curiously stretched and sticky quality; his lips moved painfully.

"Get that man in, for God's sake!"

"He's all right."

"He's not all right—take him in."

"When we get breakfast."

"You're getting breakfast. It's coming."

"Oh?" Orninski said. Slowly he looked around, at Mel Simmons, at the other convicts, as if to make sure they had heard, and then said, "I see." *I thee:* it sounded comical, almost like an imitation of a kid lisping, but more blubbery.

"Now will you take that man in?"

"Who said it's coming?"

"I say it's coming. It's coming."

Orninski considered this, then nodded to two convicts standing behind one of the boarded windows, next to a pile of wood scraps on the floor. "Okay," he said. "I think maybe they got the idea."

The two convicts climbed onto the window sill, balancing on one foot, holding on to the frame. One reached out and took hold of Cloninger's belt. The other leaned over and grabbed Cloninger's hand. Together they pulled him up and held his body horizontal to ease him inside. A third convict helped lower him to the floor. His glasses were gone, his face deeply flushed. He was wheezing and trembling, his eyes open but unfocused. One of the convicts held his arm to keep him steady.

"Let him sit down," Orninski said.

The convict untied the ropes from Cloninger's ankles and took him back to the corner and sat him down. He looked dazed.

Then Johnny saw that the other guard, Delft, next to him on the floor, had his hands tied, resting in his lap. His feet were also tied. But he looked better than he had last night. His cuts and bruises seemed less inflamed.

Next to him sat a convict, his arms crossed over his knees, his face turned from Johnny. The name on his shirt tag was *Verdun*.

"What's going on?" Johnny said.

"That's what we'd like to know," Orninski said.

"Why are you tying up these men? Why'd you board up the windows?"

"Get that one covered," Orninski told one of the convicts, motioning to the window Cloninger had been out.

The convict slid a large sheet of plywood, which had been leaning against the wall, over the window, making the room suddenly darker. The board had three eyeholes cut in it. The holes let in some light, and some came in around the edges. Johnny noticed that the lamps under the table were lighted. You could still see throughout the room but everything was dim, gray, gauzy. The room smelled more rank than it had last night; the air was almost rancid.

"What's going on?" Johnny said.

"That depends on what you're talking about, I guess. I mean, are you talking about them turning off the water? Or maybe about them turning off the lights? Or maybe about how they're trying to starve us out? I mean, which of those things are you talking about?"

Orninski was close enough to see Johnny's expression, and was obviously pleased by what he saw. Behind Orninski the convict began hammering nails through the plywood sheet to the wooden window frame. Another convict was already bent over to peer through one of the eyeholes.

"What's the matter, Mr. Mancino? You mean they didn't even tell you about all that? Whatd'ya know, heh? Is that what I gotta do when you come in here?—give you all the news, so you know what's going on?"

"Is the water back on now?"

"It's on. And you can see, the lights too. Which only just leaves the food."

"I told you—it's coming."

"It better come." He was silent a moment. "Sure, last night we get all this bullshit about offers and settling and everything, and then this morning—"

"I didn't say there'd be an offer. I was just trying to see if you'd—"

"Sure," Orninski said. "Only what happens then this morning? We go over and turn on the faucet and all that comes out is a funny noise. Then they won't even send in our goddamn breakfast. Then we look out the window and suddenly there's about ten times as many screws running around out there, and what they're carrying is all these goddamn big elephant guns that they got. Which, you know, don't look like they're thinking of making no offers, because what it looks like is they're thinking of just busting right in here. So if you wanna be brought up to date on what's going on around here, that's what's going on."

Orninski sounded strident, abrasive. He was close to rage. And in the erratic, glassily intense look of his one cyclops-like eye, Johnny could see for the first time a convincing suggestion of the man they had been talking about last night—the paranoic, the psychotic.

"If you're really interested in negotiating," Johnny said, slowly, steadying his voice, "then maybe it'd be better to take it easy . . . not to let things get out of hand."

"Talk to your friends out there about things getting out of hand."

They were standing near the boarded windows, perhaps six feet apart, talking loud enough for everybody to hear. Behind Orninski the convict remained bent over at the eyehole; further back, in the corner, Cloninger sat motionless, remote; Delft, his hands and feet tied, watched them; next to him the convict that the Warden was so interested in, Verdun, kept his head turned away, resting on his knees. Two convicts sat at the back table, keeping an eye on the guards, and maybe on Verdun too. All the convicts stationed around had knives in their belts. The ones sitting on the floor across the room were quiet, their faces indistinct in the dimness.

Johnny looked at Orninski. "Maybe the best thing to tell them would be—"

"The best thing to tell them would be we're all very sick and tired of all this fucking around with the lights and everything. Because if they just try one more thing like that, they're gonna be sorry."

"You shouldn't be making threats."

"Only I am, heh?"

Johnny paused. "Are you still interested in settling this thing? If not, there's no point in—"

"Sure, I'm interested. For them." He pulled his head back, as if pointing with his chin, indicating the men throughout the room. Under his chin, a ragged line of dried blood had turned dark. "Not for me. Because I'll tell you, the Warden out there would be a lot happier if they carried me out of here with a lot of big holes in me, because then he only has to say that this inmate Orninski, who had this gun in his hand, just got shot in self-defense, which makes everything afterward a lot simpler. So I'll tell you something, when I hear that first gun go off out there, or see those guys coming, I'm gonna know right then that this inmate Orninski is a dead duck, and don't have to worry about what he does in the time he's got left. And I ain't shitting you. I mean this. I can't do anything for me anymore. So what I'm gonna do is something for them, so when they carry me out of here full of holes, the other cons they'll say that guy there that's dead now and all covered with his own blood, at least he died doing some good for guys just like him, that nobody else in the whole fucking world ever gave a shit about doing any good for."

Johnny couldn't decide if Orninski was saying this for him, or for the other convicts. But he said it with a kind of feverish conviction, his voice thick and lisping, his one good eye stretched wide.

"Maybe if we can settle this thing," Johnny said, "there won't be any need for—"

"All right," Orninski said sharply. "And now I want you to tell the Warden there's two things we're gonna have to get in here if he wants to do any settling, and we're gonna have to get them right away. Number one is breakfast."

"I keep telling you—it's coming."

"I don't wanna be told it's coming! I want it here!"

"All right," Johnny said. He looked at his watch: five after seven. Ten minutes, Kale said, and now it was ten minutes, and where the hell was it? The only one who seemed to bother telling him anything resembling the truth was Orninski, who felt obliged to tell it from behind a gun. A great crowd to be caught in the middle of—Orninski in here and Griffing and Kale out there. "What's the other thing?"

"The other thing is I want the Warden to send in a man we can talk to about some things we want."

"You can talk to me."

"We talked to you all night, Mr. Mancino, and look where it got us. We're gonna have to have one of the Warden's own men and the one I want is Mr. Fleishman. And I want him right away, because this is their last chance. If he don't come right away, that's the end of it."

"Why didn't you just tell them this yourself?"

"We wanted you to tell them."

"All right—I'll tell them."

"Write it out," Orninski said. "Make a note for them."

"It'd be quicker if I just went out and told them."

"Mel—bring me that pad. Here," he said to Johnny, motioning to the nearest table, "you can sit right down here and write it." The table top was covered with games of tictactoe, and at the other end a stack of metal cafeteria trays were piled up. "Go ahead, sit down."

Johnny didn't move. Mel brought over a spiral pad and a pen, placed them on the table and hurried back to the door. He did not meet Johnny's eyes.

"Go ahead. Sit down."

Johnny sat at the end of the bench. The ropes they had used on Cloninger were on the floor, still tied to the table leg. He picked up the pen and opened the pad. "What do you want me to say?"

"What I just said, number one about breakfast, and number two, Fleishman, and if we don't get those two things right away, there'll be trouble. Just put it in your own words. The note's from you, not me."

Johnny hesitated. He tested the pen, drawing tight coils on the cardboard cover of the pad. It worked. He clicked the point up and down twice, looking at it. Orninski moved closer, his arms crossed, one hand tucked in, the other sticking out, pointing the gun directly down at him. He stood sideways to watch Johnny with his good eye. Johnny began writing, pausing after the first phrase, and then continuing slowly, holding the pen close to the point: *Mr. Orninski wants breakfast immediately, and wants to confer with Mr. Fleishman about the possibilities of a settlement.*

"Read it to me," Orninski said.

Johnny read it.

"Add about the trouble if we don't get it right away."

"I really don't think that'd be—"

"Add it."

Johnny wrote: *Orninski insists that there might be trouble if you don't go along on these requests.* He read it to Orninski.

"Tell them, lives will be in danger. Say it just like that—lives will be in danger."

"You don't—"

"Write it."

Johnny wrote it.

"Now read me the whole thing, from the beginning."

Johnny read it.

"Now just add one more thing," Orninski said. He looked at his wrist watch. "It's a little after seven. Put down that we have to get these two things by seven thirty. That will be the time limit."

Johnny wrote: *The time limit he has set for these two requests is 7:30.*

"Now read me the whole thing again."

Johnny read it.

"Okay," Orninski said. "And now since it's your note, I'll tell you what's gonna happen if they don't meet the time limit, and you can see if you wanna put it in or not. If we don't get these things by seven thirty, we're gonna put Mr. Cloninger there out that window again for a little more fresh air, and then shoot him. Now—you wanna put that in, or not?"

"Are you crazy?"

"I am tired of people laughing at me."

"Laughing at you?"

"If they think this is just a big joke, then that's what's gonna happen, to show them what a big joke it is."

"For God's sake, no one's laughing at you!"

"Well, now they can either listen, or they can just keep laughing if they want, which will be too bad for Mr. Cloninger, who at least won't be laughing."

Orninski was speaking quietly now, with a kind of hollow drone to his voice, his words still blubbery, sticky. His back was to the corner where Cloninger sat, staring blankly ahead, without his glasses. Cloninger gave no sign that he had heard.

"The minute you do that," Johnny said, "they'll rush you." He wet his lips. "If you kill one guard, they'll assume you're ready to kill the other, and that'll be it. You won't have anything left to threaten them with."

"We'll have you," Orninski said.

Johnny was looking up at him, staring into his lopsided face, his one good, glaring eye. Johnny shrugged; he tried to smile. "I don't think that'll stop them from coming . . ." He swallowed. "Not if you do anything to Cloninger. . . ."

"That ain't what I'm asking you," Orninski said. "I'm asking whether you want to put that in the note or not, about Mr. Cloninger."

"If I do, they might just rush right now. They might not wait."

"You wanna leave it out then?"

Johnny hesitated. He read the note over to himself: *Mr. Orninski wants breakfast immediately, and wants to confer with Mr. Fleishman about the possibilities of a settlement. Orninski insists that there might be trouble if you don't go along on these requests. Lives will be in danger. The time limit he has set for these two requests is 7:30.* He looked up. "I don't think we should say anything more."

"All right. Let me see it."

Johnny handed him the pad. His fingers were stiff; his arm moved awkwardly.

Orninski motioned for Mel, and they looked over the note together. "How does it sound to you, Mel?" he said, and then said to Johnny: "Mel here is our expert note writer."

Mel was still staring at the pad, frowning, his face darkening. He made an O with his mouth. He glanced up, first at Johnny, then at Orninski. "Is this what we're gonna say?"

"That's what Mr. Mancino's gonna say. It's his note. How does it sound?"

"I don't know."

"I mean, it sound all right to you?"

"Yeah, I guess so . . . If that's what we're gonna say . . ."

"Good. Now you just sign it, Mr. Mancino, so they'll know who it comes from."

Johnny signed it.

Orninski ripped the page out and gave it to Mel. "Just fix it up on a piece of wood now, and throw it out to them."

So he folded the paper over and picked up a piece of wood about a foot long from one of the piles. The piece was right next to the sailboat Verdun'd been sanding down when they busted in yesterday, which seemed about twenty years ago. Whatever it was that Preston'd started carving was there too, and Preston, who was watching him, yelled over, "Hey—use the statue there I made. It's a statue."

So Mel kind of shrugged and dropped the piece he had and picked up this one Preston carved on and sort of looked at it. Orninski was kind of looking too.

"What the hell kind of a statue is it supposed to be?" Orninski asked.

"It's this broad getting fucked," Preston said. "Only it ain't all finished. Go on, Mel—use it. Maybe everybody out there'll like it, and I'll be a famous artist, heh?"

So Mel took the piece up to Cloninger's desk and Scotch-taped the note to it. Preston really hadn't got too far with the carving, from what Mel could see. He tore a piece from Cloninger's clean white apron they'd found in his desk and tied it to the wood for a flag, like they did the other time. He didn't look around but could feel everybody watching him. The place was very quiet. He walked back to Orninski. Mancino was still standing there, near Orninski. They both watched him coming. Everybody in the goddamn place watched him, for Christ's sake.

"All right," Orninski said. "Throw it out."

Mel looked at all the windows boarded up.

"Throw it out the fucking door. You got the key."

So Mel went over to the door and took out the keys and looked for the right one. He found it and looked back at Orninski.

"Go on. Throw it."

He pulled open the door, with the sun suddenly so bright it practically blinded him, and gave the wood a good heave. A pretty good one, anyhow, sidearm. He could really smell the air outside. It smelled real clean and fresh. The piece flipped end over end and he watched it land and bounce and then slammed the door and locked it, and the sunlight was gone, and so was the fresh air, and the room, let's face it, really smelled pretty shitty. "Okay," he said to Orninski.

"Are they coming for it?" Orninski asked over his shoulder to Akar at the hole.

"One of the screws is," Akar said.

"Good," Orninski said. He turned to Mancino, who was still just standing there, watching everything. Mancino really towered over Orninski, who was the nearest guy. "Why don't you just sit down and make yourself comfortable, and we'll see what happens. We got, the way I figure, about fifteen-twenty minutes."

Mancino sort of shrugged.

"Go on," Orninski said. "Sit down."

So he sat down, at the same place where he made the note, like a grownup scrunched down at some little kid's desk in a schoolroom, the way his knees came up. The pen and pad were still there. Actually, although he looked kind of sore, in some ways he looked more just like some poor guy with his ass in a sling. He really did. He had this kind of empty look on his face.

Mel looked over at the hobby crew, spread out on the floor. Westerman was sitting where he was before, when Orninski was bitching to Mel about the hobby crew, and how because they all had suction somewhere they got the softest go in the whole place and so naturally wouldn't get involved in anything that could mess up their deals. That's when Orninski pointed out Westerman, and Mel remembered then that he *knew* Westerman was on the hobby crew, but somehow in all the excitement just never thought about it.

"You wanna talk to him, Mel? Go ahead—just go say hello if you want."

Shit, Mel didn't wanna talk to anybody like that. What the hell were you supposed to say to a guy like that? Actually, he didn't look like too much of a big shot, Westerman. You wouldn't pick him out of no crowd. He was older, of course, maybe fifty, and kind of moon-faced, with sort of very thin gray hair, and maybe if you saw him all spiffed up in a suit he'd look like a big shot, but just sitting with his legs crossed on the floor with the other cons, all he looked like was just another con. That really got Mel, Orninski giving orders and even, for Christ's sake, himself supposed to be the goddamn number two man, with the keys and everything, and this guy Westerman just sitting on the floor there along with everybody else and never saying a word, never even blinking a goddamn eye, but just looking kind of bored, and very cool. He was worth millions, Orninski said.

"Have you got a bathroom here?" the TV guy asked. "They ran me out so fast I couldn't get near one."

Orninski looked at him a minute. "Over there," he said, motioning with the gun to where the john was, in the other back corner. "Mel— you go with him."

"Huh?"

"Go with him."

So Mel sort of shrugged and headed over to Mancino. Mel didn't look at his face because actually, right now, he felt pretty lousy about the whole thing with the TV guy, who just came in kind of as a friend and now was really getting screwed. Mel just sort of nodded, keeping his eyes down. Mancino headed between the benches to the john and Mel walked behind. What the hell was he supposed to do anyhow, hold his goddamn hand? Christ, everything was a big production.

When Mancino got there he stopped outside, noticing there wasn't no door, and that all the guys from the hobby crew sitting on the floor on that side were naturally real interested. But then he finally just ducked under the doorway and went in. He stood sideways to the can, with his back to everybody. Mel turned around toward the guys on the floor. All of them, even Westerman, were staring real serious at the guy in there, like it was really something terrifically interesting, this guy taking a leak. Anyhow, the guy must've told the truth about not getting a chance to go, because it sounded like practically Niagara Falls. Maybe because he was so tall, it coming from so high up. It seemed to go on about five minutes. Mel looked at his watch—a quarter after now, a little more. The blood spots on his sleeve didn't seem so dark today, maybe because of the bad light.

He let Mancino walk ahead back to the table, everybody in the place still staring, and then left him sitting there and went back to the door and looked at his watch again.

Everybody in the place was real quiet. Orninski was looking out through a hole now. Maybe he was getting a little jumpy now too. Everybody else was, so Orninski might as well join the crowd. Mel just didn't have any idea in the world what was going on in that guy's head anymore.

Christ, sticking the gun right between the goddamn guy's legs! If you're gonna shoot a guy, at least do it in the head or something, not there.

But let's face it, Orninski was just really off his goddamn nut now, that's all there was to it. This morning Mel really thought Verdun for one, and then Cloninger for two, were just done for. Verdun, of course, practically asked for it. When they woke up that way, with Orninski resting his head because it hurt so much on his shoulder, everyone else was already awake and Verdun, back there in the corner but standing up with his arms folded and his head sort of tilted, was giving them this real phony, prissy kind of smile.

It must've took Orninski a minute to really come out of it, because at first he didn't move. But then he practically leaped off the floor and ran over to Verdun with the goddamn gun in his hand. "What the fuck you think you're doing?"

"Watching the show," Verdun said in that real wise-guy way.

So Orninski swung, with the gun, going right for his face. Verdun tried to duck and got it on the side of the neck, the butt of the gun. He didn't yell but it must've really hurt, and before he could move Orninski grabbed his shirt at the throat with his free hand and screamed, "Sit *down!*" and practically slammed him through the goddamn floor.

He quietened down a bit then and when Preston said he was out of tobacco and asked to grub some, Orninski said, "Wait a minute," and went back to the hobby guys on the floor and made them all get up and turn over whatever tobacco and paper they had, piling it all on the table, and then split in up for the guys from the garage. "Shit," he said, "if you guys ain't with us, then you can't expect no privileges." You could see this sort of pissed the hobby guys off, and a few of them even looked like maybe they were thinking of changing their mind now and joining in, just to keep their smokes, but none did. They'd been smoking like fiends back there—everybody had, the place really smelled crummy, and there were butts stubbed out all over the floor and everything. Orninski did all this very calm and quiet, like he'd really settled down again. And the same with the sign he had Mel make and hang out the window, saying they were waiting for breakfast. Orninski did that very calm too. But then a little later the goddamn water business just got him going again, which was when Mel thought Cloninger was gonna get it.

"What's that?" Orninski yelled when one of the guys from the hobby shop went over to the sink at around six o'clock for a drink and the faucet just sort of spit out and sputtered very loud. "What the hell is *that?*"

"Something's wrong with the water," the guy at the sink said.

Orninski shoved the guy out of the way, really sending him flying, and turned the faucet one way and then the other, twisting it back and forth as hard as he could. "Those fucking bastards!" he yelled. "Those fucking son of a bitches!" And for about a minute he was so angry he just couldn't make up his mind what the hell he wanted to do and just stood there, practically foaming at the mouth, ready to do anything, no matter how bad, if only he could think of it.

And then he scrambled as fast as he could between the tables, banging against a bench and almost knocking it over, and let out a really wild howl and grabbed Cloninger, of all people, and yanked him to his feet, holding his shirt with the one hand and sort of looping the other hand, with the gun, around the back of Cloninger's neck, all the time yelling things like "You fucking son of a bitches," and really shaking the living daylights out of the old guy.

Everybody in the place was so surprised, it happened so fast, that nobody even moved. And then Preston, who was nearest, sort of stepped toward him and said, "Hey—what the hell—maybe we better take it easy . . ."

But Orninski just whipped around and said, "Maybe *you* better shut the fuck up, is what *you* better do!"

And Preston naturally did. Because you could see, the way Orninski was carrying on, that he was really out of his goddamn skull. And then Orninski looked at Akar and Quinlan, who were the two other nearest guys, and then at all the other guys around the room. "That goes for all of you!" he yelled. "If you don't like the way I'm running this thing, what you can do about it is just shut the fuck *up!*"

Nobody moved or said anything, and you could hear the way Orninski was breathing, because he was breathing like a horse. Then he took a real big swallow and said, kind of gasping, "If that's what those son of a bitches think we mean by that sign, we'll put out another sign."

Which was when they put out Cloninger that first time, and the Warden came running out with this other guy in street clothes that nobody'd ever seen before and Orninski climbed up the window behind

Cloninger and stuck that goddamn gun between his legs and yelled to the Warden what he'd better do about the water and their breakfast if he didn't want him to pull the trigger, and also about Mancino coming in. And then when the Warden said okay, they'd do it, they pulled Cloninger back in, hauling him up and over the bottom of the window the way you'd haul in a heavy rope, but slower.

He looked at his watch again—almost twenty after. What the hell were they doing out there, fixing a goddamn twelve-course dinner? Couldn't they read English? Breakfast, that's all the hell they wanted —plain simple frigging *breakfast!* For the life of him he couldn't see why they couldn't just slop some goddamn shit on a tray like they always did and just send it in before somebody got killed.

Christ, could they really be thinking of busting in? What the hell he'd do then he just didn't know. Sure, he had a knife, right there in his pants—he touched it—but he really didn't feel much like going at anybody with a knife. Especially some guy coming at *him* with a gun.

And then Orninski, still at the little peephole, kind of let out this very strange-sounding real loud whisper, that everybody in the room could hear, like something had just surprised the hell out of him. "Well —Jesus!" And everybody in there suddenly perked up. It was like a shock going through the room—you could just feel everybody thinking *Here it comes! At last here the hell they're finally coming with the goddamn breakfast!* But nobody said this, or anything. They were all just dying to ask, but nobody did, and everybody was just like a goddamn skittery dog with his ears up. You could've heard a pin drop.

Then, still with his good eye pushed up against the hole, Orninski said it again, in the same surprised way only more so, "Well—Jesus! Jesus Christ!"

"What's happening?" Mancino finally said. He sort of barked it.

Orninski whipped around then, like he'd completely forgot about anybody being in the room there behind him. And Christ, he looked funny enough anyhow with his face all banged and swollen up and just this one crazy eye moving around, but the *look* he had, the *expression* on his face—well, it was the weirdest look Mel ever saw in his life. "It's the other guys!" he yelled, almost like he couldn't believe it himself. "They're burning down the Cell Block!"

"What?" Mancino said, barking it right out again, but Orninski was already back at the peephole and you could just see how excited he was. He could hardly hold still. He kept squirming around and scrunching up like he was trying to shove himself right through the goddamn hole to see whatever the hell was happening out there. "They *are!*" he yelled. "They're burning down the whole fucking Cell Block!"

Mancino leaped off the bench and ran over and stooped down to look out one of the other holes.

"Let us see too!" Akar said, and popped right over to grab the third hole, between the two others. And then Preston came running too and then, in a regular stampede, all the other guys from the garage except Mel himself, who was still standing by the door. Mel didn't move at all. Even some of the guys from the hobby crew jumped up and looked like they wanted to run over and look out too, but none did.

"Hey, stop pushing!" Orninski said, trying to whack off the guys crowding around him and keep looking out at the same time.

"Let us look too! What the hell's going on out there?"

"Take the fucking thing down," Preston said.

Orninski was so busy looking he didn't even answer, so Preston just ran over to the tool board over Cloninger's desk and grabbed a claw hammer and started prying off the board over the front window, nearest the door.

Orninski pulled back from his peephole and saw. "Hey—leave that up there!"

"Shit," Preston said. "We wanna see too." He had the board loose by this time and shoved it along the floor away from the window and leaned it against the wall, suddenly making the place a lot lighter with the sun blazing in. Orninski was all set to tell him to put it the hell back, but before he could open his mouth everybody crowding around the peepholes rushed over to look out the window, and he was left all alone. So he probably just figured the hell, he wanted a better look too, and hopped over himself and pushed in front of the others to get up against the glass.

"Hey," Mel said. "Nobody's watching them back there."

"Preston!" Orninski yelled. "Get back and watch those guys."

"Aw c'mon—I wanna see too."

"Watch them!"

"Aw shit," Preston said, but left the window, practically having to fight his way out. Then he got this great idea, and hopped up on the front table, where he could keep an eye on the screws and Verdun and at the same time look out over the heads of the guys at the window. "Hey—look at that fucking smoke!"

"Are they really burning it down?" some guy from the hobby crew called over. The whole bunch of them back there were sort of standing now, just itching to come over and look too, but they didn't.

"Shit yes!" Preston told them. "They're burning the fucking thing down."

From where Mel was still standing, by the door, he couldn't see anything. In some ways, it was funny, he didn't want to see. He didn't know, but the whole thing gave him a funny feeling. He could really feel it, right in his stomach. *What the hell next?*—that was what it felt like mostly. But then in some ways he kind of did want to see, so he figured the hell, and sort of moseyed over to the window, only with all those guys bunched up there he still couldn't see anything, so he just climbed on the table with Preston and looked over their heads.

And Christ—it was true. These goddamn clouds of black smoke were just pouring out of the Block, out all these little windows up there.

And then somebody at the window yelled, "Hey—open this goddamn thing up! Quiet, will you guys! Listen!" So somebody shoved up the window and they listened, and for Christ's sake, you could *hear* them, from way over in the Block, like a really loud but faraway kind of rumbling noise.

By now Orninski was practically jumping up and down. "Holy shit!" he kept saying. "Good Christ!" He grabbed Mancino's arm, who was right next to him against the window, and yelled right into his ear. "They heard about us! They're rioting in the goddamn Cell Block! They're showing those goddamn son of a bitches that they're behind us!"

The noise from out there was even louder now, and you could tell it was a lot of guys banging and screaming their heads off, only you couldn't see anything, except for the smoke, because it was all going on inside the Block.

Mancino just sort of nodded and tried to look out some more, but Orninski wouldn't let him. He grabbed his arm again. "*Now* the goddamn Warden's gonna know what kind of trouble he's started! Now everybody's gonna know!"

And then things really started happening. Suddenly a whole bunch of cons came running out from the back door of the Block, that led up from the mess hall, just running out and streaming all over the place, jumping and hollering and leaping in the air, and the guys at the window, when they saw this, just let out this terrific cheer, like the goddamn Fourth of July or something, really whooping it up, with Orninski leading the way. It was really the craziest thing Mel'd even seen, all these cons actually just running around loose like that, screaming and racing like a bunch of chickens with their head cut off. And then suddenly, like somebody out there told them to do it, they all swung around and started racing right for the goddamn hobby shop, like they were just gonna bust right in there, and for the life of him, Mel couldn't figure out what in hell they wanted to do *that* for. But just about two seconds after they all started running toward the hobby shop, some screws came charging out from the garage, heading them off, so the cons just stopped dead and swung around and headed back again as fast as they could. And then out of nowhere there were screws all over the place out there. It was like two teams on a football field, with the ball bouncing around and both teams running in all different directions at once and bumping into each other, and then the Cell Block door must have been shut because no more cons came out, and another whole bunch of screws, including Dowler, who they just caught sight of for a second, who you could tell by his suit, came barrel-assing after the cons, who all raced around the corner of the Shops Building, where they couldn't see them anymore from the window.

Then they saw a whole bunch of highway patrol guys coming from around the Block and running behind the Shops Building too, wearing these riot helmets, like white hard hats.

The guys at the window were really getting a kick out of all this—it was like watching a regular old movie, with all these cops chasing everybody around and practically falling over each other, and every time they saw another bunch go racing by they'd let out a big cheer and laugh and whoop it up. And Orninski kept shouting things like "This'll show 'em! This'll teach the son of a bitches!"

Meanwhile the smoke was getting worse and worse from the little cell windows, and suddenly they heard this really terrific crash and could actually see one of those great big huge windows in the Cell Block just explode right out into about a thousand pieces with a big gush of water shooting out right after, and then even more smoke.

"Hey—they're breaking the windows too!" Preston yelled, right next to Mel on the table. "Shit, they're really going at it."

And another window went the same way, and another, and another, and each time everybody in the room let out a big cheer. They all really seemed to be having the time of their life, especially Orninski. Mel was probably the only one who wasn't cheering or anything, who was just watching kind of quiet.

Somehow the screws must've rounded up the cons that went running behind the Shops Building, because they could see these cons being brought back now, first one batch, then another, with almost as many screws and cops around as cons. It looked like they probably caught all of them, or at least most, maybe twenty-five all together. They hadn't been out long.

Nobody cheered, of course, when the screws brought the cons back. No one said a word actually, but just watched. You could tell they really felt sorry for those poor slobs, blowing their top like that and a coupla minutes later being marched back in like a pretty sad-looking bunch of sheep.

The smoke was fading off now too, and it didn't look anymore like they were gonna burn down any goddamn Cell Block frankly, or even get to first base trying, because the building itself, which was all practically concrete, wasn't about to burn that easy. And then they saw what it was that was burning, because a bunch of screws came hustling out of the Block carrying all these smoking mattresses. They piled them on the ground out there and one screw lugged out a fire hose and started spraying them while the others kept bringing out more mattresses and tossing them on the pile, which in no time got to be about twenty feet across and higher than the screw that was spraying them. An awful lot of black smoke kept coming up from the pile—you could actually smell it now, and it really stunk—although there weren't any flames. Everything was just smoldering. It looked kind of sad, actually, all those mattresses smoking away like that and being soaked down with water, because all Mel could think of was those guys tonight who wouldn't have a mattress to sleep on. He just hoped the hell the guys did it to their *own* mattresses, not other people's.

Everyone at the window seemed kind of down in the mouth now, except Orninski. He wasn't jumping around like before, of course, but he seemed really very satisfied with everything, very chipper. "Okay now, everybody," he said, hustling them away from the windows. "The fun's over. Let's get back where we was."

So all the guys left the window and went to where they were before, and Preston and Mel climbed down from the table.

Mancino stayed at the window though. "I think Fleishman's coming," he said. He sounded different now than he did earlier. He sounded quieter, and not so quick to say things. "He's over by the garage."

"Sure, he's gonna come," Orninski said. "We asked him to, didn't we? And I'll tell you something else—breakfast is gonna come too. I think maybe it just got held up a little . . . with all those guys rioting over there." He was still talking funny from the way his mouth was all swollen up, but real cocky, like he didn't have a worry in the world. All Mel wished was that Orninski was feeling so good because he knew what the hell he was doing, not just because he was off his goddamn nut. It really got Mel before when Orninski told him he was gonna ask for Fleishman to come in too. "Your friend," he said. "We're gonna bring in your other friend now. The Fish Man."

"He ain't no friend of mine," Mel told him. "What the hell do we want him for anyway?"

"You don't want the Warden in here, do you? And who the hell else is there? Dowler? You wanna bring Dowler in here, for Christ's sake?"

"We already brung one guy in here. We brung the TV guy in. How many the hell guys we gotta bring in to settle this goddamn thing?"

"Just one," Orninski said. "Just the Fish Man, that's all."

And the way he said it, you could tell he really figured he could just wrap this Fleishman guy around his little finger. And shit, maybe he could. Mel hoped he could. Only he just hoped too Orninski knew that no matter how much of a kind of funny egg Fleishman was, that Christ knows, he was no dope.

21

"How are you, Flash?—you all right?"

"What?"

"Where's the doctor? Get the doctor in here. Sit down, Flash. Here, let me help you."

"I'm all right."

"You've got a real gash. Can you feel it? You've got a bump the size of a golf ball."

"What?"

"Where on earth is Angiotta? Is somebody getting him?"

"I'm all right. What's happening?"

"Where are your glasses? Did you lose your glasses? Flash—?"

"What?"

"Your glasses—where are they?"

"My glasses."

"Lie down now."

"Go ahead, Flash—it's the doctor. Let him look at you."

"That's it—just stretch out on the table there—ah—uhmm—uh-huh—"

"He'll fix you right up, Flash. Don't you worry."

"What?"

"Uhmmm—yes—well, let's see now—yes-s-s, we'll take care of that . . . there . . ."

"*Ouch!*"

"Can you see my fingers? How many fingers am I holding up?"

"What?"

"We can't send this man in there, Warden."

"I'm all right. *Ouch!*"

"Easy now . . . it just stings a bit . . ."

"*Ow-w-w-w!*"

"It just lasts a second."

"What?"

"Is he going to be all right?"

"Tell me how many fingers do you see?"

"What?"

"The fingers."

"What?"

□

In the Superman comic books they used to have Health and Strength Hints, and one showed how you could improve your vision by staring at telephone poles. First you stared at the closest one, then the next, then the next, on and on, ad infinitum. Only you had to do it without your glasses, and without his glasses he had trouble locating the first pole on that long road to infinity. And when he did find it, there'd be two of them, hazy and sinuous. And since that was almost forty (no!) years ago and his eyes had gotten even worse since, he couldn't exactly blame the lump that everybody insisted brightly was the size of a golf ball.

"What's going on over there?" Flash asked.

"Nothing right now," the two Griffings said in unison.

Flash held his head stiffly, preciously; it didn't exactly hurt, but a general thickening dullness throbbed rhythmically through it to produce a distant ringing. But whatever the doc pumped into his veins with his horse needle, that gallon or so of fiery, surging liquid, seemed to be working. The ringing, certainly, had lessened. And if he wasn't steady as a rock, at least no one had to hold him up. He waved and dipped a bit, that was all.

At maybe twelve or fifteen feet, he could tell somebody was there. At about five feet he could tell who it was.

"You'd better sit down, Flash."

He sat down. Both Griffings and both Kales remained standing, their four faces pretty much blurs. He put one arm on the table and sort of leaned against it, steadying himself. They were in the front end of the garage.

"Are you sure you can handle this?" Griffing said.

"Sure," Flash said. "How did I get up here?"

"Someone walked you over. Don't you remember?"

"What's happening in the dining hall now?"

"They've got everyone back in the cells. Dowler's there. Most of the mattresses are out."

"The mattresses?"

"You walked right by them. They were burning."

"I thought I smelled something. Turned into kind of a mess, didn't it? They started in the dome and the mess hall at the same time. We didn't have enough men."

"It's all right," Griffing said. "Only a few got out."

"Mr. Dowler was fantastic," Kale said.

"Good," Flash said.

"I still can't believe it," Kale said.

"What'd he do?" Flash said.

"I was right there," Kale said. "I saw it myself. Three convicts ran into the Shops Building and shut themselves into an office, right inside the door. We didn't even know whether or not they were armed, but Dowler just shoved the door open and walked in. He didn't even hesitate. Those men might have had guns, knives, whatever, for all anybody knew. One did have a knife. But he just gave it up, and Dowler marched them out. It was incredible. In about three seconds it was all over."

"That's the way to do it," Flash said.

"You must have had a few close calls yourself," Griffing said.

"I mainly served as a punching bag. Were many men hurt?"

"Some, yes. You probably got it about as bad as anybody."

"Except for Dietz," Flash said. "That's who you said it was, didn't you? Dietz?"

"That was horrible," Kale said.

No one else said anything. There wasn't a hell of a lot you could say about a guy with a wife and three kids and some twenty or so knife wounds, by rough count, which Christ knows might have been inflicted by twenty or so different inmates. Each for his own good reasons, he supposed. Flash never really knew Dietz. He wondered if any of the inmates who punctured those various soft and unprotected (how do you protect them?) parts of Dietz's body knew who he was, or cared. In some ways, he hoped they didn't know. Although if you were going to be killed by the cooperative efforts of twenty men, it probably didn't matter much whether their enthusiasm came from a personal or a symbolic hatred. (He wondered if the guy who'd put the golf ball on the back of his head knew who *he* was. Had he hoped to kill him? Would he have paused even one second if Flash had managed to turn around in time to tell him *I came into this stinking racket to help you! Can't you see that?*)

"We'll have to keep all those men in their cells until we can search them out," Griffing said. "God knows how many knives they got from the dining hall."

"What am I supposed to do in the hobby shop?" Flash said.

"Get them out of there," Kale said. "Before anyone else gets killed."

"Sure thing. Why'd they ask for me?"

"Your guess is as good as mine," Griffing said.

"Those men in there must trust you," Kale said.

Flash let this pass. That was all he needed, a resounding vote of confidence from Orninski, via Mancino and Kale. "What do you want me to say to them?"

"Nothing," Griffing said. "Orninski probably has some kind of proposal to make."

"Maybe Mancino's talked him into something," Kale said.

"I doubt that," Griffing said. "Anyhow, if he isn't ready to come out, we'll just have to move in. We can't sit here and let him make threats and wait for another blowup in the Cell Block."

"Maybe this man should have authority to accept a reasonable offer while he's in there," Kale said.

"He's in no shape to negotiate," Griffing said. "He can hardly stand up."

"I can stand up," Flash said.

"We've already had a riot," Kale said. "We've already had one man killed and another threatened right before our eyes."

"It seems to me that an hour ago you were the one who didn't want—"

"Things have changed," Kale said. "We've got to stay flexible."

"What does that mean?"

"It means we should take any reasonable way out we can get."

"We told them last night we wouldn't make any more offers," Griffing said. "I think we have to stick to that. Are you sure you can manage now, Flash?"

"Oh yes, I'm fine." He got up—too abruptly—and grabbed the table for support. He waited for the dizziness to pass.

"Don't let Mancino butt into any of this," Griffing said. "In fact, get him out of there. We don't want him in the way if we're going to have to rush. If they ask about breakfast, tell them it got sidetracked. Play down that trouble in the Block."

"If the food's all that's holding us up, I'll wave for you to send it over. All right?" He was beginning to sway a little and wished they'd start moving.

"All right."

Griffing took his arm and the three of them moved out into the sunshine, then stopped. The other two, he assumed, were looking across at the hobby shop. He also looked, but it was too far. It was like trying to locate the fourth or fifth telephone pole.

"Make it clear to them that this will be their last chance," Griffing said. "Put some pressure on."

"I'm not sure we ought to do that," Kale said.

"I'm not sending anybody over there on his knees," Griffing said.

"We should at least show some willingness to settle."

"We'll show some if he shows some," Griffing said. "Are you sure your head's all right now, Flash?"

"I guess so. Does it look all right?"

"Doc thinks you've got a concussion."

"It doesn't feel like a concussion." He touched the back of his head gingerly; a square gauze pad, somewhat damp, covered the lump.

"Can you manage without your glasses?"

"I can see things close up."

"Can you see the hobby shop?"

"Just point me. I'll be all right."

"If there's any trouble while you're over there, we'll move right in. Get down out of the way then. Try to get Mancino down too."

"Is this the right direction?"

"I'll get someone to take you over," Griffing said. "Bostick!" Someone, presumably Bostick, materialized in duo. "Will you guide Mr. Fleishman over. He's lost his glasses."

"Just point me," Flash said. "I'll find it."

The two dependable Bosticks, from their disembodied haziness, effected a kind of miraculous confluence and a single, solid, steadfast hand took Flash's arm. They started walking, and Flash felt like an idiot, aged and infirm, bandaged, myopic, blundering.

"What are you doing up here, Bostick? I thought you were on the circuit."

"Mr. Dowler brought a batch of us up before, sir." He hesitated politely. "He put one of your men on the circuit."

Naturally. Why waste a good man like Bostick flipping switches? Leave it to Jeff Dowler to figure that out. Women, children and Treatment staff first; all *men* stay behind to fight. Like Jeff Dowler, Hero, who singlehandedly cleared out a hornet's nest of armed convicts bent on riot and destruction. Jeff Dowler could see telephone poles. Jeff Dowler was Superman, the son of a bitch. And what the hell was Flash Fleishman? Little Orphan Annie, the platter-faced virgin, and scarcely able, all things considered, to handle the demands of the role.

And what the hell role was it they asked Dietz to play? And you, Dietz, Richard, Custodial Officer, Class II, husband and father, you're to take the part of raw meat. It's become one of the standard repertory roles over the years; millions of our best men have performed it, at home and abroad. Some have even gained fame from it, but not, alas, too many.

"Sure you're all right there, sir?"

"I'm all right."

"Can you see it yet?"

"It's coming." Next someone will hand him a white cane. Griffing? No—Dowler.

—We oughta maybe get you a white cane, Flash, so nobody runs you over or anything.

—Please, Jeff, no jokes. It's not your style.

"Sir—are you going to manage?"

"Just get me a little closer. How are those other men who got hurt up there? Were you up there?"

"For a while, sir, at the end. I think most of them will be all right. I hope you'll be all right."

"It's just a little bump. The size of a golf ball. Did you know Dietz, Bostick? Was he a friend of yours?"

"I knew him pretty well, sir." There was a pause as they trunched along, and Flash knew, in the awfullest depths of his soul, that there was a lump in Bostick's throat: "He was a good man, sir." It was the size of an apple, that lump, the size of the world, and it sent a shiver through Flash that well-nigh rent him asunder. Maybe someone will say the same of a certain blind man of the desert, who fell among thieves on his way to Jerusalem. But who?

Flash stopped. "I think I can see it now. That's it up ahead, isn't it? That white thing?"

Bostick still held his arm. "I'll take you to the door, sir." He was just itching. A true Security man. Like Jeff Dowler, all he wanted was to get close enough to reach Orninski with his bare hands. Leaping in with a big S on his undershirt, bullets bouncing harmlessly off his chest.

"No," Flash said. "You go back now."

"I'll wait here until you get in."

"I'll get in, don't worry." Flash started walking toward the whitish shape. It was like walking toward a building in the fog. Christ, it was like walking toward a fog. When he got closer he saw the small darker shape off to the left and veered toward it, a little wobbly without Bostick to lean on. The dark shape focused into a door and opened as he remembered just in time the small step.

"C'mon in," said a voice from behind the door.

He floated inside, steadying himself against the door frame, blinking, trying to get his bearings in the swirl, moving forward. The door slammed behind him.

"Search him," said a voice north-by-northeast.

He squinted. Somebody was there. The room was damnably dark though, which didn't help. From behind him a pair of hands slapped his pockets, not hard, almost reluctantly.

"I don't have anything."

"We just wanna make sure, Mr. Fleishman," said the voice in front.

"He's okay," said the voice in back.

It sounded familiar. He looked over his shoulder and recognized Mel Simmons. "Hello, Simmons."

"Hello, Warden . . ."

The room was quiet, and he assumed everybody was staring at him. He pretended to stare back with proper warden-like severity.

"You don't look like you are too well right at this minute," the voice in front said. It sounded almost garbled, as if the person were talking and trying to swallow his tongue at the same time.

"I'm feeling quite well, actually. How are you feeling?"

"I am not feeling so well, Mr. Fleishman. But I am feeling good enough to get by."

"Inmate Orninski, I presume."

"That's it, Warden. Inmate Orninski."

"I understand you've been hurt."

"That is exactly the truth, Warden. And it looks like maybe something happened to you too."

"Nothing worth discussing. And how is everybody else in here?"

"Everybody else in here is just fine—except they are all very hungry. In fact, they are starving."

Flash edged forward a couple of steps, blinking. He felt just a trifle woozy.

"I think maybe you will be better off just staying where you are, Warden Fleishman."

"All right." He could recognize Orninski now, and could see that he was holding something dark. "Are you planning to keep that gun pointed at me?"

"I think maybe I am planning to do that, Mr. Fleishman."

"Most wardens I know don't take kindly to having guns pointed at them."

A somewhat sharp but still mellifluous and professional voice cut in from the left, and Flash turned, vaguely distinguishing him, the goon himself, all alone at a big table. "I think we're ready to sit down and settle this thing, Warden. Mr. Orninski has said that he's—"

"That's right," Orninski said. "You see, we figured we should have somebody here official, who could talk for the Warden."

"Well, here I am. And now, if you people want to end all this foolishness, I'm sure the Warden—"

"What about all that foolishness outside before, Mr. Fleishman? When all those guys were showing how they're all behind us."

"I thought they were just hungry. Breakfast was a little slow this morning."

"We heard the noise, Mr. Fleishman. We saw the smoke. Anyhow, I hope nobody got hurt bad or anything . . . in all that foolishness."

"Oh no."

"You did."

"I slipped and fell, actually. It's just a little bump."

"Sure. Anyhow, you mentioned about how breakfast was kind of slow this morning. It has been *very* slow getting in here, and still is not here. The men are starving, Mr. Fleishman. They want their breakfast."

"If you're really ready to come out, we can manage it a lot more easily after."

"I think you will have to find a way to manage it before, Mr. Fleishman."

"Why? Once you put that gun away, we can have you sitting down in five minutes."

"I think maybe we will sit down in here, Mr. Fleishman. In five minutes."

"Do you really feel that strongly about it?"

"You got it exactly, Mr. Fleishman. I feel real strongly about it."

Flash shrugged and turned and started confidently toward what he hoped was the door.

"Hey—where you going?"

"To tell them to send breakfast in," Flash said, pausing to look back at Orninski, who was pretty fuzzy again.

"I already told them."

"But they thought you were coming out first. Now if you'll just open the door, I'll take care of it."

"Open it," Orninski said after a pause.

Flash was near the wall; he followed it to the door, which Mel Simmons unlocked and pulled open. "Thank you." Flash stepped out onto the little platform and waved vigorously several times. The glare of the sun was inordinately bright; he felt like a character in a surrealistic painting, a lone, forlorn figure in perspectiveless space, waving. He stepped back inside and Simmons locked the door. "See," he said, walking cautiously forward in the dimness as Orninski gradually clarified, "if you know the right people, you can get all sorts of things done."

"Sure," Orninski said. "And now we can just wait and see how good it works."

"Now we can start talking. This isn't a social call."

Orninski still had the gun pointed at him. "All right, Mr. Fleishman . . . I guess there is nothing wrong with a little talking while we wait for the breakfast. And I will keep it very short and simple, so there won't be any mix-up, because you see, there are only these three simple things that we will have to have before we come out—not counting breakfast, since that is already coming. The first thing is something we have already talked about last night, Mr. Mancino and us, and that is about these outside people coming in to make a study of how the prison is being run, whether for the good of the prisoners or not. Now from what Mr. Mancino said last night, the Warden said he doesn't see anything wrong with—"

"I didn't say that," Mancino said.

"With all due respect to Mr. Mancino, he wasn't authorized to speak for the Warden."

"But you are—right, Mr. Fleishman? So maybe you can tell us whether or not the Warden will okay such a study like that?"

"You said there were three things. What are the other two?"

"The second thing is really very easy, and shouldn't bother the Warden at all. It is just to give me something in here that I can make a statement on, that Mr. Mancino then can put on the air—you know . . . a tape recorder."

"A tape recorder?"

"That's right. Just to make a statement for Mr. Mancino to broadcast."

"What's the third thing?"

"The third is the most important, because it has to do not only with all my friends in here, but with all the men out there too, that got involved somehow in what you say was that little bit of trouble. And this is just a simple thing too. It's just that they don't get in any way punished for what they did."

"Who are you talking about—the men out there or the ones in here?"

"Both. They are not to get punished for what happened."

"That's out of the question."

Orninski was quiet a moment. "Are you talking directly for the Warden when you say that?"

"Yes." Flash took a deep breath and let the air out slowly. He was doing all right, although he still felt a bit woozy. He just hoped he sounded all right.

"Well . . . I don't know then, Mr. Fleishman. It don't look like you and me, we got too much to talk about then."

"Wait a minute now," the goon said. He stood up and faced Orninski from the aisle between the big tables. Flash couldn't see his expression but he sounded pretty riled up. "This wasn't at all what we talked about last night. You said then that—"

"Things have changed since then, Mr. Mancino."

"Cut it out," the goon said. "I've been trying to help you people and every time you get the chance you just add seven more things that you—"

"All *right*, Mr. Mancino!" Orninski said, swinging the gun toward him.

"Let's be careful with that thing—" Flash said.

"Let's just be careful what we say then."

"All right," Flash said. "Let's start with you. Let's hear you say something now . . . that sounds more careful than what you said before."

"Sure," Orninski said. "I'll say something real careful. I'll say—and you see here that I'm talking very slow and careful—that as far as I am concerned, my goose is cooked already, right now. Maybe Mr. Mancino here thinks I'm just kidding when I say that, because he don't know how things are run here, but you know how they are run—*Mr. Fish Man*—so you will know what I am talking about. You will notice maybe that in the three things I asked for, nothing was for me, because I know that would be just a big joke. I know what is in store for me. So what I am saying, very slow and careful, is that if the Warden won't promise not to hurt these men I am very interested in, then I can't make a promise not to hurt the men he is interested in."

"I wouldn't make any threats if I were you."

"You ain't me. And I'm making them—Mr. Fish Man."

"The name is Fleishman. F-L-E-I—"

"The time is kind of moving along, isn't it, Mr. *Fleish-man?* It don't really look like anybody is exactly breaking their hump getting any breakfast to us."

"It's coming. Now Mr. Mancino mentioned some things you had agreed to last—"

"Not agreed! Talked about!"

"Maybe we could talk about them too," Flash said.

"We tried talking. And all the Warden did was turn off the water and not give us breakfast when he promised, which maybe is what he thinks is talking. So we're finished with that. Now the Warden either says yes, or he says no."

"He may be more willing to say yes to some things than to others. If you're really serious about—"

"I'm serious about yes or no, and that's all. Because I know what the Warden would really like to do is just come in here with a lot of screws with their guns blazing so he can have a certain inmate by the name of Orninski shot all full of holes by the time the smoke clears."

"The Warden is not interested in shooting anybody."

"Meanwhile we'll get ourselves ready for it, just in case."

"What do you mean?"

"I mean—and I hope you are noticing how slow and careful I am speaking—we will first give our friend Mr. Cloninger there some more fresh air, because he has been complaining about how stuffy it is in here. And then we will take our other friend, Mr. Delft, who like you can see is all tied up there, and tie him up some more, to something solid that does not move, if you know what I mean. So if the Warden is thinking of using the tear gas he has ready out there, he should remember how Mr. Delft will be tied up, because the more gas he shoots in, the more Mr. Delft is gonna choke, which is what I understand the gas does. And then, of course, there are other things we can do, which we don't have to go into the details of now. So you can tell the Warden that, and we will see what he says about it, and the three things I mentioned to you."

"I can tell you now what he's going to say. He's going to say no. Unless you're willing to change some of—"

"Then maybe we will just start making our preparations now, if that's what he's gonna say." Orninski turned and said loudly, "Go ahead. Give our friend a little fresh air there."

"Now just wait a minute!" Flash yelled. He lurched forward furiously. Then, against the wall, clutching at it, he struggled to keep from falling down.

"That's right," Orninski said. "You just stay right where you are."

"I'm not going to let you do it," Flash said, trying to get off the wall.

"You don't look like you're gonna stop me."

"I just wouldn't try anything if I were you," Flash said. He was standing free now, drifting a bit.

"And maybe if I were you, I would just go out and tell the Warden what I said."

Flash didn't move.

"Open the door for Mr. Fleishman," Orninski said.

He heard the door being unlocked behind him. He was afraid to turn without holding on to something. "What about Mr. Mancino?"

"He can stay and wait with us, to see what the Warden says."

"He came in here voluntarily, as a favor to you. You can't force him to stay."

"We're not forcing him. We're just asking him, is all."

"It's okay," the goon said. "I'll stay."

"See, he knows he ain't got nothing to worry about. Like you can see, he's not even tied up or anything."

"The Warden's going to want to discuss with Mr. Mancino any kind of possible settlement."

"Like I said, there ain't no reason for any more discussing. Besides, we will need Mr. Mancino here to help me with the tape machine, since I am sure he understands how to use it better than me."

"He can come back for that. But he's got to come out now."

"I say he's got to stay. And you know what, Mr. Warden—what you say now don't count as much as what I say."

"It's all right," the goon said. "Go ahead."

"If I'm feeling any worse than I am now," Flash said, "I may not be able to come back. Mr. Mancino could come back then and—"

"I'm sure the doctor can fix you up enough for you to come back, if he really wants to."

"If anything happens to anybody while—"

"If anything happens to anybody, *Mr. Warden Fleish-man,* it ain't gonna be my fault. Because if anything happens it will be because of a lot of shooting or something started by the Warden. Because in all that shooting, somebody might just get hurt. Go ahead, Mel—open the door for our good friend Mr. Fleishman here. And then we'll just get busy with our preparations, starting with Mr. Cloninger."

He heard the doorknob click behind him.

"We'll be waiting to hear from you," Orninski said. "Only you really don't have to hurry, because we got plenty of things to do to keep ourselves busy. Besides, we ain't gonna be settling anything anyhow until after we get our breakfast."

"I don't see why you're so concerned with—"

"Because I told these guys they're gonna get their fucking breakfast, and they're gonna get it, that's why!"

"I'd try to stay a little calmer if I were you."

"I'm being very calm. You go on now and tell the Warden how calm I'm being."

Flash hesitated. "If you're really interested in taping a statement, I could send a machine right over. That way you could be using it while I'm explaining all these things to the Warden."

"That maybe sounds like a good idea," Orninski said after a moment. "Yeah—all right—you send the machine in. That is a real good idea, Mr. Fleishman."

"Will you leave Mr. Cloninger where he is then, until you finish with it?"

"Oh—that's the catch, heh?"

"We couldn't very well send it in while Mr. Cloninger's—"

"All right," Orninski said. "You just bring it over—yourself, don't send no one else—and we will leave Mr. Cloninger where he is for a while. Only I ain't gonna wait no sixteen hours for it, like breakfast."

"I'll be right back," Flash said. He made a cautious, flat-footed about-face and followed along the wall to the door, which opened, dazzling him with light. He stepped outside and down the step and started moving across the ground that for all he could see stretched out to the ends of the earth, trotting now, stumbling over chunks of wood, everything whirling, hoping the Good Lord in his mercy would just this once guide his feet along the Right Road, so Bostick wouldn't have to come chasing after him like a hound dog after a scared rabbit to haul him in and drop him, breathless, blind and illogical, at Griffing's feet.

22

Johnny watched Fleishman leave, watched Mel Simmons shut the door and lock it. He was standing at the middle table, perhaps ten feet from Orninski. For a minute everyone remained motionless, as if making sure Fleishman was really gone. The convict called Akar was at the peephole.

"Is he walking or running?" Orninski asked.

"Kinda running, I guess."

Orninski laughed—a short, harsh exhalation. He turned to the two convicts at the back. "O.K., let's get Mr. Delft over by the saw machine."

Johnny watched a third convict come over to help pull Delft up. Delft went limp and it was a struggle for them.

"What are we supposed to do—carry him? He ain't moving a muscle."

Orninski came up behind Delft and jabbed the gun into his back. "Move."

"I can't with my feet tied."

Orninski jabbed viciously. "Move!"

Delft let out a little cry and twisted, arching his shoulders.

"There's no need to hurt him," Johnny said.

"You just sit down, all right, and stay out of things."

Johnny hesitated, then sat down.

Delft hobbled along, an inmate holding each arm. They got him down on his side and stretched his arms along one edge of the metal base of the machine and his legs along the opposite edge, then tied his hands and feet together so that his body encircled the base, his huge stomach pressed up against it.

Orninski went back to the windows and bent down next to Akar at the peepholes. "Now we'll see how fast Mr. Fleishman gets back over here with that thing."

Johnny waited in silence along with the others.

After a few minutes one of the convicts sitting at the back table, resting his head in one hand, his elbow on that table, said without looking up: "You see any fucking food coming?"

"No, I don't see it coming," Orninski said.

"What the hell time is it anyhow?"

"It's eight thirty. It'll come, don't worry."

"I'll believe it when I taste it."

"You know what?" Akar said. He was leaning against the wall now, between two boarded windows. "I wouldn't even touch anything they sent in now. I wouldn't go near it."

Orninski looked over at him. "You wouldn't, heh?"

"You bet your sweet life I wouldn't. Not me."

"Oh?" Orninski said. "Why the hell not?"

"Because I been thinking, that's why. And I been thinking that if *I* was the fucking Warden out there, and this shit-assed bunch of cons kept bitching about sending food in, you know what I'd do? I'd put some goddamn stuff *in* the food, that's what I'd do."

Orninski stared at him. "They ain't gonna put no stuff in the goddamn food, for Christ's sake!"

"Oh yeah? Well, we'll see."

"If that's what the hell he wanted to do, why didn't he just do it last night then?"

"Maybe he didn't think of it then. But what do you think those characters been doing out there all night? They've been *thinking*, that's what they've been doing. And shit, they gotta be pretty dumb if they still ain't thought of something as simple as that."

Orninski glared at Akar. "You think he'd put stuff in when his own goddamn screws are gonna be eating it? Use your head, for Christ's sake."

"It wouldn't have to be anything that killed you. It could just be some stuff that put you out for a few hours."

"Yeah? What kind of stuff is that?"

"How am I supposed to know what kind of stuff? *Stuff!* You can put knockout drops in a drink, can't you? Well, why the hell can't you just put some in the cereal too?"

Orninski turned irritably back to the peephole, squinting through it with his one good eye. "Just don't be getting no crazy ideas, okay? We got enough to think about without a lot of crazy ideas."

For a few minutes the place was quiet.

What on earth were they doing out there?

Johnny could see the teams forming. On one side you'd have Griffing and Fleishman, the old tottering martinet feebly struggling for control in spite of his exhaustion, and the joker, the weirdo, who looked without his glasses and with that bloody bandage on his head like a huge bird that had flown head-on into a pane of glass and was now trying, cross-eyed and dizzy, to figure out what hit him. On the other side there'd be Kale, who understood nothing but the show of force, and Dowler, who believed in nothing but its actual presence.

Lives will be in danger—Orninski the wild, one-eyed prophet, with his battered face and necessary gun and hectic paranoia, at the moment more concerned about recording his testament than saving any lives, including his own. Johnny could see himself making the intro—"And now we're going to play a little tape I picked up one day under somewhat unusual circumstances . . ."

Lives will be in danger—Orninski the phrase-maker. A fine phrase, with a ring to it, a touch of madness.

It was odd realizing your own life was in danger. He had never before at any given moment thought *My life is now in danger*. It was hard to react credibly because it wasn't credible. The terms in which the awareness had to be stated were too melodramatic.

He wondered if tear gas had any permanent effect. He should probably cover his face with his handkerchief. Maybe he'd have time to get to the sink and wet it. But could you see in the gas? Didn't it blind you? He looked over at the sink, studying the route he'd have to take. Then he looked around for some protection, in case they started shooting. Under the table maybe. Or the bathroom, although it wasn't much bigger than a closet and didn't even have a door. *Get down on the floor if anything happens*—that wasn't a very comforting vision, himself stretched out on the floor as the room filled with gas and a dozen guards busted in shooting at random. Did tear gas rise or settle? Maybe the smart thing would be to watch those men back there on the floor, the spectators, and follow their lead. Do as the natives do.

He wondered what Mel Simmons was planning to do. Mel Simmons: with a knife hooked in his trousers and a ring of keys in his pocket, opening and closing the door at Orninski's bidding. He did it each time soberly, with a real sense of proprietary concern.

The more he thought about it, the more likely it seemed the rush would come, with Kale leading the way, yelling for blood and victory.

He wondered if everyone felt as queasy as he did. He'd probably jump ten feet at the first sudden noise. Maybe he was just hungry. He smiled, in spite of himself: he could see now why they were so worked up over breakfast—he was starving, his stomach ached and fluttered by turns. He'd eat anything they put in front of him, poisoned or not.

"Here he comes," Orninski said at the peephole.

"Fleishman?" Johnny asked.

"Sure, Fleishman. He's got the thing too. He's bringing it over." Orninski kept his face pressed against the plywood board. "Okay, the screw's staying behind . . . Open up when I tell you, Mel, and just take the thing. Don't let him in."

Mel waited behind the door, one hand on the key in the lock, one on the knob.

"Okay."

Mel pulled the door back a few inches. Johnny could see Fleishman's face outside in the shaft of blazing sunlight.

"Pass it in," Orninski said. He stood near the peepholes, pointing the gun at the door.

Fleishman passed in the tape recorder.

"What about breakfast?" Orninski asked.

"In a few minutes," Fleishman said.

"That's what they've been saying all morning."

"It's coming. They're doing the best they can."

"Close the door, Mel."

Mel shut and locked the door, darkening the room. Orninski peered out the hole briefly, then straightened up. "You watch here, Akar. And keep your eyes open. Anything looks funny, or they look like they're gonna try something, you just yell."

Akar bent to the peephole.

"Bring the machine over here, Mel."

Mel carried it as if it were a jewel box on a cushion. He offered it to Orninski, who seemed reluctant to touch it, and didn't. "Sure," he said finally. "Sure. There it is, eh?" He nodded and Mel placed it carefully on the table. It was the standard, familiar Wollensak, in a leatherette cover. "You know how to work this kind?"

"Let's plug it in and have a try," Johnny said.

"There's a plug up front."

Johnny carried the machine by the handle to the desk. Mel and

Orninski followed. "Let's see now." He removed the cover and studied the controls. He poked at them tentatively. "You've never used this model before either, have you?" he asked Orninski.

"No. I ain't even used any kind like that."

"You, Mel?"

"Huh? No . . . I ain't ever used anything like that."

"You're the one that's supposed to know all about it," Orninski said.

"Uh-huh," Johnny said. He fished into the pocket of the cover and brought out the microphone with its wire and jack, the power cord, an empty reel and a spool of tape. He spread everything out on the desk. "Hmmmnnnn . . ."

"You gotta plug those things in, heh?" Orninski said.

"Just have to figure out which ones go where." He turned the machine around and looked at the receptacles. "Let's see now . . . You don't happen to know the voltage in here, do you?"

"Christ, it's a regular socket, ain't it? Plug the goddamn thing in."

"Sometimes shops have two-twenty."

"Look, if you don't know how to work the—"

"I think I've got it now." He plugged in the power cord. Two other convicts drifted over to stand behind Orninski and watch. He plugged in the jack and handed Orninski the mike. Orninski held it in his left hand, his arm somewhat extended. He didn't seem to want to get too close to it. He still held the gun in his right hand.

Johnny put the empty reel on the left hub and the spool on the right. Orninski was watching closely. Johnny methodically threaded the tape through the passageway and onto the empty reel. He felt a great desire to look at his watch but didn't. A third convict came over to watch. "Let's see now . . ." He slid down the *start* switch. The tape yanked off the empty reel and snaked back onto the spool. "Oh, oh—got it backwards."

"Look, are you—"

"It'll just take a second." He reversed the wheels and began threading the tape again, working a little faster now under Orninski's one-eyed gaze. His forehead was damp; he wiped his sleeve across it.

"What the hell you gonna say in the thing?" one of the convicts asked. Johnny glanced over his shoulder: *Preston.*

"Don't you worry what I'm gonna say," Orninski told him. "I got a lot to say."

"No shit? What about?"

"About us, for Christ's sake! And it's gonna all be down there, right on that tape."

"Tell them about the food," Preston said. "Tell them the food's shitty."

"I'm gonna tell them a lot of things."

"Sure," Preston said. "You tell them."

"I'm gonna."

"Who?" Preston said. "I mean, who you gonna tell all these things?"

"Everybody," Orninski said. "This is gonna go right out on the air. Ain't it, Mr. Mancino?"

Johnny looked up. "Whatever you and the Warden agree to is all right with me."

"I want you to play it right on your show—so everybody can hear it."

"Okay," Johnny said. "I think we're about ready now."

"Yeah. Well . . . good. Let's get going then."

"Hey, can't I talk too?" Preston asked. "Let me tell them about the food part. I'll burn their fucking ears off."

"I'll do the talking," Orninski said.

"There are two speeds you can use," Johnny said. "Either 3.75 or 7.5."

"What the hell does that mean?"

"Well, the 3.75 usually is good enough for straight voice. The 7.5 is primarily for music, but you can also use it for voice. It'll give you a better-quality reproduction."

"Sure—use the better quality."

"Actually, you'll be able to say more with the 3.75. The slower speed will—"

"Just use the better one, all right? Let's get going."

"We should get a voice level first. Just talk the way you're going to after. Hold the mike about two inches away, and don't go too fast. Ready?"

"What am I supposed to say?"

"Anything. It doesn't matter. Just practice what you plan to say afterward." Johnny set the speed at 7.5 and slid the switch to *record*. Then he hesitated. The slower speed would eat up twice as much time, in case Orninski used the whole tape. "You know, I really think we'd be better off with 3.75. That way you'd have all the—"

"Look, use whatever the hell you want, all right? Let's just get going."

"Okay now . . . Go." He slid down the *start* button. The spools began to revolve in the silence. He waited. "Go ahead . . . Say something."

Orninski stared down at the mike, his head to one side, examining it with one bulging, unblinking eye.

"Hold it a little closer," Johnny said.

Orninski seemed to be trying to get his lips to move. The others watched. Mel, especially, seemed utterly absorbed.

"I thought you were gonna say so much," Preston said.

"Shut up, will you? The thing's going!"

"I see it's going! So say something, for Christ's sake!"

"I'm *gonna,* for Christ's sake, if you just shut up!"

"All right—I'll shut up. Go ahead."

The wheels revolved in silence. Everyone in the room was quiet, watching.

"Just say your name or something, if you want," Johnny said. "Anything will do."

"Orninski . . ." he croaked.

"That's it," Johnny said. "Go on now—say something else. Practice what you're going to say after."

Orninski looked at him accusingly, his eye fixed. "I don't wanna say that now—I'm gonna say that later."

"That's it," Johnny said. "A bit louder maybe. Give us a little more now."

"A little more what, for Christ's sake?"

"Just what you're doing. Just keep talking."

"I can't think of anything else."

"Tell them the food's shitty," Preston said.

"Shut up, will you? We're recording this, for Christ's sake."

"Tell them *Fuck you!*" Preston said. He leaned over Orninski's shoulder and shouted at the mike. *"Fuck you out there! The food's shitty. Fuck all of you!"*

"For Christ's sake!" Orninski said, whipping around. "Watch your language, will you? We're recording all this!"

"He said you're gonna erase it. *I wanna fuck Elizabeth Taylor.*"

Orninski pulled the mike against his chest. "You're really gonna erase all this, ain't you?"

"Sure," Johnny said. "Don't worry."

"All right—enough screwing around then. Let's hear it."

Johnny stopped the tape, reversed it, set it at *play,* and pushed the *start* button.

They listened. Orninski's face and mouth were so swollen now that he was practically unintelligible anyhow, and the microphone seemed to make it even worse. You had to listen carefully to pick up his words, and even then it was only when he was yelling that you could tell what he was saying. The clearest thing on the tape was Preston shouting *Fuck you out there!*

Johnny stopped the machine.

"Well . . . that don't sound too bad," Orninski said. "Except for this jerk here yelling his head off."

"I thought I sounded pretty good," Preston said.

"You sounded shitty was how you sounded," Orninski said. "You gonna erase all that now, heh? I mean, you're gonna take all that language and everything off, right?"

"I'll take it off." Johnny reversed the tape, set it at *record*, turned the volume all the way down and ran it through. "Just take a minute to wipe it off. Then we'll be all set. Maybe you could try to speak a little louder."

"Okay. Now you guys beat it," he told the three men behind him. "Just go over where you're supposed to be and get off my back here. Mel—you kinda take charge, all right, so I can pay attention to what I'm doing here."

"Whatd'ya mean—take charge?"

"I mean *take charge*, that's what I mean! I mean I want you over at the window there keeping an eye on things, so I can pay attention to what the hell I'm doing here."

"That ain't taking charge," Mel said. "That's keeping an eye on things."

"What is it with all you guys? Whatd'ya all giving me a hard time for? I mean, you wanna be the guy that does the talking into this thing? You another guy that got a lot to say?"

"I ain't got nothing to say," Mel said.

"You're sure now? I mean, there ain't no big message or nothing you wanna put over?"

"C'mon," Mel said. "Cut it out."

"All right. Then get the hell over there, will you, and keep a goddamn eye on things." Orninski watched Mel walk over to the window and turned to Johnny. "We're all ready to go then, heh?"

"I guess so," Johnny said, and now he looked at his watch. It was ten minutes to nine.

23

Jesus Christ, what the hell did that mean, *take over?* That's just what he needed, to be standing around sucking wind, *being in charge,* at the exact minute when the goddamn Warden out there decides to send his screws in. *Shoot the guy in charge first!* Sure.

Shit, if that didn't look stupid—all these guys holed up in here and the Warden getting ready to blow the place apart, and what the hell was Orninski doing, whose goddamn idea the whole thing was in the first place, but talking into a frigging machine?

What the hell was the point of the whole thing anymore, that's what he'd like to know. He just couldn't see anymore. He just lost track somewhere along the way. Maybe Orninski saw, and had something all worked out in his head that nobody else knew about yet. Shit, he didn't even care anymore. He'd be just as happy if the Warden *did* put something in the goddamn food, so that before you knew it you'd be fast asleep like a goddamn baby and when you woke up it'd be all over.

"Hey," Akar said. "Why can't somebody else look out this goddamn hole for a while. My eye hurts."

"I don't know," Mel said. "All right." He was standing against the wall next to Akar. Orninski was sitting at Cloninger's desk talking a mile a frigging minute into the goddamn machine, with the TV guy leaning over him diddling away at the dials. Orninski was talking real low and Mel couldn't hear him, but he really seemed to be going at it, jerking his head like he was making a big point or something, scrunching up closer and closer to the thing, with the microphone practically in his mouth now, like he just couldn't get close enough.

Mel looked around, wondering who the hell he was supposed to go ask now to look out the goddamn hole. Boy, as far as he was concerned, you could have this *being in charge* shit. He didn't wanna have to tell anyone to come over and look out the goddamn hole. What if the guy said *No, I ain't gonna look out no goddamn hole!* What the hell was he supposed to say then?

So he looked out himself. He didn't care. He didn't have nothing better to do.

It took a minute or so to really see anything, because the sun was so bright. It was really gonna be hot again today. It was like looking through a telescope, with kind of a black circle around everything, and everything real sharp and clear, like you could somehow actually see better through a hole than just looking regular.

He could see four or five screws outside the garage, and a few more just inside. He couldn't see very far into the garage, but could see the same old goddamn garbage truck there, and the Econoline and the limousine and the Fury. They hadn't moved them an inch since they were over working on them yesterday afternoon, which was like about five million years ago now.

If he leaned a little to the left, he could see the mattresses out on the ground, or at least some of them. They didn't seem to be smoking any more. Behind them he could see the Cell Block, one wing of it, and one great big broken window. There wasn't any more smoke there either.

He didn't see any sign of breakfast coming. Maybe that knockout stuff wasn't so easy to get. Where the hell would you buy it anyway?

Boy, Orninski didn't wanna let on, but Akar really knocked him for a loop with that idea. You could just see it hadn't ever occurred to him, and bothered the hell out of him because he knew Akar was right—that was exactly the kind of thing the Warden *would* think of, or even somebody like Fleishman, who after all was some kind of doctor or other and maybe knew about things like that.

It was funny, but the minute Fleishman left you could practically feel everyone in the place breathe easy again. You could see, of course, Fleishman wasn't in any shape to do anything, but still. Because a guy like Mancino, so he was a big shot on TV and everything, still he was just sort of a regular person you might meet on the street, and not a warden. When you met a warden, you jumped up and stood at attention and you said *yes sir, no sir, I'll kiss your ass sir,* and the minute Fleishman walked in you could see everybody wondering whether they oughta be standing at attention or not, or just how they should be standing. You could see even Orninski felt this, although he covered it pretty good.

Mel could see why Akar bitched to get off the goddamn job. His eye was already beginning to get squinty. Nothing was going on out there, so he backed off and looked around the room a bit, like he was sort of keeping an eye on things in there too. Orninski was still yakking away, with the goddamn wheels just spinning and spinning around, taking it all the hell down.

Nobody else seemed to be doing much. Nobody even seemed to be watching Orninski at the machine anymore.

Mel wondered if everybody in the place was just scared shit, thinking of what might happen. He was scared shit.

He looked out the peephole some more. No sign of nothing. He looked at his watch. Almost nine. Christ, it could've been three in the afternoon the way it felt. He was starving.

He heard Mancino talking and looked around. Orninski seemed to be finally finished saying all the hell he had to say. Maybe he just ran out of tape to put it on, and *had* to stop.

"Want me to play it back?" Mancino asked.

"No," Orninski said, in his regular voice again.

"Okay." Mancino started taking the tape off the machine.

"What're you doing with that?" Orninski said.

Mancino shrugged. "I can't play it if I don't have it."

Orninski just looked at him, like maybe it was a trick, like even though it was true, Orninski just did't like the idea of letting it out of his hands. "Okay," he said. "Just be careful. Just don't let nothing happen to it."

"I won't," Mancino said, and put it in the back pocket of his pants that had this shiny black stripe down the sides.

"You go back and sit down again now," Orninski said, motioning to the table where Mancino was before, but the other end of it, near the hobby crew guys instead of near the windows. Mancino went and sat, just a few feet from Westerman. Mel wondered if Mancino knew who Westerman was, or even that he was in here.

Mel noticed Orninski staring at him, so he looked out the hole again. Christ, what was he supposed to do, look everywhere at once?

It was exactly the same out there. He noticed somebody come over and look out the next hole. It was Orninski.

"Nothing happening out there, heh?" Orninski said.

"Nah," Mel said. He waited a minute. "How'd it go? With the machine and everything, I mean. You say everything you wanna say?"

Orninski sort of pulled back from the board and Mel did the same. His face was really red all over, and not just from being banged around. He looked like he was just burning up. And that one frigging eye moving around really was weird. He looked like a guy who'd just went through some kind of terrific workout and was absolutely bushed now, but at the same time feeling just great too, kind of, Mel didn't know, *satisfied.*

"It went really great," Orninski said. He was even breathing funny, like he was winded. "I'll tell you, Mel, that was the best fucking idea I ever had in my whole life."

"Really, heh? I mean, it really went all right?"

"Even better than I figured. You'll see, Mel."

"Yeah—well good," Mel said. Frankly, he didn't know *how* he'd ever see, but anyhow was glad at least Orninski felt good about it. Maybe it'd quiet him down, feeling good like that.

Mel figured this would be a good time to sort of say something about settling and everything, and so he said, very low and private, "You think maybe now, the next time the Fish Man comes in, we're gonna maybe be able to work something out?"

Orninski gave him a look. "What's the matter—you getting tight-assed, Mel?"

"It ain't that," Mel said. He could see now it really wasn't such a terrific time to bring it up, but just figured, the hell. "It's only just that, as far as I'm concerned, you could've settled it all before." The truth, actually, was that he really would've liked to walk right out that door before with Fleishman, and go right up to the Warden out there and say, *Here I am, Mel Simmons 47163. You can do whatever the hell you want with me now and it'll be all right, because I am just glad to be out of there, personally.*

"You think you can handle this thing better?" Orninski said.

"I'm just telling you how I feel, that's all."

"Do you think I like it hanging around like this?"

Mel didn't say anything. He just kind of shrugged.

"What the hell," Orninski said. "Sure, maybe none of these other guys give a shit, and can't even see what the hell I'm trying to do for them, but at least I figured maybe you'd see."

"It ain't that," Mel said. "It's just I'll be glad when it's over."

"I'll be glad too," Orninski said. "I can get my goddamn tooth fixed then. If I'm still alive."

"You'll be alive," Mel said.

Orninski looked straight at him, with that one goddamn eye of his. "Mel, I ain't gonna be alive. I'm gonna be dead."

It gave Mel the creeps, the way he said it, and they were both quiet a few minutes, looking out the peepholes, watching the screws in front of the garage. Then Mel said, "I don't want you to think I don't appreciate it. What you're doing, I mean."

"Sure," Orninski said.

Mel looked for a minute at Orninski's face while Orninski was looking out the hole. It was like a balloon that had been all blowed up out of shape and had all these colors. "Anyhow, I do appreciate it," Mel said.

"Huh?" Orninski said. "Well, good . . . I mean I'm not just looking for appreciation. Only you just don't want the guys you're breaking your hump for all turning against you, that's all."

"I ain't turning against you," Mel said.

"I never said you was," Orninski said.

They were quiet again, looking out, and then Mel said, "How you feeling now? I mean, that tooth and everything, is it getting any better?"

"It's getting worse," Orninski said. "My head feels like it's gonna blow off the top of my shoulders, if you wanna know."

"You look like you're burning up," Mel said. "You're all red."

"I feel like I'm burning up."

"You oughta drink some water. It'll cool you off."

"The water tastes shitty. Every since they turned it off before it tastes shitty."

"Yeah," Mel said. He was gonna say maybe the Warden decided to put the stuff in the water instead of the food, but then figured maybe he'd better not. Christ, he didn't know. He just couldn't keep up any more. It just wore him the hell out, even trying to think about it.

This afternoon their wing would've got out for their Saturday rec period, and their tier was supposed to play tier 4. He was hitting .326 now, with only two games left in the tourney. If he could manage, say, two hits in each game, he could bring his average up to maybe .335 or .340, which meant he might end up being number two or three hitter in the whole tourney. He was number six according to the paper last week, but except for the number one guy, who was banging away at a .421 clip, the others above him were all bunched right around the .335 mark. So with a little spurt he could catch them all, except just the number one guy. Actually, if he could just manage to catch *one* of them he'd be happy, because the paper only printed the first five so Mel, being number six, didn't get listed. Throughout the whole tourney Mel'd been hitting very consistent, but every time the paper came out he'd be just a coupla points under the guy listed number five, so never got listed. He would've really liked to get into that top five, especially now, because at the end of the tourney the top five got little certificates for being there, which along with the clipping from the paper if he made the top five would be nice to send along to Peggy and the kid.

"It's still running anyhow, the Dodge?" he asked her last time, which he always asked her, because naturally he was interested in how it was holding up.

"Oh sure," she said. "It's still running."

"I mean, you never have no trouble with it or anything?"

"Oh no," she said. "I never have no trouble. It starts and everything just fine."

That was just like Peggy. *It starts and everything.*

"It's gonna run forever, that goddamn car," Mel told her.

"Well anyhow, there's nothing wrong with it right now," she said.

"I could give you a whole list of what's wrong with that car right now," he said. "I could write you a book on what's wrong with it."

He kidded her about it then and she finally caught on and sort of laughed a little. But not much. Which was when he began to get the idea she was holding something out on him, and even came out and asked her point-blank what it was, but naturally she said what did he mean, she wasn't holding out anything. But you could tell just by looking at her she was lying. And he had some ideas about what too, and was all set next time to put it right to her and get a straight answer. Because he wasn't about to take any of that. Christ, she had a kid home and everything. Didn't that make any difference? Didn't that mean anything to her? What the hell was she doing, playing around with some guy with Chucky, for Christ's sake, right there in the next room?

The thing to do was punch the ball to right more, instead of trying to pull it. You didn't get as much power, but you got more hits.

"You see anything out there?" Orninski said.

"Huh?" Mel said. He'd been looking the whole time, along with Orninski. "No—you see something?"

"No," Orninski said. "I don't see a fucking thing." He turned and yelled to Preston, "Okay, bring him over here. We've been sitting on our ass waiting long enough."

Preston—and Larrobee, who was back there with him—just sort of looked at Orninski. You could see they weren't really too keen on putting the old guy out again.

"Come *on!*" Orninski yelled.

But before Preston or Larrobee could move, Mancino jumped up and said, "You can't put that man out there again."

"I can," Orninski said.

"At least give them time to talk over your—"

"They had their time. They're just stalling now."

Mancino started walking between the tables toward Orninski.

"You stop there!" Orninski said, and he raised the gun, right at Mancino's stomach. Then Mancino stopped.

Mel swallowed. "Stay there," he said to Mancino. "Do what he says." But he didn't really have to say it. A kind of real funny look came over Mancino's face, like he never up to this exact second really believed Orninski would shoot him.

"That's better," Orninski said. "Now just sit down again—right where you are."

Mancino sat down. He'd come about halfway along the table.

"Okay," Orninski said to Preston. "Bring him over."

So Preston and Larrobee got Cloninger to his feet and kind of half carried him over to the window. Cloninger just shut his eyes. He was sort of quivering, his lips and everything. Preston pried the board off the window and slit it to one side. The sunlight streamed right in, making the room very bright.

"Put him out," Orninski said. "Just like before."

So they put him out, Preston and Larrobee and Akar, while everyone watched. They lifted him up with his body stretched out and his face up, and then lowered him out the window upside down with his face out toward the sun and tied the ropes around his ankles again, with his legs hooked over the window, like a kid upside down on a bar in a playground.

"Now we'll see," Orninski said, looking around the edge of the window, "how the hell long it takes them to say yes or no about something."

The whole room was about as quiet as any room with that many people ever was. Mel edged over to the other side of the window to look out too. He tried not to look at Cloninger. At least he couldn't see his face, because it was down below the bottom of the window.

Over at the garage you could see that putting Cloninger out really stirred them up. He could see the Warden now, and Fleishman, right at the edge of the garage, and the screws seemed to be running around all over the place.

"Hey, Orninski," Verdun yelled from the back corner.

Orninski turned. Mel turned too.

"I gotta take a piss," Verdun said.

"Well, tie it in a knot or something," Orninski said. "Don't bother me."

"C'mon," Verdun said. "I been sitting here all morning minding my business and now I gotta piss. Whatd'ya want me to do, do it on the floor?"

"Go with him, for Christ's sake," Orninski told Preston, and turned back to the window.

Mel looked out again too. Cloninger's legs were kind of twitching, and he could hear the old guy wheezing and gasping out there.

The screws were still kind of bumbling around and running in and out of the garage. The Warden was standing still, just staring over at Cloninger.

Orninski kept looking out but Mel turned around when Verdun came out of the john with Preston behind him and walked back to the corner. Verdun didn't sit down though. He just turned the corner and started walking down toward Orninski, who was still looking out the window. It was funny but when Verdun turned the corner like that and kept walking, Preston didn't say nothing. He just looked kind of surprised. It took Mel by surprise too, and he didn't say anything either, because the way Verdun did it, so casual and everything, it was just like a regular guy turning a corner in a room to walk down another side. But then Orninski must've heard somebody coming, and sort of glanced around, not actually paying too much attention. You could see he was really interested just in what was happening over at the garage, with the Warden and everything. And when he turned, he didn't even see Verdun right away, because Verdun was coming down from the blind side. But then Orninski turned some more to see out of the good eye and saw who it was and just sort of automatically raised the gun but Verdun said, "I got something I wanna say to you, private . . ." and just kept walking, very easy and casual, like he just wanted to get close enough to whisper it, but at the same time moving along pretty quick, or at least what seemed pretty quick, because before Orninski could kind of get himself pulled together enough to tell him to stop, Verdun grabbed Orninski's hand and twisted hard and with his free hand let go with this really tremendous punch from the blind side that caught Orninski right in the face. It happened almost like it was in slow motion, but very fast. It just didn't seem to have anything to do with fast or slow. It just happened. And then for Christ's sake Mancino, the stupid son of a bitch, jumped up and was moving toward Orninski like a goddamn freight train, and then Mel was moving too, like on air, not even feeling anything, and yelling to Mancino, *"Hey!—Get back!"* and bumped right into him and felt something he thought first was in the pit of his stomach, sputtering, but then decided, no, in the chest, like the biggest kick he ever felt in his whole goddamn life.

24

How often, from out of chaos, are we led to virtue and truth, even equanimity? Not too often, truly. But it happens—one of those rarities that keep our days from becoming awful and predictable. Take for example, Flash thought, supporting himself against the fender of the garbage truck, trying to drink the foul-muck coffee, trying to keep his hand from shaking, trying to phrase, at least for himself, his thoughts more eloquently, trying to keep from falling down in the sawdust—take for example us. Will it happen to us? Would anybody be fool enough to put money on it?

I am afflicted, he decided, by moral vertigo. Abstractions waver. Where is everybody? What am I doing in all this Saturday morning madness?

But in some ways—amid the shouting, the buffeting about, the rustling of bodies racing to and fro, Kale arguing, Griffing arguing, the phone ringing, the intercom blurting and screeching—everything seemed about as clear as one could expect.

The Cell Block, at least, was under control. What else, with Jeff Dowler cleaning things up, putting people in their place?

Breakfast however, the long-awaited, the fervently desired, was still pretty iffy. It hardly mattered anymore.

"The kitchen's a real mess, sir," an officer had reported soon after Flash came back. "They really tore it apart."

"They can forget about the breakfast," Griffing told him. "We won't be needing it."

Flash closed his eyes at that point.

"What's the matter, Flash?"

He opened his eyes. "I was just thinking the breakfast might give us a little time to—"

"It's too late." Griffing turned back to the officer. "Tell Mr. Dowler to get over here. He can leave Mr. Bianco in charge."

However many minutes ago that was, they were still waiting for Dowler. They were going to rush, and Dowler was the man they needed, the man to do it. As soon as Flash reported Orninski's three demands and gave his eyewitness (a joke, that) account of life in the hobby shop, Griffing had said, "Okay, that's it. Let's get Dowler here."

"What are we going to do?" Kale asked then.

"Move in. What else can we do?"

"Mancino's still in there."

"I know," Griffing said.

"Orninski wouldn't let him out," Flash said. "So I said we'd send in the tape machine. I figured—"

"What?"

"The tape machine he wanted—I said we'd give it to him. I figured it'd keep him busy while we—"

"Have you lost your mind? What in God's name—"

Flash explained then, convincingly he thought. Griffing seemed unimpressed but grudgingly went along, and Flash brought a machine over, purloined from Philson's office who, lucky son of a bitch, was on vacation.

Flash saw Griffing now on the other side of the garbage truck, talking to Kale. They were still waiting for Dowler. Flash gulped the rest of the coffee and traced his way along the fenders and headlights to join them.

Griffing looked at him. "Sit down, Flash."

"I'm all right." His head felt like a nut about to crack open; he could feel the fissures spreading with horrible internal noises. "Did anybody find my glasses?"

"Don't you have another pair anywhere?"

"Home. I can see all right."

A shape hurried up to Griffing. "The Governor's on the phone. He wants either you or Mr. Kale."

"I'll take it," Kale said.

As Kale moved off into the blur another blue-gray form puffed up. Couriers seemed to be racing back and forth with everything except word that Birnam Wood was moving on Dunsinane. The form clarified: it was Bianco.

"Dowler?" Flash said after a moment, breaking in. "*Dowler?*"

"That's right," Bianco said. "It just happened. Just like that."

"*Dowler?*"

"Is he going to be all right?" Griffing asked.

"I don't know. They took him to the infirmary. I was standing right next to him and—well, he turned to say something to someone. He sort of hesitated, then just went down in a heap."

"*Dowler?*"

"Was it a heart attack?" Griffing asked.

"I don't know. He just gave way, just like that."

"You'll have to take over then," Griffing said. "Who's in charge up there?"

"LaSala. He'll manage."

"Okay. I want you to get twenty men over by the hobby shop, armed, along both sides, without being seen. I want another two or three on the roof. Tell them to stay on the stucco walling and make sure no one in there hears them. How long will it take to break through that roof and get some gas in?"

"A minute or so, I guess, with a couple of axes. It's just tar paper and beams."

"Give all the men masks. And three extra—no, four, in case Flash doesn't get back out. As soon as the gas gets in, the men along the sides should hit the door and the windows. They'll need axes too."

"I'll work the roof myself, if that's all right," Bianco said.

"Okay. I'll hold both arms straight out for about fifteen seconds. When I drop them, you break through."

"All right."

"The roof won't give you any protection if Orninski starts shooting. What about a steel plate to stand on?"

"It wouldn't be very quiet getting it up there."

"Maybe the men along the sides could move in as soon as you start with the ax. It'll keep him from concentrating on you."

"They should have some gas too," Bianco said.

"All right. Orninski seems to be the only one with a gun. There are eight others with knives. The ones from the hobby crew probably won't give you any trouble. Delft and Cloninger may both be tied up, and Mancino will probably still be in there, and maybe Flash too. I don't want any wild shooting. I don't want any wild anything. No firing unless it's absolutely necessary. No firing at anyone unless they're *absolutely* sure who it is."

"I'll make it clear."

"All right; tell me when you're ready."

Bianco left.

"What the hell's Kale doing on the phone?" Flash said.

"It keeps him out of the way. I want you to go back over there, Flash, and try to get Mancino out."

"Okay, I'll try."

"Tell Orninski we're ready to settle, but Mancino's got to be let out first as a show of good faith."

"I doubt if he'll buy that, Griff. Besides, do you really want me to tell him we're settling when we're getting ready to—"

"He hasn't shown any love of fair play; I don't see why we should. Mancino went in voluntarily."

"Okay. But I can't see Orninski letting him out. Not anymore."

"Well, we're going to have to try—as soon as Bianco's ready. Maybe you can talk him into it somehow. Reason with him, lie to him, I don't care. We'll give you exactly five minutes, then we'll move. If you can't get Mancino out, try to keep him from getting hurt. Lie on top of him if you have to; let the officers handle Orninski."

"I'll do my best."

"I wish to God he'd never set foot in here. He's only been trouble and more trouble."

"I know," Flash said. His wish was that the son of a bitch were a foot or so smaller, less of a target, easier to toss inconspicuously into a corner.

What a fate—risking life and limb to protect an overgrown man who smiled and read commercials. Thus the stinking, inevitable way of the world—a glib microphone clutcher bumbles into trouble and we stand ready to sacrifice Flash Fleishman, Assistant Warden in charge of TRE, without flicking an eyelash.

"I wish Dowler were here," Griffing said. "I hope he's all right." He turned abruptly as someone came trampling through the sawdust. They were still standing between the garbage truck, which smelled, and the Econoline. Why they were standing there wasn't very clear.

It was Kale, agitated and wheezing. "Griff, I think we've got—"

"We're just about ready," Griffing said. "As soon as Bianco's set, we'll move the men over."

"We may not have to. The Governor's come up with something."

A silence followed. It was an odd, hollow silence.

"I told him about the trouble in the mess hall . . . that guard being killed, and well—he's come up with something that may just do the trick. It'll be an offer directly from the Governor himself. If they come out, the Governor will personally guarantee each man fair and just treatment."

"That won't—"

"That's not all. He'll also agree to personally look into the whole situation, including any legitimate suggestions and requests by the inmates. Of course he'll naturally—"

"That won't do," Griffing said.

"What do you mean?"

"I couldn't accept anything like that," Griffing said. "It clearly implies that the inmates wouldn't get fair treatment without the Governor's intervention."

"Don't be foolish. The Governor certainly—"

"Every headline tomorrow will say the Governor got those men out by agreeing to honor their complaints against me."

"That's not what they'll say at all."

"As soon as Bianco's ready, I'm sending Flash over to get Mancino out. Then we'll move in."

"You can't—not without even trying the Governor's idea. What if something happens to Mancino? How could I go back and tell the Governor—"

"I'll tell him," Griffing said. "Now."

Kale hesitated. "All right. You do that. You see what he says."

"We won't be long," Griffing said to Flash. "Keep an eye on things."

They left and Flash moved to the open side of the garage and peered into the bright sunlit emptiness, the haze of all the world. "*Pssst!*"

The nearest officer hurried over. "Yes sir?"

"Let me know if you see anything over there."

"Excuse me?"

"I can't see that far without my glasses."

"Of course—yes sir . . . Nothing's happening there now."

"Keep watching."

Someone came over: Bianco. "Where are they?" he asked.

"Cajoling the Governor. Are you ready?"

"The men are heading over—they're swinging around the powerhouse. Have you heard anything on Dowler?"

"No," Flash said. "I'm sure he's all right. Tell me, have you ever been in that gas?"

"I got a whiff of it once. It'll burn your eyes out in two minutes; you can't see a thing."

"I can't anyhow. Is there anything I can do when it hits?"

"Get out, I guess. Do you think I should head over now?"

"No, wait."

They waited. The officer who had been faithfully keeping watch alongside Flash drifted away.

"How'd you manage in the dining hall before?" Flash asked Bianco. "I didn't even see you when I got downstairs."

"I was there. It got pretty wild for a while."

"You didn't get hurt, did you?"

"No. You did though, eh?"

"Just barely," Flash said. "Is anything happening over there—at the hobby shop?"

"No."

"He must be still at the tape machine. Thank God he's long-winded."

"What tape machine?"

Kale and Griffing returned.

"We couldn't get through," Kale said. He sounded pretty deflated. He sounded as if he wished everybody would just go away and let the whole bloody mess bring itself to whatever conclusion it wished, without his having to think one more thought or utter one more word. "We'll just have to wait, I guess . . ."

"We can't wait," Griffing said. He turned to Bianco. "Are your men ready?"

"They're on their way over."

"I want to ask you something," Kale said.

"Me?" Flash said.

"Yes. You've been in there, you've talked to that man. Do you think there's a chance he might accept the Governor's offer?"

Flash hesitated. He glanced at Griffing. He shrugged. "The guy's out of his head . . . God knows what he'd do."

"Do you think there's a chance? Any kind of chance?"

"I'm not interested whether or not he'd accept the offer," Griffing said. "I'm not making it."

"You wouldn't have to. The Governor would."

"The Governor's not Warden."

"Will you let this man answer my question?"

"I'm not stopping him."

"Do you think there's a chance?"

Again Flash hesitated.

"Go ahead," Griffing said. "Answer him."

"Well—of course there's a chance," Flash said slowly. "After all, anything's possible . . ."

"If you were Warden, would you try it?"

"I'm not Warden."

"Answer the question," Kale said.

Flash blinked. His head hurt like hell but he wasn't seeing double anymore. He'd become so used to discounting it he couldn't recall when it had stopped.

"Go ahead," Griffing said. "Answer it."

Both of them were zeroing in on him; he got the impression they were leaning down over him from some great height, ready to pounce, ready—each for his own reasons—to dismember, disembowel and macerate.

"I think maybe I might . . ." Flash said, not looking at Griffing, which meant he was looking at Kale. which made him feel even worse. He looked at his feet. "I think—well, I think the flattery of it, coming from the Governor, might somehow just hit—"

"Of course!" Kale said. "You hear that, Griff?"

"For God's sake, Flash—don't you realize what it'd mean if I let the Governor come in like that over my head?"

"I think so, Griff, but—"

"That's cowardice, Flash. That's all it is."

Flash shrugged again. His head pounded and he was sweating. "I guess I'd be willing to try anything, Griff . . . before turning people loose with guns. Someone's going to get killed if we move in."

"You'd be ready to humiliate yourself then?"

"I'm afraid I would," Flash said after a moment. His laugh was short and dry; it startled him.

"That's one of your own best men talking," Kale said. "That's not some outsider."

"Maybe you should make him Warden."

"Come on, Griff!" Flash said. "That's not what I—"

"I'm not making anyone Warden," Kale said. "You're Warden. No one's—"

"They're putting him out!" Bianco said.

They all looked over.

"Cloninger?" Flash asked.

"Yes," Griffing said. "Okay, that's it. Get on over there, Flash. You've got five minutes to get that fellow out."

"For God's sake, let him make the offer!" Kale said.

"No," Griffing said.

"We have to clear it with the Governor then."

"While that man's hanging upside down? Should we wait until Orninski puts a gun between his legs again?"

"Maybe they've located him," Kale said. "Just hold on—just one second." He tore inside.

"I'm sorry," Flash said. "I wasn't trying to contradict—"

"Forget it," Griffing said.

"Oh shit, Griff. I'm not trying to side with that—"

"I said forget it."

They waited.

"Does he seem all right?" Flash asked. "Can you tell?"

"He's conscious. He's moving."

Flash could feel the window frame cutting into the soft flesh behind his own knees. He could feel the blood rushing to his head, gagging in his throat, suffocating him.

Kale came running out. "They can't get him—the lines—"

"We can't wait any longer," Griffing said. "Either I'm handling it and I'm responsible, or you are. Which is it?"

Flash, staring, blinking in astonishment at how solid Griffing sounded, suddenly realized he was rooting for him, cheering him on, feeling enormously pleased to see him throw down the gauntlet to this barbarian, this spineless, fluttering, feeble-minded nincompoop. But then, still blinking, it occurred to him—Good Lord!—that he didn't want Griffing to win, he wanted *Kale* to win. If there really were a God, why didn't He see to it that the right people got on the right side? Why in Christ's name did anyone as long-suffering as Flash Fleishman —weary, blind, sleepless, confused, his head screeching with jagged pains—have to infuriate Griffing to agree with Kale to support the Governor to save Mancino by buttering up to Orninski? In the house that hate built. Well, it wasn't the first time he'd managed to make a complete ass of himself. At least it was for a good cause. To save a life. Whose? Did it matter? While Dietz lay dead and Cloninger hung by his feet. And Orninski expounded into a tape machine for posterity. And Long Johnny Manservant sat in there blithely waiting for Kind Fate—in the person of the nearest expendable warden—to rescue him for all his squealing fans.

"Which is it?" Griffing demanded. "Am I in charge or not?"

Flash couldn't see Kale's espression very clearly, but he could sense it as surely as he could have sensed last night, even without having noticed the round black symbol on the calendar, that there was a full moon lurking behind those rain-laden clouds. It was the pained, fragmented expression of the would-be tyrant who discovers he's nothing more than a bully. Not even a good, honest reactionary. Just a goddamned opportunist, and a frightened one to boot. (Good Christ, what did *that* mean? That when the chips were down Flash's pure and noble humanitarianism somehow emerged arm in arm with Kale's gutless corruption? No—it had to mean something else!)

Anyhow, Kale was licked, and Flash was both overjoyed and utterly dejected.

Kale gave it one more try, but his heart wasn't in it. "You've got to understand my position, Griff—I can't buck the Governor . . ."

"All right," Griffing said. "I'm out then. You're responsible for everything."

"No—it's your show . . . you're running it."

"Is that final? I don't want you changing your mind in two minutes."

"That's final. You're responsible. You've been from the beginning. I've just tried to—"

"Get moving, Flash. Five minutes."

"Breakfast is ready, sir!" an officer shouted, running up out of the sunny haze. "It's on the way."

"I told them not to bother!" Griffing snapped.

"Well, good God, let's *give* it to them!" Kale said. "We can hold them off with that and—"

"No," Griffing said.

"Warden!" an officer yelled.

"What's that noise?" Flash said.

"Good God!" Kale said.

"Get those men!" Griffing shouted. "Move!"

"What's happening?" Flash said.

"Oh my God!" Kale said.

"What is it?" Flash said.

"There he is!" Kale said. "It's him!"

"Who? What's happening?"

"Hurry!" Griffing roared. "Get over there!"

"For Christ's sake—what's going on? What's happening?"

☐

He hated to be sentimental, but the sound of Jo Ann's voice made him feel good. What the hell, if people weren't going to let you have your normal night's martinis and sleep they'd just have to accept the fact that in your weakened condition you'd probably turn sentimental.

"Flash—are you all right?"

"Of course I'm all right. Has Griff called Mrs. Cloninger?"

"Yes. Are you all right? He said you got hurt."

"Just a little bump. I'm all right, good as new."

"What do you mean, a little bump? How'd you get it?"

"It's a long story, and Griff's waiting for me, and half the reporters in the state are waiting for him. I just wanted to say hello. Hello. How'd your night go with Mrs. Cloninger? Did you get any sleep?"

"No, we drank tea. I never drank so much tea in my life. How did you get those men out of there?"

"You can read all about it in tonight's paper."

"Come on, Flash!"

"Johnny Mancino did it. The cute one."

"How can you kid about something like this?"

"He did. He brought out singlehanded, at gun point, after one of the other inmates jumped the leader in there. Made the rest of us look like a bunch of pikers. It was quite a scene, they tell me."

"Weren't you there?"

"Yes and no—it's all pretty complicated. I'll explain when I get home."

"When's that going to be?"

"In about a week probably. God only knows. Maybe tonight. I'll call again as soon as things settle down. You get on home now."

The reporters were jammed in the visitor's waiting room, still clamoring to be unleashed. He passed the open door, hurrying by with a confused and unintelligent (it was easy) look so they wouldn't think he was anybody important.

"Hey, Warden!" one yelled, trying to squeeze past the officer at the door. The others leaped up after him. Flash couldn't see them; he heard them.

"Not now—" he called back over his shoulder, fleeing. He stepped quickly into Griffing's office and moved close enough to tell that it was Kale seated behind the big desk, and Griffing standing alongside.

"What'd you find out?" Kale said. He sounded as sturdy, self-confident, efficient and obnoxious as ever. He sounded, the son of a bitch, as if everything that had happened in the last twenty hours had served only to prove once more, beyond all doubt, that where Frank J. Kale goes, there Truth and Virtue follow.

"I found out a few things," Flash said.

"So did we," Kale said. "What was this Simmons fellow doing when he got hit?"

"Mancino says he was trying to help him."

Griffing, standing alongside the desk, cleared his throat. "Orninski says he was trying to help *him.*"

"It hardly matters," Kale said. "How is Simmons? Is he going to pull through?"

"No, he's dead," Flash said. "How's Orninski?"

"He's got the flu," Kale said. "He's running one hundred and four. Practically dehydrated."

Flash shrugged. He was eager to move on, eager to watch Kale wriggling on the pin. "At any rate," he said, trying not to sound too disgracefully cheerful, "I learned something about how it all started."

"Oh?" said Kale.

"Yes. It was Walker."

"Who?"

"Walker. The Negro. The others tried to gang up on him."

Kale took this in silence. Flash wasn't close enough to see his expression.

"Are you sure?" Griffing demanded.

"Yes," Flash said. "And he was the one who bashed in Orninski's face."

There was another silence. Flash tried hard to enjoy Kale's discomfort but, disappointingly, his heart just wasn't in it. It didn't last long anyhow. Kale found his voice, and with it at least a show of his normal, bumbling *savoir faire,* as if a man in his position screwed up this badly every day of the week (true! true!) and couldn't afford to go around worrying about every teensy little disaster that he caused. "Well . . . I guess you people should look into that when things quiet down. Meanwhile, of course, let's not spread it around."

Griffing shrugged. "All right."

"What about that other business?" Kale said. "That's of more immediate importance."

"Tell me something," Griffing said, looking at Flash. His voice was flat, tired. He sounded almost bored. "What do you think of the idea of Mel Simmons as a murderer?"

"Excuse me?"

"Orninski says Simmons was keeping quiet here because he had a murder charge hanging over him."

"Orninski's looking for a fall guy."

"Obviously. Still, do you think it's conceivable? You knew Simmons pretty well."

"No," Flash said after a moment's thought. "I don't think it's conceivable."

"Give him the details," Kale said. "Let him check them out."

□

Flash called from Philson's empty office, down the hall from Griffing's. "About three months ago," he said. "On the good old Fourth of July, to be exact."

"Someone sure did," Radigan said. "Don't you read the papers?"

"Just the cheerful parts. Did you ever find the guy?"

"We never even got a lead."

"Can you tell me how much was taken?"

"Hold on." A few moments later Radigan said: "Six hundred bucks."

"Our story is four."

"The owner probably jacked up the take. It was all cash. What is it, Flash—you got the guy?"

"Maybe. Guy named Mel Simmons. You picked him up the next day —for auto theft."

"Wait a minute now—let me check." There was a longer pause this time. "Oh Christ—we *questioned* him on that too, but couldn't tie him in. Are you sure he's the guy?"

"Were there any details in the papers about the job?"

"No. We were holding that back in case—"

"Did the guy empty the cash register, leave the tray on the floor, jimmy a lock off a wooden door of a closed shelf on the back wall to grab the money box, and then beat it out the back window?"

"Hold on, hold on, I'm looking . . ." Papers rattled into the phone. "He sure did, Flash."

"Well . . . I guess he's your man then."

"Can we pin it on him? He's in for auto theft, you say?"

"He's dead," Flash said.

"Oh—was he involved in all that trouble you're having out there?"

"Sort of. Anyhow, the trouble's over."

"Well good—I knew you boys could handle it. And you know what, Flash? I got something for you too. Remember that other one you called me about that time? The big pickup at Fletcher's Drug—what was it?—sixteen dollars, something like that?"

"Oh yes. That."

"Well, we got him, about a week ago. One of the boys bumped into him coming out of another drugstore. A real haul this time—thirty-one bucks. He confessed to the other one, along with a few more. All drugstores."

"Yeah . . . well . . . I'm glad you got him."

"We get our share," Radigan said.

Flash went down the hallway and back into the Warden's office. Kale was still sitting behind the big desk. Griffing was still standing alongside.

"Did it check out?" Kale asked.

"Yes."

"Good." Kale stood up behind the desk, squaring his shoulders. "We can see those reporters now. Where's Mancino? They'll want to talk to him."

"Mancino?" Flash said.

"Yes. Where is he?"

"I let him go," Flash said.

"Why on earth did you do that?"

"I didn't see how I could stop him. He insisted on leaving. After all—he's not an inmate."

"He wouldn't see the reporters anyhow," Griffing said. "He wants the big scoop for himself."

"There's something else about that," Flash said. He hesitated. "That tape . . ."

"What tape?" Griffing snapped. "You don't mean from that fool machine you gave—"

"I'm afraid so," Flash said.

"Well, where is it? I hope you haven't left it lying around where somebody—"

"Mancino's got it . . . I didn't realize until after he'd gone."

There was a pause before Griffing spoke again. "Oh," he said. Rather coldly, Flash thought.

□

At least it got him out of having to face the reporters and, even worse, listen to Kale read his statement, with gestures. All those exploding flashbulbs, all that hubbub and bullshit. No, that was not for him. He was the original behind-the-scenes man, who desired for himself none of the glamour, the glory, the fame. Besides, he did not photograph well without his glasses.

Yes: his glasses. An officer drove him to Mountain Acres, where he could hear the cries of a few thousand local offspring playing Saturday morning ball on Rio Brava Court. Jo Ann hadn't got back yet but Janie raced across the lawn and leaped on him. "Daddy!" Marion and Jimmy clawed at him, shrieking. "Daddy—Daddy! You're all right!"

"Of course I'm all right, silly. Have you ever seen your daddy when he wasn't all right?"

"What happened to your head?"

"I bumped it. Daddy's got to get his glasses now and run off again. He lost his other ones."

He found them in his underwear drawer, and *voilà!*—there it was, the good old crystal-clear world again. Yes sir, *Shine Lovely Maid! And for thyfelf a better place prepare!* He looked in the mirror. It wasn't much, truth to tell, but it was him. The Fish Man, blinking and owl-eyed, and somewhat the worse for wear. It had been a long forty-four years.

The officer who drove him home returned to the pen with the officer who had followed them out in another car, and Flash drove the Volkswagen into town. Oh well, tonight he would drag his weary bones home and sit on his patio in the desert and drink a couple of gallons of gin and orange juice and feel sorry for himself and chatter at Jo Ann, and she, good old tubby-tub that she was, would listen to him. With her hands clasped placidly over her distended belly. That was all right: if she could love him even though he talked too much, didn't earn enough money, was unheroic, overweight, hypersensitive, near-sighted and misguided, and was referred to scornfully (by the very people he had dedicated his whole pathetic little life to helping) as the Fish Man, then he could love her even though she was pregnant. Fair was fair.

Why the hell didn't they give Jeff Dowler a sniveling condescending nickname? Didn't they also hate him?

Well, Dowler too had survived. They had all survived, except Dietz and Simmons, whom flights of angels were now no doubt singing to their rest. And Dowler was even going to get a week off, on doctor's orders, thanks to his odd little collapse which had been diagnosed, without much conviction, as a form of nervous exhaustion. (Jeff Dowler nervous? Jeff Dowler exhausted?)

In a week, at any rate, everything would be back to what hardened old jailers liked to refer to as normal. For the first few days the inmates probably wouldn't even be allowed out of their cells; they would be brought bag meals three times a day, a project in itself. Every cell and every inmate would be thoroughly searched to make sure not a single knife or fork missing from the kitchen remained at large. As a result, after every inch of the prison had been painstakingly scoured, at least twenty or thirty knives and forks would remain at large, probably forever. In a week maybe, if all went well, regular work schedules and privileges would be restored, and the inmates who burned their mattresses and were meanwhile sleeping on the cement floor might even get new ones. And during this time, of course, owing to the unstable situation at the institution, no new inmates would be sent there from any of the hundreds of jails and courthouses scattered throughout the state. That part of it, at least, would be nice. It would be, verily, like a glimpse of heaven. Even now the thought stupefied him—what would happen if suddenly, for whatever reason, people simply stopped sending other people to prison?

And in a week, Dowler would return, a little thinner perhaps, a little pale, maybe even a little less sure of himself, and Flash would tell him encouragingly, *You look great, Jeff*, because everybody would be everybody else's friend again. There would be enough other wounds to lick.

By then Griffing would even have more or less forgiven Flash for siding with Kale in that final ugly moment—when it was all over anyhow, when it didn't even make any difference, when if he had any brains he would have just shut up and waited for Verdun to give Orninski the old chop-chop and for the intrepid goon to lead the whole pack of rascals out. (What had saved them, he discovered afterward, what had kept Griffing from sending Flash barging in and from turning loose a bunch of gas-masked and trigger-happy officers, was the fact that the Treatment man who replaced Bostick on the switchboard didn't really know how to operate the thing, and screwed up the lines when Kale insisted on speaking to the Governor again.)

And in a week, or two or three, the final, official, God's-Honest-Truth report on the whole situation would be released, to be greeted with an enormous public outcry of yawns. God knows what it would say. (Would it mention the moon?) Probably that Mel Simmons, vicious murderer, started the whole thing through no fault of the penitentiary staff, who were never informed of the true nature of his crimes, and thus didn't keep him under the close surveillance that a man of his pathological violence would normally receive. What the hell, Truth was all right, in its place, although it rarely worked as well as an intelligent fib. And this fib was loaded with advantages, such as saving Kale's civil-rights crusade, and maintaining Griffing's honor, and maybe even keeping alive Flash's tottering hopes for a minimum security unit, someday, some year. My Lord is a rock in a weary land, Flash readily admitted, and I take what breaks I get, without quibbling.

He parked at the K-SUN studios, took the paper bag from the seat and trudged, dreary, footsore and bedraggled, through the glass doors into the vestibule. The same gilt-framed pictures were still on the wall, including the horrible shyly smiling one of the goon himself.

"I'd like to speak to Mr. Mancino," he told the receptionist.

"Another one—!"

"Excuse me?"

"Are you a reporter?"

"I am not a reporter."

"Sorry, I can't disturb him. Orders."

"Just say the Fish Man wishes to speak to him in the name of Law, Justice and Reason."

She eyed him dubiously, then plugged in and flicked a few times. "Johnny? I know you told me not to—but there's a gentleman here who insists you . . . well, he said just to say the Fish Man . . ."

He followed her directions: down the hall, around a corner. The door opened at his knock and there, smiling, smiled this doll, holding a pencil and a steno pad. Flash, always the *galant*, smiled back. "Come in," she said.

"Hi," Mancino said. He was at one of the two desks, behind a typewriter with a sheet of yellow paper sticking up.

"Here," Flash said. He walked over, deposited the bag on the desk, and removed from it, neatly folded, the white dinner jacket. "I *said* I'd guard it with my life."

Mancino smiled. "Much appreciated. This is June."

"I'm delighted," Flash said, nodding. And he was. She was really fine. These TV stars really got the women. It always seemed that way, that someone else had the inside track. Back during the war, when he was just a rutty teen-ager, all the ripe and beautiful virgins he pined for were being flooded with rum cokes and lured to motel rooms to debase themselves with wise-cracking guys in paratroop boots. But that was all right; he bided his time and prospered; he found Jo Ann, and she had kept him sane.

"Your head," the girl said.

"Nothing," he said. "A small bump. A lump. No larger than a golf ball."

"Sit down," Mancino said. "Something you wanted to see me about?"

"I understand you're much in demand," Flash said, sitting and crossing his legs. "I hesitate to waste your time."

"Actually, I *am* pretty busy . . ."

"Reporters hounding you and everything, eh?"

"Even the Governor called," the girl said.

She was also sitting with her legs crossed, her steno pad resting on her knee. He ogled briefly, then said, "Oh—the Governor called, did he?"

"I speak only to Governors and wardens," Mancino said.

"I assume he congratulated you on your fine performance out there."

"Something like that," Mancino said.

"I must say you look remarkably fresh, considering what you've gone through." And he did, the dog. Flash turned to the girl. "Do you know what he did out there?"

"Some of it, I guess . . . We just ran a bulletin on it."

"Kale held a press conference," Mancino said.

"I know. I left just before it."

"You don't really expect me to go along with that business about Simmons starting the whole thing, do you?"

Flash nodded at the paper stuck in the typewriter. "Is that what you're doing—preparing your exposé?"

"No exposé. I'm just going to tell what happened—what I saw— what I think of the place."

"Sure," Flash said.

"I don't expect it'll do much good—not with people like Kale and Griffing running the show. But at least it'll be the truth."

"That's right," Flash said. He paused, then cleared his throat. "By the way—I understand you still have that tape Orninski made."

Mancino smiled. "I was wondering when you'd get to that."

"We'd like to have it back. Orninski, you see, has withdrawn his permission for you to use it."

"I know what that means."

"I tried to say it with a straight face."

"I don't think you people have any legal claim on it that I can see. Since Orninski gave it to me, and since you provided the machine, implying your consent, the actual—"

"I'd have to check with our legal adviser," Flash said.

Mancino smiled. He seemed pleased as hell. "An authentic document like this . . . After all, it's one thing to report what Orninski said, but another to—"

"Orninski's in enough trouble already. He really doesn't want you to use it now."

"He was pretty sure at the time he'd be killed; it was almost a deathbed request."

"He wouldn't be the only man to have second thoughts when he found himself still alive."

"Maybe. But I feel somewhat committed."

"You know what else you'll hurt? That minimum plan I told you about—the one I had Mel Simmons lined up for."

"I guess it's too bad you had a riot just when you were pushing for reforms."

"We're always pushing for reforms."

"It'd seem to me," the girl said, "that trouble like that ought to help you *get* them."

"Unfortunately," Flash said, narrowing his gaze upon her legs, "the public's idea of reform is to make the bars of thicker steel." He turned back to the goon. "You're probably right; I can't make you give it back. So I'll just ask you. I've had a long day and a long night and a long morning, and so have you, and neither of us is in much shape for—"

Mancino stood up and walked over to a file cabinet. He pulled out the top drawer and held up the tape for Flash to see. Flash nodded, indicating that he could indeed see it. Mancino walked to a shelf and began setting up the machine that sat there. Tacked on the wall nearby was one of those imitation scrolls:

REMEMBER!

Every word you speak
Into the microphone today
Is heard by more people
Than heard President Abraham Lincoln
Deliver his Address at Gettysburg!

"Want to hear it?" Mancino said.

"Sure. Let's give the old platter a spin, as you disc jockeys say."

"Johnny never says that," the girl said.

"I meant the others."

And then, there in the room with them, was the one, the true voice of Roger Orninski, whispering hoarsely, as if leaning right up against your ear, passionately pouring out his very soul:

—*Garble-gable glum-dum rhumpfel-rhumpfel lhubb-druing dumble kampfer knockle doo . . .*

He listened for a minute or so, his eyes closed. "Does it improve . . . ?"

"There's one spot later that's a bit better—when he mentions the poison in the food."

Orninski muffled on, producing as incredible a collection of grunts and guttural blatherings as you'd ever hope to hear. He sounded as if he were chewing on the microphone rather than speaking into it.

"What poison in the food?"

"They figured you were putting knockout drops in their cereal."

"Where'd they get that idea from?"

"They were sure you must've thought of it."

"Why the hell didn't we?"

They listened. Orninski's voice became more intense, but no easier to understand. Flash caught an occasional word, a fragment of a phrase.

Mancino stopped it and rewound the tape. He took the spool off, studied it for a moment, then flipped it through the air. Flash made a stab; it glanced off his extended thumb and rolled toward the girl, who uncrossed her legs in a blink of stockinged thighs and bent forward to pick it up. Flash hopped over. She handed it to him.

"Thank you. I never was much good at catching things." He hesitated, then looked at Mancino. "One question hovers . . ."

"Yes."

"Would you give it back if it were worth anything?"

The goon smiled—fairly enigmatically.

"Well . . . thanks anyway." Flash bowed toward the girl and left, the golf ball on his head, the spool of garble in his pocket, the desert sun blazing down on him, bright, monotonous, relatively impartial.

25

Monday morning Johnny put on a dark suit and left the apartment. Downstairs Mrs. Warnsell, crouched like a brittle, spiny insect, was digging a trench for a flower bed with a forked trowel.

"There you are!" she said, pushing up her sunbonnet with the back of her wrist. "All weekend I was looking for you. You were out at the prison, heh? I saw you talking about it on television."

"That's right," Johnny said.

"In the paper too. It was a miracle you didn't get killed or something."

"It wasn't as bad as it sounded."

"I knew somebody got put in a prison once. Back in Akron, where we used to live. This man right next door, with a shotgun, was shooting at his wife. In the middle of the night the cops came and everything and put him in prison. I don't know if he ever got out; we left the neighborhood."

"Your plants are coming along very nice there," Johnny said, nodding, moving away.

"Flowers," she said. "I work on them."

There were about twenty-five people at the church, more than Johnny expected. About fifteen of these assembled at the cemetery when the cortege halted near the green crest of a hill. It was a pleasant October day, with a brilliant cloudless sky. From the graveside you could see out across the desert, past the fringes of Aurora to the San Juan Mountains.

The service was brief, almost hurried. When it ended he went over to Mrs. Simmons. She pushed her veil back. The little boy stood next to her, clutching a toy dog that looked new.

"I'm sorry," Johnny said. "I liked him . . . I'm sorry it had to happen this way."

She seemed bewildered. "I never expected you here. It was—well, it was real nice—coming like this . . ."

"I don't want to butt in," Johnny said, "but if I can help in any way—finding you a job or something . . ."

She shook her head. She smiled, almost wistfully. "I got a new job . . . I've been going to a beautician school . . ."

On the way to the car he fell into step alongside an ambling, power-ful-looking Negro. He had noticed him at the grave, standing with his huge hands clasped in front of him, his eyes down, obviously un-comfortable in his gray jacket. Johnny nodded. "Hi."

" 'Lo," the fellow said.

They walked side by side to the roadway, but the fellow didn't seem to have anything more he wanted to say, and Johnny couldn't think of anything either.